Undertones

UNDERTONES

WHERE JAZZ MEETS CRIME

BY

NANCY-STEPHANIE STONE

GALILEO PUBLISHERS, CAMBRIDGE

Galileo Publishers
16 Woodlands Road
Great Shelford Cambridge
CB22 5LW UK
www.galileopublishing.co.uk

Distributed in the USA by:
SCB Distributors
15608 S. New Century Drive
Gardena, CA 90248-2129

ISBN 978-1-912916-48-1

Printed in the EU

CONTENTS

For Marc Levin & Richard Reynolds
and
The Three Amigas

With thanks.

In memory of Barbara Davey, editor
&
Christian von Hessart, publisher of
The Mystery Review.

INTRODUCTION

"Somewhere…is the solution to the world…If we could only find it," says Coffin Ed Johnson listening to the trumpet and saxophone conversation at Big Wilt's Small Paradise Inn in Harlem.

Grave Digger Jones replies: "The emotion that comes out of experience. If we could read that language, man, we would solve all the crimes in the world."

-----Coffin Ed Johnson and Grave Digger Jones on crime and jazz in Chester Himes' Cotton Comes to Harlem (p.33).

UNDERTONES

Undertones is a reference book on jazz in crime fiction. A few ragtime and blues novels as well as a play are also included. Ragtime was a forerunner of jazz, and many of the great early jazz musicians started out playing ragtime. The blues, on the other hand, shared a common root with jazz, and developed separately into what might be considered the dark side of jazz.

As this historical overview shows, crime and jazz are soul mates in American popular culture. An early relationship began in the taverns, brothels and sporting houses of Storyville, the red-light district in New Orleans. David Fulmer's Valentin St. Cyr series: Chasing the Devil's Tail (2001), Jass (2005), Rampart Street (2006), Lost River (2009), The Iron Angel (2014), Eclipse Alley (2017) and The Day Ends at Dawn (2019) depicts this relationship during Storyville's heyday and demise. After the Navy closed Storyville in 1917, the jazz musicians went up the Mississippi River by steamboat or took the Illinois Central railroad to Chicago to play in gangster-owned clubs (Roddy Doyle, Oh, Play That Thing! 2004). A few musicians and local gangsters stayed behind in New Orleans. But as Robert Skinner's 1930s series about club owner Wesley Farrell shows (Blood to Drink (2000), Cat-Eyed Trouble (1998), Daddy's Gone A-Hunting (1999), Pale Shadow (2001), Skin Deep, Blood Red (1997) and The Righteous Cut (2002)), the jazz scene barely survived.

Jazz gave its name in the 1920s to a decade associated with excitement and lawlessness. In the Jazz Age, Americans were not going to allow the passage of the 18th Amendment in 1920, which prohibited the sale of alcohol, stand in the way of good times. While accompanied by jazz, they danced the Charleston on tabletops in gangster-owned nightclubs and drank bootleg whiskey in "speakeasies". In 1920s New York City, there were an estimated 5,000 speakeasies.

Jazz wasn't limited to a particular locality. For example, in Loren D. Estleman's Whiskey River (1990), speakeasy jazz provides the background and tempo to gangster Jack Danzig's rise and fall in the Detroit underworld. In Pamela Longfellow's China Blues (1989), the Tea Pot Dome Scandal is hatched at San Francisco's infamous Blue Canary Club where King Oliver's Creole Jazz Band provides background music.

In the 1920s jazz moved out of bars and smoky backrooms into society. At one of the legendary Long Island weekend lawn parties given by the bootlegger Jay Gatsby in F. Scott Fitzgerald's The Great Gatsby (1925), the King of Swing Vladimir Tostoff plays his composition, "The Jazz History of The World", modeled on the jazz played by Paul Whiteman at his 1924 Carnegie Hall Concert. Imogene Remus, the wife of the bootlegger George Remus in Craig Holden's The Jazz Bird (2001), hired the most popular band in Chicago, King Oliver's Creole Jazz Band, for her parties. Accompanied by a black jazz band that plays loud enough to cover the sound of a pistol shot, Catherine Jones, an Alabama socialite, does a wild Charleston in F. Scott Fitzgerald's little known short story, "The Dance" (1926).

Michael Walsh's And all the Saints (2001) is a fictional biography of gangster Owney Madden, who owned Harlem's famous Cotton Club where the Duke Ellington Orchestra was in residence. It reflects organized crime's understanding of the 1920s and their hold on the entertainment business. Aside from the financial aspects, many gangsters liked jazz. For a while, gangster Dutch Schultz "owned" Louis Armstrong. In trying to escape from the clutches of Schultz, he was shanghaied by two lesser mobsters, Tommy Rockwell and Johnny Collins. Armstrong's problems with the mob appear in Roddy Doyle's Oh! Play That Thing (2004).

On Thursday, October 24, 1929, known as "Black Thursday," the bottom fell out of the Wall Street stock market, ending the Jazz Age. An economic depression began that would eventually put one out of every four Americans out of work and would last until the Germans invaded Poland in 1939, resulting in a war and an eventual economic recovery.

In spite of economic hardship, people found the money for a night-out for dancing. In 1933, the passage of the 21st Amendment repealing Prohibition insured that there was plenty of alcohol for everyone. The Charleston gave way to the jitterbug. In New York, dancehalls and gangster owned nightclubs, like the Savoy with Chick Webb's Orchestra and the Cotton Club with the Duke Ellington Orchestra, were packed with people wanting to dance and drink their troubles away. In New York City, an entire street block on 52nd Street, known as Swing Street, was filled with jazz clubs. H. Paul Jeffers' private eye Harry McNeil (Murder On Mike, 1984), (Rubout at The Onyx, 1981) and (The Rag Doll Murder, 1987) had an office on 52nd Street above the Onyx Club. It wasn't just in New York City. Across the country, in places like Chicago (Jonathan Latimer's The Lady in the Morgue, 1936), Seattle (Harlan Reed's The Swing Music Murder, 1938), Kansas City (Lise McClendon's One O'clock Jump, 2001) and Harper Barnes' Blue Monday, 1991), clubs were packed with patrons and private detectives. As Lou Cameron's Angel's Flight (1960) shows, the mob decided which bands would get the bookings that allowed them to succeed.

In the 1940s the jazz scene changed, as did gangster control of the music business. With the exception of Duke Ellington, who was too old, and Benny Goodman, who had spine problems, most of the top jazz bandleaders disbanded their civilian bands and went to war. Artie Shaw led an all-star Navy Band, while Glenn Miller headed up a combined Army-Air Force Band. (Miller, whose song "*In the Mood*" epitomized the era, would die in an airplane over the English Channel.) A series of flashbacks in Peter Robinson's In a Dry Season (2000) shows just how important big band jazz was in the war effort. But, as Loren Estleman's Jitterbug (1998) shows, the home front still offered opportunities for gangsters to make money.

One of the casualties of World War II was big band jazz. In the war's aftermath popular taste changed. Maybe the songs that were so evocative of the era reminded people of that last dance with someone who didn't return. Whatever the reason, the difficulty of meeting a payroll along with the increasing costs of keeping a band on the road and shrinking audiences led many bandleaders like Count Basie to reduce the size of their bands. Other lesser-known orchestras simply disbanded.

An element from the big jazz bands that did survive and prosper was the band vocalist. The vocalist's role evolved from singing a few choruses to entire songs. Finally, vocalists took center stage. A few, like the skinny singer from Hoboken, New Jersey with Tommy Dorsey's band, Frank Sinatra, went on to careers in Hollywood. As was the case with the jazz bands, organized crime often decided who was going to succeed (e.g. Walker Alise in Richard Jessup's Lowdown, 1958) and who wasn't (e.g. Carl Carlson, the Carolina Crooner, in J. Madison Davis' And the Angels Sing, 1995). In one rare case, an indefinable relationship between a singer (Frank Sinatra) and organized crime figures continued throughout the singer's long career. Robert J. Randisi's light-hearted Eddie Gianelli novels (Everybody Kills Somebody Sometime (2006), Luck Be A Lady, Don't Die (2007), Hey There (You With The Gun In Your Hand) (2008), You're Nobody 'Til Somebody Kills You (2009), I'm A Fool To Kill You (2010), Fly Me to the Morgue (2011), It Was a Very Bad Year (2012), You Make Me Feel So Dead (2013),

4

The Way You Die Tonight (2014) and When Somebody Kills You (2015)) depicts Sinatra and his friends' ("the Rat Pack") antics (real and imagined) at the Sands Hotel in 1960s Las Vegas.

Organized crime also controlled the nuts-and-bolts of the recording industry. Beginning in the 1920s, record sales rather than personal appearances became the way money was made. Mobsters decided who was going to record, what songs were recorded (Richard Jessup's Lowdown, 1958), where the records would be pressed, and how they would be distributed (Lou Cameron's Angel's Flight, 1960). They set up a system that made it almost impossible to track distribution, returns and profits. As Evan Horne discovered in Bill Moody's Solo Hand (1994), variations on those schemes still exists.

A major source of income came from jukebox play rather than individual record sales. Jazz remained on the jukeboxes in black neighborhoods long after it ceased to be considered popular by the music industry. Big Joe Turner is singing on the jukebox in a 1950s Harlem tavern in the opening scene of Chester Himes' The Real Cool Killers (1985). As Peter Rabe's Murder Me for Nickels (1960) and Robert O. Greer's The Devil's Red Nickel (1997) show, organized crime's lock on the jukebox business squeezed out the smaller independent companies.

The black jazz bands experienced the same problems as their more successful white contemporaries. Many black jazz musicians went into R&B (Rhythm & Blues) and, later, soul music. But the business, financially and artistically, remained under the control of white mobsters as shown in David Fulmer's The Blue Door (2008). Even successful singers such as Dunny, in Wanda Coleman's short story "Dunny" (2008), had a limited future if they voiced any disagreement.

By the mid-1960s not even the most devoted fan could argue that jazz was America's popular music. Very few jazz clubs survived. Sales of jazz records and concert receipts were minimal compared to other areas of the music business. Even the profits from jazz festivals were chumps' change compared to the profits on the rock circuit. The sixty-years relationship between jazz and crime seemingly came undone. Jazz lives on in crime stories set after the 1960s more in the background than in the foreground.

A few words about the books covered in Undertones. The jazz world is a mystery writer's friend, offering a source for great stories. As if that isn't enough, with mention of a single song, a writer can set the mood, time, and place of a story. Memories evoked by a jazz tune can eliminate the need for pages of description and dialog.

Most of the stories in the annotated bibliography fall into two categories: those "with jazz in the foreground" and those "with jazz in the background." There are a few books and short stories included that have no jazz music but a sense of jazz is ingrained in the story's fabric. These are often set in the Jazz Age, such as Craig Holden's short story, "The P&G Ivory-Whiskey Massacree" (2004) and Max Allen Collins and Matthew V. Clemens' short story, "East Side, West Side" (2004). Both are included in Robert J. Randisi's short story anthology, Murder and all that Jazz. (2004). David Saunders' M Squad (1962), a 1960s spin-off mystery about Lieutenant Frank Ballinger's search for a cop-killer, is written in a rhythmic style that brings to mind Count Basie's jazz soundtrack from the popular American TV show. Leo Calef's 1950's crime novel, Ascenseur Pour L'Echafaud (aka Frantic), was the source for Louis Malle's classic Nouvelle Vague (New Wave) film with its soundtrack composed by Miles Davis.

The books with "jazz in the foreground" are self-evident. The protagonist may be a jazz musician like New York jazz pianist PI (Private Investigator) Johnny Staccato in Frank Boyd's Johnny Staccato (1960), an alto saxophone player like Lee Cabines in Malcolm Braly's Shake Him till he Rattles (1963) or a guitarist like Bill Cameron in James M. Cain's short story, "Cigarette Girl" (1953). Or the victim may be someone connected with jazz, usually a musician, such as singer Laurel Dane in Leigh Brackett's No Good From A Corpse (1944), bandleader Lance Grandy in Harlan Reed's The Swing Music Murder, (1938) or clarinetist Steve Sisson in Robert Avery's Murder on the Downbeat (1944). Some stories are set in jazz clubs like Robert Skinner's Wesley Farrell series and Harlan Reed and Robert Avery's books. Sometimes, something musical is stolen: music (Bart Spicer's Blues For The Prince (1951), J. R. Creech's Music And Crime (1984) and Bruce Cassidy's The Brass Shroud, (1958), three saxophones in three very different tales (Charlotte Carter's Rhode Island Red (1997), Michael Connelly's short story "Christmas Even" (2004) and Lou Jane Temple's The Cornbread Killer, (1999)) or even a jazz band (William Bankier's short story, "Concerto for Violence and Orchestra," 1997).

Books that fall into the "jazz in the background" category often have songs as their book title: "Almost Blue" (Carlo Lucarelli's Almost Blue (2001)), "Misty" (Paul Gillette's Play Misty For Me (1971)) and "Moonglow" (Kjersti Scheen's short story "Moonglow" (2007)). Sometimes, as in John Harvey's Charlie Resnick police procedurals, a book with a song as its title has a limited jazz content (the short story collection, Now's the Time, (1999)) or no jazz content (Off Minor, (1992)). But knowledge of the song title and its associations will allow one to read the book on a different level from less knowledgeable readers. Jazz establishes a sense of time and place, such as Louis Armstrong playing with the King Oliver's Creole Jazz Band in a 1920s San Francisco club in Pamela Longfellow's China Blues (1989), or his presence on the radio in 1930s Chicago in Jonathan Latimer's The Lady in the Morgue (1936).

One author's protagonist listens to jazz, and that music influences the plot. Michael Connelly's Harry Bosch books are paragons of stories with "jazz in the background." It is worth examining one to understand just how effective jazz can be in moving the story along in a seemingly non-jazz novel.

In Connelly's Echo Park (2006), the Los Angeles Police Department (LAPD) in a routine traffic check stops Raymond Waits. Body parts from two women are found in his car. Rather than get the death penalty, he agrees to trade information on a series of unsolved murders of women in exchange for a life sentence. Among his victims is Marie Gesto, whose murder haunted police detective Harry Bosch for a decade. He is suspicious of the easy answer offered to a crime that he was unable to solve.

So how does jazz fit in? Harry purchased the CD *Thelonious Monk Quartet with John Coltrane at Carnegie Hall* (2005). He listens constantly to this recently released CD of tapes that were sitting in an unlabeled box for 50 years, awaiting rediscovery. He observes: "the guy who found it had to know their sound to know what they had in that box in the archives." (p.215). Similarly, the pieces of the Marie Gesto case are waiting for Harry to rediscover and rearrange to uncover her killer.

He also listens to the 1959 Miles Davis album, *Kind of Blue*. Harry "...put on the stereo and put in the masterpiece, *Kind of Blue...* "All Blues" was the first song...and it was like being dealt blackjack at the twenty-five dollar table. It was his favorite and he let it ride." (p.270). With *Kind of Blue* playing in the background, he opens the murder book and eventually understands what he should have been looking for years ago.

Undertones is divided into two parts. The first is comprised of essays framing some of the jazz crime novels in their historical context and giving the casual reader a better understanding of the genre. Essays on ragtime and the blues offer insight into jazz roots. Other essays are regional (New York, Chicago, New Orleans, Kansas City, San Francisco, Los Angeles (black & white)), or set abroad. Four essays are topical: Private Eyes and Jazz ("Jazz Eyes"), Cops and Jazz, Jazz and Drugs, and Jazz in Spy and Thriller novels. Inevitably, there's overlap and repetition. The second part consists of an annotated bibliography of books, short stories and magazines as well as lists of: authors and their series characters, series characters and their authors, geographic locations, a chronology, a discography, a "Hot 100 list" and a list of jazz books and short stories by author.

At this point, I'd like to say something about the discography. A few books (Michael Connelly's Lost Light (2003), Rupert Holmes' Swing (2005) and Bill Moody's Looking for Chet Baker (2002)) came with jazz CDs that really enhanced the reader's experience. I wish more mysteries did, but in the absence of that, I have tried to fill the gap. I tracked down and listed the music mentioned in the books and short stories. In cases where no specific jazz was mentioned, I chose CDs that fit the mood. I really did listen to all the CDs in the jazz discography. I know the book would have been completed sooner had I not spent so many days lost in jazz.

At the 2008 Bouchercon (mystery writer's convention) in Baltimore, a friend asked how I ever found all these books. It wasn't easy and took years. With the gradual disappearance of specialized mystery bookstores, writing a book like this may be impossible in the future. When I first considered writing Undertones, I mentioned it to my friend Andy Thumauer, the owner of Spenser's Mystery Bookstore in Boston. He said he'd have a look around the store and suggested that I come in the following day. Waiting for me was a tower of books. He pulled from his shelves any book that had a musical instrument on its cover. That was the beginning of Undertones.

Vince McCaffrey of Boston's Avenue Victor Hugo Bookstore was also helpful. Aside from his books, I went through piles of old, dusty mystery magazines and eventually found a true prize, an overlooked crime jazz short story by F. Scott Fitzgerald. Sadly, both bookstores are gone.

In Cambridge, England, on the other hand, Heffers bookshop is alive and well. Without the interest of Richard Reynolds, I would never have found the English mysteries included in Undertones or gotten it published. Maxim Jakubowski of London's much-missed Murder One Bookstore was always available to answer a question.

A few other acknowledgments are due. Liz Prevett suggested the title Undertones and critically read some essays. Marietta Delehant with her Chicago Style Manual was indispensible in proof reading. Ric Bogaert offered helpful suggestions. Jim Huang kept me on the long track that ended with Undertones and almost published it. Robert Hyde of Galileo Publishers saved Undertones from oblivion with his decision to publish it. Jazz writer-critic James Isaacs always answered my questions and offered useful suggestions. Jack Woker of Stereo Jack's vintage record and CD store in Cambridge, Massachusetts was the source of much of the music I listened to and listed in Undertones. Marc Levin oversaw my business during the final months of writing when I was unreachable. Peter Brown, my attorney and life-long friend, was always there. Dorothy Dwyer and Jimmy Black looked after my homes and dogs while I was hospitalized. Harriet Lazarus guided me through the health care gauntlet. From that time emerged *Las Tres Amigas:* Doctor Jaisa Olasky pulled me back from death's door; and Doctors Katherine Esselen and Megan Shea made sure it stayed closed. And finally, Fiona Farquhar oversaw my recovery. Clearly, without these friends, Undertones could not have been written. As all writers know, those listed in acknowledgments are usually only a sampling of help in a long-term endeavor. If I listed everyone who helped me over the past fifteen years, the acknowledgements would be the size of an old Manhattan telephone directory.

In writing Undertones, I know that I am writing for two different audiences: mystery readers and jazz enthusiasts. I hope that Undertones will satisfy both.

Part 1

JAZZ ROOTS:
1. RAGTIME

Ragtime was a bridge between the music of marching bands and early jazz. It was basically a mix of marches and African rhythms. Its origins can be found in black urban communities and its years of popularity stretched between 1895-1918. Cecil Brown's fictional biography of the legendary black gangster Stagolee in I, Stagolee (2006), set in 1895 St. Louis, depicts the restless urban society receptive to ragtime. E.L. Doctorow's Ragtime (1975) offers a larger picture of a changing America (1900-1919) in which the new music was slowly accepted. That said, ragtime became the soundtrack to change in the new century.

Some of the greatest, early jazz piano players started out with ragtime. For example, Jelly Roll Morton, who credited himself with inventing jazz in New Orleans, played ragtime but adapted when he sensed its popularity fading and found "jass," as it was known, more challenging. Similarly, the Kansas City bandleader Bennie Moten studied ragtime under several of composer Scott Joplin's students, until he, too, realized the wider possibilities of improvised jazz.

Although New Orleans is considered the birthplace of jazz, it is not so easy to identify a similar city for ragtime. Sedalia, Missouri, the home of composer Scott Joplin comes to mind because of the popularity of his compositions "Maple Leaf Rag" and "The Enter-tainer." Joplin's music swept the 1890s, and he was called "the King of Ragtime." Joplin might have been remembered as just another name among legendary ragtime players, like Jess Pickett, Jack the Bear, and Sam Gordon, had not his publisher, John Stark, agreed to publish his music under his own name and pay royalties. In those days, it was unheard of for a white publisher living in segregated America to do this for a black musician.

Within six months of its publication, "Maple Leaf Rag" sold thousands of copies, making its composer financially secure for a while. From the 1899 publication of Scott Joplin's "Maple Leaf Rag" to the beginning of WWI, ragtime became America's popular music. Often songs that were not rags, such as composer Irving Berlin's "Alexander's Ragtime Band," used the word in its title as a selling point.

Larry Karp's The Ragtime Kid (2006) focuses on Joplin's struggle to get recognition for his music and have it published under his name. Joplin insisted that his compositions be played as written. His music could be interpreted by solo pianists but not improvised. He tells his young student, Brun Campbell: "My ragtime is different from ragtime you hear in hotels and saloons and parlors. Those tunes develop-usually from a melody that's been around forever… my music is composed…no different from a song by Schubert, a concerto by Mozart, or a Beethoven symphony." (p.80). To Joplin's dismay, traveling ragtime players did take his melodies and make them their own—especially in New Orleans.

In Edward D. Hoch's short story, "The Ripper of Storyville" (2003), detective Ben Snow is searching the sporting houses of Storyville for the missing daughter of a Texas businessman when he hears a different-sounding music. The story is set in 1901, so the music was an improvisation on a rag as the development of the earliest jazz was a few years away.

The changes in popular musical styles are present throughout Alan V. Hewatt's Lady's Time (1985), which spans the years between 1887 and 1919. Hewatt recounts the struggle of Alice Beaudette, a young, light-skinned Creole, who learned to play the piano from her mother's lover Brick, was stalked by a killer, and eventually moved from Storyville's sporting houses to upstate New York.

Scott Joplin has also moved to New York in Karp's second volume of his ragtime trilogy, The King of Ragtime (2008) set in 1916. For almost a decade, he has been vainly trying to get a Manhattan music publisher interested in his opera, Treemonisha. Martin Niederhoffer, a student of Joplin's and a bookkeeper at Irving Berlin's music-publishing company, convinces him to bring *Treemonisha* to Berlin. The next day he discovers a confused Joplin as a murder suspect and the opera missing. Berlin, recognized as the most famous composer-publisher of his era, claims he does not have it. The nearly destitute Joplin insists that he left his opera with him.

The final volume of Karp's trilogy, The Ragtime Fool (2010), finds Brun Campbell as an elderly man, returning to Sedalia in 1951 for a ceremony honoring his old mentor, Scott Joplin. He hopes to use Joplin's unpublished diary as an incentive for the creation of a Joplin Museum. Alan Chandler, a young ragtime enthusiast, acquired the diary for Campbell. Others, such as a New York ragtime researcher, Scotts' old Sedalia friends, and the Ku Klux Klan have different plans for the Joplin diary.

As suddenly as the ragtime craze began with the 1899 publication of "Maple Leaf Rag", the era ended in 1917 with Joplin's death. If he had not been so insistent about his music being played as it was written, ragtime might have retained its popularity; however, the possibilities of improvisation evident in early jazz seem to have intrigued musicians more than playing the same old rags. Consequently, popular music moved to New Orleans and developed into jazz. There was a brief revival of interest in Scott Joplin and his ragtime music in the 1970s when composer Marvin Hamlisch won an Academy Award for his Joplin-inspired film score for *The Sting*, and Joshua Rifkin's recording of *Scott Joplin Piano Rags* sold a million copies.

JAZZ ROOTS:
2. THE BLUES

Early jazz and blues share a common origin. Each evolved through mixing European music with African harmonies as played in the American South. Where they split is in development. Early jazz was played by schooled musicians, like the New Orleans Creole Jelly Roll Morton, who synthesized African and European musical heritages and ragtime into a written music for others to interpret. The New Orleans musicians were the heart of this new music, and the sporting houses and taverns of Storyville, the red-light district of New Orleans were its center. The blues, on the other hand, seem to have evolved through the efforts of itinerant musicians, often playing homemade stringed instruments, in various places in the rural South where there were large concentrations of black people. When urban economic opportunity beckoned, blacks moved off the land into cities, taking the blues along. David Fulmer's short story, "Algiers," recounts such a tale: that of itinerant Texas bluesman and card shark Eddie McTier, who unfortunately encounters New Orleans' detective Valentin St. Cyr. McTier explains his success at cards to his gullible victims as the result of a deal with the devil where he traded his soul for skill at cards and an ability to play the blues. But St. Cyr knows better.

Different southern locales have distinct blues sounds. For example, Mississippi blues have a harsher sound than Texas blues. In general, rural blues, usually played on a guitar, banjo or harmonica, had a more raw sound than urban blues played by groups of musicians using wind and string instruments and sometimes backing a woman singer. These backup musicians were often jazzmen. For example, jazz greats Louis Armstrong, Coleman Hawkins, Sammy Price and Benny Goodman are present on early recordings of blues singers such as Ma Rainey or Bessie Smith. However, as August Wilson's Ma Rainey's Black Bottom (1981) shows, the blending of classic blues and jazz players was not always harmonious. (Yet, nothing demolishes the invisible line between jazz and blues more than jazz vocalist Billie Holiday's recording of "Strange Fruit". After hearing it, few could deny her credentials as a blues singer.)

Jazz and blues musicians often used the same stories in their music. One of the better-known songs interpreted by blues and jazzmen across the South was that of the doomed romance of Betty and Dupree. In David Fulmer's Will You Meet Me In Heaven? (2014) set in 1920s Atlanta, Frank Dupree is a drifter who falls for Betty Andrews, a dancer. During their five-day affair, he learns that she was married but never got a wedding ring. He goes into a jewelry store to buy her a ring but things go murderously awry. Twenty years later, she returns to Atlanta and hears a blues singer singing about Betty and Dupree. Dale Curran's Dupree Blues (1948) gives a different twist to the tale. Trombone player Dupree falls for the band's young vocalist, Betty, who is only interested in having a good time. Using his winnings from a dice game, he buys her an expensive diamond ring. As his luck later changes, Dupree loses money gambling and is unable to pay the balance owed on the ring, resulting in violence.

A surprising number of early blues were recorded for the "race market." Although most of these record companies went bankrupt in the Depression, the music endured. The record business barely survived the 1930s but revived in the postwar prosperity. By the 1950s, blues records were back on jukeboxes in black communities. In the opening scene in a 1950s Harlem club in Chester Himes' The Real Cool Killers, Big Joe Turner is belting out a Kansas City blues on a jukebox.

Contemporary collectors prize the older urban and rural blues records. In Kevin Guilfoile's "O Death Where Is Thy Sting" (2007), set in Chicago, the narrator buys blues record collections from unsophisticated owners. He gets a tip about a collection owned by an elderly widow. In her late husband's collection is Jimmie Kane Baldwin's "O Death Where Is Thy Sting," the rarest blues recording. She insists she can't sell the collection until she calls her son. The next day, the narrator returns and encounters another collector. As the two blues collectors try to outwit each other, a massive snowstorm descends on Chicago trapping them in her house.

Possibly the most famous recorded bluesman was Robert Johnson. He seemed to emerge from the 1930s Mississippi Delta with an amazing guitar technique and an original repertoire of sophisticated songs with their themes of hope, love, struggle, and defeat. Johnson's life was the stuff of legend: a fast-living young man with an eye for women and a thirst for alcohol, who supposedly made a deal with the devil at a Mississippi crossroads for his music and later was poisoned by a jealous woman. At the time of his death at age 27, his fame extended beyond the Delta as the result of his records. (Johnson recorded 29 sides in five sessions between 1936 and 1937.)

In time, the crossroads of Highways 49 and 61, where Johnson made his deal, became almost as famous as the singer. Elmore Leonard set a contemporary novel in nearby Tunica. In Tishomingo Blues (2002), Dennis Lenahan witnesses a "Dixie Mafia" murder. Seemingly, he's saved from a similar fate with the arrival of Robert Taylor, in from Detroit, to assess the drug scene. The blues-loving hustler brings Lenahan to the famous crossroads and makes a similar offer.

Three contemporary mysteries deal with legendary Mississippi bluesmen and their music. Ace Atkins' first novel, Crossroad Blues (1993), is about Johnson and nine missing records from a session done before his death. Blues historian Nick Travers is asked to look for a professor of music history, who disappeared in the Mississippi Delta while on the trail of Johnson's lost recordings. Travers realizes that he was murdered for the recordings that held clues to Johnson's death. Johnson reappears in Walter Mosley's story, RL's Dream (1996) about Soupspoon Wise, an elderly, ill blues musician now living in New York City. In his youth, Wise traveled the South with the young Johnson and spends much of the novel reminiscing about their early lives together.

A third mystery about fictional Mississippi bluesmen and their music is Bill Fitzhugh's Highway 61: Resurfaced (2005). Detective Rick Shannon becomes entangled in the search for a missing blues tape made by three legendary bluesmen, Blind Buddy Cotton, Crippled Willie Jefferson, and Crazy Earl Tate. The tape, known as the Blind, Crippled and Crazy sessions, has the answers as to why the three perjured themselves to send an innocent man to the notorious Mississippi prison, Parchman Farm.

In contrast to these three stories of Delta bluesmen, David Fulmer's The Dying Crapshooter's Blues (2007) is set in 1920s Atlanta. Little Jesse Williams, an urban bluesman, pimp and crapshooter, meets a violent end. Unlike Johnson, his songs were never recorded, but he had a large, local following. As he lay dying from a drunken white policeman's gunshot, he is struggling to finish his testament (last song).

Another tale of an ill-fated bluesman is that of Junior Crudup in James Lee Burke's Last Car to Elysian Fields (2003). Crudup, a black Creole, ignored the rules of segregation that governed the South. His attitude landed him in Louisiana's Angola Prison where he disappeared. New Orleans policeman Dave Robicheaux discovers his story while on another investigation. Before his incarceration, Crudup "had made race records in Memphis, been interviewed in Downbeat magazine and performed with Cab Calloway's Orchestra in New York City all before he was thirty years old." (p.151). A white woman heard Crudup's music while he was in Angola, arranged for a recording session, and even had him sing at her home. His fatal mistake was writing a song about her. Crudup is loosely modeled on blues singer Hudie Ledbetter, known as Lead Belly, who served time in Angola for murder and supposedly secured his release after two governors heard his music and granted him a pardon. In reality, he served seven years of a 14-to-life sentence and got out with "double good time." (With help from folklorist Alan Lomax, he became a successful entertainer, giving blues concerts throughout Europe and the United States.)

Robicheaux, who unearthed the truth about Crudup's demise, had a sophisticated appreciation of the blues. Some readers may be surprised, since he's a Cajun and their music is zydeco. Early zydeco was played by black Creole musicians and influenced by the blues. His feel for the blues is evidenced early in Burke's series (The Neon Rain, 1987). Robicheaux collected classic blues and jazz records until intruders in his houseboat smashed them. After listening to an old Blind Lemon Jefferson blues recording late one evening, he "wondered why it was that only black people seemed to treat death realistically in their art. White people wrote about it as an abstraction, used it as poetic device, concerned themselves with it only when it was remote." (p. 246).

In Black Cherry Blues (1989) Robicheaux rescues a friend, Dixie Lee Pugh. He was "an honest-to-God white blues singer. He learned his music in the Baptist church, but somebody in that little cotton and pecan-orchard town rubbed a lot of pain into him, too, because it was in everything he sang..."(p. 6). His feeling for the blues and skill allowed him to cross the color line and enabled Texas bluesman Lightning Hopkins to add the finishing touches to Pugh's style. He later became a rhythm and blues star, couldn't handle that life, and slid to rock bottom. Robicheaux tries to help his friend and, in return, is framed for murder.

Like jazz, blues has managed to become a respected subject of academic interest. Blues historian Ace Atkins, who first appeared in Travers' Crossroad Blues (1998), returns in Leavin' Trunk Blues (2000). It's the story of Mississippian Ruby Walker, who was known as the "Sweet Black Angel" and one of Chicago's great blues singers until she killed her producer Billy Lyons in September 1959. Now forgotten and serving a life sentence, she agrees to grant the Tulane blues historian an interview in return for his independent investigation of Lyons' death.

In another urban blues about a wronged woman, Alberta Wright, in Chester Himes' The Big Gold Dream (1988) set in 1950s Harlem, hits the number for $36,000 and hides her lottery winnings. But she can't keep quiet about her good fortune. At a mass baptism, she speaks about cooking three pies that filled her kitchen with money. She was drugged with a Mickey Finn and seemingly half of Harlem races to her home to search for the hidden money. When she regains consciousness, Alberta can't remember where her money is. As bodies pile up and her life is endangered, Harlem police detectives Digger Jones and Coffin Ed enter the case. When she finally remembers, she takes matters into her own hands and ends up in jail, singing "Trouble In Mind."

Blues, sung by older black singers, became part of the 1950s folk music revival and acquired a wider audience. Singers, such as the long-forgotten John Hurt from rural Mississippi and the cosmopolitan Josh White, whose reputation had been damaged in the 1950s communist hysteria, became popular and had extended careers. Corrie Appleyard, a contemporary of Josh White's, plays a series of gigs on the fashionable island resort of Martha's Vineyard in Philip R. Craig's Vineyard Blues (2000). He was a close friend in the 1950s of protagonist J.W. Jackson's father. Rather than stay with J.W., he chooses to stay with the grandson of a friend and his body is later found in the ashes of a torched house. Jackson is determined to find the arsonist and killer of his friend.

Whites, and not just rednecks like Dixie Lee Pugh, began to play the blues and achieve recognition and financial success in the 1960s. These blues musicians and their audiences were young, college-educated, urban and suburban kids. That's the scene in Linda Barnes' Steel Guitar (1991), set in Boston where PI Carlotta Carlyle meets her old friend Dee Willis, now a successful blues singer. Dee confesses that a former band member is blackmailing her over songwriting credits and royalties. Carlotta locates the alleged blackmailer only to realize that the real blackmailer is within Dee's inner circle. In another contemporary story, Peggy Ehrhart's Sweet Man Is Gone (2008), jazz and blues come together. Maxx Maxwell's blues band is about to hit the big time when her guitarist "commits suicide." She knows it's murder, suspects the killer is in her band, but her investigation misses the significance of a solo once played by 1930s jazz bandleader Benny Goodman's guitarist, Charlie Christian. Sweet Man Is Gone closes the circle of jazz and blues.

While jazz would evolve into many forms during the 20th Century, blues more or less stayed the same. True, the instruments would change from broomstick and cigar box guitars to electric ones. But the themes of hope, struggle, lost love and defeat that Robert Johnson sang about underlie stories from David Fulmer's "Algiers," set in the early 1900s, to Peggy Erhart's contemporary Sweet Man Is Gone.

Jazz:
New Orleans

As descendants from French and Spanish colonialists, the Creoles were among New Orleans' first settlers. They were proud of their heritage and maintained cultural ties to Europe. Creoles spoke French, educated their children in Europe if possible, and were known for their musical abilities. As was the European custom, many wealthy Creole men took mistresses, often from other races. There was a wide choice available because of New Orleans' location in the heart of the Natchez and Choctaw Indian nations, commerce with the Caribbean, tolerant attitudes toward freed slaves and economic opportunities for immigrants. The Creoles, even the *gens de couleur* (or Black Creoles), considered themselves white if they were of mixed heritage. They lived downtown in the French Quarter, while freed blacks lived uptown in the American Quarter. Often, they were slave owners.

After the 1803 influx of Americans resulting from the Louisiana Purchase (of French territory), the Creoles were slowly pushed out of their dominant position in New Orleans' economy. Barbara Hambly's Benjamin January series set in the 1830s and 1840: Fever Season (1833), A Free Man of Color (1833), Graveyard Dust (1834), Sold Down the River (1834), Die Upon a Kiss (1835), Dead Water (1835), Wet Grave (1835), Dead and Buried (1836), Good Man Friday (1838), Crimson Angel (1838), Murder in July (1839), Cold Bayou (1839), Drinking Gourd (1839), Lady of Perdition (1840) and two short stories "Libre" (1835) and "There Shall Be Your Heart Also" (1835) depicts the changing position of the Creoles in New Orleans and their blindness to their predicament. Aside from January, only Marie Zuleika Rochier, a light skinned Creole in "Libre", who flees to Boston where she can pass as Spanish, realizes their day as a privileged minority has ended.

The increasing numbers of Americans posed a special danger to mixed race Creoles and free blacks. The Abolition Act of 1833 abolished slavery in British colonies in the Caribbean and Africa and, enforced by the British Navy, ended the slave trade when the demand for labor in the southern cotton fields and the Republic of Texas was increasing. American slave traders prowled parts of New Orleans kidnapping people and looking for "runaway" slaves. Even with the protection of his friend, fiddle player Hannibal Sefton, there were parts of the city that January was hesitant to enter. January, his family and friends had run-ins with slavers (Cold Bayou), (Dead Water), (Drinking Gourd), (Fever Season), (Good Man Friday), (Lady of Perdition) and (Sold Down the River).

January was born a slave but freed by his mother's white protector who took on the responsibilities of educating him and sending him to Paris to study medicine. Murder In July outlines his life in Paris and how those events affected a murder in New Orleans nine years later. Due to racial prejudice in France, he returned to New Orleans in 1833 but is unable to practice as a surgeon and ends up as a music teacher and amateur detective. He survives by playing the piano at octoroon or quadroon balls, Creole subscription dances, and opera companies, and through giving private lessons to children of wealthy Creoles. In Sold Down the River, January agrees to leave New Orleans and go upcountry to help his former master, Simon Fourchet, discover who is sabotaging his crops and murdered his butler. Returning to the plantation that he left 35 years earlier, January hears the field hollers, songs, and African drum rhythms that would evolve into the blues and early jazz. His classically trained mind thinks about the possibilities of this music. But it would take at least three generations and another Creole, Jelly Roll Morton in David Fulmer's Jass (2005), to blend it into jazz.

By 1860, 40% of New Orleans' population consisted of immigrants. The sheer numbers of newcomers guaranteed that the Creoles would lose their status in New Orleans. The Civil War and the Emancipation Proclamation ended their precarious existence between the races. With Reconstruction and the ensuing Jim Crow (race) laws, the Creoles found themselves classified as black. They protested and rioted to no avail. In1894, the matter was settled when a court ruling upheld the Louisiana Legislature Code III, which stated that anyone with any African blood was black. That effectively shut the door to the professions for the Creoles and ended their prosperity. As a result, many downtown Creoles were little better off than the uptown blacks. Classically trained Creole musicians, who had previously played in their own symphonies and opera company orchestras, were forced to take employment where they could find it. That often meant playing in the bars and bordellos of the city's red-light district. In Alan V. Hewat's Lady's Time (1985) set during the years 1887-1919, Obregon Vraicoeur, a classically trained violinist, is reduced to playing guitar in Buddy Bolden's jazz band and goes insane. The problems associated with race, and the desire of Creoles to pass as white, are a factor in all the novels and short stories by Hambly. They also figure in Hewat's novel, in David Fulmer's seven Valentin St. Cyr books, and Robert Skinner's six Wesley Farrell books.

Known as "The Crescent City" because of its geographic location along a bend in the Mississippi River, New Orleans had an economy as diverse as its early settlers. It began as a center of commerce for the fur, logging, tobacco, cotton, and slave trades. With its reputation as a good-time place, trappers, loggers and river men flocked to the city. Increased commerce brought shipping and an influx of sailors. Eventually, the United States Navy established a major base in New Orleans.

The city developed a large red light or "Tenderloin" District, located near the railway station on Basin Street. In 1857 prostitution was legalized and attempts were made to limit the growth of the Tenderloin District. Inevitably, gambling, prostitution, liquor and drug use got out of hand.

Consequently, in 1897, Alderman Joseph Story sponsored legislation to officially create a brothel district. It became known as Storyville, though most musicians called it "the District." They flocked to its bars and brothels, and its existence as a place for entertainment became intertwined with the birth of jazz. In 1917 the U.S. Navy, fearing for the health its sailors before they were shipped overseas to war, insisted on the closing of Storyville. With the elimination of their source of employment, musicians left Storyville, ending the Crescent City's special place in the development of jazz.

At the turn of the century, however, one of the best-known jazz musicians in Storyville was the cornet player, Buddy Bolden. Born in 1877 and the grandson of a slave, Charles "Buddy" Bolden grew up in New Orleans. As with many mythic figures, it is very difficult to separate fact from fiction.

What is known is that Bolden was a hard-living musician whose life-style facilitated a slide into insanity and eventual commitment in 1907 to the East Louisiana State Hospital in Jackson where he died in 1931. Bolden's contribution to jazz was his ability to fuse sectionalized structures and harmonics of formal Creole dance music with the urban blues as played uptown by unschooled black musicians. Unfortunately, unlike other legendary New Orleans musicians, there remains only a single photograph of Bolden with a band and no recorded examples of his music.

By the early 1900s, Bolden's music was receiving attention from other musicians, including Creoles. For the first time, people came to hear a musician, not a band. The audience was often integrated. Clearly, Bolden was a challenge to vested interests, musically, socially and politically. This threat underlies David Fulmer's first novel of his Storyville series, Chasing the Devil's Tail (2001).

As Chasing the Devil's Tail begins in 1907, Storyville's political boss Tom Anderson orders his trouble-shooter Valentin St. Cyr to investigate a series of murders of prostitutes. Normally, the killings would remain unnoticed outside of Storyville, but their increasing number and the bizarre placement of a single black rose beside each victim guaranteed problems. Known as the King of Storyville, Anderson is aware that if he can't maintain order, someone else will. Early in St. Cyr's investigation a link emerges: all of the victims knew the cornet player, Buddy Bolden. The jazz legend was at the height of his artistic powers but was also rapidly descending into insanity. King Bolden, as he was known around the Quarter, might behave irrationally, but to St. Cyr that did not make him a killer. It could, however, make him a scapegoat.

Bolden reappears in Michael Ondaatje's <u>Coming through Slaughter</u> (1979), which presents a less detailed picture of Storyville and concentrates on Bolden. The increasingly erratic trumpet player never returned home from a gig, and his old friend Webb, a detective, promises Bolden's wife Nora that he will find him. Eventually, he locates Bolden, who has given up music and is living with another woman. Bolden goes to Webb's cottage on Lake Pontchartrain to practice and then returns to New Orleans to find Nora living with his old trombone player. He turns to his other love, music, with a vengeance.

Bolden appears in a cameo in Alan V. Hewat's <u>Lady Time</u> and hires Alice Beaudette's father Obregon Vraicoeur as a replacement guitarist in his black jazz band with disastrous consequences. In another appearance in 1913, in David Fulmer's <u>Lost River</u> (2009), Bolden, now locked away in the state mental hospital in Jackson, provides the missing piece, an overheard conversation in a serial-murder case that threatens Tom Anderson's control over Storyville and enables Valentin St. Cyr to find a killer. In <u>Eclipse Alley</u> (2017), set in 1915, St. Cyr buys a recording from a session eight years earlier of Buddy Bolden's band doing the tune "Careless Love." It's expensive but St. Cyr willingly overpays to have this trace of his old friend. In the final volume of the St Cyr series, <u>The Day Ends at Dawn</u> (2019), set in 1917, Bolden's confinement in a mental hospital doesn't protect him from a killer.

Another legendary jazz musician from Storyville was Jelly Roll Morton. He was born Ferdinand La Menthe around 1885. His father F.P. La Menthe was a black Creole, who disappeared early in Ferdinand's life. His mother, a light-skinned Creole, then married a man named Morton. Jelly Roll inherited his mother's light skin that helped him pass for white. Like many lighter-skin Creoles, he looked down on those whose skin was darker than his. He grew up in a musical family and mastered many instruments but preferred piano. By the time Jelly Roll was in his mid-teens, he was making a living playing piano, gambling, and pimping in Storyville. In his piano playing, he tried to reproduce the sound of a marching band with his left hand playing the bass line while his right hand reproduced the lead of a cornet or clarinet. Morton was not the best piano player in the District but what distinguished him from other musicians was his ability to compose and arrange the music that would be known as jazz. These written arrangements allowed musicians outside New Orleans to play this new popular music. Unlike Buddy Bolden, who left no existing recorded examples of his work, Morton recorded extensively throughout his career. Between 1923 and 1939, he cut around 175 sides in varying formats including solo and with his group, the Red Hot Peppers. Sadly, however, Morton outlived his style of jazz's popularity and, unable to adapt to changing musical tastes, died unnoticed in poverty on July 10, 1941.

When David Fulmer's second Valentin St. Cyr novel, Jass, begins, it is 1909 and the young Morton is beginning to under-stand that his future is in the new music rather than hustling and pimping. He was aware that jazz challenged the existing social order, since early bands were often integrated and encouraged social interaction between the races in public places. With the murders of two black musicians, Morton feared that someone opposed to the new music, also recognized its challenge to the status quo, and was willing to kill to stop its spread. Morton shared his concerns with his friend, Creole detective Valentin St. Cyr, who dismissed the murders as an occupational hazard of fast-living musicians. Then two more musicians are murdered, making a total of four deaths within a two-weeks period. Clearly, St. Cyr could no longer pass off the murders as coincidence. He discovers that the four musicians played together in the Union Hall Jazz Band and were rumored to be involved with a white woman. To find their killers, his inquiry reaches beyond the confines of Storyville to confront the power and politics of New Orleans society and its color line.

Although jazz moves to the background in the remaining books of Fulmer's Storyville septet, it's very much a part of the fabric of his stories. In Rampart Street, Tom Anderson requests that St. Cyr look into the murder of John Benedict, a respected Rampart Street businessman. A few days later a second businessman, Charles Kane is drowned. Benedict and Harris were in the shipping business together, along with Henry Harris, who has plans to run for the Senate. Looking for a link between the three that could cause Benedict's and Kane's deaths, he discovers all were members of the Ku Klux Klan and responsible for disturbances on the New Orleans docks that forced most of the small, Italian shippers out of business. Among the casualties was St. Cyr's father. Harris manages to stay a step ahead of St. Cyr until he stumbles into a Sicilian sent to repay a family debt.

In <u>Lost River</u> (2009), set in 1913, three years after <u>Rampart Street</u>, St Cyr has left Storyville to work as private investigator for a fancy St. Charles Street law firm. But a series of murders in Storyville and debts (real and imagined) bring him back into Tom Anderson's domain. Anderson is aging badly with the unsolved, mounting numbers of murders pointing to his loss of control over Storyville. St. Cyr senses that the murders are somehow linked but fails to grasp the pattern. Then Buddy Bolden, locked away in Jackson since 1907, sends for St. Cyr. Bolden repays a debt to St. Cyr, in providing a cryptic clue before he descends into the depths of madness, never really to return. St. Cyr manages to put the pieces together to save the King of Storyville.

In <u>The Iron Angel</u> (2014), set in 1915, a serial murderer named Gregory is roaming Storyville and ritually killing prostitutes. Tom Anderson seems unable to stop him. He persuades a reluctant Valentin St. Cyr to return to Storyville and end the killing spree. St. Cyr, employed by a high-class law firm, senses Storyville's days are numbered and that his future lies elsewhere. Yet he can't refuse his old friend.

Also set in 1915 is <u>Eclipse Alley</u> (2017), in which a prominent businessman's mutilated body is discovered in a dark alley. Within days, three other well-known men are murdered. St. Cyr's friend, New Orleans police detective James McKinney, asks for assistance. St. Cyr agrees to help, knowing it will cost him the security of his private investigative work. As the investigation moves closer to the ailing Tom Anderson, St. Cyr suspects the killer to be a woman. Buddy Bolden's spirit is not far from St. Cyr-he senses his mystical presence on the streets of Storyville and purchases his only known recording, "Careless Love," from a shifty French recordist, Mr. Cyril.

In the final book of Fulmer's Storyville septet, The Day Ends at Dawn (2019), someone fires a shot through Valentin St. Cyr's bedroom window. It's the morning before the 1917 closing of Storyville and St Cyr suspects it's part of the escalating chaos. But he wonders if it's a warning related to the impending arrival from Washington of information connected to the closing of Storyville. A series of violent incidents directed against his wife Justine and his associates indicates that it is. Also, his old nemesis, the disgraced Captain Picot, has returned to New Orleans seeking revenge. Against a background of increasing disorder, St Cyr and Justine must identify an unknown killer.

Nathaniel Rich's King Zeno (2018) focuses on three characters from the dominant ethnic groups in New Orleans that emerged in the political, economic and social shake-out in 1918: Police Detective William Bastrop, an American veteran and acclaimed war hero, was in reality a coward. One of those he betrayed on the battlefield has followed him to New Orleans seeking revenge. Isadore Zeno is a scuffling black jazz musician, hoping to make a living by playing the fancy hotels and large venues. To support his jazz band, he turns to crime. Beatrice Vizzini is the widow of an Italian crime boss, determined to make a legitimate living in the wartime construction boom. The infamous "Axeman" touches the lives of all three.

A generation passes in the Crescent City before the appearance of Robert Skinner's six Wesley Farrell Stories. Due to the closing of Storyville and the economic depression, the Quarter in the 1930s is tamer than in the St. Cyr septet. By the mid-1930s, New Orleans attempted an economic recovery. But jazz was flourishing in places other than Basin Street. The city's Prince of Jazz, Louis Armstrong, (who appeared as a street tough in Fulmer's Chasing the Devil's Tail and Jass) had taken the train north to Chicago to join King Oliver's Band and later settled into a residency with Earl Hines at the Savoy's Terrace Ballroom. (Jazz's other royals were elsewhere as well: Count Basie was packing the Reno Club in Kansas City, and Duke Ellington had seemingly moved into Harlem's Cotton Club.) So when people went out night clubbing in the city where jazz was born, they listened and danced to local swing bands covering national hits.

Wesley Farrell, the owner of the Club Tristesse and Robert Skinner's protagonist in Skin Deep, Blood Red (1997) set in 1936, runs such a place. A former bootlegger, Farrell was a Creole, light enough to pass as white. He hid his past, knowing that his current life and success with the Club Tristesse would end if people knew the truth. It's this fear of discovery and its consequences that dominate Skin Deep, Blood Red. Mob-boss Emile Gans knows Farrell's secret and forces the club owner to use his sources to uncover the killer of a crooked New Orleans cop. Also investigating the murder is white Police Inspector Francis X.F. Casey. Farrell and Casey's investigations run parallel, eventually intersect and tear apart the white underworld.

Israel Daggert joins the series in Cat-Eyed Woman, (1998). A former member of the Negro Detective Squad, Daggert was framed for a murder in 1933 and spent five years in Angola State Penitentiary. He returns to New Orleans to clear his name and marry his sweetheart, Lottie Sonnier, who is killed hours before his return. Lottie's younger sister Marguerite believes the murder will be dismissed as one of many unsolved colored killings and seeks help from Savanna Beaulieu, the elegant owner of the Club Moulin Rouge, the Quarter's finest jazz club. She, in turn, passes the matter on to Farrell. His investigation snakes towards Stella Bascomb, known as the "Cat-Eyed Woman", who is the black mistress of a white mobster. A former prostitute from the Mississippi Delta, Bascomb clawed her way to the top and isn't about to step down without unleashing every man under her power against Farrell and Beaulieu.

The battle with the "Cat-Eyed Woman" proved too much for Beaulieu, who left New Orleans for a new life, running a Central Avenue club in Los Angeles. As Daddy's Gone a-Hunting (1999) begins, Farrell feels lost without her and wonders if things might have been different if they, like his parents, had gotten married in Havana. However, marrying a black woman in 1938 would mean losing everything he had achieved. His loneliness makes him vulnerable to the charms of Carol Donovan, the black owner of the Original Southport Club. Initially, she asks for help in dealing with a shakedown. Blindly, Farrell does her bidding, moving beyond the shakedown towards her ultimate goal-the undoing of a crime boss.

In March 1939 memories of an event occurring five years earlier portends consequences for Wes Farrell in Blood to Drink (2000). He briefly met Coast Guard Commander George Schoefield, who was in charge of interdicting bootlegged whiskey, and witnessed his murder. Now his younger brother, James, a fledgling Treasury agent, comes to New Orleans seeking his brother's killers. Apparently, Farrell's name was on a list of bootleggers found among his possessions. Farrell realizes that if he doesn't uncover the murderers, young Schofield may cause him problems or get him killed.

In the autumn of 1940, war in Europe is almost a foregone conclusion. But in New Orleans, as Pale Shadow (2001) begins, European events seem as distant as those on another planet. Sergeant Israel Daggett is called to the scene of the murder of Linda Blanc, who was tortured to death. Blanc was the girlfriend of Luis Martinez, a former bootlegger and partner of Farrell. Fifteen years have passed since they worked together, and Luis has apparently branched into counterfeiting. But then, things are often not what they seem to be.

In the final Wes Farrell book, The Righteous Cut (2002), the daughter of crooked New Orleans councilman Whitman Richards has been kidnapped. Richards is forced to shut down the police investigation out of concerns that his own illegal activities will be uncovered. Fearing for the life of her daughter, Richards' estranged wife Georgina asks for help from her former boyfriend, Wes Farrell.

The Fulmer books depicted a growing New Orleans on the

brink of fulfilling its musical and economic potential. Skinner's books, however, show a city trying to hold on to its identity in the midst of a national depression in spite of its being stripped of uniqueness as the source of the best jazz in the country. The postwar years changed the face of jazz into bebop, and these changes were not kind to New Orleans. Traditional New Orleans jazz and even swing became passé. Jazz clubs closed, and those that survived were more attuned to separating tourists from their money than attracting jazz musicians. While crime had always been a factor in the Quarter's existence, now the Mafia's presence added darkness to the city. The heirs of the Sicilian avenger, who saved Valentin St. Cyr in <u>Rampart Street</u>, have a more menacing presence. In the postwar years New Orleans was transformed from an easy, happy-go-lucky place into a tough town with all the characteristics and mean streets of classic noir.

A 1950s pulp story by Clark Howard and a novel by Leonce Gaiter reveal the darkness. In Howard's "Horn Man" (1980), a trumpet player named Dix has returned to New Orleans after serving 16 years for a murder committed by his girlfriend, Madge Noble. An old friend awaits his arrival and takes him to Traditional Hall where he is offered a job as well as a silver trumpet once owned by New Orleans trumpet legend Blind Ray Blount. Dix's inclination is to wave it all aside and go looking for Madge, who's living with a young doper named Le Beau. In Leonce Gaiter's novel of vengeance, <u>Bourbon Street</u> (2005), Deke Watley, a Texas gambler, arrives in New Orleans at Mardi Gras for a high stakes poker game. All of the other players are acquainted and share some relationship with blind crime-boss, August Moreau. In a bar, he encounters his old girlfriend Hannah and resumes the affair. But she is now the mistress of Moreau. Clearly, he's been lured to New Orleans for something other than poker and sex.

Moving on to the 1980s, the crime novels of James Lee Burke's Dave Robicheaux are identified with New Orleans. But there's surprisingly little jazz in Burke's Robicheaux stories. Dave Robicheaux's surrounded by zydeco, Cajun music and the blues. Why, living in the city that gave birth to jazz as he does, doesn't he listen to jazz? In The Neon Rain (1987), the reader learns that Robicheaux's family was Cajun. Cajun is short for Acadian, which refers to the Acadians, who were expelled from Nova Scotia in 1755 and settled in southwest Louisiana. They hunted and fished and were definitely not urban types. In fact, Cajun was regarded as Louisiana shorthand for "white trash." The Acadians brought with them a musical heritage of French and Acadian folk songs that mixed local folk music and Afro-Caribbean rhythms, resulting in Cajun music.

Zydeco, on the other hand, is the music of rural, usually black Creoles that mixed Louisiana plantation music with African and Caribbean rhythms. Both Cajun music and zydeco are both rural in origin and closer to the blues than to jazz that stressed wind instruments and had an urban origin. (A more detailed discussion of Robicheaux and zydeco/Cajun music is beyond the scope of this book. Interested readers are referred to three other Burke books: A Stained White Radiance (New York: Hyperion, 1992), Cadillac Jukebox (New York: Hyperion, 1996) and Jolie Blon's Bounce (New York: Simon & Schuster, 2002).

Jazz did have some appeal to Robicheaux. He liked classic jazz with its rough, earthy, unpolished sounds from New Orleans' past. In fact, Robicheaux once had a collection of early jazz recordings by Bunk Johnson, Kid Ory, and Bix Beiderbecke, et al. that were smashed when thugs tore up his houseboat in The Neon Rain. He never replaced them. As Black Cherry Blues (1989) and Last Car to Elysian Fields (2003) show, the blues, not jazz, was his thing. So while you might find Robicheaux in a New Iberia honkytonk listening to the blues (or zydeco or Cajun music), you'd never find him at Snug Harbor listening to Wynton Marsalis play jazz.

By the late 1980s, the Quarter was a faint reflection of its past. The heart of Storyville, Tom Anderson's Annex with its half-block-long bar located at the corner of Basin and Iberville Streets, was just a memory. So too were the jazz clubs like those of Wesley Farrell and Savanna Beaulieu that hung on through the Depression, only to die in the postwar years when jazz was replaced in New Orleans by other forms of music. As always, however, some neighborhood jazz bars survived. In <u>Blue Bottle</u> (1999), James Sallis' Lew Griffin gets shot in the head coming out of one that featured modern jazz rather than Dixieland played for tourists.

The jazz clubs on Basin Street were more interested in separating conventioneers and tourists from their dollars than featuring quality jazz. Fat Jack McGee, a once talented clarinetist, owns such a club in John Lutz's <u>The Right to Sing the Blues</u> (1986). His star attraction, piano player Willy Hollister, shows an interest in singer Ineida Mann, a.k.a. Collins, the sheltered daughter of a local financier with organized crime connections. To sort out things, he calls on his old friend, private investigator (PI) Alo Nudger. After Ineida is kidnapped, both men get more than they bargained for.

Pat Gallegher, a cornet player in a French Quarter bar named Holidays, temporarily hangs up his horn to become a detective in five books by Richard Helms. In <u>Joker Poker</u> (2000), Clancey Vincoeur hires Gallegher to find her missing lover, whom she fears her husband has killed. As his investigation proceeds, he realizes that her husband Lester had links to the New Orleans mob. Gallegher is framed for his murder and needs to find the killers for his own survival. In <u>Voodoo That You Do</u> (2001), Gallegher witnesses the murder of a member of Lucho Braga's Italian mob and is blackmailed into finding the killer. While looking for the killer, he stumbles into the middle of a turf war between the Vietnamese and the Italian Mafia. In <u>Juicy Watsui</u> (2002), Gallegher agrees to help the police find the killer of strippers in the French Quarter. One of the victims was the girlfriend of Gallegher's employer. He joins forces with a retired FBI profiler, Clarence "Clever" Evers, who knows more about the grisly murders than he should. A body is discovered entombed in the floor of a building next to Holiday's in <u>Wet Debt</u> (2003). Gallegher is intrigued by the seventy-years old murder of Scott Everidge, a gunsel (gunman) from Kansas City. After researching the era in the newspaper morgue and interviewing survivors, Gallegher realizes the suave Everidge tried to push his way into New Orleans society and crossed the wrong person. His understanding of the players and the stakes in 1933 prove useful when one of the current Italian crime families becomes interested in him.

In the final book of the quintet, <u>Paid in Spades</u> (2019) Gallegher repays a personal debt to a gambler that leads to a vicious Brazilian gang. At the same time, as a favor to his girlfriend, social worker Merlie Comineau, he's looking for the father of a young girl in her shelter that leads through the Louisiana oil fields to the Brazilians. But Gallegher knows there are no coincidences in his life.

In Julie Smith's contemporary Skip Langdon series, jazz is one of a several kinds of music entertainment in a city hungry for money. It competes with R&B, the blues, zydeco, and Cajun music for listeners and entertainment dollars. In the series debut, <u>New Orleans Mourning</u> (1990), jazz is in the background. The book gives readers a feel for contemporary New Orleans during Mardi Gras. The King of the Carnival, civic leader Chauncey St. Amant, is killed as the parade moves along St. Charles Street. Rookie policewoman Skip Langdon is brought in on the case as she is from a prominent family and can navigate through a social gauntlet worthy of Tennessee Williams. St. Amant was given a New Orleans send-off but it is the Neville Brothers, not the Marsalis Brothers, who play at the funeral.

Smith reaches into New Orleans history for her second Langdon book, <u>The Axeman's Jazz</u>, (1991). In 1919 a serial killer stalked New Orleans. The killings finally stopped, but the killer was never caught. Known as the "Axeman," the killer told the city via letters to the press that anyone in a house playing jazz would be spared. The Axeman apparently has returned in 1991, announced his presence to the media, and killed two people. Newly promoted to the rank of Homicide Detective, Langdon helplessly watches more bodies pile up until there are enough for her to decipher a pattern and identify the killer.

In <u>Jazz Funeral</u> (1993), the promoter-producer of the New Orleans Jazz and Heritage Festival, Hamson Brocato is discovered in his kitchen, murdered with a knife in his chest. As with Chauncey St. Amant's family in <u>New Orleans Mourning</u>, there is no shortage of suspects within Brocato's family and inner circle of friends. Again, Langdon uses her social skills to identify the killer. The only jazz present is the street band that follows Brocato's funeral cortège. Smith's Langdon series continues with other books, but the jazz content is minimal.

Aside from reflecting New Orleans contemporary multi-cultural musical heritage, Smith's books emphasize the importance of family (in society and on the street). In <u>House of Blues</u> (1995), Arthur Hebert, premier restaurateur is shot during a family dinner. When Skip Langdon arrives at the crime scene, his daughter Reed, her ex-addict husband Dennis and their baby Sally, are missing. Initially, Langdon considers a kidnapping gone awry. Hebert's other son, Grady, a fledgling writer, who finds nightly refuge at the House of Blues, relates a dysfunctional family portrait with a rogue daughter, Evie as Sally's mother. Langdon then stumbles into another family's quarrel, revealing Arthur's Mafia ties, eventually allowing politics to win out over justice.

The importance of family is also reflected in Smith's short story "Kid Trombone" (2004), featuring Talba Wallis, a young black computer geek/poetess turned private investigator. Trombone Tyrone or 'Kid Tyrone' as Tyrone Falgout was known, was from a legendary music family and had infamous drug and alcohol problems. He was murdered in his bed. He had been dealing "roofies" (Rohypnol-the date rape drug) from his trombone case while playing on the street and his activities struck a sour note with someone.

All of the books and short stories mentioned are pre-Hurricane Katrina. While the entertainment district, the French Quarter, structurally survived the storm, areas along the 17th Street Canal, such as the Lower Ninth Ward where musicians live, did not fare well. So in this post-K era, it still may be a while before jazz really returns to New Orleans and its mystery fiction.

Jazz:
Kansas City

"I'm going to Kansas City, Kansas City here I come," sang bartender-turned-blues singer Big Joe Turner at Piney Brown's famous Sunset Club, located at 18th and High Streets. The white-owned, black-managed jazz spot was one of around 50 nightclubs within a six-block area of Kansas City's nightclub district, running from 18th Street in the south to 12th Street in the north. If you were a jazz musician in the 1920s and 1930s, Kansas City was what was happening. The New Orleans scene ended in November 1917 when the War Department, fearing for the morals of its soldiers, closed down Storyville. Up the Mississippi River in Chicago, the gang wars made life chancy for musicians, whose livelihoods depended on performing in mobster-owned cabarets and jazz joints. The New York scene was dominated by a few elegant nightclubs like Harlem's Cotton Club, whose elaborate floor show featured scored music by Duke Ellington's orchestra. As for L.A., it was, in those days, little more than scattered bungalows, palm trees and celluloid dreams.

For roughly 20 years, starting with the passage of the Volstead Act in 1919, Kansas City was unique—a city run by corrupt politi-cians and gangsters with a benevolence that let it escape both the gang excesses of Chicago in the '20s and the worst of the Depression in the '30s. Political boss Tom Pendergast's tolerance and interest in bootlegging insured a flow of money into the city. After Prohi-bition was repealed, Pendergast turned to liquor wholesaling, night-clubs, and the cement business. Instead of using cement to entomb competitors as done elsewhere, Pendergast's company, Ready Mixed Concrete, built public buildings, highways and lesser roads in

Kansas City and surrounding Jefferson County. This homegrown precursor of President Franklin Delano Roosevelt's WPA (Works Progress Administration) program provided jobs for many who would be otherwise unemployed. The citizens of Kansas City with money in their pockets spent it on Pendergast liquor in Pendergast-controlled clubs.

Kansas City was more than just a place where there was employment during the Depression. It was famous for its jam sessions, in which jazz musicians would meet after work and often play to exhaustion. Blue Monday (1991), the title of Harper Barnes' book, refers to the sessions following a weekend's work that would continue into the next day. Jam sessions aside, musicians worked long hours. For example, the bands at the famous Reno Club backed four hour-long floorshows, with the first show beginning at 9 pm and the last at 4 am. Between the floorshows, the band provided dance music for the club's patrons, with only a ten-minute break every hour. On Sundays there was also a breakfast dance and jam session, so musicians would work from 9pm on Saturday night straight through until noon Sunday. The work, however, had its compensations, of which fame was high on the list. Reno Club musicians were heard live on a nightly broadcast on a shortwave radio station. Among its listeners in January 1936 was legendary Columbia record producer John Hammond, who heard a Count Basie band broadcast while he was in Chicago. In the spring of 1936, he headed to Kansas City.

The top band in KC, although initially not the best, belonged to Bennie Moten. Born in 1894, Moten started as a baritone horn player, who turned to ragtime as a teenager and studied under two of Scott Joplin's students. As ragtime went out of fashion, Moten's interests shifted to jazz. In 1921, he and his fledgling 6-piece jazz band landed a recording contract and a job at the Panama Club, one of the Pendergast-controlled cabarets. This initiated a mutually profitable relationship between Moten and the Pendergast machine. Financial success enabled him to recruit top musicians from other bands, as few could resist the combination of high wages, guaranteed employment, and a coveted recording contract. Over the years he lured a number of players away from the area's top band, the Oklahoma-based Blue Devils, including (Count) Bill Basie, Eddie Durham, Lester Young and Hot Lips Page. Moten was both a good musician and an astute businessman. When he saw something special in the young Basie, he had no qualms about signing him, although Moten's own role as a pianist was diminished.

At the time of his death in 1935, Moten had reached the top, having just negotiated a long, profitable engagement at the Rainbow Room in Denver, one of the largest ballrooms in the West. The band had gone on to Denver under the leadership of Moten's cousin Bus (and Basie) while Moten himself stayed behind for a postponed tonsillectomy. The evening before the operation, Moten and his surgeon (a longtime friend) went out on the town; the following morning, an artery in Moten's throat was severed during surgery. He drowned in his own blood on the operating table.

After learning of Moten's death, his band returned from Denver, reorganized under Basie's leadership, and continued to play the KC scene. But KC's days as the jazz capital of the Midwest were numbered. In 1938 Pendergast was indicted for income-tax fraud, and his political career ended. With it went prosperity and the jazz scene. Many KC musicians went east, including the old Bennie Moten/Count Basie Orchestra.

Incorporating an incisive knowledge of jazz with local KC history, Harper Barnes uses Bennie Moten's death as a jumping-off point for Blue Monday. His protagonist Michael Holt is a 23-year-old police reporter for the Journal-Post who dreams of following an earlier cub reporter (for the Kansas City Star) to fame and fortune, but there could only be one Ernest Hemingway, so Holt turns to jazz. Most of his evenings are spent with a young, black, college-educated teacher, listening to jazz in KC's clubs. When he reads of the death of bandleader Moten, news that even makes the three white-owned newspapers, he feels the loss personally. Just a few hours earlier, he had seen Moten shooting pool and drinking at the Sunset Club.

Holt wades through the conflicting initial reports to discover that Moten died of a botched tonsillectomy—and that the surgeon who performed the operation has disappeared. When he ends up in

43

the city morgue, Holt senses a big story. He knows that the talk in the jazz clubs is of new drugs in town and muscle from out of state. He saw Piney Brown tossing some Italian thugs out of the Sunset Club. Holt knows that Bennie Moten would close his eyes to a reefer smoked off the bandstand but was known for his opposition to heroin. His quest for truth crosses the color line and teaches an unexpected lesson in race relations.

While jazz is very much in the foreground in Blue Monday, it's in the background in Lise McClendon's One O'clock Jump (2001) and Sweet and Low (2002). It's 1939 when One O'clock Jump begins. Poland has just been invaded, but America remains at peace. At home in Missouri, Pendergast has been convicted on corruption charges and sent to jail. Most of the top jazz bands that gave the city its distinctive sound are gone. Count Basie can usually be heard over the airwaves doing his nightly radio-club gig from New York's Famous Door. But some bonds are hard to break. In One O'clock Jump, PI Dorie Lennox goes dancing at the exclusive Kansas City Club where Julia Lee is playing. Basie, Lester Young, and Jo Jones put in a surprise appearance.

Lennox is a switchblade-carrying PI who works for Sugar Moon Investigations, run by a transplanted Englishman, Amos Haddam. She failed in her first assignment and watched Iris Jackson, the girlfriend of gangster "Gorgeous" George Terranciano, jump from a bridge into the Mississippi River at 1 am. "One o'clock jump. Like the Count Basie tune," she's told by Kansas City Star reporter Harry Talbot. (p.5). Surprisingly, Jackson's boyfriend still wants to retain Lennox to look into his deceased girlfriend's background.

By Dorie Lennox's second outing (1940) in Sweet and Low, the Nazis appear to be winning the war in Europe, and FDR is seeking another term as President. Amos Haddam and Dorie Lennox have been hired to watch over Thalia Hines, the beautiful, rich and willful daughter of Haddam's old friend from WWI, Commander Eveline Hines, who is critically ill. Thalia goes out every night, partying, dancing and singing at K.C.'s jazz clubs. Initially, Haddam took the job as a courtesy to a dying friend. But after a failed kidnapping, he takes it seriously. To add to their problems, the rebellious Thalia has set her sights on a fortune-hunting Nazi sympathizer.

Andres Rodriguez' short story "Yesterday," (2012) is set in the 1970s in a music district now in decline. The owner of Milton's Tap Room, a club that plays records rather than features live jazz, has disappeared. Milton Morris had been around and ran K.C. saloons before Prohibition. After hours, a drunk bangs on a closed door until Tom, the bartender, opens it and hears a story of the mob being after Morris. Following several nights of searching, Tom approaches the indifferent police about Morris' disappearance.

A final K.C. mystery, Lou Jane Temple's The Cornbread Killer (1999) takes place twenty years later. The "historic" music district of Eighteenth and Vine has been renovated and will host a blues and jazz festival. Then the event's planner dies under suspicious circumstances and restaurateur Heaven Lee, who coordinated the catering, takes over. Before the jazz festival even begins, Charlie Parker's plastic saxophone, recently bought at a London auction for $119,000, is stolen from its display case in the new museum.

These five stories offer a history lesson in the rise (Blue Monday), decline (One O'clock Jump, Sweet and Low, and "Yesterdays,") and transformation (The Cornbread Killer) of one of jazz's foremost cities that had its own distinct and influential style of music.

CRIME AND
JAZZ IN CHICAGO

The closing of Storyville wasn't the only reason for the jazz musicians' exodus from New Orleans. By 1917 over a half million blacks, seeking economic opportunities and an escape from Jim Crow (legalized segregation), left the rural South for the urban North, especially Chicago, Detroit, Philadelphia and New York. By the end of the 1920s, a million more left in what sociologist's term, "The Great Migration." Possibly because it was the at the end of the Illinois Central Railway line, more than 50,000 blacks, mostly from the Deep South, settled in Chicago's South Side. Aside from their hopes for a new life, they also brought their taste for jazz and the blues. The entertainment area along South State Street with its clubs and nightspots, known as "The Stroll," could have competed with New Orleans in its heyday.

In July of 1922, Louis Armstrong boarded an Illinois Central train in New Orleans. He was going to join King Oliver's Creole Jazz Band, playing at Chicago's Lincoln Gardens. Oliver, who left New Orleans two years earlier, was now considered the most famous black jazz bandleader in America. With the arrival of young Armstrong, he would have the best jazz band. Oliver also encouraged a group of white high school jazz enthusiasts, later known as the Austin High Gang for the wealthy West Side neighborhood from which they came. These young white musicians were fast learners, developed their own style of jazz that was known as "Dixieland," and were soon playing clubs where black musicians couldn't even get in through the back door.

Despite this racial discrimination, there was plenty of work for both black and white bands in the gangster-owned nightclubs and "speakeasies," where bootleg liquor was available. In the spring of 1923, even the jazz wanderer, Jelly Roll Morton, turned up in Chicago. But the good times that had arrived with the passage of the 18th Amendment (Prohibition) on June 20, 1920 were not to last.

In February 1928, federal agents began raiding North Side nightspots. A new "hip flask" law held that establishments providing "set-ups" (ice, ginger ale, soda water) for patrons to mix with their own alcohol were subject to prosecution. They also raided the black-and-tan (integrated) clubs on the Southside. Seeing the handwriting on the wall, owners began closing their establishments. The kiss of death was a gang war between Al Capone and his rivals with the jazz clubs as prime targets. The Plantation Club, where King Oliver had been playing, was bombed. For jazz musicians, Chicago was no longer safe. In May of 1929, even Louis Armstrong, who was now fronting his own group at the Savoy, headed for New York City. The great days of Chicago jazz were over, yet the predominantly black South Side blues scene continued, and would even see a revival beginning in the 1950s.

Roddy Doyle's <u>Oh, Play That Thing</u> (2004) begins in 1924 Chicago. The trumpet- playing vocalist Louis Armstrong is famous but not a superstar. He hires Henry Smart, an ex-IRA gunman on the run from both the law and New York gangster Owney Madden, to deal with the white club owners and gangsters. But deadly gang rivalries force Armstrong out of work. In order to survive, Armstrong and Smart resort to petty crime. Unexpectedly, Armstrong is offered a job in New York that he can't resist but that his manager Smart should have resisted.

Four years later in Ray Celestin's <u>Dead Man's Blues</u> (2016), Pinkerton Detectives Michael Talbot and Ida Davis inadvertently become involved in the gang war when they are hired to find a thrill-seeking, club-hopping, missing heiress Gwendolyn Van Haren. Unfortunately, she saw too much and even with Ida's friend Louis Armstrong (see Celestin's <u>The Axeman's Jazz</u>, 2014) trawling the clubs for information, they're too late discovering her fate. Meanwhile Al Capone brought in from New York, his old friend

Dante Sanfelippo, a gunman and a fixer, to uncover a traitor in his organization. He learns someone is bringing in drugs from Canada along with Capone's alcohol in a gambit to break his control of the lucrative Chicago scene.

Susanna Calkins' Murder Knocks Twice (2019) and The Fate of a Flapper (2020) offers young Gina Ricci's insider's view of the speakeasy scene before the stock market crash effectively ended the Jazz Age. Her family connections get her a job as a cigarette girl at The Third Door in January 1929 in Murder Knocks Twice. Times were good and there was music, money and liquor around. Having lost her innocence ten months later, she's able to disarm a patron who lost everything in the stock market fluctuations and crash in The Fate of a Flapper.

Less than a decade later, 1930s Chicago was a very different place. The ebullience of the Jazz Age was replaced by the hopelessness of the Depression. Big band swing was replacing King Oliver's style of jazz. Chicago's native son Benny Goodman was beginning his rise to become "The King of Swing" elsewhere. Louis Armstrong managed to adapt and played in New York. The only way private eye Bill Crane of Jonathan Latimer's The Lady in the Morgue (1936) hears him is on the radio. Crane also hears local jazz as he makes the rounds of the dance halls and the surviving jazz clubs in search of an elusive trumpet player. He had been hired to see if "Alice Ross," found hanging naked in a honky-tonk hotel, was actually a missing socialite who had run off with a trumpet player from Rudy Vallee's band. Before he can make the identification, the body is stolen from the Chicago Morgue. After a rye-fueled search around town for the missing body, he realizes that she was not the missing socialite. But he's intrigued that the trumpet player was a presence in both ladies' lives.

While the Chicago jazz scene lost its steam at the end of the 1920s, the blues scene kept chugging along. Ace Atkins' novel, Leavin' Trunk Blues (2000) is set in 2000 but flashes back to the 1950s Chicago. Ruby Walker was one of those thousands who boarded the Illinois Central in Mississippi and arrived in Chicago. Known as "The Sweet Black Angel," she became one of Chicago's greatest blues singers until she killed her lover, record producer Billy Lyons, in September 1959. Now serving a life sentence in jail and forgotten by all but the most erudite blues collectors, she agrees to give Tulane University Blues scholar Nick Travers an interview in exchange for his investigation into Lyons' death. But Travers' investigation awakens old animosities and arouses a killer named Stagger Lee.

A 1980s blues short story that also flashes back to the 1950s is Libby Fischer Hellmann's "Your Sweet Man" (2007). Calvin Rollins picks up his dying father, Johnny Jay, at Joliet Prison where he spent the last thirty years, to bring him home to die. In the 1950s, Johnny Jay and his wife Inez were at the center of the blues scene until Inez left for national fame. When she eventually returned, Johnny Jay and Calvin see her, and she dies in a family dispute. Too quickly, Johnny confessed to her murder.

Stuart M. Kaminsky's short story "Blue Note" (2008), also set in 1950s Chicago, brings together the jazz and blues scenes. Gambler Pitch Noles is called "The Prince of Tell" because of his ability to read other gamblers' body language. He is forced into a poker game with three gamblers who won $20,000 in an earlier, crooked game from a drug dealer named Terrance "Dusk" Oliver. If he doesn't win $40,000 for Oliver by 5 am, Noles' mother Mae, a blues singer with the Count Basie Band, will lose a finger for non-payment of a drug debt.

In another 1950s'story, Chad Byers' Jazzman (1997), Ray Parker plays trumpet in a second-rate club. His girlfriend, a prostitute named Molly, wants to leave Chicago. Ray is too drunk on alcohol and music to realize she's serious about stealing an out-of-town monthly pay-off and skipping town. The mob thinks he's involved and goes after his fingers.

Trumpet-player Johnny Nickle is looking for a guitarist for his band when he comes upon young Connor Johnson in Brad Mengel's "The Devil You Know" (2013). Although Nickle dislikes Johnson's manager, he hires the guitar player. Belatedly, he learns that Connor has been involved with the daughter of a Chicago mobster and that his manager ran out a $1,000 gambling debt. When a Chicago gunman is seen at the club, Johnny knows trouble is on its way.

A Chicago crime story set in the 1960s is David Saunders' M Squad (1962), a pulp spin-off from the popular American television show (starring Lee Marvin) that featured an exciting Count Basie soundtrack. Chicago Police Lieutenant Frank Ballinger must find a serial killer before the killer finds him. But Ballinger's certainty of the killers' identities and their guilt blind him to the fact that there may be two cop killers prowling Chicago's mean streets. While there is no actual jazz in the plot, Saunders has captured the story with such style that the reader can almost hear the Count Basie jazz soundtrack.

By the time tenor saxophone legend Jackson Payne comes to 1970s Chicago in Jack Fuller's The Best of Jackson Payne (2000), the jazz scene is reduced to neighborhood bars. The legendary clubs like the Savoy where Louis Armstrong played or the Pershing where in the 1950s Ahmed Jamal made his name, exist only in memories. But Payne's more interested in finding his drug-addicted daughter, Michelle, than playing jazz. Unfortunately for Payne, his past reputation from L.A. as a police informant on the drug scene, followed him to Chicago.

From the 1970s on, the blues scene overshadowed jazz. The blues clubs often drew a rough clientele, but in Jack Fredrickson's "Good Evening Blues" (2007), The Crossroads seems to be an exception. The failing taproom was transformed by Saturday night open-mike sessions for aspiring, mostly young, white musicians. It's a suspicious deal as the bar owner kept all the profits. His new "partner," a promoter named Pearly Hester, plans to make his money from the aspirant's demos. But Pearly seems to favor those with fancy guitars over those with real talent.

In a 1980s blues story, Stephen Mertz's "Death Blues" (1988), Stomper Crawford, a blues legend missing for eight years, is seen going into a club called Leon's. When investigating the sighting, O'Dair, who is both a blues aficionado and a private investigator, is told that he was misinformed. Upon returning to his car, he's assaulted by two thugs and warned away from inquiring about Crawford. It seems the old blues man is believed to have witnessed a mob killing and is hiding.

In the 1990s, Chicago, like Kansas City and New Orleans, tried to cash in on its vanished jazz past through festivals. In Beth Anderson's Night Sounds (2000), keyboard player Joe Barbarello picks up Joey Bauer, a young woman in the audience at the Ravinia Summer Jazz Festival and spends the next three days with her. He is quickly returned to reality by the Chicago Police, who charge him with being an accomplice in the death of Bauer's former boyfriend. In a deadly parody of "The Producers," he sold more shares in his company than existed. Meanwhile, Barbarello's band, Night Sounds, has been offered a major label recording deal and an imminent tour. Both will be compromised by the pending murder charges.

Another 1990s mystery that reaches into Chicago's jazz past is Michael Raleigh's The Maxwell Street Blues, (1994). Private investigator Paul Whelan is hired by a black attorney to find Sam Burrell, who had a table at the Maxwell Street open-air flea market. Eventually, Burrell's body is found and police charge street punks with his death. But O.C. Brown, an old jazz musician, remains unconvinced of their guilt and encourages Whelan to continue his investigation. To discover Burrell's killer, Whelan ventures into the city's jazz past and unresolved racial problems.

A final contemporary book, Yolanda Joe's Hit Time (2002), focuses on the recording business that became a source of money for the mob after the club scene's demise. As Hit Time begins, a body is discovered floating in Lake Michigan while TV investigative reporter Georgia Barnett is at a nearby charity event. She identifies the body as Fib Weaver, the crooked boss of Hit Time Records, who had a reputation of exploiting his jazz and blues artists. There's no shortage of murder suspects. Topping the list are blues guitarist Jimmy Flamingo and Weaver's estranged son Guy. Barnett, however, suspects the killer to be someone else.

Looking back, Chicago's history of crime, jazz and blues offers writers great background and plots. Their stories provide a snapshot of the city's past, which is inseparable from its music.

JAZZ AND CRIME IN THE BIG APPLE

Every jazz musician wants a slice from the Big Apple (New York City). Jazz may have been born in New Orleans, developed different styles in Chicago, Kansas City and the West Coast, but New York has been the place where innovations happen and money made.

Many of the jazz musicians, who left New Orleans in 1917 after the navy closed Storyville, went to New York City. The city already had a reputation as jazz-friendly. It was the center of the new recording industry, the importance of which was immediately apparent. Few people saw the Original Dixieland "Jass" Band of cornet-playing Nick LaRoca and four New Orleans jazzmen but more than a million purchased the Victor Talking Machine recording of "Livery Stable Blues." With its cornet and trombone mimicking barnyard animal sounds, it was closer to variety music popular at the beginning of the century than to 1920s jazz. It was, however, very different from the polite dance music of the day. Seemingly, on the strength of record sales, the Original Dixieland "Jass" Band was booked into Reisenweber's, the famous restaurant and dancehall, located at Fifty Eighth Street and Eighth Avenue. Within a short time, the band was making over $1,000 a week. This did not escape the notice of organized crime, which understood that the recording business could become a source of income.

An additional attraction of New York for jazz musicians was Tin Pan Alley where tunesmiths turned out popular music for Broadway shows and the country. Music sales were often a substantial part of a jazz musicians' income. For example, the sale in 1923 of several

Duke Ellington compositions helped him survive through a difficult period.

Another attraction for jazz musicians was New York City's dance-halls and nightclubs. Social dancing had become a national craze, acceptable for middle class Americans, and no more so than in New York City. In 1914 the elegant English dance team of Irene and Vernon Castle toured America demonstrating "the Castle Fox-Trot." (The provocative dances of the ragtime era were not on their dance cards.) A factor in the Castles' success was the ten-piece black dance orchestra led by James Reece Europe. The Castles were fascinated by Europe's playing of W.C. Handy's "Memphis Blues" and created the fox trot to be danced to it.

After the Castles' return to England, Europe's orchestra and small groups were in demand at white society functions. His dance music was not jazz as 1920's bandleaders like Fletcher Henderson would later play. But with its unusual rhythms, riffs and solos, it helped New Yorkers become receptive to new forms in music. (Europe, who survived World War I as a commissioned officer in the 369th (the Harlem Hellfighters) brought the regimental band to an enthusiastic reception in France and opened a door for jazz. He wouldn't see his music's widespread postwar acceptance, however, as he was murdered by a mentally-ill band member in 1919).

New York's greatest attraction for jazz musicians was Harlem. New York City was another destination for blacks leaving the south during "The Great Migration." It was home to more blacks than any Northern city (including Chicago) and most lived uptown in Harlem. In the 1920s, Harlem was a middle/working class community, unlike what it later became. It was the era of the Harlem Renaissance, when writers, artists, intellectuals, and musicians flocked to live in a black community.

On January 20, 1920, the 18th Amendment, which prohibited the sale of alcohol, became law in the United States. Jazz, which had been slowly moving away from its shady past to genteel associ-ation with dancers like the Castles and concert hall performances, was thrust back to its criminal associations. The Castles' foxtrot was kicked aside by the Charleston. They danced it on the top of taxis driving down 5th Avenue, on tabletops in speakeasies, and in huge dancehalls like the Roseland or the Savoy. Over 5,000 speakeasies, serving bootleg liquor, sprung up in New York City. Owney Madden and other gangsters opened posh nightclubs, such as the Cotton Club, where Duke Ellington took up residence in the late 1920s and stayed for almost a decade.

Jazz was not limited to the nightclubs and dancehalls of Harlem. For example, in 1924 black bandleader Fletcher Henderson, with tenor saxophonist Coleman Hawkins, settled into the Roseland Ballroom in Times Square. (A few blocks away in the basement Hollywood Club, the young Duke Ellington learned his trade.) The popular white bandleader Paul Whiteman had a long stay at the Palais Royale off Broadway. Whiteman's Orchestra even played Carnegie Hall in 1924. At that famous concert, George Gershwin's "Rhapsody in Blue" had its debut.

In the speakeasies and clubs of the Big Apple, film and Broadway stars, politicians, gangsters, newspapermen and club patrons mixed freely as reflected in John Roebart's <u>Sing Out Sweet Homicide</u> (1961). In this story, a numbers runner is killed in a hit-and-run accident that is dismissed by police as a drunk-driving case. Newspaperman Scott Norris from the New York Record believes that there is more to his death than the police admit. Norris spends his time at The Charleston Club where he meets with sources and has a girlfriend, a singer named Pinky, who dances in the Charleston line. In an evening he encounters everyone from Mayor James Walker to mobster Sky Mattison (based on Owney Madden).

Owney Madden's fictional biography, <u>And All the Saints</u> (2003) by Michael Walsh, details a time when mobsters were celebrities in New York. Madden, who made his money brewing beer, was one of the founders of the Crime Commission, a group of gangsters who divided up the bounty from Prohibition. He opened the Cotton Club, which employed Duke Ellington and Louis Armstrong. With the exception of the entertainers and staff, no blacks were permitted entry, except prizefighter Jack Johnson who had sold the club to Madden. (The stars and staff went next door to 646 Lenox for a shot, a snort or a smoke). Madden remembered: "At the Cotton

Club everybody who was anybody, and everybody who wanted to be somebody, showed his face. Jimmy Walker was a regular, toddling in most nights after midnight; no wonder the press called him 'the night mayor of New York.' " (p.222). Writer Damon Runyon and gossip columnist Walter Winchell were also regulars.

A similar picture of organized crime's hold on nightlife in the Big Apple appears in Roddy Doyle's <u>Oh! Play That Thing</u> (2004). Henry Smart, an ex-IRA gunman and hustler, flees from New York City to Chicago after problems with gangsters Owney Madden and Dutch Schultz. In Chicago, he meets Louis Armstrong and becomes "his white man." He secures jobs, negotiates salaries and ensures that Armstrong got paid. When Armstrong gets an offer of work in New York that includes recording with his own group, the Hot Five, they go to New York. Working in New York meant national exposure from radio broadcasts from nightclubs like the Cotton Club. In the Big Apple, Louis would have only one manager—and it wasn't going to be Smart.

Two short stories reflect the gangster culture in which jazz flourished in 1920s Manhattan. In Max Allen Collins and Matthew V. Clemens' "East Side, West Side" (2004), private eye Mickey Ashford is about to get married when his matron of honor, actress Mae West, goes missing. He traces West, who was Owney Madden's ex-girlfriend, to the Gramercy Hotel, where she is visiting actor-gangster George Raft. In another part of Manhattan in Martin Myers' "Snake Rag," jazz musician-aspiring detective Vito Monte is hired to retrieve two diamonds stolen from gangster Legs Diamond's courier. In the course of his search, he encounters clarinetist Bix Beiderbecke and saxophonist Frank Trumbauer, known in jazz history as Bix and Tram, who are in the Big Apple to make their soon-to-be classic jazz records at the Okeh studio.

On October 24, 1929, the American stock market crashed, an event that ushered in the Great Depression. By the early 1930s, 15 million Americans, one out of every four wage earners, were out of work. Even in the Big Apple, the music business was badly hit. Dancehalls closed and half of the theatres on Broadway were dark. Most record companies ceased production. Those that survived did so, barely. If people no longer had the money to buy jazz records, they did listen to the music on the radio. For example, Duke Ellington's Orchestra was broadcast live from the Cotton Club; and Benny Goodman had a radio show.

For a while, Harlem's gangster-owned nightclubs survived. After Prohibition's repeal in 1933, they had fancier floorshows and more music to keep downtown white patrons coming to their clubs. Duke Ellington worked steadily at the Cotton Club throughout the 1930s. White jazz fans and thrill seekers still went uptown for the jazz and the atmosphere, while white musicians went there to play in late night jam sessions. White and black jazz musicians might play the same music, but never in the same band because of racial segregation. (Even top bandleaders like Benny Goodman and Artie Shaw had problems when pianist Teddy Wilson and singer Billie Holiday joined their respective bands in the 1930s.) Katherine Courtland, the missing heiress that private eye (PI) Bill Crane searches for in Jonathan Latimer's <u>The Lady in the Morgue</u> (1988), meets a white trumpet player from Rudy Valee's band named Sam Udoni in a Harlem Club. Crane observes: "...a lot of good white musicians go down to Harlem after they finish playing and practice with the black bands. They get a chance to make up variations in Harlem, while they have to stick to the straight music with commercial bands." (p.148).

People found money to go out for an evening and dance their troubles away. The largest Harlem dancehall was the Savoy, where bandleader-drummer Chick Webb and his vocalist Ella Fitzgerald headlined. It extended an entire city block on Lenox Avenue, between 140th and 141st streets. The Savoy always had two bands, so the music never stopped. New York City became home base for many of the big bands that crisscrossed America. Big band swing dances (like the jitterbug) replaced the Charleston.

Increasing racial tensions in Harlem in the 1930s caused the jazz scene to slowly shift downtown to the West Side. On 52nd Street between Fifth and Seventh Avenues were two blocks of jazz clubs, such as The Spotlite, the Yacht Club, The Three Deuces, Jimmy Ryan's, Leon and Eddie's, The Onyx and The Famous Door, where the best musicians played jazz. There never had been such a cluster of jazz clubs in New Orleans, in Chicago, or in Kansas City.

The Onyx began its life in the 1920s as a musician's speakeasy. The password for entry had been "802", the number of the white musicians' union. Harry MacNeil in H. Paul Jeffers' Rubout at The Onyx (1981) has his office above the Onyx but spends much of his time downstairs listening to Art Tatum at the piano. As former policeman-turned-private eye and clarinetist, Harry is an enthusiast with friends and roots in the jazz community. He is hired by Gloria Seldes to investigate the murder of her husband Joey, a low-level gunsel in Owney Madden's gang, who was gunned down on New Year's Eve at the Onyx Club. His investigation reveals that Joey was involved in a 3½ million dollars diamond robbery. Rubout at the Onyx is filled with 1935 atmosphere, great jazz and cameo appearances by pianist Art Tatum, bandleaders Jimmie Lunceford and Paul Whiteman, composer George Gershwin, gossip columnist Walter Winchell, Police Commissioner Lewis Valentine, and the 100th mayor of New York, James John Walker.

In MacNeil's second case, The Rag Doll Murder (1982), Harry still has his office above the Onyx Club. Art Tatum has moved on and jazz violinist Stuff Smith' group, featuring the one-armed trumpet player Wingy Malone, is the source of Harry's evening entertainment. Evelyn Procter, the sister of slain fashion model Jamey Flamingo, hires Harry to find Flamingo's killer. The police have charged a mentally limited delivery boy for the crime but Evelyn and Harry think his guilt is improbable.

His last case, Murder on Mike (1984), takes place four years later in 1939. Stuff Smith is back at the Onyx Club. But Harry has moved his office around the corner because of a fire. Changes on the jazz scene did not to portend well for its future in the Big Apple. Most striking is the move of the Cotton Club from its old location on 125th Street, where it had been for a dozen years, to a new mid-town location at Broadway and 48th Street. The entertainment is still top-notch, however, as Harry sees headliners Maxine Sullivan and Louis Armstrong. But the move was caused by economic factors related to the Depression and the increasing incidences of racial violence. The uptown blacks resented the downtown white club goers and thrill seekers. Harlem was becoming unsafe for white jazz fans. As if this wasn't enough of a problem for club owners, radio was becoming an alternative source for music and entertainment.

As Murder on Mike begins, Harry has been hired by Maggie Skeffington, the co-star of a popular radio crime show to prove the innocence of announcer David Reed, the show's announcer. Derek Worthington, the star and producer, was discovered dead in an empty studio. The show's entire cast has alibis, except Reed. Harry gets his killer, but he's disillusioned. He tells Maggie, "I'm an ex-cop who's now a private investigator who'd prefer nothing better than to play clarinet with a top jazz band and leave the detective work to guys better than me." (p.117).

The decline of the big bands is still in the future as Octavus Cohen's Danger In Paradise (1944) begins in wartime New York City. Big-Band singer-radio star Iris Drake has just returned from a U.S.O. (United Service Organization) tour of Caribbean military bases. In Cuba, she met a Cuban playboy, who asks her to bring a box of El Corsario cigars to a friend in New York. Iris decides to buy another box for her friend, Jimmy Drake. The boxes get switched inadvertently with murderous consequences.

Two other wartime mysteries, John L. Benton's Talent for Murder (1942) and Robert Avery's Murder On The Down (1944) reflect the jazz scene on the home front. In John L. Benton's Talent for Murder (1942), Hamilton Scott, a successful young construction engineer, decides that he doesn't want to marry the boss' daughter and flees from a stifling house party to drink himself into oblivion at the Alligator Club on 52nd Street. The next morning, Scott awakes to find both that he has a job as the band's piano player and is suspect in a murder. To clear himself, he enters a world of war profiteering and murder.

Robert Avery's Murder on The Downbeat (1944) is set in the jazz clubs of Harlem and 52nd Street. Newspaper columnist Malachy Bliss and his girlfriend Julie Mitchell are enjoying an after-hours jam session in a Harlem club when Steve Sisson (modeled on Benny Goodman), a popular clarinetist, is discovered at his table with a thin steel spike through his brain. The police arrest Mitchell as the killer since she was the last person to speak with him. Sisson had destroyed her career as a radio singer. To get her released, Bliss must ferret out the killer from a group of suspects that includes a Harlem gangster, a club owner, an aspiring blues singer, a famous bandleader and various musicians from within Sisson's band. Bliss does his detecting between drinking highballs, scouting for new jazz talent, and filing his newspaper column. He will remind readers of Dashiell Hammett's Nick Charles. Both <u>Talent for Murder</u> and <u>Murder on the Downbeat</u> offer memorable descriptions of the classic jazz clubs of Harlem and 52nd Street in their heyday.

Throughout the 1940s, the jazz scene was changing, reflecting the economy and American popular taste. The government was slow to remove a 30% wartime entertainment tax that affected attendance at dance halls and jazz clubs. Bandleaders faced increasing travel costs and shrinking audiences. Some bandleaders like Duke Ellington and Count Basie survived, but others like Les Brown, Tommy Dorsey, Harry James, and Benny Goodman, were forced to dissolve their bands. They were unable even to find work in the clubs along 52nd Street. Economics demanded that struggling club-owners book small groups. By the end of the 1940s, swing was no longer the thing.

Jazz was also changing into music for listening rather than dancing. In its new incarnation, it had challenging harmonic structures that were difficult for some jazz fans to understand. Young musicians, who had come out of the big bands, such as alto saxophonist Charlie Parker and trumpeter Dizzy Gillespie, played bebop. The brilliant but erratic Parker had a hard drug habit that many of his followers and fans adopted. Consequently, by the late 1940s and early 1950s, jazz was linked with hard drug use.

The jazz scene changed considerably on 52nd Street in the late 1940s when the events of Evan Hunter's <u>Quartet in H</u> (1956) occur. Although not a conventional mystery, it tells the story of a talented young trumpet player, Andy Silvera, who was the youngest member of a wartime big band. He uses marijuana and progresses on to hard drugs. Before he dies from hepatitis contracted from a dirty needle, he manages to wreck the lives of everyone around him. Hunter's story portrays the links between drugs and bebop.

Another story linking bebop and drug use is Douglass Wallop's Night Light (1953) set in New York City's declining jazz scene of the 1950s. Robert Horne's daughter Barbara was shot by a mentally disturbed man who then jumps/falls to his death. Her killer is identified as Alfie Lambert, a talented bebop drummer. Crazed by grief, Horne decides to take revenge by killing Lambert's father. Following the image of the day, the jazz musicians, especially the bebop players, are portrayed as drug-using social outcasts.

Evan Hunter was more even-handed in Streets of Gold (1974) written twenty years after Quartet in H. Ignazio "Iggy" Silvio Di Palermo was born blind in an Italian neighborhood in East Harlem in 1926. A piano protégé, he is on his way to success in the classical world until he discovers an Art Tatum record. Iggy convinces an older piano player named Biff Anderson to teach him jazz fundamentals. They frequent the clubs on 52nd Street until Anderson dies from a drug overdose. In 1955 Iggy changes his name to Dwight Jamison and records "The Man I Love," which becomes an unexpected hit. At this point, the Mafia step into his life.

In the late 1940s, the wartime truce between the Five (Mafia) Families in New York City, overseen by gangster Frank Costello, was breaking down. In Ray Celestin's The Mobster's Lament (2019), set in 1947, Gabriel Leveson, who runs the Copa for Costello, senses trouble and wants out by faking his own death. Before he can act, Costello tasks him with recovering a missing $2 million dollars. Leveson suspects one of the Families, probably Vito Genovese's, has the money. Costello wants his money back but won't support violence resulting in a gang war with Genovese and is willing to sacrifice Leveson.

1950s Manhattan frames a novel and a short story featuring private detective Pete Chambers by potboiler specialist, Henry Kane. In Until You Are Dead (1951) piano player Kermit Teshle witnesses a murder and blackmails the killer for the $100,000 he needs to open a jazz club. He wants to hire Pete Chambers to accompany him to the payoff. Chambers refuses. Teshle is murdered and the payoff money disappeared. Out of guilt, Chambers prowls the mean streets and jazz clubs looking for Teshle's killer. In Kane's short story, "One Little Bullet" (1960), Pete Chambers is sitting in a cocktail lounge when the owner, Joe Malamed, is shot during a drum roll from an Afro-Cuban jazz floorshow. The shooter was sitting at a nearby table of five people, each of whom had motive to kill Malamed.

By the 1950s, singers, mostly veterans from the big bands, dominated the music industry. William Irish (Cornell Woolrich) wrote a short story, "The Jazz Record" (1965) about a crooner's premonition of his own death that appears on an odd pressing of a record. In Frank Kane's Juke Box King (1959), singer Mickey Denton catches the ear of mobster Tony Agnelli in a Long Island Club. He becomes convinced Denton could be a significant source of money for the New York mob. They marshal their resources behind Denton, insuring jukebox hits, bookings at top clubs, and a movie deal. Agnelli planned to use Denton to break gangster Bugsy Spiegel and the Chicago mob's hold on Hollywood. In Richard Jessup's Lowdown (1958), Walker Alise sings over a stolen master tape of a song, "White Midnight" by a popular bandleader. He impresses the mob with his tape, and under their guidance, his singing career takes off in the direction of Hollywood. Like Mickey Denton in Juke Box King, Walker Alise becomes a mob asset without a safety net as he burned too many people along his way to the top.

1950s Harlem is the setting for a short story by Grace F. Edwards and the early Chester Himes novels. Gone are the glory days. It is now a very tough and depressed neighborhood with all the associated problems of poverty, unemployment, and crime. In Grace F. Edwards' short story, "The Blind Alley," tenor saxophonist Matthew Paige awakens from a disturbing dream and goes to lead his weekend combo at the Blind Alley. His gig is disrupted by the appearance of recently released ex-convict, Rhino, who is unwelcome in the neighborhood. As Matthew is leaving the club at the end of the evening, he remembers that he was murdered in his dream. Edwards incorporated this as a chapter in a novel, The Blind Alley, (2010), a realistic story of Rhino's negative impact on 7 families living in a small tenement.

Harlem in the late 1950s and early 1960s provides the background for Chester Himes' eight police procedurals, featuring Coffin Ed Johnson and Grave Digger Jones. It was a time of riots, violence, and corruption and the potent mix of competing black movements (Black Power, Black Muslims and Black Jesus).

In 1957 the French editor Marcel Duhamel of Gallimard Press approached the black American expatriate writer to create a series of detective stories set in Harlem. The French were fans of the hard-boiled school of detective fiction created by the American writers Dashiell Hammett and Raymond Chandler and enthusiasts of American black culture. Duhamel wanted his author, who had never written detective fiction but served time in jail for robbery, to write a detective series set in Harlem. It was the first time a black writer wrote a black detective series for a white audience. Unlike Grace F. Edwards' short story and novel, the resulting series bore little resemblance to the realities of life and grew more detached and violent as the series progressed. But French loved them, as have a lot of other readers.

Hines' police procedurals are about the usual subjects: murder and vengeance: (The Real Cool Killers, 1985), (The Crazy Kill, 1984) and (Blind Man with a Pistol, 1989), theft of money: (All Shot Up, 1969), (Cotton Comes to Harlem, 1985), A Rage in Harlem, 1985), and (The Big Gold Dream, 1988) and drugs: (The Heat's On, 1986). Jazz appears in the background of these books, giving the reader a sense of its place in the black community as well as adding to the plot. For example, in Cotton Comes to Harlem both men stop at Big Wilt's Small's Paradise to look for stoolies (informants), watch the dancers and listen to the band. As the saxophones and trumpets trade choruses, Grave Digger Jones says: "If we could read that language, man, we could solve all the crimes in the world." Coffin Ed Johnson agrees but wants to leave as "Jazz talks too much to me." Grave Digger adds: "It ain't so much what it says…its what you can't do about it." (p.33). Another instance where jazz sets the mood occurs in The Real Cool Killers, as a white man goes into bar looking for trouble. Big Joe Turner, the Kansas City bluesman, is wailing from a jukebox and sudden violence is just a beat or two away.

A few of the landmark jazz clubs still survived. The transformed Five Spot, now drew a predominantly white, listening crowd in 1958 rather than a participatory black one. That said, Coffin Ed and Grave Digger Jones still take witness, John Babson, to hear Thelonious Monk after the three were canvassing the area for a suspect in <u>Blind Man with a Pistol</u>. Babson slips away and is murdered in front of the club.

In the 1960s, New York City was home to a series of private eyes. One of the more famous, thanks to a short-lived, television series, was Johnny Staccato (portrayed by John Cassavetes). The front jacket blurb on Frank Boyd's <u>Johnny Staccato</u> (1960) describes him as: "A smooth man on the ivories, hot on the trigger, and cool in a jam." Staccato plays piano at Waldo's, a Greenwich Village bar and does a bit of detecting on the side. Or maybe, it's the other way around as he's licensed to carry a gun. His ex-girlfriend, Shelley Carroll, calls him after she is arrested for the murder of a music publisher-DJ named Les Miller. As a musician, Staccato knows that Miller has no shortage of enemies within the business, ranging from singers, songwriters, publishers, mobsters to family members. Another private detective slugging through the 1960s music business is Johnny Fletcher in Frank Gruber's <u>Swing Low Swing Dead</u> (1964). On a forty-dollar bet in a card game, Fletcher's friend Sam Cragg wins an unpublished song from its composer. The composer is later murdered and Cragg is offered $50,000 for its rights. The offer is a gambit in a larger game for rights to a best-selling song.

Private detective Johnny Amsterdam comes to the rescue of jazz singer Sandra Tyson in Michael Lawrence's <u>I Like It Cool</u> (1960). Tyson is the unacknowledged daughter of the famous cartoonist Mark Tyson. Her mother, now destitute, was the source of the idea of his comic strip. The singer's approach to Tyson for help ended badly. When he is murdered, she becomes suspect.

No one wrote better about 1960s New York City than columnist-jazz critic Nat Hentoff in his three novels <u>Call the Keeper</u> (1966), <u>Blues for Charlie Darwin</u> (1982), and <u>The Man from Internal</u>

Affairs, (1985). The 1960s were a time when jazz clubs were struggling to survive in a losing battle with rock music. Black power, political issues and fusion jazz sidetracked the music. Consequently, it was losing its audience. The political and social alliance between Jews and blacks was breaking down, depriving jazz of the money and management that insured its survival in earlier, difficult times, such as the Great Depression. Hentoff's protagonists are Jewish cops who are jazz fans. In his first novel, Call the Keeper (1966), a crooked NYPD detective named Harry Sanders was murdered. Detective Horowitz, who was assigned the case, knows everyone is better off with Sanders dead. Nevertheless, he focuses on Sanders' recent victims for the killer. The jazz-loving Horowitz realizes that a prime suspect is Randal, a well-regarded white jazz guitarist, who was working with a questionable cabaret card (required for work in the city). Randal had a minor narcotics problem in his past that should have kept him from getting the card. Other suspects are a young black power activist and his sister, who dates white men, as well as a psychopath named Septimus. In a memorable scene when Horowitz has dropped into a club to listen to Randal, the legendary tenor saxophonist Coleman Hawkins also stops in. Although he is from a different generation, Hawkins can appreciate the younger players' efforts. Another old-time musician, a trumpet player now working as a messenger, also stops by and expresses his bitterness about the new jazz scene.

In Blues for Charlie Darwin (1984), NYPD Detectives Noah Green and Sam McKibbon investigate the murders of two women: Kathleen Ginsberg, the wife of an NYU (New York University) professor and Emma Dixon, the owner of a small Greenwich Village bookstore. Both women were murdered in their homes. As a respite from the investigations, jazz fans Green and McKibbon go out to the few remaining clubs to see drummer Art Blakey and the Jazz Messengers and hear singer Betty Carter. In Hentoff's final volume, The Man from Internal Affairs, (1985), Detective Green's search for the killer of two prostitutes and a junkie is hampered by corruption charges leveled against him by an anti-Semitic, retired cop. Attorney Jason Mendelssohn represents Green in front of the

Internal Affairs Division. They are both Jewish, first-generation Americans, had gone to Boys High School in Brooklyn together and shared a jazz obsession.

By the 1970s, the jazz scene in New York City had been reduced further. Very few jazz clubs survived. Joey Streeter, the owner of Pal Joey's on West Fiftieth Street, in J. F. Burke's The Kama Sutra Tango, (1977) is, however, an exception. Streeter, a jazz piano player, started a neighborhood club and expanded it as the benefits of the overflow from nearby Andy Warhol's Factory became evident. He takes on a partner, jazz buff Jock. Eventually, he learns that Jock is the nephew of a powerful Mafioso. Streeter witnesses the murder of Jock. He is framed for the murder but the frame is so obvious that even the police look elsewhere for the killer. Streeter realizes that his partner was an aspiring porn filmmaker and blackmailer when he discovers a list of films starring nine patrons who were at Pal Joey's the night of the murder. Things get dangerous when someone believes Streeter has the actual films.

A second Joey Streeter novel depicts the continued reduction of the jazz scene. In the year since his partner's death, jazz pianist Joey Streeter has transformed Pal Joey's from a jazz club to a cabaret where the evening's final set is televised. As Crazy Woman Blues (1978) begins, Alice, the girl in the magician's disappearing act, fails to reappear. Concerned but not yet worried about her safety, Streeter goes looking for her. He discovers two thugs ransacking her dressing room and realizes the possibility of criminal involvement.

In the 1980s and beyond, as jazz clubs became scarcer, club owners are less often the subjects of jazz mysteries. The novels now tend either to focus on individual jazz musicians or to have jazz as a background element, such as an interest of a detective. One exception is Paul Pines' The Tin Angel, (1983) set in 1980s Manhattan. Pablo Waitz's jazz club, The Tin Angel, located in the East Village, has survived. But his partner, Miguel Ponce, has not. He is killed in a shoot-out that also claims the lives of two policemen. The police think Waitz knows the killers' identity. Waitz is determined to find out why Ponce was killed.

Artie Deemer, the reluctant detective in a series by Dallas

Murphy, makes his debut in the late 1980s. Deemer spends most of his time sitting in a Morris chair, smoking dope, listening to jazz records and watching the tugboats on the Hudson River. His lifestyle is supported by Jellyroll, the advertising "spokes-dog" for a dog food company. In Lover Man (1987), his existence is disrupted by the NYPD, who inform him that his girlfriend, Billie Burke, was discovered bound and drowned in her apartment. A posthumous message sends him after her killer. Lush Life (1992) finds Deemer falling for Crystal Spivey, a top-rated pool player and ex-wife of his law school friend, Trammell Weems. Weems has disappeared after looting a bank that laundered money for the CIA, the mob and various criminals. An angry depositor kidnaps Spivey, who is rescued by Deemer. It appears everyone is more interested a nonexistent tape than recovering their money. As with Lover Man, the title Lush Life gives the story a little more kick for readers familiar with the song.

A number of other jazz-crime series set in New York debuted in the 1990s and continued through the decade. Charlotte Carter's Nanette Hayes is a black tenor saxophone-playing musician, who finds trouble on the mean streets of the Big Apple. In Rhode Island Red (1997), she unknowingly is used in a scam to find Charlie Parker's legendary golden alto saxophone. Known as "Rhode Island Red", the saxophone was stuffed with dope and given to Parker as payment for gig on Long Island. It was stolen from him dockside before he left for a 1950s European tour.

Voodoo is a subject of Nanette Hayes' next outing in Drumsticks (2000). Hayes is given a mojo doll made by a street vendor. Her recent bad luck changes and she gets a prestige gig at an upscale eatery. Nanette seeks out the maker of the doll, Ida Williams, and invites her to the opening. In a seemingly freak accident, Williams is shot after arriving at the restaurant. During the ensuing investigation, Nanette discovers Williams was into blackmail as well as voodoo.

A second series with a black heroine is Grace F. Edwards' Mali Anderson. Anderson, the daughter of a jazz musician, lives in an area of Harlem (Striver's Row) that has managed to hold on to the dignity of its past. Her father has instilled in her an understanding of Harlem's heritage. For example, she knows where the old Savoy dancehall and the Cotton Club were located on Lenox Avenue. Her father has a job playing piano at the New Club Harlem on Malcolm X Boulevard, a supper club and an attempt to bring jazz back into the neighborhood. But jazz is very much in the background in the first book of the series, If I Should Die (1997), a story about smuggling drugs.

Jazz moves closer to the foreground in A Toast Before Dying (1998). At a popular Harlem club called the Half Moon Bar, a barmaid and singer with Mali Anderson's father's jazz band, Thea Morris, is killed in an alleyway. Kendrick Owen, her ex-boyfriend and club bartender, was in the alley and tried to run to her rescue. He is arrested as a prime suspect. Mali is determined to clear his name by finding the real killer.

No Time to Die (1999) is a story of serial murder in Harlem in which several of Mali's friends fall victim to the killer. Mali fears that she and/or her father may be the killer's next victim unless she discovers his identity. Again, there's not much jazz here. There are a few snippets of Harlem's jazz past as background. For example, Mali walks by the boarded-up site of the old clubs like Small's, where street vendors set up their wares in the once elegant club fronts.

In the final Mali Anderson story Do or Die (2000), she returns from a jazz cruise on the QEII to find that Star Hendrix, the daughter of her father's piano player and sometime singer in her father's band, was murdered. Mali scours Harlem's "three B's" (beauty parlors, barber shops, and bars) for leads in unmasking the killer. As with the earlier books, jazz is mostly in the background, framing the story with its history.

Another series that debuted in the 1990s is Reggie Nadelson's Artie Cohen police procedurals that are usually set in New York City but also have episodes in London, Paris, Moscow and Hong Kong. Cohen was born Artemy Ostalsky in Moscow, the son of a former KGB official. He immigrated to New York City via Tel Aviv. His family was forced to leave the Soviet Union because of his mother's dissident activities. Artie would become a NYPD officer, and later, a private investigator. His cases often have a Russian slant.

Artie first heard jazz through Willis Conover's Voice of America radio program. The musicians frequently featured were singer Billie Holiday, pianists Errol Garner and Oscar Peterson, trumpeter Chet Baker, and tenor saxophonists Lester Young and Stan Getz. They remained among his favorites throughout his life. His father's position in the KGB gave Artie access to such luxury items as jazz records. His most prized possession was Stan Getz's album, *The Steamer*. It remained important in his life and appears in four books. Unlike Hentoff's 1960s jazz loving, Jewish police officers Green and Horowitz, Artie doesn't go out to New York's jazz clubs. The closest he ever got to a jazz legend was sleeping with tenor player Stan Getz's ex-girlfriend in <u>Bloody London</u> (1999). His relationship with the jazz greats is through vinyl records and CDs.

Artie's cases as a police officer and a private investigator do not concern jazz. They focus on organized crime: <u>Sex Dolls</u> (2002); drugs: <u>Hot Poppies</u> (1997) and <u>Sex Dolls</u> (2002); murder: <u>Fresh Kills</u> (2007), <u>Bloody London</u> (1999), <u>Disturbed Earth</u> (2004), <u>Red Hook</u> (2006), <u>Londongrad</u>, (2009) and <u>Blood Count</u> (2010.) His most unusual case concerned the theft of nuclear material (<u>Red Hot Blues</u>, 1998). Jazz is in the background of all these stories. For him, jazz serves as lifeline to the world as well as an escape from it.

Artie's cases crisscross the city and, for example, take him from Brighton Beach (<u>Red Hot Blues</u>) to Sutton Place (<u>Bloody London</u>) and Chinatown (<u>Hot Poppies</u>) to Sugar Hill (<u>Blood Count</u>). One story that's uniquely New York is <u>Blood Count</u>, which is set in 2008 Harlem. Artie gets a confused call from his ex-girlfriend Lily, living at the historic Louis Armstrong Apartments in the Sugar Hill section of Harlem, about the death of her Russian neighbor, Marianna Simonova. He learns that several elderly residents have also recently died. Carver Lennox, an ambitious, black entrepreneur, has been pressuring older residents to sell their units to him for renovation. Artie suspects Lennox killed them for their units to pay off his debts incurred in the 2008 financial crisis. Despite Barak Obama's recent election, Artie's investigation is hampered by the color line. Even for a jazz lover, some things don't change.

A final story of jazz and crime in the Big Apple is John Harvey's In a True Light (2002). Sloane, an art forger recently released from two years in an English jail, finds a letter from American painter, Jane Graham, with who he had an affair in New York in the 1950s. Dying of leukemia, she tells him of a daughter, Connie, he never knew. She asks Sloane to find her as they have been estranged for a decade. He locates her in New York where she is singing in a mob-controlled club. (It's a long way from *The Five Spot* where Sloane heard pianist Thelonious Monk play in the 1950s.) Her abusive manager-lover Vincent Delaney may have killed his last singer and certainly beat up at least two other women. At the same time Sloane is trying to convince her to leave Delaney, the NYPD are building a murder case against him.

Clearly, New York jazz mysteries illustrate the social, political, geographic and aesthetic changes through the decades. They also reflect jazz's diminishing importance in the city. In periods when jazz flourished and the mob controlled the clubs, jazz is front and center as the subject matter of the novels and short stories. When jazz's presence wanes, it is often relegated to the background, used to set the mood of the story or to give it history.

WEST COAST: L.A. JAZZ

When the 1917 influx of jazz musicians arrived from Storyville looking for work, Los Angeles offered limited possibilities. It was still very much a seaside bungalow community surrounded by palm trees and the occasional oil well. The Creole and Black musicians were able to find some work around Central Avenue that had an active jazz scene for a decade. The new hotels on Wiltshire Boulevard with their ballrooms and the fancy clubs scattered about town offered limited opportunities for white jazz musicians and none for blacks in this segregated city. After the celluloid dreamers arrived from the East and transformed the City of Angels, the jazz scene changed.

With the 1928 production of Al Jolson's *The Jazz Singer*, movies began to talk, sing, and dance. While 1930s Hollywood was known for gangster films, it was also the era of the lavish M.G.M. musicals. The studios needed musicians, who played in jazz clubs in the evenings.

The Los Angeles jazz scene may have been separated from New York's Swing Street (52nd Street) by 3,000 miles, but live radio broadcasts from its clubs, posh hotel ballrooms and Harlem night-spots closed the gap. In fact, the distance and the three-hour time difference worked in its favor. The evening network radio broad-casts from New York usually featured three bands: a "sweet" band, a rumba or Latin band and a jazz band. The jazz bands usually were scheduled late when many people on the East Coast were asleep. But with a three-hour time difference, the evening was just beginning for listeners on the West Coast when jazz bands like

Benny Goodman's took over the radio wire at midnight in New York. After Goodman's popular 1935 "Let's Dance" show was cancelled because of a strike, the band was financially forced to go on tour. The cross-country tour went so poorly that the band intended to break up in Los Angeles. When they arrived at their last stop, L.A.'s Palomar Ballroom, it was filled with fans waiting to see the band they heard on the radio. The next day Benny Goodman and his Orchestra were stars.

Swing bands began to add Los Angeles to their tour itineraries. Recognizing a new market, the studios put bandleaders like Goodman, Artie Shaw, and the Dorsey Brothers (with their skinny singer, Frank Sinatra) in their films. They also recognized the potential of black audiences and cast Duke Ellington, Jimmy Lunceford and Louis Armstrong in films for the sepia market. The era of bandleader as movie star had begun.

Raymond Chandler's novelette, "The King in Yellow" (1938) is set in 1930s Hollywood when "swing was the thing." Hotel detective Steve Grayce is forced to evict the rowdy bandleader-trombonist King Leopardi from the Carlton Hotel for disturbing guests by playing his trombone in the hotel hallway at 1:30 am. The next day, the hotel fires Grayce, who angrily goes to the Club Shalotte to confront Leopardi. A fistfight ensues. A few hours later Leopoldi is murdered in a way to appear as suicide. While Grayce is not a suspect, he is determined to find the killer of the celebrity bandleader.

A 1940s Hollywood mystery about the relationship between the studios and the touring big bands is Sylvia Tate's Never by Chance (1947). Jazz pianist Johnny Silescy is a well-regarded Hollywood studio musician and composer. His fiancée, Corinne Tailor, is killed in a freak hit-and-run accident. A call from the coroner's office informs him that Corinne was not the woman he thought her to be. Silescy becomes obsessed with discovering her true identity, loses his studio work, and eventually goes out on tour with a big band only to lose that job as well.

By the late 1940s, the big band business was faltering and clubs began to hire smaller groups. The era of the private eye-detective

(PI) sitting in a smoke-filled jazz club listening to a cool combo had arrived. In Leigh Brackett's No Good from a Corpse (1944), singer Laurel Dane is a vocalist in a small combo at the Skyway Club in Hollywood, who asks her old friend, PI Edmund Clive, for help with a problem from her past. Before Clive can learn the details, she's murdered. A childhood friend is charged with her murder, but Clive believes the killer is within the convoluted circle of her family and their friends. The highlight of this story is a nifty nightclub scene in which Dane sings "*Blues in the Night.*" In another Hollywood PI story, John Macdonald's The Moving Target (1949), (which was brought to the screen as *Harper* with Paul Newman), Lew Archer is hired by Elaine Sampson to find her eccentric husband, Ralph, who was last seen at Burbank Airport. Archer navigates a dysfunctional family gauntlet, ending up at a shady jazz club and chatting up a junkie piano player named Betty Frawley. Betty knows what Lew is after and isn't going to tell him. In a third PI tale, Roy Huggins' The Double Take (1948), Stu Bailey is hired by industrialist Ralph Johnson to uncover anything in his wife's background that could make her vulnerable to blackmail. Bailey has a few drinks at Dino's, the jazz club next door to his office on Sunset Strip. Aside from that, there's very little jazz content. The Double Take is included because Bailey went on to fame in Huggins' late 1950s crime TV series *77 Sunset Strip* that had a memorable jazz soundtrack.

Stu Bailey reappears in three of Huggins' short stories collected in 77 Sunset Strip (1958). Again, aside from Bailey having a few drinks at Dino's, the jazz content is negligible. The stories focus on a deadly family cruise ("Death and the Skylark"), a mentally unstable client, a disappearing corpse, and a greedy family ("Appointment with Fear") and an old-fashioned locked-room murder case ("Now You See It").

While Bailey was suave in a West Coast jazzy way, he couldn't compare with the hero of another TV detective show, *Peter Gunn* (with its best-selling jazz soundtrack by Henry Mancini). No one was cooler in the late 1950s and early 1960s than Peter Gunn (portrayed by Craig Stevens). Readers knew that from the opening lines of Henry Kane's Peter Gunn (1960): "The music was cool at Mothers. Edie was singing and Peter Gunn, alone at a corner table, was tapping his foot to the jazz." (p.5). He liked jazz and wore Brooks Brothers suits from Manhattan. He was on good terms with Lieutenant Jacoby of the L.A. police force which unusual for a P.I. Gunn is hired by Steve Bain, President of the Teamster's local union, to look into the background of guitarist Sam Lockwood, who is interested in Bain's daughter, Alice. When Lockwood is discovered with a gun, standing over Bain's body, Gunn believes the guitarist's story and looks elsewhere for the killer.

A more traditional pulp detective is former cop, Mac Stewart in John Farr's The Deadly Combo, (1958). He solves the murder of his friend, trumpet legend, Dandy Mullens, who had been reduced to begging drinks at the Onyx Club. It appears that Mullens had told his story about his "solid gold horn" to the wrong person. Stewart follows a murderous trail through L.A.'s sleazy, late nightclubs, to Muscle Beach, to the fancy apartment of singer Faye Farmer and a blackmail scheme.

By the 1950s, organized crime had a strong presence in L.A. In James Ellroy's White Jazz (1992), Lieutenant Dave Klein of the L.A. Police Department (LAPD) kills a key witness in a federal boxing probe, much to the relief of the LAPD and gangster Mickey Cohen. With their boxing investigation shut down, Federal investigators decide to target corruption in the LAPD. Klein realizes that he's going to be sacrificed and hopes to divert attention by finding a saxophone-playing killer named Tommy Kafesjian. In another slice of sleaze, Ellroy's short story, "Dick Contino's Blues" (1994), a washed-up crooner decides to fake his own kidnapping and heroic escape to shed a reputation for cowardice stemming from his refusal to be drafted during the Korean War. Unfortunately, one of the kidnappers has a different agenda.

A mystery that recounts the big band era and the corruption within the recording industry in Hollywood is Lou Cameron's Angel's Flight (1960). Bassist Ben Parker witnesses the career of drummer-turned-vocalist, bandleader and movie star, Johnny Angel. Angel gets to the top by destroying people with more talent and/or stealing their work. Eventually, he tangles with Parker over his Afro-

Cuban band and almost destroys him until Federal investigators begin a payola (pay to play) investigation. A mystery that touches on a payola scandal is Ellery Queen's <u>Death Spins the Platter</u> (1962). Only a few of the big band singers, like Frank Sinatra, survived into the payola era. White singers, like Dick Contino in Ellroy's story, ended up in low-end clubs. Some black singers and jazz musicians moved over to R&B and recorded for the smaller labels that became a focus of the federal investigators. Most of the records played by Tutter King the DJ in <u>Death Spins the Platter</u> on his popular L.A. television show would have been recorded on investigated labels. <u>Death Spins the Platter</u> is not focused on jazz itself but is included to show how popular music had moved away from jazz to music for teenagers. That said, the same crooks that controlled the record market in the time of <u>Angel's Flight</u> controlled it in Tutter King's day (early 1960s).

A different view of early 1960s life in the City of Angels is offered in Peter Duchin and John Wilson Morgan's <u>Good Morning Heartache</u> (2003). Society bandleader Philip Damon has accepted a six-week residency at the Coconut Grove. Short a vocalist and a trumpet player, he hires Buddy Bixby, a Chet Baker type, who's just been released from jail where he served time on narcotics charges. When Bixby dies after a late night jam session at the Lighthouse, his death is dismissed as a drug overdose. But Hercules Platt, who recently resigned from the San Francisco police force and signed on as sax player in Damon's band, thinks it is murder.

A 1980s novel shows that things had really not changed in the recording business since the days of <u>Angel's Flight</u> is J. R. Creech's <u>Music and Crime</u> (1989). Ray the Face is a 32-year-old saxophonist scuffling to make a living in jazz. He and his partner Lonnie resort to petty crime to supplement their meager earnings from jazz. Through Lonnie, Ray meets Reggie, an attractive black singer with a blues voice and a sleazy manager named Cody. The infatuated Ray agrees to write music for her and soon discovers that Cody has stolen its copyright. All that's left for the two jazzmen is a return to crime.

Jumping a decade to the 1990s, writer-musician Bill Moody

created Evan Horne, a jazz piano-player-turned-detective, who lives in L.A. Unlike the earlier detectives, such as Peter Gunn, Lew Archer, Edmund Clive or Stu Bailey, Horne is primarily a jazz musician who reluctantly becomes a detective after injuring his hand in an automobile accident. In Horne's debut, Solo Hand (1994), his former employer, Lonnie Cole, a jazz singer turned soul singer from the slums of Central Avenue needs help with a blackmail problem. The kidnappers name Horne as the middleman. But the payoff goes awry and Horne finds himself as the prime suspect in a heist. To clear his name, he needs to uncover the identity of the blackmailer/thief and discovers a record profit scam.

In The Sound of the Trumpet (1997), Horne enters the crazy world of jazz memorabilia and unreleased tapes after his friend, Ace Buffington asks him to verify legendary trumpet player Clifford Brown's presence on a newly discovered tape from the 1950s. At that time, Hollywood was home to numerous small companies eager to record new West Coast musicians. Horne listens to the tape and believes that he's hearing Brown's sound. Buffington's friend Ken Perkins actually has two tapes and a trumpet with the initials "C.B." on it. The tapes are later stolen and Perkins is murdered. The killer overlooked the trumpet that is used as bait to uncover his identity.

Moody's third book with a L.A. is setting is Bird Lives (1999). Horne's old friend, Santa Monica Police Lieutenant Dan Cooper, requests help in solving a series of murders of prominent jazz musicians. On the wall above the body of his latest victim, smooth-jazz musician Ty Rodman, the killer wrote "Bird Lives!" Cooper thinks Horne's entry into the jazz scene could be useful in catching the serial killer. But Horne's hand had healed enough for him to record and he was trying to complete an album. At heart, Horne is a jazz musician, not a detective, and the whole experience of catching the killer is too much for him. He leaves for Europe as soon as his album is finished.

Recently returned from Europe in Fade to Blue (2011), Horne has a brush with Hollywood when he's offered a lucrative consulting job helping actor Ryan Stiles play the piano in an upcoming film as well as scoring it. Horne accepts despite reservations about its hot-tempered star. Following a row with paparazzi, an aggressive photographer is dead after his motorcycle went off a cliff. It's ruled an accident and Stiles has an alibi. Then a second photographer is strangled after blackmailing Stiles. Although Stiles is a prime suspect, Horne senses a killer in his entourage.

Moving from private eyes to police procedurals, the most popular, contemporary L.A. series is easily Michael Connelly's Harry Bosch books. Harry was born there, grew up in its institutions, and returned to its police force after service in Vietnam. The city is his beat. He lives in a house on Woodrow Wilson Drive in the Hollywood Hills above Los Angeles that he purchased after consulting on a movie. Harry spends a lot of time on his deck overlooking the city lights and freeway traffic below, thinking about various cases, and listening to jazz. The music helps him focus what's important and blocks out everything else. Because L.A. is a sprawling city connected to its various parts by a network of freeways, Harry also spends a lot of time alone driving in his car, listening to jazz on his cassette deck-CD player. The great jazz clubs of 1940s Central Avenue and 1950s Hollywood are long gone but Harry does hear jazz legend Frank Morgan whenever the alto player returns to town. In spite of his love of jazz, Harry's only musician friend is the elderly Quentin McKinzie to whom he returns an alto saxophone found in a pawnshop after a robbery in the short story "Christmas Even" (2004).

Like many cities, Harry's Los Angeles has a diverse, often conflicting, ethnic make-up with wide social and economic disparities. These differences are set against a background of other extremes: ocean, mountains and desert. In a promotional DVD that accompanied The Narrows (2004), Connelly quotes a comment made by a fellow staffer at the Los Angeles Times. Los Angeles was "…a sunny place for shady people." As Connelly's books show, it is also a deadly place.

Harry's first case, The Black Echo (1992), concerns a bank robbery based on an actual occurrence. Over a long holiday weekend, robbers in all-terrain vehicles entered the tunnels of the defunct Red Car transit system that joined the city's storm drain system and drove to their target. They dug into the bank and spent the weekend looting safe deposit boxes. Harry's door into the case is the alleged drug overdose death of Billy Turner, a former "tunnel rat", who, like Bosch, fought the Viet Cong in the dark tunnels under the battlefields in Vietnam.

Drug traffic from nearby the Mexican border is a continuing problem for the LAPD. In The Black Ice (1993), undercover narcotics cop Cal Moore, who was suspected by Internal Affairs of having crossed over, kills himself. Bosch refuses to believe his old friend would commit suicide and suspects murder. In a more recent instance, Bosch is working cold cases for the San Fernando Police Department, when called to a double murder at a drugstore in Two Kinds of Truth (2017). His experienced eye sees an execution and an investigation leads into the lucrative, illicit world of prescription drugs.

As a city cop, Harry has his share of prostitution cases. It is personal for him since his own mother was a murdered prostitute. In The Concrete Blonde (1994), Bosch deals with serial killers of prostitutes. He thought that he killed the Dollmaker, a serial killer of eleven prostitutes. Four years later, the killings start again. In another prostitution case, The Last Coyote (1995), Harry is on suspension and uses the time to investigate the unsolved murder of his mother.

After her death, Harry grew up in a series of institutions resulting in sympathy towards unwanted children. In City of Bones (2002), a dog's discovery of a human bone leads Harry to a shallow grave containing the remains of a twelve-year-old boy killed 25 years earlier. Harry is angered and saddened that a child would be missing without his absence reported. After identifying the child, he looks for his killer. In The Wrong Side of Goodbye (2016), Harry, recently retired from the LAPD, looks for ailing, billionaire Whitney Vance's possible heir. His family broke up his relationship with a Mexican girl when he was young, leaving her to deal with her pregnancy alone.

Gone are the days when the movie studios could close down a police investigation. Harry gets high profile cases involving the Hollywood crowd. In Trunk Music (1997), he is called to investigate the death of producer, Tony Aliso, who had just returned from a Las Vegas gambling jaunt. Apparently, Aliso was involved in a money-laundering scheme for organized crime interests but hadn't betrayed their trust. Consequently, Harry thinks there was a personal motive behind the killing. In another Hollywood case, A Darkness More Than Night (2001), movie director David Storey is accused of murdering actress Jody Krementz during sex and then arranging her death to look like a suicide. Harry has developed a convincing case against the director. But Storey's investigator, Rudy Tafero, comes up with a scheme to have him discredited.

Lost Light (2003) is a different sort of Hollywood case. Recently retired, Harry decides to revisit an old unsolved case involving a murdered studio employee and the theft of $2 million. The Brass Verdict (2008) is another murder case involving a movie producer. Harry works with defense lawyer Mickey Haller, a protagonist from The Lincoln Lawyer (2005), to uncover a jury-tampering scheme. They initially are on opposite sides in a case involving Hollywood producer Walter Elliot, who is accused of murdering his wife and her lover in Elliot's Malibu house. Both men independently discover the reason for Elliot's disinterest in his defense.

Starting in the 1940s on Central Avenue and continuing to the present with the Rodney King and O.J. Simpson cases, the LAPD had a confrontational relationship with L.A.'s black community. In Angel's Flight (1999), Howard Elias, a black lawyer who success-fully sued the LAPD over racism and brutality, is found murdered at the foot of Angel's Flight, the inclined railway that links downtown L.A. to Bunker Hill. Elias was about to file another suit again the LAPD. There's pressure on Harry to pin the case on a "rogue cop" and close down the investigation, but Harry doesn't think the chosen scapegoat is guilty.

In The Narrows (2004) Harry crosses tracks with a protagonist from another series. Robert Backus is a rogue FBI agent turned serial killer from The Poet (1997). Harry's friend, profiler Terry McCaleb has died under mysterious circumstances. He decides the killer's identity lies within McCaleb's files and follows a trail to Backus.

Harry returns to the LAPD to join the Open-Unsolved Unit after a three-year absence in The Closers (2005) and revisits the case of a sixteen-year-old girl, who was kidnapped from home and murdered. Recent DNA evidence points to white supremacist Roland Mackey, who had no known links to the victim. In another old case, Echo Park (2006), Raymond Waits, who was arrested with body parts from two women, will swap information on other murders in exchange for a life sentence. Included in Waits' offer was the unsolved 1993 Marie Gesto case that always haunted Harry. He was convinced of the killer, Anthony Garland, but couldn't prove it. Harry agrees to accompany the prosecutor, Waits and his lawyer to the supposed site of Gesto's murder.

Harry gets involved in a terrorism case after Stanley Kent is killed execution style in The Overlook (2007). Kent had access to radio-active materials that are missing. The FBI believes his killers to be Arab terrorists planning to make a "dirty" bomb. Cut out of the "national security" case by the FBI, Harry insists on pursuing his own investigation.

In these and other Michael Connelly books, the jazz component can be found in the music that Harry Bosch listens to as he tries to solve his cases. No jazz musician is killed or is a killer. There are no shoot-outs in jazz clubs. But Harry is always listening to jazz. He has an intimacy with his music that he is unable to have with people. Because of this relationship to his music, jazz has become his shadow soul.

WEST COAST JAZZ: THE OTHER L.A. (CENTRAL AVENUE)

"I'm in the land of sunshine, standin' on Central Avenue" sang Big Joe Turner in his classic composition, "Blues on Central Avenue." Turner was a late arrival to Central Avenue's flourishing music scene, having been waylaid in Kansas City for most of the 1930s. Jazz had actually arrived early in the 1900s on Central Avenue, the heart of the Black community in segregated Los Angeles. Nearly a decade before the Navy closed Storyville in 1915, bassist Bill Johnson and a group of New Orleans jazzmen came for a month's stay at the Red Feather Tavern. Central Avenue proved a popular place and soon there were enough New Orleans musicians to support the Creole fraternal organizations that cushioned the arrival of the Storyville jazz exiles. In 1919 Kid Ory, a top New Orleans jazz musician arrived and formed Kid Ory's Original Creole Band. Even Jelly Roll Morton spent time on Central Avenue. From 1917 to 1922, he was working on the West Coast, and almost three of those years were spent in Los Angeles. Unable to decide whether he wanted to be a pimp or a piano player, he was both: he played piano at Central Avenue's Cadillac Café and ran a string of prostitutes called "The Pacific Coast Line."

Outside of Central Avenue, the opportunities for black jazz musicians were limited. The movie studios, hotel ballrooms and most nightclubs were closed to them. In the 1920s, the Cotton Club, located across from the M.G.M. studios in Culver City, began hiring black jazz musicians. Like its New York namesake, the work involved black musicians playing for a white clientele. Louis

Armstrong played there in the 1930s. So did Duke Ellington. The famous nightclub scene of singer Ivie Anderson backed by Duke Ellington and his Orchestra from the 1937 Marx Brothers movie, *A Day at the Races,* was filmed there.

Central Avenue's jazz scene was supported by an influx of black immigrants from Texas, Louisiana and Arkansas. They came for the manufacturing jobs and the chance to buy their own homes. Because of strictly enforced housing covenants, they settled along Central Avenue and in the rural area of Watts. It was Harlem with palm trees, a community of mostly black-owned businesses. Retired Ellington band vocalist, Ivie Anderson owned the best-fried chicken restaurant.

Central Avenue was the economic and social center of this segregated city. In its middle was the elegant Dunbar Hotel where Duke Ellington, Jimmy Lunceford, Sy Oliver et al. stayed when they were in town. Next door was the Club Alabam, and during WWII, the Downbeat and Last Word opened nearby. A plethora of smaller, lesser-known clubs sprung up around the Dunbar. With great food, music and accommodations, all the black bands visited Central Avenue.

The Central Avenue's nightlife was similar to Harlem's in its heyday. Its jazz clubs attracted pianist-singer Nat Cole, vibes player Lionel Hampton, pianist Art Tatum, and bluesman T-Bone Walker as well as younger musicians, such as pianist Hampton Hawes and alto saxophonist Frank Morgan. Certain local white musicians, like the alto sax player Art Pepper or guitarist Barney Kessel, were a common sight. Musicians from the touring white swing bands, including Benny Goodman's, would go to Central Avenue after finishing their evening's work at the hotels on Wiltshire Boulevard. Hollywood celebrities, such as Humphrey Bogart, Robert Mitchum and Ava Gardner et al. came for the food and music. The jazz fellowship of Central Avenue was not, however, a two-way street: blacks that ventured away from Central Avenue did so at peril in this segregated city.

In May 1940 after the election of the "reformist" administration of Fletcher Bowron, City Hall tried to control Central Avenue by decreeing that alcohol could not be served in public establishments after 2 am. (Similar legislation had closed down Chicago clubs in the 1920s and Kansas City clubs in the late 1930s.) In spite of frequent police harassment, the nightlife continued in after-hours clubs and restaurants. Although the outbreak of World War II affected the number and quality of musicians, it actually invigorated the jazz scene by making club jobs available to younger musicians. The party on Central Avenue continued, fueled by the wartime prosperity from the continuing influx of blacks and the opening of defense industry jobs to them. Roughly, between 1930 and 1950, the black population doubled. By 1950, blacks represented around 9% of the Los Angeles population.

The end of WWII brought economic changes to Central Avenue, however, as women and black workers lost their jobs in the defense industry to returning white veterans. Blacks could no longer pay their mortgages and began to lose their homes. There was less money to be spent on entertainment. The clubs responded with smaller jazz combos, and R&B (Rhythm and Blues) groups, made up of veterans from the big band era. Instead of having large horn sections, these pared-down groups would have a single saxophone, trombone, and trumpet. Jukeboxes, which became popular in the 1930s, entirely replaced live entertainment in some clubs.

In the late 1940s, the L.A. police under Chief William H. Parker began to harass club owners who offered entertainment in an interracial environment. Mixed race couples, out for an evening of entertainment on Central Avenue, were stopped in their cars. Prominent black celebrities were harassed. For example, bandleader Billy Eckstine was arrested on Central Avenue for having a new Cadillac with New York license plates. This crackdown was not limited to the Central Avenue Area. In Glendale, blacks needed a special permit to be out after 6 pm. Residents in swanky Hancock Park tried to prevent singer-pianist Nat King Cole from buying a home.

In this racially tense atmosphere in Walter Mosley's <u>Devil in a Blue Dress</u> (1990), Easy Rawlins, who's just lost his job at the

Champion aircraft factory and has a mortgage due, accepts a job from white hustler Dewitt Albright to find a white girl named Daphne Monet. She is known to frequent the Central Avenue jazz clubs. Easy learns that she can usually be found with an elusive, black bootlegger named Frank Green. Monet is, apparently, the girlfriend of Todd Carter, a powerful white Los Angeles politician. As people connected to Monet die, Easy realizes there's a racial element in this seemingly simple job and calls in backup from Texas.

The toxic mix of race and organized crime in the late 1940s and early 1950s appears in Raymond Benson's <u>Blues in the Dark</u> (2019). Independent film producer Karissa Glover rents an old mansion in the West Adams section of L.A. ("Sugar Hill"), where black movie stars once lived between 1940s-1960s. The house belonged to a white actress, Blair Kendrick, who disappeared after making six successful films noir. Intrigued as well as searching for new material, her research reveals that Blair had been involved with black jazz pianist Hank Marley and intended to retire and marry him. But Ultimate Pictures producer, Eldan Hirsch needed her to pay off mob debts. Marley was picked up off the street by studio thugs after an evening at the Downbeat Club and never seen again. Blair was thought to have died after witnessing the mob's killing of Hirsch.

Central Avenue had always been open to all music: Dixieland, swing, R&B and bebop. Post-war jazz fans were familiar with bebop from live radio broadcasts and records brought west by enterprising Pullman railroad porters. There also were local nightspots where fans could hear the new music. Billy Eckstine took his Big Band of beboppers into the Plantation Club in Watts. Coleman Hawkins was around, playing with young beboppers. Trumpet player Howard McGhee and tenor saxophonist Teddy Edwards were playing bebop at Central Avenue's Downbeat Club. But in December 1945, when club owner Billy Berg brought Dizzy Gillespie in from New York with a group of beboppers that included Charlie Parker to play at his Hollywood supper club on Vine Street, the police took notice. Berg had insisted on integrated audiences. It was, also, evident that

Charlie Parker was a heroin user. When the group returned to New York, it was without Parker. He had disappeared while looking for dope, reappeared on Central Avenue, played a few dates, and was arrested. Thanks to the intercession of a record producer, who didn't want his newly signed star to serve hard time, he was committed to Camarillo State Hospital in Ventura. Parker wrote the jazz standard "Relaxin' at Camarillo" after his six month stay.

Beboppers studied Parker's music and copied his lifestyle. When cops saw black bebop players, they believed hard drugs and their dealers were not too far away. The jazz standard, "Moose the Mooche" was written by Charlie Parker about a drug dealer, who sold heroin and bebop records from his shoeshine stand. There was none of the artsy association of bebop musicians and Beat Literature that San Francisco cops around North Beach briefly tolerated. When L.A. cops saw jazzmen, they thought that they saw criminal drug abusers.

This connection between drugs and bop is at the heart of Jack Fuller's The Best of Jackson Payne (2000). Musicologist Charles Quinlan is interested in writing a biography of the tenor saxophonist Jackson Payne, who was a paragon of the self-destructive, brilliant jazz musician. To better understand him, Quinlan interviews the people that knew him as youth, especially the drug-dependent women who Payne abandoned early in his career. He also learns that the police turned Payne into an informant, allowing them to bust well-known musicians and catch an infamous dealer known as "the Leopard". Eventually, Payne served a short sentence in San Quentin, where he played in the band and drugs were easily available. Upon his release, he went to Paris but couldn't escape his Central Avenue past.

The 1950s spelled the end for the jazz scene on Central Avenue. In James Ellroy's White Jazz (1992), Art Pepper is still playing his saxophone at the Club Alabam when Detective Dave Klein of the LAPD is trawling the depths of the jazz world looking for a saxophone playing killer. But Pepper is an unreliable junkie; and the once elegant club is reduced to a junkie jug-joint. The musicians, their listeners and the money, had gone elsewhere. Jazz clubs, such as the Lighthouse in Hermosa Beach, The Haig and Shelly Manne's Manhole in Hollywood, were integrated for both musicians and clientele. The film studios opened their doors to black musicians and arranger/composers such as Benny Carter, Oliver Nelson and Quincy Jones. By the time of the rioters in later years, there wasn't much left to loot or burn on Central Avenue.

WEST COAST JAZZ:
SAN FRANCISCO

In 1917, fearing for the morals of their sailors before their departure to the Great War, the U.S. Navy insisted on the closure of the New Orleans' famous red-light district, Storyville. Consequently, a wave of jazz musicians, seeking new employment, headed up the Mississippi River to Memphis and Chicago, then, east to New York City, and west to Kansas City. Eventually, the jazz diaspora crossed the Rockies into California and went south to Los Angeles and north to San Francisco. It took longer for jazz to take root in California than in other parts of the country. It wasn't until the 1950s that California developed the own distinct, "cool" sound, known as West Coast Jazz.

At the time of the diaspora, Los Angeles was little more than palm trees, a bunch of bungalows and the occasional celluloid dreamer. On the other hand, in spite of the Earthquake, San Francisco had developed economically into a "money town" with clubs and hotels that would attract some of the best bands during the Jazz Age. In Pamela Longfellow's China Blues (1989), set in 1923, the house band at Rose St. Lorraine's club, the Blue Canary, is King Oliver's, with the young Louis Armstrong on trumpet and his future wife, Lil Hardin, on piano. Louis' hot trumpet provides a background to the cold political dealings that manifested into the Teapot Dome Scandal.

After the Jazz Age ended with the Great Depression, some of the lesser-known bands survived the 1930s and early 1940s by playing one-nighters. Constantly touring by railroad, they would crisscross wide areas of northern California, stopping in San Francisco to change musicians and to pick up fresh musical arrangements.

Violinist Katy Green joins the Ultra Belles, an all-female swing band on one such tour, in Hal Glatzer's Too Dead to Swing (2002). As the tour progresses and band members are murdered, Katy's survival depends on her detecting skills.

1940s San Francisco frames Rupert Holmes' Swing (2005), a book that came with a CD of musical clues. Jack Donovan's Orchestra has just landed a two-week engagement at the Hotel Claremont. Tenor star Ray Sherwood is approached by a young college student, Gail Procter, who wants him to orchestrate an avant-garde composition to be played by the Pan Pacific Orchestra radiobroadcast at San Francisco's World's Fair. War is just around the corner and the composition has more than musical interest to listeners in Tokyo.

By the early 1960s, well before the Summer of Love, San Francisco hotels still attracted big bands, while its North Beach area jazz musicians developed unique reputations and a place within the Beat Movement. In Peter Duchin and John Wesley Wilson's Blue Moon (2002), Manhattan bandleader Philip Damon opens his orchestra's residency at the swanky Fairmont Hotel with a charity gala that ends in murder. Helping Damon uncover the murderer is San Francisco's sole black detective, the saxophone-playing Hercules Platt. Sandwiched in is a nostalgic tour of 1963 San Francisco with scenes in a North Beach Beat hangout, jazz clubs, and bookstores, Fisherman's Wharf, Nob Hill, Haight-Ashbury and Chinatown. The story is filled with celebrity cameo appearances of Joe DiMaggio, Melvin Belli, Clint Eastwood, Bill Cosby, Woody Allen, Herb Caen, Alfred Hitchcock and Kim Novak.

While jazz musicians in Los Angeles, such as alto saxophonist Bud Shank, were scoring Bruce Brown's early surf movies, San Francisco's jazz musicians became a part of the North Beach Beat culture. They often provided the musical accompaniment-background for poetry and literary readings. For example, Jack Kerouac immortalized pianist George Shearing in On the Road (1957) and saxophonist Brew Moore in Desolation Angels (1965). The linkage of jazz with the North Beach Beat movement also had a potentially less salutary effect—the identification of jazz musicians with beatniks and hard drug users.

Two 1960s crime novels and a short story focus on jazz and drugs. In Beat writer Malcolm Braly's hard-boiled novel, Shake Him till he Rattles (1963), San Francisco narcotics cop Lieutenant Carver is on a crusade to clear the North Beach of Beats and drug-using jazz musicians. He's obsessed with alto player Lee Cabiness, who smokes the occasional joint but isn't a hard drug user. Carver is not, however, above planting evidence to get Cabiness. In Frank Kane's more traditional pulp potboiler, The Guilt Edged Frame, (1964) a hot, young, trumpet player, Marty Lewis, owes the mob six thousand dollars from his drug habit. He's beaten up, arranges a loan to pay off the mob but still ends up dead. His girlfriend discovers the body and is charged with his murder. She calls her old friend, private eye (PI) Johnny Liddell, who flies in from the Big Apple to discover the killer.

Jazz drummer-writer Bill Moody's short story "Child's Play" (2004), is set in a club like the Black Hawk. Miles Davis appears to offer Wilson Childs a job as John Coltrane's replacement in his band. Later that evening, piano player Quincy Simmons and Childs are stopped by the police, who find drugs and a gun in Childs' car. Not wanting his friend to miss the opportunity of playing with Miles, Simmons says belongs to him and later jumps bail.

Skipping thirty years to the 1990s, jazz is now regarded as marginal within the music industry with a very limited appeal. With the exception of the Monterey Jazz Festival, San Francisco fans hear their jazz on CDs and neighborhood bars. In Bill Pronzini's Blue Lonesome (1995), Jim Messenger is a C.P.A. who spends much of life outside of work listening to the vintage jazz of Duke Ellington. A lonely man, Messenger eats dinner nightly at the Harmony Café and notices another diner, Janet Mitchell. After she commits suicide, Messenger is determined to find out about her and why she killed herself. In Josef Skvorecky's short story "The Mathematicians of Grizzly Drive" (1988), Polish jazz singer Eve carries out a different enquiry. While singing in a San Francisco bar named The Sailor's Dream, she meets the Berkeley mathematics crowd and discovers a formula that solves a kidnapping.

A series of contemporary investigations are carried out by bass-playing, private investigator August Riorden. In Mark Coggins'

The Immortal Game, (1990), he is hired by Silicon Valley entrepreneur Edwin Bishop to recover a software program stolen by Terri McCulloch, one of his paid female companions. In another Silicon Valley tale, Vulture Capital (2002), Riordan is hired to find the missing Chief Technical Officer, who was working on a device to help spinal chord victims but could be adapted for other uses, e.g. terrorism, slave labor and crime. Back in San Francisco in Candy From Strangers (2006), he is hired to find a missing art student who had a risqué web site and enters a world of Internet sexual predators. In a uniquely San Francisco case, Riordan is hired by the Dragon Lady of Chinatown to investigate election fraud in Runoff (2007). While in The Big Wake-Up, (2009), he is hired by a wealthy Argentine family to find the grave of a woman who died in Milan but was buried under an alias in San Francisco. (Everyone but Riordan knows who is in the casket.) Riordan has abandoned his bass guitar for a Luger in No Hard Feelings (2015). It's a continuation of Vulture Capital and a return to the misuse of spinal chord technology and human robotics. Finally, in another uniquely San Francisco case, The Dead Beat Scroll, (2019), Riordan discovers "The Bee-Hive," an unknown scroll by beat writer Jack Kerouac, which is sought after by a murderous Charles Manson-like family.

Two contemporary San Francisco mysteries have to do with music rights. In the music business, rights and royalties are where money is made, and often more important than performance fees. Jazz pianist Evan Horne has returned from Amsterdam and settled in San Francisco in Bill Moody's Shades of Blue (2008). His friend and teacher Calvin Hughes has died, leaving Horne his valuable Hollywood Hills home and other possessions. While going through Hughes' belongings, Horne realizes that Hughes was possibly the composer of two tunes made famous by Miles Davis. Sorting out the latter, he encounters a crazed, unaccredited composer. In Gloria White's Death Notes (2005), San Francisco PI Ronnie Ventura is enjoying a night of jazz at one of the few surviving clubs, which is interrupted by the murder of the show's headliner, Match Margolis. Ventura is retained by Margolis' widow to recover his sax and music stolen from his home.

The remaining mysteries are a mixed lot set in the Bay area or neighboring coastal communities. In David Corbett's <u>Done For A Dime</u> (2003), the legendary baritone sax player Raymond "Strong" Carlisle is shot in the back outside his home in Rio Mirada, a deteriorating neighborhood on the tip of San Francisco Bay. Detective Dennis Murchison almost dismissed the killing as drug-related and focused his investigation on a street punk. Then a tip points Murchison in an unexpected direction.

Two other mysteries are set in coastal communities with cultural links to San Francisco. In John Daniel's convoluted <u>Play Melancholy Baby</u> (1986), jazz pianist Casey Jones reluctantly leaves the coastal town of Morro Rock to come to San Francisco to help ex-singer Dixie Arthur deal with the disappearance of her daughter, Molly. A final mystery and a personal favorite, is Paul J. Gillette's <u>Play Misty For Me</u> (1971), which is actually a novelization of the movie screenplay by Jo Helms and Dean Riesner and based on Helms' story. Carmel jazz DJ Dave Garland's life is disrupted by a woman named Evelyn Draper that he picked up for a one-night stand. He learns that she has been calling his radio show nightly requesting the Erroll Garner composition, "Misty." Once in Garland's life, however, she refuses to leave. "Misty" is so skillfully woven into the plot, that it's difficult to hear the tune without thinking of the story.

JAZZ MYSTERIES ABROAD—AN OVERVIEW

Jazz appealed to a smaller audience in Europe than in the United States. Early jazz was an acquired upper-class taste. That is not to say that its audience was less enthusiastic than in the United States—just smaller.

Ragtime, the forerunner of jazz, crossed the Atlantic Ocean not long after the craze swept the United States at the end of the 19th century. Both sheet music and recordings were readily available to European musicians. But it was the black marching bands that accompanied the American Expeditionary Force in World War I that sparked interest in American popular music. The best remembered of these black marching bands were the Seventy Black Devils of the 350th Field Artillery led by Tim Bryan and the 369th Infantry Regiment Band (known as the Hellfighters) led by James Reese Europe, with its drum-major and dancer, Bojangles Robinson. (Robinson would later go on to fame dancing with Shirley Temple in four movies). Their music was a mix of marches, ragtime, dance music and "jass".

In the 1920s black bands, such as the Southern Syncopated Orchestra, led by Will Marion Cook, toured Europe. These bands played mostly dance or show music. The first "jazz band" to visit Europe was the white, five-man Original Dixieland Jazz Band in 1919. Two years earlier, they made the first jazz recordings in New York City of "Livery Stable Blues" and "Dixieland Jass One-Step". While it wasn't the sort of jazz that King Oliver's band with Louis Armstrong would be playing in the early 1920s, their music was recognized as something different. For example, in Ian

Morson's short story, "There Would Have Been Murder," (2004) young Harry Rothstein, an English Communist Party leader, was captivated by their sound while working in the kitchen of a fancy London club.

Throughout the 1920s white jazz bands, such as that of "the King of Jazz", Paul Whiteman, toured Europe. But they too played dance or show music. Whiteman is perhaps best known in the 1920s for debuting George Gershwin's "Rhapsody In Blue" in New York's Carnegie Hall, which was a far cry from "Livery Stable Blues". By the end of the 1920s and into the 1930s, black bands led by Louis Armstrong and Duke Ellington regularly appeared in Europe playing jazz. Some black musicians and entertainers, such as Coleman Hawkins, Bricktop and Arthur Briggs, found the racial situation in Europe (excluding Germany) more conducive and settled there. By the 1930s, white jazz bands led by Benny Goodman, Mildred Bailey and others were frequently touring Europe. Their music was also available through Hollywood films and vinyl recordings.

Jazz spread beyond Europe in the interwar years. Phryne Fisher in Kerry Greenwood's The Green Mill Murder (2007) has an evening at Melbourne's best jazz club interrupted by the murder of a marathon dancer during "Bye Bye Blackbird." In Night in Shanghai (2014), American Thomas Greene is recruited to lead The Kings, a black jazz band playing in the biggest Triad (gangster owned) nightclub in Shanghai. When the Japanese take over the city, the jazz-loving administrator defies instructions and keeps the club open as long as possible.

London and Paris became the overseas centers of jazz. The English favored white jazz bands while the French preferred visiting black bands. That said, English bands sometimes included black American musicians, such as Coleman Hawkins. Even in the 1930s, when swing was the thing in the States, the European jazz audience remained small and club-based, where attendance was limited to the wealthy. Three English mysteries written in the 1940s, but set a decade earlier, give the reader a very different snapshot of life from that in Depression-era America. In James Ronald's Death Croons the Blues (1940), the American blues singer Adele Valee has been murdered. Reporter Julian Mendoza, trying to clear the man who found her body, discovers her links to business titans and prominent politicians. Her social connections distinguished her from earlier Storyville singers and the blues singers, such as Ma Raney and Bessie Smith with their traveling shows of the 1920s and 1930s. He also finds that she had no qualms about blackmail. Death Croons the Blues portrays an unpleasant view of the existing class system, including the dire conditions of the poor.

Ngaio Marsh's A Wreath for Rivera aka Swing, Brother Swing (1949), also, gives an unflattering picture of upper-class jazz fans. The eccentric Lord Pastern bullies his way into playing with Breezy Bellair's jazz band, and, accidently, kills the accordion player. Pastern behaves arrogantly towards the police, who are trying to clear him of intentional murder. During the investigation, Scotland Yard's Roderick Alleyn comes across drugs that add another dimension to his investigation. (Marijuana use by musicians crossed the Atlantic on the transatlantic ocean liners along with jazz.) Drugs also make an appearance in Ray Sonin's The Dance Band Mystery (1940). Scotland Yard had a different understanding of drugs and society than its American counterpart. The Yard is more interested in finding the English source of marijuana cigarettes for London's jazz musicians and their American gangster connection than in prosecuting users.

Across the English Channel in 1930s Paris, American jazz singer, expatriate Memphis Jones (loosely based on Josephine Baker and Bricktop) in Francine Matthews' The Alibi Club (2006) owns a fashionable nightspot. Cole Porter would have felt at home in the Alibi Club with its gathering of expatriates, businessmen and diplomats. It bears little resemblance to American speakeasies, jazz clubs or dance halls. Jones is accepted by the French but slapped in the face by racism when she tries to leave with other American expatriates as the Germans advance on Paris. Facing an uncertain fate, she makes her own way to safety in North Africa.

When the Nazis came to power in Germany in 1933, they actively discouraged jazz because of its links to Blacks and Jews as well as its stress on individuality. American jazz bands, such as that led by the American expatriate clarinetist Danny Polo, had been touring Germany since the mid-1920s. Although the arrival of dancer Josephine Baker and her revue in Berlin in 1925 created a memorable stir, the Germans, like the English, preferred white bands. By the early 1930s, the growing xenophobia inhibited even the touring white jazz bands from playing in Germany.

In 1935, Joseph Goebbels, the Reich Minister of Public Enlightenment and Propaganda, prohibited jazz as well as Jews from playing music. (The top German jazz band, the Weintraub Syncopators, whose members were mostly Jewish, left to work abroad and finally settled in Australia in 1937.) A few Berlin jazz clubs were allowed to remain open exclusively for foreign diplomats and businessmen as well as high-ranking Nazis. Hieronymus Falk, a young mixed-race trumpet player and his band, worked in those clubs in Esi Edugyan's Half Blood Blues (2011) until they fled to Paris. The Nazis and betrayal were not far behind.

Jazz went underground into secret, cellar clubs where enthusiasts danced to records smuggled into Germany during the war. Among rebellious German youth, there was a movement known as *Swing-Jugend* or Swing Youth, whose members dressed outrageously and danced to jazz records in these cellars. The Gestapo dealt very harshly with these young jazz enthusiasts when caught as Peter Bruck, a Benny Goodman fan, learned in Paul Dowswell's Auslander (2010) set in 1943 Berlin. Although Bruck escaped a Gestapo raid, one of his friends was not so fortunate and his capture would imperil an escape network for Jews.

Goebbels eventually realized the impossibility of sealing off Germans from jazz—especially from foreign radio broadcasts. So he set up Charlie and His Orchestra—his own band of the best, surviving German jazz musicians. Popularly known as Mr. Goebbels Jazz Band, it played propaganda set to jazz. But Charlie really couldn't compete with Benny, Glenn or Duke.

During World War II, Nazi-occupied Europe was isolated from the revolutionary changes in American jazz, such as bebop. As a result, wartime jazz was a continuation of 1930s musical styles.

While the Nazis regarded jazz as degenerate music, they often looked the other way when it was played outside Germany and had other problems to deal with as occupiers. Consequently, black Dixieland bandleader Chops Danielson was able to play and broadcast his weekly radio show in Copenhagen in Wm. Ellis Oglesby's <u>Blow Happy, Blow Sad</u> (1996). In Denmark, blacks were not rounded up by the Nazis and were treated as Danes. Danielson falls afoul of the Nazis for reasons other than his color.

Swing came to wartime Europe with the American military and left with them. In postwar England, musicians and fans preferred to look back to New Orleans and the roots of jazz, mostly ignoring the new bebop movement that seduced some American musicians. Even twenty years later, young fans such as Trevor Chaplin in Alan Plater's <u>The Beiderbecke Affair</u>, (1985), <u>The Beiderbecke Tapes</u>, (1986) and <u>The Beiderbecke Connection</u>, (1992) favored jazz pioneers, such as the white 1920s clarinet player Bix Beiderbecke over contemporary players.

American swing bands, such as Glenn Miller's, dominated the wartime airwaves as portrayed in Peter Robinson's <u>In a Dry Season</u> (2000). But postwar jazz was no longer popular music. The smaller audiences listened to jazz, rather than danced to it. A still smaller group, often identified as beatniks and outsiders, became interested in bebop and the hard drugs that seemed to go along with it. Consequently, in England police kept a close watch on jazz clubs as illustrated in two stories by John Harvey, "Minor Key" (2009) and "Drummer Unknown" (2004).

The French, on the other hand, welcomed the Beats and the beboppers (provided they came in small numbers). As John Harvey's short story "Minor Key" (2009) shows, they even tolerated the drug scene as long as the users were not French. With a liberal racial scene, Paris was more conducive to the jazz life than London. There were a number of clubs, such as Taboo, the Blue Note and Chat Qui Peche that offered opportunities to play jazz. These opportunities were no longer available in the States, where the few surviving clubs, such as the one in David Fulmer's <u>The Blue Door</u> (2008), now booked R&B. The French drug scene policed itself. Those who failed to follow its rules, like Valentine Collins in John Harvey's "Minor Key" (2009) or Jackson Payne in Jack Fuller's The Best of Jackson Payne (2000), were dealt with harshly.

In postwar Europe, several developments aided the spread of jazz. First was the increased availability of American jazz records that were expensive but still within the reach of musicians and devoted fans. In J.P. Smith's Body and Soul (1987), Jerzy Wozzeck, an expatriate Polish piano player living in Paris, diverts money from a drug deal to buy jazz recordings by Thelonious Monk, John Coltrane and Charlie Mingus. Norwegian writer Kjersti Scheen's short story "Moonglow" (2007) tells of four friends who used to spend weekends in a cabin in the woods drinking and listening to jazz records.

Helping the spread of jazz was the realization by the American government of its value in the cultural Cold War. Jazz ambassadors, such as Louis Armstrong, Duke Ellington, Dave Brubeck and Benny Goodman, were sponsored by the United States State Department and toured extensively, especially behind the Iron Curtain (Soviet dominated Europe). A parallel development was Willis Conover's jazz radio show on the government-sponsored Voice of America. The broadcasts reached the young Artie Cohen, living in Moscow (Reggie Nadelson's Sex Dolls 2002), making him a lifelong fan of Stan Getz and Lester Young. Similarly, a Czech police lieutenant named Boruvka heard Conover's show. He developed a love of jazz that caused trouble in Josef Skvorecky's The Mournful Demeanor of Lieutenant Boruvka, (1987), The End of Lieutenant Boruvka, (1990) and The Return of Lieutenant Boruvka, (1991).

Another postwar development was the jazz festival. In May 1949 a group of American jazz musicians flew to Paris for an international jazz festival. French fans, isolated by the war from recent changes in jazz, gave the musicians an enthusiastic reception. Included in the group was the New Orleans traditionalist Sidney Bechet, the original bebopper Charlie Parker, and the young Miles Davis. (In the 1950s, Davis would make a significant contribution to La Nouveau Vague (New Wave Cinema) with his jazz soundtrack to Louis Malle's film, Ascenseur Pour L'Echafaud (Lift to the Scaffold) that was based on Noel Calef's crime novel of the same name aka

Frantic, 1956.)

As time went on, the number of European jazz festivals increased. Musicians made jazz festivals a regular part of their summer schedules: everyone went to the North Sea Jazz Festival and then fanned out to Montreux, Nice, Cannes, Umbria, Copenhagen and elsewhere. Several mysteries use jazz festivals as a backdrop. Tessa Barclay's A Final Discord (2005) concerns a wealthy young man's desire to put together a quintet to play at the Montreux Jazz Festival in Switzerland. In Stella Whitelaw's Jazz and Die (2014), private investigator Jordan Lacey is hired to protect the 14-year-old daughter of English jazz trumpeter Chick Peters, who is headlining at a Dorset jazz festival and received threatening letters. A jazz festival in Prague in Bill Moody's Czechmate: The Spy Who Played Jazz (2013) provides cover for a drummer to become a reluctant secret agent. In James Grant's Don't Shoot the Pianist (1980), local mobsters decide to promote a jazz festival in London for their own ends.

Often musicians, who came for the jazz festivals, liked the social, work and drug scenes and remained in Europe. Tenor saxophone player Fletcher Page settles in Amsterdam in Bill Moody's Looking for Chet Baker (2002). American trumpet player Chet Baker, who became addicted to narcotics early in his career, wandered the European jazz scene for thirty years looking for drugs. They were his downfall in Looking for Chet Baker. Jazz festivals, of course, were not limited to Europe, and have become international events. The music and action in Phyllis Knight's Shattered Rhythms (1994), for example, take place at the Montreal Jazz Festival.

In the 1960s, the blues also found a receptive festival audience in Europe. Bluesmen Muddy Waters and Howlin' Wolf toured and recorded with rock musicians such as Eric Clapton, Stevie Winwood and the Rolling Stones and played the festivals. Although far from the Delta or the destinations of the Great Migration, Europeans eventually turned their hands to the blues. Massimo Carlotto's private detective, Marco "the Alligator" Buratti, was a blues musician, singing with the Old Red Alligators. Unfortunately, for Buratti, his involvement in Italian radical politics landed him a seven-year stint in jail during which time he lost his voice. After his release, he wanted to spend his time drinking Calvados at the La Cuccia blues club in Padua that he owned with his friend, Max La Memoria. But along with another acquaintance from jail, Beniamino Rossini, they became private investigators. Their cases involve drugs (<u>The Columbian Mule</u> 2001), kidnapping (<u>Bandit Love</u>, 2009), snuff films (<u>Master of Knots</u>, 2001) and murder (<u>Blues for Outlaw Hearts and Old Whores</u>, 2017). With Northeastern Italy ripe with political corruption and an economic wasteland, there's no shortage of business for a PI/bluesman.

It took about fifty years for European jazz to evolve from the small, stuffy clubs of the 1920s to the large European jazz festivals. In recent years, however, these festivals have had to prop themselves up by adding rock and soul music to attract an audience. The number of jazz clubs has also declined. The (fictitious) Blue Devil Club in Nice, serves as a backdrop for Peter Morfoot's quartet of Captain Paul Darac police procedurals (<u>Impure Blood</u> (2016), <u>Fatal Music</u> (2017), <u>Box of Bones (2018)</u> and <u>Knock 'Em Dead</u> (2020)). Sadly, even in Europe, jazz remains music for a relatively small number of enthusiastic fans. It's surprising, therefore, that Europeans are writing more mysteries than ever with jazz content.

"JAZZ EYES"

For readers from a certain generation, jazz and the private eye novel often goes together. This is a result of television and, specifically, the jazz soundtracks of the successful private eye shows of the late 1950s and early 1960s. But a literary linkage actually dates to the Jazz Age. For example, in Christopher Booth's <u>Killing Jazz: A Detective Story</u> (1928), private eye Jim Bliss solves the murder of an elderly, wealthy man whose death was induced by a jazz record.

While New Yorker Jim Bliss was conservative, the 1930s detectives were usually a very social and jolly lot, who enjoyed going out to jazz clubs. Much of their jolliness was fueled by alcohol, which was legal again. In jazz clubs narcotics, especially marijuana, were available, but seemed to have little attraction for private eyes.

Easily, the jolliest and drunkest of this early lot was Jonathan Latimer's Bill Crane, who was also the first series private investigator (PI) not to emerge from the pulps (magazines). Crane preferred to hold a drink rather than a gun and to solve cases by deduction rather than through violence. He's part of the 1930s school of fast-talking, witty, screwball detection. In Latimer's classic, <u>The Lady in the Morgue</u> (1936), Crane goes to the Chicago Morgue to see if the body of "Alice Ross" is actually that of Kathryn Courtland, a wealthy young woman, who ran off with a trumpet player from Rudy Vallee's band. The identification is complicated by disappearance of the corpse and murder of the morgue attendant. Eventually, Crane realizes "Alice Ross" was not Kathryn Courtland but becomes interested in the recurring presence of trumpet player Sam Udoni in both of these women's lives.

Dan Jordan, the PI in Harlan Reed's The Swing Music Murder (1938) is also a heavy drinker. Jordan and his girlfriend Anita are in a Seattle nightclub listening to Lance Grandy's Swing Swing Boys when the bandleader is shot. Jordan is so drunk that he's barely aware of what's going on. When the police question him regarding his presence in the club, he belligerently replies that he's "waiting for the revolution." (p.24). The following day, he sobers up enough to be hired to find Grandy's killer by a friend of the man erroneously arrested for the murder after the police learn of a quarrel over song rights. Jordan discovers that almost everyone in the club had reason to kill the bandleader. What's interesting about The Swing Music Murder is its feel for the 1930s jazz scene. Reed's book depicts characters often in a marijuana haze speaking slang (a bit dated) in jazz clubs. Sadly, this was Jordan's second and final case as his PI career ended in Seattle. (He's truly a forgotten PI, usually omitted from reference books.)

Both The Lady in the Morgue and The Swing Music Murder were written in the 1930s for a Depression era audience. On the other hand, H. Paul Jeffers' three books Rubout at The Onyx (1981), Murder on Mike (1984) and The Rag Doll Murder (1987) were written about the 1930s for an audience fifty years later. Jeffers' New York City is an exciting place, populated by glamorous people. His detective, Harry MacNeil, a former policeman, is a jazz-lover who plays the clarinet and has friendships with George Gershwin and Paul Whiteman dating back to the 1920's famous "Carnegie Hall Rhapsody In Blue Concert". Harry's office is located in the brownstone above the Onyx Club on 52nd Street, known as Swing Street. He spends his evenings downstairs drinking and listening to Art Tatum play piano or going to other jazz clubs.

In Rubout at The Onyx, Harry is hired by Gloria Seldes to investigate the murder of her husband Joey, a low-level gunman in Owney Madden's mob, on New Year's Eve at the Onyx Club. Harry discovers Joey's involvement with two of Madden's thugs in the theft of 3 ½ million dollars' worth of unrecovered diamonds. Obviously, Gloria knew about the heist and hopes that Harry will stumble upon the diamonds. Rubout at the Onyx is filled with music, atmosphere and celebrity cameo appearances (e.g. Art Tatum, Jimmy Lunceford, Paul Whiteman, George Gershwin, Walter Winchell, Jimmy Walker, Fiorello H. LaGuardia and Owney Madden).

In his next case, The Rag Doll Murder, Harry's office is still above the Onyx but Tatum is no longer playing there. Harry's evenings are now spent listening to the one-armed trumpet player, Wingy Mannone, with violinist Stuff Smith's group or going out dancing at Small's. But jazz has moved into the background. Harry has been retained by Evelyn Procter to find the killer of her sister, fashion model, Jamey Flamingo. A mentally limited delivery boy, Toby Maxwell, has been arrested by the police and "confessed" to the murder. Both Harry and Evelyn believe the real killer is in the fashion or fur trades, not deliveries.

By Harry's third and final case, Murder on Mike, the New York's jazz scene has changed. The Cotton Club, where Harry hears Louis Armstrong and Maxine Sullivan, has moved downtown to Broadway and Seventh Avenue in the heart of the theatre district, opening in time for the 1939 World's Fair. (The original club on 125th Street was forced to close by economic factors associated with the Depression, the increasing violence and racial tensions in Harlem.) On Swing Street (52nd Street), the big bands of Woody Herman, Charlie Barnet and Count Basie are playing the clubs. Although Harry saw Herman at the Famous Door, his preference is for the small groups like that of violinist Stuff Smith's at the Onyx. Harry had been known to join their jam sessions. In spite of the abundance of live music, 1930s radio was becoming an alternative source for entertainment. In Murder on Mike, Derek Worthington, the producer of the popular Detective Fitzroy's casebook crime series, is found dead in an empty radio studio. The entire cast has alibis except the announcer, David Reed, who claimed to be watching the ice-skating outside Rockefeller Center. The cops arrest Reed but Harry thinks he's innocent. He must verify Reed's alibi or establish a different time of death. Although the MacNeil trio is set in Depression New York, everyone seemed to be having a good time. Rubout at the Onyx, however, showed an awareness of international problems and war on the horizon.

The PIs of the late 1940s were not jolly. The war took care of that. If they drank a lot, it was to get drunk rather than be social. The music, too, had changed. Most of the big bands had broken up, to be replaced by smaller groups of musicians who played clubs rather than large ballrooms. On the west coast, veterans of the Stan Kenton band played "cool" jazz while in the east, high-energy bebop was becoming the sound of the day.

The paragon of the 1940s West Coast PI was John Macdonald's (who later renamed himself Ross Macdonald) Lew Archer. Archer served in the South Pacific, returned home to California, worked as a PI and married a blonde girl named Sue. Like other young couples of the time, they had gone out dancing at the clubs on Sunset Boulevard and the ballrooms of the big hotels on Wiltshire Boulevard. Bandleader Les Brown's 1944 song, "Sentimental Journey," sung by Doris Day, was their song. But the life of a PI is not conducive to marriage. In 1948 Sue filed for divorce. By 1949 in The Moving Target (1949), Archer is alone in a West Hollywood bar called the Wild Piano, listening to a junkie piano player named Betty Fraley. She once had talent but drugs and a jail term ended her career. Lew is looking for clues in the kidnapping of Ralph Sampson, a wealthy businessman last seen at Burbank airport. Betty knows enough not to talk to Lew, who's beaten up for his trouble.

Archer's office was located on Sunset Strip, near Dino's, where he could drink and listen to jazz. Sharing a very similar setup (a few doors away) was Stuart Bailey of Roy Huggins' The Double Take (1946) and 77 Sunset Strip (1958). Bailey is a war veteran with fewer social complications than Archer and runs his own successful detective agency. In The Double Take a mundane identity check turns deadly. 77 Sunset Strip was cobbled together from three earlier short stories: "Appointment With Fear", "Now You See It" and "Death and the Skylark". The short stories are about murder ("Death and the Skylark" and "Now You See It") and greed ("Appointment with Fear."). Aside from the fact that Bailey takes clients to the jazz bar next door for a few drinks, these stories have very little jazz content. They are included because Huggins' PI, Bailey, went on to phenomenal success in the late 1950s American television series, *77 Sunset Strip*, which opened the door for a number of detective shows with jazz and spin-off paperback books.

A less well-known L.A. PI is Hollywood screenwriter Leigh Brackett's Edmund Clive of <u>No Good from a Corpse</u> (1944). Singer Laurel Dane asks her old boyfriend, Clive, for help. Before she can explain further, she is murdered. Aside from the victim and a memorable nightclub scene, there's not much jazz in this tale of family jealousy and murder in 1940's L.A.

Meanwhile across the country in New York City, detectives Johnny Fletcher and Sam Cragg get a crash course in the troubled music business at the end of the Big Band Era in Frank Gruber's <u>The Whispering Master</u> (1949). Marjorie Fair, an unsuccessful vocalist, tosses a demo recording across the airshaft and through the apartment window of Johnny Fletcher before she is murdered. Johnny wants to find out about his deceased neighbor. The music business interested Gruber enough to return to it in his last mystery, <u>Swing Low, Swing Dead</u> (1964) written fifteen years later. Johnny's friend Sam wins a song in a crap game from unsuccessful songwriter Willie Waller. He dismisses claims of the song's value until Waller is murdered. Gruber was a prolific author, writing 250 short stories for the pulps in the 1930s and 34 mysteries between 1939 and 1969 (as well as numerous westerns and television and movie scripts). His Johnny Fletcher-Cragg series (14 books) are what might be termed "PI lite" and a notch or two below Bart Spicer's Carney Wilde series.

From 1949-1959 Bart Spicer wrote seven Carney Wilde PI novels. Possibly the best, and certainly the most interesting, "Jazz Eye" (PI in a jazz environment) tale is Spicer's <u>Blues for the Prince</u> (1950) set in postwar Philadelphia. Jazz is very much in the foreground, along with segregation. The legendary and beloved black trumpet player Harold Morton Prince, known as the Prince, has been murdered and police have arrested his arranger and longtime friend, Stuff McGee, as his killer. McGee claims that he composed the music that made the Prince famous. PI Carney Wilde, a white WWII veteran, is hired by the Prince's family to sort out the truth and/or protect the Prince's legacy. In the course of his investigation working for a wealthy black family, he becomes aware of the realities of segregation, such as the inability to obtain employment commensurate to one's education, refusal of medical services and housing problems. Spicer knows his jazz history and the scene of the Prince's memorial jam session at the Hot Box deals with the 1940s' jazz controversy between New Orleans and Chicago style musicians. Spicer (and Wilde) favors the New Orleans blacks over the white Chicago-style players: "They tried and tried damned hard to play as well as the Dixie Negro units, but they weren't the instrumentalists…The Chicago boys couldn't play that well, so they replaced it with a honking tenor sax…" (p.162). There's no place for bebop here.

From 1947-1972, Henry Kane turned out 32 books (28 novels and 4 volumes of short stories) featuring his pulp P.I., New Yorker Pete Chambers, another "PI lite". In Until You Are Dead (1951), piano player Kermit Teshle witnesses a murder and tries to blackmail a racketeer. Teshle plans to use the money to open his own jazz club. He wants to hire Chambers to accompany him to the payoff but Chambers refuses. Teshle is murdered and the money disappears. Chambers goes club hopping, trawling for information and drinking, until he realizes the killer's identity. In the process, Kane presents a picture of Manhattan's entertainment world of the 1950s—a place where people knew each other, got their news from the late-edition newspapers and what columnist Walter Winchell said mattered.

In the 1950s, Puerto Ricans (encouraged by the Democratic Political machine) began moving to New York City and a Latin influence, especially Afro-Cuban, became a factor in jazz. In Kane's short story, "One Little Bullet" (1953), nightclub owner Joe Malamed is shot during a drum roll in an Afro-Cuban jazz floorshow. Sitting and drinking at the bar, Chambers missed the sound of the shot. Triangulation establishes the shooter was sitting at a table with Malamed's partner, a singer, a former jockey turned entrepreneur, a critic and Malamed's widow. The murder weapon belonged to Malamed's partner, who hires Chambers to find the killer.

In Bruce Cassidy's The Brass Shroud (1958), non-series PI Johnny Midas is looking for missing bank clerk Andrew Claussen, who approved fraudulent loans. He knows of Claussen's obsessive interest in jazz and tracks him to the Willow Lake Pavilion. A jazz combo is playing there, featuring the legendary 1930s trumpet player, Buck LeGrande, who is attempting a comeback. But LeGrande dies in a car crash. Suspecting a link between LeGrande and Claussen, Midas delves into the trumpet player's life for clues. His story was common among white swing players: a small-town boy who went to college and became a successful musician. During the 1930s, he played with the top bands, made movies in Hollywood and earned lots of money. After Pearl Harbor, musicians and their fans joined the military. LeGrande returned home after the war to a changed music scene and little work. When the Korean conflict broke out, he joined the U.S.O. In a story twist that's unique to 1950s American politics, the Chinese overrun a military base and LeGrande ends up brainwashed in a prison camp. Following the armistice, he returns home "changed" and "a fellow traveler". As the result of his imprisonment, LeGrande had to learn to play jazz all over again. He constantly listened to his records, as "his lip was gone." Midas, too, listens to LeGrande's records, which eventually offer the break in the case.

A trumpet solo also provides the key for another "P.I. lite", Danny Boyd in Carter Brown's (aka Alan G. Yates) The Ever Loving Blues (1961). The Australian born Brown ground out hundreds of pulp potboilers with The Ever Loving Blues being one of his better efforts. Boyd is hired by a Hollywood studio boss to find his missing starlet, Gloria Van Raven. She disappeared in Florida along with a bankrupt Wall Street tycoon Edward Woolrich II, blues singer Ellen Fitzroy and trumpet player Muscat Mullins. Boyd finds Fitzroy's body on Woolrich's yacht and learns that she was his wife. Mullins apparently witnessed the murder but was so stoned that he doesn't remember anything. Woolrich becomes the prime suspect after revealing that his wife was heavily insured. Hearing a recording of "The Ever Loving Blues" with Fitzroy backed by Mullins' trumpet, Boyd isn't so sure. Brown's The Ever Loving Blues represents the end of a style of pulp fiction, where the writing was spare, the music was mostly Dixieland, and the PI was usually from a potboiler series. The rest of the 1960s "jazz eyes" were spin-offs from popular television series.

Henry Kane, author of the Pete Chambers series, led the way with Peter Gunn (1960). Kane wrote both the spin-off and numerous episodes for the television show. Peter Gunn was cool and wore Brooks Brothers suits in L.A. He had a beautiful jazz singer girlfriend, Edie Hart and a good relationship with Lieutenant Jacoby of the police. He is, in many ways, an updated Carney Wilde. The opening lines usher the reader into a familiar scene to television viewers: "The music was real cool at Mother's. Edie was singing and Peter Gunn, alone at a corner table, was tapping his foot to the jazz." (p.5). He is approached by teamster boss Steve Bain to check out the background of guitarist Sam Lockwood, who is seeing Bain's daughter, Alice. Gunn's interaction with Lockwood is negative. After Bain is murdered, the guitar player is suspected. But Gunn decides to look beyond Alice's love life for the killer.

On the East Coast is Greenwich Village's version of cool, Frank Kane's Johnny Staccato (played by John Cassavetes). Unlike Gunn, who was a professional PI, Staccato is a full-time musician playing at club called Waldo's. He is, however, licensed to carry a gun. In Staccato (1960), Johnny is asked for help by his ex-girlfriend, singer Shelly Carroll. She is accused of murdering DJ Les Miller. Believing her innocent, Johnny knows that Miller had no shortage of enemies and is determined to find the killer.

Although both Peter Gunn and (to a lesser degree) Johnny Staccato were successful television PIs, they were limited to single volume spin-offs. The same was true of other spin-offs from hit PI television shows with jazz soundtracks, such as *Hawaiian Eye*, *Surfside 6*, and *Mr. Lucky*. (In the 1960s, popular taste was changing and spies entranced the public. TV shows like *The Man From Uncle* (26 spin-offs) and *I Spy* (10 spin-offs) reflected reader's preferences.) As noted, Boyd's Johnny Staccato is different from all of the earlier PIs, as he was an "amateur eye". Many of the later fictional Jazz Eyes followed the Staccato model and were musicians dabbling in crime detection.

That said, however, in the 1980s, two well-regarded series detectives proved the exception and briefly ventured into jazz. John Lutz's Alo Nudger, a sometime loser, was a long way from the suave Peter Gunn. In The Right to Sing the Blues (1986), he is hired by New Orleans café owner-Dixieland clarinetist Fat Jack McGee to investigate his star attraction, piano player Willy Hollister. He has shown an interest in singer Ineida Mann aka Collins, the daughter of a local financier with criminal connections. David Collins expects Fat Jack to watch over his sheltered daughter, who has pretensions of being a blues singer. Fat Jack lives off nostalgia, with his playing days past and his club designed to attract tourists. The Italian mob, once a group of thugs on Rampart Street, now rules the city.

Another 1980s PI novel with a jazz edge is Loren Estleman's Lady Day (1987). Detroit PI Amos Walker encounters his old friend Iris, a black prostitute, who is up from the Islands and looking for her missing father, Little Georgie Favor. He played Kingston with his Moonlighters, had an affair, and left without knowing that he fathered a daughter. Through various contacts, Walker traces him to a bar, Captain Ted's Party, where "…in time the bandstand would be replaced by another booth or video game and the big old fashioned neon juke box standing next to it would be the only source of music." (p.128). Favor plays for the occasional Budweiser and one person-a young musicologist, L.C. Candy. Before he can tell Iris about her father, Walker finds himself in the middle of a drug war.

Aside from these two 1980s PIs, jazz doesn't have a presence in the professional PI novel. It is, however, present with amateur detectives, usually musicians, like Bill Moody's piano playing Evan Horne (Bird Lives! (1999), Death of A Tenor Man (1995), Fade To Blue (2011), Looking For Chet Baker (2002), Shades of Blue (2008), Solo Hand (2009), and The Sound of the Trumpet, (1997)). Mark Coggins' series about bass-playing detective, August Riordan (The Immortal Game (1999), Vulture Capital (2002), Candy from Strangers (2006), Runoff (2007), The Big Wake-Up (2009), No Hard Feeling (2015) and The Dead Beat Scroll (2019)) is another example.

The days of jazz and the professional PI may be over.

COPS AND JAZZ

In the 1950s cops and jazz musicians occupied opposite poles in a small world. A partial explanation can be found in the changes in postwar society and popular musical taste. The war with its draft of top musicians and gas rationing ended traveling big bands and America's love affair with jazz. Jazz evolved into bebop, which was difficult for some fans to understand. It was meant for listening, not dancing. Many, who did understand it, had problems with narcotics—specifically heroin.

The police, considered at the time to be guardians of society, saw themselves insiders, and regarded jazz musicians as outsiders. When cops saw jazz musicians, they saw junkies and criminals. This view is reflected in Malcolm Braly's Shake Him till he Rattles (1963), where San Francisco Police Lieutenant Carver is on a crusade to clear the Beats and jazz musicians out of San Francisco's North Beach and stop its drug traffic. He is obsessed with alto saxophonist Lee Cabines, who smokes marijuana, and ready to plant heroin on him. In John Harvey's short story "Drummer Unknown" (2004), Sergeant Arthur Neville pressures a junkie drummer for information on narcotics use in a London jazz club and kills his girlfriend. Both Carver and Neville, blinded by their hatreds, were crooked cops. In Patricia Hall's Dressed to Kill (2014), DCI Keith Jackson thinks that black, American expatriate saxophonist Muddy Abraham is involved in the murder of a young girl whose body was discovered behind a Soho jazz club. Jackson doesn't like black, jazz musicians. He's sure that, at the least, Abraham is trafficking in narcotics.

When Abraham comes up relatively clean, he instructs Detective Sergeant Harry Barnard to dig deeper into the jazz musician's past to find grounds for deporting him.

While jazz was no longer the popular music of white Americans in the late 1950s and 1960s, it always retained a hold in black communities. Nowhere is this truer than in Chester Himes' stories of two Harlem police detectives, Coffin Ed Johnson and Grave Digger Jones. Both men met overseas in the army, joined the New York Police Department (NYPD), and lived next to each other in Astoria, Long Island. Their beat is Harlem, where they are known, respected and feared. Himes writes: "The word police has the power of magic in Harlem. It can make whole houses of people disappear." (Blind Man with a Pistol (1969) p.125). They appear in eight novels, five of which The Real Cool Killers, (1959), A Rage in Harlem, (1965), Cotton Comes to Harlem (1965), The Heat's On (1966), and Blind Man With A Pistol (1969) are briefly considered for their jazz element. While none of Himes' characters are jazz musicians, a jazz scene or riff often sets the tone of the story or a key scene. In The Real Cool Killers violence suddenly begins at the bar of Dew Drop Inn on 129th Street and Lenox Avenue. With the Kansas City style bluesy, tough jazz of Big Joe Turner blaring from jukebox, the only white man in the club is killed after being accused of messing around with someone else's wife. In Heat's On, the strains of Lester Young's saxophone in the parlor of a high-class whorehouse provides a counterpoint to Coffin Ed's rage when he is looking for Grave Digger Jones' supposed killer. Jackson, who was fleeced by Imabelle in Rage in Harlem, A met her at the Undertaker's Annual Dance at the Savoy. In Blind Man With A Gun, Coffin Ed and Grave Digger's suspect/witness in the death of a white theatre producer is murdered outside the Five Spot, where they were taking in a set by Thelonious Monk.

For Coffin Ed and Grave Digger, a part of each evening is spent looking for trouble in jazz clubs and bars, such as the Shalimar, Sugar Ray's, Dickie Wells', Count Basie's, Small's, The Red Rooster and the Hotel Theresa's lounge. One night in Cotton Comes to Harlem, while searching for stoolies (informants), Coffin Ed Johnson and

Grave Digger Jones stop at Big Wilt's Small's Paradise at 135t Street and Seventh Avenue to drink a few whiskies, listen to the jazz and watch the black and white dancers. In the old days before the Savoy burned down, Grave Digger and his wife used to go out dancing there. Listening to the musical conversation between the sax and trumpet sections of the band, Grave Digger says: "If we could read that language man, we could solve all the crimes in the world…It ain't so much what it says…It's what you can't do about it." (p.34).

Expatriate Himes' increasing anger at the racial situation in the United States made his Harlem series less realistic as the violence increased in each novel. Jazz began to play a smaller role in his writing. Initially, the series had been commissioned in France in the 1950s as part of Gallimard's La Series Noire by editor Marcel Duhamel to piggyback on the popularity of detective novels and the French fascination with American black culture. Himes' Harlem and his two crusading cops bore little relation to reality, but French readers seemed not to care. His work remains in print in France whereas typically it's out of print in the U.S.

A more realistic picture of New York cops is found in the work of jazz critic Nat Hentoff, who tried his hand at crime fiction, resulting in three police procedurals that reflected the social, political and jazz scene of the 1960s. It was a time when cops were often regarded as social outsiders. His detectives are Jewish and jazz fans. Hentoff's first novel, Call for The Keeper (1966), is set in New York City during the beginning of the Black Power movement, the deterioration of the political and social alliance between Jews and blacks and the changes in jazz that evolved into fusion. NYPD Detective Horowitz is investigating the murder of a crooked black undercover detective, Harry Sanders. Looking for his killer, he focuses on Sanders' recent targets, including a white guitarist named Randal with a questionable cabaret card. Randal had a minor narcotics conviction that should have prevented him from getting a cabaret card and working in New York City. One bartender tells Horowitz that Randal is well liked as "…he doesn't try to be black…He plays what he knows….Most whiteys try to sound like they were brought up in sanctified churches. What they sound like are sons of mothers who had black maids." (p.14). Near closing time one evening, Coleman Hawkins, the idol of earlier generations and ultimate survivor, comes to listen. So, too, does an old trumpet player, who once played with in the bands of Duke Ellington and Fletcher Henderson, and is now a messenger. "He's bitter", Randal tells Horowitz of the latter. "The music has passed him by. No place in jazz for the old. Except a very few." (p.14)

In Blues for Charlie Darwin (1982), detectives Noah Green and Sam McKibbon, mix business and pleasure in the jazz club scene while looking for the killer of Kathleen Ginsburg, a New York University professor's wife and of Greenwich Village bookstore owner, Emma Dixon, who was a friend of Green's wife. Green is a second- generation New Yorker, the son of Leftist, Jewish parents. McKibbon's family, on the other hand is black, and has lived in Harlem for several generations. On his night off, Green goes to hear Art Blakey and his Jazz Messengers at the Blue Light in Greenwich Village. The tension between Jews and blacks from the Black Power movement doesn't apply to the jazz loving Green. The club owner tells him: "Catch the tenor with Art Blakey. New Blood: Nineteen goddam years old! Sure wish Mingus was still around. He would love this cat…I'll bring him over later…Always helps to know the heat." (p.97).

In Hentoff's The Man from Internal Affairs (1985), McKibbon is away fishing and listening to tapes of singer Billie Holiday and tenor saxophonists Lester Young and Ben Webster, while Green is facing corruption charges. It's a trumped-up case brought by an anti-Semitic cop. Green's defense lawyer and friend Jason Mendelssohn went to Boys High School with him, shared his obsession with jazz and once got from him some rare Kay Kyser recordings. Possibly because Hentoff, who wrote for *The Village Voice* (from 1959-2009), was a social as well as a jazz critic, his three books capture the 1960s environment.

Skipping a generation and crossing the Atlantic, another police procedural series with a jazz tinge is English author John Harvey's Charlie Resnick stories. His books and short stories span a time from Margaret Thatcher's England of the 1980s to Tony Blair's

New Labour of the 1990s and Gordon Brown's recession. They are mostly set in the English Midlands in a declining manufacturing city resembling Nottingham. The English-born Resnick is an outsider. As a son of Polish refugees, he still maintains close ties to the Polish community. When first introduced in Lonely Hearts (1989), his wife Elaine has dumped him, leaving him divorced, over forty and overweight. His life is seemingly divided into several parts—his police work and his love of jazz. Charlie also likes cats and has four of them. Each cat is named after an American jazz musician—Dizzy (Gillespie), Bud (Powell), (Art) Pepper and Miles (Davis).

Unlike Himes or Hentoff's cops, who saw the jazz greats in clubs, Resnick's relationship with legendary musicians is largely through vinyl records or CDs. It is a different intimacy than seeing them live. Harvey writes in the coda to Now's the Time (1999) that Resnick was first introduced to jazz through a pile of scratched 78s that his uncle, a tailor, brought back from the States. The 78s were mostly big band vocalists—Bing Crosby, Frank Sinatra, Ella Fitzgerald and Billie Holiday with Teddy Wilson. In the introduction to Minor Key (2009), he remembers the first song of hers that he ever heard was "I Cried for You" with Teddy Wilson and his Orchestra.

Billie Holiday has haunted Charlie and become a part of his life through the years. In Lonely Hearts (1989) he broods about her childhood and her death from narcotics. In Cold Light (1994), his life significantly improves after he buys the pricey, boxed CD set of the Collected Billie Holiday on Verve for Christmas. Jazz clearly provides an emotional refuge for Charlie in an increasingly violent world. Nowhere is this more evident than in Cold in Hand (2008). Karen Shields, who's investigating the death of Charlie's lover, Lynn Kellogg, notices his albums and CDs, asks if he had always "been into jazz?' "Pretty much. One of the things that keeps me sane. Least, it used to," he replies. (p.331). When Lynn was murdered, Charlie was listening to trombonist Bob Brookmeyer play "There Will Never Be Another You."

In the coda from Now's the Time, Harvey writes: "Charlie is pretty much locked into jazz whose roots and style are found in the '40s and '50s, the years of classic bop and swing, Lester Young,

Ben Webster, Milt Jackson. Parker, of course. Thelonious Monk."
(p.298). Charlie tried to see some of the surviving legends but he's
a long way in time and space from New York's Swing Street. In <u>Still
Waters</u> (1997), he is called away from a Milt Jackson concert when
the body of a young girl is found floating in a canal. He also heard
Art Pepper, whose beautiful alto saxophone's tone seemed unaffected
by his drug addiction until close to his end. Charlie remembers it
in the short story "Home" (2006). In "Slow Burn"(1998), a BBC
radio play turned into a novella whose title was taken from the
Charlie Parker Songbook, Charlie recalls seeing some of the second
tier jazz greats such as Nat Adderley, Teddy Edwards, Al Cohn, and
Zoot Sims at Jimmy Nolan's Jazz Club.

With all this jazz in the background, there's actually very little
jazz in the foreground. The often-overlapping themes of the Resnick
books have little to do with jazz. They are mostly straightforward
police work. Harvey writes of revenge: <u>Cutting Edge</u> (1991), <u>Wasted
Years</u> (1993), and <u>Easy Meat</u> (1996); serial murder: <u>Lonely Hearts</u>
(1989), <u>Off Minor</u> (1992) and <u>Still Waters</u> (1990); murder: <u>Wasted
Years</u>, (1993), <u>Cold Light</u> (1994), <u>Living Proof</u> (1995), <u>Easy Meat</u>
(1996), <u>Cold in Hand</u> (2008) and <u>Darkness, Darkness</u> (2014);
drugs: <u>Rough Treatment</u> (1990) and <u>Last Rites</u> (1999); jealousy:
<u>Living Proof</u> (1995); theft: <u>Still Waters</u> (1997); mental illness: <u>Last
Rites</u> (1999) and <u>Cold Light</u> (1994). In <u>Cutting Edge</u>, however,
Charlie does offer shelter to Ed Silver, a tenor saxophone player,
who drank away his career. Silver's claim to fame as far as Charlie
is concerned is that he saw Charlie Parker before he was going to
record his famous Dial sessions. Aside from this vignette, the book
is about revenge and murder.

While the titles of the eleven short stories that compose <u>Now's
the Time</u> are drawn from the Charlie Parker Songbook, only four
have jazz content upfront. "Cool Blues" is, despite its title, about
jazz. It concerns a robber who uses the names of Ellington musicians
when he picks up young girls on the London Tube and robs them.
Resnick arranges an elaborate trap for him at Ronnie Scott's jazz
club. In another, "Now's the Time," Resnick has come to London
for jazz musician Ed Silver's funeral when his wallet is stolen by a

young girl at King's Cross train station. In "Work," an elderly jazz musician is brutally beaten after he identifies a robber for Resnick. In the final story, "Slow Burn," a jazz club from Charlie's past is torched. The remaining stories are concerned with familiar subjects of police procedurals with no overt connection to jazz beyond the title and emotional tenor: theft: "Now's the Time", "Dexterity", "She Rote", "Bird of Paradise", "Cool Blues", "Stupendous" and "My Little Suede Shoes"; assault: "Confirmation" and "Work"; arson: "Cheryl" and "Slow Burn".

In the coda to <u>Now's the Time</u>, Harvey acknowledges that certain musicians influence specific books, such as Billie Holiday and Lester Young in <u>Lonely Hearts</u> and Milt Jackson in <u>Still Water</u>. Charlie Parker's influence is present in all Resnick novels and most of the short stories as he is always listening to his music. As noted earlier, <u>Now's the Time</u>, contains stories whose titles are taken from the Charlie Parker Songbook. Harvey also acknowledges the influence of pianist Thelonious Monk on all of his writing. He notes: "…its Monk whose music I've returned to again and again when writing both the books and the stories; Monk whose broken rhythms have underscored the emotional landscape of Resnick's journey and helped to suggest their form." (pps. 298-299). The final scene in the final book of the series, <u>Darkness, Darkness</u>, finds Charlie sitting on a park bench with his final thoughts about a new Monk album of concerts in Milan and Paris featuring "of Minor," and "Straight, No Chaser." He muses: "Why play the right notes…? You know the rest." (p.337). Readers familiar with Monk know the rest.

Two police series set in contemporary New Orleans attracted a serious and dedicated readership in the 1990s-James Lee Burke's Dave Robicheaux series and Julie Smith's Skip Langdon series. Storyville had long closed, and with it went New Orleans as a place of employment for large numbers of musicians. Although jazz clubs still existed on Bourbon Street, it was one of several options, along with Cajun music and R&B that vied for attention and tourist dollars. It is still surprising that James Lee Burke's Dave Robicheaux series has so little jazz as no writer can compare with his understanding of a dark side of New Orleans. The initial book, The <u>Neon</u>

Rain (1987) introduces Dave Robicheaux, a New Orleans police detective. He is a Cajun with a love of music that runs to zydeco, the blues and classic jazz. Robicheaux had a collection of historical jazz and blues vinyl records of Bunk Johnson, Kid Ory and Bix Beiderbecke that are smashed after intruders trash his houseboat.

Julie Smith's Skip Langdon is different from the other police officers discussed in this section. Langdon risked the disapproval of her socially prominent family to join the New Orleans Police Department. She's the polar opposite of Robicheaux, whose Cajun parents were uneducated and two steps from poverty. Aside from the pressures of solving a variety of crimes, she must deal with sexism, family disapproval and the resentment of colleagues. Although the Langdon books are set in New Orleans, she's not really a jazz or blues fan. Consequently, with the exception of The Axeman's Jazz (1991), jazz is very much in the background of the Langdon stories.

Returning to New York City in the late 1990s, as well as several generations of cops away from Hentoff's Green and Horowitz, is Reggie Nadelson's Artie Cohen. Born Artemy Ostalsky in Moscow, Cohen, is a NYPD cop who later became a private investigator. He arrived in New York when he was 13 via Israel. His father was a KGB officer who lost his job due to his mother's activities against the regime, forcing the family to emigrate. Artie had heard his first jazz while living in Moscow from Willis Conover's Voice of America radio program. He eagerly listened to Billie Holiday, Stan Getz, Chet Baker, Errol Garner and Oscar Peterson, whose music remains a part of his life. His father's position in the KGB also gave him access to western luxuries, such as jazz records. Cohen's most prized possession was the Stan Getz recording, *The Steamer*, which remained his favorite and appears in four books. In Sex Dolls, he muses, "Sometimes I ask myself, usually around New Year when I've had too much to drink, what I'd trade to be Stan Getz. Would I trade it all in…How would it feel…?" (p.7). His favorite wedding present was the famous jazz photographer Herman Leonard's picture of Stan Getz (Red Hook).

Artie clearly loves jazz, listening to it for pleasure and refuge. Unlike Hentoff's Green and Horowitz or even his father when he was a KGB officer in New York, Artie doesn't go to jazz clubs. The closest he got to a jazz legend was sleeping with Stan Getz's ex-girlfriend Frances Pascoe in Bloody London. After she committed suicide with Stan Getz recording of "Falling in Love" playing in the background, he takes an old eight-track tape of "Stella by Starlight" that Getz had recorded for her when they were together.

Cohen's background and language skills make him useful to the NYPD in their dealing with Russian organized crime in Brighton Beach. In Londongrad (2009), however, he's overmatched by Putin's FSB, (the successors of the KGB) but protected by their memories and respect for his father and one officer's love of jazz. His most unusual case deals with the theft of nuclear material: Red Hot Blues, (1999). Other cases are similar to those found in contemporary police procedurals: organized crime: Sex Dolls, (2002); drugs: Sex Dolls (2002); murder: Fresh Kills (2007), Bloody London (1999), Disturbed Earth (2004), Red Hook (2006), Londongrad (2009) and Blood Count (2011).

While Blood Count clearly refers to the Billy Strayhorn composition, the jazz that appears is in memories of the elderly residents at the Louis Armstrong apartment complex at Sugar Hill of Ella Fitzgerald and of Louis Armstrong and the records played during their Christmas gathering. In the laundry room, he encounters an elderly lady, who was a life-long, friend of Ella Fitzgerald (from Yonkers to Beverly Hills). Ella was Artie's father's favorite musician. He remembers a conversation with him about his time in New York: "I felt my good communist soul was being sucked out, Artyom. Not by material goods, or by the American way of life, but by the music, especially by Ella Fitzgerald." (p.95).

On the other side of the country in Los Angeles is another cop outsider, Michael Connolly's Harry Bosch, who loves much of the same jazz as Artie Cohen. If tenor player Stan Getz was Artie Cohen's man, then the lesser-known alto saxophone player Frank Morgan is Harry's Bosch's. Morgan (1933-2008) was a force on the West Coast jazz scene in the early 1950s, recording his first album in 1955. His next album came thirty years later; the long absence was due to a heroin habit. Drug free in his later life, Morgan's playing was better than ever. In the late evenings when Bosch can't sleep, he listens to Morgan's music and looks down at the city of Los Angeles from his hilltop home. When Morgan is playing L.A. clubs, Bosch is there.

In "Nighthawks," which appears in a short collection (In Sunlight or in Shadow, 2016, edited by Lawrence Block) inspired by the paintings of Edward Hopper, Harry Bosch ponders inspiration and its influence. Bosch "always thought that studying and understanding the sound of a saxophone had made him a better detective...he knew that hearing Frank Morgan play "Lullaby" somehow made him better at what he did." (p.84).

Another West Coast alto player, Art Pepper (1925-1982) is also important to Bosch. Pepper, whose career was also interrupted by drugs and jail, managed to record with surprising frequency. He was not as successful as Morgan in shaking his drug habit. Bosch listens to Pepper often in the early books and passes on his appreciation to his friend, FBI profiler, Terry McCaleb, in A Darkness More Than Night, (2001).

Aside from Morgan and Pepper, the fictional alto sax player Quentin McKenzie is a part of Bosch's jazz life. In the short story "Christmas Even" (2004), while Harry is investigating a pawnshop robbery, he finds an alto saxophone belonging to McKinzie, whom he had heard playing while on a troop ship returning home from Vietnam. Harry learns that McKinzie is now in a nursing home and returns his horn on Christmas Eve. They become friends. After his death, McKinzie leaves Harry his horn as he has been teaching Harry to play. In Lost Light (2003), Harry is able to make it through George Cables' song "Lullaby", learned from a Frank Morgan CD.

Like Artie Cohen, Harry Bosch had an unusual childhood. He was the son of a prostitute and spent his childhood in a series of state institutions. When he was old enough, he went to Vietnam as a "tunnel rat", chasing the enemy in the dark tunnels underneath the battlefields (The Black Echo, 1992). After returning to Los Angeles, he joined the police department. Because of his background, Bosch saw himself as the spokesperson for those who couldn't speak for themselves: especially unwanted children: City of Bones (2002), The Burning Room, (2014) and Wrong Side of Goodbye (2016); women: The Closers, (2005), Echo Park (2006) and The Black Box, (2012); prostitutes: The Concrete Blonde (1994) and The Last Coyote (1995). As a Los Angeles detective, he gets high profile Hollywood cases: A Lost Light (2003), Darkness More Than Night (2001), Trunk Music (1997), The Last Coyote (1995) and The Brass Verdict (2008). He also investigates racism: Angel's Flight (1999); narcotics: The Black Ice (1993), Two Kinds of Truth (2017); and terrorism: The Overlook, (2007). Often he finds himself at odds with his own police department: The Last Coyote (1997), Angel's Flight (1999), The Crossing (2015), and Two Kinds of Truth (2017); the political establishment: The Burning Room (2014) and the FBI: The Black Echo (1992) and The Overlook (2007).

With the exception of the short story, "Christmas Even", none of his cases have anything to do with jazz. But he's always listening to jazz. It provides balance in his life and helps him focus on the cases on hand. For example, in The Last Coyote he listens to Clifford Brown's "Willow Weep for Me" while remembering the death of his mother and Miles Davis' "All Blues" when trying to understand the thrill killing of David Fitzpatrick in Echo Park. In Echo Park, while listening to Thelonious Monk Quartet with John Coltrane at Carnegie Hall, a newly released album of recently discovered fifty-year-old concert tapes, Bosch decides to go through the old Marie Gesto murder casebook, looking for clues that he feels must be there. Riding out to inform a police officer's wife of her husband's death in Angel's Flight, Harry "had brought a homemade tape with him… of saxophone pieces Bosch particularly liked. He fast-forwarded it until he found the one he wanted. It was Frank Morgan's "Lullaby". It was a sweet and soulful funeral dirge… goodbye…" (p.314).

On the back cover of a promotional CD, Dark Sacred Night— The Music of Harry Bosch, Michael Connelly tried to explain the link between writing and jazz as well as between jazz and the detective. He observes: "Whenever I write a Harry Bosch novel I am usually listening to jazz. It inspires me. Maybe the improvisation of the music helps the improvisation of writing…It also helps me set the character of this detective. Invariably, the music I am listening to ends up in the books…I think the music he listens to says a lot about him." The Brass Verdict, (2008) was dedicated to Frank Morgan, who had recently died.

A different contemporary police procedural series is British author Peter Morfoot's Captain Paul Darac quartet. It's not just the Mediterranean setting in Nice, France or the Napoleonic legal code that makes it unlike other police procedurals. Captain Darac is a ranking officer in the Brigade Criminelle, not an outsider like Harry Bosch, Artie Cohen, Dave Robicheaux, etc. Also, he's not a lone wolf and freely uses the talents of his colleagues in the Brigade Criminelle to solve cases. Like Skip Langdon, he's from a respected family. Although he's separated from his partner, he's not "damaged" by life like Harry Bosch or Dave Robicheaux. In fact, as Knock 'Em Dead (2020) concludes, he's about to enter a new phase in his personal life.

Like Harry Bosch, Charlie Resnick and Artie Cohen, Darac's always listening to jazz CDs. But he's too young to have seen the jazz legends in the twilight of their careers at European jazz festivals. Unlike the other police officers, Darac is also a jazz musician. He's a guitarist, who spends his nights playing at the Blue Devil Jazz Club. Often he's called from its stage to a crime scene. That said, with one exception, jazz is mostly in the background in the Darac books.

As Impure Blood (2016) begins, a man is murdered in a Muslim prayer group and nobody seems to have seen the killer. Relations with Nice's Muslim community are tense, so Darac doesn't expect their help. To complicate matters, the Tour de France is about to begin. Then his boss, Agnes Dantier, and her father are kidnapped. Initially, Darac views the incidents separately, then eventually links them.

Jazz features prominently in Fatal Music (2017). The body of an elderly woman, Jeanne Mesnel, is discovered in her hot tub. She died several days earlier. Darac was ready to dismiss her death as natural but his curiosity was aroused by her jazz record collection and the realization of her likeness on a 1963 poster above the door to the Blue Devil Jazz Club. Later he learns of her involvement with the club's owner, his friend American Eldridge Clay. He also discovers her house was recently sold under unusual circumstances to a young American curator at the nearby Villa Rose museum.

In <u>Box of Bones</u> (2018), Darac witnesses the death of an onlooker during the Carnival Parade. It's the first of a series of deaths linked to a 19 million Euro robbery in which a reward was paid as the loot was recovered. Only Pierre Delmas, the inside man, was ever caught. Darac believes Delmas, recently released from jail, is killing gang members who double crossed him. At the same time, Darac is looking for his guitar that was stolen from a Carnival float. The trail leads to revelations of corruption in the city's government.

In the fourth Darac book, <u>Knock 'Em Dead</u> (2020), Ambroise Paillaud, an old comic actor, is killed by a train. Surveillance film of the incident indicates suicide rather than murder. When his will is discovered missing and its notary, Caroline Rosay, is murdered, Darac's team takes a closer look. While Paillaud is not the man everyone thought him to be, the killer of Rosay and the missing will becomes the focus of Darac's investigation.

In all of these police procedurals, with characters as varied as Paul Darac and Harry Bosch, or for that matter, Charlie Resnick, Artie Cohen, Noah Green and Dave Robicheaux, the reader who knows jazz, tunes into the mood and emotions of the story with a special understanding.

JAZZ AND DRUGS

Drug abuse has long been a part of jazz culture. In the 1950s, sociologists hypothesized that racial discrimination was the cause of its use among jazz musicians. While numerous black musicians (alto saxophonist Charlie Parker, trumpeter Howard McGhee, singer Billie Holiday) were addicts, there were also a lot of white addicts (alto saxophonist Art Pepper, trumpeter Chet Baker, baritone saxophonist Serge Chaloff). Some jazz musicians (drummer Stan Levey, alto saxophonist Frank Morgan) managed to "get clean", stay off drugs and have successful careers. Others (tenor saxophonist Stan Getz, trumpeter Miles Davis) used drugs on and off throughout their lives. Very few (pianist Bill Evans, trumpet player Louis Armstrong) had successful careers in spite of their continuing drug use. Some jazz musicians who overcame their addictions (guitarist Joe Pass, alto saxophonist Frank Morgan) had careers shortened by time spent in jail on drug related offenses. Others (pianist Richard Twardzik, pianist Sonny Clark) died from drug overdoses. And some (trumpeter Chet Baker, tenor saxophonist Wardell Gray) died under suspicious circumstances related to drugs. Drugs shortened lives and careers and took the lives of its users, regardless of their color.

A few explanations for drug use come to mind: In the early days of jazz, playing long hours for short money, often in gangster-controlled clubs, few musicians could resist the escape provided by easily available drugs (and alcohol). During the Big Band Era, musicians spent more hours on the road than on the bandstand and drugs offered a different travel experience. Finally, there was the belief in the 1950s that was popularized by emulators of Charlie Parker that hard drugs put one's playing on a higher level. With a few it did, but most burned out, often spectacularly.

Drug use by musicians during the Jazz Age and the Depression era was usually marijuana or "reefers" and accepted as a part of life. That acceptance is reflected in the writing of the period. In Jonathan Latimer's 1936 novel, <u>The Lady in the Morgue</u>, PI Bill Crane observes musicians having a routine reefer during a night's work at a taxi dance. The bartender tells Crane "…all them musicians hit the smoke." (134). Similarly, in Harlan Reed's 1938 novel, <u>The Swing Murder Music</u>, PI Dan Jordan discovers an unmarked door leading to the musician room and smells marijuana. In the slang of the day, musicians who used marijuana were called "vipers". Louis Armstrong was a viper and smoked a daily reefer. (He considered it safer than alcohol because it was an herb.)

Drugs crossed the Atlantic Ocean to England with the jazz musicians who worked on the transatlantic ocean liners. Two Depression Era English jazz mysteries reflect the changing views on drugs: In <u>The Dance Band Mystery</u>, (1940) by Ray Sonin, Scotland Yard's Inspector John Adams is more interested in the two American gangsters bringing drugs into the country than the English musician who is the source for London dance band musicians. Journalist Sam Underhill explains the motivation for drug use among musicians to Adams: "…the American white musicians liked the negro style of playing, so they set about copying it, and what quicker way of copying it could they find than smoking the same cigarettes as those that got the black men so excited?" (p.91) The English jazz musicians copied their American counterparts for the same reason.

A harsher view of the English jazz club scene is shown in Ngaio Marsh's <u>A Wreath For Rivera</u> (1949). Inspector Roderick Alleyn is called to investigate an accidental homicide of jazz musician Carlos Rivera that turns out to be murder. Alleyn learns that the bandleader, Breezy Bellairs had a cocaine habit, the victim was his supplier and the club was a front for the distribution of drugs. Unlike <u>The Dance Band Mystery</u>, there is no rationale offered for drug use in this story.

A tougher American attitude towards hard drug use was soon

evident. In Harper Barnes' <u>Blue Monday</u> (1991), set in 1930s Kansas City, bandleader Bennie Moten is unhappy about the increasing amount of hard drugs available to jazz musicians from white mobsters. Cub reporter Michael Holt suspects this might a reason for the bandleader's unexpected death.

In the 1930s, musicians, such as Louis Armstrong and Gene Krupa, became national icons. Their marijuana use soon came to the notice of authorities, which resulted in headline-grabbing drug arrests. The drug use of jazz musicians became an interest for the police. In a 1950's story, John Harvey's "Child's Play" (2004), two young jazz musicians, tenor saxophonist Wilson Childs and pianist Quincy Simmons, drive home from a late night San Francisco jazz club. They are caught by police during a "routine" traffic stop. The police search Childs' car and find a gun and drugs. Earlier that evening Miles Davis had seemingly offered Childs the job as John Coltrane's replacement in Davis' band. Not wanting Childs to miss an opportunity to play with Miles, Simmons says the drugs and gun belong to him.

Few musicians could withstand the publicity surrounding a drug conviction. In New York City, a conviction on drug charges meant the loss of a cabaret card without which a musician could not work in the clubs. That's why Billie Holiday was reduced to singing in a Ceres Street bar in Portsmouth, New Hampshire in Brendan Dubois' short story, "The Lady Meets the Blue" (2017). Her loss of her cabaret card was a famous case, but it also happened to other musicians. In Ernest Lehman's novella, <u>The Sweet Smell of Success</u>, (2000), publicist Sidney Falco places innuendoes about drug use in gossip columns. With planted marijuana, he sets up a police bust of a Sinatra-like singer, Steve Dallas. Dallas' career is over.

By the 1950s, fictional jazz musicians are usually hard drug users and their drug use has deadly consequences. Mystery novelist Evan Hunter (Ed McBain) wrote <u>Quartet in H</u> (1956), about Andy Silvers, a talented trumpet player, who goes on the road with a big band and is introduced to marijuana. Silvers progresses to heroin, wrecks the lives of his friends and dies from hepatitis contracted from a dirty needle. In Douglass Wallop's <u>Night Light</u> (1953), a drug-crazed drummer Alfie Landon is transformed into a sniper and kills a number of innocent people before he jumps/falls to his death.

A more realistic story about hard drug use and its consequences is Stuart M. Kaminsky's "Blue Note" (2008), set in 1950s Chicago. Gambler Pitch Noles is known as "The Prince of Tell" because of his ability to read other gambler's body language. He is forced into a poker game with three crooked gamblers who won $20,000 from a drug dealer named Terrance "Dusk" Oliver. If Noles doesn't win $40,000 for Oliver by 5am, Mae, the singer in Count Basie's band, will lose a finger for non-payment of drug debt. Mae is Noles' mother.

There is no shortage of drug-using jazz musicians for writers to incorporate into their stories. Tenor saxophonist Wardell Gray (1921-1955) is a case in point. Gray emerged as one of the top tenor players of the bop era and was famous for his musical duels with tenor player and drug user, Dexter Gordon in the black clubs along L.A.'s Central Avenue. During the 1940s, when jazz musicians started using heroin, Gray remained clean. But in the 1950s, he developed a drug habit. In May 1955, Gray was part of the band hired for the opening of the short-lived Moulin Rouge, the first interracial casino-resort in segregated Las Vegas. He died under mysterious circumstances and his body was found in the desert. Whether he was killed by the mob or died from a "hot shot" (drug overdose) has never been established. Gray's story, along with that of the short-lived, controversial Moulin Rouge, has been incorporated into three mysteries: Bill Moody's Death of a Tenor Man (1995), Charles Fleming's Ivory Coast (2002) and Richard Rayner's The Devil's Wind (2005).

In Death of a Tenor Man, researcher Ace Buffington asks his friend jazz pianist Evan Horne for help in writing a paper on Gray's death. Buffington thinks that the surviving musicians will talk more freely to Horne. Horne's investigation sparks the interest of organized crime elements whose present business dealings could be affected by the events of thirty-seven years earlier. The Ivory Coast focuses on mobster Moe Winer's secret financing of the first integrated hotel-casino, the Ivory Coast, fronted by a retired boxer. Gray's death castes a shadow over the opening of the Ivory Coast (modeled on The Moulin Rouge) and is a strand in the story, not its focus. In The Devil's Wind black tenor player Wardell Lane (loosely based on Gray) is murdered by the mob and his body is dumped in the desert. He had refused to sell heroin for the mob-connected son of a United States senator. As with The Ivory Coast, the tenor player's death is a very small part in a larger story.

Chet Baker (1929-1988) was another West Coast musician with a career-long drug problem. Baker's redeeming qualities were his James Dean good looks (that faded quickly with drug use) and the beautiful sound of his trumpet. (His singing is an acquired taste.) He spent much of his life in Europe, where access to hard drugs was easier and people were more forgiving. But he died under mysterious circumstances in Amsterdam. The Dutch police believe that he was sitting in a window, nodded off from drugs, and fell to his death. Others believe that an angry dealer pushed Baker to his death over unpaid drug debts. (In 1966, he had his teeth knocked out, allegedly over lack of payment to a dealer.) Bill Moody used the unresolved questions around Baker's death in his Evan Horne novel, Looking for Chet Baker (2002). Horne's friend, academic researcher Ace Buffington, tricks a reluctant Horne into investigating Baker's death. Although initially he begs off the investigation, Buffington hints that Horne knows more about Baker's death than he really does. Soon Horne has Baker's drug dealer's interest.

The police realized that musicians were an easy drug conviction and sometimes used their substance dependence for their own ends, as shown in two books set on opposite sides of the Atlantic Ocean. In 1960s San Francisco, jazz was associated with the North Beach Beat culture. Beat writer Jack Kerouac included cameos of pianist George Shearing and guitarist-vocalist Slim Gaillard in On the Road (1957) and tenor saxophonist Brew Moore in Desolation Angels (1965). But the jazz musicians who provided a musical accompaniment for literary readings also became identified with drug-using beatniks. In Shake Him till he Rattles (1963), written by the lesser-known Beat writer Malcolm Braly, Police Lieutenant

Carver is on a crusade to clear the North Beach clubs of beatniks and jazz musicians. He is after alto saxophone player Lee Cabiness, who smokes an occasional reefer but is not a hard drug user. To get him, Carver decides to plant evidence in advance of a raid. He uses a Beat playwright Terry Sullivan, a hard drug user whom Carver has turned into both an informant on the drug scene and a dealer to snare other users. Similarly, in John Harvey's short story "Drummer Unknown" (2004), Sergeant Arthur Neville, a crooked police officer, leans on an addict drummer for information on the London jazz-drug scene. After raiding a club that turns out to be clean, the enraged Neville kills the drummer's girlfriend.

While other Europeans seemed to have a more tolerant attitude towards drug use, the English attitude hardened by the 1950s. They were a lot tougher on drug-using jazz musicians than the police on the other side of the English Channel. Harvey offers an interesting insight into the London jazz-drug scene of the 1950s-1960s with two interrelated short stories "Just Friends" (2007) and "Minor Key" (2009). In "Just Friends", a story of a thirty-year friendship that begins in London when three lads, Jimmy, Patrick and Val, get caught up in the seductive jazz scene and form their own group. Knowing his limitations on the trumpet, Patrick becomes the group's manager until it dissolves, then Val's manager. He dabbles in drugs and profits enough to eventually end up as the owner of several West End clubs. Jimmy, the drummer, drops out to become a cop, and later, an investigator. Val, the most talented of the three, is snared into the jazz-drug world and dies an early death. Val's story is told in "Minor Key." After Val gets busted on drug charges, Patrick calls Jimmy for a favor. Patrick arranges to get Val a job in Paris, away from the London drug scene. With club and recording offers, things seem to be going well for Val in Paris until he encounters an American drummer-dealer. He falls back into drugs, crosses a drug dealer, and gets a beating from which he never really recovers.

A jazz musician with a drug habit could try to escape from the consequences by becoming an informant. Two stories of police turning jazz musicians into informants are Frank Kane's The Guilt Edged Frame (1964), a Johnny Liddell PI thriller, and Jack Fuller's

The Best of Jackson Payne (2000). In The Guilt Edged Frame set in 1960s San Francisco, Marty Lewis, a young trumpet player owes the mob thousands of dollars from his drug habit. He's beaten up as an inducement to pay his drug debt. He goes to the police with the name of his supplier in return for dropping any narcotics charges. He also arranges for a loan from his agent to pay off the mob and agrees to a three-month tour to get out of town. But his travel plans displease someone enough to kill him and frame his girlfriend for the murder. A more realistic story is Jack Fuller's The Best of Jackson Payne, covering twenty years of Payne's life. Through a series of interviews, musicologist Charles Quinn hopes to gain enough understanding to write the definitive biography of tenor saxophone genius, Jackson Payne. He realizes that the L.A. police busted Payne for drugs. Rather than destroying his career with a long jail sentence, they turned him into an informant on the Central Avenue drug scene, allowing them to bust a well-known musician named Damon Reed and catch a drug dealer nicknamed "the Leopard." In return, he served a short stretch in San Quentin, where drugs were plentiful and he played in the prison band. Upon release, he goes to Paris. Payne seems to have his life under control, until he encounters Damon Reed and the Leopard again.

Drug smuggling is another topic that, considering the amount of traveling musicians do, enters into the literature far less than one might expect. In an early short story, "Mr. Hyde-de-Ho" (1956) by Veronica Parker Johns, a smuggler adopts the identity of a jazz musician and gives a gullible young girl on a transatlantic liner the gift of a wooden box that is later found to contain drugs. While the story is forgettable, the descriptions of the New York club scene are memorable.

Far more interesting is Martin Maltese's North to Toronto (1998). Customs officials discover heroin in the saxophone case of jazz musician Dave Harrigan, who is returning to the States after a successful tour. A surprised Harrigan disavows any knowledge of the drugs and his lawyer believes him. The lawyer hires investigator Henry Kloss to discover who framed his client. His investigation results in a death and a disappearance and uncovers numerous financial motives for the drug smuggling. In Jack Batten's Straight

No Chaser (1989), saxophonist Dave Goddard has returned to Toronto after several California gigs. Goddard has become concerned that someone is following him. He hires his friend Crang who botches the surveillance job. Crang watches thieves assault Goddard and steal his saxophone. By coincidence he encounters one of the assailants at a foreign film festival and follows him back to his hotel with the intention of stealing the sax back. He is interrupted in his endeavors but not before discovering that the saxophone case is filled with heroin. Crang has stumbled into a Vietnamese drug smuggling operation.

Misuse of prescription drugs is a recent aspect of the drug problem. In Richard J. Cass' Solo Act (2017), club owner Elder Darrow investigates the illicit uses of legal drugs after the death of his girlfriend, jazz singer Alison Sommers. While in Michael Connelly's Two Kinds of Truth (2017), Harry Bosch is working cold cases when he's called to a crime scene where two pharmacists have been murdered. Bosch's experienced eye spots a hit, not a robbery. One of the victims filed a complaint against a clinic for writing too many prescriptions. Further investigation reveals a prescription drug scam using older, homeless people.

Two final books are more light-hearted. In Charlotte Carter's Rhode Island Red (1997), street musician Nanette Hayes doesn't play her tenor saxophone well enough to make a living and is supported by her boyfriend. But he's using her for bait in a scam to find Rhode Island Red, which is not an apple or a bird but, a gold saxophone stuffed with dope that was given in payment to Charlie Parker for playing at a Newport wedding. The sax was apparently stolen dockside from Parker before he was to leave on a European trip. J. P. Smith's Body and Soul (1987) is a slapstick story set in Paris. Jersey Wozzeck, a Polish jazz pianist, is recruited by his best friend into a surprisingly well-paying job of delivering packages. Of course, the packages contain drugs. Wozzeck uses the money to buy rare American jazz records of Bud Powell, Thelonious Monk, John Coltrane and Charlie Mingus. When his jazz record collection is complete, he wants out of the delivery job. But his employers, a criminal consortium called "UniRex", will not let him go easily.

JAZZ SPIES AND THRILLERS

In comparison with mysteries, jazz appears in few spy stories and thrillers. This is surprising as jazz can be effective shorthand for establishing a sense of time and place, two important elements of spy stories and thrillers. Jazz very quickly outgrew its New Orleans roots, even its American roots, to become accepted internationally. So an explanation cannot be that jazz is a music identified with American locales. When jazz does appear in spy stories and thrillers, however, it can be a major element. Prime examples are two prewar stories (Rupert Holmes' Swing (2005), and Hal Glatzer's The Last Full Measure (2006)) and five wartime stories (Wm Ellis Oglesby's Blow Happy, Blow Sad (1996), Andrew Cartmel's The Vinyl Detective: Victory Disc (2018), Ross MacDonald's Trouble Follows Me (1946), Hunton Downs' Murder In the Mood (1998) and Francine Mathews' The Alibi Club. (2006)).

Aside from their more obvious work as entertainers during World War II, musicians were often drafted into signals intelligence and code breaking because of their cognitive skills. This linkage of code-breaking and music is at the center of Swing (2005), Blow Happy, Blow Sad (1996), Murder in the Mood (1998), The Vinyl Detective: Victory Disc (2018) and Trouble Follows Me (1946). In Rupert Holmes' Swing, set in prewar San Francisco, dance band arranger Ray Sherwood discovers military secrets encoded in an avant-garde composition played by a Japanese swing band at the Golden Gate Exposition. While in Wm Ellis Oglesby's Blow Happy, Blow Sad, black cornet player Chops Danielson sends coded messages from the Danish underground to S.O.E. (the Special

Operations Executive) in London during his Thursday evening radio broadcasts from occupied Denmark. In <u>Murder in the Mood</u>, four newly discovered wartime radio broadcast discs offer clues to Glenn Miller's fate and secret information regarding the Battle of the Bulge. The Vinyl Detective in Andrew Cartmel's <u>The Vinyl Detective: Victory Disc</u> searches for old broadcast recordings by the Flare Path Orchestra containing coded, treasonous information. Similarly, in Ross Macdonald's <u>Trouble Follows Me</u>, Sue, a late-night DJ in Oahu, was broadcasting more than jazz across the Pacific to the Japanese.

A jazz club is the focal point of Francine Mathews' <u>The Alibi Club</u> (2006) set in pre-war Paris. It is a tale of expatriate habitués and their varying fates as the Germans advance on Paris. At the center of the group is the club's black owner, entertainer Memphis Jones, who is modeled on entertainers Josephine Baker and Ada "Bricktop" Smith. She has little but discrimination to look forward to with repatriation to America. After being left behind, she stays a step ahead of the Nazis in making her own way to North Africa with a suitcase of bomb-grade uranium.

Hal Glatzer's <u>The Last Full Measure</u> (2006) is set on the other side of the world. While working on a Pacific cruise liner, swing violinist and sometime detective, Katy Green realizes a Nisei (Japanese-American) passenger was framed for murder and stumbles upon the Japanese plan to attack Pearl Harbor.

Jazz recordings also create mood and recreate memories of their times, eliminating the need for descriptions and details. Possibly one of the best examples is found in John Lawton's <u>Flesh Wounds</u> (2005). Scotland Yard Inspector Troy's wartime girlfriend Kitty has unexpectedly returned to postwar London and is now married to a possible Democratic presidential nominee. She brings Troy, an accomplished pianist, two popular American jazz LPs: Erroll Garner's *Concert by the Sea* and Dave Brubeck's *Time Out*. Although it is a 1950s recording, Garner's lush and romantic *Concert by the Sea* stirs up memories of an unresolved wartime romance. Brubeck's *Time Out*, on the other hand, with its emphasis on unusual time changes, hints of major changes to come to postwar Britain with its empire in decline. Troy broods over both recordings throughout the book.

Jazz can be used very effectively to create atmosphere associated with a specific place. For example, Afro-Cuban dance music with its pulsing beat and exotic undertone of excitement is associated with crime and 1950s nightclub life in New York and Havana. In Henry Kane's "One Little Bullet" (1960), Manhattan nightclub owner Joe Malamud's murder during a mesmerizing drum solo initially goes unnoticed by PI Pete Chambers. Two novels set in revolutionary Cuba use Afro-Cuban jazz to accentuate an exotic locale and enhance the sense of danger. King Bongo, in Thomas Sanchez' King Bongo (2003) is a Cuban-American bongo player and hustler at the mob-owned Tropicana nightclub when a bomb explodes. His sister, a featured dancer, is missing and Bongo's search for her is hindered by the secret police's suspicion of his revolutionary activities. In Charles Fleming's After Havana (2004), Peter Sloan, also working at the Tropicana, gets mixed up in revolutionary politics after his girlfriend Anita is kidnapped by a rogue, rebel cell. The New York jazz clubs (Blue Note, Half Note, Five Spot, Village Vanguard, Village Gate and even the Apollo Theatre) frame Reggie Nadelson's Cold War thriller, Manhattan 62. At the Village Gate, jazz-loving KGB agent, Max Ostalsky engages Miles Davis in conversation about Russia. In return, Miles slyly plays a few bars of "Moscow Nights." On another occasion, Ostalsky and NYP Detective Pat Wynne evade a manhunt by hiding backstage at Harlem's Apollo Theatre during a dynamic James Brown show.

As popular taste began to change in the postwar era, jazz became the music of social outsiders. In spy stories, as in mysteries, jazz was often associated with drugs and subversive politics. In Martin Cruz Smith's wartime story, Stallion Gate (1986), Sergeant Joe Pena is released from the penal stockade to drive his childhood friend, Robert Oppenheimer, who is supervising development of an atomic bomb at Los Alamos. Puma, a Pueblo Indian, is the ultimate outsider. Before the war, he was a talented jazz pianist, who played bop on New York's 52nd Street and owned a jazz club. But Pena was forced to join the army or go to jail after he and other drunken musicians attempted to give a free jazz concert to black servicemen. Overseeing both Oppenheimer and Pena is Captain Augustino, who is convinced the scientist is a communist and dislikes Pena.

Alan Plater's The Beiderbecke Tapes (1986) is set in the 1980s, a decade of social unrest and political change in England. Security agents use social activist Trevor Chaplin's love of jazz for their own purpose when a local publican gives him six tapes of Bix Beiderbecke's music. One of the tapes, however, appears to contain a conversation between two government officials discussing the dumping of nuclear waste.

Jazz can be a means of withdrawal from the world. In Andrew Klavan's Hunting Down Amanda, (1999) saxophone player Lonnie Blake isn't a drug addict or a political outsider but has withdrawn into his music after the murder of his wife. He's drawn back into the world after helping a young woman, Carol Dodson, escape from her pursuer.

There are two series in which jazz as an escape is present in varying degrees. South African émigré Gillian Slovo's Kate Baeier begins her five books run in Thatcher's London as a detective and ends ups as an investigative journalist. Kate's a jazz lover who plays the alto sax for relaxation and escape. As a liberal South African, she is the outsider in a politically rigid England undergoing social change and economic unrest. She encounters bent coppers (Close Call,1995), murder, including that of her boyfriend (Catnap, 1994), South African political intimidation (Morbid Symptoms, 1984), police infiltration of a group of radical activists (Death By Analysis, 1986), and incest (Death Comes Staccato, 1988).

A contemporary spy series features Barry Eisler's John Rain, a Nisei who became a professional assassin with an international clientele after his stint in Vietnam as a sniper made it impossible for him to return to a normal life. In his "off-time," he escapes into jazz, finding refuge in the music of Bill Evans and other American modernists, as well as in contemporary Brazilian jazz. Rain is at home in jazz clubs from New York City to Sao Paulo and Tokyo. In the latter, he meets jazz pianist Midori Kawamura, whose life he changes irreparably. Eisler's books mix death and contemporary politics: political corruption in Japan (<u>Rain Fall</u>, 2002), the rising influence of the Yakuzu (the Japanese criminal syndicate) and its links to rightwing Japanese politics (<u>Hard Rain</u>, 2003), nuclear terrorism (<u>Requiem for An Assassin</u>, 2007), the international arms trade (<u>Rain Storm</u>, 2004), (<u>Killing Rain</u>, 2005) and finally Rain's own survival (<u>The Last Assassin</u>, 2006).

Lastly, jazz can frame the action as in David Terrenoire's <u>Beneath a Panamanian Moon</u> (2005). Former Special Ops (Special Operations) agent John Kirby plays piano on the Washington diplomatic circuit until he is sent down to Panama to a rundown hotel outside Panama City that is also a training ground for private military types. The hotel needs a piano player for a big New Year's Eve gala that may, in fact, be a coup.

A political coup casts a shadow in A.K. Jenkins' <u>Twice No One Dies</u> (2004). Marius, a retired Ghanaian Intelligence officer living in Togo, regularly spends his Friday nights at *Le Jazz Spot*, listening to his friend Louis, a trumpet player. One night, Louis fails to appear. A few days later, his body is found on the beach. The police claim it was a drug deal gone bad. With elections weeks away, there is constant violence to ensure the re-election of the corrupt leader known as *Le Crocodile*. But Louis was into jazz, not drugs or politics. Marius hopes to understand Louis' fate by retracing the walk from his home to *Le Jazz Spot*.

As this mix of spy and thrillers shows, jazz can fit into stories set different times and places with themes ranging from wartime intelligence to political coups. Jazz can be an integral part of the plot, add atmosphere, flesh out the story or move it along. It's surprising it's not used more often.

PART 2

Authors & their Series Characters

Books & Novellas

Author	Character
Aaronovitch, Ben	Peter Grant
Atkins, Ace	Nick Travers
Barnes, Linda	Carlotta Carlyle
Batten, Jack	Crang
Boeckman, Charles	Johnny Nickle
Boyce, Trudy Nan	Sarah "Salt" Alt
Boyd, Frank	Johnny Staccato
Brown, Carter	Danny Boyd
Burke, J.F.	Joe Streeter
Burke, James Lee	Dave Robicheaux
Calkins, Susanna	Gina Ricci
Carlotto, Massimo	Marco "the Alligator" Buratti
Charlotte Carter	Nanette Hayes
Cartmel, Andrew	The Vinyl Detective
Cass, Richard J.	Elder Darrow
Celestin, Ray	Michael Talbot & Ida Davis.
Cleverly, Barbara	Joe Sandilands
Cockery, Tim	Hitchock Sewell
Coggins, Mark	August Riordan
Colburt, Curt	Jake Rossiter
Compton, D.G.	Alec Duncan
Connelly, Michael	Harry Bosch & Mickey Haller

Kellerman, Jonathan	Alex Delaware
Knight, Phyllis	Lil Richie
Larson, Skoot	Lars Linstrom
Latimer, Jonathan	Bill Crane
Lawrence, Michael	Johnny Amsterdam
Lawton, John	Frederick Troy
Leslie, John	Gideon Lowry
Lutz, John	Alo Nudger
Macdonald, Ross	Lew Archer
McClendon, Lise	Dorie Lennox
Merrill, Joan	Casey McKie
Moody, Bill	Evan Horne
Morfoot, Peter	Captain Paul Darac
Mosley, Walter	Easy Rollins, Leonid McGill & Socrates Forlow
Moss, Stephen L.	Paul Kingston
Murphy, Dallas	Artie Deemer
Nadelson, Reggie	Artie Cohen
Ordover, Andrew	Jordan Greenblatt
Padura, Leonardo	Mario Conde
Pentecost, Hugh	Pierre Chambrun
Plater, Alan	Trevor Chaplin & Jill Swinburne
Raleigh, Michael	Paul Whelan
Randisi, Robert J.	Eddie Gianelli
Reed, Harlan	Dan Jordan
Robinson, Peter	Alan Banks
Runcie, James	Sidney Chambers
Sallis, James	Lew Griffin
Saunders, David	Frank Ballinger
Sheridan, Sara	Mirabelle Bevin
Skinner, Robert	Wesley Farrell
Skvorecky, Josef	Lieutenant Boruvka, Eve Adam
Slovo, Gillian	Kate Baeier
Smith, Julie	Skip Langdon
Spicer, Bart	Carney Wilde
Temple, Lou Jane	Heaven Lee

Vandagriff, G.G.   Catherine Tregowyn
White, Gloria   Ronnie Ventura
Whitelaw, Stella   Jordan Lacey
Williams, Kirby   Urbie Brown

SHORT STORIES

Allyn, Doug   Moishe Abrams
Beckman, Jr., Charles   Johnny Nickle
Connelly, Michael   Harry Bosch
Fulmer, David   Valentin St. Cyr
Hambly, Barbara   Benjamin January
Harvey, John   Charlie Resnick
Hentoff, Nat   Sam McKibbon
Huggins, Roy   Stu Bailey
Hoch, Edward D.   Ben Snow
Kane, Henry   Pete Chambers
Lippman, Laura   Tess Monaghan
Lutz, John   Alo Nudger
Skvorecky, Josef   Eve Adam & Lieutenant Boruvka
Smith, Julie   Talba Wallis

Series Characters & Authors

Books

Character	Author
Adam, Eve	Josef Skvorecky
Alt, Sarah "Salt"	Trudy Nan Boyce
Amsterdam, Johnny	Michael Lawrence
Anderson, Mali	Grace F. Edwards
Archer, Lew	Ross Macdonald
Bailey, Stu	Roy Huggins
Baeier, Kate	Gillian Slovo
Ballinger, Frank	David Saunders
Banks, Alan	Peter Robinson
Barnett, Devil	Teddy Hayes
Bevin, Mirabelle	Sara Sheridan
Boruvka, Lieutenant	Josef Skvorecky
Bosch, Harry	Michael Connelly
Boyd, Danny	Carter Brown
Brown, Urbie	Kirby Williams
Buratti, Marco "the Alligator"	Massimo Carlotto
Butz, Bernie	Carol S. Fowler
Cafferty & Quinn	Heather Graham
Campbell, Brun	Larry Karp
Caryle, Carlotta	Linda Barnes
Chambers, Pete	Henry Kane
Chambrun, Pierre	Hugh Pentecost

Chambers, Sidney	James Runcie
Chaplin, Trevor	Alan Plater
Cohen, Artie	Reggie Nadelson
Conde, Mario	Leonardo Padura
Cragg, Sam	Frank Gruber
Crane, Bill	Jonathan Latimer
Crang	Jack Batten
Damon, Philip	Peter Duchin
Darac, Captain Paul	Peter Morfoot
Darrow, Elder	Richard J. Cass
Davis, Ida	Ray Celestin
Deacon	Charles Fleming
Deemer, Artie	Dallas Murphy
Duncan, Alec	D.G. Compton
Farrell, Wesley	Robert Skinner
Fisher, Phryne	Kerry Greenwood
Fletcher, Jessica	Donald Bain
Fletcher, Johnny	Frank Gruber
Floyd, C.J.	Robert O. Greer
Fortlow, Socrates	Walter Mosley
Gainelli, Eddie	Robert J. Randisi
Gallegher, Pat	Richard Helms
Grant, Peter	Ben Aronovitch
Green, Katy	Hal Glatzer
Green, Noah	Nat Hentoff
Greenblatt, Jordon	Andrew Ordover
Griffin, Lew	James Sallis
Gunn, Peter	Henry Kane
Hale, Max	George Harmon Coxe
Haller, Mickey	Michael Connelly
Hayes, Nanette	Charlotte Carter
Hjelm, Paul	Arne Dahl
Horne, Evan	Bill Moody
January, Benjamin	Barbara Hambly
Jackson, J.W.	Philip R. Craig
Johnson, Coffin Ed	Chester Himes

Jones, Grave Digger	Chester Himes
Jordan, Dan	Harlan Reed
Kingston, Paul	Stephen L. Moss
Lacey, Jordan	Stella Whitelaw
Langdon, Skip	Julie Smith
Lee, Heaven	Lou Jane Temple
Lennox, Dorie	Lise McClendon
Liddell, Johnny	Frank Kane
Linstrom, Lars	Skoot Larson
Lowry, Gideon	John Leslie
MacNeil, Harry	H. Paul Jeffers
McGill, Leonid	Walter Mosley
McKie, Casey	Joan Merrill
Maxwell, Maxx	Peggy Ehrhart
Montale, Fabio	Jean Claude Izzo
Mulheisen, Fang	Jon A. Jackson
Nickle, Johnny	Charles Boeckman
Nickle, Johnny	Whit Howland
Nudger, Alo	John Lutz
Platt, Hercules	Peter Duchin
Rain, John	Barry Eisler
Rawlins, Easy	Walter Mosely
Resnick, Charlie	John Harvey
Ricci, Gina	Susanna Calkins
Riordan, August	Mark Coggins
Ritchie, Lil	Phyllis Knight
Robicheaux, Dave	James Lee Burke
Rossiter, Jake	Curt Cobert
Ryan, Frank	Brian Harvey
Sandilands, Joe	Barbara Cleverly
Sewell, Hitchock	Tim Cockey
Shannon, Rick	Bill Fitzhugh
Sloane	John Harvey
Smart, Henry	Roddy Doyle
Staccato, Johnny	Frank Boyd
St. Cyr, Valentin	David Fulmer

Streeter, Joe	J. F. Burke
Swinburne, Jill	Alan Plater
Talbot, Michael	Ray Celestin
Travers, Nick	Ace Atkins
Tregowyn, Catherine	G.G. Vandagriff
Troy, Frederick	John Lawton
Vinyl Detective, The	Andrew Cartmel
Walker, Amos	Loren D. Estleman
Whelan, Paul	Michael Raleigh
White, Gloria	Ronnie Ventura
Wilde, Carney	Bart Spicer
Winter, Erik	Ake Edwardson

SHORT STORIES

Abrams, Moishe	Doug Allyn
Adam, Eve	Josef Skvorecky
Bailey, Stu	Roy Huggins
Boruvka, Lieutenant	Josef Skvorecky
Bosch, Harry	Michael Connelly
Chambers, Pete	Henry Kane
January, Benjamin	Barbara Hambly
Monaghan, Tess	Laura Lippman
Nickle, Johnny	Brad Mengel
Nudger, Alo	John Lutz
Resnick, Charlie	John Harvey
Snow, Ben	Edward D. Hoch
Sloane	John Harvey
St. Cyr, Valentin	David Fulmer
Wallis, Taiba	Julie Smith

Books & Short Stories By Authors

Aaronovitch, Ben.
(Ben Dylan Aaronovitch)
(series: Peter Grant)

Moon Over Soho. London: Gollancz, 2011; New York: Ballantine, 2011.

Peter Grant is a police constable and a sorcerer's apprentice specializing in supernatural criminal cases for the London Met. He's called to examine the body of jazz drummer Cyrus Williams, who died in a Soho club. Grant hears the tune "Body and Soul" coming from the body and realizes that it's a case for his special skills. A few hours later, a trombone player dies and Grant hears the same tune. To him, it suggests a serial jazz vampire. Grant's boss, Detective Inspector Thomas Nightingale, the last registered wizard in England, agrees.

Allyn, Doug.

"The Sultans of Soul," In Manson, Cynthia & Halligan, Kate (eds.). Murder To Music. New York: Carroll & Graf, 1997.

Private Investigator R.B. Axton is hired to collect royalties owed to Vernon Mack, a member of the legendary Sultans of Soul. After determining the ownership of the Sultan's recording masters, he belatedly learns that jealousy and revenge were Mack's true interests rather than recouping a financial debt.

"Jukebox King, The." In <u>Alfred Hitchcock's Mystery Magazine</u>. Vol. 47. No. 6. June 2002.

(series: Moishe Abrams)

Moishe Abrams, who controls the jukeboxes in Detroit, becomes drunk at Leo Brown's Lounge, so Brownie offers to drive him home. At a deserted cross street, Abrams jumps out of the car. The next day, Brownie learns that Abrams died and the mob holds him responsible. If he can't find Abrams' killer, he's a dead man.

Anderson, Beth.

<u>Night Sounds</u>. San Diego: Clocktower, 2000.
  While working at the Ravinia, Illinois Jazz Festival, keyboard player Joe Barbarello meets Zoey Bauer and spends the next three days with her. The Chicago Police bring him back to reality by informing him that he is a suspect in the murder of Zoey's boyfriend. Meanwhile Barbarello's band, the Night Sounds, have been offered a contract and a tour, both of which would be compromised by the pending murder charges.

Asimov, Isaac.

"Mystery Tune." In Waugh, Carol-Lynn Rossel, Greenberg, Martin Harry & Asimov, Isaac (eds.). <u>Show Business Is Murder</u>. New York: Avon, 1983.
  Christopher, nicknamed "Eighty-Eight," lives along life's fringe, playing piano in second-rate nightspots and running errands for the mob. One day, he's discovered dying in an alley with a knife in his back. Although he knew his killer, he refuses to name him. In his last moments, however, he hums a few notes and taps out a musical clue.

Atkins, Ace.
(series: Nick Travers)

<u>Crossroad Blues</u>. New York: St. Martin's, 1998.

Music historian Michael Baker disappeared in the Mississippi Delta. As a favor to his department head at Tulane University, blues historian Nick Travers agrees to look for the missing scholar. In Greenwood, he learns that Baker was on the trail of nine previously unknown recordings by blues legend Robert Johnson. New Orleans entrepreneur Pascal Cruz has, also, heard about the recordings and will kill to get them.

Leavin' Trunk Blues. New York: St. Martin's, 2000.
Known as the "Sweet Black Angel," Mississippi-born Ruby Walker was one of Chicago's great blues singers until she killed her lover and producer Billy Lyons in September 1959. Now virtually forgotten and serving a life sentence for murder, she agrees to grant Tulane blues historian, Nick Travers, an interview in exchange for his investigation of Lyon's death. In meetings with elderly South Side musicians and Ruby's friends, he stirs up old animosities and a killer named Stagger Lee.

Dark End of the Street. New York: Morrow, 2002.
Blues singer Loretta Jackson asks her friend Nick Travers to find her missing brother, the legendary soul singer, Clyde James. He had been living on the streets of Memphis for twenty-five years after the murder of his wife. Travers' search takes him to Memphis, to a Mississippi casino and the rescue of a kidnap victim. He also stumbles into a gambling war between the Dixie Mafia and the rightwing Sons of the South.

Avery, Robert.

Murder On the Downbeat. New York: W.H. Wise, 1944.
While newspaperman Malachy Bliss and his girlfriend Julie Mitchell are enjoying an after-hours jam session in a Harlem club, clarinetist Steve Sisson is murdered at a nearby table. Because Julie had a public disagreement with Sisson, the police arrest her as his killer. As Bliss discovers in his attempt to clear her, almost everyone in the club from musicians to gangsters had motives to kill Sisson.

Bader, Jerry.

"Killer Jazz." In Bader, Jerry. (ed.) Noir 1. London & New York: MRPWebbmedia, 2018.

Maurice Delbourne, a jazz pianist and son of deceased reggae icon, Dickerson Delbourne, is targeted for assassination in L.A. by two Jamaican political parties, who fear the consequences if he goes into politics. The Americans are aware of the assassination plans but would rather see Delbourne dead than as a live wild card in Jamaican politics.

Bain, Donald.
(see Jessica Fletcher)

Bankier, William.

"The Dog Who Hated Jazz." In Asimov, Isaac, Greenberg, Martin H., Waugh, Carol-Lyn Rossel, (eds.). Hound Dunnit. New York: Carroll & Graf, 1987.

Blind jazz pianist Joe Benson takes a weekend job playing at Jack Danforth's Coronet Hotel. His dog, Queenie, dislikes jazz and is kept in Danforth's office while his master is working. She foils an attempted robbery and the robber is later identified by her bites.

"Concerto for Violence." In Manson, Cynthia & Halligan, Kate. (eds.). Murder To Music. New York: Carroll & Graf, 1997.

Determined to make money by playing disco music rather than jazz, trumpet player Leonard Zolf steals the Bones Cornfield Quintet away from its leader. But the moderate temperament of the swing players allows Cornfield to get back his group.

Barclay, Tessa.

Final Discord, A. London: Severn House, 2005.

Gregory Crowne, the exiled Crown Prince of Hirtenstein, lives in Geneva, Switzerland and works as a music promoter. He is asked by banker Anton Guidon to put together a jazz quintet for the Montreux Jazz Festival to be led by Crowne's clarinet-playing son, Gilles. Unfortunately, Gilles' jazz ambitions threaten his family and their bank.

Barnes, Harper.

Blue Monday. St. Louis: Patrice, 1991.

Cub crime reporter-jazz fan Michael Holt suspected foul play in the death of bandleader Bennie Moten during a tonsillectomy. Moten, a commanding figure on the Kansas City jazz scene, had opposed the increasing use of hard drugs by young musicians. Holt, also, discovers the body of Moten's doctor in the morgue. The Kansas City police, however, dismiss his death as another unsolvable black, drug- related, killing.

Barnes, Linda.
(series: Carlotta Carlyle)

Steel Guitar. London: Hodder & Stoughton, 1992; New York: Delacorte, 1991.

When Boston PI Carlotta Carlyle, who moonlights as a taxi driver, picks up singer Dee Willis, it becomes a trip into their past. Willis is looking for Davey, a former member of their music group and now a vagrant. After Dee's bass player is murdered and a blackmail note threatens to jeopardize her career, her search takes on a frantic, murderous tempo.

Batten, Jack.
(series: Crang)

Crang Plays the Ace. Toronto: Macmillan, 1987.

Financier Matthew Wansborough asks Crang, a criminal lawyer, to investigate a family holding, Ace Trash Removals, which is unusually profitable. Wansborough's cousin, Alice Brackley is a company officer, partner, and romantic interest of gangster, Charles

Grimaldi. Before Crang figures out Ace's scam and gets Wansborough's funds returned, events turn deadly.

Straight No Chaser. Toronto: Macmillan, 1989.

Someone is following saxophone player Dave Goddard, who asks Crang to identify his follower. But Crang botches the job. He watches an assault on Goddard and theft of his saxophone. By coincidence, he sees the assailant, Raymond Fenk, at a film festival and follows him back to his hotel with intention of stealing back the saxophone. Instead he discovers that someone used Dave Goddard's saxophone case to transport drugs and murdered Fenk.

Riviera Blues. Toronto: Macmillan, 1990.

Crang and his girlfriend Annie travel to the French Riviera so that she can cover the film festivals. His ex-father-in-law, Swotty Wetherhill, asks him to check on his cousin Jamie Haddon, who sent an odd postcard. Crang's ex-wife Pamela, also, has an interest in Jamie, who walked out of their affair. He finds Jamie living way above his means on the Riviera.

Blood Count. Toronto: Macmillan, 1991.

Ian Argyll, one of Crang's down-stairs neighbors, has died of AIDS. Alex Corcoran, his surviving partner, is determined to kill the man who infected Ian. Crang and his girlfriend Annie hope to intervene after identifying the man and warn him of Alex's irrational behavior. But Alex is murdered. His death forces Crang into Toronto's gay world to uncover his killer and a scandal that reaches Ontario's Provincial Government.

Beckman, Charles Jr.
(Charles Boeckman)
(series: Johnny Nickle)

Honky-Tonk Girl. New York: Falcon, 1953.

Miff Smith, the drummer in Johnny Nickle's jazz band, has been murdered. Smith was the second musician to die after the group recorded *The Ghost Album*. Knowing the police will not properly investigate Smith's murder, Johnny decides to do it himself. Because Smith was a womanizer, he mistakenly believes the key to his death lies with three women: Ruth, an avid jazz fan, Jean, a Honky-Tonk streetwalker and Raye, the mentally unstable daughter of a corrupt politician.

"Run Cat Run." In Suspense, Suspicion & Shockers. Corpus Christi: von Boeckmann Fiction Factory, 2012.

Trumpet player Johnny Nickle recorded "Jazz Date," considered one of the best jazz recordings ever made. That session was infamous as everyone involved died, except Johnny and a clarinet player. His evening plans to leave Corpus Christi are disrupted by a girl named Nona, who insists at gunpoint that he play "Jazz Date." In the audience, he spots the clarinet player.

(non-series stories)

"Afraid To Live." In Suspense, Suspicion & Shockers. Corpus Christi: von Boeckmann Fiction Factory, 2012.

Trumpet player Dan Skeel's wife Dorothy has left him for the town's big-spender, Mel Duggard. But Dorothy is unsure whether she wants to divorce Skeel and marry Duggard. He decides to frame her for murder and blackmail her into marriage. Skeel has a coward's reputation and is expected to stand aside.

"Dixieland Dirge." In Suspense, Suspicion & Shockers. Corpus Christi: von Boeckmann Fiction Factory, 2012.

Jazz trumpet legend Mizz Milner returned to New Orleans after learning that the son he never knew, Jim Williams, gave up music when his wife left him. Williams plans to kill her. But Milner kills her, so that Jim can return to music.

"Hot Lick For Doc, A." In Suspense, Suspicion & Shockers. Corpus Christi: von Boeckmann Fiction Factory, 2012.

Buddy Turner was a top clarinetist until he caught his two-timing wife with his arranger. He became an alcoholic bum, known as Doc DeFord, who ran errands for chump's change. He's asked to pick up marijuana from a hotel room and finds a dead body. DeFord takes the drugs and goes off to listen to a promising, young clarinetist named Ramon. He realizes that the club owner killed the drug courier. As he confronts him, Ramon steps in.

"Last Trumpet, The." In Suspense, Suspicion & Shockers. Corpus Christi: von Boeckmann, 2012.
    Trumpet player Earl Gerald was murdered. His half-brother Allan claimed to have written the music that made him famous and intends to sue his widow for royalties. The police are looking for Allan's wife, who was seen running from Earl's hotel room. Piano player, Big Lips, wants to find his friend's killer and insure Earl's widow security.

"Mr. Banjo." In Suspense, Suspicion & Shockers. Corpus Christi: von Boeckmann Fiction Factory, 2012.
    Roger Spencer, a wealthy attorney, returned to the Texas town where grew up as the son of the town drunk. He had been befriended by a blind street musician, named Mr. Banjo, who allegedly saved a lot of money. The town's crooked sheriff tried to beat its location from him. Roger rescued him but the old man died from his injuries. Roger took his banjo and made a meager living with it until its neck split, revealing $5,000. He used the money for his education and law school.

"Should A Tear Be Shed?" In Suspense, Suspicion & Shockers. Corpus Christi: von Boeckmann Fiction Factory, 2012.
    Gangster Jess Novell takes out a life insurance policy on Lawrence Terrace, Jr., known as "Feet," a dim-witted jazz tap dancer. After failing to kill him twice, Novell decides to take Feet hunting. But it's Novell who suffers a "hunting accident."

Bennett, Ron.

Singapore Swing. Holicong, PA: Cosmos, 2003.

Alan Chance of the Banks Detective Agency is hired by wealthy Singapore socialite Marcia Sanders to investigate three threatening letters sent to her husband, jazz musician Ted Saunders. Saunders is murdered and his body discovered by Chance, who must find the killer to clear himself of murder charges. With no apparent leads, he looks into Sanders' personal life and finds an unhappy marriage and numerous motives for murder.

Benson, Raymond.

Blues In the Dark. London & New York: Arcade, 2019.
Independent film producer Karissa Glover rents an old mansion in the West Adams section of L.A., where black movie stars and musicians lived in the 1940s-1960s. The mansion belonged to white film noir actress Blair Kendrick, who disappeared after six successful films. Glover discovers that she was involved with black jazz pianist Hank Marley and planned to give up her career. But her producer, Eldon Hirsch, needed her for another film to pay off mob debts. More than fifty years later, interest in her fate still has dangerous consequences.

Benton, John L.

Talent For Murder. London: Collins, 1967; New York: Gateway, 1942.
Hamilton Scott, a young construction engineer, walks out of a socially stifling party and away from his fiancée to find refuge in a drunken evening at 52nd Street's Alligator Club. The next morning he learns that his fiancée's father, Theodore Parson, has been murdered and that he's a suspect. Assuming the job as the band's piano player, Scott must discover the Parson's killer among the party guests.

Bird, Brandon.
(George Evans & Kay Evans)

Downbeat For A Dirge aka Dead And Gone. New York: Dodd, Mead, 1952.

Big band singer Kerry Galloway has been murdered but her body disappeared before the police arrived. The band's alto sax player, who claimed to know about her disappearance, is also missing and presumed dead. Without bodies, there can be no murder investigations. So the NYPD (New York Police Department) convinces Hamp Howe to go undercover, taking over the band's baritone sax chair. While he discovers the sax player's killer, it's his wife Carmel, who realizes Kerry has not sung her last note.

Bloch, Robert.
(Robert Albert Bloch)

"Dig That Crazy Grave!" In <u>Ellery Queen's Awards: Twelfth Series</u>. London: Collins, 1959; New York: Simon & Schuster, 1957.

Upon learning that the Jo-Jo Jones Sextet is playing at a local jazz haunt, Professor Talmadge takes his girlfriend Dorothy to hear them. He's writing a book on jazz and hopes to interview Jones. While Dorothy enjoys the jazz, she dislikes Jones and wants to leave after the interview. The next weekend, Talmadge returns to hear Jones and discovers that Dorothy has become Jones' groupie and a junkie.

Booth, Christopher B.

<u>Killing Jazz</u>. New York: Chelsea House, 1928.

Caleb Ballinger is awakened from his Sabbath meditations by the sound of jazz. He rushes out of his room to the top of the stairs where his heart stops and falls to his death. His two nephews, Paul and Loren, accuse each other of playing the phonograph recording that caused Ballinger's heart attack. Loren had a contentious relationship with his uncle. Public opinion convicts him without any evidence. Upon the urging of his daughter, Ballinger's physician, hires New York City detective Jim Bliss to uncover the killer.

Borneman, Ernest.
(Ernst Wilhelm Julius Bornemann)
<u>Tremolo</u>. London: Jarrolds, 1948; New York: Harper, 1948.

Although Chicago jazz clarinetist Mike Sommerville still plays with friends, he has given up performing to concentrate on his business of manufacturing and repairing wind instruments and raising his family. His life, however, is disrupted by a series of incidents that cause Mike and his wife Marge to suspect that their house is haunted and then to question their own as well as each other's sanity.

Boyce, David.

"Special Arrangement." In Harvey, Charles. (ed.). <u>Jazz Parody</u>. London: Spearman, 1948.
Club owner Dan O'Shay forces Jake the drummer into a smuggling operation with unexpected results.

Boyce, Trudy Nan.
(series: Sarah "Salt" Alt)

<u>Out of the Blues</u>. New York: Putnam, 2016.
Detective Sarah "Salt" Alt is given the cold case of blues singer Mike Anderson, who died from a drug overdose a decade earlier. New evidence suggests that it might have been intentional—"a hot shot." She interviews his family as well as Midas Prince of a megachurch, who is inexplicably hostile. Anderson's band, Old Smoke, is playing in Atlanta, so Salt goes to hear them. Dan Pyne, the rhythm guitarist, was one of the last people to speak with Anderson. He's shot in the back while dancing with her.

Boyd, Frank.
(Pseudonym of Henry Kane)

<u>Johnny Staccato</u>. London: Consul, 1964; New York: Gold Medal, 1960.
PI Johnny Staccato's old girlfriend Shelley Carroll made an evening visit to song publisher-DJ Les Miller's apartment, discovered him dead and ran. The police are now holding her for his murder.

Staccato knows Miller had no shortage of enemies, ranging from aspiring caste-away singers, songwriters, publishers, mobsters, and family.

Brackett, Leigh.
(Leigh Douglass Brackett)

No Good from a Corpse. New York: Coward, McCann, 1944.
Singer Laurel Dane asks PI Ed Clive for help with two problems: one regarding the blackmail of Mick Hammond, an estranged childhood friend of Clive's; the second concerns her own past. But she's murdered before explaining the latter. Clive knows that Hammond, who police are holding as her killer, is innocent and must find the real killer.

Braly, Malcolm.

Shake Him till he Rattles. London: Muller, 1964; New York: Gold Medal, 1963.
On a crusade to clean up San Francisco's North Beach, Lieutenant Carver is after alto sax player Lee Cabiness, who seems to personify the Beat Culture that he despises. But Cabiness only smokes grass and isn't into heavy drugs. Carver, however, never hesitated to plant evidence for his own ends.

Brown, Carter.
(Pseudonym of Alan Geoffrey Yates)
(series: Danny Boyd)

The Ever-Loving Blues, aka Death of a Doll. London: Horwitz, 1971; New York: Signet, 1961.
Private Investigator Danny Boyd is hired by a studio boss to find his missing starlet, who disappeared along with a Wall Street tycoon, a blues singer and a jazz musician. Boyd locates them. He, also, learns that the tycoon is broke and the recently murdered blues singer was his heavily insured wife.

Brown, Cecil.

I, Stagolee. Berkeley: North Atlantic Books, 2006.

Gangster Billy Lyons was trying to take over black businessman Stagolee's holdings and killed his friend Joe as a provocation. As Lyons grabbed Stagolee's new Stetson and dropped his hand into his knife pocket, Stagolee shot him. He was arrested by the sheriff, who was up for re-election. Judge Murphy, needing Republican black votes, released him on bail. The Democrats offered to drop all charges in return for black votes in this tale of political corruption and intrigue.

Brown, Fredric.

"Murder Set to Music." In Charteris, Leslie (ed.). The Saint Mystery Library #3. New York: Great American Library, 1959.

Ralph Oliver and Danny Bushman were childhood friends and played together in bands until they tired of the jazz life. Danny married the band's vocalist and opened a used car business with Ralph. When their old band plays a local club, Danny is inexplicably beaten up. The investigating officer, Lieutenant Andrews concludes it's a case of mistaken identity. After the band's sax player is murdered, forcing Ralph to sit in as a replacement, Andrews looks into the two friend's past for a motive.

Burke, J. F.
(series: Joey Streeter)

The Kama Sutra Tango. New York: Harper & Row, 1977.

Joey Streeter is a piano player and a part owner with jazz buff Jock Alfieri of Pal Joey's, a New York nightclub. Belatedly, he learned that his real partner is Jock's uncle, Rocco, a local Mafiosi, who added gambling upstairs. After finishing his midnight Ellington set, Joey witnesses their local bagman, Lieutenant Maginnis, set-up Jock with Streeter's gun. But the frame is too much even for Sergeant Sweeney, who is more interested in the money and pornographic films found in Jock's studio.

<u>Crazy Woman Blues</u>. London: Constable, 1979; New York: E.P. Dutton, 1978.

Joey Streeter has changed his jazz club, Pal Joey's, into a successful cabaret, where late evening performance will be televised. During the show's debut, Alice, the disappearing girl in the magician's act, fails to reappear. Concerned, Joey goes looking for her and discovers two thieves sacking her room, several dead bodies and the possibility of her criminal involvement in a robbery and a murder.

Burke, James Lee.
(series: Dave Robicheaux)

<u>The Neon Rain</u>. London: Century, 1989; New York: Henry Holt, 1987.

While fishing, Dave Robicheaux hooks the body of a young prostitute, Lovelace Deshotels. After the sheriff of neighboring Cataovatche Parish refuses his request for an autopsy and he is roughed up twice, Robicheaux knows something is wrong. Soon he's running a deadly gauntlet between the local Mafia, Nicaraguan drug dealers, Treasury agents and Contra gunrunners.

<u>Black Cherry Blues</u>. London: Century, 1990; Boston: Little, Brown, 1989.

Dave Robicheaux's old friend, former college roommate and R&B star, Dixie Lee Pugh, has fallen on hard times. He is now working for a mid-level Mafioso. Pugh overheard details of a double murder in Montana and asks Dave for help. Dave soon finds himself framed for murder and facing ten years in Angola Prison unless he can discredit a witness.

<u>Last Car to Elysian Fields</u>. London: Orion, 2003; New York: Simon & Schuster, 2003.

Dave Robicheaux returns to New Orleans after the beating of his friend, Father Jimmie Dolan, who was investigating a toxic landfill. While helping Dolan, Robicheaux learns about bluesman Junior

Crudup, who was sentenced to the penitentiary at Angola and never came out. At the same time, he is also investigating a drunk-driving accident that killed three teenaged girls and the murder of the owner of the "daiquiri window" where the under-age girls bought their liquor.

(non-series)

The Lost-Get Back Boogie Baton Rouge: Louisiana State University Press, 2004.

Guitarist Ivy Paret is released from Angola State Penitentiary after serving two years for manslaughter. He finds his father dying and his family only interested in their inheritance. He decides to go to Montana where his recently released cellmate, jazz pianist Buddy Riordan, has a ranch. Hoping to start a new life, he gets drawn into the Riordan family's problems.

Burnett, W.R.
(William Riley Burnett)

Romelle. New York: Knopf, 1946.

Romelle is a 30-year-old singer working at a 3rd rate club. Jules, who's new to L.A., comes in for a few nights and becomes infatuated. Romelle eventually accepts his marriage proposal. One day, a gangster/blackmailer named Ross, barges into their world. After Ross' body is discovered in a L.A. alleyway, their lives are endangered.

Burwell, Rex.

Capone, the Cobbs and Me. Livingston, AL.: University of West Alabama, 2015.

Al Capone invites baseball major-leaguer Mort Hart to his Arrow Head Inn resort. Capone wants Hart to give baseball super-star Ty Cobb a note regarding monies owed. He does Capone's bidding and meets Cobb's wife, Charlene. Cobb is crazed with jealousy and ready to kill Hart. Hart also knows more about the death of one of Capone's gunmen than is good for him.

Byers, Chad.

<u>Jazz Man</u>. Brooklyn: Gryphon, 1997.

Ray Parker plays the trumpet in second-rate, mob-owned jazz clubs. His girlfriend Molly works as an Ida Lupino look-alike prostitute. Molly wants to leave Chicago but Ray is too consumed with his music and alcohol to understand that she's serious. She plans to steal the monthly payoff from St. Louis and skip town. The mob takes her threat of leaving seriously enough to work him over as a warning.

Cain, James M.
(James Mallahan Cain)

"Cigarette Girl." In Spillane, Mickey & Collins, Max Allen (eds.). <u>Century of Noir, A</u>. New York: New American Library, 2002.

Bill Cameron, a guitarist with Art Lomak's band, goes to the Here's How nightclub to find that the band has the music charts for a song written by his bandleader. He is smitten with the club's cigarette girl Lydia, who is returning to Las Vegas that evening. She is fleeing from Tony Rocco, a mobster who is obsessed with her.

Calef, Noel.

<u>Ascenseur Pour L'echafaud</u>. Paris: Librairie Arthème Fayard, 1956; aka <u>Frantic</u>. New York: Gold Medal, 1961.

Julien Courtois kills Bordgris, a loan shark and fakes his suicide. Courtois becomes trapped in the elevator when the electricity is shut off for the weekend. As a teenaged couple steals his car for a Bonnie-and-Clyde caper, Courtois' neurotic wife sees a young woman getting into his car. In a jealous rage, she rushes to her brother Georges, telling him that Julien cheated in a business deal and the police become involved. Miles Davis improvised the soundtrack for the classic *Nouveau Vague* (New Wave) film by director Louis Malle based on the book.

Calkins, Susanna.

(series: Gina Ricci)

Murder Knocks Twice. New York: St. Martin's, 2019.

Gina Ricci, a cigarette girl at The Third Door, a Chicago speak-easy, learns her predecessor died under mysterious circumstances. She hopes to discover more from Marty Doyle, the club's photographer. Gina witnesses his murder, and as his killer flees, Marty hands her his camera. Although she doesn't reveal that she witnessed the murder, numerous people, including his killer, believe she has his camera.

The Fate of a Flapper, New York: Monotaur, 2020.

A woman Gina Ricci had seen drinking at the Third Door was poisoned, along with her companion, and a third patron sickened. Later the club is firebombed. The Third Door is located in a neutral zone between two gangs and the bad liquor and the bombing may be gang related. To add to the club's problems, the New York stock market crashed, ending easy money and the Jazz Age.

Cameron, Lou.

Angel's Flight. London: Gold Medal (Muller), 1962; New York: Gold Medal, 1960.

Bassist Ben Parker witnesses Johnny Angel's debut as a drummer in Daddy Holloway's band, his ruthless rise to the top of the music business and his demise at the hands of a wronged woman. While never experiencing Angel's level of success, Parker is still a target of Angel's wrath.

Cameron, Stella.

Tell Me Why. London: Zebra, 2002; New York: Kensington, 2001.

Jazz pianist Carolee Burns has given up a successful career and only plays occasional gigs at a friend's club in Seattle. Max Wolfe, a retired professional football player, is interested in both Carolee and her music. He realizes that her reclusive lifestyle is the result of her ex-husband's emotional and financial blackmail.

Campo, J.P.

On A Good Day it Just Bounces Off. Ridgewood: Books-by-Books, 2005.

Guitarist Bobby Turner experienced brief fame and no fortune. Now he is scrambling for gigs in the Big Apple. In Hollywood, George Cadwell, a second-rate actor and drug supplier to the rich-and-almost famous, crosses Columbian gangsters and the L.A. police. He flees to New York City for one last caper. Among his intended victims is Turner's estranged wife, Carol.

Carlotto, Massimo.
(series: Marco "the Alligator" Buratti)

The Columbian Mule. Rome: Edizioni E/o, as Il Corrierre, Colombiano, 2001; London: Orion, 2003; New York: Europa, 2013.

Columbian Arias Cuevas is caught smuggling cocaine through Venice Airport. He cooperates with the police in setting up a sting to catch the intended recipient that nets art smuggler Nazzareno Corradi instead. His lawyer hires Marco "the Alligator" Buratti, a former blues singer-turned-investigator, to help with his defense. Corradi's innocence in the drug matter is immaterial as the authorities are determined to punish him for a 20 year-old robbery.

The Master of Knots. Rome: Edizioni E/o, 2001, as Il Maestro di Nodi. London: Orion, 2004; New York: Europa, 2014.

Mariano Giraldi hires Marco "the Alligator" to investigate the disappearance of his wife, Helena, a S&M model. Then Giraldi and a sex slave disappear. Marco discovers all three were involved in snuff films. He tracks down the films' distributor, who points him toward the real culprit known as the Master of Knots.

Bandit Love. Rome: Edizioni E/o, 2009 as L'amore del bandito. London & New York: Europa, 2009.

Sylvie, the girlfriend of Marco's partner Beniamino Rossini, has been kidnapped because of mistaken hit on a Serbian gangster. The Serbian's girlfriend, along with Kosovan thugs, hid her in a gang-bang club on the French Rivera. Marco and Beniamino manage to free her but the son of a Kosovan gang lord and several gang members are killed. Now Marco and his friend are on a death list and must go into hiding.

Blues For Outlaw Hearts and Old Whores. Rome: Edizioni E/o, 2017 as Blues Per Cuori Furorlegge e Vecchi Puttane. London & New York: Europa Editions, 2020.

Marco and his friends, Max the Memory and Beniamin Rossini, are blackmailed by Dottoressa Angela Marino of the Italian police and their nemesis Giorgio Pellegrini into solving a double murder. They manage to play Marino and Pellegrini against drug king pin Paz Anaya Vega (the Spaniard) whose boyfriend was murdered by Pellegrini. All three are casualties in the encounter and Marco and his two friends live to fight another day. Or, in Marco's case, kick-back, drink Calvados, and listen to the blues.

Carter, Charlotte.
(series: Nanette Hayes)

Rhode Island Red. London: Mask Noir, 1997; New York: Serpent's Tail, 1998.

Nanette Hayes, a tenor saxophone player on the streets of New York, is persuaded to let Sig, another musician, spend the night on her apartment floor. But Sig is actually an undercover cop, who hid $60,000 in her saxophone and is murdered while she's asleep. Anyone she talks to about Sig ends up dead.

Coq au Vin. New York: St. Martin's, 1999.

Nanette's favorite aunt, Vivian, a wild living, jazz-loving lady, sends an S.O.S. from Paris. She needs money quickly. Nanette arrives in Paris to find her aunt missing and enlists Andre, a black violinist, in her search. Ultimately, they find Vivian but become entangled in a deadly lover's quarrel and a recording scam.

Drumsticks. New York: Mysterious, 2000.

After being given a Mojo doll by a street vendor, Nanette Hayes' luck changes. She seeks out the doll's maker, Ida Williams, and invites her to her jazz opening at an upscale eatery. When Williams is accidently killed, Nanette asks a friend in the NYPD to monitor the investigation. It appears that the doll maker was into voodoo and blackmail.

"Birdbath." In Editors of the Mysterious Press, The Mysterious Press Anniversary Anthology. New York: Warner, 2001.

Nanette Hayes witnesses a purse snatching. Later she learns that the purse-snatcher, jazz musician Richie Rice, was murdered. He had been the boyfriend of supermodel Hattie Randall. Intrigued, Hayes investigates further and discovers that Rice and Randall were blackmailing designer David Panama, who had ties with organized crime.

(non-series)

"A Flower Is A Lonesome Thing." In Harvey, John (ed.), Blue Lightning. London: Slow Dancer, 1998.

A blues singer turned nightclub entertainer, facing her own death, receives some beautiful flowers from an admirer.

Cartmel, Andrew.
(series: The Vinyl Detective)

The Vinyl Detective: Written in Dead Wax. London: Titan, 2016.

The Vinyl Detective is hired to find a rare 1950s West Coast Jazz recording on the small Hathor label by Easy Geary called *Easy Come, Easy Go*. He manages to secure a copy only to lose it to murderous rivals. Like all big collectors, he doesn't know what he owns, finds a copy among his records and delivers it to his client, who barely listens to it. Its value is a message encoded in it and in 13 other recordings on the Hathor label.

The Vinyl Detective: Victory Disc. London: Titan, 2018.
    The Vinyl Detective finds a rare 78 of the British wartime band, The Flare Path Orchestra, and lists it on the Internet. Joan Honeyland, the daughter of the bandleader, Lucky Honeyland, buys it and hires him to find as many of her father's recordings as possible. In so doing, he comes across the story of Johnny Thomas, one of Lucky's crew, who was accused of murder and executed. He also discovers a Nazi interest in the discs, as Lucky was a covert Nazi operative.

Cass, Richard J.
(series: Elder Darrow)

In Solo Time. Farmington ME: Encircle, 2017.
    The body of Timmy McGuire, a jazz guitarist, is discovered on the stage of Elder Darrow's jazz club. Boston Homicide Detective Dan Burton thinks Jacquie Robillard, Darrow's occasional girlfriend, is his killer as she had a public fight with McGuire in the club. Darrow disagrees but Burton arrests her. Darrow's sure the killer was in the club the night of the quarrel and the motive is in McGuire's past.

Solo Act. Farmington, ME: Encircle, 2017.
    Elder Darrow suspected murder when his former girlfriend, Alison Sommers, "jumped" to death from a window. She had been spending most of her time in New York City pursuing a jazz singing career. She also had been dealing with depression and on medication. After accepting the suicide verdict, Darrow decided to investigate the sleazy crowd she had been spending time with during the last months of her life and a society doctor with whom she was involved.

Burton's Solo. Farmington ME: Encircle, 2018.
    On television news, Elder Darrow's friend, Boston homicide detective Dan Burton, slugs clothing designer Antoine Bousquet, who

was suspected of killing two Chinese seamstresses. Consequently, he's suspended and Bousquet is released without bail. When Bousquet's body is discovered, Burton is the prime suspect. Boston Police's Internal Affairs inspectors, the Russian mob, the remnants of Boston's Irish Mafia and a Chinese psychopath mistakenly believe Darrow knows his whereabouts.

Last Call at The Esposito. Farmington, ME: Encircle, 2019.

Kathleen Crawford, Elder Darrow's former girlfriend and a professional thief, is in hiding. She's at Rinker's Island Prison when a casket unexpectedly opens revealing the body of a neighborhood activist, who opposed bringing the Olympic Games to Boston. Dan Burton, Elder's cop friend, is called to the crime scene and recognizes Crawford. She had stolen a briefcase from gangster Donald Maldonado containing property deeds for proposed Olympic sites. He's just as determined to kill her as retrieve the briefcase.

Sweetie Bogan's Sorrow. Farmington ME: Encircle, 2020.

During singer Lily Miller's debut at the Greenwood, formerly the Esposito, her manager Rasmussen Carter is stabbed by Alfonso Deal-Greenwood, the lover of aging jazz diva, Sweetie Brogan. Alfonso was setting up a drug deal with Edward Dare, a procurer of girls for New Orleans gangster Frank Vinson. Miller dumps Carter for Dare as her new manager. After Evangeline, a singer, disappears with Dare, Elder Darrow becomes involved. Carter and Dare are killed and their deaths linked to a cocaine deal with Brogan's nephew, Baron Loftus, who manages the Greenwood/Esposito in this convoluted tale of vendettas.

Cassiday, Bruce.

The Brass Shroud. New York: Ace D-285, 1958.

Skip-tracer Johnny Midas is asked to find missing bank teller Andrew Claussen, who approved fraudulent loans. Midas' lead in the case is a legendary jazz trumpet player, Buck Lagrande, whose attempted comeback ended in a car crash. While looking for clues about Claussen in Lagrande's past, he finds himself searching for the real Buck Lagrande.

Castle, Frank.

Hawaiian Eye. New York: Dell, 1962.

Heiress Yolanda Destin asks Tracey Steele to find her missing secretary, Mae Gamble. While unable to find her, Steele does discover the body of a naval intelligence officer floating in the hotel's pool. He realizes that Destin, the heir to one of Hawaii's oldest fortunes, is manipulated by her cousin. All of the Hawaiian Eye detective agency resources are needed to explain the missing secretary, the dead sailor, Destin's strange behavior and three murders.

Celestin, Ray.
(series: Michael Talbot & Ida Davis)

The Axeman's Jazz. London: Mantle, 2014; New York: Sourcebooks Landmark, 2015, as The Axeman.

Detective Lieutenant Michael Talbot is in charge of "the Axeman" murder investigation of Italian grocers. Newly released from Angola Prison, former detective Luca d'Andrea, is doing the same for the Mafia, who claim innocence in the matter. Ida Davis, an octoroon secretary at Pinkerton's and her young friend, Louis Armstrong, are doing their own investigation. The Axeman sent a letter to the Times-Picayune indicating that he will select his next victim from a household not playing jazz. Each investigation provides a clue leading to the unmasking of the Axeman and the motive behind the seemingly unrelated murders.

Dead Man's Blues. London: Mantle, 2016; New York: Pegasus, 2017.

Pinkerton Detectives Michael Talbot and Ida Davis are hired to find missing heiress Gwendolyn Van Haren. Ida's friend, trumpet player Louis Armstrong provides the clues leading to the apartment where Van Haren spent her final night. At the same time, Al

Capone brings in from New York City his old friend, Dante Sanfe-lippo, a rumrunner and fixer, to find a traitor in his organization. He discovers someone is piggybacking drugs on Capone's Canadian liquor shipments.

<u>The Mobster's Lament</u>. London: Mantle, 2019.
Ida Davis comes to New York City to help her former partner, Michael Talbot whose son, Tom, has been charged in the ritual kill-ing of four people in a Harlem hotel. At the same time Mafiosi Ga-briel Leveson, the manager of the Copa nightclub, is tasked by mob boss Frank Costello with recovering $2 million stolen by Benny Sie-gel, a deceased gangster from L.A. The key into both cases lies with Gene Cleveland, junkie jazz musician. As the two cases merge, Ida turns to Louis Armstrong now working in the City for help while Leveson relies on old friendships in locating Cleveland.

Chandler, Raymond.
(Raymond Thornton Chandler)

"The King In Yellow" In <u>Collected Stories</u>. London & New York: Everyman, 2002.
Detective Steve Grayce throws bandleader-trombonist King Leopardi out of the Carlton Hotel for disturbing other guests at 1:30 am by playing in the hallway. Two days later Leopardi is found murdered in the bed of his former band singer, Dolores Chiozza.

Cleverly, Barbara.
(series: Joe Sandilands)

<u>Ragtime In Simla</u>. London: Constable & Robinson, 2002; New York: Carroll & Graf, 2003.
En route to Simla, Joe Sandilands witnesses the murder of a Russian baritone named Korsovsky. He's killed at the same spot where Lionel, the brother of Alice Conyers-Sharpe, a respected resident of Simla, was killed a year earlier. Seemingly, Alice's only link to Korsovsky was an association with the opera house where he had an engagement. As

Sandilands' investigation intensifies, it appears Alice might not be the person she portends to be. She's betrayed by a jazz tune.

Cockey, Tim.
(series: Hitchock Sewell)

The Hearse Case Scenario. New York: Hyperion, 2002.
Hitchcock Sewell's old friend Lucy Taylor has been charged with the murder of jazz club owner, Shrimp Martin. While she admitted shooting him for two-timing her, she did not administer the fatal knife wound. In attempting to clear her of murder charges, Hitch-cock stumbles into a sport gambling scam as well as the killer of a college student.

Coggins, Mark.
(Series: August Riordan)

The Immortal Game. Berkeley: Poltoon, 1999.
Private Investigator-jazz musician August Riordan is hired by Silicon Valley entrepreneur Edwin Bishop to recover a software program stolen by one of his paid female companions, Terri Mc-Culloch, who sold it to a rival software company. Revenge rather than recovery appears to be Bishop's obsession.

Vulture Capital. Berkeley: Poltoon, 2002.
Jazz bassist-turned-private detective August Riordan is hired by Silicon Valley venture capitalist Ted Valmont to find Warren Nie-bur, the missing Chief Technical Officer (CTO) of the biotech firm NeuroStimix. Valmont has a personal interest as Niebuhr was working on a device to help spinal chord injury victims, such as his brother Tim. But others see different uses for the technology: slave labor, terrorism and crime.

Candy From Strangers. Madison: Bleak House, 2006.
Riordan is hired to find missing art student Caroline Stockwell, who had a risqué web site to solicit cash and gifts. He's ill at ease

in the art world and knows little about "cam girls" and Internet sexual predators. After she returns home, mysteriously tattooed, Caroline attempts to commit suicide. Then her best friend Monica is murdered and a similar tattoo is found on her body. Riordan believes he's after a pervert but the obvious suspects turn out to be red herrings.

Runoff. Madison: Bleak House, 2007.

Leonora Lee, known as the Dragon Lady of Chinatown, hires jazz bassist/detective August Riordan to investigate fraud in San Francisco's recent mayoral primary. Lee's candidate's poor showing led her to believe that someone hacked into the city's voting system. After a quick lesson in the computer science behind the system and a less than subtle introduction to the political factions and Chinese gangsters who have an interest in the election's outcome, Riordan agrees.

The Big Wake-Up. Boulder: Bleak House, 2009.

Jazz bassist-turned-detective August Riordan is hired by a wealthy Argentine family to locate the final resting place of Maria de Magistria, who died in Milan, Italy. Her body was buried in San Francisco in 1974 under an unknown alias. With help from his friend, computer whiz Chris Duckworth, Riordan thinks that he has discovered Maria's grave. He soon realizes that the grave may really be that of Argentinean dictator Juan Peron's wife, Eva.

No Hard Feelings. Lutz, FL: Down & Out Books, 2015.

Winnie, a quadriplegic, regained mobility using implants developed by a biomedical start-up. As detailed in Vulture Capital, the company failed because of sabotage by a crippled sociopath known as the Winemaker. Now out of jail, he is unable to recreate Winnie's success and is determined to get her implants. She seeks help from August Riordan.

The Dead Beat Scroll. Lutz, FL: Down & Out Books, 2019.

August Riordan returned to San Francisco after the murder of his friend Chris Duckworth. He encounters Chris' last client Angelina, who hired him to find her missing half-sister, Corrine White. Riodan finds Corrine's body as well as unknown scroll by Jack Kerouac, from his <u>On The Road</u> period. Known as "the Beat-hive," it contains writing on polyamorous families and communal living sought by a murderous Canadian Manson-like family.

Cohen, Octavius Roy.

<u>Danger in Paradise</u>. London: Robert Hale, 1949; New York: Macmillan, 1944.

Radio star and Big Band singer Iris Randall has just returned to New York City from a U.S.O. tour of Caribbean military bases. In Cuba, she was asked by a playboy named Benigno to bring a box of El Corsario Invincible cigars to his friend in New York. Not knowing anything about cigars, she decides to buy another box as a gift for her friend, Jimmy Drake. Both boxes are stolen in separate incidents, each involving murder.

Colbert, Curt.
(series: Jake Rossiter)

<u>Rat City</u>. Seattle: Ugly Town, 2001.

PI Jake Rossiter's morning begins with a bang when small-time bookie, Big Ed, bursts into his office shooting. Rossiter is the better shot but is puzzled over his attacker's motive. He mistakenly puts aside the investigation of the disappearance of Lincoln Tyree, a young, black, jazz musician, to concentrate on Big Ed's motive.

Coleman, Wanda.

"Dunny." In <u>Jazz and Twelve O'Clock Blues</u>. Jaffrey: Black Sparrow, 2008.

Although he's a successful singer with best-selling albums, Dunny is always in debt to his record label. He's tired of singing what they want him to sing and wants a change. Unfortunately, he voices his "problems" to the wrong person.

Compton, D.G.
(series: Alec Duncan)

Back of Town Blues. London: Gollancz, 1996.

Alec Duncan, formerly a Detective Chief Inspector, now plays jazz piano in a Liverpool club. He was dismissed from the police for using excessive force. Not doing well after the murder of his girlfriend, Duncan decides to visit her jailed killer, Trevor Blandon for some sort of closure. Following the visit, Blandon's mother is murdered. Duncan is the prime suspect.

Connelly, Michael.
(series: Harry Bosch, Mickey Haller)

The Black Echo. London: Orion, 2000; Boston: Little, Brown, 1992.

A body stuffed into a drainpipe on Mulholland Drive is identified as Billy Turner, a former "tunnel rat." who hunted Viet Cong in the tunnels with Harry Bosch in Vietnam. Bosch discovers that Turner was under suspicion for involvement in an unsolved bank robbery using a tunnel. The FBI seems uninterested in Bosch's findings and suggests to the LAPD that Bosch might be involved in the robbery. The FBI wants him off the investigation, and then changes course, pairing him up with Agent Eleanor Wish.

The Black Ice. London: Cassell, 2001; Boston: Little, Brown, 1993.

A suicide discovered in a sleazy L.A. motel is identified as Cal Moore, an undercover narcotic cop, who was being investigated by Internal Affairs. The LAPD wants to cover-up his death but Lieutenant Harry Bosch is not satisfied. He is vindicated after the autopsy reveals murder. But Bosch is diverted from Moore's case into clearing up the unsolved cases of Lewis Porter, a murdered, drunken cop. Bosch thinks Moore's and Porter's cases are linked to murderers in Mexico.

The Concrete Blonde. London: Orion, 2000; Boston: Little, Brown, 1994.

Although LAPD Detective Harry Bosch has been cleared of using excessive force, the widow of Norman Church, known as the Dollmaker and a serial killer of 11 prostitutes, is suing him for civil damages. She has hired high-profile lawyer Honey Chandler. As the trial begins, the body of a prostitute is discovered killed in the manner of the Dollmarker's victims. Did Bosch kill the wrong man four years ago as Chandler insists or is it a copycat killing by someone with inside knowledge of the case?

The Last Coyote. London: Orion, 1995; Boston: Little, Brown, 1995.

After being placed on suspension for striking his commanding officer, Harry Bosch decides to use the time to look into the unsolved murder of his mother, Marjorie Lowe, a prostitute. That investigation was seemingly curtailed by political pressure from the D.A.'s office. He discovers that the principals have even more to lose today than they did thirty years earlier.

Trunk Music. London: Orion, 1997; Boston: Little, Brown, 1997.

LAPD Detective Harry Bosch is called to investigate the murder of Hollywood producer Tony Aliso, who was found stuffed into the trunk of his Rolls Royce with two bullets in his head. Although it appeared to be a Mafia hit, the LAPD's Organized Crime Unit and the FBI are uninterested in the murder. Aliso spent his final weekend in Las Vegas, so Bosch heads there and into a maze of money laundering and FBI undercover operations.

Angel's Flight. London: Orion, 1999; Boston: Little, Brown, 1999.

Howard Elias, a prominent black lawyer, who made a career from suing the Los Angeles Police Department (LAPD) on civil rights issues, is murdered. LAPD homicide detective Harry Bosch is given charge of the investigation, which has potential for sparking a race riot. There is pressure for Bosch to identify a "rogue" cop as the killer.

A Darkness More Than Night, London: Orion, 2000; Boston: Little, Brown, 2001.

Film director David Storey is on trial for murdering actress Jody Krementz, and arranging her death to appear as a suicide. Retired FBI profiler Terry McCaleb is brought into the ritualistic murder case of Edward Gunn, who had been frequently questioned by Harry Bosch in the unsolved murder of a prostitute. McCaleb suspects that Bosch, who's in the spotlight with the Storey trial, may have taken justice into his own hands.

City of Bones. London: Orion, 2002; Boston: Little, Brown, 2002.
A human bone discovered by a dog leads LAPD detective Harry Bosch to a shallow grave containing the bones of a twelve-year-old boy, killed 25 years earlier in Laurel Canyon. An appeal to the media results in the identification of Arthur Delacroix. Nicholas Trent, a pedophile living in the area, is a prime suspect. While searching for Delacroix's killer, Bosch loses an unexpected chance at personal happiness.

Lost Light. London: Orion, 2003; Boston: Little, Brown, 2003.
Recently retired from the LAPD, Harry Bosch decides to revisit the unsolved murder of 24-year-old Angela Benton, who was employed at a movie studio that lost $2 million in a robbery shortly after her death. Both the LAPD and the FBI warn Bosch off the case. While checking on the backgrounds of employees from the bank that loaned the money, he learns that Linus Simonson, who had been shot during the robbery, retired with a small "confidential" financial settlement.

"Christmas Even," In Randisi, Robert J. (ed.). Murder and all that Jazz. New York: Signet, 2004.
Harry Bosch was investigating a robbery and murder at the Three Kings Pawnshop and discovered the robber dead on the floor. He also finds an alto saxophone belonging to Quentin McKinzie, whom Harry had heard playing on a troop ship when he was returning from Vietnam. Harry learns that McKinzie is in a nursing home and returns his horn to him on Christmas Eve.

<u>The Narrows</u>. London: Orion, 2004; Boston: Little, Brown, 2004.

The widow of FBI profiler Terry McCaleb asks Harry Bosch, now retired from the LAPD and a private investigator, to look into the death of her husband. Terry was assumed to have died of heart failure. She suspects the medicines that he required daily were tampered with. A review McCaleb's recent cases lead Bosch to Nevada and into an FBI investigation of the serial killer, known as the Poet, who was presumed dead.

<u>The Closers</u>. London: Orion, 2005; Boston: Little, Brown, 2005.

After his three-years retirement, Detective Harry Bosch returns to the LAPD to join Kizman Rider in the Open-Unsolved Unit. Their first case involved the 1988 killing of Rebecca Verloren, a sixteen-year old biracial girl, who was taken from her bedroom and killed. Recent DNA evidence taken from the murder weapon implicates a White Supremacist.

<u>Echo Park</u>. London: Orion, 2006; New York: Little, Brown, 2006.

The LAPD arrests Raymond Waits with body parts of two women. He agrees to swap information on a series of unsolved murders in exchange for a life sentence. Among the victims was Marie Gesto, whose death haunted LAPD's Harry Bosch a decade earlier. Although Bosch was sure that Waits was involved, he was protected by his father's money and influence. Bosch is suspicious of the easy answer offered to a crime he struggled to solve.

<u>The Overlook</u>. London: Orion, 2007; New York: Little, Brown, 2007.

LAPD's Harry Bosch is called out in the middle of the night to the murder scene of Dr. Stanley Kent, who has been killed execution style with two bullets in the head. But the FBI's Rachel Walling, Harry's ex, appears and takes the case away from him. Apparently, Kent had access to missing radioactive materials that the FBI fears are now in the hands of Arab terrorists intent on making "a dirty bomb." To Bosch, however, the case feels more like murder than terrorism.

<u>The Brass Verdict</u> London: Orion, 2008; New York: Little, Brown, 2008.

Criminal defense attorney Mickey Haller inherits the cases of a murdered colleague, Jerry Vincent. The most important case concerns Walter Eliot, a Hollywood producer, accused of murdering his wife and her lover. In reviewing Vincent's defense strategy, Haller realizes why Eliot insisted on an immediate trial rather than seeking a continuance. Working independently on Vincent's murder case, LAPD Homicide Detective Harry Bosch makes the same discovery.

<u>9 Dragons</u>. London: Orion, 2009. New York: Little, Brown, 2009.

Harry Bosch is called to a site in South L.A. where John Li, the owner of Fortune Liquors, was murdered. Li had refused to pay protection money to the Triads. As he closes in on the Triad executioner, Bosch receives an email from Hong Kong indicating that his daughter Maddie, who lives there with his ex-wife, has been kidnapped. He flies to Hong Kong to look for his daughter and discovers that she may have been kidnapped for body parts.

<u>The Drop</u>. London: Orion, 2011; New York: Little, Brown, 2011.

Harry Bosch's old nemesis, Councilman Irwin Irving, wants him to determine whether his son George was pushed or fell off the balcony of the Chateau Marmot. Initially, Bosch believes someone, who was burned in one of George's influence peddling schemes, pushed him. Later he realizes the cause of death was more personal. Harry also must explain why eight-year-old Clayton Pell's DNA was found at the scene of a twenty-year-old, unsolved murder-rape case.

<u>The Black Box</u>. London: Orion, 2012; New York: Little, Brown, 2012.

During the Los Angeles riots, Harry Bosch was called to a crime scene where Anneke Jespersen, a Danish photojournalist, was killed execution style. Twenty years later, Bosch returns to the unsolved case. He is now able to trace the gun's use in several gang executions and eventually recovers the Beretta. As the gun's last known destination was Iraq, he believes it was a war trophy. Bosch suspects the killer to be a National Guardsman, who was in L.A. during the riots and in Iraq.

Burning Room. London: Orion, 2014; New York: Little, Brown, 2014.

Harry Bosch and his new partner Lucy (Lucia) Soto are investigating the murder of Orlando Merced, a Mariachi musician, who has died of septic poisoning from a bullet shot into his spine ten years earlier. Merced may not have been the intended target. Another band member was having an affair with the wife of a well-connected political donor. Bosch realizes that his partner is obsessed with finding an arsonist, who set a fire in an unlicensed daycare center, resulting in the deaths of 20 people, mostly children.

The Crossing. London: Orion, 2015; New York: Little, Brown, 2015.

Defense Attorney Mickey Heller enlists the recently retired Harry Bosch as an investigator in the rape/murder case of Lexi Parks, a prominent City official. In spite of DNA evidence found at the scene, Haller insists that Da'Quan Foster, the prime suspect, is innocent. Initially, Bosch resists as it means "crossing over to the other side." But the thought that real killer is free and an innocent man will go to jail convinces him. Bosch's investigation leads into Vice Squad dealings.

"Nighthawks." In Block, Lawrence. (ed.). In Sunlight or in Shadow. London & New York: Pegasus, 2016.

Now retired from the LAPD and working as a PI, Harry Bosch is hired by a wealthy industrialist to find his missing daughter. He encounters her at the Chicago Museum of Art viewing Hopper's "Nighthawks." After speaking with her, he reports back to his employer that the girl in a news photo was not his daughter. Unsure as to whether he was believed, he calls her and suggests she move again.

The Wrong Side of Goodbye. London: Orion, 2016; New York: Little, Brown, 2016.

Whitney Vance, an elderly, reclusive billionaire, hires free-lance investigator Harry Bosch to find a Mexican girl that he once loved. After she got pregnant, the Vance family broke up the relationship and she disappeared. With his days numbered, Vance wants to know her fate and if he has an heir. Bosch realizes people in Vance's company are aware of the situation and have a lot to loose.

Two Kinds of Truth. London: Orion, 2017; New York: Little, Brown, 2017.
Harry Bosch is working cold cases for the San Fernando Police Department when he's called to a drug store where two pharmacists have been murdered. Bosch's experienced eye spots a hit, not a robbery. One of the victims filed a complaint against a clinic for writing too many prescriptions. The FBI convinces Bosch to go undercover. At the same time, Preston Borders, a convicted murderer, claims Bosch planted evidence. If Borders is freed, every case Bosch ever worked on will be open to question.

Conroy, Albert.
(Pseudonym of Marvin H. Albert)

Mr. Lucky. New York: Dell, 1960.
Lucky and his friend, Andamo, give a ride back to Los Angeles from Mexico to an American couple with car trouble. But no good deed goes unpunished in this pulp fiction TV spin-off. The man, Mort Connors, a small-time crook, is later murdered and Lucky's fingerprints are found on the gun's cartridge clip. To clear himself, Lucky must find Connors' girlfriend Fan and the real killers. But Fan is more interested in finding stolen jewels hidden by Connors in Mexico.

Corbett, David.

Done for a Dime. London: Orion, 2004; New York: Ballantine, 2003.
The legendary blues baritone sax player, Raymond "Strong" Carlisle is murdered in his front yard. Detective Dennis Murchison has

two suspects: Arlie Thigpen, a street punk, who works for a local drug dealer, and Toby Marchand, Carlisle's son. But a tip from a double-crossed, self-confessed arsonist points Murchison in a very different direction.

Conway, Martha.

<u>Sugarland</u>. San Francisco: Noontime Books, 2016.

Black jazz pianist Eve Riser is on the run after witnessing the killing of a white man. Her accomplice gave her money and a letter to Rudy Hardy, a bootlegger and owner of the Oaks in Chicago where her sister, Chickie, is a singer. While waiting for Rudy outside the club, she chats with Rudy's sister, Lena. As Rudy approaches, he's killed in a drive-by shooting and Eve is wounded. They decide to team up and work both sides of the color line to find Chickie and Rudy's killer.

Coxe, George Harmon.
(series: Max Hale)

<u>The Lady Is Afraid</u>. New York: Knopf, 1940.

Alan Procter hires detective Max Hale to watch over his sister, Gail. She has been seeing jazz bandleader Don Washburn, who has a reputation as a womanizer and a gambler. Washburn's fast lifestyle catches up with him and he's killed with Gail's gun. To save his client, Hale must sort through Washburn's many enemies and women to uncover the killer.

(non-series)

<u>The Ring of Truth</u>. New York: Knopf, 1966.

When Jess Flemming, a mob enforcer, is murdered, the police eventually focus their investigation on jazz trumpeter, Ralph Estey. Both men were engaged in a public argument over a hat-check girl outside a jazz club. Dr. Paul Standish, who knew both men, does not believe Estey is a killer. After he "commits suicide," the police plan to end the investigation. Convinced it's a cover-up, Standish wants to find the real killer.

Craig, Jonathan.

Frenzy aka Junkie. London: Brown, Watson, 1966; New York: Lancer, 1962.

Trumpet player Steve Harper is summoned by his friend police officer Mark Logan to the apartment of old-time trumpet player (and part-time drug dealer) Wally Hanes, who was his roommate until he got involved with Kathy Mason. Someone identified as "Kathy" reported the killing of Hanes. Harper must find Kathy before the police. He knows she was not strong enough to strangle Hanes. His search is impeded by Phyllis Connery, a former piano player in his band and ex-girlfriend, who's in love with him.

Craig, Philip R.
(series: J.W. Jackson)

Vineyard Blues. New York: Scribner, 2000.

Corrie Appleyard, an old African-American bluesman and friend of J.W.'s father, unexpectedly appears at J.W.'s home. He's visiting Martha's Vineyard to play a couple of gigs. Appleyard is staying with the grandson of a friend in a house, owned by a local slumlord. When the house burns down, a body found in the basement is identified as Appleyard. Jackson is determined to find the arsonist-killer of his father's friend.

Creech, J. R.

Music And Crime. London: Bloomsbury, 1991; New York: Putnam, 1989.

Ray The Face, a 32-year-old tenor player, is struggling to make a living playing jazz. But he and his bass player, Lonnie, are forced into petty crime to survive. Through Lonnie, Ray meets Reggie, a talented singer. Infatuated, he asks her to help him add lyrics to music he has written. But Reggie's manager, Cody Orleans, has his own plans for his singer and the music.

Curran, Dale.

Dupree Blues. New York: Knopf, 1948.
Trombone player Dupree falls for the band's young vocalist, Betty, who is more interested in having a good time than getting serious. Using his winnings from a dice game, he buys her an expensive diamond ring. Unfortunately, Dupree later loses a lot of money gambling and is unable to pay the jeweler the balance owed on the ring, resulting in violence.

Dahl, Arne.
(series: Paul Hjelm)

Misterioso. Malmo: Bra Böcker, 1999; New York: Pantheon, 2011; as The Blinded Man, London: Vintage, 2012.
Paul Hjelm, head of a national crime team (the A-Team), is tasked with stopping the serial murder of business leaders. Each victim was shot twice in the head and then the bullets were dug out of the wall while the killer listened to a recording of Thelonious Monk playing "Misterioso." Initially, Hjelm believed the murders were the result of a quarrel within the secret society. Eventually, the killer's luck runs out, forcing him to leave the recording of "Misterioso" behind.

Daniel, John.

Play Melancholy Baby. Menlo Park: Perseverance Press, 1986.
Casey Jones plays piano and sings standards weeknights at Gershwin's, a club on the California coastal peninsula. Ex-singer Dixie Arthur invites him to San Francisco, and tries to hire him to locate her missing daughter, Molly. Casey belatedly realizes that he had an affair with Molly in Europe; and that Wolf, the drug dealer who caused their problems, is back.

Davis, J. Madison.

<u>And The Angels Sing</u>. Sag Harbor: Permanent Press, 1995.

Carl Carlson, the Carolina Crooner, is on the verge of stardom when he is drafted into the army. Wounded in North Africa, the German speaking Carlson is transferred as a translator to a POW camp in western Pennsylvania. Hoping to return to singing, he contacts Cleveland mobster Ernie Musso, who had been interested in his career. But the war has changed things. Carlson must finger a rival gangster to earn Musso's help.

Deaver, Jeffrey.
(Jeffrey Wilds Deaver)

<u>Mistress of Justice</u>. New York: Doubleday, 1992.

By night, Taylor Lockwood is a jazz pianist, struggling for success in the Big Apple. By day, she works as a paralegal at a Wall Street firm. Mitchell Reece, a litigator, asks for her help in recovering a promissory note stolen from his safe. She conducts her search in the midst of a merger fight that is tearing apart the firm.

Dionne, Ron.

<u>Sad Jingo</u>. New York: Delabarre, 2012.

Jingo Dalhousie, who works as a janitor in his cousin's Greenwich Village jazz club, fantasizes about a career as a pianist playing Thelonious Monk's music. When his unusual name appears in a best selling novel by Diana Madeiros, Jingo believes that he can play like Monk. He tries to get Madeiros to listen but is tagged as a stalker.

Dobbyn, John F.
(series: Michael Knight)

"Monday, Sweet Monday." In <u>Alfred Hitchcock's Mystery Magazine</u>. Vol. 50. No. 6. June 2005.

Boston criminal defense attorney Michael Knight plays jazz piano in a Beacon Street club owned by 1950s jazz legend Charles "Daddy" Hightower. Keno Westoba, a young Haitian sax player, sits in and is hired for the week. But the Boston Police arrest Keno for arson in Philadelphia, on the strength of a witness' positive identification. Then the witness is murdered. Suspecting the involvement of the Haitian mob, Knight believes in Keno's innocence and investigates the matter.

Doctorow, E.L.

Ragtime. London: Macmillan, 1976; New York: Random, 1975.
A gang of firefighters harasses Coalhouse Walker, Jr., a ragtime piano player from Harlem, as he's driving his car back from visiting his fiancée. He leaves his car by the road to get help from the police but is rebuffed and returns to find his car trashed by the firefighters. His demands that his car be repaired are ignored. As the first in a series of revolutionary actions, he firebombs the firehouse and kills several policemen.

Dowswell, Paul.

Auslander. London: Bloomsbury, 2009.
After Peter Bruck's parents are killed, he is briefly placed in a Warsaw orphanage. He's adopted by a Nazi family because of his Aryan looks. His growing dislike of life in Berlin causes him to rebel. He listens to jazz records and visits prohibited jazz cellars, once barely escaping a Gestapo raid. Through one of his jazz friends, Peter becomes involved in helping "submarines" (Berlin Jews) escape from Germany.

Downs, Hunton.

Murder In the Mood. Southampton: Wright Books, 1998.
Four previously unknown wartime broadcast recordings of American bandleader Glenn Miller are stolen from a London

auction house. Documentary filmmaker Artie Case was offered the discs by the thief, who was later murdered. The initially indifferent Case becomes intrigued as the discs hold clues to the fate of Miller as well as suppressed secrets concerning the Battle of the Bulge.

Doyle, Roddy.
(series: Henry Smart)

Oh, Play That Thing. London: Jonathan Cape, 2004; New York: Viking, 2004.

Ex-IRA gunman Henry Smart is on the run when he lands at Ellis Island in 1924. But gangster Owney Madden's Crime Commission sidetracks his chance at a new life. He flees to Chicago where he meets Louis Armstrong, who needs a white man to deal with club owners and gangsters. Soon New York City beckons, and Henry mistakenly believes his closeness to Louis will shield him from old enemies.

DuBois, Brendan.

"The Lady Meets the Blues," In Vega, Eddie (ed.). Noir Nation 6. Middletown, DE: 2017.

Mike, a rookie police detective, is called to a Portsmouth bar over a shooting. The victim, Anguillo, was a jazz-loving Mafioso who drove up from Boston to hear Billie Holiday. She is reduced to playing waterfront bars after losing her New York City Cabaret Card. At the end of her set, Anguillo was shot at close range while sitting with three bodyguards. Mike knows the publicity would only hurt her and lets the three gangsters return to Boston after discovering the murder weapon. He calls the victim's son and relates his findings.

Duchin, Peter & Wilson, John Morgan.
(series: Hercules Platt)

Blue Moon. New York: Berkley, 2002.

At a charity benefit, inaugurating Philip Damon's orchestra's residency at San Francisco's Fairmont Hotel, the wealthy bully Terence Hamilton Collier III, who was dancing with a woman resembling Damon's late wife, is murdered. Damon joins the investigation along with Charlene Statz, the wife of Fairmont's owner and a mystery buff. As the murders mount up, San Francisco's only black detective, the saxophone playing Hercules Platt, makes it an investigating trio.

Good Morning, Heartache. London: Prime Crime, 2003; New York: Berkley, 2003.

Needing a vocalist and a trumpet player for his six-week Coconut Grove residency, bandleader Philip Damon hires Buddy Bixby, a Chet Baker-like junkie musician, recently released from jail. Hercules Platt, ex-San Francisco cop turned saxophone player, agrees to watch over him. When Buddy dies in what police deem a drug overdose, Platt disagrees. His investigation is, however, hindered by the race Watts riots.

Edugyan, Esi.

Half Blood Blues. London: Serpent's Tail, 2011; New York: Picador, 2012.

Hieronymus Falk, a young mixed race jazz trumpet player, is half-black and half-German. After fleeing from Berlin to Paris with his band, he was arrested by the Nazis and sent to Sachsenhausen concentration camp. Witnessing the arrest was Sid Griffith, the band's bassist, who recounts the incident at a 1990s Berlin retrospective honoring Falk. The other surviving band member, drummer Chip Jones, has recently heard from Falk, who is living in Poland. He has invited both men to visit him but Griffith is reluctant.

Edwards, Grace F.
(series: Mali Anderson)

If I Should Die. New York: Doubleday, 1997.

Mali Anderson witnesses the murder of her friend, Harlem Children's Chorus Director Erskine Harding, and the attempted kidnapping of a child. The police arrest a street-child as the killer. After another murder is linked to the Chorus, Mali looks for answers in the direction of Erskine's half brother, gangster Johnny Harding.

Toast Before Dying, A. New York: Doubleday, 1998.
In an alley behind the Half-Moon Bar in Harlem, Thea Morris, a popular barmaid and sometime singer in Mali Anderson's father's band, is murdered. The police hold as the killer her ex-boyfriend, a part-time actor and bartender named Kendall, who claims to have run to her defense. Teddi Lovette, the owner of a small theatre company, hires Mali to clear Kendall.

No Time to Die. New York: Doubleday, 1999.
Mali Anderson's friend Claudine Hastings is garroted in her apartment. She is the first victim in a series of killings. Mali is convinced that Claudine's soon-to-be-ex-husband was the killer. Although evidence points otherwise, she remains convinced of the killer's identity until almost becoming the killer's next victim.

Do or Die. New York: Doubleday, 2000.
Mali Anderson returns from jazz cruise on the QE2 to find Starr, the daughter of Ozzie Hendrix, the piano player and vocalist in her father's band, murdered. She had a troubled past of drug use and her old pimp and supplier, Short Change, is suspected of the murder. The suffering and physical deterioration of Ozzie adversely affects her father so much that Mali is concerned about his welfare and must quickly find the killer.

(non-series)

"The Blind Alley." In Shades of Black. Bland, Eleanor Taylor (ed.). New York: Berkley, 2004.
Waking from a nightmare and suffering from a hangover, Matthew goes to his weekend gig, playing saxophone at the Blind Alley.

Rhino's back in the neighborhood after serving a reduced murder sentence and unwelcome. He's at the Blind Alley, acting in a threatening, unbalanced manner. As Mathew's leaves the club late that night, he remembers that he was murdered in his nightmare. This episode was woven into a book with the same title.

The Blind Alley. New York: iUniverse, 2010.
    Rhino has returned after serving two years of a ten years murder sentence. He distrupts the lives of seven families living in a tenement and the patrons and performers of its basement after-hours club, The Blind Alley. Rhino attacks 15 years old Sara Martin, but is she's rescued by Matthew's 15 years old son, Theo. The residents can't call the police as Morgans are illegals from the Islands. So they must wait until Rhino does something to them before bringing in the police.

Edwardson, Ake.
(series: Erik Winter)

Sun And Shadow. Stockholm: Norstedts, 1999; London: Harvill, 2005; New York: Viking, 2006.
    Chief Inspector Erik Winter returns to Gothenberg from the Costa del Sol to a gruesome double murder. The heads of victims were switched and Black Metal rock music apparently provided a soundtrack to the crime. Black Metal is a foreign world to the jazz-loving Winter. The only clue to the murderer's identity is a paperboy's memory of a man in uniform leaving the crime scene.

Ehrhart, Peggy.
(series: Maxx Maxwell)

Sweet Man Is Gone. Waterville, ME: Five Star, 2008.
    Before blues singer Maxx Maxwell's band opens at a Greenwich Village club, her guitarist Danny Nashville commits suicide by jumping out of a window. Maxwell suspects that her former guitarist, Stan, had something to do with Danny's death. After Nashville's

girlfriend, Monique commits suicide, Maxx believes Stan committed a second murder to cover up the first.

Got No Friend Anyhow. New York: Gale, 2011.

Maxx Maxwell understands that her blues band needs a CD to get gigs. So they pay $1,000 for a master but their producer, Rick Schneider, disappears with the demo. Some band members believe that Schneider, who had financial problems, skipped town with their money. Maxwell believes otherwise and goes looking for him and the band's CD.

Eisler, Barry.
(series: John Rain)

Rain Fall. London: CreateSpace, 2013; New York: Putnam, 2002; aka A Clean Kill in Tokyo.

John Rain kills Japanese politician Yashiro Kawamura, who was going to a meeting with a western journalist. He was carrying a missing computer disc filled with incriminating information linking the Liberal Democratic Party to the Japanese criminal syndicate, the Yakazu. Dangerous people think Rain has the disc. Relaxing at jazz club, Rain meets pianist Midori Kawamura, whom he realizes is the daughter of the man he killed and that some people believe she has the disc.

Hard Rain. London: Michael Joseph, 2003; New York: Putnam, 2003.

Assassin-for-hire John Rain wants to retire and disappear in Brazil. But Tatsu, head of Japan's FBI, needs him to remove two Yakuza enforcers with ties to the corrupt Nationalist Party boss, Yamamoto. He takes out the first killer but is hesitant about the second until people in his own life are threatened and killed.

Rain Storm. London: Michael Joseph, 2004; New York: Putnam, 2004; aka Choke Point.

Former CIA assassin John Rain goes to Macau to kill arms

dealer Achille Belghazi, who is selling high tech weaponry to Arab terrorists. He soon realizes that he's not the only one hunting Belghazi and that the others may compromise his mission.

Killing Rain. London: Onyx, 2006; New York: Putnam, 2005; aka Redemption Games.
John Rain agrees to kill an arms dealer in Manila for the Israelis but freezes when the man's son interrupts the hit. Rain does kill his bodyguards, who were ex-CIA agents. The Israelis panic, believing Rain has killed CIA agents, and decide to kill him. In this heated atmosphere, everyone misses the significance of the Manila meeting.

The Last Assassin London: Michael Joseph, 2007; New York: Putnam, 2006.
Assassin John Rain learned that he has a son with Midori Kawamura. They are living in New York City where she is working as a jazz pianist. They are, however, being watched by the Chinese Triad as a favor to Yakazu (Japanese) crime boss Yamaoto who wants Rain dead. Because he has again endangered Midori, Rain understands that the only way to guarantee her safety is to kill Yamaoto.

Requiem for an Assassin. London: Michael Joseph, 2008; New York: Putnam, 2007.
John Rain's friend Dox is kidnapped by rogue CIA agent John Hilfer and will only be released if Rain kills three people. Rain suspects Hilfer has no intention of releasing Dox but kills the two people to buy time and asks the Israelis for help. But the kidnapping and murders are just a distraction to allow Hilfer to go forward with a more deadly operation.

Ellroy, James.
(Pseudonym of Lee Earle "James" Ellroy)

White Jazz. London: Century, 1992; New York: Knopf, 1992.
LAPD Lieutenant Dave Klein kills a key witness in a Federal boxing investigation, much to the relief of the LAPD and gang-

ster Mickey Cohen. Angered, the Feds decide to target corruption within the LAPD. Klein realizes that he's going to be sacrificed to contain the Federal investigation but hopes to divert attention by finding a saxophone-playing psychopath against a background of corruption, incest and madness in 1950s L.A.

"Dick Contino's Blues." In <u>Hollywood Nocturne</u>. London: Prentice Hall, 1994; New York: Penzler, 1994.

Singer Dick Contino decides to fake his own kidnapping and heroic escape in an attempt to shed his reputation of cowardice resulting from a refusal to be drafted during the Korean War. Unfortunately for Contino, one of his kidnappers has his own agenda.

Estleman, Loren D.
(series: Amos Walker)

<u>Lady Yesterday</u>. London: Macmillan, 1987; Boston: Houghton Mifflin, 1987

Detroit PI Amos Walker is asked by his old friend Iris for help in locating her father, Little Georgie Favor, a legendary trombone player, who unknowingly left behind a daughter after a Jamaican gig. Walker's investigation puts them in the middle of a vendetta between local mobsters and newly arrived Columbians.

(non-series)

<u>Whiskey River</u>. London: Scribners, 1991; New York: Bantam, 1990.

Tabloid crime writer Constantine "Connie" Minor met young Jack Danzig at Hattie Long's Bar after he convinced her to give him his first job. Minor chronicles Danzig's move up in the Detroit underworld, his fortune made as a bootlegger, the marriage to society girl Vivian Deering, his gang war with Joey Machine and betrayal. Speakeasy jazz provides the background and tempo for this Jazz age story.

<u>Jitterbug</u>. New York: Forge, 1998.

A serial killer masquerading as a soldier disrupts Detroit Police

Lieutenant Maximillian Zagreb's black-market investigation. Short of manpower, Zagreb pressures mobster Frankie Orr to have his minions search for the killer. Robert Leroy Parker Gitchfield, known as Gidgit, who runs all the black clubs, music outlets and black-market activities, is drawn into the hunt against a background of one of World War II's worst race riots.

Farr, John.
(Pseudonym of John Alfred "Jack" Webb)

The Deadly Combo, New York: Ace, 1958.

Danny Mullens, a legendary jazz trumpet player, who had fallen on hard times, is murdered in an alley behind the Onyx Club. It is thought that a disappointed robber, who believed the story of his "golden horn," beat him to death. His old friend, jazz aficionado and ex-policeman, Mac Stewart disagrees. He roams the streets of L.A. on the trail of a killer that whines from second-rate jazz clubs and Muscle Beach to the heights of the jazz world.

Fitzgerald, F. Scott.
(Francis Scott Fitzgerald)

"The Dance." In Ellery Queen's Mystery Magazine. Vol. 21. No. 112. March 1953.

In this overlooked short story by F. Scott Fitzgerald, the excitement generated by Charleston dancer Catherine Jones and the black jazz band's accompaniment to her dancing cover the sound of a murder at an Alabama country club party.

The Great Gatsby. London & New York: Scribners, 1925.

Midwesterner Nick Carraway lives next door to the mysterious Jay Gatsby, who has legendary weekend parties. He learns from golfer Jordan Baker that Gatsby and her cousin, Daisy Buchanan, once were engaged. At Gatsby's urging, Nick sets up a meeting between the unhappily married Daisy and Gatsby which has unintended consequences for everyone. Although it's always in the background, jazz music sets the tone of the parties and the era.

Fitzhugh, Bill.

Highway 61 Resurfaced. New York: Morrow, 2005.

Rick Shannon of Rockin' Vestigations and a Vicksburg classic rock D.J. is hired by an imposter of Lollie Woolfolk to find her missing grandfather. After the old man is found and murdered, the real Lollie wants answers. Shannon suspects the murder is related to blues recordings made by Blind Buddy Cotton, Crippled Willie Jefferson and Crazy Earl Tate, known as the legendary Blind, Crippled and Crazy sessions.

Fleming, Charles.
(series: Deacon)

The Ivory Coast. New York: St. Martin's, 2002.

Worried about increasing competition and decreasing profits, mobster Moe Winer hopes to make up a potential shortfall by secretly financing the first integrated hotel-casino, the Ivory Coast. It's to be fronted by the retired black boxer, Worthless Jones. To guarantee Tom Haney, Las Vegas' racist, top cop doesn't interfere, he sends a hit man to intercept a special package from Chicago. But in a mix-up, Deacon, a junkie trumpet player, and not the hit man, gets the package.

After Havana. New York: St. Martin's. 2004.

Depressed over the lost of his girlfriend Anita, Deacon left Las Vegas, and is playing the trumpet as Peter Sloan in the band at Havana's Tropicana Hotel. His gangster friend, Mo Weiner, also, left Las Vegas for Havana with the intention of buying a casino and restaurant. Anita, too, is in Havana with wealthy businessman Nick Calloway when a rogue, rebel cell, kidnaps her for ransom. Cuban policeman Luis Cardozo joins Sloan and Calloway in a rescue attempt but he has his own agenda involving the rebel leader Carlos Delgado.

Fletcher, Jessica & Bain, Donald.
(Jessica Beatrice Fletcher & Donald Sutherland Bain)
(series: Jessica Fletcher)

Murder in a Minor Key. London & New York: Signet, 2001.

In this novelization of a tv episode from *"Murder She Wrote,"* Jessica Fletcher attends a writer's meeting in New Orleans and renews a friendship with jazz critic Wayne Copely that is ended by his death. His body was discovered near the grave of an old voodoo queen with snakebite as the cause of death. Although the police regard his death as "accidental," Jessica has serious doubts. Copely had been working on a study of legendary trumpeter Little Red Le Coeur, a contemporary of Buddy Bolden, and searching for "lost" cylinder recordings.

Foehr, Stephen.

Storyville. Bro: Jiri Vanek, 2009.

Antoine, a light skinned hustler working for Storyville boss Tom Anderson, is jilted by his childhood sweetheart, an octoroon named Mary Ann, who is involved with a wealthy, white planter. During the race riots, he murders his rival, only to lose Mary Ann who is killed while out looking for her missing lover. All this occurs against a background of the power struggle between Anderson, the Italian Mafia and the New Orleans Police Chief.

Foote, Shelby.
(Shelby Dade Foote, Jr.)

"Ride Out." In Albert, Richard N. (ed.). Blues To Bebop. Baton Rouge: Louisiana State University Press, 1990.

Duff Conway, who learned to play the cornet in a rural detention center and local roadhouses, finally hits the Big Apple. With success in his grasp, a lung infection sends him back to Mississippi.

Local girl, Julie Kinship is initially excited by Conway's celebrity but soon tires of him. For excitement, she initiates a confrontation between Conway and a gambler, Chance Jackson, with deadly consequences.

Fowler, Carol S.
(series: Bernie Butz)

"And The Angels Sing." In <u>Blues in the Night</u>. Houston: Strategic Book Publishing and Rights Co., 2013.

Jazz reviewer and part time detective Bernie Butz discovers Tiny Rivers, a jazz pianist, in an Italian restaurant and gets him a job with the high-powered Wendall McCabe Quintet. Unknown to Butz, Rivers is a drunk, who manages to stay sober through the gig and a recording session. After getting his paycheck, however, he goes to a liquor store with fatal results.

"Blues in the Night." In <u>Blues in the Night</u>. Houston: Strategic Book Publishing and Rights Co., 2013.

Bernie goes to hear a new group, the Johnny Mulray Quintet. The drummer, Nicky Spinoza, fails to appear as he's involved with Johnny's wife, Marilyn. During the evening, Butz meets Laura Singer, who lives in Johnny's apartment building. Several days later, Marilyn and Nicky are murdered. Laura thought she saw the killer, who looked like Johnny, going down the fire escape. Johnny insists on his innocence.

"Born To Be Blue" In <u>Blues in the Night</u>. Houston: Strategic Book Publishing and Rights Co., 2013.

Bernie Butz goes to Dolphin Beach, Florida to write an article on trombone legend Snooky Jones, who was moving to Europe for racial reasons. He stumbles into friction between segregated black and white jazz clubs, fueled by the murder of a young black trumpet player and the white owner of a black club.

"Loverman." In <u>Blues in the Night</u>. Houston: Strategic Book Publishing and Rights Co., 2013.

A woman claims that she's pregnant by young sax sensation, Jack Goldberg. If he doesn't give her $10,000, she'll go to the press and cops about his drug habit. These revelations would end his promising career. Butz realizes its a scam and gets Goldberg off drugs as well.

"Passion Flower." In <u>Blues in the Night</u>. Houston: Strategic Book Publishing and Rights Co., 2013.

A number of Chicago jazz musicians have been strangled with piano wire and castrated. Bernie Butz realizes they all worked with a piano player named Don Flores. Flores is eventually caught and turns out to be woman—Donna Flores. She masqueraded as a man so she could play jazz.

"Blowin' Up a Storm: The Second Chronicles of Bernie Butz." Lexington, KY: CreateSpace (self-published), 2016.

The post-war edition of the Jerry Farlow Orchestra is back in Chicago and trying to deal with the changing times and music. Four of Farlow's musicians, the youngest and most talented, have drug issues. Fearing the negative publicity will destroy Farlow's struggling orchestra, critic/part-time detective Butz uses his influence with the Mafia and the police to defuse the situation.

Fredrickson, Jack.

"Good Evenin' Blues." In Hellmann, Libby Fischer. (ed.). <u>Chicago Blues</u>. Madison: Bleak House, 2007.

The narrator owns a failing Chicago bar, "The Crossroads," named after Robert Johnson's famous blues tune. Pearly Hester appears one day and suggests an open mike on Saturdays for aspiring blues musicians. He agrees to do all the promotion and let the bar keep the profits. Hester plans to make his money pressing demos for the blues aspirants. Things go well until one day the narrator sees expensive guitars belonging to several of the young singers in a nearby pawnshop.

Fuller, Jack.

<u>The Best of Jackson Payne</u>. New York: Knopf, 2000.

Through a series of interviews, white musicologist Charles Quinlan is trying to understand the career of the tenor player Jackson Payne well enough to write a definitive biography. Beginning his twenty-year career after the Korean War, Payne played hard-bebop, used and dealt drugs, and finally, was arrested. Wanting to avoid a long prison sentence, he agreed to become a L.A. police informant. Several victims caught in the resulting sting would be Payne's undoing.

Fulmer, David.
(Thurston David Fulmer)
(series: Valentine St. Cyr)

<u>Chasing The Devil's Tail</u>. Scottsdale: Poisoned Pen Press, 2001.

Storyville political boss Tom Anderson orders Creole detective Valentin St. Cyr to find the killer of prostitutes. The number of killings as well as the placement of a black rose beside each victim guarantees an interest outside of Storyville. St. Cyr discovers that all of the victims knew cornet player Buddy Bolden, then at the height of his musical powers but descending into insanity. He believes Bolden's irrational behavior doesn't make him a killer. Anderson disagrees.

<u>Jass</u>. New York: Harcourt, 2005.

Piano player Jelly Roll Morton is convinced that someone is murdering jazz musicians and asks his friend, Creole detective Valentin St. Cyr, to investigate two deaths. But St. Cyr dismisses the request until two more musicians die. All of the murdered musicians were from the Union Hall Band. He learns from its surviving member of an incident involving a young, white girl and suspects her identity is the key to the murders.

<u>Rampart Street</u>. New York: Harcourt, 2006.

John Benedict, a respected businessman, is murdered on Rampart Street. Detective Valentin St. Cyr, is asked to investigate the murder by people who really want to sweep the matter under the rug. But the dead man's daughter, Anne Marie, wants to know the identity of her father's killer. After a businessman with ties to Benedict, Charles Kane, and a third man, Henry Harris, who is New Orleans wealthiest man, are killed, St, Cyr sets about finding their killers.

"Algiers." In Smith, Julie. (ed.) <u>New Orleans Noir</u>. New York: Akasic, 2007.

Tom Anderson asks Valentin St. Cyr to go across the river to Algiers and deal with a card cheat at a friend's bar. The cheater, Eddie McTier, is a gambler and bluesman, who claimed to have traded his soul to the devil for luck at cards and the ability to play the blues. But his luck runs out when he deals a crooked hand to St. Cyr.

<u>Lost River</u>. New York: Houghton Mifflin Harcourt, 2009.

Valentin St. Cyr left Storyville to work as an investigator for a St. Charles Street law firm. But his new life is interrupted by a series of murders in or near the sporting houses of Storyville's most prominent madams, who ask for his help. St. Cyr realizes that in three years that he's been away, Storyville's political boss Tom Anderson has aged badly and is perceived to be loosing control over the district. To maintain the status quo, he must find the killers.

<u>The Iron Angel</u>. Raleigh: Bang Bang Lulu, 2014.

A serial killer named Gregory is roaming Storyville, ritually murdering prostitutes. The aging, ailing Tom Anderson is unable to stop him. He persuades a reluctant Valentin St. Cyr to return to Storyville and end the killing spree. St. Cyr, now employed by a law firm, is currently engaged in looking for the missing daughter of a client. His nemesis, Captain Picot of the New Orleans police, learns of an elderly woman, suffering from amnesia, who might be St. Cyr's missing mother. He concocts a scheme to use her to hurt the Creole detective.

<u>Eclipse Alley</u>. New Orleans: Crescent City Books, 2017.

The mutilated body of Herbert Waltham, a prominent New Orleans citizen, is discovered in Eclipse Alley in a run-down part of Storyville. St. Cyr's friend, James McKinney, asks St. Cyr, now a private detective, to come in on the case. Within days, three more men meet similar fates. St. Cyr believes the killer may be a woman, who was harmed by the men. Rebecca Marcus of the Times Picayune sees an opportunity to break through as a crime reporter. While providing some unique help, her ambition is a problem for the surprisingly sympathetic investigators.

<u>The Day Ends at Dawn</u>, New Orleans: Crescent City Books, 2019.

Early in the morning before the closing of Storyville, a shot is fired through the bedroom window of Valentin St. Cyr. He wonders if it's related to the impending arrival of information from Washington concerning the corrupt dealings of certain prominent citizens or just a freak event. A series of violent incidents directed at St. Cyr's wife and associates makes it clear that it's the former. Under someone's protection, St. Cyr's old nemesis, the revenge seeking Captain Picot, has returned to New Orleans. St. Cyr, his wife Justine and police lieutenant James McKinney must find a mysterious killer with a personal vendetta.

(non-series books)

<u>The Dying Crapshooter's Blues</u>, New York: Harcourt, 2007.

Professional thief Joe Rose arrives in Atlanta for his winter stay with Pearl Spencer and finds himself as the prime suspect in a jewel robbery that occurred during a Christmas party. He learns that Pearl was hired as extra help for the party and fears a setup. He, also, happens upon Little Jesse Williams, a pimp and a crapshooter, who has been inexplicably shot by a drunken policeman. As Jesse is slowly trying to finish a deathbed blues, Rose is determined to find out why he was shot.

<u>The Blue Door</u>. New York: Harcourt, 2008.

Former boxer Eddie Cero stops a fight between two punks and private eye Sal Giambroni and is offered a job. His first assignment for Giambroni is to catch a bartender suspected of theft at The Blue Door, a club that had seen better days. The club's singer, Valerie Page, was formerly a member of the Excels, whose leader was her brother Jimmy Pope. He mysteriously disappeared after a recording session. Cero decides to use his new investigative skills to discover Pope's fate.

Will You Meet Me In Heaven? Raleigh: Bang Bang Lulu, 2014.
Frank Dupree, a drifter, meets Betty Anderson, a dancer, in the lounge of her Atlanta hotel where she is playing the piano. He's infatuated with her and that infatuation turns into a five-day affair. She tells him that she separated from her husband and he never gave her a wedding ring. Determined to get her a ring, Dupree goes into a jewelry store but things go awry. He shoots two people and takes the ring. But Betty refuses it as it is stolen.

Gailly, Christian.

An Evening at The Club. New York: Other Press, 2003. Also as Soir au club. Paris: Editions de Minuit, 2001.
After being overwhelmed by the jazz life-style, pianist Simon Nardis retired to a subdued existence with his wife, Suzanne. One evening, a business associate takes him to dinner and a jazz club before his evening train to Paris. After a few drinks while listening to the jazz trio, he approaches the piano and plays the night train and Suzanne out of his thoughts. Deborah, the club's owner and a well-regarded singer, has plans for him that doesn't include Suzanne.

Gaiter, Leonce.

Bourbon Street. New York: Carroll & Graf, 2005.
Texas gambler Deke Watley arrives in New Orleans during Mardi Gras for an invitational poker game. He discovers the other players knew each other and had some relationship with blind crime boss,

August Moreau. In The Ten Spot, a downtown jazz club, he encounters an ex-girlfriend named Hannah. Watley realizes that he has been lured to New Orleans and trapped into a deadly revenge scheme.

Garcia, Vee Williams.

The Jazz Flower. New York: iUniverse, 2006.

Rosa Johnson Stills grew up wanting to be a jazz singer. She also wanted Alan Covington, who is trapped in an arranged marriage with socialite Iris Haywood. Moving to New York City, Rosa gets a job singing at the Blue Phoenix nightclub and becomes entangled with the hot-tempered gangster, Jackson Parker. Covington, who continued seeing Rosa after his marriage, is murdered. Parker seems the likely killer.

Gillette, Paul.
(Paul J. Gillette)

Play Misty for Me. London: Tandem, 1972; New York: Award, 1971.

Upset over his breakup with Tobe Williams, jazz DJ Dave Garland picks up Evelyn Draper at a bar after his late night radio show. Unfortunately, what he considered a one-night stand becomes an obsession for Draper with unpleasant consequences for Garland and anyone else in his life.

Gilmer, Byron.

Felonious Jazz. Durham: Laurel Bluff Books, 2009.

Legal investigator J.D. Swain is sent to the home of one of his firm's clients after the client, developer Mickey Reuss, found his house burglarized and the family dog killed. The new Mrs. Reuss thinks Mickey's first wife is responsible but Swain suspects otherwise. Parked nearby is jazz bassist Leonard Noblac, who has decided to take revenge on the inhabitants of the new development of Rocky Falls.

Glatzer, Hal.
(series: Katy Green)

<u>Too Dead to Swing</u>. London: Daniel & Daniel, 2004; Santa Barbara: Perseverance Press, 2002.
Swing alto saxophone and violin player Katy Green joins the Ultra Belles, an all-girl band, touring California by train. She replaced a violinist who fell to her death from the Santa Monica pier. Other musicians in the band meet violent ends as the tour continues. Unless she finds the killer, Katy suspects that she will become the next victim.

<u>A Fugue in Hell's Kitchen</u>. London: John Daniel, 2004; Palo Alto: Perseverance, 2004.
Swing violinist Katy Green ventures into the classical music world when her friend, cellist Amalia Chen, loses a valuable manuscript of a Paganini string quartet used in a radio broadcast. The manuscript is later discovered by Chen, inexplicably stuffed in a magazine, and returned to its owner. But the returned manuscript is a forgery. Chen is arrested and might be deported unless Green finds the missing original.

<u>The Last Full Measure</u>. Santa Barbara: Perseverance, 2006.
Jazz violinist Katy Green accepts a holiday cruise job with Ivy Powell's Quartet on the luxury liner, S.S. Luriline, sailing between San Francisco and Honolulu. Once on board, she learns the real reason for her presence is to help Hawaiian band singer, Roselai Akau, find and transport a buried family treasure. While she doesn't find the treasure, she does stumble on the Pearl Harbor conspiracy.

Goldsmith, Martin.
(Martin M. Goldsmith)

<u>Detour</u>. London: Black Mask, 2008; New York: Macaulay, 1939.
Jazz violinist Alexander Roth leaves New York to hitchhike to Los

Angeles. In New Mexico, he is picked-up by Mr. Haskell, who buys him a steak dinner and later slumps dead in the passenger seat. Initially, Roth panics but then strips the body, takes his money and belongings to assume Haskell's identity. After crossing the Arizona line, he picks up a woman hitchhiker named Vera and decides to treat her to steak dinner. During their meal, she tells him that she knew Haskell.

Goodis, David.
(David Loeb Goodis)

<u>Shoot The Piano Player</u>. London: Prion, 1999; New York: Gold Medal, 1956.
   Eddie Lynn plays the piano at a bar named Harriet's Hut. Once an accomplished pianist who played Carnegie Hall, Lynn found the price of success too high and sought safety and respite in anonymity. But his brother Turley, who doubled-crossed the mob and now needs shelter, disturbs even this. Eddie helps him escape and must face the consequences.

<u>Street of No Return</u>. London: Black Lizard, 1994; New York: Gold Medal, 1961.
   Eugene Liddell, a former big-band singer, is a skid row bum known as "Whitey." His career-ending downfall resulted from infatuation with a racketeer's girlfriend, a prostitute named Celia. He sees Sharkey, the racketeer, on the street and follows him, hoping to see Celia again. Instead, he finds violence, murder and a race riot.

Gorman, Ed.
(Edward Joseph Gorman, Jr.)

"The Reason Why." In Spillane, Mickey and Collins, Max Allen (eds.), <u>A Century of Noir</u>. New York: New American Library, 2002.
   At a 25th high school reunion, Karen tells her friend Dwyer that she sent a note to three classmates, regarding the death of a fourth

at Pierce Point years ago. Did he jump or was he was pushed? Karen had overheard a conversation that pointed to the latter and wanted to know the truth. She challenged them at a meeting at Pierce Point.

"Muse." In Randisi, Robert J. (ed.). <u>Murder and all that Jazz</u>. New York: Signet, 2004.

Dave Osborne, a former reporter, returns to his old newsroom to flaunt his success as a songwriter and an author. His former editor Dulcy Tremont asks reporter Jason Manning to set up a dinner meeting with Osborne who is later murdered. The prime suspect is Dulcy's jealous boyfriend, newspaper owner Cal Rawlins. Manning was inexplicably sent a manila envelope containing songs that people are willing to kill for.

Gosling, Paula.

<u>Solo Blues</u> aka <u>Loser's Blues</u>. New York & London: Coward, McCann & Geoghegan, 1981.

Johnny Cosatelli, now a successful jazz pianist, abandoned his classical career. A prominent classical promoter offers him a second chance. Then Cosatelli's ex-girlfriend Lisa is murdered and both the police and her current boyfriend, a well-established antique dealer, think Johnny is her killer. Claverton, the boyfriend, decides to take the matter into his own hands as the police seem to standby.

Graham, Heather.
(series: Caffery & Quinn)

<u>The Dead Play On</u>. Don Mills, Ontario: Mira, 2015; New York: Thorndike, 2015.

Tyler Anderson inherited his friend Arnie's saxophone. While playing it, he has a new understanding of friend's death. He asks Dani Cafferty, an old friend, to investigate. She turns to her partner, Michael Quinn, a former cop, who realizes that Arnie was the first in a number of murdered New Orleans musicians who were school friends. Cafferty and Quinn suspect the killer is looking for Arnie's "magic sax" that allegedly bestowed unusual musical abilities.

Granelli, Roger

Out of Nowhere. Bridgend, Wales: Seren, 1995.

Frank Magnani is a Welsh guitarist, who arrives in New York City to make his mark in the Big Apple's jazz scene. Unfortunately, one of the first people he encounters is Johnson, a drug dealer and gofer. He gets Magnani locked into an unchallenging but profitable gig that he loses as the result of drugs provided by Johnson. Eventually, he and Johnson get into a fight. Magnani thinks that he killed Johnson and goes on the run.

Grant, James.

Don't Shoot the Pianist. London: Piatkus, 1980.

In this noir comedy, Lew Jackson, an aging musician and partner in a run-down Battersea jazz club, hopes to save his club by promoting a jazz festival during the August bank holidays. After his backer drops out, the local criminal syndicate comes to his rescue with funds and enough influence to sign hitherto unattainable jazz groups. The festival venue, Town Hall, is located between two banks. Crime boss Jack Reeder hopes the festival will cover the noise of blowing bank vaults.

Green, George Dawes.

The Caveman's Valentine. London: Little, Brown, 1994; New York: Warner, 1994.

Romulus Leadbetter, a Juilliard-trained classical pianist, lives in a cave in New York City's Inwood Park. After the body of Scotty Gates, the former model of photographer David Leppenraub, is dumped in front of his cave, Romulus is determined to find his killer. He heard that Leppenraub was considered untouchable because of his status in the art world and tortured Gates to death in a snuff video.

Greenwood, Kerry.
(Kerry Isabelle Greenwood)
(series: Phryne Fisher)

The Green Mill Murder. London: Allen & Unwin, 2012; Scottsdale: Poisoned Pen Press, 2007.

Phryne Fisher's evening of dancing to Tintgel Stone's Jazzmakers at Melbourne's best jazz club is interrupted by a murder in the midst of "Bye Bye Blackbird." Charles Freeman, her escort, panics and disappears. Consequently, he is considered a prime suspect. His mother hires Phryne to find her son, clear his name and also find his missing brother Vic, who disappeared after the war. The murder victim, Bernard Stevens, was a blackmailer and Freeman one of his gay victims.

Greer, Robert O.
(series: C.J. Floyd)

The Devil's Red Nickel. New York: Mysterious, 1997.

Clotilde Polk, the daughter of the famous Chicago DJ LeRoy, known as Daddy Doo-Wop, asks C.J. Floyd to investigate the death of her father. The Polks intended to open an oldies store and resurrect Polk's soul recording company. Floyd's investigation unexpectedly expands to Chicago and into organized crime's control of the record business. He discovers no shortage of suspects with reasons to kill Polk.

Gruber, Frank.
(series: Johnny Fletcher & Sam Cregg)

The Whispering Master. London: Panther, 1956; New York: Signet, 1949.

Just before her murder, failed singer Marjorie Fair tossed a phonograph record across the airshaft into Johnny Fletcher and Sam Cregg's apartment window. Initially, the police consider Fletcher a suspect. To clear himself, he is determined to examine Fair's life to find the answer to her murder.

Swing Low Swing Dead. London: Five Star, 1972; New York: Belmont, 1964.

On a $40 bet in a crapgame, PI Johnny Fletcher's friend, Sam Cragg wins a song, titled "Apple Taffy," from songwriter, Willie Waller. His claim that the song is worth thousands of dollars is dismissed until he is murdered. After they are offered $50,000 for the song, Fletcher learns the same song with the title "Lollipops," allegedly by composer Al Donnelly, is the hottest selling record. Donnelly makes his own deadly offer.

(non-series)

"Words and Music." In Brass Knuckles. Los Angeles: Sherbourne, 1966.

While having a few beers, Oliver Quade and Charlie Boston encounter a drunken songwriter named Billy Bond, who insists that the piano player play his just published song, "Cottage By The Sea." He quarrels with the pianist, takes a drink of beer spiked with hydrocyanic acid and dies instantaneously. After the police interrogation, Quade decides to check out Billy's room and discovers all of his music missing. A few days later he hears Billy's song with a different title and composer credited.

Guilfoile, Kevin.

"O Death Where is Thy Sting?" In Hellmann, Libby Fischer H. (ed.). Chicago Blues. Madison: Bleak House, 2007.

The narrator is a blues records collector, who buys collections from unsophisticated owners. He gets a tip about a collection belonging to a 70-year-old widow. Among Mrs. Walker's records is "Death Where Is Thy Sting?" a rare blues recording made in 1938 by killer on the run, Jimmie Kane Baldwin. He offers to buy the collection from the unsuspecting widow, who needs to check with her son in Arizona before its sale and is told to return the next day. When he does, another blues aficionado is also there.

Gwinn, William.

<u>Jazz Bum</u>. New York: Lion, 1957.

Vic Ravenna, a talented young clarinet player from an Italian immigrant family, is obsessed with Zora Zato, a second-rate singer and musician. He takes a year's sentence on drug charges to shield her, but she is indifferent to his sacrifice. Following his release, his jazz career blossoms while Zora's career stalls. After twenty years and past offers of help, Vic realizes that he no longer cares when she asks for a singing job.

Hall, Patricia.
(Pseudonym of Maureen O'Connor)

<u>Dressed To Kill</u>. London: Severn House, 2014.

Detective Sergeant Harry Barnard investigates the death of a 15-year-old girl whose body was found behind a Soho jazz club. His boss wants to close the club as he's sure it's a center for drugs and prostitution. He also thinks a black, American expatriate saxophone player named Muddy Abrahams is involved with drugs. Barnard's girlfriend, Kate O'Donnell, was working as a fashion photographer where the victim was a model. When a second girl dies, Barnard and O'Donnell work together to find a killer.

Hambly, Barbara.
(series: Benjamin January, Hannibal Sefton)

<u>A Free Man of Color</u>. New York: Bantam, 1997.

Benjamin January is playing the piano at the Salle d'Orleans when he encounters a former music student, Madeleine Trapagier, who is trying to crash a quadroon ball to confront her late husband's mistress, Angelique Crozat, over missing jewelry. January convinces her to leave before she is discovered. But Crozat is murdered and her jewelry disappears. As a free black man, January is a useful suspect in the increasingly segregated, recently Americanized New Orleans.

Fever Season. New York: Bantam, 1998.

Although Benjamin January, a free black man, has been trained as a doctor in Paris, he cannot practice medicine in New Orleans. So he teaches music to the daughters of the Creole elite for his living. After he agrees to take a message from a runaway slave to a servant of one of his employers, he becomes aware of the kidnapping of free blacks and slaves during the annual summer yellow fever epidemic and their transport by slave traders to the Missouri Territory.

Graveyard Dust. New York: Bantam, 1999.

Benjamin January's sister, Olympe, a voodooiene, is arrested for supplying the poison that killed Issak Jumon, whose body has not been found. January must navigate quickly and carefully through Creole and free-black society to uncover the real killer so his sister can be released from jail where summer diseases, especially yellow fever, are rampant.

Sold Down the River. New York: Bantam, 2000.

Simon Fourchet, the former owner of Benjamin January and his mother Livia, asks for help in solving a murder and the sabotage of his cotton crop. With fears of a slave uprising running high, January reluctantly agrees to pose as a field hand to discover the trouble-makers. After Fourchet is poisoned, January is in personal danger. He suspects that the killer is within the slave owner's family.

Die Upon a Kiss. New York: Bantam, 2001.

Benjamin January saves Italian opera impresario, Lorenzo Belaggio from an assault. The hysterical Belaggio identifies January's friend, John Davis, the owner of a financially failing rival French opera company as his assailant. Although there's no shortage of suspects within Belaggio's opera company, January thinks the up-coming production of Othello may be a factor in the impresario's attack. Inadvertently, he stumbles upon Belaggio's involvement in slave smuggling and Italian Nationalist politics.

<u>Wet Grave</u>. New York: Bantam, 2002.

The body of Hesione LeGros, once the mistress of one of Jean Lafitte's pirate captains, is found in the roughest part of New Orleans. Although she was reduced to living off the street, Benjamin January remembered meeting her in 1812 when she was beautiful. The police have no inclination to investigate a murder whose only clue is a strange boot print. After a case of guns is wrongly delivered to Artois St. Chinian, the young octoroon is murdered. The same boot print is found at the crime scene. The police's dismissal of both the matters forces January to discover the killers.

<u>Dead Water</u>. New York: Bantam, 2004.

Benjamin January learns from Hubert Granville, President of the Bank of Louisiana, that the bank's manager, Oliver Weems, absconded with $100,000, including $4,000 of January's money. Granville is afraid the bank will collapse. Weems was seen purchasing a steamship ticket. Granville asks January to follow him north and recover the money. January is aware that by leaving New Orleans, he could easily be kidnapped and sold into slavery. But loss of the money will undercut the life he and his wife Rose have created together.

"Libre." In <u>Ellery Queen's Mystery Magazine</u>. November 2006.

Benjamin January's mother asks him to find Marie Zuleika Rochier, a friend's missing daughter, who is to be "placed" with wealthy, nasty, drunken, white businessman, Jules Dutuille. Nicholas Saverne, not quite as wealthy as Dutuille, is also interested in her. January realizes that the light skinned Marie Zuleika has planned a different life for herself.

"There Shall Be Your Heart Also." In Smith, Julie. (ed.). <u>New Orleans Noir</u>. New York: Akashic, 2008.

After an attempted theft, Benjamin January discovers that a family bible belonging to saloon owner Kentucky Williams holds half of the key to the site of treasure stolen during Vice President Aaron

Burr's treachery. January manages to determine the thief's identity, steal his part of the map, and substitute a false trail in Williams' bible that the thief is allowed to steal.

Dead and Buried. London & New York: Severn House, 2010.
As Benjamin January and Hannibal Sefton are playing at a funeral, the casket slides open revealing the body of a white man, Patrick Derryhick, that Hannibal knew at Oxford. Viscount Gerry Foxford is arrested for the murder. He has an alibi, which he refuses to reveal, involving Isobel Deschamps. Her mother sends her away from New Orleans and sells Isobel's maid/companion, fearing what she might reveal. Despite the dangers of slave hunters, January goes up country to inform her of Pierrette's sale, Foxford's plight and confirm suspicions of her heritage.

Ran Away. London & New York: Severn House, 2011.
Pasha Huseyin is accused of killing his two concubines and tossing their bodies out of a window. January, who knew him twenty years earlier in Paris, has doubts. But Oliver Breche, the pharmacist across the road, claims to have witnessed the murders. A xenophobic public is sure of Pasha's guilt. While investigating the murders, January learns that the Pasha's gold was stolen and gradually taken from the house by the concubines and Breche had a sexual relationship with one of them.

Good Man Friday. London & New York: Severn House, 2013.
Needing money after the bank failures, Benjamin January agrees to accompany sugar planter Henri Viellard and his wife Chloe (along with his January's sister and her child with Viellard) to Washington to look for Viellard's missing friend, accountant Selwyn Singletary. He's presumed dead after January discovers his valuables, clearly stolen from a grave, at pawnshop. He had been sent by Rowena Bray's father to investigate theft of monies from her father's London bank. She's implicated in stealing secrets from her husband, who was employed by the Navy Department.

Crimson Angel. London & New York: Severn House, 2014.

Benjamin January's wife Rose's white half-brother appears at their home with a story about the family's lost treasure in Haiti and tries to enlist him in going to Haiti-January refuses. Her brother is murdered and someone tries to kill Rose. She and Benjamin decide to leave New Orleans for refuge in the bayou at Rose's family's sugar plantation. But they aren't safe there either. January believes the only way to insure his family's safety is to retrieve certain papers and the treasure in Haiti to trade for his family's safety.

Drinking Gourd. London & New York: Severn House, 2016.

Benjamin January and Hannibal Sefton go to Vicksburg to help a wounded "conductor" on the Underground Railway. The head conductor, Reverend Ezekias Drummond was murdered and the prime suspect is slave dealer Jubal Cain, who is actually the Mississippi coordinator of the Railroad. While trying to clear Cain, January is mistaken for a runaway slave and rescued by Hannibal. But he is soon on the run after being sold to a slave dealer after Hannibal is almost killed. Meanwhile, a hidden group of fugitive slaves are waiting to "follow the drinking gourd" north.

Murder In July. London & New York: Severn House, 2017.

British spymaster Sir John Oldmixton offers Benjamin January a hundred dollars to uncover the murderer of an Englishman, Harry Brooke. A friend of January's sister, Jacquette Filoux, who owned the house where Brooke was staying, is accused of the murder. It brings back memories of January's life in Paris during the 1830 insurrection when Anne Ben-Gideon was falsely charged with her husband's murder and sent to the guillotine. Her alibi and lover, Gerry O'Dwyer disappeared and has reappeared 9 years later in New Orleans.

Cold Bayou. London & New York: Severn House, 2018.

Benjamin January agrees to play the piano at the wedding of elderly French landowner Veryl St-Chinian and 18-year-old Irish bargirl, Ellie Trask. She would become heir to 300,000 acres of cotton producing land. Her uncle Mick plans to call-in old mortgages on every slave and former slave (such as January and his mother) and sell them. He's determined to move quickly before it can be established whether the mortgages were paid off. Hannibal races against time and bad weather to return from New Orleans with evidence of payment.

Lady of Perdition. London & New York: Severn House, 2019 & 2020.

Benjamin January and Hannibal Sefton are searching for Selena Belliger, a spoiled willful student from Rose's school, who eloped with Seth Javal to Texas only to be sold to a slave dealer. With Abishay Shaw's help, they steal her back. Along the way, they encounter Valentina Taggart, the wife of the wealthy landowner of Rancho Perdition, who aids their escape. Valentina's husband is killed and she is the accused killer. She brought land to her marriage that her late husband's family wants. January and Sefton delay their return to uncover Taggart's killer.

Harvey, Brian.
(series: Frank Ryan)

Beethoven's Tenth. Victoria, B. C.: Orca, 2015.

Frank Ryan spends his days tuning pianos and his nights playing jazz at The Loft, owned by his friend Kaz Nakamura. An eccentric, elderly Austrian lady, Miss P., has a piano that needed tuning. In payment she gives Ryan a hand-written old manuscript, which is actually Beethoven's Tenth, stolen by her Nazi father. She has three parts and her brother Pfiffner has the fourth. He was willing to kill his sister for the missing parts, so having Ryan killed is no obstacle.

Tokyo Girl. Victoria, B.C.: Orca, 2016.

Canadian jazz musician Frank Ryan is reduced to teaching Tokyo housewives to play the piano. One of his students is a stylish young woman named Akiko, the mistress of Goto, a *yakuza* boss. He likes jazz and offers Ryan a lucrative job at one of his clubs. On the train returning from weekly lessons with Akiko, Ryan encounters Momo. She tells him that her brother was kidnapped by the *yakuza* and forced into the Fukushima cleanup. Loneliness has blinded him to the consequence of believing her.

Harvey, John.
(series: Charlie Renick)

Lonely Hearts. London: Viking, 1989; New York: Putnam, 1989.

In Charlie Resnick's debut, Shirley Peters is brutally murdered and the police are holding her common law husband, who had a history of violence. Then a second woman, Mary Sheppard, is murdered. Both women may have communicated with their killer through a local "lonely hearts" column.

Rough Treatment. London: Viking, 1990; New York: Henry Holt, 1990.

Thieves break into the home of television director Harold Roy and find two surprises: his wife is at home and a kilo of heroine is in the safe. The thieves decide to sell the cocaine back to Roy, a move that brings in Inspector Charlie Resnick as he is investigating the cocaine trade as well as the increase in robberies among the affluent.

Cutting Edge. London: Viking, 1991; New York: Holt, 1991.

Three hospital workers with varying skills and responsibilities are attacked with a scalpel. One victim, a young university student, who worked as an anesthetist's assistant, dies. Police Detective Charlie Resnick must determine if the three incidents are linked or separate crimes before he can discover who is responsible for them.

Off Minor. London: Viking, 1992; New York: Holt, 1992.

Six-year-old Gloria Summers disappeared from a local park and is discovered dead eight weeks later in a pile of rubble. Emily Morrison, also six, disappears from her yard. Inspector Charlie Resnick hopes that by finding Summers' killer, he can prevent the same fate for

Morrison. But what if the two crimes are not linked?

Wasted Years. London: Viking, 1993; New York: Holt, 1993.

A psychopath, who Police Inspector Charlie Resnick jailed ten years earlier, is unexpectedly granted parole. At the same time, a series of robberies vie for Resnick's attention. The participants are all linked to Resnick's past and a time when his personal life irreversibly changed.

Cold Light. London: William Heinemann, 1994; New York: Holt, 1994.

Social worker Nancy Phelan was missing for 19 hours before Detective Charlie Resnick learns of her disappearance. The investigation focuses on her ex-boyfriend, Robin Hidden, who has been unable to accept their breakup. As the investigation progresses, however, it becomes evident they are dealing with a psychopath out to challenge Resnick directly.

Living Proof. London: William Heinemann, 1995; New York: Holt, 1995.

The organizers of a mystery writers conference ask Police Inspector Charlie Resnick to watch over their guest, the American PI writer, Cathy Jordan, who had been receiving threatening letters. Their fears of an incident prove correct. Resnick's attention, also, focuses on a series of robberies by a prostitute that end in murder.

Easy Meat. London: William Heinemann, 1996; New York: Holt, 1996.

Nicky Snape, a punk with a string of juvenile arrests, commits suicide in a detention home. Charlie Resnick is unhappy with the answers he receives from authorities regarding Snape's death. The official investigation is given to Bill Ashton, a passed-over and soon-to-retire officer. After Ashton is murdered, Resnick wonders if the two deaths are connected.

Still Waters. London: William Heinemann, 1997; New York:

Henry Holt, 1997.

Police Inspector Charlie Resnick is forced to leave a Milt Jackson concert after the body of a young, unidentified woman is discovered floating in a canal. Three months later, second body is found floating in the canal but this time it is identified as Jane Peterson, a friend of Charlie's girlfriend, Hannah. He learns that Jane was terrorized by her husband. Two paintings by Herbert Dalziel are stolen by Jerzy Grabinski, who cooperates with the police in cracking an art theft/forgery ring involving the painter Sloane (the subject of In a True Light, 2001).

"Cool Blues" In Blue Lightning. London: Slow Dancer, 1998.

A man, using the names of various musicians from the Duke Ellington band, picks up women on the London underground and robs them. Police Inspector Charlie Resnick sets up a plan to trap him when Joe Temperley is playing at Ronnie Scott's club.

Last Rites. London: William Heinemann, 1998; New York: Holt, 1999.

Michael Preston, who was incarcerated for killing his father, escapes custody while attending his mother's funeral. He wants his sister Lorraine to go away with him but she's married with two young children. While Police Inspector Charlie Resnick is hunting for Preston, a drug war is breaking out in Nottingham.

Now's the Time. London: Slow Dancer Crime, 1999.

See short stories in collection below.

"Bird of Paradise." In Now's the Time. London: Slow Dancer, 1999.

Art thief Jerzy Grabinski is in Nottingham to steal two Dalziel landscapes, when he stops an attack on a nun. Sister Teresa had been counseling a woman whose husband had objected. Grabinski pays a visit to the husband, notices stolen merchandise, and tells DI Charlie Resnick. He leaves town without stealing the paintings.

"Cheryl." In Now's the Time. London: Slow Dancer, 1999.

Cheryl is a deliverer of meals to Nottingham's elderly residents. She learns that a stroke-victim is terrorized by a loan shark's collector. She tries to intervene and is beaten for her effort. DI Charlie Resnick learns of the situation and visits the loan shark, as the debt should have been nullified by the woman's husband's death. He finds evidence to convict the man of arson.

"Confirmation." In Now's the Time. London: Slow Dancer, 1999.
Thieves, who brutally beat two of Charlie Resnick's police officers, purposely humiliate a fence of stolen goods named Terry Cooke. Cooke reveals their identity to Resnick.

"Dexterity." In Now's the Time. London: Slow Dancer, 1999.
Nicky Snipe twice stole a CD player from neighbor who takes justice into his own hands with a petrol bomb.

"My Little Suede Shoes." In Now's the Time. London: Slow Dancer, 1999.
The family Doberman trips up a small Elvis impersonator/second-story man when the dog grabs a blue suede shoe.

"Now's the Time." In Now's the Time. London: Slow Dancer, 1999.
Charlie Resnick comes to London for the funeral of his friend, musician Ed Silver and gets his wallet stolen by a young girl at the King's Cross train station. After the funeral he goes looking for her, saves her from a severe beating, and sends her home on a train.

"She Rote." In Now's the Time. London: Slow Dancer, 1999.
Charlie Resnick recovers stolen fax machines from a shop where perennial trouble-maker Ray-O has got his boss's daughter into trouble.

"Slow Burn." In Now's the Time. London: Slow Dancer, 1999.
Jimmy Nolan's jazz club burns down and Charlie Resnick suspects arson. It becomes a murder case when the body of a young boy is found among the ashes. The club survived only through the financial intervention of businessman Russell Vener who was married to

Nolan's daughter. Vener is discovered dead from a shotgun in his car. Initially the death is ruled a suicide but is later changed to a murder.

"Stupendous." In Now's the Time. London: Slow Dancer, 1999.

After the death of Cooke, a dealer in stolen goods, his business associates get into a violent fight. His daughter Sarah and common-law wife Eileen benefit from the will. News of Sarah's miscarriage is also revealed.

"Work." In Now's the Time. London: Slow Dancer, 1999.

Terry Cooke beats up an elderly musician who identified him to DI Charlie Resnick for a particularly vicious robbery. Now confined to a wheelchair, Ronnie also lost an eye. Resnick harasses Cooke to the point where he is driven to suicide.

"Home." In Jakubowski, Maxim (ed.). The Best British Mysteries IV. London: Allison & Busby, 2006.

After listening to alto saxophonist Art Pepper and remembering seeing him at the end of his career, Charlie Resnick thinks about the contemporary Nottingham drug epidemic. His thoughts are interrupted by a telephone call relating the shooting death of fifteen-year-old girl returning from a party with her brother. He suspects her death to be drug related but runs into a wall of silence.

Trouble In Mind. Nottingham: Crime Express, 2007.

PI Jack Kiley is hired to find Sergeant Terry Anderson, who has gone AWOL, so that he will not have to return to Iraq when his unit is redeployed. Kiley is afraid that Anderson will hurt himself or his estranged wife and their two children. He asks for help from DI Charlie Resnick to search the family house in Nottingham. The family is absent but evidence indicates they were taken away against their will.

Cold In Hand. London: William Heinemann, 2008; New York: Harcourt, 2008.

Charlie Resnick has been partly in charge of the investigation of a young girl murdered during a fight and the shooting of Detective Inspector Lynn Kellogg. The girl's father claims that Kellogg shielded herself with his daughter's body. At the same time, Stuart Daines of the national Serious and Organized Crime Agency has shown unusual interest in Kellogg and one of her cases involving an Eastern European criminal syndicate.

Minor Key. Nottingham: Five Leaves, 2009.
See short story collections.

"Well, You Needn't." In Minor Key. Nottingham: Five Leaves, 2009.
On his birthday Charlie Resnick thinks of the past—specifically the Miner's Strike a decade earlier and people on both sides, and his role enforcing Margaret Thatcher's policies. Peter Waites, formerly a striking miner and on the dole for 10 years, is ashamed of his son Jack, who has joined the police. He's ready to arrest Barrie Shorter, who continued to work during the strike and eventually lost his job and his family and turned to theft. Charlie goes along on the arrest and then goes home to listen to *Thelonious Monk at The Jazz Workshop* that he found that morning in a thrift shop—specifically, to "Well You Needn't."

A Darker Shade of Blue. London: Arrow, 2010.
See short story collections for details of 18 stories by John Harvey.

"Billie's Blues." In A Darker Shade of Blue. London: Arrow, 2010.
Eileen Cooke, an old acquaintance of Charlie's, calls in the murder of a 15-year-old. Initially, she claimed to have found the body, then admitted seeing two men in a van pick her up. A few days later, she tells Charlie she saw one of the men, who's a vice squad cop, at a party.

"The Sun, the Moon and the Stars." In A Darker Shade of Blue. London: Arrow, 2010.
Eileen Cooke is now living with Michael Sherwood aka Mikhail Sharminov, who made a fortune in bootleg dvds and CDs. One

night 2 gunmen come through a window and kill him but spare her. Lynne and (Charlie) get the case that goes nowhere as it was a contract hit.

Darkness, Darkness. London: William Heinemann, 2014; New York: Pegasus, 2014.

The bones of a woman, who died 30 years earlier, are unearthed during the demolition of some old miners' residences. She's identified as Jenny Hardwick, who was active in the 1984 Miners' Strike. At that time, Charlie was running an intelligence unit. Now he's in semi-retirement and recruited to help with the investigation. The easy conclusion is that her hot-tempered husband, Barry, a non-striking miner or a known sexual predator, killed her. But Charlie thinks her death was tied to union activities.

(non-series)

In a True Light. London: William Heinemann, 2001; New York: Carroll & Graff, 2002.

Just released from a two-year sentence for art forgery, Sloane finds a letter from Jane Graham, a famous American painter with whom he had an affair forty years earlier. She tells him that she is dying and reveals that he has a daughter, Connie, who lives in New York City. Graham asks him to find her. Sloane discovers that Connie is a singer working in mob-controlled clubs and that her manager, Vincent Delany, murdered his last singer.

"Drummer Unknown." In Randisi, Robert J. (ed.). Murder and all that Jazz. New York: Signet, 2004.

Crooked policeman Arthur Neville leans on a junkie drummer for narcotics information and threatens his addicted girlfriend, Ethel. Neville raids a club, finds it clean, and then kills Ethel. The drummer contacts another policeman, Tom Holland, who sets up a sting for Neville.

"Just Friends." In Jakubowski, Maxim (ed.). The Penguin Book of

<u>Crime Stories</u>. Robinson, Peter. (ed.). London & New York: Penguin, 2007.

Patrick, Jimmy, and Val are on the fringes of the 1950s London jazz scene. Patrick trades in his trumpet to become the band's manager, then Val's manager, and eventually ends up as the owner of several London clubs. Jimmy abandons his drums to become a London police officer, and later, a private investigator. Val, the most talented of the three, gets caught up in the drug scene and dies young. (See Harvey's short story "Minor Key").

"Minor Key." In Jakubowski, Maxim. (ed.). <u>Paris Noir</u>. London: Serpent's Tail, 2009.

Val Collins, a talented alto sax player, is busted for drugs. His friend and sometime manager, Patrick gets him a job in Paris, away from the London drug scene. At first things go well, the gig is extended, and recording date set up. But then Val encounters an American dealer/drummer involved in the Paris drug scene.

"Favor." In <u>A Darker Shade of Blue</u>. London: Arrow, 2010.

PI Jack Kiley gets his friend Derek Becker a gig with singer Dianne Adams and her quartet at Ronnie Scott's. Their version of "A Ghost of Chance" creates a sensation and possibility of a future tour for Becker. Kiley manages to defuse a situation when compromising photographs of Adams and actress Virginia Pride appear. But at the club Pride's gangster husband tries to intimidate Adams and Becker forces him to leave. After the gig ends, thugs jump Becker in Soho.

Haut, Woody

<u>Cry for a Nickel, Die for a Dime</u>. Concord, MA: Concord ePress, 2014

Abe Howard, a freelance news photographer, took crime scene photos of murdered jazz musician, Little Jimmy Estes. Surprisingly, the photos are not saleable and for his efforts, he's beaten by two of gangster Mickey Cohen's goons. Howard's curiosity is peaked about Estes. He was working on early blues reissues for a mobbedup independent record company with Kim Jones, a glamorous Lana Turner look-alike. While visiting Estes' father, Abe learns Jimmy was a photographer and among his jazz pictures are photos of interest to Cohen.

Hayes, Teddy.
(series: Devil Barnet)

<u>Wrong as Two Left Feet</u>. London: Xpress, 2003.

Devil Barnett's good friend Honey Lavelle asks him to find a missing friend of hers, songwriter Wood Henry Taylor. Ever since his wife's death, Taylor has been with a greedy, crazy prostitute. Taylor, who also worked as a courier at a Wall Street brokerage house, has disappeared along with four million dollars in bearer bonds.

<u>Blood River Blues</u>. London: Justin, Charles, 2004; Boston: Kate's Mystery Books, 2004.

Former CIA agent Devil Barnett returns to Harlem after the murder of his father and takes over the legendary Be-Bop Tavern. But Barnett can't escape his past. He is asked to use his skills to find the killer of six people in a Harlem brothel. One of the victims was a prominent Japanese diplomat.

<u>Dead by Popular Demand</u>. London: Justin, Charles, 2005; Boston: Kate's Mystery Books, 2005.

Two young English rap stars working in New York City die violently on the same night. An uncle of one of the boys asks jazz club owner Devil Barnett to investigate their deaths. Members of the group Dancehall Dogz continue to die as Barnett enters the violent world of rap, encountering a Harlem minister and English drug lords as well as the usual slimy, music business people.

Hellmann, Libby Fischer.

"Your Sweet Man." In <u>Chicago Blues</u>. Madison: Bleak House, 2007.

Calvin Rollins picks up his father Jimmy Jay at Joliet Prison and brings him home to die. In the 1950s, Jimmy Jay and his wife Inez were at the center of the Chicago Blues scene. Then Inez went off with a white promoter only to be murdered when she returned to Chicago. Although Jimmy Jay went to jail for her murder, they both know the killer's identity.

Helms, Richard.
(series: Pat Gallegher)

Joker Poker. Lincoln: Writer's Showcase, 2000.

Clancey Vincoeur hires cornet player PI Pat Gallegher to find her missing lover Sammy Cain, whom she fears has been killed by her husband, Lester. Gallegher's investigation is complicated by Lester's link to the New Orleans mob. When Gallegher goes to talk with Lester, he discovers his body and knows that he's been set up.

VooDoo That You Do. Back Alley, 2001.

Cornet player Pat Gallegher witnessed the murder of Hotshot Spano, an elderly member of Lucho Braga's mob, by Haitian punks. Braga blackmails Gallegher into finding Spano's killer. Gallegher befriends a ten-year old runaway, Louise, who was found rummaging for food in the dumpster behind Holiday's where Gallegher works. She is the stepdaughter of Jimmy Binh, a dangerous Vietnamese gangster. She witnessed the murder of a prostitute and fears for her life. In helping her, he discovers Spano's killer and finds himself in the middle of a gang war.

Juicy Watsui. Back Alley, 2002.

A killer is stalking the strippers of the French Quarter. One of his victims is Lucy Nivens, the girlfriend of Pat Gallegher's employer. New Orleans Police Department (NOPD) Detective Farley Nuckolls bribes Gallegher with a box of Cuban cigars to put aside his cornet and help after a prominent FBI profiler appears to decline the case. Gallegher is to be the investigation's "public face."

Wet Debt. Back Alley, 2003.

Construction workers uncover a body in the cement floor of a building next to Holiday's jazz club. Gallegher's boss, Shorty, is worried that the "crime scene" will delay the completion of construction on his club. Gallegher gets the work curfew removed but is intrigued by the seventy-year-old murder of Scott Everidge, who was a hoodlum from Kansas City.

Paid in Spades. Franklin, TN: Clay Stafford Books, 2019.
Pat Gallegher is looking for two missing people: Cabby Jacks, who helped him with his gambling problem and Garry Sharp, the father of a girl in a shelter run by Gallegher's girlfriend. While looking for Sharp, he stumbles on a scam of substituting cheap Chinese oil pipes for quality American oil pipes run by a Brazilian gang. Coincidentally, the Brazilians may be involved in Cabby's disappearance. But Gallegher knows there are no coincidences in life.

Hentoff, Nat.
(series: Noah Green)

Blues For Charlie Darwin. London: Constable, 1983; New York: Morrow, 1982.
New York police detectives Noah Green and Sam McKibbon investigate the murder in her home of Kathleen Ginsburg, the wife of a NYU (New York University) professor. Shortly, thereafter, the black owner of a small Greenwich Village bookstore Emma Dixon, is, also, murdered in her home. The two murders appeared to be linked to a black crime boss.

Call the Keeper . London: Secker & Warburg, 1967; New York: Viking, 1966.
Sanders, a crooked, black, New York Police Detective, is murdered. Although NYPD Detective Horowitz knows everyone is better off without Sanders, he must find his killer and squeezes Sanders' victims for information. A black psychopath named Septimus, who Horowitz once sent to jail, seems the likely killer.

The Man From Internal Affairs. New York: Mysterious, 1985.

The upper torsos of two prostitutes and a junkie are discovered stuffed in trashcans. An elderly labor organizer, Moishe Kagan, is the prime suspect. Police detective Noah Green believes he's innocent and gets him a good criminal defense attorney. But his search for the real killer is hampered by an Internal Affairs investigation.

Hewat, Alan B.

Lady's Time. London: Heinemann, 1986; New York: Harper & Row, 1985.

Ragtime piano player Alice Beaudette was the daughter of Mimi Beaudette and Obregon Vraicoeur, both victims of the 1890s race laws, which stripped the Creoles of their special status in New Orleans. Mimi adapts to her lower status, becoming a laundress. But Obregon, a classically trained violinist, snaps while being forced to play jazz for his living in Buddy Bolden's band. Obregon sees his family's only salvation in ridding it of its black bloodline.

Himes, Chester.
(Chester Bomar Himes)
(series: Coffin Ed Johnson & Grave Digger Jones)

Cotton Comes to Harlem. London: Muller, 1966; New York: Putnam, 1965.

Freshly released from jail, con-man Deke O'Hara is promoting a Back-To-Africa scam, promising each $1,000 investor, transportation back to Africa, 5 acres of land, seed, etc. But his Harlem rally is disrupted by masked white gunmen, who make off with $87,000 hidden in a bale of cotton. NYPD Detectives Coffin Ed Johnson and Grave Digger Jones are determined to find the missing cotton bale and return the money to the fleeced investors.

The Heat's On. London: Frederick Muller, 1966; New York: Putnam, 1986.

Grave Digger Jones and Coffin Ed Johnson of the NYPD answer

a false fire alarm set off by an albino giant named Pinky and see a dwarf, who is a known drug dealer, running away. They catch him and force him to cough up swallowed drugs. But he was hit too hard, resulting in his death and suspension of both men for brutality. While searching for Pinky, Digger Jones is shot. Believing his partner dead, Coffin Ed goes on rampage through Harlem looking for the killer and finds a French heroin smuggling operation.

All Shot Up. London: Panther, 1969; New York: Berkeley, 1960.
Harlem political boss Casper Holmes is robbed of $50,000 from the National Committee and his Pinkerton bodyguard and a bystander killed. Coffin Ed and Grave Digger suspect the crooked Harlem politician of complicity. He's double-crossed by the robbers and rescued by the two detectives. They know he's too well connected to pay for his crime and the $50,000 ends up as an anonymous donation to a charity. All Shot Up is the only series' novel not set in the summer.

Blind Man with a Pistol. London: Hodder & Stoughton, 1969; New York: Vintage, 1989.
A dead white man was found without his trousers and with his throat slit. Eventually, he's identified as Richard Henderson, a producer of off-Broadway plays, who lived near Washington Square and used to hang-out at the Five Spot jazz club. Coffin Ed Johnson and Grave Digger Jones find a witness/suspect, John Babson, who is killed outside of the Five Spot. The murders occur against a background of widespread violence and riots.

The Crazy Kill. London: Allison & Busby, 1984; New York; Berkeley, 1959.
While watching a robbery, stoned-out Reverend Short falls from a third story window into a large bread delivery basket. While he's unharmed, the basket's other occupant, Valentine Hanes, is dead. Grave Digger Jones and Coffin Ed Johnson know his killer is within a small group of his family, friends and red herrings. The prime suspect is Johnny Perry, who is married to Val's sister, Dulcy, and may have tired of having him around his house. Was he going to

give Val $10,000 to start a business or was it blackmail?

A Rage in Harlem. aka For the Love of Imabelle. London: Allison & Busby, 1985; New York: Avon, 1965.

Dim-witted Jackson entrusts his life savings of $1500 to a con-man friend of his girlfriend, Imabelle. He tells Jackson that he can change $10 into $100 but the money disappears in an explosion and Jackson is arrested for counterfeiting. Jackson steals some money from his employer to bribe a "marshal" and loses the remainder in a dice game. With his money and Imabelle gone, he turns to his hustler brother for help.

The Real Cool Killers. London: Allison & Busby, 1985; New York: Avon, 1959.

A white man named Galen is chased out of a Harlem jazz club and killed on the street. But the gun used by the apparent killer only fires blanks. Sonny, the gunman, manages to escape and is sheltered by a gang known as The Real Cool Muslims, who have their own use for him. Meanwhile Harlem police officer, Grave Digger Jones learns of a possible motive for the killing: Galen liked to beat up young black girls.

The Big Gold Dream. London: Allison & Busby, 1988; New York: Thunder's Mouth Press, 1996.

Alberta Wright hit the number for $36,000. She attends a mass baptism with her latest man Rufus and, in a religious frenzy, tells the gathering about cooking three pies that filled her kitchen with money and then she seemingly dies. Rufus races home, searches, finds nothing and sells her furnishings. But Alberta didn't die and can't remember where her money is hidden. As bodies pile up and her life is endangered, Digger Jones and Coffin Ed enter the case. When she does remember, she takes matters into her own hands, singing "Trouble In Mind."

Hoch, Edward D.
(Edward Dentiger Hoch)
(series: Ben Snow)

"The Ripper of Storyville." In The Ripper of Storyville. Norfolk: Crippen & Landau, 2003.
    Texas oilman Archer Kinsman asks Ben Snow to find his daughter Bess, who ran away to New Orleans six years earlier. Kingman is dying and wants to leave her his money but hasn't heard from her in several years. Snow thinks that he has located her and fears for her life as someone is killing Storyville sporting girls.

Holden, Craig.

The Jazz Bird. New York: Simon & Schuster, 2001.
    On October 6, 1927 bootlegger George Remus killed his society wife, Imogene, known as "the Jazz Bird" for her taste in music and life-style. After Remus was sent to jail in 1924 on bootlegging charges, Imogene took up with Prosecutor Frank Dodge and stole an estimated $80 million from Remus. Upon his release, Remus tried to recover his property and wife. Charlie Taft of Cincinnati, the son of the former President, is prosecuting a seemingly straightforward murder case.

"The P&G Ivory Whiskey Massacree." In Randisi, Robert J. (ed.). Murder and all that Jazz. New York: Signet, 2004.
    When Al Capone tries to move in on Cincinnati bootleggers by shooting up one of their liquor refineries, local mobsters John Marcus and George Connors retaliate.

Holmes, Rupert.
(David Goldstein)

Swing. London: Allison & Busby, 2007; New York: Random, 2005.
    In San Francisco at the fashionable Hotel Claremont, Ray

Sherwood, an arranger and tenor sax player with Jack Donovan's Orchestra, finds a note from a young Berkeley music student. She has written an award-winning avant-jazz composition, "Swing Around The Sun" which will be played by a Japanese jazz band at the Golden Gate Exposition. Entranced by Gail Prentice, he agrees to arrange the piece and is ensnared in an unexpected scenario.

Howard, Clark.

"Horn Man." In Gorman, Ed, Pronzini, Bill & Greenberg, Nathan, (eds.). American Pulp. New York: Carroll & Graf, 1997.

After serving sixteen years for murder, jazz trumpet player Dix returns to New Orleans looking for his old girlfriend Madge Noble, who had convinced him to take the rap for her. Fearful of the future consequences of their meeting, his old friends try to tempt him away from his mission with a silver trumpet and a steady job. But Dix learns Madge's address.

Howie, Elizabeth.

The Band Played Murder. London: Boardman, 1948; New York: M.S. Mill, 1946.

It's a dream come true for small-town radio singer Connie Waring, who is recruited by the famous bandleader, Gale Ullman, to replace vocalist, Anne Kent. She soon learns that Kent was fired for pulling a knife on the band's other vocalist Mandy Martin with whom she must share hotel accommodations. Waring returns from a walk and discovers Martin dead and the entire band suspect.

Howland, Whit.

Trouble Follows. Bearsville, AZ: Pro Se, 2015.

As their final gig before returning to L.A., Johnny Nickle and the Daybreakers play the little Nevada town of Aragusa. Three drifters, who disrupted his gig in St. Louis, enter the bar and cause trouble.

The owner of the local boarding house, where Johnny's band is stay-ing, realizes that the three have come to town to rob a weekly ar-mored truck pick-up.

Huggins, Roy.

The Double Take. London: Cassell, 1947; New York: Morrow, 1946.

After receiving an ominous telephone call regarding his wife, Margaret, industrialist Ralph Johnson hires PI Stuart Bailey. Dismiss-ing blackmail as the motive, Bailey goes to Seattle to investigate her background and returns with more questions than answers. It's still all rather low-key until the bodies start to appear. The Double Take was the inspiration for the television show, "77 Sunset Strip", which had more jazz than the book.

77 Sunset Strip. New York: Dell, 1958.

Capitalizing on the popularity of the television show, "77 Sun-set Strip," Huggins strung together three previously published short stories, "Death and the Skylark", "Appointment With Fear" and "Now You See It" that are linked only by the appearance of PI Stuart Bailey and his girlfriend Betty Callister. The stories focus on a deadly family cruise ("Death and the Skylark"), a mentally unstable client, a disappearing corpse, and a greedy family ("Ap-pointment With Fear") and an old-fashioned locked-room murder case ("Now You See It").

"Appointment With Fear." In 77 Sunset Strip. New York: Dell, 1958.

Back from Hawaii, Bailey receives a $700 check and request for help to go to the Desert Inn in Phoenix to meet with D.C. Hallor-an. He discovers a mentally unstable client, a disappearing corpse, a murder suspect and a greedy family.

"Death and the Skylark." In 77 Sunset Strip. New York: Dell, 1958.

Bailey is hired by Glen Callister, who suspects that his young wife and the first mate aboard The Skylark, are having an affair and plan to kill him during a Hawaiian cruise. Bailey joins the cruise. A few mornings later, Bailey discovers Glen dead and his wife Eilene, Owen the first mate, and Glenn's daughter Betty all suspect.

"Now You See It." In 77 Sunset Strip. New York: Dell, 1958.

Gordon Trust hires Bailey but is murdered before he can explain why his services are needed. Bailey was present in Trist's study along with his business partner, his worthless son, and his wife when Trist was stabbed and the murder weapon disappeared.

Hughes, Dorothy B.
(Dorothy Belle Flanagan)

"The Black and White Blues." In Gorman, Ed, Pronzini, Bill & Greenberg, Martin H. (eds.). American Pulp. New York: Carroll & Graf, 1997.

A white girl at a dance is jealous of another girl's new dress and marcelled hair. Her friend tells her that the black band members make good money and have fancy cars. At the dance's end, she convinces the clarinet player to drive her home, which is a dangerous thing to do in a southern border state.

Hunter, Evan.
(aka Ed McBain)

Quartet In H. London: Constable, 1956; New York: Simon & Schuster, 1956.

Andy Silveria, a talented trumpet player, joins a local band and is watched over by his older friend, piano player Bud Donato. After Bud and the band are drafted, young Andy goes on the road with a big band and finds an escape from his loneliness in drugs with destructive results for everyone.

Streets of Gold. New York: Harper, 1974. London: Macmillan, 1975.

Ignacio "Iggy" Silvio Di Palermo was born blind into an Italian immigrant family in East Harlem in 1926. He studied piano and was on the verge of a classical career when he discovers an Art Tatum record in his brother's jazz collection. Iggy switches to jazz and is successful enough to attract the mob's attention.

Irish, William.
(aka Cornell Woolrich)
(Cornell George Hopley-Woolrich)

"The Dancing Detective." In The Dancing Detective. New York: Lippincott, 1946; London: Hutchinson, 1947.

Dime-a-dance girl Ginger Allen is concerned when her friend Julie Bennett is late for work at Joyland. Two cops appear and tell her that Julie was murdered by a sadist, who has killed three dance-hall girls. He stabbed them and placed dimes in their eyes. Little else is known about the killer, except that his favorite song is "Poor Butterfly." One night, someone dances with Ginger and requests the band play "Poor Butterfly."

"The Jazz Record" In The Saint Mystery Magazine Vol. 22. No. 3. July 1965.

Ceil, the narrator's record collecting daughter, who torments her family by constantly playing a new record each week, brings home one that reveals the fate of singing idol Matt Madden.

Izzo, Jean-Claude.
(series: Fabio Montale)

Total Chaos. London & New York: Europa Editions, 2005; Paris: Editions Gallimard, 1995 (as Total Keops).

Three friends, Ugo, Manu and Fabio grew up on the streets of Marseilles. After a robbery turned violent, Fabio took a different road, joined the colonial army, and later became a policeman, working in La Paternelle, the Arab ghetto. Ugo and Manu remained in the criminal underworld until they were murdered by the mob and police respectively. Montale is determined to find his friends' killers.

<u>Chourmo</u>. London & New York: Europa, 2006; Paris: Editions Gallimard, 1996.

Fabio Montale's wealthy cousin Gelou asks for help finding her missing son, who turns up dead. He was with his girlfriend in her apartment when an outside noise caused him to open the door and see the assassin sent to kill an Algerian intellectual. Serge, a friend from Montale's police days, is killed in a drive-by shooting. He had been investigating the rise of militant Islam in the *bidonvilles*. Both cases come together in a mix of militant Islamic and rightwing fascism.

<u>Solea</u>. London & New York: Europa Editions, 2007; Paris: Editions Gallimard, 1998.

The Mafia is after Montale's friend, investigative reporter-journalist Babette Bellini, who learned too much about their operations in southern France. He ignores their threats until they kill Sonia, a woman he just met, and start killing his friends. Now that they have his attention, he realizes where Babette's computer discs are hidden. He tries to convince Babette to deal with the Mafia.

Jackson, Jon A.
(series: Fang Mulheisen)

<u>Man With an Axe</u>. New York: Atlantic Monthly, 1998.

Tenor sax player Tyronne Addison and his wife Vera rescued teamster-boss, Jimmy Hoffa from hit men. They agreed to hide him at Turtle Lake, a black resort in northern Michigan, until he straightened out a "misunderstanding" with the mob. Twenty years later, Detroit homicide detective Fang Mulheisen discovers enough information in notebooks left by his mentor, the legendary Groot-ka, to reopen the Hoffa investigation.

Jeffers, H. Paul.
(series: Harry McNeil)

<u>Rubout at the Onyx</u>. New York: Ticknor & Fields, 1981.

Joey Seddes, a small-time crook and member of Owney Madden's gang, is murdered on New Year's Eve 1935 at the Onyx Club on 52nd Street. His widow Gloria hires PI Harry MacNeil to find Joey's killers. MacNeil discovers that Gloria is more interested in finding 3 ½ million dollars' worth of diamonds from a robbery in which Joey may have been involved than finding his killers.

Murder on Mike. New York: St. Martin's, 1984.

Derek Worthington, the star and producer of a popular crime series, is found dead in an empty radio studio. Worthington had no shortage of enemies. The show's cast has alibis, except for its announcer, David Reed, who had a public fight with him before his death. But the show's co-star, Maggie Skeffington, convinces PI Harry MacNeil of Reed's innocence and hires him to find the real killer.

The Rag Doll Murder. New York: Ballantine, 1987.

A mentally limited delivery boy, Toby Maxwell, has been arrested and confessed to the murder of fashion model, Jamey Flamingo. Her sister, actress Evelyn Proctor, believes Maxwell innocent as Jamey's dog Fala, who always barked at the delivery boy, was silent on the afternoon of the killing. She hires PI Harry MacNeil to find the killer.

Jenkins, A.K.

Twice No One Dies. Canberra: Equine Press, 2015.

Marius, a retired Ghanaian Intelligence officer living in Togo, regularly spends his Friday nights at Le Jazz Spot, listening to his friend Louis, a trumpet player. One night, Louis fails to appear. Marius later learns that Louis was murdered. The police claim it was a drug deal gone bad. With elections weeks away, there is constant violence to insure the re-election of the corrupt leader known as *Le Crocodile*. But Louis wasn't into drugs or politics.

Jessup, Richard.

<u>Lowdown</u>. London: Pan, 1961; New York: Dell, 1958.

Walker Alise, a talented vocalist impatient for success, pirates a master tape from a popular bandleader and overdubs a vocal. He takes the demo recording to Sweets York, a well-known middle-man, who uses it to get money from small-time gamblers to jump-start Alise's career. But the singer double-crosses York and uses the money to get himself in a position to deal with organized crime. He rockets to the top of the music and movie businesses but burned so many people that no one holds a safety net to stop his eventual fall.

Joe, Yolanda.

<u>Hit Time</u>. New York: Simon & Schuster, 2002.

A body is discovered in Lake Michigan while TV investigative reporter Georgia Barnett is covering a nearby charity event. She is able to identify the victim as Fab Weaver, the crooked, former boss of Hit Time Records. There's no shortage of suspects, including her sister's friend, blues guitarist, Jimmy Flamingo and Weaver's drug-gie son, Guy.

Johns, Veronica Parker.

"Mr. Hyde-de-Ho." In Queen, Ellery, (ed.). <u>Ellery Queen's Awards:</u> <u>Eleventh Series</u>. London: Collins, 1958; New York: Simon & Schuster. 1956.

Jean works for a small jazz record company in Manhattan. She gets a call from Peg, a wealthy college friend, who is returning from a European vacation. Peg met a jazz musician named Marvin Duffy on board the ship and wants Jean to meet him. She isn't impressed and Peg responds with hostility. Jean is suspicious of Duffy's inter-est in Peg.

Jones, Arthur E.

<u>It Makes You Think</u>. London: Long, 1958.

Bandleader Raymond Stack asks Felix Holiday to his weekend retreat. On the way, they spot an automobile in a gully belonging to Eve Hartley, the vocalist in Stack's band, who has been missing for several days. Although the front seat is bloody, there's no body in sight. Holiday must find her body and the killer. There's no shortage of suspects in the band, including its leader.

Kaminsky, Stuart M.

"Blue Note." In Hellmann, Libby Fisher. (ed.). <u>Chicago Blues</u>. Chicago: Bleak House, 2008.

Pitch Noles is known as "the Prince of Tell" for his ability to read the body language of other gamblers. He is told by drug dealer Terrance "Dusk" Oliver that the blues singer with the visiting Basie Band will lose a finger for nonpayment of a drug debt unless Noles plays poker with three gamblers, who cheated him out of $20,000. If Noles doesn't win $40,000 by 5 am, his mother will lose her finger.

Kane, Frank.
(series: Johnny Liddell)

<u>Juke Box King</u>. New York: Dell, 1959.

Mickey Denton is a young crooner imitating Dean Martin, when mobster Tony Agnelli hears him in a Long Island club. Agnelli is convinced Denton could be a source of money for the New York mob as well as their entry into Las Vegas and Hollywood. Denton exchanges his struggling career for a successful one as a mob asset, mistakenly assuming that his public success will later be enough to buy him his freedom.

<u>The Guilt-Edged Frame</u>. New York: Dell, 1964.

Trumpet player Marty Lewis has an expensive drug habit. After being severely beaten over an unpaid drug debt, he identifies his supplier to police in return for dropping narcotics charges against him. He arranges for a loan from his agent to repay the mob and plans to leave town on tour, much to the consternation of his girlfriend, club owner Lee Carr. When she's discovered in a hotel room with his body, only her friend, PI Johnny Liddell believes in her innocence.

Kane, Henry.
(series: Peter Gunn, Pete Chambers)

Until You Are Dead. New York: Simon & Schuster, 1951.

After witnessing a murder, piano player Kermit Teshle appears to have successfully blackmailed the killer into giving him the $100,000 he needs to open a jazz club. Afraid of a double cross at the payoff site, he attempts to hire PI Pete Chambers to accompany him. But Chambers refuses. Teshle is murdered and the payoff money disappears. Pete searches for the killer among Teshle's acquaintances.

"One Little Bullet." In The Name Is Chambers. New York: Pyramid, 1960.

Private investigator Pete Chambers realizes that nightclub owner Joe Malamed was shot during a drum roll in the Afro-Cuban floorshow. From the bullet's angle, the killer was at a table with Malamed's partner Melvin Long, singer Ruth Benson, former jockey and loan shark Frankie Hines, critic Charles Morse and the widow Claire Malamud. Chambers' task of identifying the killer is difficult as each suspect had a motive.

Peter Gunn. New York: Dell, 1960

In this spin-off from the popular 1960s television series, PI Peter Gunn is hired to investigate the musician boyfriend of the daughter of Steve Bain, a powerful union leader. After Bain is murdered, Gunn is honor-bound to find his killer and discovers an extensive list of potential killers

Karp, Larry.
(series: Brun Campbell)

The Ragtime Kid. Scottsdale: Poisoned Pen Press, 2006.

15-year-old Brun Campbell, a ragtime vagabond, ran away to study under pianist Scott Joplin. On his first morning in Sedalia, he stumbles upon a woman's body, and finds a locket and a money clip holding $25. Campbell discovers that the locket holds a picture of the man trying to steal Joplin's music and that the money clip belongs to Joplin. When a friend is arrested for the murder, Campbell decides to find the real killer.

The King of Ragtime. Scottsdale: Poisoned Pen Press, 2008.

It's 1916 and for almost a decade Scott Joplin has been vainly trying to get a Manhattan music publisher interested in his opera, *Treemonisha*. Martin Niederhoffer, a student of Joplin's and a bookkeeper at Irving Berlin's music publishing company, convinces Joplin to bring his opera to Berlin. The following day he discovers a confused Joplin standing over a body in Berlin's office. Berlin claims not to have the opera that Joplin says he left the previous day.

The Ragtime Fool. Scottsdale: Poisoned Pen Press, 2010.

In this final volume of Karp's ragtime trilogy, Brun Campbell, now an elderly man, returns to 1951 Sedalia for a ceremony honoring his old mentor, Scott Joplin. He hopes to acquire Joplin's unpublished diary to use in the creation of a Joplin Museum. Alan Chandler, a ragtime enthusiast, gets the diary for Campbell. But others, such as a New York ragtime researcher, Scott's old Sedalia friends and the Ku Klux Klan have different plans for the Joplin diary.

First, Do No Harm. Scottsdale: Poisoned Pen Press, 2004.

Trying to dissuade his son Martin from going to medical school, painter Leo Firestone recounts the summer of 1943 when he worked as his father's extern. He saw his father perform abortions, sell black market babies and pharmaceuticals, and supply narcotics to an addict. When he thought his father is covering up a murder, he and his saxophone-playing neighbor, Harmony, decided to investigate and followed a trail with deadly consequences for everyone.

Kellerman, Jonathan.
(series: Alex Delaware)

A Cold Heart. London: Headline, 2003; New York: Ballantine, 2003.

Blues guitarist Baby Boy Lee is murdered behind a L.A. blues club. Eighteen years earlier, he had a hit with "A Cold Heart" and then fell on lean times, only to be murdered on the verge of a comeback. His death is one in a series of talented, upcoming performers and artists that psychologist, sleuth Alex Delaware links together. Lee had his guitars serviced by Robin Castagna, Delaware's ex, which makes his death personal and brings a psychopath into his home.

Klavan, Andrew.

Hunting Down Amanda. New York: Morrow, 1999.

After a late-night gig, saxophone player Lonnie Blake encounters Carol Dodson on a Manhattan street. She begs him to hide her from an unidentified pursuer. After she leaves the following morning, Blake wants to know more about her. He tries to track her down and realizes that professionals, who will not hesitate at murder, are hunting Carol and her daughter Amanda.

Knight, Phyllis.
(series: Lil Ritchie)

Shattered Rhythms. New York: St. Martin's, 1994.

Bass player Ernie West hires PI Lil Ritchie to find missing jazz guitarist Andre Ledoux, who had recently turned his life around, abandoning drugs and alcohol. She discovers him frightened by a recent LSD incident and hiding at a relative's home. Lil convinces him to return to performing, resulting in triumph and tragedy at the Montreal Jazz Festival.

Koenig, Joseph.

Really The Blues. London & New York: Pegasus, 2014.
Creole expatriate Eddie Piron plays jazz trumpet at La Caverne Negre, a favorite hangout of the SS. When his drummer disappears, then reappears floating in the Seine, Eddie is dragged into a murder investigation. To add to his troubles, an American grifter and former cop, tries to blackmail him. The Nazis become interested in him when it turns out that his drummer was a saboteur. With his apolitical existence shattered, he joins an anti-Nazi plot.

Lamp, C.O.

The Return of Glenn Miller. Lakeville, Minn: Galde Press, 1999.
Alex Barca buys failing small-town radio stations and sells as many shares in them as possible before skipping town. But in Clarinda, a shrewd seller blocked the scam. So he illegally increases the broadcast strength to sell advertising time beyond the usual radius and pockets the revenue. His idea of playing Glenn Miller's music to draw in his listeners is more successful than anyone anticipated.

Larson, Skoot.
(series: Lars Lindstrom)

The No News is Good News Bad News Blues. Bloomington & London: Author House, 2007.
Jazz musician Lars Lindstrom discovers the body of a Middle Eastern man on his patio chair. He takes his wallet for identification purpose and then calls the police. When they arrive, the body is gone. They dismiss Lindstrom's call as a "nuisance." But the Feds are interested because of fears of a dirty bomb entering San Pedro's

container port. They believe that the terrorists, based in Oslo, were trying to contact Lindstrom.

Real Gone Horn Gone Blues. Bloomington & London: Author House, 2007.

Lars Lindstrom's saxophone player, Lucien Bezich, known as "Loose," believes that he bought Art Pepper's Martin alto saxophone for $3,000 on the Internet. He asks Lindstrom to accompany him to pick up the saxophone. When they arrive at the seller's house, they find a corpse, no saxophone and the police. They are eventually cleared of any part in the murder but have stumbled into a container theft operation.

The Dig You Later, Alligator Blues. Bloomington & London: Author House, 2009.

Several exotic dancers disappear in the South Bay area and the girlfriend of Lars Lindstrom's saxophone player is frightened. The disappearances coincide with the appearance of a six-foot alligator in a channel. Captain Tom Cheatham of the LAPD, a jazz fan, tells Lindstrom that Louis Munoz, a crooked cop who once tried to frame him on drug charges, is a suspect in the case.

Latimer, John.
(Jonathan Wyatt Latimer)
(series: Bill Crane)

The Lady in the Morgue, London: Methuen, 1957; New York: Doubleday, 1936.

The body of "Alice Ross," an apparent suicide, is missing from the Chicago Morgue and the morgue attendant murdered. The police try to hold Bill Crane, a private investigator, responsible. He is in Chicago to find out whether the suicide is actually Kathryn Courtland, a wealthy socialite, who was estranged from her family. Apparently, Kathryn left New York City with a trumpet player from Rudy Vallee's dance band.

Lawrence, Michael.
(Lawrence Lariar)
(series: Johnny Amsterdam)

I Like it Cool. New York: Popular, 1960.

Jazz singer Sandra Tyson confides to PI Johnny Amsterdam that she is the unacknowledged daughter of well-known cartoonist and womanizer, Mark Tyson. Her mother actually developed the concept of the Tyson's comic strip but was left destitute after the comic strip gained popularity. Amsterdam agrees to accompany Sandra when she confronts her father. The next day Tyson is found murdered. The police arrest Sandra and Amsterdam must find the real murderer.

Lawton, John.
(series: Frederick Troy)

Flesh Wounds. London: Weidenfield & Nicolson, 2004. New York: Atlantic, 2005; aka Blue Rondo.

Frederick Troy's American wartime girlfriend Kitty Stilton returns to London after an eighteen-years absence. Because she is now married to Democratic Party Presidential hopeful Calvin Mc-Cormick, PI Joey Rork tails her at the behest of politicians concerned with her past sexual escapades. After Rork is murdered, Troy belatedly realizes that he stumbled into a gang war.

Lehman, Ernest.
(Ernest Paul Lehman)

Sweet Smell of Success. In The Short Fiction of Ernest Lehman. Woodstock: Overlook, 2000.

Publicist Sidney Falco is consumed with success. To maintain his lifestyle and profession, he is dependent on gossip columnist J.J. Hunsecker to mention the names of his clients in his column. When Hunsecker's sister Susan falls for a singer Steve Dallas, he demands that Falco destroy Dallas' reputation by planting negative gossip with other columnists about his marijuana use and sets up a drug bust.

Leonard, Elmore.
(Elmore John Leonard, Jr.)

<u>Tishomingo Blues</u>. London: Viking, 2002; New York: William Morrow, 2002.

Daredevil High-Diver Dennis Lenahan witnesses a "Dixie Mafia" murder. He is saved from a similar fate by the arrival of Robert Taylor, a black hustler from Detroit, who's in town to evaluate the drug scene for a potential takeover. The blues-loving hustler brings Lenahan to the famous crossroads at Highways 49 and 61 where blues legend Robert Johnson allegedly swapped his soul to the devil for immortality and makes Lenahan a similar deal.

Leslie, John.
(series: Gideon Lowry)

<u>Killing Me Softly</u>. New York: Pocket, 1994.

Gideon Lowry plays the piano in Key West clubs and takes an occasional PI job. When Virginia Murphy returns to Key West after almost a lifetime's absence, she hires Gideon to find the killer of her sister, Lila, forty years earlier. After Virginia falls to her death, the Key West establishment, including Gideon's brother, close ranks in an attempt to shut down any investigation.

<u>Night and Day</u>. New York: Pocket, 1995.

MTV pop star Asia hires jazz pianist-turned detective Gideon Lowry to find her missing husband, writer Frank Maguire, whom she wishes to divorce. Because it is the Hemingway Day Festival, Lowry easily enlists the Key West literati to help find the elusive Maguire, who once wrote a book on Hemingway. Maguire is discovered dead at the Hemingway house. An elderly Hemingway sparing partner and friend of Lowry is charged with the murder.

<u>Love for Sale</u>. New York: Pocket, 1997.

A lonely Gideon Lowry resorts to a Key West escort service and has a surprising evening with Katy Moran. The next day she hires him to help her deal with a jewel encrusted chalice salvaged from a sunken Spanish galleon. After she allegedly commits suicide in her trailer and the chalice disappears, Lowry is determined to uncover her killer and recover the chalice.

<u>Blue Moon</u>. New York: Pocket, 1998.

Gideon Lowry's old girlfriend Gabriella Wade, the owner of the Blue Moon restaurant, is engaged to Ray Emerson, a recent arrival at Key West. Realizing just how little she knows about Emerson, she asks Lowry to do a background check. Gideon is, also, facing a major change in his life as a real estate developer that Emerson works for, is pressuring him to sell his Duval Street home.

Lippman, Laura.
(series: Tess Monaghan)

"The Shoeshine Man Regrets." In Randisi, Robert J. (ed.). <u>Murder and all that Jazz</u>. New York: Signet, 2004.

Tess and her friend Whitney notice a spot on a man's shoe while they are waiting for valet parking. An elderly, black shoeshine man appears, and offers to clean the man's shoe. Its owner accuses him of putting the spot there and a fight ensues. When the police are called, they discover the old man is wanted on a forty-year-old murder charge.

Longstreet, Pamela.

<u>China Blues</u>. London: Grafton, 1989; New York: Doubleday, 1989.

Heiress Libby Stratford Hamilton decides to fix her unfaithful husband James by having an affair with the Chinese criminal Li Kwan Won. But James, a crooked DA with eyes on the White House, couldn't care less about Libby's infidelity and has his own plans for the Chinese bootlegger and his adopted mother Rose

St. Lorraine, who runs San Francisco's infamous Blue Canary Club.

Loustal-Paringaux, Jacques de.

<u>Barney and the Blue Note</u>. Netherlands: Rijperman, 1988.
 Barney is a French musician who plays with expatriates and touring jazzmen. While working with Art Blakey and the Jazz Messengers in Paris, he begins to think about playing in the States. Around this time, he also becomes addicted to heroin. After a successful gig at New York's Five Spot, he decides to go to California. He disappears into the competitive West Coast jazz scene, only to re-emerge as a junkie, who doesn't remember killing his dealer.

Lucarelli, Carlo.

<u>Almost Blue</u>. London: Harvill, 2003; San Francisco: City Lights Noir: 2001;
 Grazia Negro of the Serial Crimes Unit believes that a psychopath is killing university students in Bologna and stripping their corpses. The police establishment prefers to regard the killings as unrelated. Simone Martini, a young blind man, who spends his time at home listening to jazz and to the sounds of the city on his radio scanner, can identify the killer. The killer, unfortunately, also, can identify Martini.

Lutz, John.
(series: Alo Nudger)

<u>The Right to Sing the Blues</u>. New York: St. Martin's, 1986.
 PI Alo Nudger is hired by New Orleans restaurant owner and clarinet legend Fat Jack McGee to investigate his star attraction, piano player, Willy Hollister. He's interested in the band's vocalist, Ineida Mann, the daughter of a powerful, local crime boss. Only McGee knows the girl's real identity. Nudger discovers that Willy's past girlfriends have disappeared.

<u>The Right to Sing the Blues</u>. In Manson, Cynthia & Halligan, Kate. (eds.). <u>Murder To Music</u>. New York: Carroll & Graf, 1997.

Jazz club owner Fat Jack McGee hires Alo Nudger to check the background of piano player Willy Hollister, who is interested in the group's vocalist Ineida Mann. Unknown to Hollister, she is the daughter of a powerful New Orleans' businessman. Nudger discovers that McGee has reason to be concerned. Lutz turned this short story into a novel.

(non-series)

"Chop Suey." In Randisi, Robert J. (ed), <u>Murder and all that Jazz</u>. New York: Signet, 2004.

An aspiring blues singer named Lauralee and Jabelle, a singer from Harlem, are eating together at Kim's Chinese restaurant. She meets Jabelle's boyfriend Jefferson and advises her to drop him. Much later, Jabelle goes to Jefferson's room and discovers him asleep with Lauralee. Angered, she kills them both with a ceremonial sword from Kim's restaurant.

Macdonald, Ross
(aka Kenneth Millar, John Macdonald)
(series: Lew Archer)

<u>The Moving Target</u>. London: Cassell, 1951; New York: Knopf, 1949.

On the recommendation of former D.A., turned councilor-to-the-rich, Albert Graves, Elaine Sampson hires private eye Lew Archer to find her missing husband, Ralph. Everyone but Archer seems more interested in Sampson's money than his fate. Archer learns that Ralph, recently obsessed with astrology, has been associating with a rough crowd on the fringe of the entertainment world. After the arrival of a ransom note, he senses an inside job has sealed Ralph's fate.

(non-series)

<u>Trouble Follows Me</u> aka <u>Night Train</u>. New York: Dodd, Mead & Co., 1946.

Ensign Sam Drake meets Mary, a late-night DJ, who plays jazz for the Pacific Fleet. They decide to check up on her distraught co-worker Sue, who just broke up with her boyfriend. She apparently committed suicide or is it murder? A black sailor, Hector Lamb, was a prime suspect but had an alibi. He had, however, sent a large amount of money to his wife in Detroit. Sue may have been broadcasting more than jazz across the Pacific.

Maltese, Martin.

<u>North to Toronto</u>. New York: Manor, 1978.

Returning home after a successful Canadian tour, jazz musician Dave Harrigan is detained by customs when heroin is discovered in his saxophone. Harrigan claims that he was framed. His lawyer believes him and dispatches investigator Henry Kloss to Canada. Kloss uncovers a number of suspects, no shortage of motives, and at least one, possibly two murders in this 70s caper.

Marks, Paul D.

<u>The Blues Don't Care</u>. Lutz, FL: Down & Out Books, 2020.

White piano player Bobby Saxon gets a job in Booker Taylor's black band working on a gambling ship, the Apollo, when James Christmas, an aggressive band member, has an altercation with a guest. Later the guest is murdered and police arrest Christmas. He insists on his innocence and Taylor asks Saxon to find the killer. The victim had an import/export company that traded with Nazi Germany before the embargo. Saxon is soon caught up in a world of spies where no one is whom they portend to be.

Marsh, Ngaio.

(Edith Ngaio Marsh)

A Wreath For Rivera. Boston: Little, Brown, 1949; aka Swing, Brother Swing. London: Collins, 1949.

On opening night at the Metronome, the eccentric Lord Pastern, who is playing in Breezy Bellair's jazz band, is supposed to shoot the piano player, Carlos Rivera, as part of their act. Rivera is a hot-tempered Latin, disliked by everyone except Pastern's daughter, Felicite. He is actually killed, leaving no shortage of motives and suspects, ranging from Pastern's family to the band members for Scotland Yard's Roderick Alleyn to shift through to find the killer.

Mask, Ken.

Murder at The Butt. Los Angeles: Milligan Books, 2003.

Former Assistant District Attorney turned private investigator, Luke Jacobs, finds himself as the alibi for Iris French in the murder of real estate agent Pepper Louise at New Orleans' Funky Butt jazz club. Aware something is wrong with French, he is determined to find the killer.

Mathews, Francine.

The Alibi Club. New York: Bantam, 2006.

As the Nazis advance towards Paris, a group of American expatriates, who spend time at The Alibi Club that is owned by American jazz singer Memphis Jones, see their lives crumble. Sally King's fiancée, lawyer Philip Sitwell, "commits suicide" under sordid conditions but she thinks it was murder. Diplomat Joe Hurst, who is concerned for her safety, agrees. Knowing the Nazis' racial policies, club owner Jones joins the exodus to North Africa with something special for the Allied war effort in her baggage.

McClendon, Lise.
(series: Dorrie Lennox)

One O'Clock Jump. New York: St. Martin's, 2001.

It's a routine surveillance job for Kansas City PI Dorrie Lennox until Iris Jackson, the girlfriend of small-time hoodlum "Gorgeous" George Terraciano, jumps into the Missouri River. Surprisingly, she is asked to stay on the case and find about the late Miss Jackson. Meanwhile Lennox's boss is framed for a murder and Jackson reappears from the dead.

Sweet And Low. New York: Thomas Dunne, 2002.

PI Amos Haddam and his assistant Dorie Lennox are surveilling Thalia Hines, the young, beautiful, and willful daughter of Eveline Hines. Commander Hines, as she is known from her days as a nurse in WWI, is dying and has hired them to keep Thalia out of trouble. Thalia goes out nightly to dance and drink in Kansas City's jazz joints. Things take a deadly turn, however, after she sets her sights on a fortune hunter.

Mengel, Brad.
(series: Johnny Nickle)

"The Devil You Know." In White, David. (ed.). Charles Boeckman Presents Johnny Nickle. Batesville, AZ: Prose Productions, 2013.

Johnny Nickle needed a new guitar player when Captain Manning approaches him about Connor Johnson, who plays well enough for the band. But Connor has a weakness for women and Manning gambles. Connor had been involved with the daughter of a Chicago mobster and is currently infatuated with the band's singer. Manning ran out on a $1,000 gambling debt. Johnny expects trouble as Chicago gunmen were seen in the club.

Merrill, Joan.
(series: Casey McKie)

And All That Madness. London: iUniverse, 2010. New York: iUniverse, 2009.

San Francisco jazz singer and club owner Dee Jefferson asks her friend, PI Casey McKie to investigate the death of club owner, Milton Brown. The police accepted a suicide ruling. Then someone shoots blues singer Big Ruby, which is passed off by the police as a violent domestic disturbance. After jazz promoter Max Greenfield is shot in Palm Springs and it's dismissed as a gay shooting, McKie is convinced someone has a deadly grudge.

And All That Sea. London & Bloomington: iUniverse, 2010.

PI Casey McKie is invited on a Caribbean jazz cruise by her friend, singer Dee Jefferson. But her vacation is interrupted with the disappearance of a wealthy passenger, a French countess named Lien Boudreaux. The ship's captain wants a discreet investigation and is more fearful of negative publicity than interested in the woman's fate. Casey wonders whether the Countess was thrown overboard at sea or murdered at a tourist port.

And All That Stalking. Bloomington: iUniverse, 2012; London: CreateSpace, 2012.

PI Casey McKie is asked by her friend, jazz singer/club owner Dee Jefferson to investigate the death of a young singer. She believes the prime suspect, her boyfriend, drummer Greg Sanderson, is innocent. McKie learns the crime scene was cleaned of forensic evidence. Looking further, she realizes Terilynn Walter's murder is the most recent in a series of killings of aspiring jazz singers. Dee's young protégée, Lara Vale may be next on the killer's list.

And All That Madness. London & New York: CreateSpace 2013.

The New York Jazz Society has come into possession of a letter implying jazz diva Georgia Valentine died from a self-administered heroin overdose. Casey McKie's best friend, jazz club owner/singer Dee Jefferson begs her to go to New York City to clear her name. In New York, McKie is quickly convinced that Valentine was murdered and has a credible list of suspects including a jilted lover, a shiftless husband, a crooked manager, organized crime elements and anti-drug crusaders.

And All That Motive. London & New York: CreateSpace, 2014.
Vocalist Sid Satin is murdered in his RV at the Pacific Coast Jazz Festival. Singer Dee Jefferson owned the murder weapon and they had a public argument. She turns to her friend San Francisco PI Casey McKie for help. McKie realizes that the police have already decided Jefferson's guilt and the only way she can avoid being charged is by finding the killer. Unfortunately, a lot of people had motives to kill him.

Merril, Judith.
(Judith Josephine Grossman)

"Muted Hunger." In Charteris, Leslie & Santesson, Hans. (eds.). The Saint Magazine Reader. Garden City: Doubleday, 1966.
A jazz groupie named Cindy is nearly beaten to death. The band has its suspicion of her assailant's identity but no one is talking. The narrator, the daughter of the band's founder, realizes that any of them are capable of violence. By listening to the band, she identifies the killer through his playing.

Mertz, Stephen.

"Death Blues." In Gorman, Ed (ed.). The Second Black Lizard Anthology of Crime Fiction. Berkeley: Black Lizard, 1988.
Carl Hensman, a blues collector, tells his friend P.I. O'Dair that he saw Stomper Crawford going into a club. But the blues legend disappeared eight years earlier. At the club, O'Dair is told that Hensman was mistaken. Upon returning to his car, he's attacked by two thugs and then rescued by Crawford's son, Isaac. He's taken

to meet Stomper and learns that gangsters mistakenly believe he witnessed a murder and fears for his life.

Meyers, Martin.

"Snake Rag." In Randisi, Robert J. (Ed.). <u>Murder and all that Jazz</u>. New York: Signet, 2004.

Vito Monte, a struggling jazz musician, is hired to retrieve two diamonds belonging to Legs Diamond that were stolen from a courier. Vito is looking for the courier Snake Gardella, who finds him and Legs.

Millar, Kenneth
(see Ross Macdonald)

Molina, Antonio Munoz.

<u>Winter In Lisbon</u>. London: Granta, 1999; aka <u>El Invierno en Lisboa</u>. Madrid: Seix Barral, 1987.

Expatriate jazz pianist Santiago Biraldo, who plays at The Lady Bird in San Sebastian, Spain, is infatuated with Lucretia, the wife of Malcolm, a small-time art dealer and thief. Unexpectedly, the couple goes to Berlin, leaving Santiago obsessed by memories of Lucretia. Three years later, thugs come after Santiago, assuming he knows where Lucretia is. Apparently, she has left Malcolm and took a Cezanne. She eventually contacts Santiago, whose main concern is to warn her of trouble.

Mones, Nicole.

<u>Night in Shanghai</u>. London & New York: Houghton Mifflin, 2014.

Black pianist Thomas Greene accepts a job offer in Shanghai leading The Kings, a black jazz dance band. The classically trained Greene has little feel for jazz and is dependent on written scores. But the other band members are good cover for him. A struggle for Shanghai is being waged between the Nationalists, the Communists, and the Japanese. After the Japanese take control, the Nationalists plan to use Greene to lure the jazz-loving administrator into a deadly trap.

Moody, Bill.
(series: Evan Horne)

Solo Hand. London: Slow Dancer, 1999; New York: Walker, 1994.

Soul singer Lonnie Cole asks his former piano player Evan Horne, who is recovering from an automobile accident that injured his right hand, to investigate a blackmail problem before the American Music Awards. Horne is the chosen middleman. After losing the payoff money, however, he is suspected of involvement and can only clear himself by finding the real blackmailers. Along the way, he uncovers a scam that costs Cole more than the blackmail.

Death of a Tenor Man. New York: Walker, 1995.

Ace Buffington asks his friend, musician Evan Horne for help researching a paper on tenor player Wardell Gray, who died under suspicious circumstances in May 1955, two days after the opening of the first integrated hotel-casino in Las Vegas, The Moulin Rouge. Buffington believes that the surviving musicians would talk freely to another musician. But Horne's investigation has stirred up organized crime elements whose present business dealings could be affected by the events thirty-seven years earlier.

The Sound of the Trumpet. New York: Walker, 1997.

Record collector Ken Perkins hires private investigator and jazz musician Evan Horne to listen to two newly discovered jazz tapes from the 1950s to verify Clifford Brown as the trumpet player. Perkins also claims to have Brown's trumpet. Initially convinced of the tape's veracity, Horne's doubts grow after Perkins is murdered, the tapes disappear and a vengeful killer stalks him.

Bird Lives. New York: Walker, 1999.

Santa Monica police Lieutenant Dan Cooper calls his friend, jazz pianist Evan Horne to the murder scene of jazz musician Ty Rod-man. His killer had written "Bird Lives" in blood on the wall above the body. Rodman's murder is one of a series of prominent jazz musicians that puzzle the FBI. Cooper thinks that Horne's insight into the jazz world might help in catching a serial killer.

Looking for Chet Baker. New York: Walker, 2002.

While in London, his first stop in a European club tour, Evan Horne encounters his friend, academic Ace Buffington, who tries to convince him to help research a book on trumpet player Chet Baker's death. Horne refuses. Although his next gig in Amsterdam with expatriate Fletcher Page goes well, Horne is upset by Buffington's arrival and disappearance. Fearing the worst, Horne searches for his missing friend and stumbles into the Dutch drug world that snared Baker.

Shades of Blue. Scottsdale: Poisoned Pen Press, 2008.

Just back from Amsterdam, jazz pianist Evan Horne learns that his old friend and teacher Calvin Hughes has died, leaving him his Hollywood Hills home, his possessions and his money. Sorting through the possessions, Horne finds a note and photograph leading to the unsettling discovery that Hughes was his father and the possible composer of two jazz standards associated with Miles Davis.

Fade To Blue. Scottsdale: Poisoned Pen Press, 2011.

Jazz pianist Evan Horne is offered a lucrative gig of teaching movie star Ryan Stiles to appear to be playing the piano in an upcoming film as well as scoring it. Horne accepts despite reservations about Stiles. Following a row with paparazzi, an aggressive photographer is found dead after his motorcycle went off a cliff. It's ruled an accident and Stiles has an alibi. Then a second photographer is strangled after blackmailing Stiles. Although Stiles is a prime suspect, Horne senses the killer is in his entourage.

(non-series)

"The Resurrection of Bobo Jones." In Harvey, John. (ed.). <u>Men From Boys</u>. New York: HarperCollins, 2003.

Tenor sax player Brew Daniels' antics have made it impossible for him to find work. His agent offers him a job at a gangster-owned club near Greenwich Village called The Final Bar. He's to play with the once-great pianist Bobo Jones, who had a breakdown on stage and almost killed his last sax player. Daniels' brilliant playing revitalizes Jones but the sax player fears for his life.

"Childs' Play." In Randisi, Robert J. (ed.). <u>Murder and all that Jazz</u>. New York: Signet, 2004.

During a late evening encounter, trumpet legend Miles Davis appears to offer tenor sax player Wilson Childs a job as John Coltrane's replacement in his band. Later, Childs and his piano player Quincy Simmons are stopped by police and during a routine traffic check. Marijuana and a gun are discovered in Childs' car. Not wanting Childs to miss an opportunity to play with Miles, Simmons says it all belongs to him. He jumps bail and resurfaces 25 years later.

"Camaro Blue" In Philips, Gary. (ed.) <u>Cocaine Chronicles</u>. New York: Akashic, 2005.

Musician Robert Ware's 1989 Chevy Camero Sport and his tenor sax were stolen by Raymond Morales, who is killed by police after a highspeed chase and a shoot-out. Ware gets his car back but his horn is missing. He goes to Morales' funeral and realizes he went to school with his sister. She tells him she has the horn.

"File Under Jazz." In Bishop, Claude & Bruns, Don. (eds.) <u>A Merry Band of Murderers</u>. Scottsdale: Poisoned Pen Press, 2006.

Jazz pianist Ray Fuller hears a tune on his car radio and calls the radio station to learn its title, "D Minor Hues" by Lou Harris and that he was murdered, possibly by his girlfriend. Fuller goes to an oldies store and finds a copy of *Lou's Blues* and meets a woman looking for the same album. Her name is Emily Parker and she claims Harris wrote the song for her. He gives her the album after he's taped it and later realizes that she killed Harris.

Czechmate: The Spy Who Played Jazz. Lutz, Fla: Down And Out
Books, 2013.
American drummer Gene Williams has been invited to play at
the 1968 Prague Jazz Festival. The apolitical Williams is oblivious
to a possible Russian invasion. The CIA knows an invasion is imminent. Their Czech source, Josef Blaha, fears that he has been
compromised and wants a clean courier. The CIA decides to use
Williams but the jazzman is initially unwilling and only reluctantly
agrees. After making contact with Blaha, the Czech is murdered
leaving the inexperienced Williams in trouble.

"Jazz Line." In Mood Swings. Lutz, Fl: Down & Out Books, 2015.
Late night jazz disc jockey Tim Weston has been getting calls
from a smoky voiced woman named Madeline. He has fantasized
about her but is surprised when she suggests a meeting after his
show one night. Her calls were interspaced with those of another
listener, an aggressive bigot with a smoker's cough. After entering
her apartment, he hears her voice as well as a smoker's cough.

Morfoot, Peter.
(series: Captain Darac)

Impure Blood. London: Titan, 2016.
No one sees a killing in the midst of a Muslim prayer group. To
complicate the investigation, the Tour de France is about to begin.
Then Captain Darac's boss, Agnes Dantier, the Commissaire of the
Brigade Criminelle and her father Vincent, the former Commissaire, are kidnapped. Initially, Darac supervises two separate investigations, briefly links them and separates them again. Once Darac
understands the motive, he knows time is running out for the Dan-
tiers.

Fatal Music. London: Titan, 2017.
The body of Jeanne Mesnel, an elderly lady, was discovered in

her hot tub. She died several days earlier. Darac was ready to dismiss her death as natural but his curiosity was aroused by her jazz record collection and the discovery of her likeness on a 1963 poster above the door to the Blue Devil Jazz Club where Darac often plays. He learns that the Mesnel house was recently sold to a young American curator at the nearby Matisse Museum under unusual circumstances.

Box of Bones. London: Titan: 2018.
Captain Darac witnesses the death of a spectator during the Carnival Parade. The death is eventually linked to a 19 million Euro robbery case in which a substantial reward was paid as the loot was recovered. Delmas, the inside man, was arrested and served jail time. His daughter was to receive part of the reward. Darac suspects Delmas was double-crossed and is killing gang members.

Knock 'Em Dead. Cambridge: Galileo, 2020.
Ambroise Paillaud, a retired comic actor, is killed by a train. Surveillance film indicates suicide rather than murder. When his recent will is discovered missing and his notary murdered, Darac's team take a closer look. While the victim wasn't the man everyone presumed him to be, the killer of the notary and the missing will becomes the focus of Darac's investigation.

Morson, Ian.

"There Would Have Been Murder." In Ashley. Mike, (ed.). The Mammoth Book of Roaring Twenties Whodunnits. New York: Carroll & Graf, 2004.
Special Branch has received a tip that the British Communist Party plans to take advantage of the postwar social unrest with some sort of action. Sergeant John Banks is sent to party headquarters and determines there is no threat as they are "still British first." Their leader, Harry Rothstein, joined the Party to divert money to buy expensive jazz records that he plays on his home gramophone. The supposed action was actually a diversion to occupy the police during a robbery.

Mosley, Walter.
(Walter Ellis Mosley)
(series: Easy Rawlins, Leonid McGill & Socrates Fortlow)

Devil In a Blue Dress. London: Serpent's Tail, 2001; New York: Norton, 1990.

White hustler Dewitt Albright hires recently unemployed Easy Rawlins to find Daphne Monet, a white woman known to frequent Watts' black jazz clubs. His inquiries result in enough dead bodies for Easy to call Houston gunman Mouse for backup. He learns that some of Daphne's hunters want the $30,000 she has stolen from the politically prominent Todd Carter while others want revenge by embarrassing him.

RL's Dream. London: Serpent's Tail, 1995; New York: Norton, 1995.

Soupspoon Wise, an elderly, ill black man, was evicted from the apartment where he lived for 28 years. A young white woman, Kiki Waters took him in. Soupspoon is diagnosed with advanced cancer but lacks the insurance needed to get medical care, so Kiki forges the required documents. Soupspoon, who learned the blues as a child and once played with the legendary bluesman Robert Johnson, reminisces about his life.

"Blue Lightning." In Harvey. John, (ed.). Blue Lightning. London: Slow Dancer, 1998.

Socrates Fortlow is awakened by a trumpet in an adjacent lot, playing a slow blues. That night, after work, Socrates stakes out the abandoned lot and confronts the horn player, Hoagland Mars. They go back to Socrates' room and drink brandy while Hoagland plays his horn. Later, he robs Socrates.

Trouble Is What I Do. London & New York: Mulholland/Little Brown, 2020.

PI Leonid McGill is hired by Philip "Catfish" Hunter, a 94-year-old Mississippi bluesman (and Ernie Eckles, an old "associate" of

McGill's) to give a letter to Justine Sternman, a wealthy heiress, revealing her black lineage as Catfish's granddaughter. Her father, Charles Sternman, Catfish's son, is a powerful, corrupt bigot. He won't hesitate to kill to prevent public knowledge of his black heritage.

Moss, Stephen L.
(series: Paul Kingston)

<u>Autumn Leaves</u>. West Lafayette, Indiana: Northside Press, 2014.
Bassist Paul Kingston gets a gig in trumpet player Clive Peterson's band. Peterson is considered the best jazz musician in Milwaukee. The next morning, he learns that the trumpet player was murdered. The police regard it as a case of mistaken identity or gang activity. But Peterson's widow Marian disagrees and asks Kingston to investigate. A series of violent incidents convince Kingston that she was right. But then, inexplicably, she asks him to stop his investigation.

Murphy, Dallas.
(series: Artie Deemer)

<u>Lover Man</u>. New York: Scribner's, 1987.
Artie Deemer, who is supported by his celebrity dog, Jellyroll, spends his life in his Morris chair listening to jazz and smoking dope. This idyllic life is disrupted by the NYPD who inform him that his former girlfriend, Billie Burke, was discovered bound and drowned in her apartment. A posthumous note sends him on a search for the killer that winds through Mafia wars, turf fights between the NYPD and the FBI and ends in a bizarre tale of family revenge.

<u>Lush Life</u>. New York: Pocket, 1992.
The new love of Artie Deemer's life is Crystal Spivey, a top ranked pool player and ex-wife of his law school acquaintance, Trammell, who runs a bank that specializes in money laundering. When Tram-

mell disappears, angry depositors kidnap Crystal in hopes of flushing him out. Deemer rescues her but learns that there is more interest in an incriminating tape than recovering the missing money.

Don't Explain. New York: Pocket, 1996.

Artie Deemer, the jazz-loving recluse, who lives off the earnings of his celebrity dog, Jellyroll, has his world shaken by a publicity hungry stalker who threatens Jellyroll. Deemer, his girlfriend, ace pool player Crystal Spivey and Jellyroll find refuge in a cabin off the Maine coast. Their solitude is disrupted by the arrival of religious pilgrims and a serial killer.

Nadelson, Reggie.
(series: Artie Cohen)

Red Mercury Blues. London: Faber & Faber, 1995; aka Red Hot Blues. New York: St. Martin's, 1998.

Moscow born Artie Cohen, now a New York City cop, decides to investigate the murder of an ex-KGB General Gennadi Ustinov, who was a family friend. His unofficial search for Ustinov's killer takes him to Brighton Beach where he stumbles onto the radioactive trail of a nuclear smuggler of "Red Mercury", the heart of a miniaturized atomic bomb. He reluctantly follows the trail to Moscow.

Hot Poppies. London: Faber & Faber, 1997; New York: St. Martin's, 1999.

Diamond merchant Hillel Abramsky discovers a dead Chinese girl in his shop and calls Artie Cohen. Artie's Chinese friends, the Taes, ask him to look after their daughter, Dawn, whom they suspect of having a drug problem. Meanwhile, Artie's girlfriend Lily Hanes goes to China to adopt a child but things go wrong. When Artie goes to Hong Kong to discover the identity of the Chinese crime boss known as the Debt Collector, the three stories' strands come together.

Bloody London. London: Minotaur, 1999; New York: St. Martin's, 1999.

Thomas Pascoe, an elderly investment banker and philanthropist, is murdered at his Sutton Place apartment co-operative, Middlemarch. As the co-op heads, Pascoe and his wife Francis angered many people. After the death of an elderly Russian resident and opponent of Pascoe, Artie's investigation adopts a Russian focus. It uncovers the surprising extent of Russian ownership of prime New York real estate. When Frances is murdered after pointing Cohen's investigation towards England, he discovers a similar Russian presence in London.

Sex Dolls. London: Faber & Faber, 2002; aka Skin Trade. London: Arrow, 2006.

Artie gets a forgery case that takes him and his girlfriend, Lily Hanes to London and Paris. Someone has tried to forge a check on a long dormant account of a dead man, Eric Levesque. Artie's has to stop in London but Lily insists on going ahead to Paris alone. When he eventually arrives, he discovers Lily badly beaten and near death. While hunting for her attackers, he realizes that her attack might be related to his case.

Disturbed Earth. London: Heinemann, 2004; New York: Walker, 2004.

Artie interrogates a young Russian woman who found a pile of bloody children's clothes and it leaves him uneasy. When May Luca's naked body is found, the police assume the clothes were hers. She was a friend of Artie's godson Billy, who is also missing. After a third child disappears, Artie suspects the cases are unrelated and thinks that Billy was abducted by a retarded child named Hersey Shank.

Red Hook. London: Heinemann, 2006; New York: Walker, 2006.

On the day before his wedding, Artie Cohen receives a confused telephone call for help from his old friend, Sid McKay, who was once a respected journalist. He goes to Red Hook to see a suddenly evasive McKay. Feeling that he had wasted his time, Artie ignores

McKay's continuing calls until McKay is murdered. Looking for his killer, Artie finds McKay's legendary files wanted by many people, including his friend Tolya Sverdloff.

Fresh Kills. London: Heinemann, 2006; New York: Walker, 2007.
Artie Cohen offers to take care of his nephew Billy Farone, who has a two-week furlough from the Florida institution where he has been living since stabbing to death a retarded child, Hersey Shank. Artie has been assured that Billy has been cured. He is so busy shielding Billy from Hersey's revenge seeking brother that he misses the warning signs of more trouble.

Londongrad. London: Atlantic, 2009; New York: Walker, 2009.
Artie discovers a dead girl wrapped in duct tape on a park swing. After identifying her, he notices her resemblance to his friend Tolya Sverdloff's daughter, Valentina, and fears the killers went after the wrong girl. Unfortunately, he's right and eventually, they realize their error and kill Valentina. Tolya incorrectly believes she was killed because of his anti-Putin activities. He knows the killer's identity and goes after him. But he becomes critically ill in Russia and needs Artie's help.

Blood Count. London: Atlantic Books, 2011; New York: Walker, 2010.
Artie gets a call from his ex-girlfriend, Lily. She's living at the Louis Armstrong Apartments at Sugar Hill (Harlem) and irrationally fears responsibility in the death of Marianna Simonova, an elderly Russian resident. Artie learns that several residents have recently died. Carver Lennox, an ambitious black entrepreneur, who's in trouble financially, has been pressuring older residents to sell him their apartments for renovation and resale, emerges as a prime suspect.

Manhattan 62. London: Corvus, 2014; New York: Atlantic, 2014.
NYPD Detective Pat Wynne encounters Soviet exchange student Max Ostalsky, who loves Greenwich Village with its folk and jazz

clubs. He introduces him to Nancy Rudnick, a wealthy "red diaper" baby. Pat is called out to Pier 46 where a young Cuban has been murdered and discovers a charm belonging to Nancy. Belatedly he realizes Ostalsky is both involved with Nancy and KGB. Against a background of increasing tension of the Cuban Missile Crisis, he tracks down Ostalsky and learns the outline of an assassination plot.

Nemac, John.

Canary's Combo. Hollywood: Nite-Time, 1964.
Bandleader Joe Falcon is determined to find the killer of his young piano player, Pete Sullivan. While exhausting all of the suspects on both sides of the color line, Joe learns that Sullivan was bisexual. Then he asks too many questions and arouses a killer willing to kill again to protect his sexual preference.

Nielsen, Helen.

"You Can't Trust a Man." In Pronzini, Bill & Muller. Marcia, (eds.) The Deadly Arts. New York: Arbor, 1985.
Crystal Coe has done well for herself in the seven years since Tony took the rap for her and went to jail. Now she's a successful singer, married to a very wealthy man. But Tony's reappearance threatens it all as she's still married to him. So she shoots him in her car, claiming that he was trying to rob her.

Novak, Robert

B-Girl. New York: Ace, 1956.
Irene Malloy, a small-town singer, is given a chance by trumpet player Chuck Duval when his band plays a local roadhouse and joins the band.. Chuck's temper and selfishness eventually cost them their jobs. Unable to play because of a damaged lip, he forces Irene to become a B-Girl until his abuse results in their breakup. After hard times, just as she is finding success as a radio singer and

personal happiness, Chuck tries to re-enter her life.

Nuckel, John.

Harlem Rhapsody. New York: Independent, 2019.
   Charles Merritt, a decorated veteran from the Harlem Hellfighters and trumpet player, is recruited by a secret group of businessmen headed by J.P. Morgan in their effort to clean up Tammany Hall. His job is to ferret out illegal dealings overheard in conversations at the Cotton Club. His ally is Belle Turner, Harlem's most beautiful woman. Cotton Club owner Owney Madden is pressured into accepting the operation by threats of closure.

Oglesby, Wm Ellis.

Blow Happy, Blow Sad. Edmonton: Commonwealth, 1996.
   Dixieland bandleader Chops Danielson works for the Danish Resistance, encoding German military intelligence into his cornet solos broadcast to London during his weekly radio show. After the Gestapo arrested his girlfriend Svenya, he may have to betray his comrades to secure her freedom.

Ondaatje, Michael.
(Philip Michael Ondaatje)

Coming Through Slaughter. London: Marion Boyars, 1979; New York: Norton, 1976.
   Buddy Bolden works as a barber by day and a jazz musician by night. When he disappears, his childhood friend, a detective named Webb, finds him and convinces him to return to New Orleans.

Ordover, Andrew.
(series: Jordan Greenblatt)

Cool For Cats. Seattle: C4C Books, 2011.
   Jordan Greenblatt is a bass player and a private investigator. He

gets a call from the father of a girl whom he dated in high school to investigate the hit-and-run accident that killed her. The police investigation was inadequate and Greenblatt suspects political interference. Too hastily, he goes public with his findings, so that no one will listen when he finally gets it right.

The Cat Came Back. Middletown, DE: Creating-A-Life Books, 2016.
   Chris, a young college student, approaches Jordan Greenblatt about a "problem" on campus. Because Chris isn't specific, Greenblatt forgets about Chris until his death. Feeling guilty, Greenblatt accepts an undercover assignment as music graduate student. He is aware of campus drug use but unable to find their source until Chris' friend Maddy Taylor is endangered.

Padura, Leonardo.
(Leonardo de la Caridad Padua Fuentes)
(series: Mario Conde)

Havana Fever. London & New York: Bitter Lemon Press, 2009.
   No longer a Havana policeman, Mario Conde now makes his living as a used book dealer. He stumbles upon a library of rare books that has been untouched since its owner fled to Florida 43 years earlier. Inside one book is a newspaper clipping about the death of the legendary singer Violeta del Rio. Conde is intrigued as he realizes that she was romantically involved with the library's owner. The more he learns, the more certain he is that she was murdered.

Patchett, Ann.

Taft. Boston: Houghton Mifflin, 1994.
   To provide stability in his family's life, jazz drummer John Nickel gives up his career to manage a bar named Mandy's and put his girlfriend Marion through school. But it's not enough for Marion,

who takes their son and moves to Florida. Nickel hires a young girl named Fay Taft as a waitress and soon is dealing with her infatuations as well as taking on her troubled brother Carl's problems.

Pentecost, Hugh

(Judson Pentecost Philips)
(series: Pierre Chambrun)

Murder Goes Round and Round. London: Robert Hale, 1989; New York: Dodd Mead, 1988.

Toby March, the internationally famous masked impersonator of jazz stars, disappears after his show's opening at the Blue Lagoon, a club in New York's elegant Hotel Beaumont. A search has uncovered blood in March's room and the body of a Scotland Yard detective in the hotel's basement. Then hotel manager Pierre Chambrun is shot. Chambrun believed March had criminal connections. But the police cannot find him, as no one knows what he looks like.

Phillips, Gary.

"The Performer" In Vega, Eddie. (ed.). Noir Nation N6. Middletown, DE: Noir Nation, 2017.

Avery Randolph plays piano at the Seaside Lounge in Los Amitos. Aside from Carlson the bartender and Emily, a General's widow who always sat by the window with a martini, Randolph seemingly didn't know anyone. Then Lori, who worked at the PX, picks him up. After a few nights together, she enlists him in a scheme to rob her kinky, former boss. The heist goes off perfectly except Lori decides to kill her ex-boss and Carlson would kill Randolph. But they failed to take account of Randolph's partner, Emily.

Pines, Paul.

The Tin Angel. New York: Morrow, 1983.

Pablo Waitz is the half-owner of the East Village jazz club, The Tin Angel. His partner, Miguel Ponce, is killed in a routine traffic stop that turned violent and claimed the lives of two policemen. The police want to find the killers and lean on Waitz. He wants to find the reason behind his friend's death. Was it a drug deal gone badly? Or betrayal by an ex-girlfriend? Or a revenge killing or a hit?

Plater, Alan.
(series: Trevor Chaplin & Jill Swinburne)

The Beiderbecke Affair. London: Methuen, 1985.
  Trevor Chaplin stumbles upon a "white market" operation while trying to get a four-volume set of Bix Beiderbecke recordings. This brings Trevor and his girlfriend Jill Swinburne to the attention of the local police. To distract the overly eager Sergeant Hobson, they guide him towards the corruption between big business interests and Leeds government officials.

The Beiderbecke Tapes. London: Methuen, 1986.
  Trevor Chaplin, a jazz collector, gets six Bix Beiderbecke tapes from John, his local publican. One of the tapes, however, appears to be a conversation between government officials regarding the illegal dumping of nuclear waste. After John disappears, Chaplin's housemate Jill Swinburne, a conservation activist, thinks they should investigate the tape. Their efforts are met with intimidation.

The Beiderbecke Connection. London: Methuen, 1992.
  Trevor and Jill are asked by their sometime associate Big Al to shelter a refugee named Ivan and then take him to the Yorkshire border. While Ivan is a fan of both Bix Beiderbecke and Duke Ellington, he is also a sophisticated thief and subject of an international manhunt.

Pronzini, Bill.

Blue Lonesome. New York: Walker, 1995.
  CPA Jim Messenger's only interest outside of his work is jazz.

He eats at the Harmony Café every evening and becomes obsessed with a woman, who brushes off his attempted introduction. After she commits suicide, he learns that no one knew her true identity. Messenger decides to find out who she was and why she chose death over life.

Queen, Ellery.
(Richard Deeming)

Death Spins the Platter. London: Gollancz, 1975; New York: Knopf, 1962.

Popular L.A. disc jockey Tutter King has lost his television show following payola (play for money) revelations during a Senate investigation. Newsman Jim Layton goes to KZZX to cover the final show and finds his body. He discovers that others at the station, who took payola, didn't lose their jobs and the women in King's life were unhappy with him.

Rabe, Peter.
(Peter Rabinowitsch)

Murder Me for Nickels. New York: Gold Medal, 1960.

Jack St. Louis, who owns a small jazz label, also works for gangster Walter Lippit. Lippit controls all the jukeboxes within a thirty-mile radius. When the Chicago syndicate moves in, St. Louis realizes the magnitude of their problem but Lippit doesn't, until it's too late. To save him, St. Louis reluctantly offers him his record pressing facilities and goes to Chicago to obtain needed masters. He returns to discover Lippit cutting him out of his own business.

Raleigh, Michael.
(series: Paul Whelan)

Maxwell Street Blues. New York: St. Martin's, 1994.

Private Investigator Paul Whelan is hired by black attorney Dave Hill to find Sam Burrell, who operated a table at the Maxwell Street open-air flea market. After Burrell's body is discovered, the police charge street punks with the crime. But O.C. Brown, an old jazz musician friend of Burrell's, asks Whelan to continue his investigation. To find the killer, Whelan ventures into Chicago's jazz past and confronts the race problem.

Randisi, Robert J.
(Robert Joseph Randisi)
(series: Eddie Gianelli)

Everybody Kills Somebody Sometime. New York: Thomas Dunne, 2006.
Frank Sinatra, Dean Martin, Sammy Davis, Jr., Peter Lawford and Joey Bishop are in Las Vegas for the filming of the movie *Oceans 11* and working at the Sands at night. Sinatra asks Sands' pit boss, Eddie Gianelli, ("Eddie G.") to find the source of the threats Martin has been receiving. After Eddie is beaten up, Sinatra has Mob backup flown in from New York. The threats to Martin turn out to be the least serious part of a problem.

Luck Be a Lady, Don't Die. New York: Thomas Dunne, 2007.
Frank Sinatra and his friends have returned to Las Vegas for the premiere of the film, *Ocean's 11*. But his new girlfriend, Mary Clarke, who is also gangster Sam Giancana's girlfriend, has disappeared. Sinatra asks his friend, Sands' pit boss Eddie Gianelli, to find her before the premiere. Unknown to Sinatra and Giancana, Mary and her sister Lily stole $100,000 from the Chicago mob who followed her to Las Vegas.

Hey There, You With The Gun In Your Hand. New York: Thomas Dunne, 2008.
Singer Frank Sinatra asks Eddie Gianelli to help Sammy Davis Jr., who is being blackmailed over an embarrassing photograph of his wife, actress May Britt. Gianelli agrees to be the middleman in the $25,000 payoff but discovers a dead body and no photographs at the payoff site. After someone contacts Davis asking for a higher

price, Gianelli suspects that there are two different groups of black-mailers.

You're Nobody 'til Somebody Kills You. New York: Minotaur, 2009.
Dean Martin asks Eddie G. if he could help Marilyn Monroe who insists she's being followed, and not by the usual fans or paparazzi. Negative press also torments her after Clark Gable's death follow-ing the filming of *The Misfits*. Eddie stashes Marilyn in Sinatra's Palm Springs home and with help from his friend PI Danny Bardini and Brooklyn torpedo Jerry Epstein uncover a FBI operation, using thugs for hire. He also assures Marilyn that Kay Gable doesn't hold her responsible for her husband's death.

I'm a Fool to Kill You. London & New York: Severn House, 2010.
Ava Gardner was seen hurriedly leaving the lobby of the Sands. Frank Sinatra wants to know what was going on with his ex-wife and asks Eddie G. to find her. He traces her back to L.A. and the Beverley Hills Hotel where she's staying as Lucy Johnson. Ava's drinking excessively and upset over aging. She confesses to blacking out in Chicago for three days. Apparently she was with the son of a gangster who was killed in a mob hit and fears her problems will rub off on Frank.

Fly Me to the Morgue. London & New York: Severn House, 2011.
Eddie G. and his friend Jerry join Dean Martin and Bing Crosby for racing at Del Mar. Jerry does well enough to impress Bing, who asks him to look at a racehorse in Las Vegas that he's thinking of buying as his regular trainer failed to show. At the Red Rock Canyon Ranch, they discover the horse's owner dead and Eddie's friend PI Danny later finds the missing trainer dead. The Arnold family is heavily into debt, gambling and the mob and there's disagreement over selling the horse to Crosby.

It Was a Very Bad Year. London & New York: Severn House, 2012.
Eddie Gianelli helps comedian Joey Bishop's tv wife Abby Dal-ton deal with blackmail. For $5,000, he secures photos and nega-

tives of a very young Dalton. The exchange occurs on the day JFK is killed and Sinatra, a Kennedy friend, is distraught. Then Frank Jr. is kidnapped & held for $240,000 ransom, which Sinatra pays. While working on the Dalton case, Gianelli found a list of dates and names that matched some of those heard by Frank Jr. 's kidnappers that is their undoing.

You Make Me Feel so Dead. London & New York: Severn House, 2013.

Col. Parker, Elvis Presley's manager, asks his friend Frank Sinatra to watch over his singer, who's in Las Vegas for the opening of *Viva Las Vegas*. Presley has been associating with an unsavory crowd, known as the Memphis Mafia. Sinatra passes the task on to Eddie G., who after initial misgivings allows Elvis to join the investigation of a blackmail/murder case. In a frame-up, Eddie G.'s friend, PI Danny Bardini, is accused of murdering the blackmailer of his secretary, Penny.

The Way You Die Tonight. London & New York: Severn House, 2013.

Jack Entratter's secretary Helen appears to have committed suicide in a locked bathroom. Both Entratter and Eddie G. suspect murder. Entratter tasks Eddie G. with finding her killer. With the Sands' tight security, it had to be an inside job. At the same time, Howard Hughes, who's eyeing Las Vegas, tries to hire Eddie G. away from the Sands. Also, Hollywood icon and frequent guest at the Sands, Edward G. Robinson, is coming to town to research a poker movie, *The Cincinnati Kid*. Eddie G. gets him a dealer/instructor as well as entry in a high-stakes game.

When Somebody Kills You. London & New York: Severn House, 2015.

Someone has put out an open contract on Eddie G. that's attracting both amateurs and professionals. Frank Sinatra asks Eddie G. to go to L.A. to help his friend Judy Garland with a problem of stalking and blackmail. Eddie convinces Judy that she's not being stalked but that her managers were blackmailing her and skimming. Frank (and mobster Sam Giancana) help uncover the origin of the contract—Robert

Maheu, who's angered by Eddie G.'s decision to stay at the Sands.

(non-series)

"The Listening Room." In Murder and all that Jazz. New York: Signet, 2004.

Truxton Harris goes to a St. Louis jazz club named The Listening Room that is owned by his friend Billy Danvers. Billy wanted to speak with him but was killed with a letter-opener before they could meet. Lewis finds two cigarette butts on Danvers' office floor and two more beside drummer Hal Joseph.

Murder and all that Jazz. New York: Signet, 2004.

Randisi edited this collection of thirteen short stories about crime and jazz.

Rayner, Richard.

The Devil's Wind. London: HarperCollins, 2005; New York: Atlantic Monthly, 2005.

Maurice Valentine, a Hollywood architect, married to the daughter of a Nevada Senator, is the designer of casinos and hotels for the mob. He learns that success can be short-lived when he is sexually involved with ambitious and talented Mallory Walker. His obsession drags him into a deadly vendetta against Las Vegas mobster Paul Martilini.

Reed, Barbara

Harmonic Deception. San Bernardino: Rare Sound Press, 2010.

Jazz pianist Liz Hanlon is on the verge of wider recognition. She signs a recording contract and plays in the house band in Los Angeles' hottest club, where she is celebrating. Three teenage girls disrupt the party with a violent robbery, wounding several people and killing one. Unlike the police, Hanlon rejects the random robbery theory and thinks the event was specifically targeted.

Reed, Harlan.
(series: Dan Jordan)

The Swing Music Murder. New York: Dutton, 1938.

A very drunk private eye named Dan Jordan and his girlfriend Anita are at a night club featuring Lance Grandy's Swing Swing Boys when the bandleader is murdered during a break. Songwriter Harry Evans, who claims Grandy stole a song from him, is arrested for Grandy's murder. Evans' friend, Stanley J. Leighton hires Jordan to find the murderer and clear Evans.

Reeves, Robert.

"Danse Macabre." In Penzler. Otto, (ed.). Pulp Fiction: The Dames. London: Querus, 2008.

Firpo Cole is a small-time pickpocket, who hangs around the Tango Palace dance hall and is in love with Ruth Bailey. But she's infatuated with Juggar Callahan, the bandleader and club owner, who's interested in torch singer, Mona Leeds. Bailey allows Cole to escort her home nightly. After a public fight with Leeds, she confides to him that someone put $500 in her pocketbook. The next morning Bailey is dead and he's a murder suspect. He thinks Callahan is the killer.

Rich, Nathaniel.

King Zeno. London: MCD, 2018; New York: Farrar, Straus & Giroux, 2018.

Americans, blacks and Italians were the dominant ethnic groups in 1918 New Orleans. American Police Detective William Bastrop returned from the war a public hero but in reality had been a coward. One of the men he betrayed followed him to New Orleans seeking revenge. Isadore Zeno is a black trumpet player trying to make a living with his jazz band playing fancy hotels and large venues. But to finance himself, he turns to crime. Beatrice Vizzini is the widow of an Italian crime boss and owner of a large construction company. She's determined to become a legitimate business-woman but her son might be the axe murderer.

Rieman, Terry.

<u>Vamp Till Ready</u>. London: Gollancz, 1955; New York: Harper, 1954.
Radio singer Gerda Leedon was once a protégée of diva Sari Aranyi and remains a part of her life. When three people connected to Aranyi are murdered, her problems become Leedon's problems. While trying to unwind in the midst of an intense police investigation, Gerda, her boyfriend Nicky, a celebrity-gangster Max and his lawyer Abner catch a late-night set by Turk Murphy's jazz band at the Italian Village.

Roberts, Les.

"Jazz Canary." In Randisi. Robert J., (ed.). <u>Murder and all that Jazz</u>.. New York: Signet, 2004.
Singer Kate O'Dwyer asks PI Milan Jacovitch for protection from her ex-husband, Charlie Hapgood, who is pressuring her for money. O'Dwyer unexpectedly reverses herself and tells him everything is settled with Charlie. Jacovitch suspects that it isn't.

Robinson, Peter.
(series: Alan Banks)

<u>A Necessary</u> End. London: Viking, 1989; New York: Scribners, 1989.
An anti-nuclear demonstration in the quiet town of Eastvale turns violent, resulting in the stabbing death of a police officer. London dispatches Superintendent "Dirty Dick" Burgess of the anti-terrorism squad to find the killer. Chief Inspector Alan Banks remembers and dislikes Burgess from his London days. Burgess is sure that the killer is at "Maggie's Farm," an isolated farm where the demonstration planners live. Meanwhile, Banks looks into the slain officer's past for a motive.

In a Dry Season. London: Macmillan, 2000; New York: Morrow, 1999.

A summer drought dried the Thornfield Reservoir revealing the abandoned village of Hobb's End, flooded forty years earlier to build the Reservoir. A child playing in the area discovers a skeleton, later identified as Gloria Shackleton, a "land girl" from London. She worked on a local farm and married Matthew Shackleton, who never returned from the war in Burma. Detective Chief Alan Banks interviews the former residents of Hobb's End and the American soldiers once stationed at the nearby base to uncover the killer's identity.

Aftermath. London: Macmillan, 2001; New York: Morrow, 2001.

Two young police constables (PC) respond to a domestic violence call, and discover Lucy Paine unconscious in the hallway. Her husband, Terence, is hiding in the basement near a staked-out body. PC Dennis Morrissey is killed by Paine. PC Janet Taylor can only subdue him with deadly force. Payne is later confirmed to be the serial killer known as "the Chameleon." Chief Inspector Alan Banks is unsure of Lucy's role in events and questions are raised about the police's use of excessive force.

Playing With Fire. London: Macmillan, 2004; New York: Morrow, 2004.

Two houseboats burn on a lonely stretch of the Eastvale Canal, killing their occupants. After arson is established, Chief Inspector Alan Banks has no shortage of suspects, including a member of his own investigative team. A second incident seemingly establishes art forgery as the arsonist's motive. But Banks isn't satisfied and his doubt almost costs him his life.

(non-series)

"The Magic of Your Touch." In Randisi. Robert J., (ed.). Murder and all that Jazz. New York: Signet, 2004.

The narrator, a Toronto jazz musician, hears an elderly black man playing a song near an outside brazier. He kills him for the song that becomes popular and the base of his career. He becomes obsessed by his song and seeking relief, goes for a walk in the Toronto night.

Rodriguez, Andres.

"Yesterdays." In Paul. Steve, (ed.). <u>Kansas City Noir</u>. London and New York: Akashic, 2012.

Milton Morris, the owner of Milton's Tap Room, a bar that had been open since Prohibition, has disappeared. The Tap Room no longer featured live music but played jazz recordings. By closing time, Tom, the long-time bartender, becomes concerned. A drunk bangs on the door to tell Tom a doubtful story that the mob is after Morris. After a few weeks pass, Tom concludes that Morris chose to disappear.

Roeburt, John.

<u>Sing Out Sweet Homicide</u>. New York: Dell, 1961.

Reporter Scott Norris doesn't believe the death of numbers runner Charles "Soapy" Durant was a simple case of hit-and-run by a drunk driver. His discovery that the widow, a dancer named Phyllis, was once the girlfriend of gang boss Sky Matson and that the Durants had seven bank accounts brings blackmail into the picture.

Ronald, James.

<u>Death Croons the Blues</u>. London: Hodder & Stoughton, 1934; New York: Phoenix, 1940.

Billy Cuffy stumbles upon the body of American blues singer Adele Valee while robbing her apartment. Terrified, he noisily races down the fire escape, alerting neighbors and the police. He seeks refuge in a boarding house inhabited by crime reporter Julian Mendoza, who convinces him to surrender to the police on burglary charges. Meanwhile, Mendoza seeks the murderer of the blues diva who was also a blackmailer.

Runcie, James.
(James Robert Runcie)
(series: Sydney Chambers)

"A Matter of Time." In <u>Sidney Chambers and the Shadow of Death</u>. London & New York: Bloomsbury, 2012.

Sidney Chambers, the vicar of Grantchester, hears American jazz singer, Gloria Dee, at a Soho jazz club owned by his sister Jennifer's boyfriend, Johnny Johnson's family. He's charmed by Johnny's younger sister, Claudette who works as a waitress. Gloria's music captivates Sidney until it's interrupted by the discovery of Claudette's body. She had just broken up with her boyfriend who emerges as the prime suspect. But Chambers is convinced of the boy's innocence.

Sallis, James.
(series: Lew Griffin)

<u>Blue Bottle</u>. London: No Exit, 1999; New York: Walker, 1999.

Lew Griffin is shot in the head as he is leaving a music club with an older, white woman. It takes him about a year to regain his sight but he still has little memory of the shooting incident. Was the shooter after him or the woman? Paralleling his search for understanding is his investigation into the disappearance of a writer who knew the woman.

Sanchez, Thomas.

<u>King Bongo</u>. New York: Knopf, 2003.

King Bongo, a Cuban-American hustler and dynamic bongo player, is celebrating New Year's Eve 1957 at the Tropicana Nightclub when a bomb goes off, killing his girlfriend, Mercedes. His sister, a featured dancer known as the Panther, is missing. A powerful secret policeman, Humberto Zapata, suspects Bongo's involvement with the anti-Batista opposition and his interest hinders Bongo's search for his sister.

Saunders, David.
(series: Frank Balliger)

M Squad. New York: Dell, 1962.

In this spin-off from the 1960s jazz-laced television show, Police Lieutenant Frank Ballinger must uncover a serial cop killer before he becomes a victim. Ballinger's certainty of the killer's identity blind him to the fact that there may be more than two cop killers on the streets of Chicago.

Scheen, Kjersti.

"Moonglow." In Hutchings, Janet. (ed.). Passport to Crime. New York: Carroll & Graf, 2007.

PI Margaret Moss is hired to eavesdrop on an annual dinner of Herman and three friends at the Theatre Café. Someone stole a collection of jazz 78s from Herman during a country weekend in 1967. He believes the thief is finally ready to confess and wants Moss as a witness. But the suspected thief collapses from possible shellfish poisoning that actually is murder. It seems the record theft was only a minor matter in the events of that weekend 40 years ago.

Sheridan, Sara.
(series: Mirabelle Bevin)

London Calling. London: Polygon, 2013.

Lindon Claremont, a young black sax player, is the prime suspect in the disappearance from a Soho jazz club of Rose Bellamy Gore, an eighteen-year-old debutante. He flees to Brighton to seek help from his friend Vesta and her boss Mirabelle Bevan, a former secret agent. They convince him to surrender to the police. Shortly thereafter, he's discovered dead in his jail cell, an apparent suicide. Convinced of his innocence in Rose's disappearance, Mirabelle turns her detecting skills to uncover the truth.

Shurman, Ida.

<u>Death Beats the Band</u>. New York: Phoenix, 1943.

Bandleader Andy Parker is shot while singing his hit song, "Headlined In My Heart" at the Long House Casino. Bass player Jack Coler, an amateur detective, tries to uncover the killer among the musicians and guests isolated at the club by a blizzard. Then tenor player Tony Carezzi, the band's marijuana supplier, is murdered. Coler has a surplus of suspects as both men were disliked by the band.

Skinner, Robert.
(series: Wesley Farrell)

<u>Skin Deep, Blood Red</u>. New York: Kensington, 1998.

Wesley Farrell, a Creole club owner passing as white in New Orleans, is blackmailed by gangster Emile Gans into finding the murderer of crooked cop, Chance Tartaglia. Also investigating the murder is Police Inspector Francis Casey, who suspected Tartaglia's corruption. As they work both sides of the color line, Casey knows they have more in common than finding a killer.

<u>Cat-Eyed Trouble</u>. New York: Kensington, 1998.

Black Detective Israel Daggert has been released from Angola prison after serving five years for the murder of drug dealer Junior Obregon. He was innocent and is determined to find the real killer. When Daggert's fiancée, Lottie Sonnier is murdered, jazz club owner Savanna Beaulieu asks Wesley Farrell to find her killer. Frank Casey, Chief Detective of the New Orleans Police, thinks the two murders are linked. Both men follow a deadly trail leading to Stella Bascomb, known as "the Cat-Eyed Woman".

<u>Daddy's Gone A-Hunting</u>. Scottsdale: Poisoned Pen Press, 1999.

Ernie LeDoux returns to New Orleans after serving a ten-year sentence in Angola prison for a $75,000 armored car robbery. But the man who held the loot for LeDoux is dead and his widow is clearly living above her means. Also interested in the stolen money is Archie Badeaux, the muscle for mobster Jonathan Lincoln, whose daughter was LeDoux's girlfriend. Club owner Carol Donovan claims to have been threatened by Badeaux and goes to Wes Farrell for help. Her real target is, however, Lincoln.

Blood to Drink. Scarsdale: Poisoned Pen Press, 2000.

Towards the end of Prohibition, jazz club owner Wes Farrell was riding in a car with Coast Guard Commander George Schofield, who was killed by a shotgun blast. Five years later, Schofield's younger brother, James, a U.S. Treasury Agent, arrives in New Orleans with a list of suspects. Farrell realizes that if he doesn't uncover George's killer, James will blunder into trouble and cause problems for him. At the same time, Frank Casey, the Chief of The Detective Bureau, is investigating the death of a black detective.

Pale Shadow. Scottsdale: Poisoned Pen Press, 2001.

Linda Blanc, the girlfriend of Wesley Farrell's old bootlegging partner, Luis Martinez, is tortured to death. A similar fate befalls Martinez cousin, Wisteria Mullins. Luis apparently branched out into counterfeiting and is hunted by a blonde Spaniard named Santiago Compasso. But Martinez is an organizer, not the boss of the ring. Regardless, Farrell knows Luiz is in over his head.

The Righteous Cut. Phoenix: Poisoned Pen Press, 2002.

The daughter of corrupt New Orleans councilman Whitman Richards has been kidnapped. He is forced to shut down police Captain Frank Casey's investigation out of fear that his illegal activities will be uncovered. Richards' estranged wife Georgina, asks her old boyfriend, jazz club owner Wesley Farrell, for help in finding her daughter.

Skvorecky, Josef.
(series: Lieutenant Boruvka, Eve Adam)

"That Sax Solo." In <u>The Mournful Demeanor of Lieutenant Boruvka</u>, Toronto,: Lester & Orpen Dennys, 1973; New York: Norton, 1987.
Lieutenant Boruvka's past as a saxophone player helps him break an alibi and discover the killer of the vocalist in a band.

<u>Sins for Father Knox</u>. London: Faber & Faber, 1989; New York: Norton, 1988.
A collection of short stories, two of which feature Czech police Lieutenant Boruvka, and all of which involve Eve Adam, a night club singer with a talent for crime solving, who travels the world earning hard currency for the State Concert Agency. Each of the ten stories violates one of the set rules of writing detective stories established by Father Ronald Knox in 1929.

"A Question of Alibis." In <u>Sins for Father Knox</u>. London: Faber & Faber, 1989; New York: Norton, 1988;
Sitting at the bar, Mr. Jensen tells singer Eve Adam that he is going to be murdered. Later in the evening, after Jensen is killed along with the hotel clerk and nosey Mrs. Ericson, Eve wonders if there are two Mr. Jensens.

"An Atlantic Crossing." In <u>Sins for Father Knox</u>. London: Faber & Faber, 1989; New York: Norton, 1988.
Returning to Europe from New York by sea, singer Eve Adam encounters a Japanese man responsible for the wartime murder of one passenger's brother and another's family. He disappears.

"Intimate Business, An." In <u>Sins for Father Knox</u>. London: Faber & Faber, 1989. New York: Norton, 1988.
Using singer Eve Adam's intuition, police Lieutenant Boruvka clears Adam, who was convicted of murdering a movie producer.

Boruvka hopes Adam will join the police but she opts to work abroad as a singer, earning hard currency for the regime.

"Just Between Us Girls" In <u>Sins for Father Knox</u>. London: Faber & Faber, 1989; New York: Norton, 1988.

Singer Eve Adam, who's now working in Paris, has a new boy-friend, "Cool Jean". But he turns out to be someone's husband.

"The Man Eve Didn't Know From Adam," In <u>Sins for Father Knox</u>. London: Faber & Faber, 1989. New York: Norton, 1988.

While working in Italy, singer Eve Adam and a friend are having a mountainside picnic when she observes the driver of a white sports car pick up a Danish hitchhiker, who is later murdered.

"The Mathematicians of Grizzly Drive," In <u>The Sins for Father Knox</u>. London: Faber & Faber, 1989; New York: Norton, 1988.

While singing in a San Francisco bar named The Sailor's Dream, Eve Adams meets the Berkeley mathematics crowd and discovers a formula that is the answer to a kidnapping.

"Miscarriage of Justice." In <u>Sins for Father Knox</u>. London: Faber & Faber, 1989. New York: Norton, 1988.

Singer Eve Adam is working in upstate New York when she is charged with arson. She knows the identity of the real arsonist, Bob Cornhill, who was trying to kill his mother-in-law. After clearing herself of the crime, she has difficulty proving Cornhill's guilt.

"Mistake in Hitzungee." In <u>Sins for Father Knox</u>. London: Faber & Faber, 1989. New York: Norton, 1988.

Eve Adam is singing in Sweden when she encounters Mr. Mac, who mistakes her for the woman who hired him to kill a blackmailer. But someone has beaten Mr. Mac to his target and Eve's friend, Zuzka, an exotic dancer, is the prime suspect. Eve must find the real killer to clear Zuzka.

"The Third Tip of the Triangle." In <u>Sins for Father Knox</u>. London:

Faber & Faber, 1989; New York: Norton, 1988.

Back in Prague, singer Eve Adams helps Lieutenant Boruvka solve a murder involving homosexual jealousy.

"Why So Many Shamuses?" In <u>Sins for Father Knox</u>. London: Faber & Faber, 1989; New York: Norton, 1988.

Singer Eve Adam, now working in Manhattan, chats up PI Mc-Grogan, who's tailing Connie Starrett and several admirers. Mc-Grogan, Connie, an ex-actor named Leary, and two detectives, end up dead. Adam's detecting skills assist New York Police Detective Raglin in solving the case.

"Pirates." In <u>The End of Lieutenant Boruvka</u>. London: Faber & Faber, 1990; New York: Norton, 1990.

Lieutenant Borovka learns of a plan to spirit a child, whose parents fled during the Soviet invasion, out of the country. He allows the escape and ends up in jail only to be helped by his old friend, singer Eve Adam.

<u>The Return of Lieutenant Boruvka</u>. London: Faber & Faber, 1990; New York: Norton, 1991.

After singer Eve Adam arranged his escape from a Prague jail, former police Lieutenant Boruvka is living in exile in Toronto and working as a parking lot attendant. But he uses his detecting skills to find the murderer of Heather Donby, a promiscuous young woman. The story fills out the relationship between Adam and Boruvka-but other than that, there is no jazz content.

Slovo, Gillian.
(series: Kate Baeier)

<u>Morbid Symptoms</u>. London: Pluto, 1984; New York: Dembner, 1985.

Kate Baeier, an alto sax playing, free-lance writer and researcher, is hired by the surviving members of the African Economic Reports collective to investigate the death of Tim Nicholson, who died in an elevator shaft. The wealthy, left wing playboy, who financed the AER, was researching ties between South Africa and Argentina and a joint "secret project." While officially Richardson's death is dismissed as an accident, others have reason to doubt this finding.

Death Comes Staccato. London: Women's Press, 1987; New York: Doubleday, 1988.

Marion Weatherby hires Kate Baeier to discover the identity of a man always in the audience when her young daughter, Alicia, a talented violinist and pianist, gives a performance. The man is James Morgan, a music impresario, who specializes in developing young musicians. At a concert's end, Baeier discovers Alicia standing over Morgan's body in a stairwell, babbling that she killed him. Baier manages to get Alicia away from the crime scene but is later suspected of the murder and reluctantly released only to find Mrs. Weatherby no longer requiring her services.

Death by Analysis. London: The Woman's Press, 1986; New York: Doubleday, 1988.

Kate Baeier's ex-therapist Franca asks her to look into the death of her friend, psychoanalyst Paul Holland, who died in a hit-and-run accident. She concludes that he was murdered and that his killer could be found among a group of patients who share a radical, political past.

Catnap. London: Michael Joseph, 1994; New York: St. Martin's, 1996.

Kate Baier's brief return to London is extended when she experiences unexpected harassment. She had spent five years as a war correspondent after the death of her lover Sam in a hit-and-run accident. Sensing that the source of her current difficulties might lie in the past, she re-examines her old cases that were abandoned when she hastily closed up her detective agency. At the back of her mind is the fear that Sam's death might have been connected to her work.

Close Call. London: Michael Joseph, 1995.

Kate Baeier is asked to find policewoman Janet Morris, who called in a rape complaint, and then disappeared from the same police station where Baier is writing a personality piece on Chief Superintendent Rodney Ellis. While wandering around the station looking for the elusive Morris, she stumbles upon the body of James Shaw. Shortly thereafter, the police raid Baeier's house and discover a planted bag of heroin.

Smith, C. W.

"The Plantation Club." In Breton, Marcela. (ed.). Hot and Cool Jazz Stories. New York: Plume, 1990.

After hearing bebop coming from the Plantation Club, a night-club in the town's small black ghetto, two high school jazz enthusiasts befriend alto player Curtis "Stoogie" Goodman. He encourages their music and they become self-styled beatniks. When they are busted for two marijuana cigarettes, they fearfully identify their source, "Stoogie" Goodman, who has already served time on drug charges.

Smith, J. P.

Body and Soul. New York: Grove, 1987.

Jazz pianist Jerzy Wozzeck has a marginal existence playing at "the Club" in Paris. He is recruited by his best friend, Andrej Kupki into a mysterious scheme of delivering packages for Unirex that contain drugs. To ensure his loyalty, Unirex entrap and frame him for murder. Hoping to escape to London, Wozzeck finds his only way out is through cold-blooded murder.

Smith, Julie.
(series: Skip Langdon)

New Orleans Mourning. New York: St. Martin's, 1990.

It's Mardi Gras in New Orleans and the King of the Carnival, civic leader Chauncey St. Amant, is shot during the Rex Parade. Rookie

Policewoman Skip Langdon, who grew up in New Orleans society, is grudgingly brought into the case. Probing the secrets of Chauncey's life and his dysfunctional family, she suspects his killer may be a former secretary. After being stalked by the killer, she realizes her mistake.

The Axeman's Jazz. New York: St. Martin's, 1991.
A serial killer terrorized New Orleans in 1919. In notes to the press, he claimed that he would spare the lives of those who played jazz in their homes. Seemingly, in 1991, the Axeman has returned. Assigned to this baffling murder case, Detective Skip Langdon realizes that the victims and their killer became acquainted in self-help therapy groups.

Jazz Funeral. New York: Ballantine, 1993.
The producer of the New Orleans Jazz and Heritage Festival Hamson Brocato is murdered and his sixteen-year-old sister Melody is missing. Did she kill her brother or see his killer? New Orleans police officer Skip Langton knows Melody holds the key to the killing and must find her among the runaways in the French Quarter before the killer.

House of Blues. London: Books Brimble, 2013; New York: Fawcett, 1995.
During a Monday night family dinner, Arthur Hebert, a famous restaurateur, is shot. When Skip Langton appears at the crime scene, his daughter Reed, her husband Dennis and their daughter Sally are missing. Initially, she believes it to be a kidnapping gone awry. After a night of booze and blues at the House of Blues, Hebert's son Grady decides to take Langdon through the family labyrinth to understand the case. At the same time, she stumbles into another deadly family quarrel involving the Mafia.

(series: Talba Wells)

"Kid Trombone." In Randisi, Robert J. (ed.) Murder and all that Jazz. New York: Signet, 2004.

Singer Queenie Feran tells Talba Wells that her ex-husband Dupree Howell was murdered because of "what he knew." Her investigation reveals knowledge about the street drug trade and an understanding of family pride.

Smith, Martin Cruz.

Stallion Gate. London: Collins Harvill, 1986; New York: Random, 1986.

Sergeant Joe Pena, a talented jazz pianist, is released from the army stockade to provide security for his childhood friend, Robert Oppenheimer, who is supervising the development of the atomic bomb at Los Alamos. Pena is supposed to inform Captain Augustino of Oppenheimer's activities as the Captain is convinced that "Oppie" is a Soviet agent. Pena uncovers the treachery of Klaus Fuchs, a Soviet agent. But that is of no interest to Augustino who is obsessed with Oppie.

Sonin, Ray.

The Dance Band Mystery. London: Kimsley, 1940.

Drummer Nick Lomas is murdered during a recording session of George Grayson's band. Tipped to the story, Dance Band News' reporter and former jazz pianist Sam Underhill sneaks into the studio crime scene and encounters Scotland Yard's John Adams. Their shared investigation unexpectedly expands beyond the murder into narcotics and involvement of American gangsters.

Spicer, Bart.
(series: Carney Wilde)

Blues For the Prince. London: Collins, 1951; New York: Dodd, Mead, 1950.

The famous black trumpet player Harold Morton Prince, known as "The Prince," was murdered and police are holding his arranger, Stuff McGee, as his killer. McGee claimed that he, not the Prince, composed the music that made the Prince legendary. PI Carney Wilde is retained by the Prince's family to investigate his death and uncover his killer.

Steele, Colleen.

"Them There Eyes." In The Ladies Killing Circle, (eds.). <u>Bone Dance</u>. Toronto: Rendezvous, 2003.

Harry Finley plays trumpet in a swing band that works in summer resorts. He is aware of an attractive young woman watching and following him from gig to gig. Every time he leaves the bandstand to try and talk, she leaves. Finally, after loosing his concentration and his job, he catches up with her, only to uncover a case of mistaken identity.

Stevens, Kevin.

<u>Reaching The Shining River</u>. Paris: Betimes, 2014.

County prosecutor Emmet Whelan, who married into a socially and politically prominent Kansas City family, is urged to investigate the murder of a black jazz musician. The K.C. ruling families, who were pushed out of power by the Pendergast political machine, hope to tie Pendergast to the murder. Blinded in pursuit of his investigation, Whelan is unaware of how many lives will be jeopardized by its outcome.

Tate, Sylvia.

<u>Never By Chance</u>. New York: Harper, 1947.

Jazz pianist Jerry Silesc is a highly regarded Hollywood studio musician, arranger and composer. While he was walking early one morning with his fiancée Corinne Taylor, a speeding car kills her. His grieving is disrupted by a call from the coroner's office, informing him that Corinne was not the woman that he believed her to be. He becomes obsessed with discovering her true identity.

Temple, Lou Jane.
(series: Heaven Lee)

The Cornbread Killer. New York: St. Martin's, 1999.

Heaven Lee, a Kansas City restaurateur-chef is coordinating the food for the gala opening of the renovated Eighteenth and Vine Historic Music District, the accompanying jazz and blues festival and the dedication of the Negro Leagues Baseball Museum. Evelyn Edwards, the event planner, is murdered. Then Charlie Parker's famous plastic saxophone is stolen from the museum. Lee takes over some of Edward's responsibilities but is burdened with a suspicion of the thief's identity.

Terrenoire, John.

Beneath a Panamanian Moon. New York: Dunne, 2005.

John Kirby learns that there's no such thing as an ex-spy. His former boss, the mysterious Mr. Smith, pressures him into forsaking the Washington diplomatic-cocktail circuit to take a job playing jazz piano at a seedy hotel outside Panama City where the guests may be planning a New Year's coup.

Vandagriff, G.G.

Murder in the Jazz Band. Salt Lake City: Orson Whitney Press, 2020.

The brother of Oxford tutor Catherine Tregowyn and his girlfriend are arrested for the murder of James, an Oxford saxophonist and jazz bandleader. Both are eventually released but the police charge Joe, a jazz trombonist in James' band, with the murder. At the same time, one of Catherine's best students, Beryl Favringham is undergoing a personal crisis and disappears. She had been secretly involved with James.

Vining, Keith.

Keep Running. Chicago: Chicago Paperback House, 1962,

Jack Norman had one of the best bands in New Orleans until

he got involved with a singer named Gerry. She was actually the mistress of mob boss Tony Reik, who is slowly taking over the club scene. Before Jack understands what's going on, he's a part of Tony's operation. When he wants out, he's framed for murder and forced to flee for his life. In Gulf City, Florida he takes a job at a resort club, only to realize that Tony's mob has targeted it and that Gerry is the band's new vocalist.

Wainwright, John.
(John William Wainwright)

<u>Do Nothin' till You Hear from Me</u>. London: Macmillan, 1977; New York: St. Martin's, 1977.

Bandleader Lucky Luckhurst receives a severed ear and a ransom note for his wife, Shirley. It's a mistake as his wife is standing beside him with both her ears. He takes the ear and note to the police, who release him after a thorough questioning. Luckhurst is determined to find the person for whom the ear and ransom note were intended.

Wallop, Douglas.

<u>Night Light</u>. New York: Norton, 1953.

On her way home from school, Robert Horne's young daughter, Barbara is shot by a sniper, who jumps or falls to his death. Horne becomes obsessed with his daughter's killer, a jazz drummer, and a need for revenge.

Walsh, Michael.

<u>And all the Saints</u>. New York: Warner, 2003.

A fictional memoir of New York gangster Owney Madden who made a fortune as a bootlegger during prohibition and became a founding member of the "Crime Commission," the governing group of organized crime. Madden owned Harlem's fabulous Cotton Club, which employed Duke Ellington and his Orchestra. His memoir provides a picture of the crime world's hold on entertainment in the Big Apple for over twenty years.

Warren, Vic.

Hong Kong Blues. San Diego: Turning Heads, 2014.
A body falling from a low-flying helicopter disrupts the wedding of Chris Girolami and jazz singer Megan Deschamps on board a ship in Victoria Harbor. The dead man, Chen Zongze, the financial head of a triad, was attempting to stop the trade in shark fins. Chris hears Zongze's dying words and forgets them. The triads, however, believe Chris knows Zongze's final words and are willing to kill for them.

Watson, I.K.

Wolves Aren't White. London: Allison & Busby, 1995.
Lennie Webb, the vocalist with Wolves Aren't White jazz band flirts with Julie Delaney, the sister of Paddy, a vicious gang lord who mysteriously reappeared from his South American exile. Webb is warned off Julie and beaten up. After an unexpected apology from Delaney, Webb discovers Julie's serious mental problems and past. He also learns that Paddy, who is dying, returned to England to expose the mob's reach into the establishment.

White, Gloria.
(series: Ronnie Ventura)

Death Notes. London: Severn House, 2005.
San Francisco PI Ronnie Ventura was present at the murder of tenor sax legend Match Margolis, who was beginning a comeback. No one in the jazz club saw the killer. His greedy, young widow, all of his friends, and music associates, seemed supportive of Margolis' attempted comeback. Ventura decides to look into his past for his killer.

White, Richard.

"Notes in the Fog." In White, David. (ed.). Charles Boeckman

Presents Johnny Nickle. Batesville, AZ: Prose Productions, 2013.

At the end of an evening's work, Johnny is approached by Julie Dominguez, who was the widow of Johnny's sax player, Phil. She tells him that Phil was murdered. Later, two thugs warn Johnny away from Julie and beat him up. Phil's brother Alan asks him to help Julie by collecting something from a locker in the Salinas bus depot. Shortly thereafter, Alan is murdered.

Whitelaw, Stella.
(series: Jordan Lacey)

Jazz and Die. London: Hale, 2014.

Jordan Lacey, a former policewoman turned private investigator, was hired on the recommendation of DCI James, to safeguard Maddy Peters, the spoiled 14-year-old daughter of the famous jazz trumpeter, Chuck Peters. Maddy's father is headlining at a jazz festival in Dorset at an outside venue. Meanwhile James is preoccupied with the recent discovery of the body of another young girl. She was killed three years earlier and had attended Maddy's school.

Wiley, Richard.

Soldiers in Hiding. London: Chatto & Windus, 1986; New York: Atlantic Monthly, 1986.

Teddy Maki and his friend Jimmy Yamamoto, Nisei (California-Japanese) jazz musicians, are stranded in Tokyo after Pearl Harbor. Drafted into the Japanese Army, Teddy Maki is ordered to shoot an American prisoner after Jimmy has refused and is killed. Haunted by the incident, Teddy, who became a Japanese television personality after the war, sees a chance for revenge on the man who ordered the senseless execution that killed Jimmy.

Williams, Kirby.
(series: Urby Brown)

<u>Rage in Paris</u>. Wainscott N.Y.: Pushcart, 2014.

Urby Brown is a Creole musician playing clarinet in Paris and working as a PI after the failure of his jazz club. He is hired by American fascist Barnet Robinson III to find his missing daughter, Daphne. She ran away from school with drummer Buster Thigpen, who Brown remembered as a thug from their shared New Orleans youth. Daphne has been kidnapped and is being held for $100,000 ransom or possibly its all been staged so she could get the money to go to Nazi Germany and marry Hitler.

<u>The Long Road from Paris</u>. Wainscott N.Y.: Pushcart Press, 2018.

Urby Brown has seemingly overcome his personal problems and reconciled with his girlfriend, Hannah Korngold. They reopened their jazz club, which has survived the economic depression. But the political strife between the fascists and the leftists, and French political instability portends a dark future when the Nazis take over Paris.

Wilson, August.

<u>Ma Rainey's Black Bottom</u>. London: Penguin, 1985; New York: Plume, 1981.

Ma Rainey and her entourage arrived at a Chicago studio to record blues standards. But the blues diva keeps everyone waiting. The tension within the band between the younger, more modern players (trumpeter Levee) and the old band members (Cutler and Toledo) reaches a boiling point. Rainey believes Levee is a troublemaker and fires him. Then Sturdyvant, the studio owner, reneges on an implied agreement decides to record Levee and his new band. In frustration, Levee turns to violence.

SHORT STORY COLLECTIONS

Albert, Richard N. (ed.).

From Blues to Bebop: A Collection of Jazz Fiction. Baton Rouge: Louisiana State University Press, 1990.
Shelby Foote's 1954 story "Ride Out" is included in this collection.

Ashley, Mike. (ed.).

The Mammoth Book of Roaring Twenties Whodunits. New York: Carroll & Graf, 2004.
A collection of 23 short stories by a mix of Anglo-American crime writers set in the 1920s. English author Ian Morson's "There Would Have Been Blood" about a feared communist uprising is included.

Asimov, Isaac, Greenberg, Martin H. & Waugh, Carol-Lynn Rossel (eds.).

Show Business is Murder. New York: Avon, 1983.
Isaac Asimov's "Mystery Tune" is included among the eighteen show business stories.

Hound Dunnit. New York: Carroll & Graf, 1987.
William Bankier's "The Dog Who Hated Jazz" is found in this collection of 17 mystery short stories having to do with dogs.

Bishop, Claude & Bruns, Don (eds.)

A Merry Band of Murderers. Scottsdale: Poisoned Pen Press, 2006.
Bill Moody's "File Under Jazz" appears in this collection of 13 stories.

Bland, Eleanor Taylor. (ed.).

Shades of Black. New York: Berkley, 2004.
   Included in this collection of 22 stories of crime and mystery written by African-American writers is Grace F. Edwards' "The Blind Alley".

Beckman, Charles.

Suspense, Suspicion & Shockers. Corpus Christi: Von Boekman Fiction Factory, 2012.
   Seven stories out of this anthology of twenty-four are about jazz. They are: "Mr. Banjo," "Run Cat Run," "A Hot Lick For Doc," "Dixieland Dirge," "The Last Trumpet," "Should A Tear Be Shed?" and "Afraid To Live."

Breton, Marcela. (ed.).

Hot and Cool: Jazz Short Stories. New York: Plume, 1990.
   C.W. Smith's "The Plantation Club" is included in this collection of jazz short stories.

Chandler, Raymond.

Collected Stories. New York: Everyman, 2002.
   Chandler's novella "The King In Yellow" appears in this collection of short fiction.

Charteris, Leslie. (ed.).

The Saint Mystery Library # 3. New York: Great American Library, 1959.
   "Murder Set to Music" by Fredric Brown is one of three stories by three authors.

Coleman, Wanda.

Jazz and Twelve O'clock Tales. Jaffrey: Black Sparrow, 2003.

Taking its title from a line in Billy Strayhorn's "Lush Life, this collection of 13 stories of lonely, lost people includes "Dunny."

Fowler, Carol S.

Blues in the Night. Houston: Strategic Book Publishing and Rights Co., 2013.
A collection of five jazz stories ("Loverman," "Born to be Blue," "And the Angels Sing," "Passion Flower," and "Blues in the Night") that feature jazz reviewer-private detective Bernie Butz.

Gorman, Ed (ed.).

The Second Black Lizard Anthology of Crime Fiction. Berkeley: Black Lizard, 1988.
Included in this collection of 37 short stories and one novel is Steve Mertz's story, "Death Blues."

Gorman, Ed, Pronzini, Bill & Greenberg, Martin. (eds.).

American Pulp. New York: Carroll & Graf, 1997.
A collection of 35 classic short stories drawn mostly from the pulps. Dorothy B. Hughes' "The Black and White Blues" is actually one of the few stories in this collection that did not originally appear in the pulps. Its source is New Copy-A Book of Stories and Sketches. New York; Columbia University Press, 1959.

Gruber, Frank.

Brass Knuckles. Los Angeles: Sherbourne, 1966.
"Words and Music" can be found in this collection of ten original stories.

Harvey, Charles. (ed.).

Jazz Parody. London: American Jazz Society, 1947.

A collection of English postwar jazz fiction that includes David Boyce's "Special Arrangement."

Harvey, John. (ed.).

Blue Lightning. London: Slow Dancer, 1998.
A collection of eighteen short stories edited by John Harvey about different kinds of music. Harvey's "Cool Blues," Charlotte Carter's "A Flower Is A Lonesome Thing" and Walter Mosley's "Blue Lightning" are among them. .

Men From Boys. New York: HarperCollins, 2003.
A collection of seventeen short stories edited by John Harvey that includes Bill Moody's jazz tale, "The Resurrection of Bobo Jones."

Minor Key. Nottingham: Five Leaves, 2009.
The story "Well, You Needn't," originally written as a give-away at the Helsinki Book Fair, appears in this signed, limited edition collection of miscellaneous stories ("Billie's Blues," "Minor Key," etc.) that were scattered in other places. Also included are six jazz poems.

Now's the Time. London: Slow Dancer, 1999.
The individual short story titles in this collection of stories by Harvey are taken from compositions by alto saxophonist Charlie Parker. The novella "Slow Burn" was adapted from a BBC Chanel 4 radio program. A suggested list of related music for listening is included at the end.

A Darker Shade of Blue. London: Arrow, 2010.
16 short stories, many from other collections, including "Billie's Blues," "Trouble in Mind," and "Favor."

Hellmann, Libby Fischer. (ed.).

Chicago Blues. Chicago: Bleak House, 2008.

Stuart Kaminsky's "Blue Note" and Kevin Guilfoile's "O Death Where is thy Sting?" are found in this collection of short stories by 21 contemporary Chicago authors.

Hoch, Edward D.

The Ripper of Storyville. Norfolk: Crippen & Landau, 2003.
A collection of 14 stories about 19th century gunman Ben Snow. The title story, "The Ripper of Storyville" is set in the redlight district of New Orleans.

Hutchings, Janet. (ed.).

Passport To Crime. New York: Carroll & Graf, 2007.
Kjersti Scheen's "Moonglow" is one of the 26 stories from 15 countries collected from Ellery Queen's Mystery Magazine.

Irish, William.

The Dancing Detective. New York: Lippincott, 1946.
"The Dancing Detective" is included in Irish's eight stories.

Jakubowski, Maxim. (ed.).

The Best British Mysteries IV. London: Allison & Busby, 2006.
Thirty British mysteries that include John Harvey's "Home" featuring Charlie Resnick.

Paris Noir. London: Serpent's Tail, 2007.
John Harvey's "Minor Key" is included in this collection of eighteen dark tales set in "The City of Light".

Kane, Henry.

The Name is Chambers New York: Pyramid, 1960.
"One Little Bullet" is included in this collection of six short

stories featuring PI Pete Chambers.

Ladies Killing Circle, The (eds.).

<u>Bone Dance</u>. Toronto: Rendezvous, 2003.
Colleen Steele's "Them There Eyes" can be found in this crime collection of stories with music themes by Canadian women authors.

Lehman, Ernest.

<u>Sweet Smell of Success</u> by Ernest Lehman. Woodstock: Overlook, 2000.
A collection of Ernest Lehman's short fiction about Hollywood and Broadway. Along with two novelettes, <u>Sweet Smell of Success</u> and <u>The Comedian</u>, it also contains thirteen short stories.

Manson, Cynthia & Halligan, Kate (eds.)

<u>Murder to Music</u>. New York: Carroll & Graf, 1997.
A selection of short stories that originally appeared in the Ellery Queen Mystery Magazine and the Alfred Hitchcock Mystery Magazine which have to do with music and mystery. Three stories, Doug Allyn's "The Sultans of Soul," William Bankier's "Concerto for Violence and Orchestra" and John Lutz's "The Right to Sing The Blues" are jazz related.

Moody, Bill.

<u>Mood Swings</u>. Lutz, Fl: Down & Out Books, 2015.
<u>Mood Swings</u> is a collection of nine of Bill Moody's short stories, most of which have been published in other places. Included are "The Resurrection of Bobo Jones," "Camaro Blue," "File Under Jazz," "Jazzline" and "Child's Play."

Mysterious Press Editors, The.

The Mysterious Press Anniversary Anthology. New York: Warner, 2001.
Charlotte Carter's "Birdbath" is one of the editor's choices.

Paul, Steve. (ed.)

Kansas City Noir. New York: Akashic, 2012.
Andres Rodriguez's story "Yesterdays" appears in this collection of fourteen short stories about Kansas City.

Penzler, Otto. (ed.).

Pulp Fiction: The Dames. London: Quercus, 2007.
Robert Reeves' story "Dance Macabre" is included in the twenty-three collected stories.

Queen, Ellery. (ed.).

Ellery Queen's Awards: Eleventh Series. New York: Simon & Schuster, 1956.
Veronica Parker's "Mr. Hyde-de-Ho" was among the Second Prize winners in this annual Ellery Queen Mystery Magazine contest collection.

Ellery Queen's Awards: Twelfth Series. New York: Simon & Schuster, 1957.
Robert Bloch's classic "Dig That Crazy Grave!" for which he won a second prize is included in this collection of stories from the annual Ellery Queen Mystery Magazine contest collection.

Randisi, Robert J. (ed.).

Murder and all that Jazz. New York: Signet: 2004.
A collection of thirteen short stories, eleven of which deal with jazz while the other two are set in the Jazz Age. Themes run the gamut from stolen aspirations to stolen drugs; and the settings are as varied as Jazz Age Cincinnati, and 50s London, to contemporary

L.A. Authors included in this collection are Craig Holden, John Lutz, Martin Meyers, Max Allen Collins and Matthew V. Clemens, John Harvey, Peter Robinson, Bill Moody, Michael Connelly, Les Roberts, Julie Smith, Ed Gorman, Laura Lippman and Robert J. Randisi. The idea for the anthology came to Randisi while watching the movie, *Chicago*.

Robinson, Peter. (ed.).

Penguin Book of Crime Stories. New York: Penguin, 2007.
John Harvey's "Just Friends" is included in this international collection by 15 crime writers.

Runcie, James.

Sidney Chambers and the Shadow of Death. London & New York: Bloomsbury.
"A Matter of Death" is one of six stories in this Grantchester collection.

Skvorecky, Josef.

The End of Lieutenant Boruvka. New York: Norton, 1975.
Five short stories reflect the increasing disenchantment of jazz loving Lieutenant Boruvka until he reaches his breaking point after the Soviet invasion. Singer Eve Adam, whom he rescued from jail, repays the favor.

The Mournful Demeanor of Lieutenant Borouvka. New York: Norton, 1987.
A collection of a dozen short stories that feature the crime solving skills of the jazz loving Prague policeman, Lieutenant Boruvka. Only one story, "That Sax Solo" has to do with jazz.

Sins For Father Knox by Josef Skvorecky. New York: Norton, 1988.

A collection of 10 crime stories, featuring Czech singer (and amateur sleuth), Eve Adam, who travels around the world earning hard currency for the Polish government.

Smith, Julie. (ed.).

New Orleans Noir. New York: Akashic, 2007.

A collection of eighteen pre-K and post-K (Katrina) short stories about New Orleans. David Fulmer's "Algiers" and Barbara Hambly's "There Shall Be Your Heart Also" are the two historical stories included in this volume.

Spillane, Mickey & Collins, Max Allen (eds.).

A Century of Noir. New York: American Library, 2002.

A collection of 32 noir classics that includes one jazz story, James M. Cain's "Cigarette Girl" and a second one by Ed Gorman, "The Reason Why" which has a character who likes jazz, especially Dakota Staton.

Vega, Eddie. (ed.)

Noir Nation International Crime No. 6. Middletown, DE: Noir Nation, 2017.

Vega edited this uneven collection of 14 jazz short stories that included Brendan DuBois' "The Lady Meets the Blues" and Gary Phillips' "The Performer."

White, Steve. (ed.).

Charles Boeckmann Presents Johnny Nickle. Batesville, AZ: Prose Productions, 2013.

Two novellas or long short stories are collected that feature Charles Boeckmann's character Johnny Nickle: Brad Mengel's "The Devil You Know" and Richard White's "Notes in the Fog."

Jazz
Discography

This jazz discography lists the music mentioned in the short stories and novels that comprise <u>Undertones</u>. When specific music has not been mentioned, I have attempted to find music that reflects the story. Almost everything listed is in compact disc (CD) format. Jazz CDs go out of print faster than other forms of music, so some listings may not be available or may have been replaced by newer compilations by the time of publication of <u>Undertones</u>. Consequently, I have listed the label but not specific catalog numbers. Regard this as a guide; it's the best I can offer. Happy listening....

Aaronovitch, Aaron. <u>Moon Over Soho</u>. London: Gollancz, 2011; New York: Ballantine, 2011.

Coleman Hawkins. *Body and Soul Revisited* (Verve, 1992).

Constable Peter Grant hears strains of "Body and Soul" coming from murdered musicians. Coleman Hawkins recorded the definitive version in October 1939 and numerous other times in his career. *Body and Soul Revisited* contains the 1939 version as well as one recorded in January 1956.

Allyn, Doug. "The Jukebox King," In *Alfred Hitchcock's Mystery Magazine*. Vol. 47. No.6. June 2002.

John Lee Hooker performs on stage in Brownie's Lounge.

John Lee Hooker: *The Ultimate Collection 1948-1990* (Rhino, 1991).

"The Sultans of Soul," In Manson, Cynthia & Halligan, Kate (eds.).

Murder To Music. New York: Carroll & Graf, 1997.

Nothing specific is mentioned but the Flamingos sang the sort of music in the story. *The Best of the Flamingos* (Rhino, 1990).

Anderson, Beth. Night Sounds. San Diego: Clocktower, 2000.

Larry Willis' quartet is a bit older than Joe Barbarello's group but they play his kind of jazz. Larry Willis: *The Offering* (High Note, 2008).

Asimov, Isaac. "Mystery Tune." In Waugh, Carol-Lynn Rossel, Greenberg, Martin Harry & Asimov, Isaac (eds.). Show Business is Murder. New York: Avon, 1983.

Eighty-eight plays second-rate jazz clubs. King Fleming's style seems similar to that of the murdered piano player.

King Fleming: *The King Fleming Songbook* (Southport, 1996).

Atkins, Ace. Crossroad Blues. New York: St. Martin's, 1998.

Blues historian Nick Travers is after nine lost Robert Johnson recordings that have already cost one collector his life.

Robert Johnson: *King of the Delta Blues Singers* (Columbia, 1998).

_____. Dark End of the Street. New York: Morrow, 2002.

Ace Atkins is looking for Clyde James, a once-famous soul singer, who sounded like Otis Redding.

Otis Redding: *The Dock of the Bay* (Elektra/Warner, 1991).

Carla Thomas: *The Best of Carla Thomas: The Singles Plus 1968-1973* (Stax, 1993).

_____. Leavin' Trunk Blues. New York: St. Martins, 2000.

Muddy Waters, Little Walter, and Etta James were all on Southside jukeboxes.

Muddy Waters: *The Chess Box* (Chess, 1989).

Little Walter: *His Best* Chess 50th Anniversary Collection (Fontana/MCA, 1997).

Etta James: *The Best of Etta James* (MCA, 1999).

Avery, Robert. <u>Murder on the Downbeat</u>. New York: W.H. Wise, 1944.

Bobby Gordon and Dave McKenna: *Clarinet Blue* (Arbors, 2000) features the sort of jazz that murdered clarinetist Steve Sisson would have played. Newspaper man Malachy Bliss and his girlfriend, Julie Mitchell frequented 52nd Street jazz clubs and would have heard both Dizzy Gillespie and Charlie Parker.

Dizzy Gillespie Big Band: *Showtime at The Spotlite* (Uptown, 2008).

Charlie Parker: *Bird at The Roost* (Savoy, 1988).

Bader, Jerry. "Killer Jazz." In <u>Noir 1</u>. London & New York: MRP-WEBMEDIA, 2018.

Jazz pianist Maurice Delbourne's father, reggae icon Dickerson, was a Bob Marley-like musician. Marley is best featured on the 2 CD set, *Bob Marley Live!* (Tuff Gong, 2017). Reggae frames the story.

Bankier, William. "Concerto For Violence and Orchestra." In Manson, Cynthia & Halligan, Kathleen (eds). <u>Murder To Music</u>. New York: Carroll & Graf, 1981.

American Al Cohn and his Dutch sidemen play standards that catches the mood, if not the precise music of Bones Cornfield.

Al Cohn: *Rifftide* (Timeless, 2010).

_____. "The Dog Who Hated Jazz". In Asimov, Isaac, Greenberg, Martin H., Waugh, Carol-Lynn Rossel (eds.). <u>Hound Dunnit</u>. New York: Carroll & Graf, 1987.

Oscar Peterson, Art Tatum and Teddy Wilson influenced blind pianist Joe Benson.

Oscar Peterson: *Oscar Peterson Plays Standards* (Verve, 1987).

Art Tatum: *The Piano Starts Here* (Columbia, 1995).

Teddy Wilson: *Teddy Wilson at the Piano: Mr. Wilson* (Sony, 1990).

Barclay, Tessa. <u>A Final Discord</u>. London: Severn House, 2005.

Italian-American tenor sax player Joe Lovano, who regularly plays the European jazz festival circuit, is the sort of musician Gilles would want for his group.

Joe Lovano: *Joyous Encounter* (Blue Note, 2005). Lovano leads the group used during the 2005 European jazz festival summer season.

Gilles loved 50s jazz and would have listened to such classic albums as: Dizzy Gillespie: *Sittin' In* (Verve, 2005); and Stan Getz: *Jazz Giants '58* (Verve, 2008).

Barnes, Harper. Blue Monday. St. Louis: Patrice, 1991.

Bennie Moten, Count Basie and Andy Kirk were the top jazz musicians in Kansas City at the time of the story.

Bennie Moten: *Bennie Moten's Kansas City Orchestra (1929-1932)* (RCA Bluebird, 1990).

Count Basie and His Orchestra: *One O'clock Jump* (Decca, 1990).

Andy Kirk: *1936-1937, 1937-1938* (Classics, 1990).

Barnes, Linda. Steel Guitar. London: Houghton & Stoughton, 2002; New York: Delacorte, 1991.

Bonnie Raitt has a similar style to Carlotta Carlyle's friend, singer Dee Willis.

Bonnie Raitt: *Road Tested* (Capitol. 1995).

Batten, Jack. Blood Count. Toronto: Macmillan, 1991.

Duke Ellington: *...And His Mother Called Him Bill* (RCA, 1987), Ellington's tribute to his friend and collaborator, Billy Strayhorn contains "Blood Count."

During much of the book, Crang is reading singer Mel Torme's biography. The four- volume set, Mel Torme: *Jazz and Velvet* (Properbox, 2004) and *Mel Torme and the Marty Paich Dek-Tetete* (Concord, 1986) offers a musical overview of Torme's career.

Birk Robinson's father is listening to Bud Powell's "Polka Dots and Moonbeams" when Crang stops by looking for him. "Polka Dots and Moonbeams" can be found on Bud Powell: *The Amazing Bud Powell Volume 2* (Blue Note, 1989).

_____. Crang Plays The Ace. Toronto: Macmillan, 1987.
While at home drinking vodka, Crang listens to Bill Evans.
Bill Evans: *You Must Believe in Spring* (Warner, 2004).
He's also a fan of 1950s Lester Young:
Lester ("Pres") Young, Roy Eldridge, Harry Edison: *Laughin' to Keep from Cryin'* (Verve, 2000) and Lester Young and Teddy Wilson: *Pres and Teddy* (Verve, 1991) are two of Pres' better albums from that period.

_____. Riviera Blues. Toronto: Macmillan 1990.
Crang listens to 1950s Billie Holiday songs.
Billie Holiday: *Music for Torching* (Verve, 1995).

_____. Straight No Chaser. Toronto: Macmillan, 1991.
Crang is a fan of tenor saxophonists Zoot Sims' and Stan Getz's early work.
Zoot Sims: *Swing King!* (Proper, 2004).
Stan Getz: *Une Anthologie 1952/1955* (Bojazz, 2007).

Beckman, Charles, Jr. "Afraid To Live." In Suspense, Suspicion & Shockers. Corpus Christi: von Boeckmann Fiction Factory.
Mamber, the blind piano player, was playing "Body and Soul" when Dan Skeel comes to talk to him about cowardice. An interesting version of that evergreen can be found on Coleman Hawkins' *Body and Soul Revisited* (Decca, 1993) with Tommy Flanagan on piano.

_____. "Dixieland Dirge." In Suspense, Suspicion and Shockers. Corpus Christi: von Boeckmann Fiction Factory, 2012.
Trumpet legend Mizz Milner had Freddie Keppard's style. His vintage recordings can be heard on Freddie Keppard: *1920 Jazz Classics* (Master Classics, 2012).

_____. Honky Tonk Girl. New York: Falcon, 1953.
Johnny Nichol's fictional group plays both "Basin Street Blues" and "Muskrat Raskrat Ramble". The arrangements on the Pete Fountain's album were, no doubt, similar to those usually played by

Nichols band while those on veteran Jack Teagarden's album were closer to *"The Ghost Album."*

Pete Fountain. *Basin Street Blues* (Ranwood, 1997).

Jack Teagarden. *Muskrat Ramble* (Just a Memory, 2002).

Drummer Miff Smith was killed while listening to early Gene Krupa recordings.

Gene Krupa. *Ballads & Bebop: Best of Columbia 1945-49* (Collectables. 2002).

_____. "A Hot Lick for Doc." In <u>Suspense, Suspicion & Shockers</u>. Corpus Christi: von Boeckmann Fiction Factory, 2012.

Ramon the young clarinetist plays "What Is This Thing Called Love." Artie Shaw's version can be found on Artie Shaw: *The Swing Era: The Music of 1937-1938, Vol. 1.* (Hallmark, 2008).

_____. "The Last Trumpet," In <u>Suspense, Suspicion & Shockers</u>. Corpus Christi: von Boeckmann, 2012.

No specific music is mentioned but Bobby Hackett had a career that ran from jazz's early days through the 1950s and beyond.

Bobby Hackett: *What A Wonderful World* (Sony, 1990).

_____. "Mr. Banjo." In <u>Suspicion, Suspense & Shockers</u>. Corpus Christ: von Boeckmann Fiction Factory, 2012.

The style of banjo that Roger Spencer learned from Mr. Banjo, the street corner musician, can be found in *Altemont, Black Stringband Music from The Library of Congress* (Rounder, 1998).

_____. "Run Cat Run." In <u>Suspense, Suspicion & Shockers</u>. Corpus Christi: von Boeckmann Fiction Factory, 2012.

Johnny Nickle just finishes playing Bix's classic "Riverboat Shuffle" when Nona hands him a note requesting "Jazz Date." "Riverboat Shuffle" can be found on Bix Beiderbecke: *Riverboat Shuffle* (Charly Classic, 1993).

_____. "Should A Tear Be Shed?" In <u>Suspense, Suspicion & Shockers</u>. Corpus Christi: von Boeckmann Fiction Factory, 2012.

Lawrence "Feet" Terrace, Jr. tap dances to "Back Home in Indiana." The Original Dixieland Jazz Band first recorded the tune but many other versions exist. One of the best is Art Tatum: *Back Home in Indiana* (Dance Plant Records, 2012).

Bennett, Ron. Singapore Swing. Holicong: Cosmos, 2003.

Ruby Braff has a sound similar to that of trumpet playing, fictional, Singapore bandleader Ted Sanders.

Ruby Braff & Ellis Larkins: *Ruby Braff & Ellis Larkins Duets Vol. 2* (Vanguard, 2000).

Benson, Raymond. Blues in the Dark. London & New York: Arcade, 2019.

Blair hears music on the set of *The Jazz Club* that reminds her of some favorite tunes. Cab Calloway doing "Minnie the Moocher" and Louis Armstrong playing "I'll Be Glad When You're Dead, You Rascal You."

"Minnie the Moocher" can be found on *Cab Calloway & The Cotton Club Orchestra* (Phoenix, 2006). "I'll Be Glad When You're Dead, You Rascal You" is on *Louis Armstrong: The Best of the Decca Years, Vol. 1: The Singer* (Verve, 2007).

Blair was also a Fats Waller fan: Fats Waller: *The Very Best of Fats Waller* (Sony 2010).

Hank Marley's signature tune was "Blues in the Dark" which can be heard sung by Jimmy Rushing on *Rushing Sings, Basie Swing* (Essential, 2017).

Earle Hagen's "Harlem Nocturne" was another Marley favorite found in a dozen versions on *Harlem Nocturne* (Kipepeo, 2019).

Benton, John L. Talent for Murder. London: Collins, 1967; New York: Gateway, 1942.

Hamilton Scott spent a drunken evening on 52nd Street. He might have heard alto saxophonist Charlie Parker, tenor saxophonist Allen Eager and/or pianist Al Haig, all of whom were playing clubs at the time of the story.

Charlie Parker: *Bird at The Roost: The Savoy Years. Volume Four.* (Savoy, 1998).

Allan Eager: *An Ace Face* (Giant Steps, 2008).

Al Haig: *Al Haig Meets the Master Bop Saxes* (Definitive, 1999).

Bird, Brandon. <u>Downbeat For a Dirge</u>. a.k.a. <u>Dead and Gone</u>. New York: Dodd, Mead, 1952.

Irene Kral. *The Band and I and Steveireno w. Herb Pomeroy and Al Cohn Orchestras* (Fresh Sounds, 2011) consists of two sessions featuring vocalist Irene Kral that were recorded at the time singer Kerry Galloway was trying to make her mark.

Block, Robert. "Dig That Crazy Grave!" In Queen, Ellery (ed.). <u>Ellery Queen's Awards: Twelfth Series</u>. London: Collins, 1959; New York: Simon & Schuster, 1957.

Jo Jones: *The Essential Jo Jones* (Vanguard, 1995) and *Jo Jones Special* (Phantasm Imports, 2010) by Count Basie's great drummer that cover the period when his fictional counterpart, Jo-Jo Jones, played.

Booth, Christopher. <u>Killing Jazz: A Detective Story</u>. New York: Chelsea, 1928.

The Grossman Jazz Orchestra's recording of "the Hula Hula Blues," which shocks Caleb Ballinger is fictional.

Similar jazz age tunes played by white musicians can be found on three anthologies: *Nipper's Greatest Hits-The 20's* (RCA, 1990); *The Naughty 1920s* Volume *1* (Grammercy, 2012); and *The Naughty 1920s Volume 2* (Grammercy, 2012).

Borneman, Ernest. <u>Tremolo</u>. London: Jarrolds, 1948; New York: Harper, 1948.

Mike picks up his clarinet and plays along with the recording of Bessie Smith's "One and Two Blues," coming in behind Joe Smith's cornet solo. "One and Two Blues" can be found on *Bessie Smith Sings the Blues-Volume 2* (Sound Vision, 2008).

Boyce, David. "Special Arrangement." In Charles, Harvey. (ed.). <u>Jazz Parody (Anthology of Jazz Fiction)</u>. London: Spearman, 1948.

Benny Goodman kept away from drugs but his small groups often played in clubs where narcotics were present. Benny Goodman: *The Complete Small Group Recordings* (RCA, 1997).

Boyce, Trudy Nan. Out of the Blues. New York: G.P. Putnam, 2016.
Front inscription is from Robert Johnson's "Hellhound On My Trail" which can be found on Robert Johnson: *King of the Delta Blues Singers* (Sony, 1998).

The Mavis Staples song that Salt hums as she works is "Step Into The Light" which is on Mavis Staples: *Have a Little Faith* (Alligator, 2004).

Mike's band plays the Kansas City staple "Every Day I Have the Blues" which can be found on Jimmy Rushing's *Every Day I Have the Blues* (Polygram, 1990).

Mike Anderson listened to Blind Willie McTell with blues favorite being "Bell Street Blues," "Band O' Blues" and "Statesboro Blues." These songs can be found on Blind Willie McTell, *Classic Years 1927-1940* (JSP, 2003).

Boyd, Frank. Johnny Staccato. London: Consul, 1960; New York: Gold Medal, 1960.
Al Haig Trio: *03/13/54 One Day Session* (Fresh Sound Records, 2007) was from a marathon recording session that resulted in two albums for the under-recorded 31-year-old bebop pianist. It's the paragon of East Coast cool jazz and definitely Johnny Staccato's style.

Brackett, Leigh. No Good from a Corpse. New York: Coward, McCann, 1944.
No one sings Harold Arlen's timeless "Blues in the Night" better than Ella Fitzgerald.
Ella Fitzgerald: *The Very Best of the Harold Arlen Songbook* (Verve, 2007).

Braly, Malcolm. Shake Him till he Rattles. London: Muller/Gold Medal, 1963. New York: Gold Medal, 1963.

The feeling of early Miles Davis' music is very much in evidence even though Lee Cabiness plays an alto saxophone and not a trumpet. Recommended: Cannonball Adderley with Miles Davis: *Somethin' Else* (Blue Note, 1985); Miles Davis All-Stars: *Walkin'* (Prestige, 1966) and *Miles Davis Vol. 2* (Blue Note, 1995).

Brown, Carter. The Ever-Loving Blues, a.k.a. Death of a Doll. London: Horwitz, 1971; New York: Signet, 1961.
Like the fictional Muscat Mullins, trumpet player Pete Candoli is a Hollywood veteran.
The Candoli Brothers Sextet: *2 For the Money* (Mercury, 2004).

Brown, Cecil. I, Stagolee. Berkeley: North American Books, 2006.
At the time, ragtime was the music for entertainment and Scott Joplin is the piano player at Stagolee's Cake Walk. Scott Joplin: *King of the Ragtime Writers* (Biograph, 2003) features his original hits on piano rolls.
Blues also has a lesser presence in I Stagolee, especially Lonnie Johnson's "Crowin' Rooster Blues" found on Lonnie Johnson: *Vol. 2, 1940-1942* (Document, 1992).

Brown, Fredric. "Murder Set to Music." In Charteris, Leslie (ed.). The Saint Mystery Library. New York: Great American Library, 1959.
Ralph sits in and plays "Body and Soul." In 1936 Coleman Hawkins played the definitive version of "Body and Soul" which, along with a 1956 version, can be found on Coleman Hawkins: *Body and Soul* (RCA, 1996).
After Lieutenant Andrews enquires about the gambling habits of various band members, the conversion shifts to talk and Dave Brubeck.
Dave Brubeck/Paul Desmond. *Jazz at the Black Hawk/Jazz at Storyville* (Fantasy, 1990) is early 1950s Brubeck jazz.

Burke, J.F. Crazy Woman Blues. London: Constable, 1979; New York: E.P. Dutton, 1978.
Jazz pianist Joey Streeter was forced to change his jazz club, Pal Joey's, into a cabaret in order to survive financially. So there's not

much jazz here. He does play a midnight set of Ellington tunes similar to those found on Duke Ellington: *Piano Reflections* (Capitol, 1989).

_____. The Kama Sutra Tango. New York: Harper & Row, 1977.
Joey Streeter is a piano player like Hal Schaefer.
Hal Schaefer: *June 1st* (Summit, 2001).

Burke, James Lee. Black Cherry Blues. Boston: Little, Brown, 1989; London: Century, 1990.
Dixie Lee Pugh was a blues & R&B star. Ronnie Earl and the Broadcasters: *Radio Hope* (Stony Plain, 2007) is an example of white, contemporary blues.
Pugh visited the black, Texas bluesman Lightnin' Hopkins who helped him with his distinctive style. Lightnin' Hopkins: *Country Blues* (Rykodisc (Disc 1), 1986) is representative of Hopkins' early playing.

_____. Last Car to Elysian Fields. London: Orion, 2002; New York: Simon & Schuster, 2003.
James Crudup is loosely based on blues singer Leadbelly, whose guitar and songs gained him early release from the notorious Angola Prison where he was serving time for murder. Leadbelly: *Where Did You Sleep Last Night* (Smithsonian Folkways, 1996).

_____. The Lost Get-Back Boogie. Baton Rouge: Louisiana State University Press, 2004.
Lenny Breau, like Ivry Paret, could play just about everything on the guitar.
Lenny Breau: *One Way* (OW, 1994).

_____. The Neon Rain. Holt, 1987; London: Century, 1989.
Dave Robicheaux had a collection of classic jazz recordings by Bix Beiderbecke, Bunk Johnson and Kid Ory. Music by these jazz pioneers can be found on *Jazz Early Days* (As Good as it Gets, 2000).

Robicheaux thinks about death while listening to Blind Lemon Jefferson's "See That My Grave Is Swept Clean". It can be found on Blind Lemon Jefferson: *The Best of Blind Lemon Jefferson* (Yazoo, 2000).

Burnett, W.R. Romelle. New York: Knopf, 1946.
Although Ruth Price sings with Johnny Smith's Quartet rather than accompanies herself on the piano, the album *Ruth Price Sings with The Johnny Smith Quartet* (Fresh Sound, 1989) has a set of standards Jules would have heard Romelle LaRue do in a 1950s Los Angeles club.

Byers, Chad. Jazz Man. Brooklyn: Gryphon, 1997.
Gerry Mulligan Quartet. *Reunion With Chet Baker* (EMI, 1988).
Although Chet Baker's trumpet on Jerome Kern's standard, "All the Things You Are" is in a quartet rather than a trio, it smokes with the same passion (fueled by alcohol) that Ray Parker felt, making him oblivious to the danger signs all around him.

Burwell, Rex. Capone, the Cobbs and Me. Livingston AL.: University of West Alabama, 2015,
Mezz Mezzrow can be heard on *Mezz Mezzrow Collection 1928-1955* (Fabulous, 2016).
Because of segregation in the 1920s, Bix Beiderbecke and Louis Armstrong never recorded together.
Bix is best heard on: *Bix Beiderbecke and The Chicago Cornets* (Milestone, 1992).
Mort Hart and Charlene Cobb listened the Paul Whiteman Orchestra play "Hot Lips" which is on *Paul Whiteman & His Famous Orchestra* (Jazz Essentials, 2016).
Louis Armstrong started every show with "Back Home in Indiana" which can be found on *Satchmo the Great* (Sony, 1994).
Aside from being a top clarinetist, Mezz Mezzrow was Louis Armstrong's (and others) marijuana ("muggles") supplier. Armstrong had a hit song, "When I Got trouble, I Got My Muggles" which is

on Vol. 4 of *Louis Armstrong: The Complete Hot Five & Seven Recordings* (Columbia Legacy, 2016).

Cain, James M. "Cigarette Girl." In Spillane, Mickey & Collins, Max Allen (eds.). A Century of Noir. New York: New American Library, 2002.
 Joe Pass. *Virtuoso Live!* (Pablo, 1992). Recorded live at the Vine Street Bar and Grill in Hollywood in 1991, this set of solo guitar by Joe Pass contains many of the standards that would have been played in a 1950s club setting.

Calef, Noel. Ascenseur pour l'echafaud. Paris: Librairie Arthème Fayard, 1956; aka Frantic. New York: Gold Medal, 1961.
 La Nouvelle Vague (New Wave) film director Louis Malle approached Miles Davis to do the soundtrack for *Ascenseur pour l'echafaud*. It was so successful that French film noir directors employed American expatriate jazz players for many of their films. Davis' soundtrack was released as a 10" record and enjoys strong sales (as a cd) to this day. Miles Davis: *Ascenseur pour l'echafaud.* (Fontana, 1957).

Calkins, Susanna. The Fate of a Flapper. New York: Minotaur, 2020.
 Charleston: Hit Songs of the 1920s (Past Perfect, 2008) offers background music ranging from Fred Astaire's "Fascinating Rhythm" to Roger Wolfe Kahn's "Crazy Rhythm." Most of the tunes were popularized in the Big Apple and crossed the Hudson to Chicago.

_____. Murder Knocks Twice. New York: St. Martin's, 2019.
 No specific orchestras or tunes are identified. *Vintage Charleston* (Bygone, 2012) features tunes by popular orchestras of the time (1924-1928), such as Roger Wolfe Kahn, Jack Hylton and Paul Whiteman for background listening.

Cameron, Lou. Angel's Flight. London: Gold Medal, 1962; New York: Gold Medal, 1960.
 Bob Cooper: *Group Activity* (Fresh Sound, 2006). The Stan Kenton band's tenor sax player, Bob Cooper's first album as a leader

reflects the cool West Coast sound that underlay the Hollywood music scene.

Singer Johnny Angel is a successful Hollywood bandleader when Ben Parker arrives from the east for a film job. Bandleaders were in demand as reflected on Tommy & Jimmy Dorsey: *Swinging in Hollywood* (Rhino, 1998).

Victor Feldman: *Latinsville* (Contemporary, 2003). Latin tinged standards that were popular in the late 1950s and would have been played by Ben Parker's Afro-Cuban band in New York City.

Cameron, Stella. <u>Tell Me Why</u>. New York: Kensington, 2001.

Joanne Brackeen: *Popsickle Illusion* (Arkadia 70372, 2000).

This solo recording by Brackeen, mixing standards and originals, offers a program Carolee Burns might have played.

Campo, J.P. <u>On A Good Day it Bounces Off</u>. Ridgewood, N.J.: Books-by-Booksends, 2005.

Jazz guitarist Bobby Turner loves Wes Montgomery's sound.

Before he recorded the big band albums, there were the small group sessions in which display Wes' distinct, crisp sound such as Wes Montgomery: *Movin' Along* (Riverside, 2007). He was at his best here with James Clay, Victor Feldman, Sam Jones and Louis Hayes.

Wes Montgomery. *Fingerpickin'* (Pacific Jazz, 1996). Originally recorded in 1957, Wes is first heard as a leader in a group that included his two brothers.

Carlotto, Massimo. <u>Bandit Love</u>. London & New York: Europa, 2010.

Relaxing in his club, Marco hears Jimmy Witherspoon singing "Money's Gettin' Cheaper" coming through on the speakers. It's on at least 3 different albums, among them *Spoon Calls Hootie* (Hallmark, 2010).

At a girlfriend's apartment, Marco spies Alberta Adams' *Born with the Blues* (Cannonball, 1999) among her CDs and plays his favorite tune on it, "Searchin'."

Leaving a blues bar, he puts on the Elmore James CD *Baby Please Set a Date* (Wolf, 2010).

_____. Blues For Outlaw Hearts and Old Whores. London & New York: Europa, 2020.

Marco likes white women singers. In the morning, he listens to Cowboy Junkies' Margo Timmins singing "Post Card Blues" and "Walkin' After Midnight." Both can be found on Cowboy Junkies: *The Trinity Sessions* (RCS, 1988).

Edith, the former prostitute, dances to Natalie Merchant for Marco. Her earliest (and best) album is *Tigerlily* (Elektra, 1995).

Starting a new life with Edith, Marco remembers an old blues song by James Carr, "At the Dark End of the Street." While recorded by many singers, such as Linda Ronstadt (*Heart Like a Wheel*, Capitol, 1985), the original can be found on James Carr: *The Complete Goldwax Singles* (Ace, 2011).

_____. The Columbian Mule, London: Orion, 2003; New York: Europa, 2013.

Marco "the Alligator," Buratti, former blues singer, listens to a lot of blues both on record and live in his club.

To get ready for an evening at his club, he listens to Joe Louis Walker singing "My Dignity", which can be found on Joe Lewis Walker: *Blues Survivor* (Verve, 2000).

Driving on the autostrada, he plays a cassette of Taj Mahal singing "Lovin' in my Baby's Eyes" that is on *The Essential Taj Mahal* (Columbia, 2005).

The resident singer in Marco's club, Eliosa Deriu, sings two Billie Holiday standards, "God Bless the Child" and "Fine and Mellow." The original "God Bless the Child" can be found on Billie Holliday: *God Bless the Child* (MCA, 1995).

"Fine and Mellow" is on *Billie Holiday* (Collectables, 1990).

_____. The Master of Knots, London: Orion, 2004; New York: Europa, 2014.

It's a grim book and the only music Buratti listens to is Van Morrison's "Moondance." Van Morrison. *Moondance* (Warner, 2008).

Carter, Charlotte. "Birdbath." In Editors of the Mysterious Press. The Mysterious Press Anniversary Anthology. New York: Warner, 2001.
Nanette Hayes is listening to Etta Jones sing at the Charlie Parker jazz fest when jazz musician Richie Rice snatches the purse that will cost him his life. Etta Jones' *Easy Living* (High Note, 2000) is a sample of her classic style.

_____. Coq au Vin. New York: Mysterious, 1999.
Nanette enlists Andre, a young black violinist, to help her find her missing aunt. Andre plays old-fashioned swing violin like Stephane Grappelli did with Django Reinhardt.
Django Reinhardt: *The Indispensible Django Reinhardt (1949-1950)* (RCA, 1992).

_____. Drumsticks. New York: Mysterious, 2000.
Nanette admires Sonny Rollins' tenor sax skills which are evident on Dizzy Gillespie, Sonny Rollins, Sonny Stitt: *Sunny Side Up* (Verve, 1997).
Singer Jimmy Scott is another favorite. Jimmy Scott: *Moonglow* (Milestone, 2003).

_____. "Flower is a Lonesome Thing, A." In Harvey, John, (ed.). Blue Lightning. London: Slow Dancer, 1998.
Two albums fit the mood of the story:
Etta Jones. *Don't Go to Strangers* (Prestige, 2006).
Dinah Washington. *What A Difference A Day Makes* (Polygram, 2000).

_____. Rhode Island Red. London: Mask Noir, 1997; New York: Serpent's Tail, 1998.
Nanette Hayes plays the tenor saxophone and would be a fan of Hank Mobley. Hank Mobley: *Hank Mobley Quintet* (Blue Note, 1998).

Cartmel, Richard. The Vinyl Detective: Victory Disc. London: Titan, 2018.

The tension breaker in the Vinyl Detective's house is one of Nevada's favorites, a lesser known *bossa* session: *Luiz Bonfa Composer of Black Orpheus Plays and Sings Bossa Nova* (Verve, 1963).

The Flare Path Orchestra, of course, was fictional, but Glenn Miller played the two tunes on the 78, "Blues in the Night" and "Elmer's Tune."

Miller's "Blues in the Night" was only available as a radio air check but is found on *Glenn Miller: America's Bandleader* (RCA Bluebird, 2003).

"Elmer's Tune" by the Miller band is readily available on CDs such as *The Best of Glenn Miller* (RCA, 1966) or *The Essential Glenn Miller* (RCA, 2005).

Annette Hanshaw, a 1920's star, whose singing captivated Nevada and the Vinyl Detective and ended her songs with "That's all," can be heard on *Annette Hanshaw: The Personality Girl, 1926-1927* (Sensation, 2014) or *Annette Hanshaw: Twenties Sweetheart* (Jasmine, 2004).

The Sonny Rollins disc that's on the turntable when love-struck Leo arrives isn't identified, so *Sonny Rollins: Way Out West* (Contemporary, 1957) will do.

Tinkler's folkie girlfriend Opal likes John Martyn and listens to *John Martyn-Live at Leeds* (Island, 1975).

_____. The Vinyl Detective: Written in Dead Wax. London: Titan, 2016.

The Vinyl Detective is listening to the Gil Mille Sextet on Blue Note during an early morning encounter with a stranger outside his window. The album is *Complete Blue Note 50s Sessions* (EMI, 2008).

In a charity shop, he comes across the Phillips' recording by Duke Ellington of *Anatomy of a Murder*. It's reissued as *Duke Ellington: Anatomy of a Murder-Soundtrack of the 1959 Motion Picture* (Sony, 1999). He also finds a bunch of Woody Herman albums from the 1960s. An example is *1963: Swingin' Big Band Ever 25th Year* (UMVD, 2002).

At Tinkler's house, the Vinyl Detective listens to the Claude Thornhill Orchestra playing "Snowfall." It can be found on *Claude Thornhill & His Orchestra* (Hindsight, 1997). The Vinyl Detective finds his "friend" Stinky listening to the motion picture soundtrack from Lalo Schifrin's *Bullitt*. It's available as *Bullitt 1968* (Aleph Records, 2017).

Ree's grandmother had a rare Russ Garcia session. Something similar can be found in *Russ Garcia's Wigville Band* (Fresh Sounds, 2005).

Cass, Richard J. <u>Burton's Solo</u>. Farmington, ME: Encircle, 2018.

If there's no live music in the Esposito Bar, Elder Darrow listens to CDs for background. Among those played are:

The Beach Boys: "Pet Sounds" on *Pet Sounds* (Capitol, 2001).

Blossom Dearie: "Everything I Got" on *Blossom Dearie* (Verve, 1985).

Bobby Bland: "St. James Infirmary" on *Two Steps from The Blues* (Geffin, 2001).

Dave Brubeck-Paul Desmond: *Brubeck-Desmond: The Duets 1975* (Verve, 2009) as no "early" tunes specified.

Tommy Flanagan: "Peace" on *Something Borrowed, Something Blue* (OJC, 1990).

Johnny Hartman: "Lush Life" on *John Coltrane, Johnny Hartman* (GRP, 1963).

Milt Jackson: "Bags' Groove" on *Bags' Groove: Greatest Hits* (Atlantic-Warner, 2019).

Keith Jarrett: *Paris/London Testament* (ECM, 2009).

Chris McBride: *Superbass Live at Scullers* (Telarc, 2006). (No tune specified from it.).

Wes Montgomery: "California Dreamin'" on *California Dreamin'* (Verve, 1989).

Marcus Roberts: "It Aint Necessarily So" on *Gershwin for Lovers* (Sony, 1994).

_____. <u>In Solo Time</u>. Farmington, ME: Encircle, 2017.

Timmy McGuire's trio plays "How Insensitive" and "Straight No Chaser." "How Insensitive" can be found on Jacob Fischer Trio: *Black Orpheus* (Venus, 2013).

"Straight No Chaser" is on Wes Montgomery's *Echoes of Indiana Avenue* (Resonance, 2012).

When no one is in the club, Elder Darrow listens to *Mose Allison London Sessions, Vol. 1* (Blue Note, 2001).

After Dan Burton set up Jacquie Robillard, he drinks to "Suicide Is Painless" (the theme from M.A.S.H.). It's on numerous albums but a memorable version is Harry Allen/Jan Lundgren Quartet: *Quietly There* (Stunt, 2014).

_____. Last Call at The Esposito. Farmington, ME: Encircle, 2019.

The jazz Elder Darrow plays at the Esposito is mostly on CD rather than live. Some of the tunes are:

Miles Davis: "Autumn Leaves" on *In Person Friday & Saturday Nights at The Black Hawk* (Columbia, 2008).

Duke Ellington: "Take The A Train" (long version) on *The Essential Duke Ellington* (Columbia, 1987).

Tommy Flanagan: "Peace" on *Something Borrowed, Something Blue* (OJC, 1990).

Charlie Haden: "Body and Soul" on *Charlie Haden & Jim Hall* (Blue Note, 2014).

Johnny Hartman: "Lush Life" on *John Coltrane & Johnny Hartman* (GRP, 1963).

Wes Montgomery: "California Dreamin'" on *California Dreamin'* (Verve, 1989) &

"Road Song" on *Road Song* (A&M, 1989).

Joe Pass: "I Got It Bad and That Ain't Good" on *After Hours* (Telarc, 1989).

_____. Solo Act. Farmington, ME: Encircle, 2017.

Elder Darrow listens to Wes Montgomery's *California Dreaming* (Verve, 1989) as he tries to understand Alison's Death.

He's listening to Paul Desmond's *Skylark* when he opens an envelope containing a photo of Alison leaving the Fenway Pharmacy. Paul Desmond: *Skylark* (King, 2013).

Darrow listens to Charlie Parker's solo of the bop standard

"Cherokee." It's available on numerous CDs, including Charlie Parker: *Cherokee* (Masters of Jazz, 2000).

Laverne Baker's *Blues in The City* (MazJazz, 1999) seems like the sort of set Alison Sommers would do.

_____. Sweetie Brogan's Sorrow. Farmington ME: Encircle, 2020.

"Misty" was Sweetie Brogan's signature song and can be heard on *Sarah Vaughan's Golden Hits* (Polygram, 2006).

Lily sings "Misty" much to Sweetie's dismay and "Sunny Side of the Street." The latter by Ella Fitzgerald can found on *Ella and Basie* (Verve, 1997).

In her debut at the Greenwood, Evvie sings "Our Love is Here to Stay." A new collection of out-takes with various backings can be found on Ella Fitzgerald's *Love Letters from Ella* (Concord, 2007).

Evvie also sings "The Girl from Ipanema" that is Astrud Gilberto's calling card and is on *Astrud Gilberto's Finest Hour* (Verve, 2001).

When the Greenwood returns to Elder Darrow's control as the Esposito, he plays two favorites Keith Jarrett's *Koln Concert* (ECM, 1999) and Wes Montgomery's *California Dreamin'* (Verve, 1989).

Cassidy, Bruce. The Brass Shroud. New York: Ace, 1958.

Ruby Braff, like the legendary trumpet man Buck Lagrande, can play any style of jazz. Ruby Braff: *Me, Myself And I* (Concord, 1989).

Castle, Frank. Hawaiian Eye. New York: Dell, 1962.

Arthur Lyman: *Leis of Jazz* (HiFi, 1998). Recorded live in 1959 at Henry Kaiser's Hawaiian Village Motel, Lyman's group played music that the Hawaiian Eye detectives would hear in the lounge as they relaxed after a day of detecting.

Celestin, Ray. The Axeman's Jazz, London: Mantle 2014; aka The Axeman. New York: Sourcebooks Landmark, 2015.

One of the best overviews of early New Orleans jazz is *New Orleans: Cradle of Jazz 1917-1946* (Charley, 1999).

_____. <u>Dead Man's Blues</u>. London: Mantle, 2016; New York: Pegasus, 2017.

Louis Armstrong & Earl Hines are continually playing tunes throughout the book such as "West End Blues," "Muskat Ramble," & "Basin Street Blues." They can be heard on *Louis Armstrong on Okeh* (Sony Legacy, 2012) and *Louis Armstrong, Vol. 4* (Columbia, 1989).

_____. <u>The Mobster's Lament</u>. London: Mantle, 2019.

Carmen Miranda is headlining at the Copa. She is featured on *Carmen Miranda: The Brazilian Bombshell* (RETSP, 2014).

While looking for information, Gabriel wanders into a bar where King Oliver is on the turntable. King Oliver: *Shake It & Break It* (Blaricum, 2011).

Ida hears Charlie Parker playing "Relaxin' at Camarillo" and "Anthropology." "Relaxin'" can be found on *The Best of Charlie Parker* (AAO Music, 2014) and "Anthropology" on *The Complete Live Performances (at the Roral Roost, 1949)* (Savoy, 1998).

Armstrong plays "Cornet Chop Suey" at his comeback concert. The 1926 original is on *Louis Armstrong and his Hot Five, Vol. 1* (Columbia, 1988).

Chandler, Raymond. "King In Yellow, The." In <u>Collected Stories</u>. London & New York: Everyman, 2002.

Bandleader/trombonist King Leopoldi wasn't quite in Tommy Dorsey's class but then few people were.

Tommy Dorsey: *The Seventeen Number Ones* (RCA, 1990).

Cleverly, Barbara. <u>Ragtime In Simla</u>. London: Constable & Robinson, 2002; New York: Carroll & Graf, 2002.

Joe Sandilands meets Alice Conyers while she is listening to "Tiger Rag" and recalls seeing the Original Dixieland Jazz Band play the Hammersmith Palais. "Tiger Rag" can be found on *Original Dixieland Jazz Band* (Avid, 2006).

Alice's toe tapping to "St. Louis Blues" on board ship gives her away. It's also on that album.

Cockey, Tim. The Hearse Case Scenario. New York: Hyperion, 2002.

Vocalist Lee Cromwell sings standards with the Edgar Jonz Experience at a jazz club owned by the late Shrimp Martin.

Like Lee Cromwell, Irene Kral was an under-appreciated singer throughout her career. Irene Kral. *Just For Now* (Jazzed Media, 2004).

Coggins, Mark. The Big Wake-Up. Boulder: Bleak House, 2009.

John Coltrane. *Giant Steps* (Atlantic, 1990). Riordan actually unwinds to this Coltrane classic.

Bass player Paul Chambers is Riordan's idol. His early albums fit the tone of the story-*Eight Classics* (101 Distribution, 2012). See below (Candy from Strangers) individual albums.

_____. Candy From Strangers. Madison: Bleak House, 2006.

As noted earlier Paul Chambers is bassist August Riordan's favorite jazz musician. Chambers' *Eight Classic Albums* (101 Distribution, 2012) that includes classic albums such as: *Bass on Top, Chamber's Music, Whims of Chambers, Paul Chambers Quintet, We Three, 1st Bassman, Go* and *Shades of Red* are always in play.

Riordan also finds *Birth of the Cool* (Blue Note, 2001), the old Miles Davis Capitol classic (reissued on Blue Note), mixes well with bourbon during an evening at home.

While driving to a gig, Riordan gets in the mood by listening to Coleman Hawkins' bossa album, *Disafinado* (Impulse, 1997), and Cannonball Adderley's classic quartet: *Cannonball Takes Charge* (Blue Note, 1997).

_____. The Dead Beat Scroll. Lutz, FL: Down & Out Books, 2019.

August Riordan has swapped his bass for a Lugar pistol, and there's no specific music mentioned. He plays pop, jazz and standards, so Steve Rodby's albums with Ross Traut were my background choices. Traut & Rodby: *The Double Life* (Columbia, 1991) and *The Great Lawn* (Columbia, 1989).

_____. The Immortal Game. Berkeley: Poltroon, 1999.

Riordan, a bass playing PI, has photographs of Paul Chambers and Jimmy Blanton on his office wall. Albums featuring Chambers and Blanton are:

Paul Chambers Sextet: *Whims of Chambers* (Blue Note, 1996)
Duke Ellington: *The Blanton-Webster Band* (RCA Bluebird, 1986).
Riordan also listen to Benny Carter's *Jazz Giant* (OJC, 1990).

_____. No Hard Feelings. Lutz, FL: Down & Out Books, 2015.

August Riordan has swapped his bass for a Lugar pistol, so there's no specific music mentioned. He plays pop, jazz and standards, so again Steve Rodby's albums with Ross Traut were my background choices. Traut & Rodby: *The Double Life* (Columbia, 1991) and *The Great Lawn* (Columbia, 1989).

_____. Runoff. Madison: Bleak House, 2007.

Trying to impress a girl during a gig, bassist/detective August Riordan imagines he's George Duvivier playing "Love Walked In" on Carol Sloane's early classic album. Carol Sloane. *Live at 30ᵗʰ Street.* (CBS SONY/Japan, 1962).

_____. Vulture Capital. Berkeley: Poltoon, 2002.

There's no specific jazz mentioned in Riordan's caper but Ron Carter's tribute to Miles Davis reflects the story's mood.

Ron Carter. *Dear Miles* (Blue Note, 2007).

Cohen, Octavus Roy. Danger In Paradise. New York: Macmillan, 1944; London: Robert Hale, 1949.

Iris Randall is a popular Big Band radio singer like June Christy. June Christy: *Early June* (Fresh Sounds, 1991).

Colbert, Curt. Rat City. Seattle: Ugly Town, 2001.

Although their leader was a piano player, the Count Basie Band always had a strong sax section. Count Basie: *1947-Brand New Wagon* (RCA Bluebird, 1990).

Coleman, Wanda. "Dunny," In <u>Jazz and Twelve O'clock Blues</u>. Jaffrey: Black Sparrow, 2008.

Dunny has the voice and temperament of soul singer, David Ruffin.

David Ruffin: *The Ultimate Collection* (Motown, 1998).

Collins, Max Allen & Clemens, Matthew V. "East Side, West Side." In Randisi, Robert J., (ed.). <u>Murder and all that Jazz</u>. New York: Signet, 2004.

Duke Ellington: *The Okeh Ellington* (Columbia C, 1991) and Roger Wolfe Kahn: *1925/1928,* Jazz Oracle, 2000) reflect the Jazz Age music scene in New York City at the time of this short story.

Compton, D.G. <u>Back of Town Blues</u>. London: Orion, 1996.

Alec Duncan plays solo piano. He would have enjoyed Dave McKenna: *Giant Stride* (Concord, 1999).

Duncan is also a fan of Erroll Garner and Teddy Wilson. Erroll Garner: *Solitaire.* (Mercury, 1993) and Teddy Wilson: *Teddy Wilson at the Piano: Mr. Wilson.* (Sony, 1990) are both top-notch solo outings from these jazz masters.

Connelly, Michael. <u>9 Dragons</u>. London: Orion, 2009; New York: Little, Brown, 2009.

Harry listens to "Seven Steps to Heaven" after a satisfying day at work and thinks about how Carter's work is so distinctive as a leader and a sideman. Relating Carter's music to his own case, he knows that he has now become a sideman and is dependent on others. Ron Carter. *Dear Miles* (Blue Note, 2007).

While a fan of the masters, Bosch is open to new talent as well. He listens to Tomasz Stanko, a Polish trumpet player who, "sounded like the ghost of Miles Davis" (p.100), while he's on a stakeout. Tomasz Stanko. *Soul of Things* (ECM, 2002).

_____. <u>Angel's Flight</u>. Boston: Little, Brown, 1999. London: Orion, 1998.

Driving out to tell Margie Sheehan about the death of her husband, Frank, Harry Bosch fast forwards the tape of saxophone music until he comes to Frank Morgan's "Lullaby".

"Lullaby" is on Frank Morgan: *Jazz 'Round Midnight* (Verve, 1987). It's Morgan in a mellow mood.

Another Morgan album that Bosch would like is Frank Morgan/ Bud Shank: *Quiet Fire* (Contemporary, 1991). Bud Shank, the paragon of west coast cool jazz, is reborn as a bebopper when he joins bopper Morgan in this live set from Seattle's Blues Alley.

_____. The Black Box. London: Orion, 2012; New York: Little, Brown, 2012.

Bosch listens to jazz in the evenings, often over dinner, with his daughter, Maddie. He muses that his favorite jazz musicians are: Frank Morgan, George Cables, Art Pepper, Ron Carter and Thelonious Monk.

Frank Morgan: *Jazz 'Round Midnight*. (Verve, 1997), which contains *"Lullaby."*

George Cables: *Person to Person*. (SteepleChase, 1995)-a solo outing.

Art Pepper: *Art Pepper Meets the Rhythm Section*. (Contemporary, 1998)-possibly Pepper's best session, helped by Miles Davis' rhythm section. It's always been a Bosch favorite.

Ron Carter. Dear Miles (Blue Note, 2007)-a tribute to his former boss by Miles' bassist.

Thelonious Monk: *Thelonious Monk Plays Duke Ellington* (Riverside, 1987). Monk and his rhythm section's (1955) classic salute to Duke Ellington.

Over a special birthday dinner with his daughter, Bosch listens to Cables' play the standard "Helen's Song," and wonders about Helen. It's found on George Cables: *Cables Fables* (SteepleChase, 1991).

For his birthday, Mattie gets Harry the six-volume set of previously unreleased concerts by Art Pepper that she found on the Internet and that he didn't know about. He puts on *Vol. 1. The Complete Abashiri Concert* (Widow's Taste, 2006).

On another evening while working his way through his birthday Art Pepper CDs, he puts on Vol. III *The Croydan Concert* (Widow's Taste, 2008). It contains a stunning version of "Patricia" which Pepper wrote for his daughter. Bosch thinks that, like Pepper, he's not at home a lot with his daughter.

Although Bosch listens to mostly classic musicians, he's open to listening to younger players. Also, he hopes to stimulate his daughter's growing interest in jazz by uncovering players of a different generation. A jazz friend at the firing range suggests that he listen to Danny Grisset and in return, he recommends Gary Smulyan.

Danny Grissetti. *Form* (CrissCross, 2009). Pianist Grisetti and his quintet/sextet explore a mix standards and originals.

Gary Smulyan. *Hidden Treasures* (Reservoir, 2005). Baritone saxophonist Smulyan is Bosch's most recent discovery among the younger players. Each tune on the album is based on chord changes of better-known composition.

_____. The Black Echo. Boston: Little, Brown, 1992; London: Orion, 1992.

Harry Bosch was in what might be termed his "angry young tenor stage" and preferred tenor saxophonists who took the listener to the edge. In later books, he'll mellow out with alto players. Two tenor saxophone players that he listens to are Wayne Shorter and Sonny Rollins.

Sonny Rollins: Way Out West (OJC,1991). Rollins, who never liked pianos, omits one in this trio album of songs with a western theme.

Wayne Shorter: *Speak No Evil* (Blue Note. 1964). A solid quintet date with Freddie Hubbard joining Shorter.

_____. The Black Ice. London: Cassell, 2001; Boston: Little, Brown, 1993.

Bosch spends New Year's Eve listening to the music of alto saxophonist Frank Morgan with the widow of the murdered, undercover cop Cal Moore.

Frank Morgan's compilation, *Jazz' Round Midnight* (Verve, 1997) contains two of Bosch's favorite tunes, "Helen's Song" and "Lullabye".

Frank Morgan: *Listen to the Dawn* (Antilles, 1994) has guitarist Kenny Burrell joining Morgan for the haunting "Remembering," "I Didn't Know About You" and "Goodbye".

_____. The Brass Verdict. London: Orion, 2008; New York: Little, Brown, 2008.

Attorney Mickey Haller's father had defended alto saxophonist Frank Morgan on drug charges. Morgan is Harry Bosch's favorite west coast jazz musician. And he's always listening to his music on his iPod or at home. For a change, he did switch over to Ron Carter. Morgan was also a favorite of author Michael Connelly's, who dedicated this book to him.

Ron Carter: *Stardust* (Blue Note, 2001). Carter joins tenor saxophonist Benny Golson in a session of standards.

Frank Morgan: *Frank Morgan* (GNPD, 1991) was recorded in the late 1950s, around the time Haller's father would have defended him for drug charges.

Frank Morgan with the Cedar Walton Trio: *Easy Living* (Contemporary, 1985) is a relaxing outing by two jazz veterans that is Harry's kind of jazz.

Frank Morgan: *Jazz 'Round Midnight* (Verve, 1997) contains "Lullaby", a Bosch favorite.

_____. The Burning Room. London: Orion, 2014; New York: Little, Brown, 2014.

Bosch stops at the Blue Whale and hears Grace Kelly play "Over The Rainbow." It's on *Every Road I Walk* (Pazz, 2006).

At the airport he listens to Frank Morgan tribute film soundtrack that's unavailable. The closest thing is Frank Morgan All Stars. *Reflections* (OJC, 2000).

Bosch listens to Ron Carter's "Seven Steps To Heaven" and "Stella By Starlight" while reading the Bonnie Brae murder book. These tunes, as well as others associated with Miles Davis, can be found on the tribute album by Ron Carter. *Dear Miles* (Blue Note, 2007).

_____. "Christmas Even." In Randisi, Robert, (ed.). <u>Murder and all that Jazz</u>. New York; Signet, 2004.

Frank Morgan: *Jazz 'Round Midnight* (Verve, 1997) includes "Lullaby" which Harry Bosch learned to play on the alto saxophone that he found in a pawnshop and returned to its original owner Quentin McKenzie and was later willed to him.

_____. <u>City of Bones</u>. London: Orion, 2002; New York: Little, Brown, 2002.

Three albums that Julia Brasher and Harry Bosch play during their short time together are:

Miles Davis: *Kind of Blue* (Columbia, 1997).

Clifford Brown: *Jazz 'Round Midnight* (Verve, 1993).

Bill Evans: *Bill Evans at the Village* Vanguard (Riverside, 1987).

_____. <u>The Closers</u>. London: Orion, 2005; New York: Little, Brown, 2005.

Harry Bosch listens to Boz Scaggs' "For All We Know" after coming home from work and learning about a possible skinhead connection in the death of Rebecca Verloren. It can be found on Boz Scaggs: *But Beautiful* (Gray Cat, 2003).

Harry is listening to Miles Davis' *Kind of Blue* at home when reviewing the murder book again for something that he might have missed when Chief Irvin's minion, McClellan, comes to tell him that there are no security files on the Chatsworth Eights' alibis. Miles Davis: *Kind of Blue.* (Columbia,1997).

_____. <u>The Concrete Blonde</u>. Boston: Little, Brown, 1994; London: Orion, 2000.

Harry Bosch listens to a quartet playing Billy Strayhorn's music while watching his partner Edgar meet with the high-priced attorney Honey Chandler, who's after Bosch.

Billy Strayhorn: *The Peaceful Side of Billy Strayhorn* (United Artists, 1996).

_____. The Crossing. London: Orion, 2015; New York: Little, Brown, 2015.
As he's working on his motorcycle, Bosch listens to John Handy's "Naima," the 1967 an ode to John Coltrane, which appears on John Handy Quintet, *New View* (Koch 1997).
While reading the Lexi Parkes' murder book, he listens Ron Carter backed by two guitars playing "Bags Groove" which is on Ron Carter, *In Memory of Jim.* (Somethin' Else, UCCD, 2014).
Bosch is listening to Wynton Marsalis' "The Majesty of the Blues" when he walks into a trap but the music also blocked out the sound of his rescuer. "The Majesty of the Blues" can be found on Wynton Marsalis, *The Majesty of the Blues,* (Sony, 1989).

_____. Darkness More Than Night, A. Boston: Little, Brown, 2001; London: Orion, 2001.
Art Pepper: *Art Pepper Meets The Rhythm Section* (Contemporary, 1988). Harry Bosch lives to Art Pepper's music and listens with FBI profiler Terry McCaleb to this classic album that joins Pepper with Miles Davis' rhythm section.
Chet Baker: *Picture of Heath* (Pacific Jazz, 1990). Originally issued as "Playboys", Chet Baker's trumpet and Art Pepper's alto sax play off each other making this a successful duet that captured the west coast sound of its time (1956) and became timeless.

_____. The Drop. London: Orion, 2011; New York: Little, Brown, 2011.
Chet Baker: *Night Bird,* (Giants 2000). While reading "the murder book" on George Irving, Chet Baker's "Nightbird" comes on Harry's CD player and he remembers seeing him live in San Francisco in 1982. Twenty years later in a Venice Beach restaurant, he heard John Harvey read his poem on Baker's death. The tune prompts him to think about the similarities of both men's deaths: each died under questionable circumstances by either falling or being pushed to their deaths.

Harry puts on a Frank Morgan CD when he brings Hannah back to his home in the Hollywood hills. Frank Morgan: *Jazz Round Midnight* (Verve 2000).

When Harry comes home late from work he is pleased to find his daughter listening to an Art Pepper CD. Art Pepper: *Art Pepper Meets the Rhythm Section* (Contemporary, 1988).

Gary Smulyan. *Hidden Treasures* (Reservoir, 2006). With bassist Christian McBride and drummer Billy Drummond, baritone saxophonist Smulyan plays ten lesser-known compositions by well-known musicians based on the chord changes of standards and jazz classics.

While driving to Modesto after the rogue Guardsmen, Bosch listens to more from the unreleased Art Pepper set. On *Vol. 5, The Stuttgart Concert* (Window's Taste, 2010), he listens to Pepper's theme "Straight Life" but it's his version of "Over the Rainbow" that catches Bosch, fixes Anneke Jespersen in his mind, and results in a replay.

_____. Echo Park. London: Orion, 2006; New York: Little, Brown, 2006.

Thelonious Monk: *Thelonious Monk Quartet with John Coltrane at Carnegie Hall* (Blue Note, 2005). Harry Bosch listens to this newly discovered album, the tapes of which were sitting for fifty years undiscovered in a box.

To sharpen his senses before opening the murder file, he listens to Miles Davis' *Kind of Blue* (Columbia, 1997).

Much of the book's action took place around Chavez Ravine. Harry listens to Ry Cooder: *Chavez Ravine* (Nonesuch, 2005).

_____. The Last Coyote. Boston: Little, Brown, 1995; London: Orion, 1995. Harry Bosch listens to trumpet player Clifford Brown while relaxing and working on his house. "Willow Weep for Me," a Bosch favorite, can be found on *Clifford Brown: Jazz 'Round Midnight* (Verve, 1993).

Abbey Lincoln comes on Bosch's car radio. She joins alto saxophonist Frank Morgan on *Frank Morgan: Jazz 'Round Midnight* (Verve, 1997).

_____. Lost Light. Boston: Little, Brown, 2003; London: Orion, 2003.

Art Pepper joins Lee Konitz on "The Shadow of Your Smile". Art Pepper: *The Hollywood All-Star Sessions. Vol. 5.* (Galaxy, 1997).

Throughout the book, Harry Bosch is trying to learn the Frank Morgan song "Lullaby". It can be found on Frank Morgan: *Jazz 'Round Midnight* (Verve, 1997).

Another Bosch favorite is Frank Morgan's *Listen to The Dawn* (Antilles, 1994) with guitarist Kenny Burrell.

When the book opens, Harry Bosch is listening to Frank Morgan playing "All Blues" on *City Nights* recorded live from the Jazz Standard in New York. Frank Morgan: *City Nights* (High Note, 2004).

Harry listens to Ron Carter while driving. Ron Carter: *Stardust* (Blue Note, 1995).

_____. The Narrows. Boston: Little, Brown 2004; London: Orion, 2004.

George Cables is a favorite of author Connelly and Bosch. He composed the music on the promotional DVD *Blue Neon Night* that was included with the book.

George Cables Trio: *Alone Together* (Grove, 1995).

Harry's music taste is not limited to jazz. Lucinda Williams: *World Without Tears* (Lost Highways, 2003).

_____. "Nighthawks." In Block, Lawrence (ed.). In Sunlight or in Shadow. London & New York: Pegasus, 2016.

Harry Bosch muses about inspiration and the Frank Morgan tune "Lullaby." A version appears on Frank Morgan's CD with George Cables, *Montreal Memories* (HighNote, 2018).

_____. Trunk Music. London: Orion, 1997; Boston: Little, Brown, 1997.

Although the story is set in L.A., the East Coast sound of Al Cohn rather than that of West Coast tenor saxophones fit the book's mood: Al Cohn & Zoot Sims: *Easy as Pie* (Label M, 2000); Al Cohn: *The Al Cohn Quintet with Bob Brookmeyer* (Verve, 2005);

Al Cohn: *Rifftide* (Timeless, 1957).

_____. <u>Two Kinds of Truth</u>. London: Orion, 2017; New York: Little, Brown, 2017.

Bosch listens to several older albums as he reviews the Preston Borders' murder case. For Bosch, the tenor sax brings the past into focus.

Houston Person & Ron Carter: *Chemistry.* (High Note, 2016) is a series of duets between Person's tenor sax and Carter's bass. It's their 5th meeting and Bosch has seen them live and has their earlier albums on vinyl.

Frank Morgan: *Mood Indigo* (Antilles, 1989) features one of Bosch's favorite tunes, "Lullaby" and it's in the background as he reviews his interview with convicted murderer Preston Borders.

Convoy, Albert. <u>Mr. Lucky</u>. New York: Dell, 1960.

Henry Mancini: *Mr. Lucky* (RCA, 2007) is the television show's soundtrack.

Gerry Mulligan: *The Gerry Mulligan Quartet. Complete Studio Recordings* (Lonehill, 2005) epitomizes the Los Angeles environment of the 1960s series.

Conway, Martha. <u>Sugarland</u>. San Francisco: Noontime, 2016.

Eve Riser played in small groups much like Lil Armstrong who was working with her husband Louis in Chicago at the time of the story. Louis Armstrong: *Louis Armstrong: The Hot Fives, Vol. 1* (Columbia, 1982).

Eve heard a recording of James P. Johnson playing "Harlem Strut"—one of her favorite stride piano tunes. It's on James P. Johnson: *Carolina Shout* (Fabulous, 2015).

Corbett, David. <u>Done For a Dime</u>. London: Orion, 2004; New York: Ballantine, 2003.

Raymond "Strong" Carter, a baritone sax player, is murdered in his front yard. Either *Lee Konitz and the Gerry Mulligan Quartet* (Pacific Jazz, 1988) or Pepper Adams: *Critic's Choice* (EMI, 2005) are both fine west coast baritone sax albums.

Coxe, George Harmon. <u>The Lady Is Afraid</u>. New York: Knopf, 1940.

The hard drinking Elman Band came together at the end of the Big Band era and because of this bad timing never had a real chance of success. It was a fine dance band like Dan Washburn's band. Ziggy Elman: *Ziggy Elman and His Orchestra 1947* (Circle, 1984).

_____. <u>Ring of Truth, The</u>. New York: Knopf, 1966.

Ruby Braff is a journeyman trumpet player like the fictional Ralph Estey.

The Ruby Braff Trio: *Me, Myself and I* (Concord, 1989).

Craig, Jonathan. <u>Frenzy</u>. New York: Lancer, 1962; as <u>Junkie</u>. London: Wilder, 2013.

Phyllis Connery, Steve Harper's old girlfriend, has a stride piano style similar to that of Judy Carmichael. Judy Carmichael: *Judy* (C&D, 1994). Harper, who plays the trumpet in a successful club band, listens to J.A.T.P. (Jazz at The Philharmonic) trumpet battles. *J.A.T.P. The First Ten Years* (Properbox, 2005) features a trumpet battle on disc 4.

Craig, Philip R. <u>Vineyard Blues</u>. New York: Scribner, 1960.

Corrie Appleyard was a contemporary of Josh White and played similar music.

Two Josh White albums from that era are: Josh White: *Empty Bed Blues* (Sepia Tone, 2003) and *Josh White Stories Vol. 1 & 2* (Jasmine, 2020).

Creech, J.R. <u>Music And Crime</u>.

Clean-living Bob Cooper was a long way from the fictional tenor player, Ray the Face. But they both played the same sort of cool, west coast jazz.

Bob Cooper: *Group Activity* (Fresh Sounds, 2006).

Curran, Dale. <u>Dupree Blues</u>. New York: Knopf, 1948.

Chuck Willis: *I Remember Chuck Willis/The King of The Stroll* (Collectable, 2001) has the popular version of "Betty and Dupree".

Trombonist Jack Teagarden, like Dupree, worked with a lot of small bands before achieving success. Jack Teagarden: *Jack Teagarden and His All-Stars* (Jazzology, 1990).

Dahl, Arne. <u>Misterioso</u>. Malmo: Bra Böcker, 1999; London & New York: Pantheon, 2011.

Two members of the A-Team are jazz fans and immediately recognize the tape that was left behind at the murder scene as coming from Thelonious Monk's gig at the Black Hawk in New York City and released as *Misterioso*.

Thelonious Monk. *Misterioso* (Riverside, 1991).

Daniel, John. <u>Play Melancholy Baby</u>. Menlo Park: Perseverance Press, 1986.

The fictional Casey Jones sings and plays like the early Harry Connick Jr. as featured on *20 By Harry Connick Jr.* (Sony, 1990).

Davis, J. Madison. <u>And the Angels Sing</u>. Sag Harbor, N.Y.: The Permanent Press, 1995.

The great trumpet star from the Benny Goodman and Harry James bands wrote the book's title song, "And the Angels Sing." Sadly, the Big Band era was over when Elman tried to form a post war band and go out on his own. Ziggy Elman: *Ziggy Elman and His Orchestra 1947.* (Circle, 1991).

Easily the two biggest bands during WWII were the Dorsey Brothers with Frank Sinatra and the Glenn Miller Band. Carl Carlson, the Carolina crooner, would hear them on the radio and know their material well, especially Sinatra's.

Tommy Dorsey-Frank Sinatra: *The Song Is You* (RCA, 1994).
Glenn Miller: *The Popular Recordings 1938-1942* (RCA, 1989).

Deaver, Jeffrey Wild. <u>Mistress of Jazz</u>. New York: Doubleday, 1992.

Taylor Lockwood makes her living playing piano. Her taste runs to 1950s & 1960s jazz. Among her favorites are Billy Taylor, Cal Tjader, Paul Desmond, Dave Brubeck and Miles Davis.
Dave Brubeck & Paul Desmond: *The Duets* (Horizon, 2002).
Billy Taylor: *The Billy Taylor Trio* (Riverside OJCCD, 1997).
Cal Tjader: *Tjader Plays Jazz* (Fantasy OJCCD, 1988).
Miles Davis: *Kind of Blue* (Columbia/Legacy, 1997).

Dionne, Ron. Sad Jingo. New York: Delabarre, 2012.
Numerous versions of "Crepuscule with Nellie," the tune Jingo keeps struggling to play, can be found on the two-disc set: Thelonious Monk. *The Complete 1957 Riverside Recordings* (Riverside, 2006).

Doctorow, E.L. Ragtime. New York: Random, 1975; London: Macmillan, 1976.
"Wall Street Rag," and "Mapleleaf Rag" which are played by Coalhouse Walker Jr. for the family can be found, along with other rags, on John Arpin, *Complete Piano Music of Scott Joplin* (Nashville Catalog, 1997).

Dowswell, Paul. Auslander. London: Bloomsbury, 2009.
When Peter thinks he's alone, he dances around the house to Benny Goodman's "Sing, Sing, Sing." That tune can be found on most Benny Goodman anthologies but a good one is *The Very Best of Benny Goodman* (RCA, 2000).
Goebbels tried to counter the influence of jazz with his own jazz band, Charlie and His Orchestra (that was popularly referred to as "Mr. Goebbels' Jazz Band"). Approved and unapproved jazz recordings can be found in *Swing Tanzen Verboten* (Proper, 2003).

Doyle, Roddy. Oh, Play That Thing. New York: Viking, 2004; London: Jonathan Cape, 2004.
In Chicago, Louis Armstrong recorded with Earl Hines: *Hot Five, Hot Seven* (Columbia, 1990) and Louis Armstrong: *"Sugar" The Best of the Complete RCA Victor Recordings* (RCA, 1990). Henry

would have been present during these sessions, or, later, heard them on the radio.

Woody Guthrie: *Early Masters* (Tradition, 1996) is a collection of depression era songs sung by Woody Guthrie and his friend Cisco Houston that were sung in the hobo camps that Henry inhabited when he was on the road.

DuBois, Brendan. "The Lady Meets the Blues." In Vega, Eddie. (ed.). Noir Nation 6. Middletown, DE: 2017.

Mikey learns about Billie Holiday and the song "Strange Fruit" from George the bartender. It can be found on *Best of Billie Holiday: 20th Century Masters* (MCA, 2002). Another overview with mostly smaller groups from 1945-1959 is *Billie Best* (Verve, 1992).

Duchin, Peter & Wilson, John Morgan. Blue Moon. New York: Berkley, 2002.

Lester Lanin was still a top society bandleader in the 1960s. *Best of the Big Bands: Lester Lanin* (Epic, 1990) is representative of the era when bands played foxtrots non-stop at society events

_____. Good Morning, Heartache. London: Prime Crimes, 2003; New York: Berkley, 2003.

Peter Duchin's father, Eddie, had a society dance band similar to Philip Damon's. Eddie Duchin: *Best of The Big Bands* (Columbia, 1990).

Edugyan, Esi. Half Blood Blues. London: Serpent's Tail, 2011. New York: Picador, 2012.

Bill Coleman did actually live in Paris at the time of the recording sessions in Half Blood Blues. He escaped internment by returning to the States and then came back after the war to Europe where he lived until his death in 1981.

Bill Coleman: 1929-1940 (Jazz Archives, 1995); and *Bill Coleman A Paris.* (Hallmark, 2010) both feature the swing trumpet player, alongside European and American expatriate jazz musicians playing standards of the time.

Edwards, Grace F. "Blind Alley, The." In Bland, Eleanor Taylor, (ed). Shades of Black: Crime and Mystery Stories by African American Writers. New York: Berkley, 2004.

An Erroll Garner recording was played in the club to restore a sense of order after Rhino's threatening appearance. Erroll Garner: *Erroll Garner Plays Misty* (Mercury, 1992).

Matthew Paige listens to tenor saxophonist Illinois Jacquet on the radio to relax.

Illinois Jacquet: *Flying Home: The Best of the Verve Years* (Polygram, 1994). He also likes the more mellow tenor saxophonist Paul Quinichette.

Paul Quinichette: *The Vice Pres* (Verve, 2000).

_____. The Blind Alley. New York: iUniverse, 2010.

"The Blind Alley" was expanded into a book, so the previously cited CDs of Erroll Garner, Illinois Jacquet and Paul Quinichette are all applicable.

_____. Do or Die. New York: Doubleday, 2000.

Mali and her boyfriend Tad listen to Cyrus Chestnut. His debut album is Cyrus Chestnut Trio: *The Nutman Speaks Again* (Alfa, 1992). *Kenny Davern & Joe Temperly* (Chiaroscuro, 2002) was recorded on the Queen Elizabeth II and is representative of jazz cruise music they would have heard.

_____. If I Should Die. New York: Doubleday, 1997.

Marvin Gaye's 1970 album, *What's Going On* (Tamla, 1971), captures the essence of the book better than any urban jazz album.

_____. No Time to Die. New York: Doubleday, 1999.

There's not much jazz as the old clubs like Small's are boarded up and have street vendors set up in their fronts. An album representative of what was once around is Dizzy Gillespie Big Band: *Showtime at The Spotlite* (Uptown, 2008).

_____. Toast Before Dying, A. New York: Doubleday, 1998.

Alvin Queen: *I Ain't Looking at You* (Enja, 2006) and Terrill Stafford Quartet: *Taking Chances: Live at The Dakota.* (Maxjazz, 2007) are two contemporary albums with young, New York jazz musicians. It's the sort of jazz Mali Anderson would hear at clubs like Harlem's Half Moon Bar.

Edwardson, Ake. <u>Sun and Shadow</u>. Stockholm: Norstedts, 1999. London: Harvill, 2005; New York: Viking, 2006.
Erik Winter listens to John Coltrane with Red Garland's trio playing "Soft Lights and Sweet Music" which can be found on Red Garland with John Coltrane: *Traneing In* (Prestige, 2004).
He also listens to Charlie Haden. Charlie Haden: *The Best of Quartet West* (Verve, 2007).

Ehrhart, Peggy. <u>Got No Friend Anyhow</u>. New York: Gale, 2011.
Maxx Maxwell is doing her best imitation of Big Mama Thornton singing "Little Red Rooster" as the story begins. The original can be heard on Big Mama Thornton: *Ball 'n' Chain* (Arhoolie, 2011).
Blues singer Bonnie Raitt provides great background music while reading about Maxx Maxwell. Bonnie Raitt: *The Best of Bonnie Raitt* (Capitol, 2003).

_____. <u>Sweet Man Is Gone</u>. Waterville, ME: Five Star, 2008.
The Rounder anthology *Any Woman's Blues* is a collection of modern women blues singers, any one of whom could be a model for Maxx Maxwell. *Any Woman's Blues* (Rounder, 2001).
Charlie Christian's guitar styling identifies a killer. Charlie Christian: *Guitar Wizard* (LeJazz, 1993).

Eisler, Barry. <u>Hard Rain</u>. London: Michael Joseph, 2003; New York: Putnam, 2003.
John Rain's Japanese wife, Midori, plays a jazz piano much like that of Toshiko Akiyoshi: *Toshiko Akiyoshi at Maybeck. Vol. 36* (Concord, 1995).

_____. Killing Rain. New York: Putnam, 2005 aka Redemption Games. London: Onyx, 2006.

For relaxation, it's usually Bill Evans that John Rain listens to. A trio club date is *Bill Evans: The 1960 Birdland Sessions.* (Fresh Sounds, 2006). Recorded 3 years before his death, *I Will Say Goodbye* (OJC, 1996) is haunting.

And of course, Toshiko Akiyoshi's playing reminds him of his wife—a trio album is *Interlude* (Concord, 2007).

_____. Last Assassin. London: Michael Joseph, 2007; New York: Putnam, 2006.

Rain listens to Toshiko Akiyoshi, who like his wife Midori, fuses her Japanese heritage into jazz. Toshiko usually recorded with her big band, so small group sessions are few. An early (reissued) recording is *Her Trio, Her Quartet—Recordings from 1956-58* (Storyville, 2006).

He relaxes to Bill Evans. Two club dates are *Sunday at the Vanguard* (Riverside, 2008) and *Bill Evans Live at Art D'Lugoff's Top of the Gate* (Resonance, 2012).

_____. Rain Fall. London & New York: Putnam, 2002.

Rain relaxes in a jazz club, listening to a young Japanese woman pianist who plays like Toshiko Akiyoshi. An early quintet album, *Toshiko at the Top of The Gate* (Denon, 1968) captures her subtle style.

_____. Rain Storm. Putnam, 2004; aka Choke Point. London: Michael Joseph, 2004.

Rain listens to Marisa Monte in Brazil. Marisa Monte: *Rose and Charcoal* (Blue Note, 1994).

He also listens to various Bill Evans albums and to singer Eva Cassidy at Blues Alley.

Bill Evans: *The Best of Bill Evans Live* (Verve, 1997).

Eva Cassidy: *Eva Cassidy at The Blues Alley* (Blix Street, 1998) was recorded after she learned that she was dying from cancer.

_____. Requiem For an Assassin. London: Michael Joseph,

2008; New York: Putnam, 2007;

John Rain seeks solace and equilibrium in Bill Evans' jazz. Two trio albums recorded just before Evans' death in 1980 are Bill Evans Trio: *The Brilliant* (Timeless, 1990) and *Consecration II* (Timeless, 1990).

Ellroy, James. "Dick Contino's Blues." In <u>Hollywood Nocturne</u>. New York: Penzler, 1994.

Dick Contino/On Stage (Dot, 1959) Typical of the easy listening records put out by Contino in the 1950s.

_____. <u>White Jazz</u>. London: Century, 1992; New York: Knopf, 1994.

Lieutenant Dave Klein hears alto saxophonist Art Pepper playing on Central Avenue when he's looking for leads on the robbery of drug dealer, J.C. Kafesjian. His son Tommy plays alto sax.

Art Pepper: *Art Pepper Meets the Rhythm Section* (Contemporary, 1986).

Chet Baker and Art Pepper: *The Complete Playboy Sessions* (Fresh Sounds, 2007).

Warne Marsh Quartet: *Music for Prancing* (V.S.O.P, 1992).

All three of the above albums are representative of the cool, west coast, 1950s sounds prevalent at the time.

Estleman, Loren D. <u>Jitterbug</u>. New York: Forge, 1998.

During the 1930s Big Band jazz from New York City or Chicago dominated Detroit's radio sounds. Both white and black bands were popular in the Motor City.

Louis Armstrong and His Orchestra 1932-1933 (Classics, 1990).

Benny Carter and His Orchestra 1933-1936 (Classics, 1990).

Jimmy Dorsey and His Orchestra 1940 (Circle, 1993).

Ivie Anderson with Duke Ellington's Famous Orchestra (Jazz Archives, 1991).

Billie Holiday: *Lady Day* (Columbia, 2007).

Johnny Mercer's songs were at the height of their popularity during the war years. *Johnny Mercer: Blues in the Night* (Verve, 1997) has Mercer standards interpreted by jazz's greatest musicians.

Charlie Caranicas & Tom Roberts: *Move Over* (Black Knight, 2007) is a varied program of classic jazz from 1907 to 1951.

_____. Lady Yesterday. London: Macmillan, 1987; Boston: Houghton Mifflin, 1987.

PI Amos Walker's friend Iris reminds one of the singer/pianist Carmen McRae. Carmen McRae: *Fine and Mellow* (Concord, 1988).

Charlie Green was a trombonist in Fletcher Henderson's band and a bit more upscale than Iris' father. He did, however, play the same type of early jazz. Green can be heard on Vol. 1 of *The Fletcher Henderson Story* (Columbia, 1994).

_____. Whiskey River. London: Scribners, 1991; New York: Bantam, 1990.

Based in Chicago and broadcasting over WGN, the Coon-Sanders Band was one of the most popular 1920s white jazz bands. Everyone in the Middle West listened to it and tried to book the band for their parties. Mel Torme made his professional debut at age 4 with the band.

The Coon Sanders Band: *The Best of Coon Sanders* (Retrieval, 1999) contains the tunes played during their residency at the posh Nighthawk Restaurant.

Farr, John. The Deadly Combo. New York: Ace, 1958.

Don Fagerquist Octet: *Eight by Eight* (V.S.O.P., 1987) features Fagerquist, a cool but underrated trumpet player.

Faye Farmer was a popular 1950s singer with a style and following similar to smokey voiced Julie London. Julie London: *Julie Is her Name/Julie Is her Name, Vol. 2* (Liberty, 1992).

Fitzgerald, F. Scott. "The Dance." In *Ellery Queen's Mystery Magazine.* March 1953. Vol. 21. No. 112.

King Oliver's Orchestra, the Duke Ellington Orchestra and Roger Wolfe Kahn's Orchestra would play country clubs. Fitzgerald, who was not all that interested in jazz, probably heard Roger Wolfe Kahn's Orchestra playing in New York City, and may have heard the other two at parties.

King Oliver: *King Oliver and his Orchestra* (RCA, 1992).

Duke Ellington: *The Okeh Ellington* (Columbia, 1991).

Roger Wolfe Kahn: *1925/1928* (Swingtime, 1992).

A fine jazz age anthology is *Hot Dance Bands from Okeh 1923-1931* (Retrospective, 2007).

_____. The Great Gatsby. London & New York: Scribners, 1992.

Jazz and other dance music would have been played at bootlegger Jay Gatsby's infamous weekend parties on Long Island.

Duke Ellington: *The Okeh Ellington* (Columbia, 1991).

Roger Wolfe Kahn: *1925/1928* (Swingtime, 1992).

Leo Reisman: *Maestro Sophisticate* (Flare, 2006).

King Oliver: *King Oliver and his Orchestra* (RCA, 1992).

Various Artists: *Hot Dance Bands from Okeh 1923-1931* (Retrospective, 2007).

Fitzhugh, Bill. Highway 61 Resurfaced. New York: Morrow, 2005.

Nobody catches the time better than B.B. B.B. King: *How Blue Can You Get?* (MCA, 1996).

Fleming, Charles. After Havana. New York: St. Martin's, 2004.

Nat King Cole: *Nat King Cole at The Sands* (Capitol, 2002). Although this album was recorded at another mob venue in Las Vegas, the show is virtually identical to those Cole performed during his frequent visits to Havana.

Machito & His Afro-Cuban Orchestra: *The Complete Columbia Masters* (Columbia, 2002). Machito's album is the sort of music that featured in the Tropicana floorshows as well as on the dance floor.

Perez Prado: *Mambo Mania/Havana 3 am* (Bear Family, 1990). This CD, containing two of Prado's 1950s albums, is the music that drew Americans to Havana's hotels and casinos.

_____. The Ivory Coast. New York: St. Martin's, 2002.
Nat King Cole: *Nat King Cole at The Sands* (Capitol, 2002). Cole often played the Sands when his friend Frank Sinatra had an interest in the club.
Chet Baker Quartet: *Live—Out of Nowhere* (Pacific Jazz, 2001). Typical Chet before the drugs took their toll. The fictional trumpet player Deacon is modeled on the young Chet Baker.

Fletcher, Jessica & Bain, Donald. Murder In a Minor Key. London & New York: Signet, 2001.
Jessica's favorite artist at the Jazz Fest is pianist Oliver Jones. A live set similar to that which she heard is featured on Oliver Jones, *Just in Time.* (Justin Time, 2007).
It was impossible for Jessica to miss the Marsalis family at their hometown jazz festival. The Marsalis Family: *Music Redeems* (Marsalis, 2010).

Foehr, Stephen. Storyville. Bro: Jiri Vanek, 2009.
Any early New Orleans recording will do. Preservation Hall Jazz Band: *Songs of New Orleans* (Preservation Hall, 2005) is great background for this story.

Foote, Shelby. "Ride Out." In Albert, Richard N. (ed.). From Blues to Bebop: A Collection of Jazz Fiction. Baton Rouge: Louisiana State University Press, 1990.
Roy Eldridge's 1930s sound was similar to that of the fictional, black trumpet player, Duff Conway. Roy Eldridge: *Roy Eldridge with The Gene Krupa Orchestra* (Columbia, 1990).

Fowler, Carol S. "And The Angels Sing." In Blues in the Night. Houston: Strategic Book Publishing and Rights Co., 2013.
The Wendall McCabe Quintet plays "Bernie's Tune," "Time and Again" and "Fine and Mellow." The West Coast chestnut, "Bernie's Tune" can be found on Stan Getz & Chet Baker *Live at the Haig 1953* (Fresh Sounds, 2015).
Stuff Smith's "Time and Again" is in *Stuff Smith, Dizzy Gillespie,*

Oscar Peterson (Verve, 1994).

An instrumental version of Billie Holiday's "Fine and Mellow" can be found on Gene Ammons' *Fine and Mellow* (Prestige, 2003).

_____. "Blues in the Night." In <u>Blues in the Night</u>. Houston: Strategic Book Publishing and Rights Co., 2013.

Bernie listens to a new group, the Johnny Mulray Quintet that plays "Summertime." An instrumental version can be found on Eric Alexander: *Gentle Ballads III* (Verve, 2008).

Mulray's playing Woody Herman's "Blues in the Night" when Bernie interviews him at his home. "Blues in the Night" is on Woody Herman *Blues on Parade* (Verve, 1991).

Bernie is playing Ray Berle's "Skylark" when entertaining his girlfriend. Ray Eberle's version of "Skylark" is on *Ray Eberle Orchestra Plays Glenn Miller Favorites* (Simitar, 1997).

_____. "Born To Be Blue." In <u>Blues in the Night</u>. Houston: Strategic Book Publishing and Rights Co., 2013.

The band is playing "Willow Weep for Me" when Butz enters Polson's Lounge. Houston Person has an eight-minute bluesy version on *I'm Just a Lucky So And So* (High Note, 2019).

_____. "Loverman." In <u>Blues in the Night</u>. Houston: Strategic Book Publishing and Rights Co., 2013.

Jack Goldberg is out of the "cool" jazz school, very much like Stan Getz. Butz hears him play "Autumn Leaves," "Budo" and "Loverman," which are on *Stan Getz Complete Roost Recordings* (Parlophone, 1997).

"Loverman" is on *Stan Getz at The Shrine* (Verve, 2009).

Butz plays 2 jukebox tunes featuring Helen Forrest with Benny Goodman singing "How High the Moon" and Stan Getz playing "Early Autumn" with Woody Herman's Orchestra.

"How High the Moon" is on *Complete Helen Forrest with Benny Goodman* (Collector's Choice, 2002).

Stan Getz's "Early Autumn" with Herman's band is on numerous collections among them, *The Definitive Stan Getz* (Verve, 2002).

_____. "Passion Flower." In <u>Blues in the Night</u>. Houston: Strategic Book Publishing and Rights Co., 2013.
Bernie hears a set by the Stan Dickman quartet while waiting for a killer. The tunes played are "Pennies from Heaven," "It Might as Well Be Spring," "Move," and "Passion Flower."
Both "Pennies from Heaven" and "Move" are on Stan Getz: *At Storyville* (Roulette, 1990).
"It Might as Well Be Spring" is on Frank Morgan: *Listen to the Dawn* (Antilles, 1993).
"Passion Flower" can be found on John Hicks & Frank Morgan: *Twogether* (HighNote, 2010).

_____. "Blowin' Up a Storm: The Second Chronicles of Bernie Butz." CreateSpace, 2016.
Jerry Farlow's big band is similar to Woody Herman's and played tunes popularized by the various "herds."
Woody Herman: *Road Band 1948 vol. 1 & 2.* (Hep, 2005) has a classic line-up and tunes. *Four Brothers: Together Again* (RCA, 1995) brings back the famous sax line-up of Zoot Sims, Al Cohn, Herbie Steward and Serge Chaloff.

Fuller, Jack. <u>The Best of Jackson Payne</u>. New York: Knopf, 2000.
Jackson Payne admired tenor saxophonists Hank Mobley and John Coltrane, and especially liked the latter's album, *A Love Supreme*.
Hank Mobley: *The Jazz Message of Hank Mobley* (Savoy, 1998).
John Coltrane: *A Love Supreme* (Impulse, 2003).
Jimmy Giuffre was the only clarinetist that Jackson Payne could tolerate.
Jimmy Giuffre: *The Easy Way* (Verve, 2003).

Fulmer, David. "Algiers." In Smith, Julie (ed.), <u>*New Orleans Noir*</u>. New York: Akashic, 2007.
These songs by Texas bluesman Lightning Hopkins were recorded after bluesman/gambler Eddie McTier dealt his last crooked

card, but they do capture the spirit of the man. Lightnin' Hopkins: *Lightnin' Hopkins* (Smithsonian Folkways, 1990).

_____. The Blue Door. London & New York: Harcourt, 2008.

Philadelphia's soul singer Jerry Butler was a survivor, unlike Jimmy Pope, who had a similar sound. Jerry Butler: *The Iceman: The Mercury Years* (Mercury, 1993).

_____. Chasing The Devil's Tail. Scottsdale: Poisoned Pen Press, 2001.

Breaking Out of New Orleans (JSP, 2004) is a 4 CD set that was recorded after the period of the story but contains music that would have been heard earlier in New Orleans.

_____. The Day Ends at Dawn. New Orleans: Crescent City Books, 2019.

Because Storyville is closing, most of the jazz musicians left New Orleans. But the Original Dixieland Jazz Band's recording of "Livery Stable Blues" was played around town and across the country. It can be found on Original Dixieland Jazz Band: *The 75th Anniversary* (RCA, 1992).

St Cyr hears a blues, "Careless Love," in an underground room about to be closed with the rest of Storyville. A later version by Bessie Smith is on *Careless Love* (Snapper 2017).

_____. The Dying Crapshooter's Blues. London: Houghton Mifflin Harcourt, 2007; New York: Harcourt, 2007.

Blues singer Blind Willie McTell wrote a song about a crooked gambler and pimp Little Jessie Williams, who is dying from a gunshot wound and trying to finish his own final song. Blind Willie McTell: *The Definitive Blind Willie McTell* (Columbia, 1994).

_____. Eclipse Alley. New Orleans: Crescent City Books, 2017.

Although several members of Bolden's band remember recording "Careless Love," no recordings exist. The song, however, went on to become a vocalist's favorite. Two different versions are by Bessie Smith (1925) and by Madeleine Peyroux (2004).

Bessie Smith: *Careless Love Blues* (Blues Classics, 2011).

Madeleine Payroux: *Careless Love* (Rounder, 2004).

_____. The Iron Angel. Raleigh, N.C: Bang Bang Lulu, 2014. Several albums by Kid Ory containing recordings from the early 1920s and reflecting the music heard in Storyville before King Oliver dominated jazz are: *Kid Ory 1922-1947* (Document, 1997) and *Kid Ory 1922-1925* (Chronological Classics, 1999). A slightly different take on the period, featuring Jelly Roll Morton, is *New Orleans Rhythm Kings and Jelly Roll Morton* (Milestone, 1991).

_____. Jass. New York: Harcourt, 2005.

No recordings of the jazz originator, trumpeter Buddy Bolden exists.

Jelly Roll Morton was the most popular musician in Storyville after Buddy Bolden was sent away to a mental institution. Two of his albums are Jelly Roll Morton: *The Library of Congress Recordings, Vol. 1.* (Solo Art, 1990) and *Birth of the Hot* (RCA Bluebird, 1995).

_____. Lost River. New York: Houghton Mifflin Harcourt, 2009.

The four-volume set, *Breaking Out of New Orleans 1922-1929* (JSP, 2004) was recorded almost a decade after the events of the story but contains much of the jazz played in the previous decade.

_____. Rampart Street. New York: Harcourt, 2006.

Buddy Bolden is now in a mental hospital and Jelly Roll Morton has gone upriver.

Ida Cox with the Coleman Hawkins Quintet: *Blues for Rampart Street* (Riverside OJCCD, 1990). Ida Cox, who was born in 1896 and started singing at 14, knew her way around Rampart Street as is evident in this album made in 1961, six years before her death. While her voice isn't what it once was, the feeling is still there.

_____. Will You Meet Me in Heaven? Raleigh, N.C.: Bang Bang Lulu, 2014.

Upon returning to Atlanta twenty years after Dupree's death, Betty heard a street singer about her doomed romance with Dupree. There are numerous versions available by various artists from different eras:

Harry Belafonte. *The Many Moods of Belafonte/Ballads, Blues & Boasters* (Sony, 2004).

Cookie and the Cupcakes: *King of Swamp Pop* (Ace, 2004).

Nick Drake: *Family Tree* (Island, 2007).

The Grateful Dead: *Rare Cuts and Oddities.* (Grateful Dead Records, 2005).

Taj Mahal: *Blues with a Feeling.* ((RCA, 2003)

Dave Von Ronk: *The Folkways Years 1959-1961.* (Smithsonian Folkways, 1992).

Chuck Willis: *I Remember Chuck Willis/The King of the Stroll* (Collectable, 2001).

Gailly, Christian. An Evening at The Club. New York: Other Press, 2003. Also, Soir au club. Paris: Editions de Minuit, 2001.

Simon Nardis has an identifiable style much like Alan Broadbent's. Alan Broadbent Trio: *Personal Standards* (Concord, 1977).

Irene Kral is backed by Alan Broadbent's piano on this haunting session. It's very much the same relationship club owner/singer Deborah hoped to achieve with pianist Simon Nardis. Irene Kral: *Where Is Love* (Choice, 2001).

Gaiter, Leonce. Bourbon Street. New York: Carroll & Graf, 2005.

Gambler Deke Watley arrives in New Orleans at Mardi Gras. *A Celebration of New Orleans Music* (Rounder, 2005), the Musicians Hurricane Relief 2005 album, features Mardi Gras music. At the Ten Spot bar, where he encounters his lost love, Hannah, Dinah Washington is singing "Blue Gardenia" on the jukebox. "Blue Gardenia" is on *Compact Jazz: Dinah Washington Sings the Blues* (Mercury, 1978).

He also hears Horace Silver's "Lonely Woman," which can be

found on Horace Silver: *Song for my Father* (Blue Note, 1999). Alex Moreau tries to kill him to the beat of Charlie Mingus' bass on "Gunslinging Bird." That can be found on The Mingus Big Band: *Gunslinging Birds* (Dreyfus, 1995).

Garcia, Vee Williams. The Jazz Flower. New York: iUniverse, 2006. Diahann Carroll sings the sophisticated New York club music that Rosa Johnson Stills would sing at the Blue Phoenix in New York and Chez Joline in Paris. Diahann Carroll and the Andre Previn Trio *Porgy and Bess* (DRG, 2006).

Gillette, Paul. Play Misty for Me. London: Tandem, 1972; New York: Award, 1971.

Erroll Garner: *Erroll Garner Plays Misty* (Mercury, 1998) is the album that insured Garner's reputation for the remainder of his career. He owned the instrumental version of "Misty".

Benny Goodman: *Benny Goodman at Carnegie Hall 1938* (Columbia, 1999) features "And the Angels Sing."

Gilmer, Byron. Felonious Jazz. Durham: Bluff Books, 2009.

Wilbur Ware's bass solo on "Softly as in a Morning Sunrise" can be found on the Sonny Rollins' album, A *Night at The Village Vanguard* (Blue Note, 1999).

Glatzer, Hal. Fugue in Hell's Kitchen, A. London: John Daniel, 2004; Palo Alto: Perseverance, 2004.

Although the book has a classical music setting, Katy Green is a swing violinist-and Eddie South and Stuff Smith were the two top American swing violinists of their time.

Eddie South: *1937-1941* (Classics, 1993). South plays period songs.

Stuff Smith: *Hot Jazz Violin: 1930-1940* (JAZ, 2004). A sampling of the best of Stuff Smith recorded during his heyday. Trumpet player Jonah Jones compliments Smith on tunes that would have been included in their Onyx Club gigs.

Stephane Grappelli and Yehudi Menuhin: *The Best of Grappelli*

& Menuhin (Angel, 1998). A nice collection of swing jazz violin by two top players, one jazz and the other classical. Neither played on Swing Street but the songs are period classics.

Louis Jordan is playing at Small's during the time of the story. Louis Jordan: *The Best of Louis Jordan* (MCA, 1989) is a great overview of Jordan and his band.

_____. The Last Full Measure. McKinleyville: Perseverance Press, 2006.

Swing jazz violinist Katy Green has a job with an all-girl band on a holiday cruise ship bound for Honolulu when she hears surfer Bill Apapane playing his Hawaiian guitar. *Ki ho alu Christmas: Hawaiian Slack Key Guitar* (Dancing Cat, 1997) is a Christmas slack key guitar album of music that Hawaiian Apapane would play.

Ina Ray Hutton & Dolly Dawn: *Girls Night Out* (Sony, 2001) features Depression era all-girl jazz bands that offered Green work.

_____. Too Dead to Swing. London: John Daniel 2004; Santa Barbara: Perseverance, 2002.

All-Girl bands were popular even before the WWII draft took musicians from the big bands. Ina Ray Hutton & Dolly Dawn: *Girls Night Out* (Sony, 2001).

Goldsmith, Martin. Detour. London: Blackmask, 2008; New York: Macaulay, 1939.

Jazz violinist Alexander Roth played in the style of Joe Venuti. Eddie Lang and Joe Venuti: *1920s & 1930s* (JSP 1986).

Goodis, David. Shoot The Piano Player aka Down There. London: Prion, 1999; New York: Gold Medal, 1956.

Eddie has sophisticated taste and likes both bebopper Bud Powell and the more traditional Art Tatum. Bud Powell: *Jazz Giant* (Verve, 2001) is a classic 1940s trio session. Recorded between 1933 and 1949, Art Tatum: *Piano Starts Here* (Columbia, 1995) has standards and technical excellence that would have attracted Eddie.

_____. Street of no Return. London: Black Lizard, 1994; New York: Gold Medal, 1961.

1950s vocalist Mark Murphy sings material that would appeal to the fictional Eugene Liddell. Mark Murphy: *Rah!* (Riverside OJC. 1994).

Gorman, Ed. "The Reason Why." In Spillane, Mickey and Collins, Max Allen (eds.). Century of Noir, A. New York: New American Library, 2002.

While most of the music played at the 25th reunion is 1950s pop, Dwyer always liked jazz and Dakota Staton's "Street of Dreams" was his favorite song. While numerous 1950s Dakota Staton CDs are available, none have "Street of Dreams." Other versions can be found on Lee Wiley: *Music of Manhattan 1951* (Uptown, 2007) or Sarah Vaughan: *Complete Columbia Singles A&B 1949-53* (Acrobat, 2019).

A typical Dakota Staton session backed by Sid Feller's orchestra is the 1959 Capitol recording, *More Than the Most* (Collectables, 1991).

"Muse." In Randisi, Robert J. (ed.). Murder and all that Jazz. New York: Signet, 2004.

The 1970s were the decade of the singer-song writer. Two of the best were Joni Mitchell and Dory Previn. Listen for background to Joni Mitchell *Hits* (Warner, 1996), which has the expected songs, such as "Urge for Going," "Chelsea Morning," "Circle Game," etc. Oddly, "Blue" is omitted. The less known Dory Previn's *In Search of Mythical Kings: UA Years* (EMI, 2006) contains subtle, wistful songs from her first few albums.

Gosling, Paula. Solo Blues. London & New York: Coward, McCann & Geoghegan, 1981.

Pianist Dave Catney plays the sort of introspective jazz that would interest the fictional Johnny Cosatelli. Dave Catney: *Reality Road* (Justice, 1994).

Graham, Heather. The Dead Play On. Don Mills, Ontario: Mira, 2015.

Although it's set in New Orleans, the musicians play contemporary music not specifically identified with the Big Easy. *Smooth Jazz No. 1* (Concord, 2009) contains top smooth jazz hits by musicians such as Boney Jones and George Benson.

Granelli, Roger. Out of Nowhere. Bridgend, Wales: Seren, 1995.

Welsh guitarist Frank Magnani played a different style of guitar from the boppers then in vogue in New York. His style is resembles Wes Montgomery's in the mid-1950s. Wes Montgomery. *Far Wes* (Pacific Jazz, 1999).

Grant, James. Don't Shoot the Piano Player. London: Piatkus, 1980.

With unknown help from organized crime, Lew Jackson has an impressive line-up (Art Blakey, Scott Hamilton, Clark Terry, Kenny Davern and Dave McKenna) for the Battersea Jazz Festival.

Art Blakey and the Jazz Messengers: *The Witch Doctor* (Blue Note, 1999).

Kenny Davern: *I'll See You in My Dreams* (Musicmasters, 1989).

Scott Hamilton: *Signatures* (Concord, 2001) was recorded on tour at Wimbledon.

Dave McKenna: *Easy Street* (Concord, 1994).

Clark Terry: *In Orbit* (OJC, 1991). Thelonious Monk joins Ellington veteran Clark Terry on this session.

Green, George Dawes. The Caveman's Valentine. London & New York: Warner International, 1994.

Keith Jarrett: *Facing You* (ECM, 1972). A moody session that frames a moody book.

Greenwood, Kerry. The Green Mill Murder. London: Allen & Unwin, 2012; Scottsdale: Poisoned Pen Press, 2007.

Gene Austin made famous "Bye Bye Blackbird," which was a hit song in 1926. The marathon dancer is murdered in the middle of that song which is found on Gene Austin: *Gene Austin #1* (M.C. Productions, 2011).

Reisman's white society dance band played jazz similar to Tintgel Stone's Jazzmakers at the Green Mill jazz club. Leo Reisman. *Putting on The Ritz.* (Flare, 2007).

Greer, Robert O. <u>The Devil's Red Nickel</u>. New York: Mysterious, 1997.

C.J. Floyd listened to Muddy Waters after returning from Vietnam. Muddy Waters: *Muddy Waters at Newport* (Chess, 2001).

A good overview of the R&B (Rhythm and Blues) scene, which provided work for many former big band musicians, is the *Mercury R&B (1946-1962)* (Mercury, 1989).

Gruber, Frank. <u>Swing Low Swing Dead</u>. London: Five Star, 1972; New York: Belmont, 1964.

Singer-song writer Bobby Darin resembles both Willie Walter and Al Donnelly. Bobby Darin: *As Long As I'm Singing* (Rhino/ Warner, 1995).

_____. <u>The Whispering Masters</u>. London: Panther, 1956; New York: Signet, 1949.

Tony Pastor had a late 1940s big band with various singers, including the young Rosemary Clooney and her sister Betty. *Tony Pastor and his Orchestra 1945-1950* (Circle, 1995).

_____. "Words and Music." In <u>Brass Knuckles</u>. Los Angeles: Sherbourne, 1966.

The song that murdered songwriter claimed as his was "Cottage by the Sea." The closest tune is Larry Conley & Willard Robinson's "A Cottage for Sale." The 1930 single by the Revelers appeared on *The Reveler's #3. Recorded 1928-1931* (M.C. Productions, 2013).

Guilfoile, Kevin. "O Death Where Is Thy Sting? In <u>Chicago Blues</u>. Hellmann, Libby Fischer. (ed.). Madison: Bleak House, 2007).

Two anthologies of Chicago blues that would be in the basement/

garage collections of unsophisticated owners are *Essential Blues Anthology* (Not Now, 2009) and *Essential Delta Blues* (Not Now, 2005).

Gwinn, William. <u>Jazz Bum</u>. New York: Margood, 1954.
Vic Ravenna was a talented clarinetist from an Italian family with a tone like clarinetist Buddy DeFranco. *Buddy DeFranco and Oscar Peterson Play George Gershwin* (Verve, 1998) and *Autumn Leaves* (Verve, 1998) catch Buddy DeFranco at his peak.

Hall, Patricia. <u>Dressed to Kill</u>. London: Severn House, 2014.
Dexter Gordon lived in Europe at the time of the story. He didn't spend that much time in England but his recordings would be similar to the jazz Muddy Abraham played.
Three Dexter Gordon albums from that period are:
A Swingin' Affair (Blue Note, 1962).
Our Man in Paris (Blue Note, 1963).
One Flight Up (Blue Note, 1964).

Hambly, Barbara. <u>Cold Bayou</u>. London & New York: Severn House, 2018.
Benjamin January hears the music of the plantation slaves of St. Chinan that reminds him of his childhood. Similar music can be found on: *Negro Blues and Hollers* (Rounder, 1997) and *Deep River of Song: Mississippi: The Blues Lineage: Musical Geniuses of the Fields, Leves and Jukes* (Rounder, 1999).

_____. <u>Crimson Angel</u>. London & New York: Severn House, 2014.
While seeking temporary safety with his family at Rose's family sugar plantation in the bayou, Benjamin January hears slaves singing in the fields that remind him of his childhood. *Negro Blues and Hollers* (Rounder, 1997) offer a selection of this music. Also, in Haiti, he hears music that's a mix of African, Creole and Delta blues. An example is *Creole Songs of Haiti* (Smithsonian-Folkways, 2004).

_____. <u>Dead and Buried</u>. London & New York: Severn

House, 2010.

While heading up country to Isobel Deschamps' planation, January hears work songs on the steamboat and in the cotton fields. In the latter, he hears "Wade in the Water" which tells him to jump in the water as slavers are on his trail with dogs. Ramsey Lewis Trio had a jazz hit with "Wade in the Water" in 1966 on *Wade in the Water* (Cadet, 1966) and the Staple Singers had a vocal version on *Freedom Highway* (Sony, Legacy, 1991).

_____. Die Upon a Kiss. New York: Bantam, 2001.
There's no jazz here. Any 19th century opera will do.

_____. Drinking Gourd. London & New York: Severn House, 2016.

Richie Havens sings "Follow the Drinkin' Gourd," about the celestial roadmap to freedom on *Songs of The Civil War* (Sony Legacy, 1991).

Odetta's *One Grain of Sand* (Vanguard, 1963) with its songs, such as "Cotton Fields," "Boll Weevil" and "Moses, Moses," captures the mood of the story.

_____. Fever Season. New York: Bantam, 1998.

Benjamin January, a classically trained black pianist, hears the work songs of the slaves in the fields and considers playing them on a piano. *Mississippi: The Blues Lineage* (Rounder, 1999) features music that worked its way into early jazz.

_____. A Free Man of Color. New York: Bantam, 1997.

There's no real jazz here as the book's main purpose is to give the reader a picture of New Orleans society in the 1830s and a Creole's place within it. Any classical music from the period will suffice.

_____. Good Man Friday. London & New York: Severn House, 2013.

It's set mostly in Washington D.C. rather than New Orleans where the music was Piedmont blues which is similar to ragtime guitar. The thumb plays the bass line and two or three fingers pick the melody or harmony—it's known as "finger-picking." Its more complex blues would have appealed to Benjamin January rather than Delta Blues. Any Blind Boy Fuller will do but *Rough Guide to Blind Boy Fuller* (World Music Network, 2015) and *Blind Boy Fuller: East Coast Piedmont Style* (Sony, 1991) are favorites. Another example, *Classic Piedmont Blues* (Smithsonian Folkways, 2017) mixes urban and rural blues.

_____. Lady of Perdition. London & New York: 2019 & 2020.

No jazz here. Listen to Odetta's two blues albums, *Odetta and The Blues* and *Sometimes I Feel Like Cryin,'* now available on the compilation, *Odetta Sings The Blues* (Fresh Sound, 2014).

_____. "Libre." *Ellery Queen's Mystery Magazine.* November 2006.

No jazz here. As with other January stories, Odetta's blues albums (*Odetta Sings The Blues,* Fresh Sound, 2014) capture their essence.

_____. Murder in July. London & New York: Severn House, 2017.

No jazz here. I listened to Odetta's two blues albums, *Odetta and The Blues* and *Sometimes I Feel Like Cryin,'* now available on the compilation, *Odetta Sings The Blues* (Fresh Sound, 2014).

_____. Ran Away. London & New York: Severn House, 2011.

Too early for jazz. Benjamin January hears gospel and spirituals during a Protestant church service, reminding him of field songs and ring shouts from his plantation childhood. *Classic American Gospel from Smithsonian Folkway* (Smithsonian Folkways, 2008) is a fine example. Another is Odetta's *The Tin Angel* (Fantasy, 1993) which captures the story's mood and contains the classic warning to runaways, "Wade in the Water," meaning 'the Man is coming with dogs".

_____. Sold Down the River. New York: Bantam, 2000.

Hambly's Benjamin January mysteries predated jazz. They are included so the reader has an insight to the people whose descendants created jazz. The 1830s field hollers and songs used in the story eventually evolved into blues and jazz played by New Orleans musicians descended from slaves, freemen and Creole musicians. The Library of Congress Archive of Folk Culture has collected much of this music that can be found on various CDs such as *Negro Blues and Hollers* (Rounder, 1997).

_____. "There Shall Be Your Heart Also." In New Orleans Noir. Smith, Julie (ed.). New York: Akashic, 2007.
Too early for jazz. As noted elsewhere, Benjamin January played Creole and slave songs for his own pleasure. Examples can be found in Library of Congress: *Negro Blues and Hollers* (Rounder, 1997).

_____. Wet Grave. New York: Bantam, 2002.
To relax and think, pianist Benjamin January played the classical compositions of Mozart, Bach, and Vivaldi. But sometimes he played the Creole and slave songs that he heard on the New Orleans docks or remembered from his childhood on a plantation. Library of Congress: *Negro Blues and Hollers* (Rounder, 1997).

Harvey, Brian. Beethoven's Tenth. Victoria, B.C,: Orca 2015.
Frank plays Sinatra's "Fly Me to The Moon" when tuning Miss P.'s piano. It can be heard on Frank Sinatra & Count Basie, *It Might as well be Swing,* (Reprise, 1964).
He was playing "I've Got You Under My Skin" when he first gets roughed up at The Cellar. It's on Oscar Peterson: *Plays the Cole Porter Songbook* (Verve, 1959).
Frank plays a duet with Kaz on "My Funny Valentine." A solo version is on George Cables: *Person to Person* (SteepleChase, 1995).

_____. Tokyo Girl. Victoria. B.C.: Orca, 2016
Yakuza boss Goto requests Frank Ryan to play the standards "My Funny Valentine," "The Man I Love" and "Night Train."
"My Funny Valentine" can be found on George Cables' *Person to*

Person (SteepleChase, 1995).

Alan Broadbent does a memorable version of "The Man I Love" on *'Round Midnight* (Artistry, 2015).

The Oscar Peterson's jazz standard "Night Train" is found on Oscar Peterson: *Night Train* (Verve, 1997).

Harvey, John. "Billie's Blues." In <u>Darker Shade of Blue</u>. Arrow, 2010.

There are numerous recordings of Billie Holidays classic composition "Billie's Blues," written and first recorded in 1936. A vintage favorite by Billie Holiday is on *Billie's Blues* (Blue Note, 2006).

_____. "Bird of Paradise." In <u>Now's the Time</u>. London: Slow Dancer, 1999.

"Bird of Paradise" can be found in the anthology *Charlie Parker: Verve Jazz Masters 15* (Verve, 2007).

_____. "Cheryl." In <u>Now's the Time</u>. London: Slow Dancer, 1999.

Charlie Parker's "Cheryl" can be found on *Savoy's Charlie-Vol. 2* (Savoy, 2018).

_____. <u>Cold In Hand</u>. London: William Heinemann, 2008; New York: Harcourt, 2008.

Charlie listened to Thelonious Monk's trio playing "Bemsha Swing" which can be found on *Thelonious Monk Trio* (Prestige, 2007).

He also strays away from his east coast beboppers to listen to west coast jazz.

Bud Shank & Laurindo Almeida: *Brazilliance, Vol 1* (Blue Note, 1991).

He was listening to trombonist Bob Brookmeyer play "There Will Never Be Another You" when Lynn was shot. It's included in the album *The Modernity of Bob Brookmeyer* (Fresh Sounds, 2008).

_____. <u>Cold Light</u>. London: William Heinemann, 1994;

New York: Holt, 1994.

Charlie Resnick's Christmas gift to himself was the boxed set *Billie Holiday: The Verve Studio Masters* (Verve, 2005).

_____. "Confirmation." In <u>Now's the Time</u>. London: Slow Dancer, 1999.

Parker's "Confirmation" is on *Genius of Charlie Parker #3* (Verve, 1996).

_____. "Cool Blues." In <u>Blue Lightning</u>. London: Slow Dancer, 1998.

A robber uses as an alias the names of sidemen in Duke Ellington's band. Duke Ellington: *The Duke's Men: Small Groups* (Columbia, 1989).

Charlie Resnick lays a trap when Joe Temperley is playing at Ronnie Scott's.

Dave McKenna/Joe Temperley: *Sunbeam and Thundercloud* (Concord 1998) features Temperley in a relaxed duo setting.

_____. <u>Cutting Edge</u>. London: Viking, 1991; New York: Henry Holt, 1991.

Clifford Brown's trumpet provides temporary solace for Charlie Resnick.

Clifford Brown: *Clifford Brown Memorial Album* (Blue Note, 1990).

Resnick offers shelter to Ed Silver, a tenor sax player down on his luck, who saw Charlie Parker before he cut his famous Dial recordings.

Charlie Parker: *Charlie Parker on Dial* (Definitive, 2005).

_____. <u>Darkness, Darkness</u>. London: William Heinemann, 2014; New York: Pegasus, 2014.

When Charlie got the phone call informing him about a vacancy as a civilian investigator, he was listening to Thelonious Monk's "Smoke Gets in Your Eye" which is on *Monk* (Prestige, 2009).

Thinking about Lynne's murder, he listens to Eric Dolphy & Booker Little's "Aggression" that's on Eric Dolphy/Booker Little

Quintet *Live at The Five Spot. Vol.1"* (OJC, 1991).

At the time of her death, he was listening to Bob Brookmeyer's "There Will Never Be Another You" which is on *The Modernity of Bob Brookmeyer* (Fresh Sounds, 2008).

Resnick was thinking about Miles Davis' version of "Bag's Groove" with Thelonious Monk with Monk's odd solo. It's on Miles Davis, *Bag's Groove* (OJC, 1991).

Catherine Njoroge, Resnick's Kenyan investigation partner stops by his house when Charlie's listening to Cannonball Adderley's "Autumn Leaves" on *Somethin' Else* (Blue Note, 1999).

Thinking about Spike Robinson, Resnick remembers seeing him play "Now's the Time" in memory of alto saxophonist Ed Silver. A version of it by Houston Person and Ron Carter appears on *Now's the Time* (Muse, 1990). Returning from London after a trip to London, he relaxes to a Spike Robinson Gershwin cd: *The Gershwin Collection* (Hep, 1995).

After an interrogation, Resnick has Charlie Mingus' "I Can't Get Started" in his mind. This solo tune by Mingus on piano can be found on: *Mingus Plays Piano* (Impulse, 1964).

Resnick's final thoughts are about the new Thelonious Monk album of live concerts in Paris and Milan that featured "Off Minor" and Straight No Chaser," etc, titled *Two Hours with Thelonious Monk-European concerts complete-Milan and Paris* (Fresh Sounds, 2013).

_____. "Dexterity." In Now's the Time. London: Slow Dancer, 1999.

"Dexterity" is on *Complete Savoy & Dial Master Takes* (Savoy, 2007) disc 3.

_____. "Drummer Unknown." In Randisi, Robert J. (ed.). Murder and all that Jazz. New York: Signet, 2004.

Two Tubby Hayes albums, *Tubs* (Fontana, 2005), and *Jazz at The Flamingo* (Jasmine, 2001) reflect the 1950s London jazz scene.

_____. Easy Meat. London: William Heinemann, 1996; New York: Holt, 1996.

Thelonious Monk's music is always in the background of Charlie Resnick's life. Thelonious Monk: *Monk* (Columbia, 2002).

_____. "Favor." In Darker Shade of Blue, A. London: Arrow, 2010.

Derek Becker and singer Dianne Adams have a surprise hit with "Ghost of a Chance." A version by Billie Holiday with Benny Carter on alto sax can be found on *Music for Torching-Billie Holiday Story Vol. 5* (Polygram, 2007).

_____. "Home." In Jakubowski, Maxim. (ed.). The Best British Mysteries IV. London: Allison & Busby, 2006.

While thinking about the Nottingham drug problem, Resnick was listening to Art Pepper and remembering seeing him. A favorite album was *Art Pepper Meets the Rhythm Section* (Contemporary, 1988) in which Pepper plays with Miles Davis' rhythm section.

_____. In A True Light. London: William Heinemann, 2001; New York: Carroll & Graf, 2002.

When he was a young artist in New York, Sloane often went to the Five Spot to hear Thelonious Monk. The Thelonious Monk Quartet featuring John Coltrane. *Live At The Five Spot* (Blue Note, 1993) is classic. Another album recorded with tenor saxophonist Johnny Griffin, *Thelonious Monk In Action: Recorded at The Five Spot Café* (Riverside, 1990) is also rewarding.

Beginning in the summer of 1957, Monk spent 6 months at the Five Spot, playing with various musicians. When his residency ended, he was a star.

_____. "Just Friends." In Robinson, Peter. (ed.). The Penguin Book of Crime Stories. London & New York: Penguin, 2007.

Two albums featuring English jazz musicians from the early part of the story are: The New Don Rendall Quartet: *Roarin'* (BGR,

2004) and *Jazz at The Flamingo* (Jasmine, 2001).

Two albums featuring the title tune "Just Friends" are: Chet Baker: *Burnin' at Backstreet* (Fresh Sounds, 1991) and Bill Perkins and Richie Kamuca: *Just Friends* (Lonehill, 2006).

_____. Last Rites. London: William Heinemann, 1998; New York: Henry Holt, 1999.

Charlie Resnick listens to an old favorite, *Thelonious Monk Plays Duke Ellington* (Riverside OJCCD, 1987).

_____. Living Proof. London: William Heinemann, 1995; New York: Holt, 1995.

Charlie listens to the Art Tatum/Ben Webster album: *The Art Tatum Group Masterpieces. Vol. 8* (Pablo, 1975).

He heard singer Betty Carter at Ronnie Scott's London jazz club. Betty Carter: *Feed the Fire* (Verve, 1993) was recorded at London's Royal Festival Hall during the time of the story.

_____. Lonely Hearts. London: Viking, 1989; New York: Holt, 1989.

Resnick listens to Johnny Hodges throughout the book.

Jazz Masters 35: *Johnny Hodges* (Verve, 1994) features Hodges in various formats with and without Duke's men.

_____. "Minor Key." In Jakubowski, Maxim. (ed.). Paris Noir. London: Serpent's Tail, 2007.

Val Colins, a British alto sax player, shared the drug problems of alto players Frank Morgan and Art Pepper as well as baritone sax player Gerry Mulligan and the infamous trumpet player Chet Baker. Mulligan and, eventually, Morgan cleaned up their drug habits while Pepper and Baker had drug problems throughout their lives as did Val.

Chet Baker/Art Pepper: *The Route* (Capitol/Pacific Jazz, 1989).

Frank Morgan: *Frank Morgan* (Crescendo, 1991).

Gerry Mulligan: *The Gerry Mulligan Quartet. Complete Studio Recordings* (Lonehill, 2005).

Val also saw Lester Young during the final period in his life. He died shortly after his return to the States. It's on *Lester Young in Paris* (Universal, 2006).

Val's songbook favorites on the jukebox at a breakfast place on Wardour Street were by Ella Fitzgerald, "Manhattan" and "Every Time We Say Goodbye."

"Manhattan" can be found *Ella Fitzgerald Sings the Rodgers and Hart Songbook* Verve, 1997.

"Every Time We Say Goodbye" is on *Ella Fitzgerald Sings The Cole Porter Songbook (Expanded edition)* Verve, 1997.

_____. "My Little Suede Shoes." In <u>Now's the Time</u>. London: Slow Dancer, 1999.

"My Little Suede Shoes" can be found in *The Complete Charlie Parker on Verve* (Verve, 1990).

_____. <u>Now's the Time</u>. London: Slow Dancer, 1999.

The individual short story titles in this collection of stories by Harvey are taken from compositions by alto saxophonist Charlie Parker. The novella "Slow Burn" was adapted from a BBC Chanel 4 radio program. A suggested list of related music for listening is included with each story.

_____. "Now's the Time." In <u>Now's the Time</u>. London: Slow Dancer, 1999.

Resnick listened to "Theme of No Repeat" on the *Clifford Brown Memorial Album* (OJC, 2007) with Ed Silver. After Silver's death, Charlie Resnick remembers Spike Robinson at Ronnie Scott's dedicating "Now's the Time" to his memory. "Now's the Time" is on *Genius of Charlie Parker, Vol. 3* (Verve, 1996).

_____. <u>Off Minor</u>. London: Viking, 1992; New York: Henry Holt, 1992.

Thelonious Monk's "Off Minor" can be found on numerous

albums. Two examples are *Thelonious Monk with John Coltrane*: (Riverside, 1998) and *Thelonious Monk in Copenhagen* (Storyville, 1996).

_____. Rough Treatment. London: Viking, 1990; New York: Henry Holt, 1990.

Charlie listens to Thelonious Monk and Duke Ellington.

Thelonious Monk: *The Complete Prestige Recordings* (Prestige, 2002) features early Monk playing tunes that made him famous.

Duke Ellington: *Duke Ellington and Johnny Hodges Play The Blues Back To Back* (Verve, 1997) is a small group setting for the Duke and his famous alto player.

Duke Ellington: *Money Jungle* (Blue Note, 1987)-the 1920s big bandleader holds his own in a trio with two modern jazz giants, Max Roach and Charlie Mingus.

_____. "She Rote." In Now's the Time. London: Slow Dancer, 1999.

"She Rote" can be found on *Complete Charlie Parker, The* (Verve, 1990). Disc #6.

_____. Slow Burn. In Slow Burn. London: Slow Dancer, 1999.

Unable to sleep, Resnick listening to Monk's "Bemesha Swing" when the call comes about the fire at Jimmy Nolan's jazz club. Thelonious Monk's trio playing "Bemsha Swing" can be found on *Thelonious Monk Trio* (Prestige, 2007).

Resnick was listening to Art Pepper's *So In Love* (Analog, 2007) while reading Russell Vener's suicide/murder. He remembers seeing Pepper at Jimmy's club.

_____. Still Waters. London: William Heinemann, 1997; New York: Henry Holt, 1997.

Charlie Resnick is called away from a Milt Jackson concert by the discovery of a young woman's body. Milt Jackson: *Statements* (Impulse, 1993).

He hears pianist Jessica Williams in a north London club. In Jessica Williams: *This Side Up* (MAXJAZZ, 2002), an album of original compositions, her trio pays tribute to the major influences in her jazz life-Miles Davis, Milt Hinton and Dexter Gordon-all were also a part of Charlie's life and music education.

And always, when Charlie's confused, he turns to his beloved Thelonious Monk. Thelonious Monk: *Thelonious Monk Trio* (Prestige, 1988).

_____. "Stupendous." In Now's the Time. London: Slow Dancer, 1999.

"Stupendous" can be found on *Charlie Parker: Complete Savoy & Dial Master Takes* (Savoy, 2007).

_____. "The Sun, the Moon and the Stars," in A Darker Shade of Blue. London: Arrow, 2010.

No specific jazz mentioned. I listened to Gerry Mulligan & Thelonious Monk's *Mulligan Meets Monk* (Riverside, 1957), especially "Straight No Chaser" and "'Round Midnight."

_____. Trouble In Mind. Nottingham: Crime Express, 2007.

Jack Kiley listens to pianist Mose Allison and alto saxophonist Cannonball Adderley.

Mose Allison: *Trouble In Mind* (Prestige, 1988) and Cannonball Adderley: *Somethin' Else* (Blue Note, 1985).

When Kiley is with Charlie Resnick, they listen to pianist Art Tatum, tenor saxophonist Ben Webster, and of course, Resnick's favorite pianist, Thelonious Monk.

Art Tatum & Ben Webster: *The Art Tatum Group Masterieces, Vol. 8* (Pablo, 1975).

Thelonious Monk Plays Duke Ellington (Riverside, 1987).

_____. Wasted Years. London: Viking, 1993; New York: Henry Holt, 1993.

Charlie Resnick's listening is usually predictable but the addition of baritone saxophonist Serge Chaloff was unexpected.

Serge Chaloff: *Blue Serge* (Capitol, 1998).

Duke Ellington: *Duke Ellington at Newport Complete* (Columbia, 1999).

Ella Fitzgerald singing "Every Time We Say Goodbye" can be found on Ella Fitzgerald: *Gold: Her Greatest Hits* (Universal Jazz, 2003).

_____. "Well, You Needn't." In <u>Minor Key</u>. Nottingham: Five Leaves, 2009.

Charlie bought *Thelonious Monk Live at The Jazz Workshop*, recorded in San Francisco, 1957, at a charity shop. Along with "Well, You Needn't" are old favorites "'Round Midnight," "Misterioso," and "Blue Monk."

Haut, Woody. <u>Cry For A Nickel, Die For A Dime</u>. Concord, MA: Concord ePress, 2014.

Jimmy Estes became a collector of old blues 78s after hearing Robert Johnson singing "Kind Hearted Woman." It can be found on Robert Johnson: *King of The Delta Blues* (River Records, 2008).

Charles Brown was on the jukebox at Minnie's when Abe stopped in for information. Early Charles Brown can be heard on *Cool Blues of Charles Brown* (Jasmine, 2002).

Nat Cole Trio was playing on the sound system at gangster Billy Stiles' club. Early Cole recordings for radio broadcast can be found on *Nat King Cole Transcriptions* (Blue Note, 2005). Cole was replaced by Bird and Diz playing the classic "A Night In Tunisia"which can be found on *Jazz at Massey Hall* (OJC/Debut, 1989).

On his first date with Alice, Abe took her to hear Willie "the Lion" Smith at the Imperial. Late Smith can be found on Willie "the Lion" Smith: *Lucky and the Lion* (Good Time Jazz, 1999).

A favorite of Felix, the blues collector, was Charlie Patton's "Shake It Or Break It." It's collected on *The Best of Charlie Patton* (Yazoo, 2005).

A mix up between Jimmy Estes and blues singer Sleepy John Estes will cost Felix his life. Sleepy John Estes can be heard on *I Ain't Gonna Be Worried No More* (Yazoo, 1992).

Abe and girlfriend Kim hear Dinah Washington singing her hit "What A Difference A Day Makes," Jesse Belvin's "Good Night My Love," and Ray Charles' "Night Time is the Right Time" on his car radio. Along with Dinah's other 1950s hits, "What A Difference A Day Makes is on *What a Difference a Day Makes* (Jazz Images, 2018).

"Good Night My Love" is on Jesse Belvin: *The Casual* (Screenland Records, 2013). Ray Charles' "Night Time Is the Right Time" is on *Best of Ray Charles: The Atlantic Years* (Rhino, 1994).

Jimmy Estes got into jazz by hearing Dave Brubeck's alto player Paul Desmond and then Charlie Parker's "Confirmation."

Desmond's *Take Ten* (Sony 2015) features the alto saxophonist without Brubeck.

Charlie Parker's "Confirmation" is on *Now's the Time: The Genius of Charlie Parker, Vol. 3* (Verve, 2018).

Abe's friend, Moseley, seemingly the only honest cop in L.A. kills himself listening to "Angel Eyes" on Frank Sinatra's *Only the Lonely* (Capitol, 1998).

Hayes, Teddy. <u>Blood Red Blues</u>. Boston: Kate's Mystery Books, 2004; London: Justin, Charles, 2004.

Devil Barnett listens to CDs of Miles Davis' playing "My Funny Valentine" and Sarah Vaughan singing "Moonlight in Vermont."

Miles Davis Plays for Lovers (Prestige, 2003) has as its opening track, "My Funny Valentine". It originally appeared on the classic album, *Cookin' with the Miles Davis Quintet* (Prestige, 2002). It's Miles at his best.

"Moonlight in Vermont" can be found on *Sarah Vaughan's Golden Hits* (Mercury, 1990).

_____. <u>Dead By Popular Demand</u>. Boston: Kate's Mystery Books, 2005; London: Justin Charles, 2005.

Although Rap dominates the story, Devil Barnett's father had been a jazz drummer at the legendary 1940s Harlem club, Minton's, and Devil often listens to music of the period. Thelonious Monk: *After Hours at Minton's* (Definitive, 2004), Dizzy Gillespie and Charlie Christian: *After Hours* (OJC, 2000), *The Genius of Charlie Christian* (Columbia, 1990) and Charlie Christian: *Live Sessions at Minton's* (Musicdisc, 1999) all feature music from Minton's Playhouse.

_____. Wrong As Two Left Feet. London: Xpress, 2003.
The Jazz Crusaders' Complete Live at The Lighthouse '62 with its two-horn front line mixing hard bop with R&B offers jazz background to the urban crime tale.

Hellmann, Libby Fisher. "Your Sweet Man." In Chicago Blues. Chicago: Bleakhouse, 2007.
A good overview of the Chicago Blues scene can be found in *The Best of Chicago Blues* (Vanguard, 1990).

Helms, Richard. Joker Poker. Lincoln: Writer's Showcase, 2000.
Chet Baker & Paul Desmond: *Together* (Epic, 1993).
Recordings from several sessions that featured Chet Baker and Paul Desmond together in 1975 and 1977. Desmond wasn't well and died a week later. Both horn players were Gallegher favorites.

_____. Juicy Watsui. Back Alley, 2001.
New York Trumpet Ensemble: *Trumpets in Stride* (Summit, 1990). Some basic horn blues—very much the sort that Gallegher would play with his pianist, Sockeye Sam.

_____. Voodoo That You Do. Back Alley, 2001.
Pat Gallegher listens to traditionalist Sidney Bechet and mid 20th century masters, Paul Desmond and Jim Hall.
Sidney Bechet: *The Complete Sidney Bechet Vol. 1/2* (RCA, 1992).
Paul Desmond: *Concerto* (CBS, 1995) with Jim Hall.

_____. Paid In Spades. Franklin, TN: Clay Stafford Books, 2019.

Gallegher's new guitarist, Chick Kasey warms up by playing Jim Hall's "the Answer Is Yes" which can be found on Jim Hall, *Concierto* (CTI, 1975).

Chick also plays Chick Corea's "Spain" from *Light as a Feather* (Verve, 1990) while sourcing some rosewood from a luthier.

_____. Wet Debt.

Ruby Braff & Ellis Larkins: *Duets. Vol. 2* (Vanguard, 2000). Pat Gallegar and his friend Sockeye Sam would have similar cornet-piano conversations.

Hentoff, Nat. Blues for Charlie Darwin. London: Constable, 1983; New York: Morrow, 1982.

Art Blakey and the Jazz Messengers: *Meet You at The Jazz Corner of The World* (Blue Note, 2002) features a young tenor player very much like the one Noah Green heard playing with Blakey at The Blue Light in Greenwich Village.

_____. Call the Keeper. London: Constable, 1983; New York: Morrow, 1982.

Randal plays guitar and listens to Jim Hall.

Jim Hall: *Jazz Guitar* (Pacific Jazz, 1988). This is Hall's first guitar album as a leader and would be a Randal favorite.

Grachan Moncur III was popular with the Black Power crowd and is found on Jackie McLean: *Destination Out* (Blue Note, 2002).

Coleman Hawkins, who drops in for the late set, could play with musicians of any generation as evidenced on Coleman Hawkins & Friends: *Bean Stalkin'* (Pablo, 1988) and Coleman Hawkins: *The Hawk Relaxes* (Prestige, 2006).

_____. The Man From Internal Affairs. New York: Mysterious, 1985.

Noah Green gives some old Kay Kyser big band records that he found in a used record store to his childhood friend and fellow record collector Jason Mendelssohn, now a defense attorney who gets him out of trouble.

Kay Kyser: *Sentimental Favorites* (Columbia, 1987).

At the same time, Green found some recordings of singer Billie Holiday at Boston's Storyville that interest Wilfred Mulvaney of NYPD's Internal Division.

Billie Holiday: *Billie Holiday at Storyville* (1201 Music, 1999).

Hewatt, Alan V. Lady's Time. London: William Heinemann, 1986; New York: Harper & Row, 1985.

Eubie Blake: *Memories of You* (Biograph, 1990). Blake's ragtime years parallel Lady Winslow's. He was the composer of many of the tunes that she played.

Daniel Blumenthal: *Scott Joplin: Rags & Waltzes* (Pavane, 1994).

James P. Johnson: *Parlor Piano Solos from Rare Piano Roll* (Biograph, 1997).

Oddly, while racial prejudice slowed recording opportunities, black musicians, such as Lady Winslow, did make piano rolls used to demonstrate popular hits of the day.

Himes, Chester. All Shot Up. London: Panther, 1969; New York: Berkeley, 1960.

Unlike the other series' titles, All Shot Up is set in the winter and has a different feel about it. Since no specific jazz was mentioned, I listened to Marvin Gaye's *What's Goin' On* (Tamla, 1971) and the Crusaders' *Street Life* with Randy Crawford (MCA, 1979).

_____. The Big Gold Dream. London: Allison & Busby, 1988; New York: Thunder's Mouth Press, 1996.

After settling her score with Sweet Prophet, Alberta Wright sings the Richard M. Jones blues standard, "Trouble in Mind." There are numerous recordings of "Trouble In Mind," but the most fitting is by Nina Simone on *Nina Simone at Newport* (Colpix, 1960).

_____. Blind Man with a Pistol. London: Hodder & Stoughton,

1969; London: Vintage, 1989.

Thelonious Monk is headlining at the Five Spot in 1958 at the time of John Babsin's murder. Two live recordings of Thelonious Monk's Quartet at the Five Spot in 1958, feature different tenor sax players, John Coltrane and Johnny Griffin.

Thelonious Monk: *Discovery-at the Five Spot Live with Thelonious Monk and John Coltrane* (Blue Note, 2000).

Thelonious Monk: *Thelonious in Action: Thelonious Monk Quartet with Johnny Griffin at the Five Spot* (OJC, 2006).

_____. Cotton Comes to Harlem. London: Frederick Muller, 1966; New York: Putnam, 1965.

Lester Young, Roy Eldridge, Harry Edison: *Laughin' to Keep from Cryin'* (Verve, 2000), and Count Basie: *1947/Brand New Wagon* (RCA Bluebird, 1990) features music that would be on the radio and jukeboxes in Harlem.

_____. The Crazy Kill, The. London: Allison & Busby, 1984; New York: Berkeley, 1959.

Dulcy Perry constantly plays a recording of Bessie Smith singing "Backwater Blues" throughout the story. It can be found on *The Essential Bessie Smith* (Columbia Legacy, 2014).

_____. The Heat's On. London: Frederick Muller, 1966; New York: Putnam, 1966.

Ed hears Lester Young recordings in a whorehouse while looking for supposed Digger's killers. *Lester Young with the Oscar Peterson Trio* (Verve, 1952) features tunes from the Great American Songbook.

_____. Rage In Harlem, A. London: Allison & Busby, 1985; New York: Avon, 1965.

Count Basie: *1947/Brand New Wagon* (Bluebird 2292-2-RB, 1990). Basie's band survived (barely) the end of the Big Band era and their music would be on Harlem jukeboxes.

_____. The Real Cool Killers. London: Allison & Busby,

1985; New York: Avon, 1959.

Big Joe Turner is playing on the jukebox at the Dew Drop Inn when Digger Jones inquired about the murder of a white man named Galen.

Big Joe Turner: *Greatest Hits* (Atlantic, 1989).

Hoch, Edward D. "The Ripper of Storyville." In The Ripper of Storyville. Norfolk: Crippen & Landru, 2003.

Although he came on the scene a generation later and was King of the Jazz Age stride piano players, James P. Johnson: *Parlor Piano Solos* (Biograph, 1997) captures the sound and spirit of earlier times.

Holden, Craig. The Jazz Bird. New York: Simon & Schuster, 2001.

The rebellious Imogene enjoys black jazz at the Magnolia Club where she meets George Remus. She hires the new popular King Oliver Jazz Band from Chicago to play at the Sinton Hotel. King Oliver: *King Oliver and His Orchestra (1929-1930)* (RCA, 1992), a double CD set, recorded after Louis Armstrong left the band, contains all of the tunes that would have been played at parties given and attended by Imogene.

White jazz bands, such as the Coon-Sanders Orchestra, also, were prevalent in the Middle West. Based in Chicago and broadcasting over WGN, the Coon-Sanders Night Hawk Orchestra (1924-1932) was one of the most popular 1920s jazz bands. Everyone in the Middle West listened to their radio show and tried to book it for their parties. *The Best of Coon-Sanders* (Retrieval, 1999) contains tunes played during their residency at the posh Nighthawk Restaurant.

_____. "The P&G Ivory Cut-Whiskey Massacree." In Randisi, Robert J. Murder and all that Jazz. New York: Signet, 2004.

Eddie Condon recreates the sounds that he and his friends made famous in Chicago. The Eddie Condon All-Stars: *Dixieland Jam* (Columbia, 1989).

Holmes, Rupert. Swing. London: Allison & Busby, 2007; New

York: Random, 2005.

Benny Goodman and Red Norvo's orchestras were similar to those booked into San Francisco's Hotel Claremont.

Benny Goodman and His Orchestra: *Wrappin' It Up* (RCA, 1995).

Red Norvo and His Orchestra with Mildred Bailey: *1938* (Circle, 1980).

The book also comes with its own CD of musical clues.

Howard, Clark. "Horn Man" In Gorman, Ed, Pronzini, Bill & Greenberg, Martin H. (eds.). American Pulp. New York: Carroll & Graf, 1997.

Bunk Johnson offers an alternative to Louis Armstrong. *Bunk Johnson 1944/1945* (American Music, 1993).

Howie, Edith. The Band Played Murder. New York: M.S. Mill Co., 1946.

Stan Kenton: *Jazz Profile* (Blue Note, 1997). Kenton's band was the paragon of a jazz band that played a variety of venues from small clubs to large hotel ballrooms.

Howland, Whit. Trouble Follows. Bearsville: Pro Se, 2015.

Johnny Nickle is a west coast trumpet player like Jack Sheldon. The jazz on Jack Sheldon''s The California Cool Quintet, *It's What I Do* (Butterfly 2007) captures Nickles' probable sound.

Huggins, Roy. The Double Take. London: Cassell, 1947; New York: Morrow, 1946.

77 Sunset Strip (Collector's, 2001) is the Warner Brothers television soundtrack that is a combination of original music written by Mack David-Jerry Livingston and jazz standards.

Most of the small L.A. groups played at Dino's where Stu Bailey went to cool out. *Modern Sounds from California 1954-1957* (Fresh Sounds, 2005) features many of these groups.

_____. 77 Sunset Strip. New York: Dell, 1958.

77 Sunset Strip (Collector's Music, 2001). This is the soundtrack from the Warner Brother's television show, a combination of original music by Mack David-Jerry Livingston and jazz standards.

Most of the good local L.A. groups played at Dino's where Stu Bailey relaxed. *Modern Sounds from California 1954-1957* (Fresh Sounds, 2005) has a number of groups playing Sunset Strip in the mid-1950s.

Hughes, Dorothy B. "The Black and White Blues" In Gorman, Ed, Pronzini, Bill & Greenberg, Martin (eds.). <u>American Pulp</u>. New York: Carroll & Graf, 1997.

Although based in Chicago, Earl Hines' band toured extensively, playing large and small venues, like the one where the black clarinetist finds trouble.

Earl Hines: *Earl Hines and His Orchestra 1945-1947* (Classic, 1999).

Hunter, Evan. <u>Quartet in H</u> aka <u>Second Ending</u>. London: Constable, 1956; New York: Simon & Schuster, 1956;

Andy takes Bud to a 52nd Street club after the war to hear and see the changes in jazz brought about by musicians such as Charlie Parker, Dizzy Gillespie and Stan Kenton. Charlie Parker: *Bird on 52nd Street* (Fantasy, 1994) and *Bird After Dark* (Savoy, 2002) are representative of Parker's playing during this period.

Dizzy Gillespie Big Band: *Showtime at The Spotlite* (Uptown, 2008) features beboppers like pianist Thelonious Monk, drummer Kenny Clarke and tenor saxophonist James Moody.

Andy listens to Stan Kenton's *Artistry in Rhythm* when he needs an escape and shoots up with heroin. Stan Kenton: *Artistry in Rhythm* (Dutton Vocalion, 2000).

_____. <u>Streets of Gold</u>. London: Macmillan, 1975; New York: Harper & Row, 1974;

Iggy changes from a classical to jazz career after hearing Art Tatum play piano.

Art Tatum: *1935-1943 Transcriptions* (Music & Arts, 1991) contains music recorded for radio play. Haunting 52nd Street to hear its piano players, Iggy's also interested in Oscar Peterson's skill and George Shearing's style.

Oscar Peterson: *This Is Oscar Peterson* (Bluebird, 2002).

George Shearing Original Quintet: *September in The Rain* (Verve, 2000). Iggy eagerly copies blind pianist George Shearing's style and rides to fame on it. These songs and arrangements were played in the 52nd Street Clubs.

Irish, William. "The Dancing Detective." In Irish, William. (ed.). The Dancing Detective. New York: Lippincott, 1946.

The favorite song of the dance hall girl killer is "Poor Butterfly," which he requests when dancing with his victims.

Two versions popular at the time are by Benny Goodman and Leo Reisman.

Benny Goodman on *The Big Band Era: 18 Greatest Hits* (Michele, 1994).

Leo Reisman. *Maestro Sophisticate* (Flare, 2006).

_____. "The Jazz Record." In *The Saint Mystery Magazine*. July 1965. Vol. 22. No. 3.

Early in his career, Mel Torme became dissatisfied with the life of a popular crooner and switched over to jazz. Mel Torme: *The Bethlehem Years* (Bethlehem, 2005).

Izzo, Jean-Claude. Chourmo. Paris: Editions Gallimard, 1996; London & New York: Europa, 2013.

When Montale thinks of his old friend Lole in Seville, he pulls out Miles Davis' *Sketches of Spain* (Columbia, 1997) and listens to "Solea" and "Saeta."

Driving around and looking for his friend Serge, Montale listens to the Art Pepper album *More for Les* that was recorded live at the Village Vanguard in 1977.

Art Pepper: *At The Village Vanguard, Vol. 4: More For Les* (Contemporary, 1992).

He stops for a drink at Hassan's bar, Les Maraichers, where the Sonny Rollins-Jim Hall tune "Without A Song "from Sonny Rollins & Jim Hall album *The Bridge* (RCA Bluebird, 1982) is playing.

Montale keeps a cassette with Lightnin' Hopkins' "Your Own

Fault, Baby, to Treat Me The Way You Do" on it. It's from the album *Lightnin' Hopkins in New York* (Candid, 1989).

_____. Solea. Paris: Editions Gallimard, 1998; London & New York: Europa editions, 2007.

The book title is taken from the tune "Solea" found on Miles Davis' *Sketches of Spain* (Columbia, 1997).

Hassan always puts on John Coltrane's "Out of This World" as a closing night tune at his bar. It's on John Coltrane: *Coltrane (GRP, 1997).*

As the pressure from the Mafia increases, Montale listens to the blues as he drives along the coast. He plays the Pinetop Perkins tape of "After Hours" that is on Pinetop Perkins: *After Hours* (Blind Pig, 1992). It's followed by an old favorite, Lightnin' Hopkins singing "Darling, Do You Remember Me" on Lightnin' Hopkins: *Double Blues* (Fantasy, 2006).

Montale telephones Hassan looking for a friend with computer skills. In the background he hears Duke Ellington and John Coltrane playing "In A Sentimental Mood" from *Duke Ellington & John Coltrane* (Impulse, 1995). When he's trying to remember where Babette might be hiding he listens to Johnny Dyani and Abdulah Abrahim playing "Zikr" (remembrance of Allah) on Abdulah Abrahim: *Echoes of Africa* (Enja, 1979).

_____. Total Chaos. Paris: Editions Gallimard, 1995; London & New York: Europa Editions, 2005.

Fabio Montale is always listening to jazz. He falls asleep listening to an unnamed Thelonious Monk album. Monk's 1955 debut on Riverside, *Thelonious Monk Plays Duke Ellington,* is evening listening.

Montale also likes blues and listens to "Last Night Blues" with his friend Babette. It's on Lightnin' Hopkins and Sonny Terry: *Last Night Blues* (Prestige Bluesville, 1993).

He listens to French jazz, especially an early Michel Petrucciani album, *Estate* (IRD, 1982).

Montale is open to the mixing of west coast cool, alto saxophone of Gerry Mulligan, with the Brazilian bandoneon of Astor Piazzolla on *Buenos Aires, Twenty Years After* (Summit Caroselle, 1971).

Driving to a deadly rendezvous, Montale listens to Dizzy Gillespie and his big band play the Afroc-Cuban standard, "Manteca," a mix of jazz and salsa on *Manteca* (Verve, 1999).

Jackson, Jon A. Man with an Axe. New York: Atlantic Monthly, 1998.

Soul, not jazz, dominated the 1970s airwaves in the Motor City. Yet in jazz circles, Charles McPherson's alto sax was the sound in town. Charles McPherson: *First Flight Out* (Arabesque, 1994).

Jeffers, H. Paul. Murder on Mike. New York: St. Martin's, 1984.

Harry MacNeil's detective agency was located above the Onyx Club on 52nd Street. The one-armed trumpet player, Wingy Malone, as well as the Woody Herman Band played there. MacNeil also heard Louis Armstrong at the Cotton Club.

Louis Armstrong And His Orchestra: *1935-1938* (Classic, 1990).

New York Jazz Combos 1935-1937 (Hep, 2005) features Wingy Malone.

Woody Herman and His Orchestra 1937 (Circle, 1994).

_____. The Rag Doll Murder. New York: Ballantine, 1987.

Harry goes out dancing at the Onyx with Ernestine Parish and hears Stuff Smith.

Stuff Smith: *Cat On A Fiddle* (Verve, 2004). While recorded in 1959, the music is representative of Smith's repertoire that stayed pretty much the same since his sextet debuted at the Onyx Club on 52nd Street in late 1935.

_____. Rubout at The Onyx. New York: Ticknor & Fields, 1981.

The Jimmie Lunceford Orchestra: *Stomp It Off* (Decca, 1992). Lunceford's band was playing in New York City at the time of the story. Some people thought it was better than Ellington or Basie's band.

Stuff Smith: *Hot Jazz Violin: 1930-1940* (JAZ, 2004) captures

Stuff Smith in his heyday. Trumpet Jonah Jones compliments Smith's violin on tunes probably played during their Onyx gigs.

Art Tatum: *The Standard Transcriptions. 1935-1943 New York Sessions* (Music & Arts, 1991) captures Tatum at his peak in these radio transcriptions.

Jenkins, A.K. <u>Twice No One Dies</u>. Canberra: Equine Press, 2015.

Much of the music heard at *Le Jazz Spot* is contemporary standards. Most of the CDs are not titled, just the artist given, so I have chosen a few:

Michael Brecker: *Michael Brecker* (Impulse –Verve, 2018).

Stan Getz: *Spring Is Here* (Concord, 1992).

Thelonious Monk: *Thelonious Monk with John Coltrane* (Jazzland-OJCCD, 1987).

The band at *Le Jazz Spot* plays covers of the following tunes: "Wonderful World," "There Will Never Be Another You," "St. Louis Blues," and "Take Five."

The originals can be found on:

"Wonderful World:" *Louis Armstrong What A Wonderful World* (MCA, 1988).

"There Will Never Be Another You:" Bob Brookmeyer: *The Modernity of Bob Brookmeyer* (Fresh Sounds, 2008).

Louis Armstrong's signature tune, "St. Louis Blues" is on *Louis Armstrong Plays W.C. Handy* (Columbia, 1997).

"Take Five" is on Dave Brubeck's classic *Take Five* (Columbia, 1997).

Jessup, Richard. <u>Lowdown</u>. London: Pan, 1961; New York: Dell, 1958.

Tony Bennett shares a post-war, big band background with the fictional Walker Alise, the major difference between the two being that Bennett is one of jazz's gentlemen. Tony Bennett: *Cloud 7* (Columbia, 2004).

Joe, Yolanda. <u>Hit Time</u>. New York: Simon & Schuster, 2002.

The Bluesville Years: Feelin' Down on The Southside (Prestige, 1995) captures the 1950s Chicago Southside Blues sound.

Johns, Veronica Parker. "Mr. Hyde-de-Ho." In Queen, Ellery. (ed.) Ellery Queen's Awards: Eleventh Series. London: Collins, 1958; New York: Simon & Schuster, 1956.

Ruby Braff came of age in the postwar 1940s New York jazz club scene and displayed a preference towards the older swing trumpet style rather than bebop.

Ruby Braff: *Ruby Braff and Ellis Larkins Play Rogers and Hart* (Vanguard, 2000).

Jones, Arthur E. It Makes You Think Twice. London: John Long, 1958.

Raymond Stack is a mid-level bandleader rather like Art Mooney: *Art Mooney and His Orchestra 1945-1946* (Circle, 2002).

Kaminsky, Stuart. "Blue Note." In Hellmann, Libby Fisher. (ed.). Chicago Blues. Chicago: Bleak House, 2008.

Joe Williams sang "Every Day I Have the Blues" with the Count Basie Band at the Blue Note. It can be found on Count Basie & Joe Williams: *Every Day I Have the Blues* (Polygram, 1993).

Billie Holiday seems a lot like the blues singer Mae, except she never had a son. She did sing with the Basie band in the early days of her career. But in the 1950s, she was doing small group sessions like the two albums listed:

Billie Holiday: *All or Nothing at All* (Verve, 1996) and *Recital By Billy* (Verve, 1994).

Kane, Frank. The Guilt Edged Frame. New York; Dell, 1964.

Both Chet Baker and Tony Fruscella were white trumpet players with drug habits, like the fictional Marty Lewis.

Chet Baker: *Chet Baker Sextet* (Pacific Jazz, 2004). A life-long drug user, Baker seemed to be a survivor until he died under mysterious circumstances in Amsterdam.

Tony Fruscella: *Pernod* (Disconforme, 1999). Fruscella was a cool trumpet player with a drug habit and a "hot shot" (heroin overdose) ended his career.

_____. Jukebox King. New York: Dell, 1959.

Dean Martin: *Some Enchanted Evening* (Hallmark, 1999). A collection of favorites from the 1950s that crooners such as Martin, Perry Como, Buddy Greco and the fictional Michael Denton would sing.

Kane, Henry. "One Little Bullet." In <u>The Name Is Chambers</u>. New York: Pyramid, 1960.
   Machito & His Afro-Cuban Orchestra: *Vacation at The Concord* (Coral, 2004). Machito's big band played New York's clubs in the 1950s, and his drummers could easily cover a rifle shot.
   Machito Plays Mambos & Cha Cha (Palladium, 1989) features music that would be heard in New York or Havana nightclubs.

_____. <u>Peter Gunn</u>. New York: Dell, 1960.
   The original TV soundtrack: Henry Mancini. *The Music From Peter Gunn,* (Buddha, 1989).
   Shelly Manne: *Shelly Manne & His Men Play Peter Gunn* (Contemporary OJCCD, 1997) and *Shelly Manne & His Men Play More from Peter Gunn: Son of Gunn!* (Contemporary, 2005). Drummer Shelly Manne often played in the television series and his music is identified with the suave detective.
   Pepper Adams: *Critics Choice* (EMI, 2005). Although not part of the soundtrack, Adams' baritone captures the balance of moodiness and tension in *Peter Gunn.*

_____. <u>Until You Are Dead</u>. New York: Simon & Schuster, 1951.
   Jess Stacy & The Famous Sidemen: *Tribute To Benny Goodman* (Atlantic, 1987) recalls the sounds of the 1940s Goodman Band a decade after jazz was not America's popular music.

Karp, Larry. <u>First, Do No Harm</u>. Scottsdale: Poisoned Pen Press, 2004.
   There's always popular music playing in the background. A representative selection can be found on *Greatest Hits of the 1940s* (AAO, 2012).

_____. The Ragtime Kid. Scottsdale: Poisoned Pen Press, 2006.

Daniel Blumenthal's *Scott Joplin the Ragtime Dance* (Pavane, 1994) contains many of the rags and waltzes published by John Stark and played by both Joplin and his student, Brun Campbell.

Other examples of Joplin's style and compositions can be found on: Scott Joplin: *King of the Ragtime Writers* (Biograph, 2003); and Scott Joplin: *The Entertainer* (Biograph, 2003). Recordings by Brun Campbell can be found on *Joplin's Disciple* (Delmark, 2001).

_____. The King of Ragtime. Scottsdale: Poisoned Pen Press, 2008.

Joplin playing ragtime along with others, such as Jelly Roll Morton, can be found on *Elite Syncopations* (Biograph, 2003).

_____. The Ragtime Fool. Scottsdale: Poisoned Pen Press, 2010.

Brun Campbell's ragtime can be found on the previously cited *Joplin's Disciple* (Delmark, 2001). Also, *The Entertainer* (Biograph, 2003) features ragtime.

Kellerman, Jonathan. A Cold Heart. New York: Ballantine, 2003.

As no specific bluesmen were mentioned, John Lee Hooker and Muddy Waters fit into the story. John Lee Hooker: *Whiskey & Wimmen: John Lee Hooker's Finest* (Vee-Jay, 2017) and *It Serves You Right To Suffer* (MCA, 1966). Also Muddy Waters: *Muddy Waters Live at Newport 1960* (Chess, 1960) and *Best of Muddy Waters* (Chess 2013).

Klavan, Andrew. Hunting Down Amanda. New York: Morrow, 1999.

Promoter Arthur Topp thought that Lonnie Blake's style reminded him of John Coltrane. John Coltrane's *Blue Train* (Blue Note, 1997) and Tadd Dameron with John Coltrane on *Mating Game* (Riverside, 1992) reflect the story's mood.

Knight, Phyllis. Shattered Rhythms. New York: St. Martin's, 1994.

Missing guitarist Andre Ledoux played with Lee Wilder. Larry Coryell's album with Emily Remler, *Together* (Concord, 1990) captures their sound.

Koenig, Joseph. <u>Really The Blues</u>. London & New York: Pegasus, 2014.
Most of the story occurs at La Caverne Negre where Eddie's band plays standards. When the SS takes his piano player, Eddie's band plays a slow version of "Didn't He Ramble" that can be found on *Louis Armstrong at The Pasadena Civic Auditorium* (GNP Crescendo, 1994).
Because Django, a gypsy was making himself scarce, Eddie and His Angels settled for another guitarist on tunes that would have featured Django. Django's theme, "Manoir De Mes Reves" or "Django's Castle" can be found on *The Essential Django Reinhardt* (Legacy, 2011); another Django favorite, Al Jolson's "Avalon" is on Django Reinhardt: *The Classic Early Recordings in Chronological Order* (JSP, 2000).
Before the SS took his piano player, the band played "Someday Sweetheart" found on Benny Goodman: *The Complete RCA Small Group Recordings* and "Wrap Your Troubles in Dreams" that's on Roy Eldridge: *In Paris* (Disque Vogue, 1996).
Other tunes Eddie's band plays are:
"Memories of You" on Benny Goodman *Don't Be That Way* (Phoenix, 1999).
"Nobody Knows You When You're Down and Out" is best known by Bessie Smith but an instrumental version as would have been played by Eddie's group is: *Eddie Condon (1930-1944),* (Phoenix, 2007).
Tommy Ladnier's "Really the Blues" is on *The Best of '30s Victor* (Doxy, 2011).
Al Jolson's "Swanee" is on *The Best of Al Jolson* (Geffen, 2001).
"Apex Blues" played by the band is found on *Jimmy Noone's The Best Sessions 1929-1940* (Jazz Essential, 2017).
"Chinatown, My Chinatown" and "Stardust" by Louis Armstrong is on *Stardust* (Sony Legacy, 1988) and "Between The Devil and the Deep Blue Sea" on *Louis Armstrong Greatest Hits, Vol. 2* (Modern Art, 2017).

Lamp, C.O. The Return of Glenn Miller. Lakeville, Minn.: Galde Press, 1999.

Alex Barca plays Glenn Miller on his radio station. A good selection of classic Miller can be found on *Glenn Miller: Golden Years 1938-1942* (Proper, 2000).

Larson, Skoot. The Dig You Later, Alligator Blues. Bloomington & London: Author House, 2007.

Lindstrom favors hard bop when he's playing at Blondie's club. Baritone sax player Pepper Adams is a favorite and Pepper Adams Quintet's *10 to 4 at The Five Spot*. (Riverside, 1993) is a set Lindstrom might play.

On another evening, Lindstrom does a tribute to Billy Strayhorn that includes "Isafahan," "Upper Manhattan Medical Group" and "Lush Life." *Lush Life: The Billy Strayhorn Songbook* (Verve. 1996) features these tunes by a variety of musicians: Joe Henderson "Isfahan," Dizzy Gillespie "Upper Manhattan Medical Group," and Sarah Vaughan "Lush Life."

Lindstrom stops by KUVO where DJ Ed Danielson is playing Lars Gullin's "Soho." The Swedish baritone sax player is one Lindstrom's favorites. "Soho" is on Lars Gullin. *Danny's Dream. 1953-1955. Vol. 8.* (Dragon 2010).

Looking for some tunes to play on his new alto horn, Lindstrom revisits some old Don Elliot albums. Representative of Elliot's 1950's work is *Don Elliott Octet & Sextet* (Fresh Sounds, 2010).

_____. The No News is Bad News Blues. Bloomington & London: Author House, 2007.

While in Oslo, Lars Lindstrom gets to play with Norwegian jazz pianist Dag Arnesen. Arnesen can be heard on: Dag Arnesen. *Norwegian Song* (Resonant, 2007).

_____. Real Gone, Horn Gone Blues. Bloomington & London: Author House, 2007.

Lucien Bezich thought that he bought Art Pepper's Martin alto saxophone on-line that he used in many of the Contemporary recording sessions. Pepper is at his best with his alto on *Art Pepper Meets The Rhythm Section* (Contemporary, 2010).

In his evening gig at Blondy's Waterfront dive, Lars Lindstrom plays classic west coast tunes by Shorty Rogers and His Giants such as the set on *The Swingin' Mr. Rogers* (Poll Winners, 2011).

Lindstrom closes an evening set with Richard Twardzik's "The Girl From Greenland." It can be found on the Chet Baker CD *Chet In Paris. Vol. 1.* (Emarcy, 1988) with Twardzik on piano, recorded just before his death from a drug overdose.

In New York Lindstrom and his band-mates buy some rare recordings, including Quincy's Jones' Henry Mancini album that featured multi-reed man Roland Kirk.

Quincy Jones: *Explores the Music of Henry Mancini* (Verve, 2009).

Latimer, Jonathan. <u>The Lady in the Morgue</u>. New York: Doubleday, 1936; London: Methuen, 1957.

Louis Armstrong and his band were on the radio at the party that PI Bill Crane crashes. Louis Armstrong: *Louis Armstrong and His Orchestra 1932-1933* (Classic, 1990).

Although this CD was recorded ten years after the time of the story, the program is what Sam Udoni, the trumpet player from Rudy Vallee's band, might play in a small group setting. Max Kaminsky & Pee Wee Russell: *Max Kaminsky & Pee Wee Russell at the Copley Terrace Boston 1935* (Jazzology, 1996).

Lawrence, Michael. <u>I Like It Cool</u>. New York: Popular, 1960.

Sandra Tyson is a throaty, smokey voiced singer like Chris Connor or Irene Kral. Chris Connor: *A Portrait of Chris* (Critics Choice, 2001), and Irene Kral: *Where Is Love?* (Candid/Choice, 1996).

Lawton, John. <u>Blue Rondo</u>. London: Weidenfield & Nicolson, 2004; As <u>Flesh Wounds</u>. New York: Atlantic Monthly Press, 2005.

Kitty brings Troy two popular jazz albums from the States that he plays constantly throughout the book, Erroll Garner's *Concert by the Sea* and Dave Brubeck's *Time Out* that contains "Take Five". Another tune on *Time Out* is "Rondo A La Turk" which provides the title <u>Blue Rondo</u> for the English edition.

Dave Brubeck: *Time Out* (Columbia, 2000).

Erroll Garner: *Concert by the Sea* (Columbia, 2000).

Troy, himself, is a good piano player and listens to the playing of Hoagy Carmichael, Art Tatum and, even, Thelonious Monk.

Hoagy Cramichael: *Hoagy Sings Carmichael* (Blue Note, 2000).

Art Tatum: *Solo Masterpieces. Vol. 8* (Pablo, 1992).

Thelonious Monk: *Thelonious Monk Trio* (Prestige, 1998).

Lehman, Ernest. <u>Sweet Smell of Success</u>. In <u>Short Fiction of Ernest Lehman</u>. Woodstock: Overlook, 2000.

John Pizzarelli has the polished New York club sound that singer Steve Dallas sought. John Pizzarelli: *After Hours* (RCA, 1995).

Leonard, Elmore. <u>Tishomingo Blues</u>. London: Viking, 2002; New York: William Morrow, 2002.

<u>Tishomingo Blues</u> is set in Tunica, Mississippi, just 37 miles from the crossroads where bluesman Robert Johnson made his deal with the devil for immortality as outlined in his song "Cross Road Blues." *Robert Johnson: The Complete Recordings.* (Sony, 1990).

Dennis Lenahan and Robert Taylor listen to a radio recording of "High Water Everywhere," the Charley Patton's blues about the great flood of 1927 that geographically changed the Mississippi Delta. It can be found on *The Best of Charley Patton* (Yazoo, 2003).

Leslie, John. <u>Blue Moon</u>. New York: Pocket, 1998.

BeeGee Adair plays sophisticated solo piano renditions of standards and originals that Gideon Lowry included in his nightly repertoire. BeeGee Adair: *Quiet Romance* (Village Square, 2006).

_____. <u>Killing Me Softly</u>. New York: Pocket, 1994.

Dave McKenna has two club dates of standards that would appeal to Gideon Lowry. They are Dave McKenna, *Cookin' at Michael's Pub* (Prevue, 1999) and *An Intimate Evening with Dave McKenna* (Arbors, 2002).

_____. Love For Sale. New York: Pocket, 1997.

Like the fictional Gideon Lowry, during his career, Dave McKenna played more than his share of piano bars. Dave McKenna: *Cookin' at Michael's Pub* (Prevue, 1999). Two interesting journeymen piano players are Dick Hyman and Lou Stein who can be heard back-to-back on a CD: Dick Hyman. *Genius at Work*/Lou Stein *Solo* (Audiophile, 2002).

_____. Night and Day. New York: Pocket, 1995.

Journeyman jazz pianist Dave McKenna provides a great background of tunes that Gideon Lowry might play during his piano bar engagements.

Dave McKenna: *Left Handed Complement* (Concord, 1980) and *My Friend The Piano* (Concord, 1987).

Lippman, Laura. "The Shoeshine Man Regrets," In Randisi, Robert. (ed.). Murder and all that Jazz. New York: Signet, 2004.

Cole Porter's composition "Miss Otis Regrets" reveals the killer's identity. It can be found on Ella Fitzgerald: *First Lady of Song (Verve, 1990)*.

Longfellow, Pamela. China Blues. London: Grafton, 1989; New York: Doubleday, 1989.

The French RCA double CD, *King Oliver and His Orchestra* (RCA, 1992), contains much of the music that King Oliver's Orchestra with Louis Armstrong would play as the house band at the San Francisco club, The Blue Canary.

Louistal-Paringaux, Jacques de. Barney and the Blue Note. Netherlands: Rijperman, 1988.

French jazz musician Barney Wilen recorded the soundtrack to the book—all of the tunes as well as the chapter titles are featured on Wilen's IDA album. Barney Wilen: *Barney and the Blue Note* (Ida, 2009). Both the graphic (comic) book and the CD share a common jacket.

Lucarelli, Carlo. Almost Blue. London: Harvill, 2003; San Francisco: City Lights, 2001; Torino: Giulio Einaudi, 1997.

Lucarelli's title is taken from the Elvis Costello composition "Almost Blue", found on Chet Baker: *Chet Baker Sings & Plays from the film Let's Get Lost Soundtrack* (Novus, 1989).

Simone Martini, the young blind man, who aids Grazia Negro in identifying the psychopath killer, spends his days at home listening to jazz—especially to Chet Baker. That said, Enrico Rava was my choice on this one.

Enrico Rava: *Tati* (ECM, 2005). Rava's haunting, lonely trumpet makes this trio album of originals and one standard (The Man I Love) ideal listening while reading Lucarelli's tale of alienation and murder in contemporary Bologna.

Lutz, John. "Chop Suey." In Randisi. Robert J., (ed.). Murder and all that Jazz. New York: Signet, 2004.

Lauralee, a white singer, aspires to imitate Jabelle, a 1920s black singer. *Sammy Price and the Blues Singers* (Wolf, 1990) features a number of blues singers that the great pianist accompanied from 1929-1950.

_____. The Right to Sing the Blues. New York: St. Martin's, 1986.

Ineida Mann is a "wannabe" blues singer. *Any Woman's Blues* (Rounder, 2001) is a sampler of the talents of 14 contemporary women blues singers.

_____. "The Right to Sing the Blues." In Manson, Cynthia & Halligan, Kathleen. (eds.), Murder To Music. New York: Carroll & Graf, 1997.

Lutz's story is a shorter, 1983 version of the novel. The same music applies: *Any Woman's Blues* (Rounder, 2001).

Macdonald, John R. The Moving Target. London: Cassell, 1951; New York: Knopf, 1949.

Betty Fraley is a stride piano player like Judy Carmichael.

Judy Carmichael: *Judy Carmichael* (C&D, 1994). Along with guitarist Chris Flory, Carmichael plays popular songs from the first half of the 20th Century.

Maltese, Martin. <u>North To Toronto</u>. New York: Manor, 1978.
Scott Hamilton is a tenor saxophone player like the fictional Dave Harrigan. The Scott Hamilton Quintet: *The Right Time* (Concord, 1987).

Macdonald, Ross aka Kenneth Millar. <u>Trouble Follows Me</u> aka <u>Night Train</u>. New York: Dodd, Mead & Co., 1946.
Ensign Sam Drake selects "Ain't Misbehavin'" by Fats Waller as background for talking with Mary. Fats Waller: *Ain't Misbehavin'* (Sony 2016).
Sam searches Detroit bars for Hector's wife against a background of boogie-woogie. Albums representative of the 1940s are *Boogie Woogie Boys 1938-1944* (Magpie, 1994) and *Blues Piano Artistry of Meade Lux Lewis* (Riverside, 1990).

Marks, Paul D. <u>The Blues Don't Care</u>. Lutz, FL: Down & Out Books, 2020.
Booker Taylor's black band with vocalist Herb Jeffries plays covers of the big band hits by Duke Ellington ("Take the A Train"), Artie Shaw ("Blues in the Night") and Harry James ("Sing, Sing, Sing").
Jeffries is on most 1930s Duke Ellington recordings but can also be heard on the 1950s album Herb Jeffries: *Say It Isn't So* (Bethlehem, 2007).
The Ellington hits can be heard on what is regarded as the best Ellington band, *Blanton-Webster* (RCA, 2007).
Harry James can be heard on Benny Goodman and His Orchestra: *Harry James Years, Vol 1* (RCA Bluebird, 1993).
Artie Shaw: *Essential Artie Shaw* (Sony Legacy, 2005) has his hits of the period and more.

Marsh, Ngaio. <u>Wreath For Rivera, A</u>. Boston: Little, Brown, 1949; aka <u>Swing, Brother Swing</u>. London: Collins. 1949.
Arranger Ray Noble had the best British band of its time called

the New Mayfair Dance Orchestra. In spite of its name, it did play Dixieland jazz and blues along with the usual dance fare. It's all captured on Ray Noble: *The Hot Sides 1929-1943* (Great Moments, 2007).

Mask, Ken. Murder at the Butt. Los Angeles: Milligan, 2003.
No one represents contemporary New Orleans jazz better than the Marsalis family. *The Marsalis Family: A Music Celebration* (Marsalis Music/Rounder, 2002).

Mathews, Francine. The Alibi Club. New York: Bantam, 2006.
Eddie South: *Eddie South in Paris 1929 & 1937* (Disques Swing, 1985). Using guitarist Django Reinhardt and violinist Stephane Grappelli as well as the better expatriate musicians in his band, Smith's salon jazz rather than swing was in demand in the clubs of Montmartre.
Americans in Paris, Vol. 4 1935-1939 (Jazz Time, 1990) highlights expatriate American jazz musicians playing in a big band format.

McClendon, Lise. One O'clock Jump. New York: St. Martin's, 2001.
Kansas City was still a center of jazz when Dorie Lennox prowled its mean streets. A good overview of the era is *Jazz Kansas City Style* (Topaz, 1996).
Two Count Basie albums capture the sound and feeling of 1930s Kansas City.
Count Basie and His Orchestra: *One O'clock Jump* (Decca, 1992) is vintage Basie.
Count Basie: *Kansas City Suite* (Vogue, 1992) has arrangements by Benny Carter that recreates the feeling of Kansas City in its heyday.

_____. Sweet and Low. New York: Thomas Dunne, 2002.
Thalia drinks nightly at clubs, such as the Reno, and dances to the music of the Count Basie, Andy Kirk and Marylou Williams. A

sampling of these sounds can be found on Count Basie: *One O'clock Jump* (Decca, 1992), *Kansas City 1926-1939* (Jazz Classics BBC CD, 1992), and Andy Kirk: *1936-1937, 1937-1938* and *1938* (Classics 573, 581 and 598, 1992).

Mengel, Brad. "The Devil You Know." In White, David. (ed.). Charles Boeckman Presents Johnny Nickle. Batesville AZ: Productions, 2003.

Guitarist Connor Johnson accompanies the band's singer doing "Cry Me A River."

The classic version is by Julie London and Barney Kessel on Julie London: *Julie Is Her Name* (EMI, 2010). It's also on other Julie London collections.

Johnny Nickle is a bit like jazz trumpeter Tony Fruscella. His music can be found on Tony Fruscella: *Tony's Blues* (Cool & Blue, 2005).

Merrill, Joan. And All That Madness. London: iUniverse, 2010; New York: iUniverse, 2009.

Jazz singer Dee Jefferson's style is similar to Shirley Horn. She also shares Horn's love of Miles Davis' music.

Shirley Horn: *Softly* Audiophile (1988) and *I Remember Miles* Verve (1998).

Dee Jefferson has Miles Davis playing when she asks Casey McKie to investigate Milt Brown's death. Miles Davis. *Kind of Blue.* Columbia (1997).

Big Ruby sings in the style of Etta James. Etta James: *Call My Name* (Kent, 2011).

_____. And All That Sea. Bloomington & London: iUniverse, 2010.

Casey McKie's friend, San Francisco singer Dee Jefferson is reminiscent of another San Francisco singer, Inez Jones, who would have had a more popularity if she had toured. Their repertoires are similar: Inez Jones. *Have You Met Inez Jones?* (Fresh Sounds, 2012).

_____. And All That Stalking. Bloomington: iUniverse, 2012; London: CreateSpace, 2012.

Three young singers with careers similar to Lara Vale and the murder victims are Dianne Reeves, Stacey Kent and Madeleine Peyroux.

Dianne Reeves: *That Day* (Blue Note, 1997).

Stacey Kent: *Breakfast on the Morning Tram* (Blue Note, 2007).

Madeleine Peyroux: *The Blue Room* (Universal, 2012).

_____. And All That Madness. London & New York: CreateSpace, 2013.

Georgia Valentine is modeled on Billie Holiday.

Billie Holiday: The Complete Verve Studio Master Takes. Verve, (1993).

These recordings were done towards the end of her career after drugs; alcohol and hard living had taken their toll. Her loss of range is replaced by emotion.

_____. And All That Motive. London & New York: CreateSpace, 2014.

Dee opens her set with "You're Just Too Marvelous" which can be found on Margaret Whitings' *Too Marvelous For Words* (Audiophile, 1980).

McKie catches a spare bossa nova set featuring "Meditation" and "Girl From Ipanema." An early version of "Meditation" can be found on Joao Gilberto & Antonio Carlos Jobim's *Gilberto and Jobim* (Odeon, 1973). The album that introduced "The Girl From Ipanema" to American jazz fans was Stan Getz and Joao Gilberto's *Getz/Gilberto* (Verve, 1964).

McKie hears a young piano sensation, Perry Cole, play "As Time Goes By." A version updated from Dooley Wilson's in *Casablanca* is by the Eddie Higgins Trio on *Essential Ballads Best* (Venus, 2009).

Dee sings "The Nearness of You" which can be found on Chris Connor's *Classic* (Contemporary, 1987).

She also sings "It Never Entered My Mind," that is associated with June Christy on *The Intimate Miss Christy* (Capital, 1963).

Merril, Judith. "Muted Hunger." In Charteris, Leslie & Santesson, Hans (eds.). The Saint Reader. New York: Doubleday, 1965.

Tenor player Scott Hamilton's group of old friends is similar to the group featured in the story. Scott Hamilton and Friends: *Across the Tracks* (Concord, 2008).

Mertz, Stephen. "Death Blues." In Gorman, Ed. (ed.). The Second Black Lizard Anthology of Crime Fiction. Berkeley: Black Lizard, 1988.

Any good Chicago blues album will do here. I recommend Muddy Waters & Memphis Slim: *Chicago Blues Masters Vol. 1* (Capitol, 1995).

Meyers, Martin. "Snake Rag." In Randisi. Robert J., (ed.). Murder and all that Jazz. (Signet, 2004).

Fletcher Henderson's Orchestra was the top band in New York City at the time of the story. *Fletcher Henderson* (Topaz, 1994).

Molina, Antonio Munoz. Winter In Lisbon. London: Granta, 1999; El Invierno en Lisboa. Madrid: Seix Barral, 1987.

Dizzy Gillespie. *Winter In Lisbon*. (Milan Records, 1990).

Dizzy Gillespie wrote the moody, bleak film soundtrack that features small group pieces with George Mraz (bass) and Danilo Perez (piano) and some orchestral pieces.

Miles Davis*: Sketches of Spain* (Columbia, 1990). Miles' classic collaboration with Gil Evans captures the mood of the Iberian Peninsula.

Mones, Nicole. Night in Shanghai. London & New York: Houghton, Mifflin, Harcourt, 2014.

The theme song of The Kansas City Kings, Greene's group, was "Exactly Like You," made famous by Benny Goodman. It and other tunes played by the Kings can be found on: *Benny Goodman: The Complete RCA Small Group Recordings* (RCA, 1997).

On New Year's Eve 1937, Greene leads his group in an unexpected offering of "Rhapsody in Blue." Gershwin's 1924 version on piano rolls can be heard on: *Gershwin Plays Rhapsody in Blue* (Shout, 2003).

Admiral Morioka, the Japanese administrator of Shanghai is a jazz fan and gives Thomas Greene a copy of Count Basie's "One O'clock Jump" with Lester Young's saxophone solo. It can be found on *Count Basie: The Complete Decca Recordings (1937-1939)* (Decca, 1990).

Buck Clayton, who later joined Count Basie, was working in Shanghai at the time of the story. Examples of his later playing in the States in the 1930s can be found on: *Buck Clayton: The Swing Era* (Best of Jazz, 1997).

Moody, Bill. <u>Bird Lives!</u> New York: Walker, 1999.

Evan Horne aids the police looking for a serial killer who listens to bebop. Alto saxophonist Charlie Parker (Bird) and bassist Charlie Mingus are representative of that era. Charlie Parker: *Burnin' Bird* (Savoy Jazz, 2002) and Charles Mingus: *New York Sketchbook.* (CD Charley, 1986) are two early bop albums.

Horne and FBI agent Andie Lawrence hear pianist Dave McKenna at a jazz club. Both *A Celebration of Hoagy Carmichael* (Concord, 1994) and *Easy Street* (Concord, 1997) are vintage McKenna.

_____. "Camaro Blue." In Phillips, Gary & Tervalon, Jervey. (eds.). <u>Cocaine Chronicles</u>. New York: Akashic, 2005.

The club singer where Robert Ware works sings "Lover Man" and "Just Friends."

The Billie Holiday classic "Lover Man" can be found on Billie Holiday: *Lover Man* (Prime Cuts, 1995); Another version by Carmen McRae is on *Carmen McRae Sings Lover Man & Other Billie Holiday Classics* (Prime Cuts, 1995).

"Just Friends" is on the Helen Merrill-Stan Getz album, *Just Friends* (Emarcy, 1990).

_____. "Child's Play." In Randisi. Robert J., (ed.). <u>Murder and all that Jazz</u>. New York: Signet, 2004.

Wilson Childs hoped to replace tenor saxophonist John Coltrane in Miles Davis' 1961 band. The classic Miles Davis album *Cookin' with The Miles Davis Quintet* (Prestige, 2002) features Coltrane. Hank Mobley, who ended up as Coltrane's replacement, can be heard on *Miles Davis at Carnegie Hall* (Columbia, 1998).

_____. Czechmate: The Spy Who Played Jazz. Lutz, Fla: Down and Out Books, 2013.
Kenny Clarke-Francy Boland Big Band. Live in Prague 1967. (Impro-Jazz, 1967) and *Now Hear Our Meaning* (Collectibles 2001). Kenny Clarke-Francy Boland Big Band has a similar sound to Jan Pavel's Big Band. The Clarke-Boland band was international, having musicians from several European countries as well as expatriate Americans. Pavel's is an all-Czech group with American jazz drummer Gene Williams as a guest artist.

_____. Death of a Tenor Man. New York: Walker, 1995.
Wardell Gray is best remembered for his "chase" albums with Dexter Gordon. Dexter Gordon-Wardell Gray: *Citizen Bop* (Black Lion, 2000) is an example of their hard-blowing encounters.
Gray, who had a persistent drug problem, died under mysterious circumstances in May 1955 after coming to Las Vegas with Benny Carter's big band to open the first racially integrated hotel-casino, the Moulin Rouge. Benny Carter: *Aspects* (Blue Note, 1996) was recorded in late summer of 1958.

_____. Fade To Blue. Scottsdale: Poisoned Pen Press, 2011.
Russ Freeman was a L.A. musician who left jazz for studio work. While a bit dated, *Russ Freeman Trio & Quartet* (Fresh Sounds, 2010) still has that cool, California sound.

_____. "File Under Jazz." In Bishop, Claude & Bruns, Don. A Merry Band of Murderers. Scottsdale: Poisoned Pen Press, 2006.
Like the fictional pianist Ray Fuller, trumpet player Lee Morgan was killed by his jealous girlfriend. Lee Morgan: *Candy* (Blue Note, 2007).

_____. "Jazzline." In <u>Mood Swings</u>. Lutz, Fl: Down & Out Books, 2015.

DJ Tim Weston plays a number of tunes of his late-night show, such as Stan Getz' "Stella by Starlight," Oscar Peterson Trio's, "Live at The London House," and Woody Herman's "Four Brothers," as well as miscellaneous late night Keith Jarrett and Miles Davis.

"Stella By Starlight" is on Stan Getz *Stella by Starlight* (Back up, 2006); Oscar Peterson Trio is on *Live at The London House in Chicago* (Verve, 1962); Woody Herman's "Four Brothers" on *Essence of Woody Herman* (Columbia, 1994); Keith Jarrett & Charlie Haden *Last Dance* (ECM, 2014) and Miles Davis' *Plays For Lovers* (Prestige, 2007).

_____. <u>Looking For Chet Baker</u>. New York: Walker, 2002.

The Definitive Chet Baker (Blue Note, 2002) is an overview of Chet's work with emphasis on his earlier career but also present is one cut from a 1983 Stockholm concert.

Les Liasons Dangereuses (Collectables, 1999). With Duke Jordan's classic "No Problem", this moody, noirish soundtrack from Roger Vadim's film is the sort of soundtrack that expatriate jazz players, such as the fictional Fletcher Paige, composed. Soundtrack composition was not available to black jazz musicians in the States.

_____. "The Resurrection of Bobo Jones." In Harvey, John, (ed.). <u>Men From Boys</u>. London: Heinemann, 2003; New York: Morrow, 2003.

Red Garland: *The Red Garland Trio & Eddie "Lockjaw" Davis* (Prestige Moodsville OJCCD, 1989) is a less volatile tenor-piano combination than that in the story.

_____. <u>Shades of Blue</u>. Scottsdale: Poisoned Pen Press, 2008.

Kind of Blue (Columbia, 1997) is Miles Davis' most famous and influential jazz recording of the 1950s. Pianist Bill Evans, who had left Miles' sextet, returns for the recording date.

Miles Davis: *Birth of The Cool* (Capitol, 1989). With arrangements by Gil Evans, Gerry Mulligan, et al., this influential New

York album moved away from the harshness associated with bop and helped open the way to West Coast cool jazz.

Evan Horne's father, Calvin Hughes, played in a lot of small groups like pianist Al Haig's. *Al Haig Meets Master Bop Saxes:* (Definitive, 1999) reflects the New York scene at the time (1948-1949). Al Haig Trio: *03/13/54 One Day Session* (Fresh Sounds, 2007) was recorded a few years later but captures the early cool New York scene. Haig is at his peak at this marathon recording session that produced two albums.

_____. Solo Hand. New York: Walker, 1994

Pianist Evan Horne strayed from his bop roots into soul-jazz. The sort of music he'd have been playing when working with soul singer Lonnie Cole is found on Joe Sample: *Soul Shadows* (Verve, 2004).

_____. The Sound of the Trumpet. New York: Walker, 1997.

Clifford Brown's music and trumpet are the focus of Evan Horne's case. Clifford Brown: *Jazz 'Round Midnight* (Verve, 1990).

Clifford Brown & Max Roach: *Study in Brown* (Emarcy, 2000.) is a Japanese reissue of the classic album that has the music mentioned throughout the story.

Morfoot, Peter. Impure Blood. London: Titan, 2016.

There's a mix of CDs and tunes listened to by Darac and played by his band (or Dinah Graham's trio) at the Blue Devil jazz club.

Darac listens to "Naima" from *Giant Steps* (Atlantic, 1959).

Duke Ellington's "Solitude" on *The Essential Duke Ellington* (Columbia, 1987) is played by Dinah Graham's trio as is "Far Eastern Suite" on *Far Eastern Suite* (Sony, 2017).

A morning starter for Darac is "West End Blues" from *Louis Armstrong & Earl Hines-Vol. IV* (Columbia, 1989).

Charlie Mingus' "Goodbye Pork Pie Hat" is a Darac favorite found on the classic CD *Mingus Ah Um* (Columbia, 1959).

Dinah Graham's band also plays:

"All The Things You Are" which can be found on Paul Desmond

& Gerry Mulligan *Two of a Mind* (RCA, 2011).

"Blue In Green" is on Bill Evans *Blue In Green* (Milestone, 2011).

"Just Squeeze Me" is on *Miles Davis Quintet* (Prestige, 2009).

_____. Fatal Music. London: Titan, 2017.

Darac is always listening to classic jazz. Some of the tunes mentioned are:

The Didier Musso Quintet plays the rarely performed and hugely difficult Thelonious Monk tune 'Brilliant Corners', as well as the Basie tune, 'L'il Darlin'.

Chet Baker. "Look For the Silver Lining" from *Let's Get Lost* (Blue Note, 1990).

Count Basie. "Little Darlin'" from *Atomic Basie* (Parlophone, 1994).

Duke Ellington. "Anatomy of A Murder" from *Anatomy of A Murder* (Columbia, 1999).

Bill Evans. "You Must Believe in Spring" from *You Must Believe In Spring* (Warner, 1990).

Shelly Manne. *Shelly Manne at The Black Hawk, Vol. 3* (OJC, 1991)-one of Darac's favorite albums.

Sonny Rollins. "A Night in Tunisia" from *at The Village Vanguard* (Blue Note, 1999).

_____. Box of Bones. London: Titan, 2018.

Three standards provide background for Darac's conversation with his father:

"Night and Day" is on *Oscar Peterson Plays The Cole Porter Songbook* (Verve, 1986).

"They Can't Take That Away From Me" is on *Complete Clef/Mercury Studio Recordings of the Oscar Peterson Trio.* (Mosaic).

Leo Reisman's "Puttin' On The Ritz" is on *Irving Berlin: Say It With Music vol. 2* (American Songbook Classic, 2010).

John Coltrane's "All or Nothing at All" is a Darac favorite on *Ballads* (Impulse, 1963).

Bobby Watson's "Love Remains" and "Blues for Alto" on *Love Remains* (Red, 2008) reminds him of his former lover Angeline.

Dexter Gordon's "Stairway to The Stars" is on *Our Man In Paris*

(Blue Note, 2003) and played on the Blue Devil Jazz Club's sound system.

"I Am in Love" on *Shelly Manne at The Black*hawk, *Vol. 3* (OJC, 1959) was Darac's drummer, Marco's favorite tune.

_____. <u>Knock 'Em Dead</u>. Cambridge: Galileo, 2020.
The author has provided a listening list (indeed a Spotify playlist with QR code) for music referenced in <u>Knock 'Em Dead</u>.
Some favorite tunes are:
Kenny Barron. "Minor Blues" from *Minor Blues* (Venus, 2014).
John Coltrane: "My Favorite Things" from *My Favorite Things* (Atlantic, 1987).
Bill Evans with Stan Getz: "But Beautiful" from *But Beautiful* (Milestone, 1974).
Django Reinhardt: "Menilmontant" from *Djangology* (Sony, 2002).
Dianne Reeves: "I'm In Love Again" on *When You Know* (Blue Note, 2008).
Sonny Rollins: "Asiatic Raes" from *Newk's Time* (Blue Note, 2004).
Bobby Watson: "Love Remains" from *Love Remains* (Red, 1974),

Morson, Ian. "There Would Have Been Murder." In Ashley, Mike. (ed.). <u>The Mammoth Book of Roaring Twenties Whodunits</u>. New York: Carroll & Graf, 2004.
British Communist Party boss Harry Rothstein's attention was diverted from proletarian revolutionary activities into jazz after hearing the Original Dixieland Jazz Band while washing dishes in a club. Their music can be found on the French two-disc collection, *Complete Original Dixieland Jazz Band* (RCA, 1995).

Mosley, Walter. "Blue Lightning." In Harvey. John, (ed.). <u>Blue Lightning</u>. London: Slow Dancer, 1998.
Backed by the best session men in 1950s L.A., Pete Candoli plays a mix of traditional blues such as "Careless Love" and "Frankie and

Johnny" as well as late night heartbreakers like "Willow Weep for Me" and "Blues in the Night".

_____. Devil in a Blue Dress. London: Serpent's Tail, 2001; New York: Norton, 1990.

The film soundtrack, *Devil in a Blue Dress* (Columbia, 1995) captures the Central Avenue sounds in the late 1940s. Another album, by Johnny Moore's Three Trail Blazers: *Los Angeles Blues 1949-1950* (West Side, 1998) also reflects the times on Central Avenue.

_____. RL's Dream. London: Serpent's Tail, 1995; New York: Norton, 1995.

Guitarist Soupspoon Wise played with the legendary Mississippi bluesman Robert Johnson.

Robert Johnson: *King of The Delta Blues Singers* (Columbia, 1998).

_____. Trouble Is What I Do. London & New York: Mulholland, 2020.

Mississippi John Hurt has a style similar to fictional blues man Catfish Worry. Two of Hurt's albums are: Mississippi John Hurt: *Avalon Blues: The Complete 1928 Okeh Recordings.* (Columbia Legacy, 2008), and *The Best of Mississippi John Hurt* (Vanguard, 1987).

Moss, Stephen L. Autumn Leaves. West Lafayette: Northside Press, 2014.

Bass guitarist Paul Kingston's first tune with the Clive Peterson Quartet is "A Night in Tunisia." An interesting small group version can be found on Donald Byrd-Barney Wilen. *Jazz In Camera* (Sonorama, 2012).

Clive's group plays "In A Sentimental Mood" as on the Duke Ellington/John Coltrane album, *Duke Ellington, John Coltrane* (GRP, 1995).

"Autumn Leaves" was one of Clive's favorite tunes and is played at the memorial gig. It can be found on Freddie Hubbard & Jimmy

Heath. *Live at The Left Bank* (Label M, 2000).

Clive's group plays "You Leave Me Breathless." A small group version can be found on Junior Cook: *You Leave Me Breathless* (SteepleChase, 1992).

Dante sits in with the group for "Take Five." The tune still belongs to the Dave Quartet and is on *Take Five* (Columbia. 1997).

While thinking of missed opportunities, Kingston hears Frank Sinatra sing "Let's Fall in Love" from the album, *Ring-a-ding-ding* (Reprise, 1996).

Murphy, Dallas. <u>Don't Explain</u>. New York: Pocket, 1996.

Artie Deemer, the jazz-loving recluse, who lives off his celebrity dog's income, spends his time listening to jazz.

The title song, "Don't Explain" can be found on Billie Holiday: *Don't Explain: A Jazz Hour with Billie Holiday* (Verve, 2008).

Billie Holiday's "Stormy Weather" can be found on *Recital by Billie Holiday* (Verve, 1964).

_____. <u>Lover Man</u>. New York: Scribners, 1987.

"Lover Man", the Ram Ramirez standard, is on Nancy Wilson: *Lush Life* (Blue Note, 1995).

Artie Deemer listens to standards on albums by Ellington, Parker, Young, Peterson.

Duke Ellington: *Uptown* (Columbia, 1989).

Charlie Parker: *The Cole Porter Songbook* (Verve, 1991).

Lester Young: *Lester Young with the Oscar Peterson Trio* (Verve, 1997).

_____. <u>Lush Life</u>. New York: Pocket, 1992.

Billy Strayhorn's "Lush Life" can be found on Duke Ellington's tribute to his friend and colleague, *And His Mother Called Him Bill* (RCA, 1987). Other vocal versions of this Strayhorn standard can be found on Carmen McRae: *Some of the Best.* (Laserlight, 1996) and Nancy Wilson: *Lush Life* (Blue Note, 1995).

Ben Webster is Artie Deemer's favorite jazz musician. He can be heard on Ben Webster: *See You at The Fair* (Impulse, 1993) and Art Tatum/Ben Webster: *The Art Tatum Group Masterpieces Vol. 8* (Pablo, 1975).

Myers, Martin. "Snake Rag." In Randisi, Robert J., (ed.). <u>Murder and all that Jazz</u>. New York: Signet, 2004.

Fletcher Henderson's Orchestra was the top band in New York City at the time of the story. *Fletcher Henderson* (Topaz, 1994).

Nadelson, Reggie. <u>Blood Count</u>. London: Atlantic, 2011; New York: Walker, 2010.

Artie hears Louis Armstrong singing "Winter Wonderland" on the apartment's lobby sound system. It can be found on *Louis & Ella Christmas* (Verve, 2016).

En route to the Christmas party, he plays "West End Blues" in his car. It's on Louis Armstrong: *The Hot 5 & Hot 7 Recordings* (Columbia Legacy, 2002).

In the apartment laundry room, he encounters an elderly lady who knew Ella Fitzgerald and was listening to "Skylark." It's on *Ella Fitzgerald Sings the Johnny Mercer Songbook* (Verve, 2020) and then a MP3 of old Decca recording of Ella and Ellis Larkins. It can be found on Ella Fitzgerald & Ellis Larkins: *The Complete Piano Duets* (Verve Reissues, 2020).

Among Artie's favorite recent tunes are "People Time" with Kenny Barron from *People Time* (Sunnyside, 1991) and *Blood Count* on *Pure Getz* (Concord, 1982).

At Sugar Hill Club, Oscar Peterson doing "I'll Be Home for Christmas" from *Christmas* (Telarc, 2006) was on the sound system.

_____. <u>Bloody London</u>. London: Minotaur, 1999; New York: St. Martin's, 1999.

Frances Pascoe had an affair with Stan Getz and a tape that he made especially for her of "How About You" that Artie Cohen takes from her apartment after her death. When Artie gets briefly involved with her, "Stella by Starlight" is playing. Both songs can be found on *The Very Best of Stan Getz* (Verve, 2001). Frances also plays Artie's favorite Stan Getz album, *The Steamer* (Verve, 1999). She commits suicide with Getz's "Falling in Love" in the background and it's still playing when Artie finds her. "Falling In Love" is on Stan Getz: *Café Montmartre* (Universal, 2003).

_____. <u>Disturbed Earth</u>. London: Heinemann, 2004; New York: Walker, 2004.

Artie Cohen listens to his longtime favorite album: Stan Getz: *The Steamer* (Verve, 1999). Stan Getz and Joao Gilberto: *Getz/Gilberto* (Verve, 1980) is another of his favorites despite its being overplayed when it first came out. At a party, Artie hears Charlie Parker's "Autumn In New York". It's on *Charlie Parker Big Band* (Verve, 1999).

_____. <u>Fresh Kills</u>. London: Heinemann, 2006; New York: Walker, 2007.

Artie Cohen listens to Clifford Brown, Stan Getz and Bill Evans.

Clifford Brown & Max Roach: *A Study in Brown* (Emarcy, 1990).

Stan Getz's "Spring is Here" can be found on Stan Getz: *Blue Skies* (Concord, 1995).

Bill Evans' "I Should Care" is on Bill Evans: *Bill Evans at Town Hall. Vol. 1* (Verve, 1986).

_____. <u>Londongrad</u>. London: Atlantic, 2009; New York: Walker, 2009.

Artie listens to Erroll Garner's *Concert by the Sea* (Legacy, 2015) on his car CD player.

At Brighton Beach with Val, he hears summer pop—Stevie Wonder ("Castles in The Sand") and & the Drifters ("Under the Boardwalk"):

Stevie Wonder: *Stevie at the Beach* (Universal, 2008).

The Drifters: *Under the Boardwalk* (BMG 2020).

Artie listens to Clifford Brown's "Joy Spring" in the shower. It's on *The Definitive Clifford Brown* (Verve, 2002).

Throughout <u>Londongrad</u>, Artie listens to Frank Sinatra. "They Can't Take That Away from Me," & "Night and Day" are on *Classic Sinatra: His Greatest Performances 1953-1960* (Capitol, 2000). "Moonlight in Vermont" & "Come Fly with Me" are on *Come Fly with Me* (Capitol, 1985).

Ella sings two tunes from the Songbooks: "Manhattan" from *Ella Fitzgerald Sings the Rodgers and Hart Song Book* (Verve, 1957) and

"Someone to Watch Over Me" from *Ella Fitzgerald Sings the George and Ira Gershwin Songbook* (Verve, 2017).

Stan Getz's "Spring Is Here" on *Stan Getz Plays for Lovers* (Fantasy, 2006), a CD Artie gave Val, was the last music she listened to before her murder.

Tolya has the Rolling Stones playing at his party. Songs in the background are "Jumpin' Jack Flash," "You Can't Always Get What You Want," "Ruby Tuesday" and "Satisfaction" on *Hot Rocks 1964-1971* (ABKO, 2002) and "Wild Horses" on *Sticky Fingers* (Ume, 2009).

Artie encounters a KGB agent who knew his father and learned about jazz from him. He slides the MJQ's "Fontessa" into his car's CD player. "Fontessa" is on *Fontessa* (Atlantic, 1990).

_____. Manhattan 62. London: Corvus, 2014; New York: Atlantic, 2014.

Max Ostalsky is in Greenwich Village during the peak of the folk scene and goes to various clubs with Nancy Rudnick. An overview of the time is *The Greenwich Village Folk Scene* (NOT NOT3CD168, 2014).

He also hears jazz legends like Stan Getz at the Village Gate and Miles Davis at the Vanguard. *Stan Getz at the Village Gate* (Verve, 2019) captures Getz just before bossa nova took hold of his career. There is no recording of Miles Davis at the Vanguard but his weekend at the Blackhawk in 1961 contains his standard sets: *Miles Davis in Person at the Blackhawk Complete* (Columbia, 2003). Davis never recorded "Moscow Nights," a tune that he played for Ostalsky.

_____. Red Hook. London: Heinemann, 2006; New York: Walker, 2006.

Stan Getz: *The Steamer* (Verve, 1999). Stan Getz remained Artie Cohen's favorite jazz musician from the first time he heard him on a radio broadcast. Throughout his life in Russia, Israel and New York, *The Steamer* remained his favorite album. A good overview of Getz's career in the 1950s-1960s can be found on *The Essential Stan Getz: The Stan Getz Songbook* (Verve, 1992).

_____. Red Hot Blues. New York: St. Martin's, 1998; a.k.a. Red Mercury. London: Faber & Faber, 1995.

Artie Cohen grew up listening to Willis Conover's jazz program on Radio Free Europe and developed a taste for 1950s jazz, especially Stan Getz, Chet Baker and Billie Holiday.

Stan Getz: *The Steamer* (Verve, 1999). Stan Getz was his favorite musician and *The Steamer* was his favorite jazz album.

Chet Baker: *Young Chet* (Pacific Jazz, 1995).

Billie Holiday: *Music for Torching* (Verve, 1995).

_____. Sex Dolls aka Skin Trade. London: Faber & Faber, 2002.

Artie Cohen listens constantly to Stan Getz. Stan Getz and Gerry Mulligan: *Getz Meets Mulligan in Hi-Fi* (Verve, 1991); Stan Getz: *The Steamer* (Verve, 1999) are favorites. Johnny Smith: *Spring Is Here/The Genius of Johnny Smith* (Five Four, 2006) has the memorable cuts with Stan Getz, such as "Moonlight in Vermont."

Nemac, John. Canary's Combo. Hollywood: Nite-Time, 1964.

Teddy King with Al Cohn and his Orchestra: *Bidin' My Time.* (RCA, 1997) features a medium sized band with its vocalist is similar to Joe Falcon's band.

Nielsen, Helen. "You Can't Trust a Man." In Pronzini, Bill & Muller, Marcia (eds.). The Deadly Arts. New York: Arbor, 1985.

No specific tunes by singer Crystal Coe are mentioned. A 1959 vocal album by June Christy titled *Ballads for Night People* (Capitol, 2005) fits an L.A. mood.

Novak, Robert. B-Girl. New York: Avon, 1956.

Ziggy Elman. *And The Angels Sang & Body and Soul.* (Jazz Band, 1947) and Les Brown: *Les Brown's in Town* (Jazzbeat, 2007). Both of these big bands had lots of radio airtime and played roadhouses. They provided background music for anyone's dreams.

Nuckel, John. Harlem Rhapsody. New York: Independent, 2019.

Harlem Rhapsody spans several decades (1920s & 1930s). A good overview of musicians who played at the Cotton Club (Duke Ellington, Adelaide Hall & Ivie Anderson with the Ellington Orchestra as well as Cab Calloway, Ethel Waters, etc.) can be found on *Cotton Club* (Yesterday, 2006). Another CD featuring the Ellington Orchestra in the 1930s is *Duke Ellington at The Cotton Club* (Storyville, 2011).

Oglesby, Wm Ellis. Blow Happy, Blow Sad. Edmonton: Commonwealth Publications, 1996.
   Arthur Briggs was a trumpet player very much like Chops Danielson, who spent most of his life, including WWII, living in Europe.
   Arthur Briggs: *Hot Trumpet in Europe* (Jazz Archives, 1995).

Ondaatje, Michael. Coming Through Slaughter. London: Marion Boyars, 1979; New York: Norton, 1976.
   Breaking Out of New Orleans 1922-1929 (JSP, 2004) is a 4 volume set recorded later than the period of the story and is more polished than the earlier music.

Ordover, Andrew. Cool For Cats. Lexington: C4C Books, 2011.
   Bassist Jordan Greenblatt's group plays Chet Baker's version of "Imagination." It can be found on *The Best of Chet Baker Plays* (Blue Note/Pacific Jazz, 1992).
   No other specific jazz tunes are mentioned, so bassist Paul Chambers' *Paul Chambers Quintet* (Blue Note, 2009) provides interesting listening.

_____. The Cat Came Back. Middletown, Del.: Crafting-A-Life, 2016.
   Glenn Miller's "Little Brown Jug" is Lydia's audition tune for the band. It's on Glenn Miller: *Little Brown Jug* (Four Star, 1994).
   The Band works up a spare arrangement of Ray Charles' "You Don't Know Me." The original is on Ray Charles *Modern Sounds in Country & Western Music* (Concord, 2019). They also do "Won't

You Come Home Bill Bailey?" a version of which is Patsy Cline *Gold* (Decca, 2005).

Jordan ponders three different versions of "Why Don't You Do Right?"

Peggy Lee: *The Best of Miss Peggy Lee* (Capitol, 1998).

Lil Green: *Romance in the Dark* (Membron, 2003).

Sinead O'Connor: *Am I Not Your Girl* (EMI, 1993).

Padura, Leonardo. Havana Fever. London & New York: Bitter Lemon Press, 2009.

Omara Portuondo is a singer from Violeta del Rio's generation. She can be heard on *The Buena Vista Social Club Presents Omara Portendo* (Nonesuch, 2000).

Patchett, Ann. Taft. Boston: Houghton Mifflin, 1994.

Memphis jazz & blues comes and goes but the music of Elvis Presley and W.C. Handy remain on the scene.

Louis Armstrong: *Louis Armstrong Plays W.C. Handy* (Columbia, 1997).

Elvis Presley: *Elvis Presley* (RCA, 1999).

Drawing from Stax, Sun and Hi Records music catalogues, *The Memphis Box* (Icehouse IHR, 1999) offers a good overview of Memphis soul, R&B, country and rock music.

Pentecost, Hugh. Murder Goes Round and Round. New York: Dodd, Mead, 1988; London: Robert Hale, 1989.

No specific music is mentioned but Tommy Flanagan's piano captures New York sophistication in the 1980s. Tommy Flanagan: *Nights at The Vanguard* (Uptown, 1987).

Phillips, Gary. "The Performer." In Vega, Eddie. (ed.). Noir Nation N6. Middletown, DE: Noir Nation, 2017.

Dave McKenna, like Avery Randolph, was very much at home playing clubs and bar rooms. Three albums that fit the story's mood are:

Dave McKenna: *Solo* (Chiaroscuro, 1984).

Dave McKenna: *Cooking at Michael's Pub* (Prevue, 1999)
Dave McKenna: *In Madison* (Arbors, 2018).

Pines, Paul. The Tin Angel. New York: Morrow, 1983.
Always the consummate musician, tenor saxophonist Zoot Sims
would play jazz festivals and small New York clubs like the fictional
East Village club, The Tin Angel.
Zoot Sims: *I Wish I Were Twins* (Pablo, 1998).

Plater, Alan. The Beiderbecke Affair. London: Methuen, 1985.
Interesting Bix can be found on *Bix Beiderbecke and the Chicago
Cornets* (Milestone, 1992).

_____. The Beiderbecke Tapes. London: Methuen, 1986.
Bix Beiderbecke's dazzling cornet can be heard on *Bix Beiderbecke and the Chicago Cornets* (Milestone, 1992).

_____. The Beiderbecke Connection. London: Methuen,
1992.
Ivan the fugitive likes Bix Beiderbecke and Duke Ellington. The
best of Bix can be found on *Bix Beiderbecke and the Chicago Cornets* (Milestone, 1992). An interesting small group session featuring
Duke with the great Coleman Hawkins is Duke Ellington Meets
Coleman Hawkins (MCA/Impulse, 1986).

Pronzini, Bill. Blue Lonesome. New York: Walker, 1995.
Messenger listens to a lot of 1930s Ellington, especially "Perdido"
after he hears of Janet Mitchell's suicide. "Perdido" can be found on
Duke Ellington Masterpieces *1926-1949* (Properbox 25, 2001).
He also listens to a tape in Nevada of Louis Armstrong with Earl
Hines.
Louis Armstrong: *Louis Armstrong and Earl Hines Vol. IV* (Co-
lumbia, 1989).

Queen, Ellery. Death Spins the Platter. London: Gollancz, 1975;
New York: Pocket, 1962.

Jazz musicians adapted to the changing times of the 1950s by playing R&B. Ray Charles: *Ray Charles at Newport* (Atlantic, 1998) is a great example. It smokes!!!

Rabe, Peter. Murder Me for Nickels. New York: Gold Medal, 1960.

Herman Lubinsky's Savoy Record Company was a small company like the one the fictional Jack St. Louis owned and struggled to maintain its independence. It recorded the beboppers when the larger record labels were hesitant. A good example is Dexter Gordon: *Settin' the Pace* (Savoy Jazz, 1996).

Raleigh, Michael. Maxwell Street Blues, The. New York: St. Martin's, 1994.

PI Paul Whelan listens to guitarist Kenny Burrell while driving, pianist Bill Evans while thinking, and organist Jimmy Smith while relaxing.

Kenny Burrell: *Blue Lights* (Blue Note, 1997).

Bill Evans & Jim Hall: *Undercurrent* (Blue Note, 1988).

Jimmy Smith: *Six Views of The Blues* (Blue Note, 1999).

Randisi, Robert J. Everybody Kills Somebody Sometime. New York: St. Martin's, 2006.

Frank Sinatra: *Frank Sinatra at The Sands* (Reprise, 1966).

Dean Martin: *Some Enchanted Evening* (Hallmark, 1999).

Both of these albums capture the style and sounds of Sinatra and Martin in the 1960s.

_____. Fly Me to The Morgue. London & New York: Severn House, 2011.

Bing Crosby's career stretched for 40 years—a good overview (50 songs) is *Too Marvelous for Words* (Jasmine, 2002).

Frank Sinatra's ballad album, *Nice 'n' Easy* (Capitol, 2020) with its charts by Nelson Riddle is full of late-night songs that mix well with memories and the last scotch of the evening—songs like "Nearness of You," "I've Got a Crush on You," and "You Go To My Head."

_____. Hey There (You With The Gun In Your Hand). New York: St. Martin's, 2008.

Laurindo Almeida is opening for Sammy Davis Jr. at Lake Tahoe. *Sammy Davis Jr. Sings/Laurindo Almeida Plays* (Reprise, 1991) was recorded a few years after the fictional Tahoe engagement.

Despite its title, this really is a good overview of his career. Sammy Davis, Jr.: *The Wham of Sam* (Warner, 1994).

Frank Sinatra at the Sands (Reprise, 1966) contains the program Frank sang at the Sands during the 1960s.

_____. I'm A Fool to Kill You. London & New York: Severn House, 2010.

Two of Sinatra's collaborations with Nelson Riddle fit the story's mood of loss.

In The Wee Small Hours (Capitol, 1998) contains the version of "When Your Lover Has Gone" that evoked such strong memories of Ava Gardner that reportedly, Sinatra fell apart after recording it.

Songs For Only the Lonely (Capitol, 1987) contains saloon singer classics such as "Angel Eyes," "Guess I'll Hang My Tears Out to Dry," "What's New?" and the classic version of "It Never Entered My Mind."

_____. It Was a Very Bad Year. London & New York: Severn House, 2012.

Frank Sinatra obviously overshadowed his son's singing career, so Frank Jnr. ended up as his father's musical director for his last 20 years. An interesting album by Frank Jr is his tribute to his father, *As I Remember it* (Angel, 2006), which includes songs such as "Nothing at All," "All the Way," "Night and Day," and "In the Wee Small Hours."

Songs by Sinatra friend and composer Jimmy Van Heusen, "High Hopes," "All the Way," "Call Me Irresponsible" can be found on *Sinatra's Sinatra* (Reprise, 2014).

_____. "Listening Room, The." In Murder and all that Jazz. New York: Signet, 2004.

The late Nancy LaMott sang in a style similar to Carla Jenkins, who is headlining with her quartet at Billy Danvers' club.

Nancy LaMott: *What's Good About Goodbye?* (Middor, 1996).

_____. Luck Be a Lady, Don't Die. New York: St. Martin's, 2007.

Frank Sinatra was his prime in these three albums from the 1960s:

Frank Sinatra: *Frank Sinatra at The Sands* (Reprise, 1966).

Frank Sinatra: *Sinatra's Swinging Session* (Capitol, 1960).

Frank Sinatra/Count Basie: *It Might as Well be Swing* Reprise, 1964).

_____. Way You Die Tonight, The. London & New York: Severn House, 2014.

Eddie G.'s real friend in "the Rat Pack" is Dean Martin. At the time of the story, he's got a #1 song, "Everybody Loves Somebody Sometime" which can be found on *Essential Dean Martin* (Legacy, 2014). Also, *Dean Martin Live at The Sands* (Prism, 2006) captures a typical show in the 1960s.

Any of the Capitol-Reprise albums of the era are great background. *Sinatra: Best of the Best* (EMI, 2011) has many of the songs of the Sinatra era, such as "My Funny Valentine," "My Way," "It Was a Very Good Year" and "Night and Day."

_____. When Somebody Kills You. London & New York: Severn House, 2015.

Judy Garland had just finished a number of successful concerts at the time of the story. Easily, her best concert album is *Judy at Carnegie Hall* (Capitol, 1961) that includes such heartbreakers as "You Go to My Head," "The Man That Got Away" and "Stormy Weather."

Frank Sinatra's melancholy 1955 classic, *In the Wee Small Hours* (Capitol, 1955) with its Nelson Riddle arrangements, goes well with it. Among the Songbook Classics are "Last Night When We Were Young," "I'll Never Be the Same" and "I Get Along Without You Very Well."

_____. You're Nobody 'til Somebody Kills You. New York: Minotaur, 2009.

Frank Sinatra's classic albums provide 1960s atmosphere:

Frank Sinatra: *Nice 'N' Easy*. (Capital, 1960) features tunes from early in his career ("You Go to My Head," "Fools Rush In," etc) with updated arrangements by Nelson Riddle.

Frank Sinatra: *No One Cares* (Capitol, 1959). Gordon Jenkins provides the charts for this album of torch songs ("I Don't Stand a Ghost of a Chance," "Stormy Weather" etc.).

Frank Sinatra: *Ring-a-ding-ding* (Reprise, 1960). For his debut on his own label, Frank mixes Songbook tunes ("A Foggy Day," "A Fine Romance") with pop fillers. Johnny Mandel did the charts.

_____. You Make Me Feel So Dead. London & New York: Severn House, 2013.

Elvis was in town for the opening of *Viva Las Vegas* with Ann Margaret. Elvis Presley: *Viva Las Vegas* (Sony 2009) features Elvis, along with the occasional Ann- Margret duet.

Frank Sinatra-Count Basie: *Sinatra at The Sands* (Reprise, 2014) captures Sinatra at 50. Although recorded in 1966, vintage Sinatra rarely changed throughout the decade.

Rayner, Richard. Devil's Wind, The. New York: Harper & Row, 2002.

Architect Maurice Valentine listened to jazz, especially Art Pepper.

Art Pepper: *Art Pepper Meets the Rhythm Section* (Contemporary, 1986).

Chet Baker and Art Pepper: *The Route* (Pacific Jazz, 1989).

The murdered tenor saxophonist Wardell Lane is based on Wardell Gray.

Wardell Gray: *The Wardell Gray Story* (Properbox, 2003).

Reed, Barbara. Harmonic Deception. San Bernardino, CA., 2010.

Jazz pianist Reed released her own soundtrack for the book: *High Notes Are Murder*. (Rare Sounds, 2011).

Reed, Harlan. Swing Music Murder, The. New York: Dutton, 1938.
Seattle may be a long way from New York's jazz scene but its clubs, thanks to radio broadcasts, were hip to what was happening in "the Big Apple."
Tenor saxophonist Chu Berry is featured on Teddy Wilson: *Teddy Wilson & His All-Stars. Vol. 1* (Columbia, 1993).

Reeves, Robert. "Danse Macabre." In Penzler, Otto (ed.). Pulp Fiction: The Dames. London: Quercus, 2008.
Two good big band dance albums are combined on Billy May: *A Band Is Born/Big Band Bash* (Collector's Choice, 2001). They are a bit above Juggar Callahan but do provide atmosphere.

Rich, Nathaniel. King Zeno. London: MCD, 2018; New York: Farrar, Straus & Giroux, 2018.
Although recorded a few years later, *Breaking Out of New Orleans 1922-1929* (JSP, 2004) contains similar music to what would have been heard post WWI New Orleans.
Also, Kid Ory dominated the New Orleans' trumpet scene until King Oliver (with Louis Armstrong) came along.
Kid Ory: *Kid Ory 1922-1929* (JSP, 2004).

Rieman, Terry. Vamp Till Ready. London: Gollancz, 1955; New York: Harper, 1954.
Although Polly Bergen never initially trained as an opera singer as Gerda Leedon did, she had a radio (and later television) variety show and sang standards as well as popular tunes of the day.
Polly Bergen. *My Heart Sings* (Columbia, 2004) is representative of her 1950s career.
Gerda and her friends listen to the Turk Murphy Jazz Band that was based in San Francisco but would go east to New York City to clubs, such as the Italian Village, for lucrative gigs.
Turk Murphy. *Turk Murphy's Jazz Band* (Fantasy, 1991).

Roberts, Les. "Jazz Canary." In Randisi, Robert J. (ed.). Murder and all that Jazz. Signet, 2004.

Kate O'Dwyer is a jazz/pop singer. Chris Connor is jazzier in this collection of standards that catches the story's mood. Chris Connor: *A Portrait of Chris* (Collector's Choice, 2001).

Robinson, Peter. Aftermath. London: Macmillan, 2001; New York: Morrow, 2001.

There's very little jazz present. That said, Alan Banks does, however, relax listening to Duke Ellington's "Black, Brown and Beige". Duke Ellington: *Black Brown and Beige* (RCA, 1998).

He also listens, with Annie Banks, to Van Morrison's rock-blues classic album, *Astral Weeks*. Van Morrison: *Astral Weeks* (Warner, 1987).

_____. In a Dry Season. New York: Morrow, 1999; London: Macmillan, 2000.

Much of the action occurs in wartime England when the popular music heard at the American military bases was swing, with Glenn Miller being everyone's favorite, followed by Tommy Dorsey and Benny Goodman.

Major Glenn Miller & The Army Air Force Band, 1943-1944 (RCA, 1987).

Tommy Dorsey: *The Seventeen Number Ones* (RCA Bluebird, 1990).

Benny Goodman and His Orchestra: *Sing, Sing, Sing* (RCA Bluebird, 1987).

Inspector Alan Banks has a large CD collection and plays an Etta James album during his first time alone with Annie Cabot. Etta James: *The Chess Sampler* (Chess, 2000).

He also listens to the classic women jazz singers. Billie Holiday singing "Ill Wind" is a favorite and can be found on Billie Holiday: *All or Nothing at All* (Verve, 1995). Although not specifically cited, three albums by June Christy, Ella Fitzgerald, Dinah Washington and fill out the story's mood.

June Christy: *The Ballad Collection* (Capitol 72435 24479 2 3, 2000).

Ella Fitzgerald: *These Are The Blues* (Verve 829-536-2, 1994).

Dinah Washington: *Dinah Washington Sings The Blues* (Verve Compact Jazz, 1987).

_____. "Magic of Your Touch, The." In Randisi. Robert J., (ed.). Murder and all that Jazz. New York: Signet, 2004.
Before the drugs took their toll, Chet Baker sang a lot of songs on *Jazz Masters* (EMI, 1995) that stayed with listeners.

_____. Necessary End, A. London & New York: Viking, 1989.
Alan Banks listens to American bluesmen such as Muddy Waters and Walter Davis as well the great jazz/blues singer Billie Holiday.
Muddy Waters: *Muddy Water at Newport* (Chess, 2001).
Walter Davis: *The Essential Walter Davis* (Classic Blues, 2001).
Billie Holiday: *Jazz Master 12* (Verve, 1994) includes "God Bless the Child".

_____. Playing With Fire. London: Macmillan, 2004; New York: Morrow, 2004.
As Banks ages and his life changes, he listens to more jazz (Bud Powell) than in the past and acknowledges a preference for female jazz vocalists. That said, however, he still listens to classic rock (Van Morrison) and remains a folkie (Jesse Winchester).
A favorite of Banks is the Cassandra Wilson album with Bob Dylan's "Shelter from The Storm" which is mentioned in the quote.
Cassandra Wilson: *Belly of The Sun* (Blue Note, 2002).
"Night in Tunisia" can be found on Bud Powell: *'Round About Midnight at The Blue Note* (Dreyfus, 1991).
Banks often plays the classic Van Morrison album, *Astral Weeks* (Warner, 1987).
Jesse Winchester: *Live From Mountain Stage* (Blue Plate, 2001) sounds as good as he did when his voice seduced the folkie crowd in the 1960s.

Rodriguez, Andres. "Yesterdays." In Paul, Steve (ed.), Kansas City Noir. London & New York: Akashic, 2012.

Ted, the bartender and narrator, puts on a recording of Clifford Brown's "Yesterdays" after owner Milton Morris fails to return in the late evening to Milton's Tap Room.

Clifford Brown's "Yesterdays" can be found on *Compact Jazz: Clifford Brown,* (Polygram, 1990).

Although they stopped live music and played only records, *Real Kansas City 20s, 30's & 40's.* (Sony, 1996) gives the reader a sense of the music played at the Tap Room in its Prohibition heyday when Tom Pendergast and his chums used to stop in.

Roeburt, Joe. <u>Sing Out Sweet Homicide</u>. New York: Dell, 1961.

1920s jazz provides the background in this book that was a tie-in to the early 1960s TV show, *The Roaring Twenties.* A few period albums for listening are: *Louis Armstrong and His Orchestra 1928-1929* (Classics, 1991); *The Best of the Coon Sanders Original Nighthawk Orchestra* (Retrieval, 1999); Duke Ellington: *The Okeh Duke Ellington* (Columbia, 1991) and *The Fletcher Henderson Story* (Columbia, 1994).

Ronald, James. <u>Death Croons the Blues</u>. London: Hodder & Stoughton, 1934; New York: Phoenix, 1940.

In her youth, blues singer Alberta Hunter toured England and sang "St. Louis Blues" as did Adele Valee. It's included on *Alberta Hunter with Lovie Austin's Blues Serenaders* (Riverside, 1984). It was recorded in the 1960s but recaptured her earlier sound and charm.

Runcie, James. "A Matter of Time." In <u>Sidney Chambers and the Shadow of Death</u>. London & New York: Bloomsbury, 2012.

Singer Gloria Dee, who entrances Sidney Chambers, seems like Carmen McRae.

Two live sets can be found on Carmen McRae: *Woman Talk: Live at the Village Gate & The Half Note.* (Fresh Sound, 2010).

Sallis, James. <u>Blue Bottle</u>. London: No Exit, 1999. New York: Walker, 1999.

Lew Griffin was shot while coming out of a bar that featured contemporary New Orleans music like that played by pianist Dr. John. Dr John: *The Dr. John Anthology* (Rhino, 1993).

Griffin heard bluesman Lonnie Johnson in his mind before he went into surgery after being shot. Lonnie Johnson: *Another Night to Cry* (Prestige/Bluesville, 1992).

Sanchez, Thomas. <u>King Bongo</u>. New York: Knopf, 2003.

Ry Cooder & Manuel Gabon: *Mambo Sinuendo* (Nonesuch/ Perro Verde, 2003). Ry Cooder joins the Cuban guitarist Manuel Galban in an album of sensuous, noirish music. Darkness shimmies off their strings.

Sabu: *Palo Congo* (Blue Note, 1999). Sabu is the sort of bongo player that King Bongo emulates.

Saunders, David. <u>M Squad</u>. New York: Belmont, 1962.

Benny Carter's arrangements and Stanley Wilson's music on the soundtrack reflects the tone of the television show and action of the book. *The Music From Stanley Wilson's M Squad* (RCA, 1996).

Scheen, Kjersti. "Moonglow." In Hutchings, Janet (ed.). <u>Passport To Crime</u>. New York: Carroll & Graf, 2007.

The original "Moonglow," heard by Herman Hof Jiverson and his three friends during their country weekends is on the small group part of Disc 2 of *The Essential Benny Goodman* (Columbia/ Bluebird, 2007).

Sheridan, Sarah. <u>London Calling</u>. London: Polygon, 2013.

Rose's favorite singer was Nat King Cole and her cigarette case was engraved with the first two notes from the song "Too Young." But Chet Baker, deemed cooler, is a new favorite.

The original version of "Too Young" can be found on *The World of Nat King Cole* (Capitol, 2005). A representative collection of Chet Baker's 1950s vocals is *Best of Chet Baker Sings* (Blue Note, 1989).

Shurman, Ida. <u>Death Beats The Band</u>. New York: Phoenix, 1943.

Sammy Kaye and His Orchestra 1944/Les Elgart and His Orchestra 1946 (Circle, 1988). Both bands had a sound like Andy Parker's and played roadhouses like the Long Island Casino.

Skinner, Robert. <u>Blood To Drink</u>. Scottsdale: Poisoned Pen Press, 2000.

All of the top bands had left New Orleans but were on the radio. The music of Louis Armstrong, Duke Ellington, Jimmy Lunceford, Benny Goodman and Count Basie filled the airwaves.

Louis Armstrong and His Orchestra 1932-1939: *Laughing Louis* (RCA, 1969).

Duke Ellington: *Masterpieces 1926-1949* (Properbox 25, 2001).

Jimmy Lunceford and His Orchestra: *Stomp It Off* (Decca, 1992).

Benny Goodman: *Sing, Sing. Sing* (RCA Bluebird, 1987).

_____. <u>Cat-Eyed Trouble</u>. New York: Kensington, 2008.

There's lots of background music heard on records and the radio.

Louis Armstrong: *Hot Fives and Sevens* (JSP, 2001).

Duke Ellington: *Masterpieces 1926-1949* (Properbox, 2001).

Lady Day singing "Can't Help Lovin' That Man of Mine" is found on Disc 3 of Billie Holiday: *Lady Day: The Master Takes and Singles* (Columbia, 2007).

_____. <u>Daddy's Gone A-Hunting</u>. Scottsdale: Poisoned Pen Press, 1999.

The top bands are long gone from New Orleans but there's still music everywhere thanks to radio and records. Louis Armstrong and His Orchestra 1932-1939:

Laughing Louis (RCA, 1969); Duke Ellington: *Masterpieces 1926-1949* (Properbox, 2001); Count Basie: *One O'clock Jump* (Decca, 1990); Benny Goodman and His Orchestra: *Sing, Sing, Sing.* (RCA Bluebird 5630-2-RB, 1987); The Jimmie Lunceford Orchestra: *Stomp It Off* (Decca, 1992) and Fletcher Henderson: *Fletcher Henderson and His Orchestra 1932-1934* (Classics, 1990).

_____. Pale Shadow. Scottsdale: Poisoned Pen Press, 2001.
Marcel likes Benny Goodman with Charlie Christian as well as Billie Holiday and Duke Ellington.
Charlie Christian: *Broadcasts with The Old Benny Goodman Sextet 1939* (JSP, 2002).
Duke Ellington: *The Duke's Men: Small Groups, Vol. 1* (Columbia, 1991).
Billie Holiday: *Lady Day. The Master Takes and Singles* (Columbia, 2007).

_____. Righteous Cut, The. Scottsdale: Poisoned Pen Press, 2002.
By 1941 all the top bands were long gone from New Orleans. On the radio, however, the national bands prevailed. Because of his politics and music, Charlie Barnet was one white musician who effortlessly crossed the color line. Charlie Barnet had the blackest sounding white band around. Charlie Barnet & His Orchestra: *Drop Me Off in Harlem* (Decca, 2013).
Duke Ellington's 1940 date in Fargo, North Dakota represented the band at its peak.
Duke Ellington at Fargo, 1940 (Storyville, 2011).
The Basie sound remained eternal: Count Basie: *The Complete Decca Recordings 1937-1939* (Verve, 1992).

_____. Skin Deep, Blood Red. New York: Kensington, 1997.
The jazz heard in New Orleans was no longer just local but also came via radio broadcasts from New York and Chicago. Filling the airwaves were the sounds of Armstrong, Ellington, and Goodman: *Louis Armstrong and His Famous Orchestra 1928-1929* (Classics, 1991); *Ivie Anderson with Duke Ellington and His Famous Orchestra.* (Jazz Archives, 1991); Benny Goodman with Helen Ward on Benny Goodman & His Orchestra: *Sing, Sing, Sing* (RCA Bluebird, 1987).
Count Basie: *One O'clock Jump* (Decca, 1990).

Skvorecky, Joseph. End of Lieutenant Boruvka, The. New York: Norton, 1990; London: Faber & Faber, 1990.

The Kenny Clarke-Francy Boland Big Band, made up of expatriate musicians, played jazz that was heard via radio broadcasts and live in Central Europe. The Kenny Clarke-Francy Boland Big Band: *All Blues & Sax No End* (MPS, 1994).

_____. Mournful Demeanor of Lieutenant Boruvka, The. New York: Norton, 1987.

The Kenny Clarke-Francy Boland Big Band: *All Blues & Sax No End* (MPS, 1994). This primarily expatriate big band played jazz that was heard via radiobroadcasts and live appearances throughout central Europe.

_____. Return of Lieutenant Boruvka, The. London: Faber & Faber, 1990; New York: Norton, 1991.

The Kenny Clarke-Francy Boland Big Band: *All Blues & Sax No End* (MPS, 1994).

This primarily expatriate big band played music that was heard via radio broadcasts and live performances in central Europe.

_____. Sins For Father Knox. New York: Norton, 1988; London: Faber & Faber, 1989.

Kendra Shank: *Afterglow* (Mapleshade, 1994). Backed by a small group, Shank sings a cosmopolitan program that globetrotting Eve Adam would do in small clubs.

Slovo, Gillian. Catnap. London: Michael Joseph, 1994; New York: St. Martin's, 1996.

Although no specific music is mentioned, Kate Baeier is a tenor saxophone player as well as a detective. Joe Lovano's album *I'm All for You* (Blue Note, 2004) reflects the balance of inside and outside jazz that would appeal to her.

_____. Close Call. London: Michael, Joseph, 1995.

Kate Baeier hears tenor saxophonist Sonny Rollins in Gavin Dowd's car. Sonny Rollins: *Sonny Rollins Meets Hawk* (RCA, 1999) is an interesting meeting between masters of different generations and styles, Sonny Rollins and Coleman Hawkins.

_____. Death By Analysis. London: The Women's Press, 1986; New York: Doubleday, 1988.

Kate listens to alto sax, so Frank Morgan's music would appeal to her. Frank Morgan Quartet: *Yardbird Suite* (Contemporary, 2001). At one point, she also listens to Al Green. Al Green: *I'm Still In Love With You* (HI, 1993).

_____. Death Comes Staccato. London: Women's Press, 1987; New York: Doubleday, 1988.

At the end, Kate picks up her alto and plays "Backwater Blues" to cleanse the unpleasantness of the case from her life. "Backwater Blues" can be found on Horace Parlan & Archie Shepp: *Trouble in Mind* (SteepleChase, 1980).

Smith, C.W. "Plantation Club, The." In Breton, Marcella (ed.). Hot and Cool Jazz Short Stories. New York: Plume, 1990.

Like Curtis "Stoogie" Goodman, Alto saxophonist Frank Morgan had his problems with drugs. Frank Morgan: *Yardbird Suite* (Contemporary, 2001).

Smith, J.P. Body and Soul. New York: Grove, 1987.

Tempted by the large sums of money he was handling, jazz musician Jerzy Wozzeck diverted money from drug deals into jazz records by Bud Powell, Thelonious Monk and John Coltrane. Three desirable albums are:

Bud Powell: *The Amazing Bud Powell Vols. 1 & 2* (Blue Note, 1989).

Thelonious Monk: *Thelonious Monk and John Coltrane* (Riverside, 1998).

Smith, Julie. Axeman's Jazz, The. New York: St. Martin's, 1991.

A sampling of the modern New Orleans music scene can be found in the box set *City of Dreams* (Rounder, 2007).

_____. Jazz Funeral. New York: Fawcett, 1993.

Johnny Adams: *The Verdict* (Rounder, 1995). Adams is a mellow New Orleans R&B singer who can sing jazz standards with the best of the heartbreakers.

The Neville Brothers: *Walking in The Shadow of Life* (WMI, 2005). The Nevilles have personified New Orleans R&B for decades.

Wynton Marsalis: *Standards & Ballads*. (Columbia, 2008) represents contemporary New Orleans jazz at its best.

_____. House of Blues. New York: Fawcett, 1995.

There's actually no jazz and just a modicum of blues in House of Blues. Grady Hebert, the son of murdered restaurateur Arthur Hebert, spend his evenings away from his dysfunctional family in a haze of booze and blues listening to Buddy Guy at the House of Blues.

Buddy Guy. *A Man and The Blues*. (Vanguard, 1990) is representative of Guy in the 1990s.

_____. "Kid Trombone." In Randisi, Robert J. (ed.), Murder and all that Jazz. New York: Signet, 2004.

The Marsalis family has a lock on contemporary New Orleans jazz and the Neville family has a similar hold on R&B. Wynton Marsalis: *Standards and Ballads* (Columbia, 2008). Marsalis band member and the trombone player, Wycliffe Gordon captures the city's sound with *The Search* (Nagel Hayer, 2000). The Neville Brothers provide another side of New Orleans' musical background with *Walking In The Shadow of Life* (EMI, 2005).

_____. New Orleans Mourning. New York: St. Martin's, 1990.

Smith's novel takes place in New Orleans during Carnival. The anthology *Music on A Celebration of New Orleans: Music To Benefit Musicares Hurricane Relief* (Rounder, 2005) contains the varied sorts of music (traditional and modern jazz, second-line brass band, gospel, R&B and Native American) heard during Mardi Gras. With a few exceptions, all of the players are still active.

Smith, Martin Cruz. Stallion Gate. New York: Random, 1986; London: Collins, Harvill, 1986.

Before joining the army, Sergeant Joe Pena played jazz piano on 52nd Street with Charlie Parker, Dizzy Gillespie and the other bop pioneers. Dodo Marmarosa's piano style seems close to that of the fictional Joe Pena. Dodo Marmarosa: *Dodo's Dance* (Proper Intro, 2004).

Sonin, Ray. Dance Band Mystery, The. London: Quality Press, 1940.
Ray Noble: *The Hot Sides 1929-1934* (Retrieval, 2007) features a British arranger and a scattering of American musicians.
Danny Polo: *Danny Polo and his Swing Stars* (Retrieval, 2007). An American expatriate, Polo was far more successful in England than in his own country.

Spicer, Bart. Blues for The Prince. London: Collins, 1951; New York: Dodd, Mead, 1950.
At the memorial jam session for the black trumpet player Harold Prince, both black New Orleans and white Chicago style players are represented. Wilde's preference is for the older, New Orleans style.
Bunk Johnson and His New Orleans Band (1945-1946) (Document, 1996) was recorded around the time of the story and showed the old New Orleans trumpet player still had his chops and lots of music in him.
Johnny Dodds: *Blue Clarinet Stomp/The Legendary Classic Clarinetist* (Columbia Bluebird, 1990) was recorded in the late 1920s and features New Orleans legends Jelly Roll Morton, Lil Armstrong and Baby Dodds.
The Eddie Condon All-Stars: *Dixieland Jam* (Columbia, 1989) was originally recorded in the mid-1950s when many Chicago style players, like guitarist Condon, were still playing.

Steele, Coleen. "Them There Eyes." In Pike, Sue & Boswell, Joan (eds.). Bone Dance. Toronto: Rendevous, 2003.
Two white swing bands that toured frequently (like the one Harry Finley played trumpet in) were Sammy Kaye and Les Elgart: *Sammy Kaye and His Orchestra 1944/Les Elgart and His Orchestra 1946* (Circle, 1995).

Stevens, Kevin. <u>Reaching The Shining River</u>. Paris: Betimes, 2014.

No two musicians represented the Kansas City scene in the 1930s better than Count Basie and Lester Young. Although no specific tunes are mentioned, two albums representative of the era are Count Basie, *America's #1 Band*, (Columbia Legacy, 2003) and Lester Young, *The Kansas City Sessions* (GRP). The Basie Band dominated radio airplay and can be heard on Count Basie, *The Best of The Small Groups, 1936-1944* (Essential, 2016).

Big Joe Turner was in the bar where Arlene Gray worked and sang "Going To Chicago" that is found on *Blues Legends* (Mag Music), 2011.

"Lady Be Good" was Arlene Gray's signature tune. It can be found on_*The Complete Billie Holiday Remastered, Vol. 10* (Jazz Co. 2000). Gray sang standards of the era that became Billie's songs:

"All of Me": Billie Holiday *All of Me*. (Bela, 2009).

"If You Were Mine"– Billie Holiday: *The Best of Billie Holiday* (AAO Music, 2014).

"Body and Soul"– Billie Holiday: *Body and Soul* (Verve, 2009).

"Strange Fruit"– Billie Holiday: *The Best of Billie Holiday* (AAO Music, 2014).

"Loverman" – Billie Holiday: *Loverman*. (S.D.E.G. records, 2011).

"Willow Weep For Me" – Billie Holiday: *Lady Sings The Blues*. (Verve 2007)

"They Can't Take That Away From Me" – Billie Holiday: *I Only Have Eyes For You*. (Fantastic Voyage, 2006)

Tate, Sylvia. <u>Never By Chance</u>. New York: Harper, 1947.

Hollywood studio musician, jazz pianist Johnny Silesc played in small groups like those of alto saxophonist Lennie Niehaus and big bands like those led by Bill Holman.

Lennie Niehaus: *Complete Fifties Recordings* (Lonehill, 2006) and Bill Holman: *Big Band Jazz Orbit* (V.S.O.P., 1987).

Temple, Lou Jane. <u>Cornbread Killer, The</u>. New York: St. Martin's, 1999.

Ralph Sutton: *Eye Opener* (Solo Art, 1991) and Ralph Sutton and Jay McShann *The Last of The Whorehouse Piano Players*

(Chiaroscuro, 1989) recalls the sounds of Kansas City's past.

The anthology *Jazz Kansas City Style* (Topaz, 1996) offers a twenty-year overview of the Kansas City jazz scene.

Count Basie: *Kansas City Suite* (Disque Vogue, 1992), the Basie Band's retrospective album, recorded in the 1960s, recaptures a feeling of vintage Kansas City.

Terrenoire, David. Beneath A Panamanian Moon. New York: St. Martin's, 2005.

Dave McKenna's album of solo piano fits in quite nicely. Dave McKenna: *Giant Stride* (Concord, 1999).

Also, *Dick Hyman: Genius at Play/Lou Stein: Solo* (Audiophile, 2002) is a double album by two fine piano players whose style John Kirby would be familiar with.

Vandagriff, G.G. Murder in the Jazz Band. Salt Lake City Press, 2020.

Although the Pasadena Roof Orchestra is larger than James' group, these tunes probably would be played & the group (although American) captures the musical spirit of the 1930s.

Pasadena Roof Orchestra: *As Time Goes by* (metro, 2016) & *Rhythm Is Our Business* (Pasadena, 2011).

Vining, Keith. Keep Running. Chicago: Chicago Paperback House, 1962.

Jack Norman plays a jazz-country piano much like that of Mose Allison in the 1950s. Two of Allison's 1957 Prestige albums fit the mood of the story and can be found on Mose Allison: *Back Country Suite/Local Color* (Ais, 2010).

Sally's Gulf City club has a relaxed, southern feel and features older style dance numbers for their guests. Although Gene Austin was a wimpy "crooner," his band played the sort of music from 1925-1936 that would be featured at the club on Saturday evenings. Gene Austin: *Time to Relax.* (Take Two, 2011).

Wainright, John. Do Nothin' Till You Hear From Me. London: Macmillan, 1977; New York: St. Martin's, 1977.

English Big Band leader Lucky Luckhurst is a fan of 1940s American Big Band music—with Count Basie and Glenn Miller as favorites. Count Basie and His Orchestra: *1944 and 1945* (Circle, 1992); and Glenn Miller: *The Popular Recordings 1938-1942* (RCA Bluebird, 1989) are two of their many albums.

Wallop, Douglas. <u>Night Light</u>. New York: Norton, 1953.

Looking into the background of the deranged jazz musician who killed his daughter, Robert Horne enters the world of 1950s New York bebop. Three albums representative of that time are: Dizzy Gillespie Big Band: *Showtime at The Spotlite* (Uptown, 2008); Charlie Parker: *Bird After Dark* (Savoy, 2002); and Charlie Parker and Dizzy Gillespie: *Bird & Diz* (Polygram, 1997).

Walsh, Michael. <u>And All The Saints</u>. New York: Warner, 2003.

52nd Street Swing: New York in the 1930s (GRP, 2007) offers a view of the music and club scene from Swing Street i.e. clubs not controlled by Owney Madden.

Madden owned The Cotton Club, which was home base for the Ellington band and to a lesser degree, Cab Calloway. Two representative CDs are *at The Cotton Club* (Yesterdays, 2006) and *Duke Ellington at The Cotton Club* (Storyville, 2010), which are live 1930s radio broadcasts.

Warren, Vic. <u>Hong Kong Blues</u>. San Diego: Turning Heads, 2014.

Jazz singer Megan Deschamps sings numerous standards during her evening performance. A few of the songs she sings are:

"Violets For Your Furs:" Shirley Horn: *Violets For Your Furs* (SteepleChase, 1991).

"A Nightingale Sang In Berkeley Square": Dakota Staton: *Ms Soul* (Simitar, 1997).

"Body and Soul:" Anita O'Day: *Sings The Winners* (Verve, 1958).

"Stolen Moments:" Mark Murphy: *Timeless* (Savoy, 2003).

<u>Hong Kong Blues</u> is divided into 29 chapters each of which has a song title to set the mood. A few examples are:

"What A Difference A Day Made:" Dinah Washington: *What A Difference A Day Made* (Verve, 2018).

"Route 66:" Natalie Cole: *Unforgettable with Love* (Concord, 1991).

"Strangers in the Night:" Frank Sinatra: *Strangers in the Night*"

(Reprise, 2016).

"'Round Midnight:" Betty Carter: *'Round Midnight* (Rhino, 2005).

Watson, I.K. <u>Wolves Aren't White</u>. London: Allison & Busby, 1995.

Singer Lennie Webb reminded me of American singer Mark Murphy, who has maintained a European following long after being forgotten in the States.

Mark Murphy: *Midnight Mood* (Universal, 2005).

Webb's band backed Ronnie Scott. Scott can be heard on Ronnie Scott's Quintet: *Never Pat A Burning Dog* (Ronnie Scott's Jazz, 1995).

White, Gloria. <u>Death Notes</u>. London: Severn House, 2005.

Joe Lovano: *I'm All for You* (Blue Note, 2004) is an album of standards that tenor sax legend Match Margolis would play when attempting a comeback.

White, Richard. "Notes in the Fog." In White, David (ed.). <u>Charles Boeckman Presents Johnny Nickle</u>. Batesville, AZ: Prose Productions, 2013.

An L.A. session representative of 1950s cool jazz is trumpet player Shorty Rogers' *Swings* (RCA, 1991).

Whitelaw, Sarah. <u>Jazz And Die</u>. London: Hale, 2014.

English jazzman Steve Waterman plays trumpet in the style of the fictional Chuck Peters in both small and big band formats:

In Steve Waterman Quintet & Sextet: *Stablemates* (Mainstem, 2004) the group plays Benny Golson bop classics.

Steve Waterman Jazz Orchestra. (Hydrojazz, 2005) is an 18-piece jazz ensemble.

Wiley, Richard. <u>Soldiers In Hiding</u>. London: Chatto & Windus, 1986; New York: Atlantic Monthly Press, 1986.

Teddy Maki has a band that plays Duke Ellington's "Mood Indigo" note for note and other of the era's songs. The classic version of "Mood Indigo" can be found on *Ivie Anderson and Duke Ellington and His Famous Orchestra* (Jazz Archives, 1991).

Williams, Kirby. Rage In Paris. Wainscott, N.Y.: Pushcart, 2014.

Urby Brown is playing "Tiger Rag" at La Belle Princesse when Sidney Bechet joins him on stage. Bechet's version of "Tiger Rag" can be found on Sidney Bechet: *Jazz Icons from the Golden Era* (DWK, 2013).

_____. Long Road from Paris, The. Wainscott, N.Y.: Pushcart, 2018.

Jelly Roll Morton was playing "King Porter Stomp" when young Urby Brown came to Madame Lala's. It can be found on Jelly Roll Morton: *1913/1924* (Fantasy, 1992).

In Paris, Urby's band played clarinet jazz similar to that by Sidney Bechet. Tunes from that era can be found on *Legendary Sidney Bechet Petite Fleur* (Phoenix, 2011).

The last sounds Urby hears is the band playing "Oh, Didn't He Ramble," a version of which is on *Pete Kelly's Blues* (Decca, 1955).

Wilson, August. Ma Rainey's Black Bottom. London: Penguin, 1985; New York: Plume, 1981.

The album *Ma Rainey's Black Bottom* (Yazoo 1991) has the title song as well as other tunes associated with the classic blues singer. Jazz legends pianist Fletcher Henderson, guitarist Tampa Red and trombonist Kid Ory back Ma Rainey.

CHRONOLOGY

1820-1829

Hambly, Barbara. <u>Ran Away</u>.

1830-1839

Hambly, Barbara. <u>Cold Bayou</u>.
_____. <u>Crimson Angel</u>.
_____. <u>Dead and Buried</u>.
_____. <u>Dead Water</u>.
_____. <u>Die Upon a Kiss</u>.
_____. <u>Drinking Gourd</u>.
_____. <u>Free Man of Color, A</u>.
_____. <u>Good Man Friday</u>.
_____. <u>Graveyard Dust</u>.
_____. "Libre."
_____. <u>Murder in July</u>.
_____. <u>Ran Away</u>.
_____. <u>Sold Down the River</u>.
_____. "There Shall Be Your Heart Also."
_____. <u>Wet Grave</u>.

1840-1849

Hambly, Barbara. <u>Lady of Perdition</u>.

1890-1899

Brown, Cecil. <u>I, Stagolee</u>.
Hewat, Alan V. <u>Lady's Time</u>.
Karp, Larry. <u>Ragtime Kid, The</u>.

1900-1909

Doctorow, E.L. <u>Ragtime</u>.
Foehr, Stephen. <u>Storyville</u>.
Fulmer, David. "Algiers."
_____. <u>Chasing The Devil's Tail</u>.
_____. <u>Jass</u>.
Hewat, Alan V. <u>Lady's Time</u>.
Hoch, Edward D. "Ripper of Storyville, The."
Ondaatje, Michael. <u>Coming Through Slaughter</u>.

1910-1919

Celestin, Ray. <u>Axeman's Jazz, The</u> aka <u>Axeman, The</u>.
Cleverly, Barbara. <u>Ragtime In Simla</u>.
Doctorow, E.L. <u>Ragtime</u>.
Fulmer, David. <u>Day Ends at Dawn, The</u>.
_____. <u>Eclipse Alley</u>.
_____. <u>Iron Angel, The</u>.
_____. <u>Lost River</u>.
_____. <u>Rampart Street</u>.
Hewat, Alan V. <u>Lady's Time</u>.
Karp, Larry. <u>King of Ragtime, The</u>.
Rich, Nathaniel. <u>King Zeno</u>.
Williams, Kirby. <u>Long Road From Paris, The</u>.

1920-1929

Booth, Christopher B. <u>Killing Jazz: A Detective Story</u>.
Burwell, Rex. <u>Capone, the Cobbs, and Me</u>.
Calkins, Susanna. <u>Fate of a Flapper, The</u>.
_____. <u>Murder Knocks Twice</u>.
Celestin, Ray. <u>Dead Man's Blues</u>.
Cleverly, Barbara. <u>Ragtime In Simla</u>.
Collins, Max Allen & Clemens, Matthew V. "East Side, West Side."
Conway, Martha. <u>Sugarland</u>.

Doyle, Roddy. <u>Oh, Play That Thing</u>.
Estleman. Loren D. <u>Whiskey River</u>.
Fitzgerald, F. Scott. "Dance, The."
_____. <u>Great Gatsby, The</u>.
Fulmer, David. <u>Dying Crapshooter's Blues, The</u>.
_____. <u>Will You Meet Me In Heaven</u>.
Greenwood, Kerry. <u>Green Mill Murder, The</u>.
Holden, Craig. <u>Jazz Bird, The</u>.
Holden, Craig. "P&G Ivory Cut-Whiskey Massacre, The."
Longstreet, Pamela. <u>China Blues</u>.
Lutz, John. "Chop Suey."
Morson, Ian. "There Would Have Been Murder."
Myers, Martin. "Snake Rag."
Nuckel, John. <u>Harlem Rhapsody</u>.
Roeburt, John. <u>Sing Out Sweet Homicide</u>.
Walsh, Michael. <u>And All The Saints</u>.
Wilson, August. <u>Ma Rainey's Black Bottom</u>.

1930-1939

Atkins, Ace. <u>Crossroad Blues</u>.
Barnes, Harper. <u>Blue Monday</u>.
Beckman, Charles, Jr. "Mr. Banjo."
Cameron. Lou. <u>Angel's Delight</u>.
Chandler, Raymond. "King In Yellow, The."
Doyle, Roddy. <u>Oh, Play That Thing</u>.
Edugyan, Esi. <u>Half Blood Blues</u>.
Foote, Shelby. "Ride Out."
Garcia, Vee Williams. <u>Jazz Flower, The</u>.
Glatzer, Hal. <u>Fugue In Hell's Kitchen, A</u>.
Goldsmith, Martin. <u>Detour</u>.
Gwinn, William. <u>Jazz Bum</u>.
Jeffers, H. Paul. <u>Murder On Mike</u>.
_____. <u>Rubout at The Onyx</u>.
_____. <u>Rag Doll Murder, The</u>.
Latimer, Jonathan. <u>Lady In The Morgue, The</u>.

436

McClendon, Lise. One O'Clock Jump.
Mones, Nicole. Night In Shanghai.
Nuckel, John. Harlem Rhapsody.
Reed, Harlan. Swing Music Murder, The
Ronald, James. Death Croons The Blues.
Skinner, Robert. Blood To Drink
_____. Cat-Eyed Trouble.
_____. Daddy's Gone A-Hunting.
Sonin, Ray. Dance Band Mystery, The.
Stevens, Kevin. Reaching The Shining River.
Vandagriff, G.G. Murder In The Jazz Band.
Walsh, Michael. And All The Saints.
Williams, Kirby. Rage In Paris.
_____. Long Road from Paris, The.

1940-1949

Avery, Robert. Murder On The Downbeat.
Beckman, Charles, Jr. "Afraid To Live."
_____. "Run Cat Run."
Benson, Raymond. Blues In The Dark.
Benton, John L. Talent For Murder.
Borneman, Ernest. Tremolo.
Boyce, David. "Special Arrangement."
Brackett. Leigh. No Good from a Corpse.
Burnett, W.R. Romelle.
Cameron, Lou. Angel's Flight,
Celestin, Ray. Mobster's Lament, The.
Colbert, Curt. Rat City.
Cohen, Octavus. Danger In Paradise.
Coxe, George Harmon. Lady Is Afraid, The.
Curran, Dale. Dupree Blues.
Davis, J. Madison. And The Angels Sing.
Dowswell, Paul. Auslander.
Doyle, Roddy. Oh, Play That Thing.
Estleman, Loren D. Jitterbug.

Garcia, Vee Williams. Jazz Flower, The.
Glatzer, Hal. Last Full Measure, The.
_____. Too Dead To Swing.
Goldsmith, Martin. Detour.
Gruber, Frank. Whispering Master, The.
_____. "Words and Music."
Gwinn, William. Jazz Bum.
Holmes, Rupert. Swing.
Howie, Edith. Band Played Murder, The.
Huggins, Roy. 77 Sunset Strip.
_____. Double Take, The.
Hunter, Evan. Quartet In H.
_____. Streets of Gold.
Irish, William. "Dancing Detective, The."
Karp, Larry. First, Do No Harm.
Koenig, Joseph. Really The Blues.
MacDonald, John. Moving Target, The.
Macdonald, Ross. Trouble Follows Me aka Night Train.
McClendon, Lise. Sweet and Low.
Marks, Paul D. Blues Don't Care, The.
Marsh, Ngaio. Wreath For Rivera, A.
Mathews, Francine. Alibi Club, The.
Mosley, Walter. Devil In A Blue Dress.
Novak, Robert. B-Girl.
Oglesby, Wm. Ellis. Blow Happy, Blow Sad.
Reeves, Robert. "Danse Macabre."
Shurman, Ida. Death Beats The Band.
Skinner, Robert. Pale Shadow.
_____. Righteous Cut, The.
Smith, Martin Cruz. Stallion Gate.
Sonin, Ray. Dance Band Mystery, The.
Tate, Sylvia. Never By Chance.
Williams, Kirby. Long Road From Paris, The.

1950-1959

Atkins, Ace. Leavin' Trunk Blues
Beckman, Charles, Jr. "Dixie Dirge."
_____. Honky-Tonk Girl.
_____. "Hot Lick for Doc, A."
_____. "Last Trumpet, The."
_____. "Should A Tear Be Shed?"
Bird, Brandon. Downbeat For a Dirge a.k.a. Dead And Gone.
Bloch, Robert. "Dig That Crazy Grave."
Brown, Frederic. "Murder Set to Music."
Byers, Chad. Jazz Man.
Cain, James M. "Cigarette Girl."
Calef, Noel. Ascenseur pour l'echafaud aka Frantic.
Cameron, Lou. Angel's Flight.
Cassidy, Bruce. Brass Shroud, The.
Clark, Howard. "Horn Man,"
Craig, Jonathan. Frenzy a.k.a. Junkie
Du Bois, Brendan. "Lady Meets The Blue, The."
Edugyan, Esi. Half Blood Blues.
Edwards, Grace F. "Blind Alley, The."
_____. Blind Alley, The.
Ellroy, James. "Dick Contino's Blues."
_____. White Jazz.
Farr, John. Deadly Combo, The.
Fleming, Charles. After Havana.
_____. Ivory Coast, The.
Fowler, Carol S. "And The Angels Sing."
_____. "Blowin" Up A Storm: The Second Chronicles Of
Bernie Butz."
_____. "Blues in the Night."
_____. "Born To Be Blue."
_____. "Loverman."
_____. "Passion Flower."
Fuller, Jack. Best of Jackson Payne, The.

Gaiter, Leonce. Bourbon Street.

Garcia, Vee Wiiliams. Jazz Flower, The.

Goodis, David. Shoot The Piano Player (Down There).

_____. Street of No Return.

Granelli, Roger. Out of Nowhere.

Harvey, John. "Drummer Unknown."

_____. "Just Friends."

_____. "Minor Key."

Haut, Woody. Cry For A Nickel, Die For A Dime.

Himes, Chester. Blind Man With A Pistol.

_____. Cotton Comes To Harlem.

_____. Crazy Kill, The.

_____. Rage In Harlem, A.

_____. Real Cool Killers, The.

Howland, Whit. Trouble Follows.

Huggins, Roy. 77 Sunset Strip.

Hughes, Dorothy B. "Black and White Blues, The."

Hunter, Evan. Streets of Gold.

Irish, William. "Jazz Record, The."

Jessup, Richard. Lowdown.

Johns, Veronica Parker. "Mr. Hyde-de-Ho."

Jones, Arthur E. It Makes You Think.

Kane, Frank. Juke Box King.

Kane, Henry. "One Little Bullet."

_____. Until You Are Dead.

Karp, Larry. Ragtime Fool, The.

Lawton, John. Flesh Wounds.

Lehman, Ernest. Sweet Smell of Success.

Loustal-Paringaux, Jacques de. Barney and the Blue Note.

Mengel, Brad. "Devil You Know. The."

Nielsen, Helen. "You Can't Trust A Man"

Rieman, Terry. Vamp Till Ready.

Robinson, Peter. "Magic of Your Touch, The."

Runcie, James. "Matter of Time, A."

Sanchez, Thomas. King Bongo.

Sheridan, Sarah. London Calling.

Smith, J. P. "Plantation Club, The."
Spicer, Bart. Blues For The Prince.
Steele, Colleen. "Them There Eyes."
Wallop, Douglass. Night Light.
White, Richard. "Notes In The Fog."

1960-1969

Allyn, Doug. "Jukebox King, The."
Braly, Malcolm. Shake Him till he Rattles.
Brown, Carter. Ever-Loving Blues, The.
Boyd, Frank. Johnny Staccato.
Castle, Frank. Hawaiian Eye.
Conroy, Albert. Mr. Lucky.
Duchin, Peter & Wilson, John Morgan. Blue Moon.
_____. Good Morning, Heartache.
Fuller, Jack. Best of Jackson Payne, The.
Fulmer, David. Blue Door, The.
Gruber, Frank. Swing Low Swing Dead.
Hall, Patricia. Dressed To Kill.
Hentoff, Nat. Blues For Charlie Darwin.
_____. Call The Keeper.
_____. Man From Internal Affairs, The.
Himes, Chester. All Shot Up.
_____. Big Gold Dream, The.
_____. Heat's On, The.
Hunter, Evan. Streets of Gold.
Kane, Frank. Guilt Edged Frame, The.
Kane, Henry. Peter Gunn.
Lawrence, Michael. I Like It Cool.
Merril, Judith. "Muted Hunger."
Moody, Bill. "Child's Play."
_____. Czechmate: The Spy Who Played Jazz.
Nadelson, Reggie. Manhattan '62.
Nemac, John. Canary's Combo.
Queen, Ellery. Death Spins The Platter.

Rabe, Peter. <u>Murder Me For Nickels</u>.

Randisi, Robert J. <u>Everybody Kills Somebody Sometime</u>.

_____. <u>Fly Me To The Morgue</u>.

_____. <u>Hey There (You With The Gun In Your Hand)</u>.

_____. <u>I'm A Fool To Kill You</u>.

_____. <u>It Was A Very Bad Year</u>.

_____. <u>Luck Be A Lady, Don't Die</u>.

_____. <u>Way You Die Tonight, The</u>.

_____. <u>When Somebody Kills You</u>.

_____. <u>You Make Me Feel So Dead</u>.

_____. <u>You're Nobody Til Somebody Kills You</u>.

Saunders, Doug. <u>M Squad</u>.

Skvorecky, Josef. <u>End of Lieutenant Boruvka, The</u>.

_____. <u>Mournful Demeanor of Lieutenant Boruvka, The</u>.

_____. <u>Sins For Father Knox</u>.

Vining, Keith. <u>Keep Running</u>.

1970-1979

Burke, J. F. <u>Crazy Woman Blues</u>.

_____. <u>Kama Sutra Tango, The</u>.

Daniel. John. <u>Play Melancholy Baby</u>.

Gillette, Paul J. <u>Play Misty for Me</u>.

Gorman, Ed. "Reason Why, The."

Jackson, Jon A. <u>Man With an Axe</u>.

Maltese, Martin. <u>North To Toronto</u>.

Rodriguez, Andres. "Yesterdays."

Skvorecky, Josef. <u>Return of Lieutenant Boruvka, The</u>.

Wainwright, John. <u>Do Nothin' Till You Hear From Me</u>.

1980-1989

Asimov, Isaac. "Mystery Tune."

Bankier, William. "Dog Who Hated Jazz, The."

_____. "Concerto for Violence and Orchestra."

Batten, Jack. <u>Crang Plays The Ace</u>.

_____. Straight No Chaser.
Burke, James Lee. Black Cherry Blues.
_____. Lost Get-Back Boogie, The.
_____. The Neon Rain, The.
Creech, J. R. Music And Crime.
Estleman, Loren D. Lady Yesterday.
Grant, James. Don't Shoot The Pianist.
Gosling, Paula. Solo Blues.
Harvey, John. Darkness, Darkness.
_____. Lonely Hearts.
Lutz, John. Right To Sing The Blues, The.
_____. "Right To Sing The Blues, The."
Mertz, Stephen. "Death Blues."
Molina, Antonio Munoz. Winter in Lisbon.
Moody, Bill. "Child's Play"
Murphy, Dallas. Lover Man.
Pentecost, Hugh. Murder Goes Round And Round.
Pines, Paul. Tin Angel.
Plater, Mark. Beiderbecke Affair, The.
Robinson, Peter. Dedicated Man, A.
_____. Necessary End, A.
_____. Hanging Valley, The.
Slovo, Gillian. Death By Analysis.
_____. Death Comes Staccato.
_____. Morbid Symptoms.
Smith, J.P. Body And Soul.

1990-1999

Allyn, Doug. "Sultans of Swing, The."
Atkins, Ace. Crossroad Blues.
Anderson, Beth. Night Sounds.
Barnes, Linda. Steel Guitar.
Batten, Jack. Blood Count.
_____. Riviera Blues.
Burke, James Lee. Sunset Limited.

Coggins, Mark. Immortal Game, The.
Carter, Charlotte. Coq au Vin.
_____. Drumsticks.
_____. Rhode Island Red.
Compton, D. G. Back of Town Blues.
Connelly, Michael. Angel's Flight.
_____. Black Echo, The.
_____. Black Ice, The.
_____. "Christmas Even."
_____. Concrete Blonde, The.
_____. Trunk Music.
Dahl, Arne. Misterioso.
Deaver, Jeffrey Wilds. Mistress of Justice.
Downs, Hunton. Murder In The Mood.
Edwards, Grace F. Toast Before Dying, A.
_____. If I Should Die.
Edwardson, Ake. Sun And Shadow.
Green, George Dawes. Caveman's Valentine, The.
Greer, Robert O. Devil's Red Nickel, The.
Harvey, John. "Bird of Paradise."
_____. "Cheryl."
_____. Cold Light.
_____. "Confirmation."
_____. "Cool Blues."
_____. Cutting Edge.
_____. "Dexterity."
_____. Easy Meat.
_____. "Just Friends."
_____. Last Rites.
_____. Living Proof.
_____. "My Little Suede Shoes"
_____. Now's the Time.
_____. "Now's the Time."
_____. Off-Minor.
_____. Rough Treatment.
_____. "She Rote."

_____. "Slow Burn."

_____. "Stupendous."

_____. Wasted Years.

_____. "Work."

Hayes, Teddy. Blood Red Blues.

Helms, Richard. Joker Poker.

_____. Juicy Watsui.

_____. Voo Doo That You Do.

_____. Wet Debt.

Izzo, Jean-Claude. Total Chaos.

_____. Chourmo.

_____. Solea.

Jackson, Jon A. Man With An Axe.

Klevan, Andrew. Hunting Down Amanda.

Lampe, C.O. Return of Glenn Miller, The.

Leslie, John. Blue Moon.

_____. Killing Me Softly.

_____. Love For Sale.

_____. Night and Day.

Lucarelli, Carlo. Almost Blue.

Moody, Bill. Bird Lives!

_____.. Death of a Tenor Man.

_____. "Resurrection of Bobo Jones, The."

_____. Solo Hand.

_____. Sound of The Trumpet, The.

Mosley, Walter. "Blue Lightning."

_____. RL's Dream.

Murphy, Dallas. Don't Explain.

_____. Lush Life.

Nadelson, Reggie. Bloody London.

_____. Hot Poppies.

_____. Red Hot Blues. (Red Mercury Blues)

Patchett. Ann. Taft.

Plater, Alan. Beiderbecke Connection, The.

Pronzini, Bill. Blue Lonesome.

Raleigh, Michael. Maxwell Street Blues, The.

Robinson, Peter. In A Dry Season.
Sallis, James. Blue Bottle
Slovo, Gillian. Catnap.
_____. Close Call.
Smith, Julie. Axeman's Jazz, The.
_____. House of Blues.
_____. Jazz Funeral.
_____. "Kid Trombone."
_____. New Orleans Mourning.
Temple, Lou Jane. Cornbread Killer, The.

2000-2009

Atkins, Ace. Dark End of The Street.
_____. Leavin' Trunk Blues.
Barclay, Tessa. Final Discord, A.
Bennett, Ron. Singapore Swing.
Burke, James Lee. Last Car to Elysian Fields.
Campo, J.P. On Good Days It Just Bounces Off.
Cameron, Stella. Tell Me Why.
Carlotto, Massimo. Bandit Love.
_____. Blues For Outlaw Hearts and Old Whores.
_____. Columbian Mule, The.
_____. Master of Knots, The.
Carter, Charlotte. "Birdbath."
Cockey, Tim. Hearse Case Scenario, The.
Coggins, Mark. Big Wake-Up, The
_____. Candy From Strangers.
_____. Runoff.
_____. Vulture Capital.
Corbett, David. Done For A Dime.
Connelly, Michael. 9 Dragons.
_____. Brass Verdict, The.
_____. City of Bones.
_____. Closers, The.
_____. Darkness More Than Night, A.

Leonard, Elmore. <u>Tishomingo Blues</u>.
Lippman, Laura. "Shoeshine Man Regrets, The."
Mask, Ken. <u>Murder at The Butt</u>.
Merrill, Judith. <u>All That Murder</u>.
Moody, Bill. "Camaro Blue."
_____. "File Under Jazz."
_____. <u>Looking For Chet Baker</u>.
_____. <u>Shades of Blue</u>.
Nadelson, Reggie. <u>Blood Count</u>.
_____. <u>Disturbed Earth</u>.
_____. <u>Fresh Kills</u>.
_____. <u>Londongrad</u>.
_____. <u>Red Hook</u>.
_____. <u>Sex Dolls/Skin Trade</u>.
Randisi, Robert J. "Listening Room, The."
Roberts, Les. "Jazz Canary, The."
Robinson, Peter. <u>Aftermath</u>.
_____. <u>In A Dry Season</u>.
_____. <u>Playing With Fire</u>.
Scheen, Kjersti. "Moonglow."
Terrenoire, David. <u>Beneath A Panamanian Moon</u>.
Watson, I.K. <u>Wolves Aren't White</u>.
White, Gloria. <u>Death Notes</u>.

2010-2019

Aaronovitch, Ben. <u>Moon Over Soho</u>.
Bader, Jerry. "Killer Jazz."
Benson, Raymond. <u>Blues in The Dark</u>.
Boyce, Trudy Nan. <u>Out of The Blues</u>.
Cartmel, Andrew. <u>Vinyl Detective, The: Victory Disc</u>.
Cass, Richard J. <u>Burton's Solo</u>.
_____. <u>In Solo Time</u>.
_____. <u>Last Call at the Eposito</u>

_____. Solo Act.

_____. Sweetie Brogan's Sorrow.

Coggins, Mark. No Hard Feelings

Connelly, Michael. Black Box, The.

_____. Burning Room, The.

_____. Crossing, The.

_____. Drop, The.

_____. "Nighthawks."

_____. Two Kinds of Truth.

_____. Wrong Side of Goodbye, The.

Dionne, Ron. Sad Jingo.

Ehrhardt, Peggy. Got No Friend Anyhow.

Graham, Heather. Dead Play On, The

Harvey, Brian. Beethoven's Tenth.

_____. Tokyo Girl.

Harvey, John. Darkness, Darkness.

Helms, Richard. Paid In Spades.

Merrill, Joan. And All That Maddness.

_____. And All That Motive.

_____. And All That Sea.

_____. And All That Stalking.

Moody, Bill. Fade To Blue.

_____. "Jazz Live."

Morfoot, Peter. Box of Bones.

_____. Fatal Music.

_____. Impure Blood.

_____. Knock 'Em Dead.

Mosley, Walter. Trouble is What I Do.

Moss, Stephen L. Autumn Leaves.

Ordover, Andrew. Cat Came Back, The.

_____. Cool for Cats.

Phillips, Gary. "Performer, The."

Reed, Barbara. Harmonic Deception.

Warren, Vic. Hong Kong Blues.

Whitelaw, Stella. Jazz and Die.

Locations

ALABAMA

DAVIS (FICTIONAL)
Fitzgerald, F. Scott. "Dance, The"

ARIZONA

DESERT
Goldsmith, Martin. <u>Detour.</u>

LOS ALAMOS
Smith, Martin Cruz. <u>Stallion Gate.</u>

PHOENIX
Huggins, Roy. "Appointment With Fear."

CALIFORNIA

DESERT
Goldsmith, Martin. <u>Detour.</u>

LOS AMITOS
Phillips, Gary. "Performer, The."

LOS ANGELES (& HOLLYWOOD)
Bader, Jerry. "Killer Jazz."
Benson, Raymond. <u>Blues in the Dark.</u>

Brackett, Leigh. No Good from a Corpse.

Burnett, W.R. Romelle.

Cameron, Lou. Angel's Flight.

Campo, J.P. On a Good Day it Just Bounces Off.

Chandler, Raymond. "King in Yellow, The."

Connelly, Michael. 9 Dragons.

_____. Angels Flight.

_____. Black Echo, The.

_____. Black Ice, The.

_____. Black Box, The.

_____. Brass Verdict, The.

_____. Burning Room, The.

_____. "Christmas Even."

_____. City of Bones

_____. Closers, The.

_____. Crossing, The.

_____. Concrete Blonde, The.

_____. Darkness More Than Night, A.

_____. Drop, The.

_____. Echo Park.

_____. Last Coyote, The.

_____. Lost Light.

_____. Narrows, The.

_____. Overlook, The.

_____. Trunk Music.

_____. Two Kinds of Truth.

_____. Wrong Side of Goodbye, The.

Conroy, Albert. Mr. Lucky.

Creech, J.R. Music and Crime.

Duchin, Peter & Wilson, John Morgan. Good Morning, Heartache.

Ellroy, James. "Dick Contino's Blues."

_____. White Jazz.

Farr, John. Deadly Combo, The.

Fuller, Jack. Best of Jackson Payne, The.

Haut, Woody. Cry For A Nickel, Die For A Dime.

Huggins, Roy. 77 Sunset Strip.

_____. And All That Madness.

_____. And All That Stalking.

Moody, Bill. "Child's Play."

_____. Shades of Blue.

Pronzini, Bill. Blue Lonesome.

Skvorecky, Josef. "Mathematicians of Grizzley Drive, The."

White, Gloria. Death Notes.

White, Richard. "Notes In The Fog."

SAN FRANCISCO PENINSULA

Corbett, David. Done For A Dime.

Daniel, John. Play Melancholy Baby.

Glatzer, Hall. Too Dead To Swing.

Gillette, Paul J. Play Misty For Me.

SAN PEDRO

Larson, Skoot. Dig You Later, Alligator Blues, The.

_____. No News Is Bad New Blues, The.

_____. Real Gone Blues, The.

SILICON VALLEY

Coggins, Mark. No Hard Feelings.

_____. Vulture Capital.

COLORADO

DENVER

Greer, Robert O. Devil's Red Nickel, The.

CONNECTICUT

DANBURY

Nemac, John. Canary's Combo.

FLORIDA

Dolphin Beach (fictional)
Fowler, Carol S. "Born To Be Blue."

Fort Lauderdale
Brown, Carter. Ever-Loving Blues, The.

Gulf City
Vining, Keith. Keep Running.

Key West
Leslie, John. Blue Moon.
_____. Killing Me Softly.
_____. Love For Sale.
_____. Night and Day.

GEORGIA

Atlanta
Boyce, Trudy Nan. Out of The Blues.
Burwell, Rex. Capone, the Cobbs and Me.
Fulmer, David. Dying Crapshooter's Blues, The.
_____. Will You Meet Me In Heaven?
Ordover, Andrew. Cat Came Back, The.
_____. Cool For Cats.

HAWAII

Hawaiian cruise
Glatzer, Hal. Last Full Measure.
Huggins, Roy. "Death and the Skylark."

Honolulu
Castle, Frank. Hawaiian Eye.

ILLINOIS

CHICAGO

Atkins, Ace. <u>Leavin' Trunk Blues</u>.

Anderson, Beth. <u>Night Sounds</u>.

Boyce, David. "Special Arrangement."

Byers, Chad. <u>Jazz Man</u>.

Calkins, Susanna. <u>Fate of a Flapper, The</u>.

_____. <u>Murder Knocks Twice</u>.

Celestin, Ray. <u>Dead Man's Blues</u>.

Connelly, Michael. "Nighthawks."

Conway, Martha. <u>Sugarland</u>.

Doyle, Roddy. <u>Oh! Play That Thing</u>.

Fowler, Carol S. "And the Angels Sing."

_____. <u>Blowin' Up A Storm: The Second Chronicles of Bernie Butz</u>.

_____. "Blues in the Night."

_____. Passion Flower."

Fredrickson, Jack. "Good Evening Blues."

Fuller, Jack. <u>Best of Jackson Payne, The</u>.

Guilfoile, Kevin. "O Death Where Is Thy Sting?"

Hellmann, Libby Fischer. "Your Sweet Man"

Joe, Yolanda. <u>Hit Time</u>.

Kaminsky, Stuart M. "Blue Note."

Latimer, Jonathan. <u>Lady in the Morgue</u>.

Mengel, Brad. "Devil You Know, The."

Mertz, Stephen. "Death Blues."

Raleigh, Michael. <u>Maxwell Street Blues, The</u>.

Saunders, David. <u>M Squad</u>.

Wilson, August. <u>Ma Rainey's Black Bottom</u>.

DOWNSTATE

Burwell, Rex. <u>Capone, the Cobbs and Me</u>.

Howie, Edith. <u>Band Played Murder, The</u>.

UPSTATE

Gorman, Ed. "Muse."

_____. "Reason Why, The."

IOWA

CLARINDA

Lamp, C.O. <u>Return of Glenn Miller</u>.

LOUISIANA

NEW ORLEANS

Atkins, Ace. <u>Crossroad Blues</u>.

Beckman, Charles Jr. "Dixieland Dirge."

Burke, James Lee. <u>Black Cherry Blues</u>.

_____. <u>Last Car To Elysian Fields</u>.

_____. <u>Neon Rain, The</u>.

Celestin, Ray. <u>Axeman's Jazz, The</u>.

Howard, Clark. "Horn Man."

Fletcher, Jessica & Bain, Donald. <u>Murder in a Minor Key</u>.

Foehr, Stephen. <u>Storyville</u>.

Fulmer, David. "Algiers."

_____. <u>Chasing The Devil's Tail</u>.

_____. <u>Day Ends at Dawn, The</u>.

_____. <u>Eclipse Alley</u>.

_____. <u>Iron Angel, The</u>.

_____. <u>Jass</u>.

_____. <u>Lost River</u>.

_____. <u>Rampart Street</u>.

Gaiter, Leonce. <u>Bourbon Street</u>.

Graham, Heather. <u>Dead Play On, The</u>.

Hambly, Barbara. <u>Cold Bayou</u>.

_____. <u>Crimson Angel</u>.

_____. <u>Dead Water</u>.

_____. <u>Dead and Buried</u>.

_____. <u>Die Upon A Kiss</u>.

Williams, Kirby. <u>Long Road from Paris, The</u>.

MAINE

KEMPSHALL ISLAND (FICTIONAL)
Murphy, Dallas. <u>Don't Explain</u>.

PORTLAND
Knight, Phyllis. <u>Shattered Rhythms</u>

MARYLAND

BALTIMORE
Cockey, Tim. <u>Hearse Case Scenario</u>.
Lippman, Laura. "Shoeshine Man Regrets."

RURAL
Cain, James M. "Cigarette Girl."

MASSACHUSETTS

BOSTON
Barnes, Linda. <u>Steel Guitar</u>.
Cass, Richard J. <u>Burton's Solo</u>.
_____. <u>In Solo Time</u>.
_____. <u>Last Call at The Eposito</u>.
_____. <u>Solo Act</u>.
_____. <u>Sweet Bogan's Sorrow</u>
Coxe, George Harmon. <u>Lady is Afraid, The</u>.
Dobbyn, John. "Monday, Sweet Monday."

Martha's Vineyard

EDGARTOWN
Craig, Philip R. <u>Vineyard Blues</u>.

MOUNT GREEN (FICTIONAL)
Borneman, Ernest. Tremolo.

MICHIGAN

DETROIT
Allyn, Doug. "Jukebox King, The."
_____. "Sultans of Soul, The."
Estleman, Loren D. Jitterbug.
_____. Lady Yesterday.
_____. Whiskey River.
Jackson Jon A. Man With an Axe.

MISSISSIPPI

GREENWOOD & THE DELTA
Atkins, Ace. Crossroad Blues.
Fitzhugh, Bill. Highway 61 Resurfaced.
Foote, Shelby. "Ride Out."
Leonard, Elmore. Tishomingo Blues.
Mosley, Leonard. RL's Dream.

MISSOURI

KANSAS CITY
Barnes, Harper. Blue Monday.
McClendon, Lise. One O'Clock Jump.
_____. Sweet and Low.
Rodriguez, Andres. "Yesterdays."
Stevens, Kevin. Reaching The Shining River.
Temple, Lou Jane. Cornbread Killer, The.

ST. LOUIS
Brown, Cecil. Stagolee.
Lutz, John. "Chop Suey."

Randisi, Robert J. "Listening Room, The."

SEDALIA

Karp, Larry. <u>Ragtime Fool, The</u>.

_____. <u>Ragtime Kid, The</u>.

RURAL

Hughes, Dorothy B. "Black and White Blues, The."

MONTANA

Burke, James Lee. <u>Black Cherry Blues</u>.

_____. <u>Lost-Get Back Boogie, The</u>.

NEVADA

ARAGOSA

Howland, Whit. "Trouble Follows."

BEULAH

Pronzini, Bill. <u>Blue Lonesome</u>.

LAS VEGAS

Connelly, Michael. <u>Trunk Music</u>.

Fleming, Charles. <u>Ivory Coast, The</u>.

Kane, Henry. <u>Juke Box King</u>.

Moody, Bill. <u>Bird Lives!</u>

_____. <u>Death of a Tenor Man</u>.

_____. <u>Sound of The Trumpet, The</u>.

Randisi, Robert J. <u>Everybody Kills Somebody Sometime</u>.

_____. <u>Fly Me To The Morgue</u>.

_____. <u>Hey There (You With The Gun In Your Hand.)</u>

_____. <u>I'm a Fool to Kill You</u>.

_____. <u>It Was a Very Bad Year</u>.

_____. <u>Luck Be a Lady, Don't Die</u>.

_____. <u>Way You Die Tonight, The</u>.

_____. <u>When Somebody Kills You</u>.

_____. You Make Me Feel So Dead.
_____. You're Nobody 'Til Somebody Kills You.
Rayner, Richard. Devil's Wind, The.

NEW HAMPSHIRE

PORTSMOUTH
DuBois, Brendon. "Lady Meets The Blue, The."

NEW JERSEY

UPSTATE
Karp, Larry. First Do No Harm.
Sherman, Ida. Death Beats The Band.

NEW ROCHELLE
Doctorow, E.L. Ragtime.

NEW MEXICO

Smith, C.W. "Plantation Club, The."

LOS ALAMOS
Smith, Martin Cruz. Stallion Gate.

NEW YORK

ENDICOTT (FICTIONAL)
Booth, Christopher B. Killing Jazz: A Detective Story.

LONG ISLAND
Fitzgerald, F. Scott. Great Gatsby, The.

NEW YORK CITY
Avery, Robert. Murder on The Downbeat.
Asimov, Isaac. "Mystery Tune."

Beckman, Jr., Charles. "Last Trumpet, The."
Benton, John L. Talent for Murder.
Bird, Brandon. Dead and Gone aka Downbeat for a Dirge.
Boyd, Frank. Johnny Staccato.
Burke, J.F. Crazy Woman Blues.
_____. Kama Sutra Tango, The.
Cameron, Lou. Angel's Flight.
Campo, J.P. On A Good Day It Just Bounces Off.
Carter, Charlotte. "Birdbath."
_____. Drumsticks.
_____. "Flower is a Lonesome Thing, A."
_____. Rhode Island Red.
Celestin, Ray. Mobster's Lament, The.
Cohen, Octavus. Danger In Paradise.
Coleman, Wanda. "Dunny."
Collins, Max Allen & Clemens, Matthew V. "East Side, West Side."
Deaver, Jeffrey Wilds. Mistress of Justice.
Dionne, Ron. Sad Jingo.
Doyle, Roddy. Oh, Play that Thing.
Edwards, Grace F. "Blind Alley, The."
_____. Do Or Die.
_____. If I Should Die.
_____. No Time To Die.
_____. Toast Before Dying, A.
Eisler, Barry. Last Assassin, The.
Ehrhart, Peggy. Got No Friend Anyhow.
_____. Sweet Man Is Gone.
Fowler, Carol S. "Loverman."
Fuller, Jack. Best of Jackson Payne, The.
Garcia, Vee Williams. Jazz Flower, The.
Glatzer, Hal. Fugue in Hell's Kitchen, A.
Green, George Dawes. Caveman's Valentine, The.
Granelli, Roger. Out of Nowhere.
Gruber, Frank. Swing Low, Swing Dead.
_____. Whispering, Master, The.
_____. "Words and Music."

Gwinn, William. Jazz Bum.

Harvey, John. In A True Light.

Hayes, Teddy. Blood Red Blues.

_____. Dead By Popular Demand.

_____. Wrong As Two Left Feet.

Hentoff, Nat. Blues For Charlie Darwin.

_____. Call The Keeper.

_____. Man From Internal Affairs, The.

Himes, Chester. All Shot Up.

_____. Big Gold Dream, The.

_____. Blind Man With A Pistol.

_____. Cotton Comes To Harlem.

_____. Crazy Kill, The.

_____. Heat's On, The.

_____. Rage In Harlem, A.

_____. Real Cool Killers, The.

Hunter, Evan. Quartet in H.

_____. Streets of Gold.

Irish, Willam. "Dancing Detective, The."

_____. "Jazz Record, The."

Jeffers, H. Paul. Murder On Mike.

_____. Rag Doll Murder, The.

_____. Rubout at The Onyx.

Jessup, Richard. Lowdown.

Johns, Veronica, Parker. "Mr Hyde-de-Ho."

Kane, Frank. Juke Box King.

Kane, Henry. "One Little Bullet."

_____. Until You Are Dead.

Karp, Larry. King of Ragtime, The.

Klavan, Andrew. Hunting Down Amanda.

Lawrence, Michael. I Like It Cool.

Lehman, Ernest. Sweet Smell of Success.

Loustal-Paringaux, Jacques de. Barney and the Blue Note.

Merrill, Joan. And all that Madness.

Moody, Bill. "Resurrection of Bobo Jones."

_____. Shades of Blue.

Mosley, Walter. <u>RL's Dream</u>.
_____. <u>Trouble Is What I Do</u>.
Murphy, Dallas. <u>Lover Man</u>.
_____. <u>Lush Life</u>.
Myers, Martin. "Snake Rag."
Nadelson, Reggie. <u>Blood Count</u>.
_____. <u>Bloody London</u>.
_____. <u>Disturbed Earth</u>.
_____. <u>Fresh Kills</u>.
_____. <u>Hot Poppies</u>.
_____. <u>Londongrad</u>.
_____. <u>Manhattan 62</u>.
_____. <u>Red Hook</u>.
_____. <u>Red Hot Blues</u>.
Nuckel, John. <u>Harlem Rhapsody</u>.
Pentecost, Hugh. <u>Murder Goes Round and Round</u>.
Pines, Paul. <u>Tin Angel, The</u>.
Reeves, Robert. "Danse Macabre."
Rieman, Terry. <u>Vamp Till Ready</u>.
Roeburt, John. <u>Sing Out Sweet Homicide</u>.
Skvorecky, Josef. "Why So Many Shamuses?"
Thompson, Brian. "Life's Little Mysteries."
Wallop, Douglas. <u>Night Light</u>.
Walsh, Michael. <u>And All The Saints</u>.

Upstate New York

Cassiday, Bruce. <u>Brass Shroud, The</u>.
Coxe, George Harmon. <u>Ring of Truth, The</u>.
Rabe, Peter. <u>Murder Me for Nickels</u>.
Skvorecky, Josef. "Miscarriage of Justice."

NORTH CAROLINA

Raleigh-Durham

Gilmer, Byron. <u>Felonious Jazz</u>.

OHIO

CINCINNATI
Holden, Craig. <u>Jazz Bird, The</u>.
_____. "P&G Ivory Cut-Whiskey Massacre, The."

CLEVELAND
Roberts, Les. "Jazz Canary."

PENNSYLVANIA

PHILADELPHIA
Fulmer, David. <u>Blue Door, The</u>.
Goodis, David. <u>Street of No Return</u>.
_____. <u>Shoot The Piano Player</u>.
Merril, Judith. "Muted Hunger."
Spicer, Bart. <u>Blues for The Prince</u>.

UPSTATE
Bloch, Robert. "Dig That Crazy Grave!"
Davis, J. Madison. <u>And The Angels Sing</u>.

TENNESSEE

MEMPHIS
Atkins, Ace. <u>Dark End of The Street</u>.
Patchett, Ann. <u>Taft</u>.

RIVERVIEW
Curran, Dale. <u>Dupree Blues</u>.

TEXAS

CORPUS CHRISTI
Beckman, Jr. Charles. "Hot Lick For Doc, A."
_____. <u>Honky Tonk Girl</u>.

_____. "Run Cat Run."

Caribbean
Merrill, Joan. And All That Sea.

AUSTRIA

Vienna
Carlotto, Massimo. Blues for Outlaw Hearts and Old Whores.

AUSTRALIA

Melbourne
Greenwood, Kerry. Green Mill Murder, The.

CANADA

British Columbia
Harvey, Brian. Beethoven's Tenth.

Ontario
Bankier, William. "Dog Who Hated Jazz, The."
Steele, Coleen. "Them There Eyes."

Montreal
Knight, Phyllis. Shattered Rhythms.

Toronto
Battan, Jack. Blood Count.
_____. Crang Plays The Ace.
_____. Straight, No Chaser.
Maltese, Martin. North To Toronto.
Robinson, John. "Magic of Your Touch, The."
Skvorecky, Josef. Return of Lieutenant Boruvka.

CHINA

SHANGHAI
Mones, Nicole. <u>Night In Shanghai</u>.

CUBA

HAVANA
Fleming, Charles. <u>After Havana</u>.
Padura, Leonardo. <u>Havana Fever</u>.
Sanchez, Thomas. <u>King Bongo</u>.

CZECHOSLOVAKIA

PRAGUE
Moody, Bill. <u>Czechmate: Spy Who Played Jazz, The</u>.
Skvorecky, Josef. "Intimate Business, An."
_____. <u>End of Lieutenant Boruvka, The</u>.
_____. <u>Mournful Demeanor of Lieutenant Boruvka, The</u>.
_____. "Third Tip of the Triangle, The."

DENMARK

COPENHAGEN
Wm. Ellis Oglesby. <u>Blow Happy, Blow Sad</u>.

ENGLAND

EASTVALE & ENVIRONS, YORKSHIRE (FICTIONAL)
Robinson, Peter. <u>Aftermath</u>.
_____. <u>Dedicated Man, A</u>.
_____. <u>Hanging Valley, The</u>.
_____. <u>In A Dry Place</u>.
_____. <u>Necessary End, A</u>.
_____. <u>Playing With Fire</u>.

DORSET
Whitelaw, Stella. Jazz and Die.

GRANTCHESTER (CAMBRIDGE)
Runcie, James. "Matter of Time, A."

LEEDS
Plater, Alan. Beiderbecke Affair, The,
_____. Beiderbecke Connection, The.
_____. Beiderbecke Tapes, The.

LIVERPOOL
Compton, D.C. Back of Town Blues.

LONDON
Aaronovitch, Ben. Moon over Soho.
Bankier, William. "Concerto for Violence and Orchestra."
Cartmel, Andrew. Vinyl Detective, The: Victory Disc.
_____. Vinyl Detective, The: Written In Dead Wax.
Compton, D.G. Back of Town Blues.
Downs, Hunton. Murder In The Mood.
Grant, James. Don't Shoot the Pianist.
Gosling, Paula. Solo Blues.
Hall, Patricia. Dressed to Kill.
Harvey, John. "Cool Blues."
_____. "Drummer Unknown."
_____. "Favor."
_____. "Just Friends."
_____. In A True Light.
_____. "Now's the Time."
Jones, Arthur E. It Makes You Think.
Lawton, John. Flesh Wounds aka Blue Rondo.
Marsh, Ngaio. Wreath for Rivera, A.
Morson, Ian. "There Would Have Been Murder."
Nadelson, Reggie. Londongrad.
Roland, James. Death Croons the Blues.

Runcie, James. "Matter of Time, A."
Sheridan, Sarah. London Calling.
Slovo, Gillian. Catnap.
_____. Close Call.
_____. Death By Analysis.
_____. Death Comes Staccato.
_____. Morbid Symptoms.
Sonin, Ray. Dance Band Mystery, The.
Wainwright, John. Do Nothin' Till You Hear From Me.
Watson, I.K. Wolves Aren't White.

NOTTINGHAM

Harvey, John. "Billie's Bounce."
_____. "Bird of Paradise."
_____. "Cheryl"
_____. Cold Light.
_____. Cold In Hand.
_____. "Confirmation."
_____.. Cutting Edge.
_____. Darkness, Darkness.
_____. "Dexterity."
_____. Easy Meat.
_____. "Home."
_____. Last Rites.
_____. Living Proof.
_____. Lonely Hearts.
_____. "My Little Suede Shoes."
_____. Now's the Time.
_____. Off Minor.
_____. Rough Treatment.
_____. "She Rote"
_____. "Slow Burn."
_____. Still Waters.
_____. "Stupendous."
_____. "Sun, the Moon and the Stars, The."
_____. Trouble In Mind.

_____. <u>Wasted Years</u>.
_____. "Well, You Needn't."
_____. "Work."

Oxford
Vandagriff, G.G. <u>Murder in the Jazz Band</u>.

FRANCE

Marseilles
Izzo, Jean-Claude. <u>Chourmo</u>.
_____. <u>Solea</u>.
_____. <u>Total Chaos</u>.

Nice
Morfoot, Peter. <u>Box of Bones</u>.
_____. <u>Fatal Music</u>.
_____. <u>Impure Blood</u>.
_____. <u>Knock 'Em Dead</u>.

Paris
Calef, Noel. <u>Ascenseur pour L'echafaud</u> aka <u>Frantic</u>.
Carter, Charlotte. <u>Coq au Vin</u>.
Edugyan, Esi. <u>Half Blood Blues</u>.
Fuller, Jack. <u>Best of Jackson Payne, The</u>.
Hambly, Barbara. <u>Murder in July</u>.
Harvey, John. "Minor Key."
Koenig, Joseph. <u>Really the Blues</u>.
Loustal-Paringaux, Jacques de. <u>Barney and the Blue Note</u>.
Mathews, Francine. <u>Alibi Club, The</u>.
Nadelson, Reggie. <u>Sex Dolls</u> aka <u>Skin Trade</u>.
Skvorecky, Josef. "Just Between Us Girls."
Smith, J.P. <u>Body and Soul</u>.
Williams, Kirby. <u>Long Road from Paris, The</u>.
_____. <u>Rage In Paris</u>.

Riviera

Battan, Jack. Riviera Blues.
Gailly, Christian. Evening at The Club, An.

GERMANY

Berlin

Dowswell, Paul. Auslander.
Edugyan, Esi. Half Blood Blues.

Munich

Carlotto, Massimo. Blues For Outlaw Hearts and Old Whores.

HONG KONG

Connelly, Michael. 9 Dragons.
Eisler, Barry. Killing Rain aka Redemption Games.
Warren, Vic. Hong Kong Blues.

INDIA

Simla

Cleverly, Barbara. Ragtime in Simla.

INDONESIA

Eisler, Barry. Requiem for an Assassin.

ITALY

Bologna

Lucarelli, Carlo. Almost Blue.

Countryside

Skvorecky, Josef. "Man Eve Didn't Know from Adam, The."

Padua

Carlotto, Massimo. <u>Bandit Love</u>.

_____. <u>Master of Knots</u>.

Venice

Carlotto, Massimo. <u>Columbian Mule, The</u>.

JAPAN

Tokyo

Eisler, Barry. <u>Hard Rain</u>

_____. <u>Rain Fall</u>.

Harvey, Brian. <u>Tokyo Girl</u>.

Wiley, Richard. <u>Soldiers in Hiding</u>.

MACAU

Eisler, Barry. <u>Rain Storm</u>.

NETHERLANDS

Amsterdam

Moody, Bill. <u>Looking for Chet Baker</u>.

NORWAY

Oslo

Larson, Skoot. <u>No News is Bad News Blues, The</u>.

Scheen, Kjersti. "Moonglow."

PANAMA

Panama City

Terrenoire, David. <u>Beneath A Panamanian Moon</u>.

PORTUGAL

LISBON

Monina, Antonio Munoz. <u>Winter In Lisbon</u>.

RUSSIA

MOSCOW

Nadelson, Reggie. <u>Londongrad</u>.
_____. <u>Red Hot Blues</u>.

SINGAPORE

SINGAPORE

Bennett, Ron. <u>Singapore Swing</u>.

SWEDEN

Gothenburg

Edwardson, Ake. <u>Sun and Shadow</u>.

HITZUNGEE

Skvorecky, Josef. "Mistake in Hitzungee."

STOCKHOLM

Dahl, Arne. <u>Misterioso</u>.
Skvorecky, Josef. "A Question of Alibis."

SWITZERLAND

GENEVA

Barclay, Tessa. <u>Final Discord, A</u>.

TOGO
LOME

Jenkins, A.K. <u>Twice No One Dies</u>.

Hot One Hundred
(Personal Favorites)

⌒⌒⌒

Atkins, Ace. <u>Crossroad Blues</u>.
_____. <u>Dark End of The Street</u>.
Avery, Robert. <u>Murder On The Downbeat</u>.
Barnes, Harper. <u>Blue Monday</u>.
Benson, Raymond. <u>Blues In The Dark</u>.
Benton, John L. <u>Talent For Murder</u>.
Bloch, Robert. "Dig That Crazy Grave!"
Booth, Christopher B. <u>Killing Jazz: A Detective Story</u>.
Boyce, Trudy Nan. <u>Out of The Blues</u>.
Boyd, Frank. <u>Johnny Staccato</u>.
Brackett, Leign. <u>No Good From A Corpse</u>.
Braly, Malcolm. <u>Shake Him till he Rattles</u>.
Brown, Carter. <u>Ever-Loving Blues, The</u> aka <u>Death of A Doll</u>.
Burke, J.F. <u>Kama Sutra Tango, The</u>,
Burke, James Lee. <u>Neon Rain, The</u>.
Cain, James M. "Cigarette Girl."
Carter, Charlotte, <u>Rhode Island Red</u>.
Celestin, Ray. <u>Axeman's Jazz</u>.
Chandler, Raymond. "King In Yellow, The."
Cleverly, Barbara. <u>Ragtime In Simla</u>
Connelly, Michael. <u>Black Echo, The</u>
_____. "Christmas Even."
_____. <u>Echo Park</u>.
Craig, Jonathan. <u>Frenzy</u> aka <u>Junkie</u>.
Curran, Dale. <u>Dupree Blues</u>.

Dahl, Arne. <u>Misterioso</u> aka <u>Blinded Man, The</u>.
Davis, J. Madison. <u>and The Angels Sing</u>
Dobbyn, John F. "Monday, Sweet Monday.
Dowswell, Paul. <u>Auslander</u>.
Doyle, Roddy. <u>Oh, Play That Thing</u>.
DuBois, Brendan. "The Lady Meets The Blue."
Edwards, Grace F. "Blind Alley, The."
_____. <u>If I Should Die</u>
Eisler, Barry. <u>Last Assassin, The</u>.
Ellroy, James. <u>White Jazz</u>.
Estleman, Loren D. <u>Lady Yesterday</u>.
Farr, John. <u>Deadly Combo</u>.
Fitzgerald, F. Scott. "Dance, The."
Fleming, Charles. <u>After Havana</u>.
_____. <u>Ivory Coast, The</u>.
Foote, Shelby. "Ride Out."
Fuller, Jack. <u>Best of Jackson Payne, The</u>.
Fulmer, David. "Algiers,"
_____. <u>Chasin' The Devil's Tail</u>.
_____. <u>Dying Crapshooter's Blues, The</u>.
Gillette, Paul J. <u>Play Misty For Me</u>.
Glatzer, Hal. <u>Too Dead To Swing</u>.
Goodis, David. <u>Shoot The Piano Player</u>.
_____. <u>Street of No Return</u>.
Gosling, Paula. <u>Solo Blues</u>.
Greer, Robert O. <u>Devil's Red Nickel, The</u>.
Hambly, Barbara. <u>Free Man of Color, A</u>.
_____. "Libre."
Harvey, John. <u>Darkness, Darkness</u>.
_____. <u>Lonely Hearts</u>.
_____. <u>In A True Light</u>.
Hentoff, Nat. <u>Blues For Charlie Darwin</u>
Hewat, Alan V. <u>Lady's Time</u>.
Himes, Chester, <u>Cotton Comes To Harlem</u>.
Holmes, Rupert. <u>Swing</u>.
Howard, Clark. "Horn Man."

Howie, Edith. <u>Band Played Murder, The</u>.
Hughes, Dorothy B. "Black and White Blues, The."
Hunter, Evan. <u>Quartet In H</u>.
Irish, William. "Dancing Detective, The."
Jeffers, H. Paul. <u>Rubout at The Onyx</u>.
Johns, Veronica Parker. "Mr. Hyde-de-ho."
Kane, Henry. <u>Peter Gunn</u>.
Karp, Larry. <u>Ragtime Kid</u>.
Latimer, Jonathan. <u>Lady In The Morgue</u>.
Lawton, John. <u>Flesh Wounds</u> aka <u>Blue Rondo</u>.
Leonard, Elmore. <u>Tishomingo Blues</u>.
Lucarelli, Carlo. <u>Almost Blue</u>.
Macdonald, Ross. <u>The Moving Target</u>.
Maltese, Martin. <u>North To Toronto</u>.
Marsh, Ngaio. <u>A Wreath For Rivera</u> aka <u>Swing Brother Swing</u>.
Mathews, Francine. <u>Alibi Club, The</u>.
Molina, Antonio Munoz. <u>Winter In Lisbon</u>.
Moody, Bill. <u>Looking For Chet Baker</u>.
Morfoot, Peter. <u>Fatal Music</u>
Mosley, Walter. <u>Devil In The Blue Dress</u>.
Murphy, Dallas. <u>Lover Man</u>.
Nadelson, Reggie. <u>Red Hot Blues</u> aka <u>Red Mercury Blues</u>.
Oglesby, Wm Ellis. <u>Blow Happy, Blow Sad</u>.
Patchett, Ann. <u>Taft</u>.
Pines, Paul. <u>Tin Angel, The</u>.
Rabe, Peter. <u>Murder Me For Nickels</u>.
Randisi, Robert J. <u>Murder and all that Jazz</u>..
Reed, Harlan. <u>Swing Music Murder, The</u>.
Rich, Nathaniel. <u>King Zeno</u>.
Ronald, James. <u>Death Croons the Blues</u>.
Shurman, Ida. <u>Death Beats The Band</u>.
Skinner, Robert. <u>Skin Deep, Blood Red</u>.
Skvorecky, Josef. <u>Sins For Father Knox</u>.
Slovo, Gillian. <u>Morbid Symptoms</u>.
Smith, Julie. <u>Axeman's Jazz, The</u>.
Smith, Martin Cruz. <u>Stallion Gate</u>.

Sonin, Ray. <u>Dance Band Mystery, The</u>.
Spicer, Bart. <u>Blues For The Prince</u>.
Tate, Sylvia. <u>Never By Chance</u>.

JAZZ BOOKS BY AUTHORS

Aaronovitch, Ben. <u>Moon Over Soho</u>. London: Gollancz, 2011; New York: Ballantine, 2011.

Anderson, Beth. <u>Night Sounds</u>. San Diego: Clocktower, 2000.

Atkins, Ace. <u>Crossroad Blues</u>. New York: St. Martins. 1998.

_____. <u>Dark End of The Street</u>. New York: St. Martins, 2002.

_____. <u>Leavin' Trunk Blues</u>. New York: St. Martins, 2000.

Avery, Robert. <u>Murder On The Downbeat</u>. New York: W.H. Wise, 1944.

Barclay, Tessa. <u>Final Discord, A</u>. London: Severn House, 2005.

Barnes, Harper. <u>Blue Monday</u>. St. Louis: Patrice, 1991.

Barnes, Linda. <u>Steel Guitar</u>. London: Hodder & Stoughton, 1992; New York: Delacorte, 1991.

Batten, Jack. <u>Blood Count</u>. Toronto: Macmillan, 1991.

_____. <u>Crang Plays The Ace</u>. Toronto: Macmillan, 1987.

_____. <u>Riviera Blues</u>. Toronto: Macmillan, 1990.

_____. <u>Straight, No Chaser</u>. Toronto: Macmillan, 1989.

Beckman, Charles, Jr. <u>Honky-Tonk Girl</u>. New York: Falcon, 1953.

Bennet, Ron. <u>Singapore Swing</u>. Holicong: Cosmos, 2003.

Benson, Raymond. <u>Blues In The Dark</u>. London & New York: Arcade, 2019.

Benton, John L. <u>Talent For Murder</u>. London: Collins, 1967; New York: Gateway, 1942.

Bird, Brandon. <u>Dead and Gone</u> aka <u>Downbeat For A Dirge</u>. New York: Dodd, Mead, 1952.

Booth, Christopher B. <u>Killing Jazz: A Detective Story</u>. New York: ChelseaHouse, 1928.

Borneman, Ernest. <u>Tremolo</u>. London: Jarrolds, 1948; New York: Harper, 1948.

Boyce, Trudy Nan. Out of The Blues. New York: Putnam, 2016.

Boyd, Frank. Johnny Staccato. London: Consul, 1964; New York: Gold Medal, 1960.

Brackett, Leigh. No Good From A Corpse. Tucson: McMillan, 1999.

Braly, Malcolm. Shake Him till he Rattles. London: Muller, 1964; New York: Gold Medal, 1963.

Brown, Carter. Ever Loving Blues, The aka Death of A Doll. London: Horwitz, 1971; New York: Signet, 1961.

Brown, Cecil. I, Stagolee. Berkeley: North Atlantic Books, 2006.

Burke, J.F. Crazy Woman Blues. London: Constable, 1979; New York: E.P.Dutton, 1978.

_____. Kama Sutra Tango, The. New York: Harper & Row, 1977.

Burke, James Lee. Black Cherry Blues. London: Century, 1992; New York: Little, Brown, 1989.

_____. Last Car To Elysian Fields. London: Orion, 2003; New York: Simon & Schuster, 2003.

_____. Lost Get-Back Boogie, The. Baton Rouge: Louisiana State University Press, 2004.

_____. Neon Rain, The. London: Century, 1989; New York: Holt, 1987.

Burnett, W.R. Romelle. New York: Knopf, 1946.

Burwell, Rex. Capone, the Cobbs and Me. Livingston Alabama: University of West Alabama, 2015.

Byers, Chad. Jazz Man. Brooklyn: Gryphon, 1997.

Calef, Noel. Ascenseur pour l'echafaud aka Frantic. Paris: Librairie Arthème Fayard, 1956; New York: Gold Medal, 1961.

Calkins, Susanna. Fate of A Flapper, The. New York: Minotaur, 2020.

_____. Murder Knocks Twice. New York: St. Martins, 2019

Cameron, Stella. Tell Me Why. New York: Kensington, 2001.

Campo, J.P. On A Good Day It Just Bounces Off. Ridgewood, N.J.: Books-by-Books, 2005.

Carlotto, Massimo. Bandit Love. London & New York: Europa, 2010. Rome: Edizioni e/o, 2009 as L'amore del bandito.

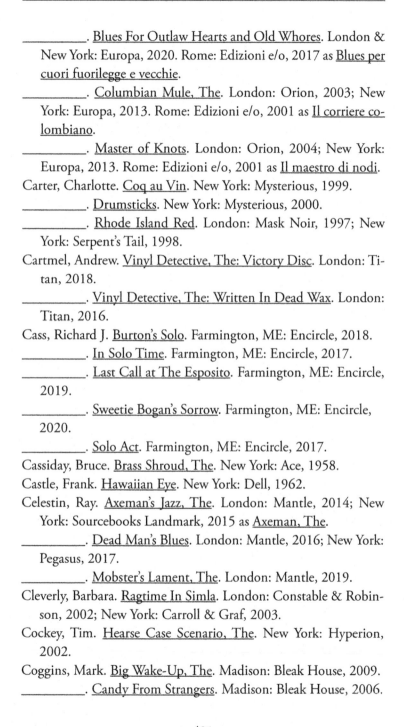

_____. Blues For Outlaw Hearts and Old Whores. London & New York: Europa, 2020. Rome: Edizioni e/o, 2017 as Blues per cuori fuorilegge e vecchie.

_____. Columbian Mule, The. London: Orion, 2003; New York: Europa, 2013. Rome: Edizioni e/o, 2001 as Il corriere colombiano.

_____. Master of Knots. London: Orion, 2004; New York: Europa, 2013. Rome: Edizioni e/o, 2001 as Il maestro di nodi.

Carter, Charlotte. Coq au Vin. New York: Mysterious, 1999.

_____. Drumsticks. New York: Mysterious, 2000.

_____. Rhode Island Red. London: Mask Noir, 1997; New York: Serpent's Tail, 1998.

Cartmel, Andrew. Vinyl Detective, The: Victory Disc. London: Titan, 2018.

_____. Vinyl Detective, The: Written In Dead Wax. London: Titan, 2016.

Cass, Richard J. Burton's Solo. Farmington, ME: Encircle, 2018.

_____. In Solo Time. Farmington, ME: Encircle, 2017.

_____. Last Call at The Esposito. Farmington, ME: Encircle, 2019.

_____. Sweetie Bogan's Sorrow. Farmington, ME: Encircle, 2020.

_____. Solo Act. Farmington, ME: Encircle, 2017.

Cassiday, Bruce. Brass Shroud, The. New York: Ace, 1958.

Castle, Frank. Hawaiian Eye. New York: Dell, 1962.

Celestin, Ray. Axeman's Jazz, The. London: Mantle, 2014; New York: Sourcebooks Landmark, 2015 as Axeman, The.

_____. Dead Man's Blues. London: Mantle, 2016; New York: Pegasus, 2017.

_____. Mobster's Lament, The. London: Mantle, 2019.

Cleverly, Barbara. Ragtime In Simla. London: Constable & Robinson, 2002; New York: Carroll & Graf, 2003.

Cockey, Tim. Hearse Case Scenario, The. New York: Hyperion, 2002.

Coggins, Mark. Big Wake-Up, The. Madison: Bleak House, 2009.

_____. Candy From Strangers. Madison: Bleak House, 2006.

_____. Deadbeat Scroll, The. Lutz, FL: Down & Out Books, 2019.

_____. Immortal Game. Berkeley: Poltroon Press, 1999.

_____. No Hard Feelings. Lutz, FL: Down & Out Books, 2015.

_____. Runoff. Madison: Bleak House, 2007.

_____. Vulture Capital. Berkeley: Poltroon, 2002.

Cohen, Octavus. Danger In Paradise. London: Robert Hale, 1949; New York: Popular Library, 1944.

Colbert, Curt. Rat City. Seattle: Ugly Town, 2001.

Compton, D.G. Back of Town Blues. London: Gollancz, 1996.

Connelly, Michael. 9 Dragons. London: Orion, 2009; New York: Little, Brown, 2009.

_____. Angels Flight. London: Orion, 1998; New York: Little, Brown, 1999.

_____. Black Box, The. London: Orion, 2012; New York: Little, Brown, 2012.

_____. Black Echo, The. London: Orion, 2000; New York: Little, Brown, 1992.

_____. Black Ice, The. London: Cassell, 2001; New York: Little, Brown, 1993.

_____. Brass Verdict, The. London: Orion, 2008; New York: Little, Brown, 2008.

_____. Burning Room, The. London: Orion, 2014; New York: Little, Brown, 2014.

_____. Closers, The. London: Orion, 2005; New York: Little, Brown, 2005.

_____. City of Bones. London: Orion, 2002; New York: Little, Brown, 2002.

_____. Concrete Blonde, The. London: Orion, 2000; New York: Little, Brown, 1994.

_____. Crossing, The. London: Orion, 2015; New York: Little, Brown, 2015.

_____. Darkness More Than Night, A. London: Orion, 2001; New York: Little, Brown, 2001.

_____. Drop, The. London: Orion, 2011; New York: Little, Brown, 2011.

_____. Echo Park. London: Orion, 2006; New York: Little, Brown, 2006.

_____. Last Coyote, The. London: Orion, 1995; New York: Little, Brown, 1995.

_____. Lost Light. London: 2003; New York: Little, Brown, 2003.

_____. Narrows, The. London: Orion, 2004; Little, Brown, 2004.

_____. Overlook, The. London: Orion, 2007; New York: Little, Brown, 2007.

_____. Trunk Music. London: Orion, 1997; New York: Little, Brown, 1997.

_____. Two Kinds of Truth. London: Orion, 2017; New York: Little, Brown, 2017.

_____. Wrong Side of Goodbye, The. London: Orion, 2016; New York: Little, Brown, 2016.

Conroy, Albert. Mr. Lucky. New York: Dell, 1960.

Conway, Martha. Sugarland. San Francisco: Noontime Books, 2016.

Corbett, David. Done For A Dime. London: Orion, 2004; New York: Ballantine, 2003.

Coxe, George Harmon. Lady Is Afraid, The. New York: Knopf, 1940.

_____. Ring of Truth, The. New York: Knopf, 1966.

Craig, Jonathan. Frenzy aka Junkie. London: Brown, Watson, 1966; New York: Lancer, 1962.

Craig, Philip R. Vineyard Blues. New York: Scribners, 2000.

Creech, J.R. Music and Crime. London: Bloomsbury, 1991; New York: G.P. Putnam, 1989.

Curran, Dale. Dupree Blues. New York: Knopf, 1948.

Dahl, Arne. Misterioso aka Blinded Man, The. Malmo: Bra Brocker, 1999. New York: Pantheon, 2011.

Daniel, John. Play Melancholy Baby. Menlo Park: Perseverance Press, 1986.

Davis, J. Madison. And The Angels Sing. Sag Harbor: Permanent Press, 1995.

Deaver, Jeffrey Wilds. Mistress of Justice. New York: Doubleday, 1992.

Dionne, Ron. Sad Jingo. New York: Delabarre, 2012.

Doctorow, E.L. Ragtime. London: Macmillan, 1976; New York: Random, 1975.

Dowswell, Paul. Auslander. London & New York: Bloomsbury, 2009.

Downs, Hunton. Murder In The Mood. Southampton: Wright Books, 1998.

Doyle, Roddy. Oh, Play That Thing. London: Jonathan Cape, 2004; New York: Viking, 2004.

Duchin, Peter &Wilson, John Morgan. Blue Moon. New York: Berkley, 2002.

_____. Good Morning, Heartache. London: Prime Crime, 2003; New York: Berkley, 2003.

Edugyan, Esi. Half Blood Blues. London: Serpent's Tail, 2011; New York: Picador, 2012.

Edwards, Grace F. Blind Alley, The. New York: iUniverse, 2010.

_____, Do Or Die. New York: Doubleday, 2000.

_____. If I Should Die. New York: Doubleday, 1997.

_____. No Time To Die. New York: Doubleday, 1999.

_____. Toast Before Dying, A. New York: Doubleday, 1998.

Edwardson, Ake. Sun and Shadow. London: Harvill, 2005; New York: Viking, 2006; Stockholm: Norstedts, 1999.

Ehrhart, Peggy. Got No Friend Anyhow. New York: Gale, 2011.

_____. Sweet Man Is Gone. Waterville, ME: Five Star, 2008.

Eisler, Barry. Blood From Blood. London: Michael Joseph, 2003 aka Hard Rain. New York: Putnam, 2003.

_____. Choke Point. London: Michael Joseph, 2004 aka Rain Storm. New York: Putnam, 2004.

_____. Last Assassin. London: Michael Joseph, 2007; New York: Putnam, 2006 aka Clean Kill in Tokyo, A. London: Thomas & Mercer, 2014.

_____. One Last Kill aka Redemption Games. London: Onyx, 2006; Killing Rain. New York: Putnam, 2005.

_____. Rain Fall. New York: Putnam, 2002.

_____. _Requiem For An Assassin_. London: Michael Joseph, 2008; New York: Putnam, 2007.

Ellroy, James. _White Jazz_. London: Century, 1992; New York: Knopf, 1992.

Estleman, Loren D. _Jitterbug_. New York: Forge, 1998.

_____. _Lady Yesterday_. London: Macmillan, 1987; New York: Houghton Mifflin, 1987.

_____. _Whiskey River_. London: Scribners, 1991; New York: Bantam, 1990.

Farr, John. _Deadly Combo, The_. New York: Ace, 1958.

Fitzgerald, F. Scott. _Great Gatsby, The_. London: Scribner, 2004; New York: Scribner, 1992.

Fitzhugh, Bill. _Highway 61 Resurfaced_. New York: Morrow, 2005.

Fleming, Charles. _After Havana_. New York: St. Martins, 2004.

_____. _Ivory Coast, The_. New York: St. Martins, 2002.

Fletcher, Jessica & Bain, Donald. _Murder in a Minor Key_. London & New York: Signet, 2001.

Foehr, Stephen. _Storyville_. Bro: Jiri Vanek, 2009.

Fowler, Carol. _Blowin' Up A Storm: Second Chronicles of Bernie Butz, The_. CreateSpace, 2016.

Fuller, Jack. _Best of Jackson Payne_. New York: Knopf, 2000.

Fulmer, David. _Blue Door, The_. London & New York: Harcourt, 2008.

_____. _Chasing The Devil's Tail_. Scottsdale: Poisoned Pen Press, 2001.

_____. _Day Ends at Dawn, The_. New Orleans: Crescent City Books, 2019.

_____. _Dying Crapshooter's Blues, The_. London & New York: Houghton Mifflin Harcourt, 2007.

_____. _Eclipse Alley_. New Orleans: Crescent City Books, 2017.

_____. _Iron Angel, The_. Raleigh, N.C.: Bang Bang Lulu, 2014.

_____. _Jass_. New York: Harcourt, 2005.

_____. _Lost River_. New York: Houghton Mifflin Harcourt, 2009.

_____. <u>Rampart Street</u>. New York: Harcourt, 2006.

_____. <u>Will You Meet Me In Heaven?</u> Raleigh, N.C.: Bang Bang Lulu, 2014.

Gailly, Christian. <u>An Evening at The Club</u>. New York: Other Press, 2003 aka <u>Soir au club</u>. Paris: Editions de Minuit, 2001.

Gaiter, Leonce. <u>Bourbon Street</u>. New York: Carroll & Graf, 2005.

Garcia, Vee Williams. <u>Jazz Flower, The</u>. New York: iUniverse, 2006.

Gillette, Paul J. <u>Play Misty For Me</u>. London: Tandem, 1972; New York: Award, 1971.

Gilmer, Byron. <u>Felonious Jazz</u>. Durham: Laurel Bluff Books, 2009.

Glatzer, Hal. <u>Fugue in Hell's Kitchen, A</u>. London: John Daniel, 2004; Palo Alto: Perseverance, 2004.

_____. <u>Last Full Measure, The</u>. McKinleyville: Perseverance Press, 2006.

_____. <u>Too Dead To Swing</u>. London: Daniel & Daniel, 2004; Santa Barbara: Perseverance Press, 2002.

Goldsmith, Martin. <u>Detour</u>. London: Black Mask, 2008; New York: Macaulay, 1939.

Goodis, David. <u>Shoot The Piano Player</u> aka <u>Down There</u>. London: Prion, 1999. New York: Fawcett, 1956.

_____. <u>Street of No Return</u>. London: Black Lizard, 1994; New York: Gold Medal, 1961.

Gosling, Paula. <u>Solo Blues</u>. London & New York: Coward, McCann & Geoghegan, 1981.

Graham, Heather. <u>Dead Play On</u>. Don Mills Ontario: Mira, 2015.

Granelli, Roger. Bridgend, Wales: Seren, 1995.

Grant, James. <u>Don't Shoot The Pianist</u>. London: Piatkus, 1980.

Green, George Dawes. <u>Caveman's Valentine, The</u>. London: Little Brown Warner International, 1994. New York: Warner, 1994.

Greenwood, Kerry. <u>Green Mill Murder, The</u>. London: Allen & Unwin, 2012; Scottsdale, Poisoned Pen Press, 2007.

Greer, Robert O. <u>Devil's Red Nickel, The</u>. New York: Mysterious, 1997.

Gruber, Frank. <u>Swing Low, Swing Dead</u>. London: Five Star, 1972; New York: Belmont, 1964.

_____. <u>Whispering Master, The</u>. London: Panther, 1956; New York: Signet, 1949.

Gwinn, William. Jazz Bum. New York: Lion. 1954.

Hall, Patricia. Dressed To Kill. London: Severn House, 2014.

Hambly, Barbara. Cold Bayou. London & New York: Severn House, 2018.

_____. Crimson Angel. London & New York: Severn House, 2014.

_____. Dead and Buried. London & New York: Severn House, 2010.

_____. Dead Water. New York: Bantam, 2004.

_____. Die Upon A Kiss. New York: Bantam, 2001.

_____. Drinking Gourd. London & New York: Severn House, 2016.

_____. Fever Season. New York: Bantam, 1998.

_____. Free Man of Color. New York: Bantam, 1997,

_____. Good Man Friday. London & New York: Severn House, 2013.

_____. Graveyard Dust. New York: Bantam, 1999.

_____. Lady of Perdition. London & New York: Severn House, 2019.

_____. Murder In July. London & New York: Severn House, 2017.

_____. Ran Away. London & New York: Severn House, 2011.

_____. Sold Down The River. New York: Bantam, 2000.

_____. Wet Grave. New York: Bantam, 2002.

Harvey, Brian. Beethoven's Tenth. Victoria, B.C.: Orca, 2015.

_____. Tokyo Girl. Victoria B.C.: Orca, 2016.

Harvey, John. Cold In Hand. London: Heinemann, 2008; New York: Harcourt, 2008.

_____. Cold Light. London: Heinemann, 2008; New York: Harcourt, 2008.

_____. Cutting Edge. London: Viking, 1991; New York: Henry Holt, 1991.

_____. Darkness, Darkness. London: Heinemann, 2014; New York: Pegasus, 2014.

_____. Easy Meat. London: Heinemann, 1996; New York: Henry Holt, 1996.

_____. In A True Light. London: Heinemann, 2001; New York: Carroll & Graf, 2002.

_____. Last Rites. London: Heinemann, 1998; New York: Henry Holt, 1999.

_____. Living Proof. London: Heinemann, 1995; New York: Henry Holt, 1995.

_____. Lonely Hearts. London: Viking, 1989; New York: Henry Holt, 1989.

_____. Off Minor. London: Viking, 1992; New York: Henry Holt, 1992.

_____. Rough Treatment. London: Viking, 1990; New York: Henry Holt, 1990.

_____. Still Water. London: Heinemann, 1997; New York: Henry Holt, 1997.

_____. Wasted Years. London: Viking, 1993; New York: henry Holt, 1993.

Haut, Woody. Cry For A Nickel, Die For A Dime. Concord, MA: Concord ePress, 2014.

Hayes, Teddy. Blood Red Blues. London: Justin Charles, 2004.

_____. Dead By Popular Demand. Boston: Kate's Mystery Books/Justin Charles, 2005.

_____. Wrong As Two Left Feet. London: Xpress, 2003.

Helms, Richard. Joker Poker. Lincoln: Writer's Showcase, 2000.

_____. Voodoo That You Do. Barbadoes Hall:Back Alley Books, 2001.

_____. Juicy Watusi. Barbadoes Hall: Back Alley Books, 2002.

_____. Wet Debt. Barbadoes Hall: Back Alley Books, 2003.

_____. Paid In Spades. Franklin TN: Clay Stafford Books, 2019.

Hentoff, Nat. Blues For Charlie Darwin. London: Constable, 1983. New York: Morrow, 1982.

_____. Call The Keeper. London: Secker & Warburg, 1967. New York: Viking, 1966.

_____. Man From Internal Affairs. New York: Mysterious, 1985.

Hewatt, Alan V. Lady's Time. London: William Heinemann, 1986; New York: Harper & Row, 1985.

Himes, Chester. <u>All Shot Up</u>. London: Panther, 1969; New Jersey: Chatham, 1973.

_____. <u>Big Gold Dream, The</u>. London: Allison & Busby, 1988; New York: Thunder Mouth, 1996.

_____. <u>Blind Man With A Pistol</u>. London: Allison & Busby, 1986; New York: Vintage, 1989.

_____. <u>Cotton Comes To Harlem</u>. London: Frederick Muller, 1966; New York: Putnam, 1966.

_____. <u>Crazy Kill, The</u>. London: Allison & Busby, 1984; New York: Chatham, 1973.

_____. <u>Heat's On, The</u>. London: Frederick Muller, 1966; New York: Putnam, 1965.

_____. <u>Rage In Harlem, A</u>. aka <u>For the Love of Imabelle)</u> London: Allison & Busby, 1985; New York: Avon, 1965.

_____. <u>Real Cool Killers, The</u>. London: Allison & Busby, 1985; New York: Avon, 1959.

Holden, Craig. <u>Jazz Bird, The</u>. New York: Simon & Schuster, 2001.

Holmes, Rupert. <u>Swing</u>. London: Allison & Busby, 2007. New York: Random, 2005.

Howie, Edith. <u>Band Played Murder, The</u>. London: Boardman, 1948; New York: M.S. Mill Co. 1946.

Howland, Whit. <u>Trouble Follows</u>. Bearsville, AZ: Pro Se, 2015.

Huggins, Roy. <u>Double Take, The</u>. London: Cassell, 1947; New York: Morrow, 1946.

_____. <u>77 Sunset Strip</u>. New York: Dell, 1958.

Hunter, Evan. <u>Quartet In H</u> aka <u>Second Ending</u>. London: Constable, 1956; New York: Simon & Schuster, 1956.

_____. <u>Streets of Gold</u>. London: Macmillan, 1975; New York: Harper & Row, 1974.

Izzo, Jean-Claude. <u>Chourmo</u>. Paris: Editions Gallimard, 1996; London & New York, 2013.

_____. <u>Solea</u>. Paris: Editions Gallimard, 1998; London & New York: Europa, 2007.

_____. <u>Total Chaos</u>. Paris: Editions Gallimard, 1995 as <u>Total Kheops</u>. London & New York: Europa, 2005.

Jackson, John A. <u>Man With An Axe</u>. New York: Atlantic Monthly, 1998.

Jeffers, H. Paul. Murder On Mike. New York: St. Martins, 1984.

_____. Rag Doll Murder, The. New York: Ballantine, 1987.

_____. Rubout at The Onyx. New York: Ticknor & Fields, 1981.

Jenkins, A.K. Twice No One Dies. Canberra: Equine Press, 2015.

Jessup, Richard. Lowdown. London: Pan, 1961; New York: Dell, 1958.

Joe, Yolanda. Hit Time. New York: Simon & Schuster, 2002.

Jones, Arthur E. It Makes You Think. London: John Long, 1958.

Kane, Frank. Guilt Edged Frame, The. New York: Dell, 1964.

_____. Juke Box King. New York: Dell, 1959.

Kane, Henry. Peter Gunn. New York: Dell, 1960.

_____. Until You Are Dead. New York: Simon & Schuster, 1951.

Karp, Larry. First Do No Harm. Scottsdale: Poisoned Pen Press, 2004.

_____. King of Ragtime., The Scottsdale: Poisoned Pen Press, 2008.

_____. Ragtime Fool, The. Scottsdale: Poisoned Pen Press, 2010.

_____. Ragtime Kid, The. Scottsdale: Poisoned Pen Press, 2006.

Kellerman, Jonathan. Cold Heart, A. London: Headline, 2003; New York: Ballantine, 2003.

Klavan, Andrew. Hunting Down Amanda. New York: Morrow, 1999.

Knight, Phyllis. Shattered Rhythms. New York: St. Martins, 1994.

Koenig, Joseph. Really The Blues. London & New York: Pegasus, 2014.

Lampe, C.O. Return of Glenn Miller, The. Lakeville, Minn.: Galde Press, 1999.

Larson, Skoot. Dig You Later Alligator Blues, The. Bloomington: Author House, 2009.

_____. No News Is Bad News Blues, The. Bloomington: Author House, 2007.

_____. Real Gone, Horn Gone Blues. Bloomington: Author House, 2007.

Latimer, Jonathan. Lady In the Morgue, The. London: No Exit, 1988; New York: Doubleday, 1936,

Lawrence, Michael. I Like It Cool. New York: Popular, 1960.

Lawton, John. Flesh Wounds. New York: Atlantic Monthly, 2005; aka Blue Rondo. London: Weidenfield & Nicolson, 2004.

Leonard, Elmore. Tishomingo Blues. London: Viking, 2002; New York: Morrow, 2002.

Leslie, John. Blue Moon. New York: Pocket, 1998.

_____. Killing Me Softly. New York: Pocket, 1994

_____. Love For Sale. New York: Pocket, 1997.

_____. Night And Day. New York: Pocket, 1995.

Longfellow, Pamela. China Blues. London: Grafton, 1989; New York: Doubleday, 1989.

Loustal-Paringaux, Jacques de. Barney and the Blue Note. Netherlands: Rijperman, 1988.

Lucarelli, Carlo. Almost Blue. London: Harvill, 2003; San Francisco: City Lights, 2001.

Lutz, John. Right To Sing The Blues, The. New York: St. Martins, 1986.

Macdonald, Ross. Moving Target, The. London: Cassell, 1951; New York: Knopf, 1949.

Macdonald, Ross. Trouble Follows Me aka Night Train. New York: Dodd Mead, 1946.

Maltese, Martin. North To Toronto. New York: Manor, 1978.

Marks, Paul D. Blues Don't Care, The. Lutz: FL.: Down & Out Books, 2020.

Marsh, Ngaio. Swing Brother Swing. London: Collins, 1949; aka A Wreath For Rivera. Boston: Little Brown, 1949.

Mask, Ken. Murder at The Butt. Los Angeles: Milligan Books, 2003.

Mathews, Francine. Alibi Club, The. New York: Bantam, 2006.

McClendon, Lise. One O'Clock Jump. New York: St. Martins, 2001,

_____. Sweet and Low. New York: Thomas Dunne, 2002.

Merrill, Joan. And All That Madness. London & New York: CreateSpace, 2012.

_____. And All That Motive. Charleston: CreateSpace, 2014,

_____. And All That Murder. New York: iUniverse, 2009.

_____. And All That Sea. London & Bloomington: iUniverse, 2010.

_____. And All That Stalking. London & Bloomington: CreateSpace, 2012.

Molina, Antonio Munoz. Winter In Lisbon. London: Granta, 1999; as El Invierno en Lisboa. Madrid: Seix Barral, 1987.

Mones, Nicole. Night In Shanghai. London & New York: Houghton Mifflin, 2014.

Moody, Bill. Bird Lives! New York: Walker, 1999.

_____. Czechmate: The Spy Who Played Jazz, Lutz, Fl.: Down and Out, 2013.

_____. Death of A Tenor Man. New York: Walker, 1995.

_____. Fade To Blue. Scottsdale: Poisoned Pen Press, 2011.

_____. Looking For Chet Baker. New York: Walker, 2002.

_____. Shades of Blue. Scottsdale: Poisoned Pen Press, 2008.

_____. Solo Hand. New York: Walker, 1994.

_____. Sound of The Trumpet, The. New York: Walker, 1997.

Morfoot, Peter. Box of Bones. London: Titan, 2018.

_____. Fatal Music. London: Titan, 2017.

_____. Impure Blood. London: Titan, 2016.

_____. Knock 'Em Dead. Cambridge: Galileo, 2020.

Mosley, Walter. Devil In A Blue Dress. London: Serpent's Tail, 2001; New York: Norton, 1990.

_____. R.L.'s Dream. London: Serpent's Tail, 1995; New York: Norton, 1995.

_____. Trouble Is What I Do. London: Orion, 2020. New York: Mulholland/Little Brown, 2020.

Moss, Stephen L. Autumn Leaves. West Lafayette Indiana: Northside Press, 2014.

Murphy, Dallas. Don't Explain. New York: Pocket, 1996.

_____. Lover Man. New York: Scribners, 1987.

_____. Lush Life. New York: Pocket, 1992.

Nadelson, Reggie. Blood Count. London: Atlantic Books, 2011; New York: Walker, 2010.

_____. Bloody London. London: Minotaur, 1999; New York: St. Martins, 1999.

_____. Disturbed Earth. London: Heinemann, 2004; New York: Walker, 2004.

_____. Fresh Kills. London: Heinemann, 2006; New York: Walker, 2007.

_____. Hot Poppies. London: Faber & Faber, 1997; New York: St. Martins, 1999.

_____. Londongrad. London: Atlantic, 2009; New York: Walker, 2009.

_____. Manhattan 62. London: Corvus, 2014; New York: Atlantic, 2014.

_____. Red Hook. London: Heinemann, 2006; New York: Walker, 2006.

_____. Red Mercury Blues. London: Faber& Faber, 1995; aka Red Hot Blues. New York: St, Martins, 1998.

_____. Sex Dolls aka Skin Trade. London: Faber & Faber, 2002. New York: Gardners, 2002.

Nemac, John. Canary's Combo. Hollywood: Nite-Time, 1964.

Novak, Robert. B-Girl. New York: Ace, 1956.

Nuckel, John. Harlem Rhapsody. New York-independent (self).

Oglesby, Wm. Ellis. Blow Happy, Blow Sad. Edmonton: Commonwealth Publications, 1996.

Ondaatje, Michael. Coming Through Slaughter. London: Marion Boyars, 1979; New York: Norton, 1976.

Ordover, Andrew. Cat Came Back, The. Middletown, De.: Creating-A-Life Books, 2016.

_____. Cool For Cats. Lexington, Kentucky: C4C Books, 2011.

Padura, Leonardo. Havana Fever. London & New York: Bitter Lemon Press, 2009; as La neblina del ayer. Barcelona: Tusquets Editores, S.A., 2005.

Patchett, Ann. Taft. Boston: Houghton Mifflin, 1994.

Pentecost, Hugh. Murder Goes Round and Round. London: Robert Hale, 1989; New York: Dodd Mead, 1988.

Pines, Paul. Tin Angel, The. New York: Morrow, 1983.

Platter, Alan. Beiderbecke Affair, The. London: Methuen, 1985.

_____. Beiderbecke Connection, The. London: Methuen, 1992.

_____. Beiderbecke Tapes, The. London: Methuen, 1986.

Pronzini, Bill. Blue Lonesome. New York: Walker, 1995.

Queen, Ellery. Death Spins The Platter. London: Gollancz, 1975; New York: Pocket, 1962.

Rabe, Peter. Murder Me For Nickels. New York: Gold Medal, 1960.

Raleigh, Michael. Maxwell Street Blues, The. New York: St. Martins, 1994.

Randisi, Robert. Everybody Kills Somebody Sometime. New York: St. Martins, 2006.

_____. Fly Me To The Morgue. London & New York: Severn House, 2011.

_____. Hey There (You With the Gun in Your Hand). New York: St. Martins, 2008.

_____. Luck Be A Lady, Don't Die. New York: St. Martins, 2007.

_____. You're Nobody 'Til Somebody Kills You. New York: Minotaur, 2009.

_____. I'm A Fool To Kill You. London & New York: Severn House, 2010.

_____. It Was A Very Bad Year. London & New York: Severn House, 2012.

_____. Way You Die Tonight, The. London & New York: Severn House, 2013.

_____. When Somebody Kills You. London & New York: Severn House, 2015.

_____. You Make Me Feel So Dead. London & New York: Severn House, 2013.

Rayner, Richard. Devil's Wind, The. New York: Harper Collins, 2005.

Reed, Barbara. Harmonic Deception. San Bernardino: Rare Sound Press, 2010.

Reed, Harlan. Swing Music Murder, The. New York: Dutton, 1938.

Rich, Nathaniel. King Zeno. London: MCD, 2018; New York: Farrar, Straus & Giroux, 2018.

Rieman, Les. Vamp Till Ready. London: Gollancz, 1955; New York: Harper, 1954.

Robinson, Peter. Aftermath. London: Macmillan, 2001; New York: William Morrow, 2001; Toronto: McClelland & Stewart, 2001.

_____. In A Dry Season. London: Macmillan, 2000; New York: Morrow, 1999.

_____. Necessary End, A. London & New York: Viking, 1989.

_____. Playing With Fire. London: Macmillan. 2004; New York: Morrow, 2004.

Roeburt, John. Sing out Sweet Homicide. New York: Dell, 1961.

Ronald, James. Death Croons The Blues. London: Hodder & Stoughton, 1934; New York: Phoenix, 1940.

Sallis, James. Blue Bottle. London: No Exit, 1999; New York: Walker, 1999.

Sanchez, Thomas. King Bongo. New York: Knoopf, 2003.

Saunders, David. M Squad. New York: Belmont, 1962.

Sheridan, Sarah. London Calling. London: Polygon, 2013.

Shurman, Ida. Death Beats The Band. New York: Phoenix, 1943.

Skinner, Robert. Blood To Drink. Scottsdale: Poisoned Pen Press, 2000.

_____. Cat-Eyed Trouble. New York: Kensington, 1998.

_____. Daddy's Gone A-Hunting. Scottsdale: Poisoned Pen Press, 1999.

_____. Pale Shadow. Scottsdale: Poisoned Pen Press, 2002.

_____. Righteous Cut, The. Scottsdale: Poisoned Pen Press, 2002.

_____. Skin Deep, Blood Red. New York: Kensington, 1997.

Skvorecky, Josef. Return of Lieutenant Boruvka. London: Faber & Faber, 1990. New York: Norton, 1991.

Slovo, Gillian. Catnap. London: Michael Joseph, 1994; New York: St. Martins, 1996.

_____. Close Call. London: Michael Joseph, 1995.

_____. Death By Analysis. London: Women's Press, 1986; New York: Doubleday, 1988.

_____. Death Comes Staccato. London: Women's Press, 1987; New York: Doubleday, 1988.

_____. Morbid Symptons. London: Pluto, 1984; New York: Dembner, 1985.

Smith, J.P. Body and Soul. New York: Grove, 1987.

Smith, Julie. Axeman's Jazz, The. New York: St. Martins. 1991.

_____. House of Blues. New York: Fawcett, 1995.

_____. Jazz Funeral. New York: Fawcett Columbine, 1993.

_____. New Orleans Morning. St. Martins, 1990.

Smith, Martin Cruz. Stallion Gate. London: Collins, Harvill, 1986; New York: Random, 1986.

Sonin, Ray. Dance Band Mystery, The. London: Kemsley, 1940.

Spicer, Bart. Blues For The Prince. London: Collins, 1951; New York: Dodd, Mead, 1950.

Stevens, Kevin. Reaching The Shining River. Paris: Betimes, 2014.

Tate, Sylvia. Never By Chance. New York: Harper, 1947.

Temple, Lou Jane. Cornbread Killer, The. New York: St. Martins, 1999.

Terrenoire, David. Beneath A Panamanian Moon. New York: St, Martins, 2005.

Vandagriff, G.G. Murder In The Jazz Band. Salt Lake City: Whitney Press, 2020.

Vining, Keith. Keep Running. Chicago: Chicago Paperback House, 1962.

Wainwright, John. Do Nothin' Till You Hear From Me. New York: St. Martins, 1977.

Wallop, Douglass. Night Light. New York: Norton, 1953.

Walsh, Michael. And All The Saints. New York: Warner, 2003.

Warren, Vic. Hong Kong Blues. San Diego: Turning Heads, 2014.

Watson, I.K. Wolves Aren't White. London: Allison & Busby, 1995.

White, Gloria. Death Notes. London: Severn House, 2005.

Whitelaw, Stella. Jazz and Die. London: Hale, 2014.

Williams, Kirby. Long Road From Paris, The. Wainscott: Pushcart Press, 2018.

_____. Rage In Paris. Wainscott: Pushcart Press, 2014.

Wiley, Richard. <u>Soldiers in Hiding</u>. London: Chatto & Windus, 1986; New York: Atlantic Monthly, 1986.

Wilson, August. <u>Ma Rainey's Black Bottom</u>. London: Penguin, 1985; New York: Plume, 1981.

NOVELLAS/SHORT STORIES BY AUTHORS

Allyn, Doug. "Jukebox King, The." In *Alfred Hitchcock's Mystery Magazine.* Vol 27. June 2002.

_____. "Sultans of Soul, The." In Manson, Cynthia & Halligan, Kate (eds.). <u>Murder To Music</u>. New York: Carroll & Graf, 1997.

Asimov, Isaac. "Mystery Tune." In Waugh, Carol-Lynn Rossel & Greenberg, Martin Harry & Asimov, Isaac (eds). <u>Show Business Is Murder</u>. New York: Avon, 1983.

Bader, Jerry. "Killer Jazz." In <u>Noir 1</u>. London & New York: Mrpweb media, 2018.

Bankier, William. "Concerto for Violence and Orchestra." In Manson, Cynthia & Halligan, Kathleen (eds.). <u>Music To Murder</u>. New York: Carroll & Graf, 1981.

_____. "Dog Who Hated Jazz, The." In Greenberg, Martin & Waugh, Carol Lynn Rossel (eds). New York: Carroll & Graf, 1987.

Beckman, Charles, Jr. "Afraid To Live." In <u>Suspense, Suspicion & Shockers</u>. Corpus Christi: Von Boeckman Fiction Factory, 2012.

_____. "Dixieland Dirge." In <u>Suspense, Suspicion & Shockers</u>. Corpus Christi: Von Boeckman Fiction Factory, 2012.

_____. "Hot Lick For Doc, A." In <u>Suspense, Suspicion & Shockers</u>. Corpus Christi: Von Boeckman Fiction Factory, 2012.

_____. "Last Trumpet, The." ." In <u>Suspense, Suspicion & Shockers</u>. Corpus Christi: Von Boeckman Fiction Factory, 2012.

_____. "Mr. Banjo." In <u>Suspense, Suspicion & Shockers</u>. Corpus Christi: Von Boeckman Fiction Factory, 2012.

_____. "Run Cat Run." In <u>Suspense, Suspicion & Shockers</u>. Corpus Christi: Von Boeckman Fiction Factory, 2012.

_____. "Should A Tear Be Shed?" ." In <u>Suspense, Suspicion & Shockers</u>. Corpus Christi: Von Boeckman Fiction Factory, 2012.

Bloch, Robert. "Dig That Crazy Grave!" In Queen, Ellery. (ed). <u>Ellery Queen's Awards: Twelfth Series</u>. New York: Simon & Schuster, 1957.

Boyce, David. "Special Arrangement." In Harvey, Charles (Ed.). <u>Jazz Parody (Anthology of Jazz Fiction.)</u>. London: Spearman, 1948.

Brown, Fredric. "Murder Set To Music." In Charteris, Leslie (ed.). <u>Saint Mystery Library</u>. New York: Great American Library, 1959.

Cain, James M. "Cigarette Girl." In Spillane, Mickey & Collins, Max Allen (eds.). <u>A Century of Noir</u>. New York: New American Library, 2002.

Carter, Charlotte. "Birdbath." In Mysterious Press (eds.) <u>Mysterious Press Anniversary Anthology</u>. New York: Warner, 2001.

_____. "<u>Flower Is A Lonesome Thing, A</u>. In Harvey, John. <u>Blue Lightning</u>. London: Slow Dancer, 1998.

Chandler, Raymond. "King In Yellow, The." London & New York: Everyman, 2002.

Coleman, Wanda. "Dunny." In <u>Jazz and Twelve O'Clock Blues</u>. Jaffrey: Black Sparrow, 2008.

Connelly, Michael. "Christmas Even." In Randisi. Robert, (ed.). <u>Murder and All That Jazz</u>. New York: Signet, 2004.

_____. "Nighthawks." In Block, Lawrence (ed.). <u>In Sunlight or in Shadow</u>. London & New York: Pegasus, 2016.

Dobbyn, John F. "Monday, Sweet Monday." In Alfred Hitchcock's Mystery Magazine. June 2005. Vol. 50. No. 6.

DuBois, Brendan. "Lady Meets The Blue, The." In Vega, Eddie (ed.). <u>Noir Nation 6</u>. Middletown, DE: 2017.

Edwards, Grace F. "Blind Alley, The." In Bland, Eleanor Taylor (ed,). <u>Shades of Black</u>. New York: Berkley, 2004.

Elroy, James. "Dick Contino's Blues." In <u>Hollywood Nocturnes</u>. London: Prentice Hall, 1994; New York: Penzler, 1994.

Jazz Books by Authors

Fitzgerald, F. Scott. "Dance, The." In *Ellery Queen's Mystery Magazine*. March 1953. Vol. 21, No. 112.

Foote, Shelby. "Ride Out." In Albert, Richard N. (ed,). Collection of Jazz Fiction, A. Baton Rouge: Louisana State University Press, 1990.

Fowler, Carol S. "And The Angels Sing." In Blues in the Night. Houston: Strategic Book Publishing Co., 2013.

_____. "Blues in the Night." In Blues in the Night. Houston: Strategic Book Publishing Co., 2013.

_____. "Born To Be Blue." In Blues in the Night. Houston: Strategic Book Publishing Co., 2013.

_____. "Lover Man." In Blues in the Night. Houston: Strategic Book Publishing Co., 2013.

_____. "Passion Flower." In Blues in the Night. Houston: Strategic Book Publishing Co., 2013.

Fredrickson, Jack. "Good Evenin' Blues." In Hellmann, Libby Fisher. (ed.) Chicago Blues. Madison: Bleak House, 2007.

Fulmer, David. "Algiers." In Smith, Julie (ed.). New Orleans Noir. New York: Akashic, 2007.

Gorman, Ed. "Reason Why, The" In Spillane, Mickey & Collins, Max Allen. (eds.). Century of Noir, A. New York: New American Library, 2002.

_____. "Muse." In Randisi, Robert. (ed.). Murder And All That Jazz. New York; Signet, 2004.

Gruber, Frank. "Words and Music." In Brass Knuckles. Los Angeles: Sherbourne Press 1966.

Hambly, Barbara. "Libre." In *Ellery Queen's Mystery Magazine*. November 2006.

_____. "There Shall Be Your Heart Also." In Smith, Julie (ed.). New Orleans Noir. New York: Akashic, 2007.

Harvey, John. "Billie's Blues." In Darker Shade of Blue. London: Arrow, 2010. Also, in Minor Key. Nottingham: Five Leaves, 2009.

_____. "Bird of Paradise." In Now's the Time. London: Slow Dancer, 1999; Chester Springs: Dufour, 1999.

_____. (ed.) Blue Lightning. London: Slow, 1998.

_____. "Cheryl." In Now's the Time. London: Slow Dancer,

1999; Chester Springs: Dufour, 1999.

_____. "Child's Play." In Moody, Bill (ed.). <u>Mood Swings</u>. Lutz: FL: Down & Out Books, 2015. Also, in Randisi, Robert J. <u>Murder and all that Jazz</u>. New York: Signet, 2004.

_____. "Confirmation." In <u>Now's the Time</u>. London: Slow Dancer, 1999; Chester Springs: Dufour, 1999.

_____. "Cool Blues." In <u>Blue Lightning</u>. London: Slow Dancer, 1998.

_____. <u>Darker Shade of Blue</u>. London: Arrow, 2010.

_____. "Dexterity." In <u>Now's the Time</u>. London: Slow Dancer, 1999; Chester Springs: Dufour, 1999.

_____. "Favor." In <u>Darker Shade of Blue</u>. London: Arrow, 2010.

_____. "Home" In Jakubowski. Maxim, (ed.) <u>Best British Mysteries IV</u>. London: Allison & Busby, 2006.

_____. "Just Friends." In Robinson, Peter. (ed.). <u>Penguin Book of Crime Stories</u>." London & New York, 2007.

_____. <u>Minor Key</u>. Nottingham; Five Leaves, 2009.

_____. "Minor Key." In Jakubowski, Maxim. (ed.). <u>Paris Noir</u>. London: Serpent's Tail, 2007. Also in <u>Minor Key</u>. Nottingham: Five Leaves, 2009.

_____. "My Little Suede Shoes." In <u>Now's the Time</u>. London: Slow Dancer, 1999; Chester Springs: Dufour, 1999.

_____. <u>Now's the Time</u>. London: Slow Dancer, 1999; Chester Springs: Dufour, 1999.

_____. "Now's the Time." In <u>Now's the Time</u>. London: Slow Dancer, 1999; Chester Springs: Dufour, 1999.

_____. "Sack O'Woe." In <u>Darker Shade of Blue</u>. London: Arrow, 2010.

_____. "She Rote." In <u>Now's the Time</u>. London: Slow Dancer, 1999; Chester Springs: Dufour, 1999.

_____. "Slow Burn." In <u>Now's the Time</u>. London: Slow Dancer, 1999; Chester Springs: Dufour, 1999.

_____. "Stupendous." In <u>Now's the Time</u>. London: Slow Dancer, 1999; Chester Springs: Dufour, 1999.

_____. "Sun, the Moon and the Stars, The." In <u>Minor Key</u>. Nottingham: Five Leaves, 2009.

_____. Trouble In Mind. Nottingham: Crime Express, 2007.

_____. "Well, You Needn't." In Darker Shade of Blue. London: Arrow, 2010; Also in Minor Key. Nottingham: Five Leaves, 2009.

_____. "Work." In Now's the Time. London: Slow Dancer, 1999; Chester Springs: Dufour, 1999.

Hellmann, Libby Fischer. "Your Sweet Man." In Hellmann, Libby Fischer (ed.). Chicago Blues. Chicago: Bleak House, 2007.

Hoch, Edward D. "Ripper of Storyville, The." In Ripper of Storyville, The. Norfolk: Crippen & Landru, 2003.

Holden, Craig. "P&G Ivory Cut Whiskey Masacree, The." In Randisi, Robert J. Murder and all that Jazz. New York: Signet, 2004.

Howard, Clark. "Horn Man." In Gorman, Ed, Pronzini, Bill & Greenberg, Martin H. American Pulp. New York: Carroll & Graf, 1997.

Huggins, Roy. "Appointment With Fear." In 77 Sunset Strip. New York: Dell, 1958.

_____. "Death and the Skylark." In 77 Sunset Strip. New York: Dell, 1958.

_____. "Now You See It." In 77 Sunset Strip. New York: Dell, 1958.

Hughes, Dorothy B. "Black and White Blues, The." In Gorman, Ed, Pronzini, Bill & Greenberg, Martin. American Pulp. New York: Carroll & Graf, 1997.

Irish, William. "Dancing Detective, The." In Irish, William (ed.) Dancing Detective, The. New York: Lippincott, 1946.

_____. "Jazz Record, The." In Saint Mystery Magazine. July 1965. Vol.22. No. 3.

Johns, Veronica Parker. "Mr. Hyde-de-Ho." In Queen, Ellery (ed.). Ellery Queem's Awards: Eleventh Series. New York: Simon & Schuster, 1956.

Kaminsky, Stuart M. "Blue Note." In Hellmann, Libby Fischer (ed.). Chicago Blues. Chicago: Bleak House, 2008.

Kane, Henry. "One Little Bullet." In Name Is Chambers, The. New York: Pyramid, 1960.

Lippman, Laura. "Shoeshine Man Regrets, The." In Randisi, Robert J. (ed.). Murder and all that Jazz. New York: Signet, 2004.

Lutz, John. "Chop Suey." In Randisi, Robert J. Murder and all that Jazz. New York: Signet, 2004.

_____. "Right To Sing The Blues." In Manson, Cynthia & Halligan, Kathleen (eds.). Murder To Music. New York: Carroll & Graf, 1997.

Mengel, Brad. "The Devil You Know." In White, David (ed.). Charles Boeckman Presents Johhny Nickle. Batesville, AZ: Prose Productions, 2013.

Merril, Judith. "Muted Hunger." In Charteris, Leslie & Santesson, Hans (eds.). Saint Reader, The. New York: Doubleday Crime Club, 1965.

Mertz, Stephen. "Death Blues." In Gorman, Ed. (ed.). Second Black Lizard Anthology of Crime Fiction. Berkeley: Black Lizard, 1988.

Meyers, Martin. "Snake Rag." In Randisi, Robert J. (ed.). Murder and all that Jazz. New York: Signet, 2004.

Moody, Bill. "Camero Blue." In Mood Swings. Lutz, Fl.: Down & Out Books, 2015. And also Phillips, Gary & Tervalon, Jervey (eds). Cocaine Chronicles. New York: Akashic, 2005.

_____. "Child's Play." In Randisi, Robert J. (ed.). Murder and all that Jazz. New York: Signet, 2004.

_____. "File Under Jazz." In Mood Swings. Lutz, FL.: Down & Out Books, 2005; Also in Bishop, Claude & Bruns, Don. (eds.). Merry Band of Murderers, A. Scottsdale, Poisoned Pen Press, 2006.

_____. "Jazz Line." In Mood Swings. Lutz, Fl.: Down & Out Books, 2015. Also in Ellery Queen's Mystery Magazine, March, 1991.

_____. "Resurrection of Bobo Jones." In Harvey, John. (ed.). Men From Boys. London: Heinemann, 2003; New York: Harper Collins, 2003.

Morson, Ian. "There Would Have Been Murder." In Ashley, Mike (ed.). Mammouth Book of the Roaring Twenties, The. New York: Carroll & Graf, 2004.

Mosley, Walter. "Blue Lightning." In Harvey, John (ed.). Blue Lightning. London: Slow Dancer, 1998.

Nielsen, Helen. "You Can't Trust A Man." In Pronzini, Bill & Muller, Marcia. Deadly Arts, The. New York: Arbor, 1985.

Phillips, Gary. "Performer, The." In Vega, Eddie (ed.). Noir Nation N6. Middletown, DE: Noir Nation N, 2017

Randisi, Robert J. "Listening Room, The." In Murder and all that Jazz. New York: Signet, 2004.

_____. Murder and all that Jazz. New York: Signet, 2004.

Reeves, Richard. "Danse Macabre." In Penzler, Otto (ed.). Pulp Fiction: The Dames. London: Querus, 2008.

Roberts, Les. "Jazz Canary," In Randisi, Robert J. Murder and all that Jazz. Signet, 2004.

Robinson, Peter. "Magic of Your Touch." In Randisi, Robert J. Murder and all that Jazz. New York: Signet, 2004.

Rodriguez, Andres. "Yesterdays." In Paul, Steve (ed.) Kansas City Noir. New York: Akashic, 2012.

Runcie, James. "Matter of Death, A." In Sidney Chambers and the Shadow of Death. London & New York: Bloomsbury, 2012.

Scheen, Kjersti. "Moonglow." In Hutchings, Janet (ed.). Passport To Crime. New York: Carroll & Graf, 2007.

Skvorecky, Josef. "Atlantic Romance, An." In Sins For Father Knox. London: Faber & Faber, 1989; New York: Norton, 1988.

_____. "Intimate Business, An." In Sins For Father Knox. London: Faber & Faber, 1989; New York: Norton, 1988.

_____. "Just Between Us Girls." In Sins For Father Knox. London: Faber & Faber, 1989; New York: Norton, 1988.

_____. "Man Eve Didn't Know From Adam, The." In Sins For Father Knox. London: Faber & Faber, 1989; New York: Norton, 1988.

_____. "Mathematicians of Grizzley Drive, The." In Sins For Father Knox. London: Faber & Faber, 1989; New York: Norton, 1988.

_____. "Miscarriage of Justice." In Sins For Father Knox. London: Faber & Faber, 1989; New York: Norton, 1988.

_____. "Mistake In Hitzungee." In <u>Sins For Father Knox</u>. London: Faber & Faber, 1989; New York: Norton, 1988.

_____. "Pirates." In <u>End of Lieutenant Boruvka, The</u>. London: Faber & Faber, 1990; New York: Norton, 1990.

_____. "That Sax Solo." In <u>Mournful Demeanour of Lieutenant Boruvka</u>. London: Lester Orpen Dennys, 1973; New York: Norton, 1987.

_____. "Third Tip of The Triangle, The." In <u>Sins For Father Knox</u>. London: Faber & Faber, 1989; New York: Norton, 1988.

_____. "Question of Alibis, A." In <u>Sins For Father Knox</u>. London: Faber & Faber, 1989; New York: Norton, 1988.

_____. "Why So Many Shamuses?" In <u>Sins For Father Knox</u>. London: Faber & Faber, 1989; New York: Norton, 1988.

Smith, C.W. "Plantation Club, The." In Breton, Marcella (ed.). <u>Hot and Cool Jazz Short Stories</u>. New York: Plume, 1990.

Smith, Julie. "Kid Trombone." In Randisi, Robert (ed.). <u>Murder and all that Jazz</u>. New York: Signet, 2004.

Steele, Coleen. "Them There Eyes." In Ladies Killing Circle, The (eds.). <u>Bone Dance.</u> Toronto: Rendezvous, 2003.

White, Richard. "Notes In The Fog." In White, David. <u>Charles Boeckman Presents Johnny Nickle</u>. Batesville, AZ: Prose Productions, 2013.

Addenda

Books & Short Stories by Authors

Kinsey, T E
(series: "Skins" & Ellie Maloney, "Barty" Dunn)

Deadly Mystery of the Missing Diamonds, The. Seattle: Thomas & Mercer, 2021.
"Skins" Maloney and "Barty" Dunn's jazz band, the Dizzy Heights, have a residency at the Aristippus Club in Mayfair. Superintendent Sunderland asks for help identifying a club member, Arthur Grant, an army deserter, who stole £25,000. Matters move beyond a lark, when band member Blanche Adams is murdered. They sift through the background of a short list of suspects until they identify the ringer and his partner, who almost skip the country with the diamonds.

Baffling Murder At The Midsummer Ball, A. Seattle: Thomas & Mercer, 2021.
The Dizzy Heights jazz band plays the Midsummer Ball at an Oxfordshire country house owned by John Bilverton, who ran a successful biscuit company. They are unable to return to London because of heavy rains. Bilverton commits suicide in his locked study. But Skins, Dunn and Ellie suspect murder because of the absence of powder burns. Then a guest dies from a suspicious drug overdose. There's no shortage of suspects in the dysfunctional Bilverton family.

Khan, Vaseem

"Bombay Blues" In Edwards, Martin (ed.). Music Of The Night. London & New York: Flame Tree Press, 2022.
Don Rollins, a black jazz pianist and leader of a nine piece band at the prestigious Taj Hotel, is killed by two bullets fired into the

back of his head. Police Inspector Persis Wadia suspects the killer is a woman because of fragment of an Elizabeth Barrett Browning poem found in his pocket. Akanksha Sen, one of his students is overly distraught by Rollins' death.

Short Story Collections

Edwards, Martin (ed.)

Music of the Night. London & New York: Flame Tree Press, 2022.
Vaseem Khan's short story "Bombay Blues" is included in this anthology of music related stories by 25 authors from the British Crime Writer's Association.

Discography

Kinsey, T E. Deadly Mystery of the Missing Diamonds, The. Seattle: Thomas & Mercer, 2021.
Bix Beiderbecke's 1924 recordings, such as "Fidgety Feet" had crossed the Atlantic and became part of the Dizzy Heights standard book played at the Aristippus Club. It's on Bix Beiderbecke and the Chicago Cornets (Milestone, 1992).

_____. Baffling Murder at the Midsummer Ball, A. Seattle: Thomas & Mercer, 2021.
Tunes on Bix Beiderbecke and the Chicago Cornets (Milestone, 1992) as well as those played by New York Society bandleader Roger Wolfe Kahn on Roger Wolfe Kahn 1925-1932 would be played by the Dizzy Heights jazz band. Paul Whiteman's recording of Gershwin's "Rhapsody in Blue" provides a key to the murder. It can be found on numerous recordings such as Paul Whiteman & His Orchestra's Rhapsody in Blue and Other Great Favorites (Reader's Digest, 1989).
Khan, Vaseem. "Bombay Blues." In Edwards, Martin (ed.). Music

<u>of the Night.</u> London & New York: Flame Tree Press, 2022.

Like Don Rollins, Teddy Wilson was an elegant, black piano player who had residencies as a single or with a group at the finest hotels and clubs throughout a long career. He freely mixed Songbook and jazz standards. The Touch of Teddy Wilson (Verve, 1957(is a trio session of Songbook chestnuts while Teddy Wilson and his All Stars (Chiaroscuro, 1996) is an example of his small jazz ensembles.

Chronology

1920-1929
Kinsey, T.E. <u>Baffling Murder at the Midsummer Ball, A.</u>
_____. <u>Deadly Mystery of the Missing Diamonds, The.</u>

1950-1959
Khan, Vaseem. "Bombay Blues."

Locations

ENGLAND

London:

Kinsey, T.E. <u>Deadly Mystery of the Missing Diamonds, The.</u>

Oxfordshire:

Kinsey, T.E. <u>Baffling Murder at the Midsummer Ball, A.</u>

INDIA

Bombay:

Khan, Vaseem. "Bombay Blues."

"